A SEARED SKY

An adult epic fantasy trilogy

Book 3

CONVERGENCE

by

STUART AKEN

First Published 2014 by Fantastic Books Publishing

Cover design by Heather Murphy

ISBN: 978-1-909163-56-0

DEDICATION

This trilogy is dedicated to Kenneth Burden, who died before I was born: the father I never knew.

Book three is dedicated to May Allison (nee Whyman) my gifted artist mother who was also my best friend until she died two days after my 16th birthday.

ACKNOWLEDGEMENTS

Books are never the work of the author alone. Fantasy trilogies make special demands on their creators. Although I wrote this book, without the help of the following people, it would never have achieved publication.

I give a great 'thank you' to Dan Grubb and his editorial team locked in his cellars. In spite of their imprisonment, they made the final edit of this book, removing those errors that elude even the most careful author.

Many thanks to cover designer, Heather Murphy, for her imaginative and stylish evocation of the book.

My thanks to Hornsea Writers, a supportive group of professional authors who provided constant encouragement, contributed ideas and acted as beta readers for parts of the text.

I could attempt to list all authors who've influenced me during my life, but I've read and absorbed so much wonder and creativity during those centuries, that I'd be bound to forget someone. I'll simply thank all the authors I've read and enjoyed.

Finally, and most importantly, I thank Valerie, my wonderful wife, for her constant support with food and other domestic necessities. But, much more than this, she employed her excellent memory, sound grounding in English language, and ability to spot clichés, inconsistencies, repetitions, and anachronisms at seven leagues to coax me into vital changes. She made the antepenultimate edit, before I read aloud the printed text. I then felt confident enough to rip the MS from my computer and send it to the publishers. For her attention to detail and her dedication in reading this tome, I thank her most warmly.

CONTENTS

Death in the square - 1

Taken - 11

After the announcement - 17

An escape attempt - 27

Quandaries - 37

A new voice - 45

In the caves - 55

Of dragons and fire - 63

Matters of leadership - 71

A tour of the island - 79

Trapped in Ov-Bebna - 87

Mehrrhyphrol - 95

Death in the desert - 103

A dark place - 111

Mindtalking - 119

A cool beginning - 127

Exposed - 135

Tensions - 143

Cold - 151

Snowfall - 157

Out of the mountains - 165

A sort of madness - 173

Disclosure of intent - 181

Trouble now and to come - 191

Thoughts - 201

Meetings - 211

Mindtalk - 219

Prisoners - 227

Trotnahn - 233

Krohtl - 243

Evil minds - 251

Sacrifice - 257

Injuries and plots - 265

Godwood moving - 273

The hardest question - 281

Across lake qonahn - 289

Seeking evil - 297

The first killing - 305

Entering the dark space - 313

The island tour begins - 321

Forming the circle - 329

An act of theft - 335

A convenient victim - 343

Justifications - 351

Powerseekers in peril - 359

An accusation - 367

At the monument - 375

Arrival - 383

Into the monolith - 391

Within - 399

Battle - 407

Trial - 415

Endings - 423

A promise fulfilled - 431

Maps - 443

About the author - 447

Alphabetical list of all characters - 449

Mythical and legendary characters, and titles in use - 457

Appendices - 459

The first great knowing - 461

The flood - 465

The legend of vaarkil and Mythanpho - 469

The confession of Gadhallah - 475

The epic of Gadhallah - 491

Sacred verses - 515

Priest's declaration at the wedding ceremony - 517

Responses due at time of coming of the skyfire - 519

Chapter 1

DEATH IN THE SQUARE

Aklon-Dji entered his father's house with Phildrad close behind. Both had their hunting knives drawn and ready. But staggering complacency had allowed Wendarah Kaz to sleep unguarded, in spite of her recent experience on The Point. When he woke her by pulling back the cover, she was slow to recognise the threat, assuming her current lover had arrived to share more pleasure.

'Going to take me…? Mhortag's balls! Aklon-Dji, how dare you invade my…?'

'Get up, Wendarah. Now. And without excessive noise or fuss, if you will.'

The temporary High Priestess rose slowly from the bed and stood, awaiting his move. If she feared him, it didn't show. 'Not going to join with me, then, Aklon? Not going to share with me those delights your many women claim you provide?'

'I would sooner join with a terzet-horn. And whether you ever experience delight again depends on your next actions.'

'Tell your friend…don't I know you?' She studied Phildrad but was unable to call to mind where she'd met him, it seemed. 'Can't recall the name. Tell him to leave, and let me show you what real pleasure can be had with a woman of experience.'

'As ever, you fail to understand your situation, Wendarah. I am here to either make use of your position on Muhnilahm or to kill you. I have little interest in which. But I give you the choice, since I find unnecessary violence distasteful.'

She bent to pick up the tabard, draped over the chair where he'd discovered her predecessor abusing another woman. That provisional High Priest he'd left hanging naked upside-down from the rafters, the lifeblood draining from his fat carcass.

Aklon swept the garment from her hands with the tip of his sword. 'You will remain as you are.'

'So you do want to join with me, after all.'

'No, Wendarah, I intend to humiliate and shame you.'

A low whistle from outside signalled that his other colleague needed to tell him something. Before he could respond, Phildrad left the room to discover what it might be. He turned to Wendarah again. 'You know the fate my father planned for me, Wendarah. It is what awaits you, should you decide against giving me the help I require.'

For all her bravado, she paled at the picture of such an agonising death. Pleasure and power were her drives. Pain was for others. Suffering was to be inflicted, not endured. Aklon had no intention of exacting such punishment, but, too steeped in her own cruelty,

1

she didn't recognise this.

'Tell me what you'd have me do.'

Phildrad returned. 'Small troop o' guards coming, Aklon.'

'Right. Come with me, Wendarah. Your first task is to make your men do as I say.'

He indicated she should precede him and she walked, upright and proud, to the front entrance of the High Priest's house to stand in the doorway as her men approached.

Most of her soldiers had either died on the disastrous foray at The Point, or been converted to the side of Aklon's Few. But the troop contained more soldiers than Aklon had at his immediate disposal. Nevertheless, she was wise enough to understand that made little difference to her situation.

'Stay. I've no need of you here. Go back to…'

'No, Wendarah. Tell them to gather all the people in the square and await your arrival.'

She passed on his whispered message. Without an officer, these simple men were used to doing as they were told. But one had the sense to understand that she wouldn't normally appear outside the house or address them in her current state.

'Is everything alright, Wendarah Kaz?'

Her natural haughtiness came to Aklon's aid. 'You question my orders?'

'No, Paltra. I just thought…'

'You don't need to think, man. Just do as I say. Is that clear?'

He shrugged, saluted and turned to go. But he stopped and turned again, unsure.

'Sorry, Wendarah Kaz. We'll need the whole garrison to collect all the citizens. Is that alright?'

Aklon whispered his full requirements as he stood in shadow at her back, his sword tip in her flesh.

'All the garrison. All the citizens. No one is excused. You have until midday.'

The soldiers went to do exactly as she required, her reputation for cruelty to those who displeased her ensuring their obedience.

Delbon re-emerged from his hiding place and Phildrad took up his position at the rear of the house, as arranged. Members of the Few, summoned by Delbon, slowly surrounded the house in case of further disturbance.

Aklon urged the High Priestess back inside the house in which he'd been raised and took her to the entrance of the Secret Pit. 'Bring everything up here. We are going to show the people the lies they have been told to keep them in the ways of Followers.'

Wendarah stared down into the small opening. 'You can't do that. They'll…'

'Yes, Wendarah, I imagine they will. Now, we have a limited amount of time at our disposal and, since I cannot trust you on your own, I will be forced to help you in the task.

Please do as I say.'

'I'm not a slave. I'm High Priestess. I won't be treated…'

He bent her over and slapped her bottom twice, humiliating rather than harming her. 'Obey me, or I will hurt you.'

'Never, never have I…'

'No. Had you ever been disciplined, you would have been a better person. Now, to the task. If you prove willing to begin with, I might free a slave to help, should he or she be so inclined.'

'Free my slaves…?'

He smiled at her. 'You cannot believe this was not organized, Wendarah. I have been planning this part of my Cause ever since my father named me Renegade and disowned me. It was inevitable once he set off on his fool's errand to Choshinahm. Now, on with the task.'

The reality of her situation clouded her face as it dawned on her at last. There would be no dramatic rescue, no intervention from outside. She was alone and defenceless against a man she'd sworn to kill in agony. Her shoulders slumped and she put her hand to her mouth.

'Finally, you understand, Wendarah. Finally, you know. No more prevarication. The time for action has come and I will have my day. Let us empty the Chamber and bring your guilty secrets up to show the people.'

She entered the dark space at last.

'Wendarah. Should you try to harm a single item, I will make you very, very sorry. I require only that you carry the foul history to the surface. Any damage to an item will result in similar damage to your skin.'

She emerged after him with her first bundle of parchments and dropped them at his feet, beside those he'd placed with care. 'Don't think this means you've won, Aklon. I've all my soldiers and the Holy Ones. The people won't be easily converted to your lies. We'll win in the end. As we always have.'

'No, Wendarah. Your reign, and that of Dagla Kaz, the man who follows false signs, is over. You are finished. But whether, and how, you live after the changes I propose, depends on how you behave during the transition. Remember that. Now, let us finish this job.'

Dagla Kaz brushed the gnats from his face for the hundredth time. The forest seemed to grow more dense with every step. Would the trail never end? The women they sought must surely have slowed down their captors enough for the hunting party to be close behind them by now.

'Caarl, is there still no sign?'

The soldier turned, irritation rapidly disguised by patience. 'I'm sorry, Dagla Kaz, but we move as swiftly as possible through the unknown. The tracks suggest we're close on their heels. But we can go no quicker than the slowest in our party.'

The High Priest knew this slight was aimed at himself and the Chief Astronomer, neither of them young or athletic. Perhaps it was time to admit this was a fit man's task. What mattered was that the Virgin Gifts were rescued before any harm came to them, before they could be violated.

He looked back along the route they'd already travelled, as far as the dense foliage allowed. Their path to this point was easy to follow. But the deeper they ventured into the forest, the more difficult it would be to return unaided.

'Very well, Caarl. Jhonaht and I, with the less able women, will return to the campsite and allow the rest of you to continue at greater speed.'

Relief was writ large on the soldier's face. 'As you suggest, Dagla Kaz. We'll wait for the rest to catch up and then select who should return with you. We need only the fit and strong to defeat these wild Vagboh. Anyone unused to swinging a sword will be more hindrance than help.'

It took little time to make the selection, and he sent Caarl ahead with the reduced team. He, and a much relieved Jhonaht, turned about and retraced their steps with three of the women and one of the young men who'd suffered a slight injury that slowed him down.

He hated handing over responsibility to the soldier, but knew him to be a trustworthy and loyal servant of the faith. This really was the most sensible solution.

'I'm tough as any man, Dagla Kaz. An' as fast on me feet. I should be with the huntin' party.'

He looked down at the portly woman and nodded. 'You do a good job of guiding our young virgins, Corphanda. But you're not as fleet of foot as you wish. Let the soldiers and younger ones rescue our girls. You can take care of them again when they return, as they surely will.'

She'd be dissatisfied with his decision until the women returned unharmed, but her presence was no real help to the hunting party.

The returners would have a night in the trees before they reached the point where they'd first been robbed of their women. But the chances of rescue improved without the rest of them tagging along. In fact, from what Caarl had said, it seemed likely that his group might even catch up with the kidnappers before evening made the forest too dark.

Oh, why was his sacred pilgrimage beset with so many problems? Was it punishment from Ytraa for his revenge on Tumalind and that damned husband of hers? Surely this

4

sort of trouble hadn't been the fate of any of the earlier pilgrimages?

'You can't be sure, Dagla Kaz. The records are so thin, details so sketchy. Perhaps there have always been troubles.' Jhonaht's words were well meant but little comfort until he had the Virgin Gifts back, unmolested and intact. Vital to the mission, their virginity was his prime concern and, kidnapped by those wild men, he couldn't help but worry over their fate.

Darkness slowly forced the party to a halt in a small clearing, where they made camp as best they could. The cooked meat gifted them by the soldier would feed them for this night. By midday on the morrow, they'd be back at the river and have the opportunity to find fresh food. None of those left were real hunters but, if the ship's captain and crew had remained as instructed, he should be able to recruit some of them for the task of providing something to eat. Ytraa alone knew how they would come by a new boat to take them on their way, though.

Sleep was long in coming, and he had no companion to share his sleep sack and take his mind off his worries. He could take Corphanda, of course, but she held no delight for him. The question that kept him awake more than any other was how the wild men had come to be aware they were camped on the edge of the forest. Their main settlement was supposed to be many leagues away. How had such savages learned of their presence?

Tumalind ached from the speed and length of their day's ride. Resting with Okkyntalah, she welcomed his gentle embrace as they ate meat he and the troop leader had caught earlier. They'd covered a great distance from the dessert city on swift, tireless camels so that they were now camped under the outliers of the great fire mountain. It's ever-present plume of smoke and ash rose above them, hiding many early stars and polluting the air with its acrid smell. Tomorrow they'd enter the city of these strange Followers and discover how best to reach the High Priest's party, a meeting she dreaded with every particle of her being.

'We won't be alone this time, Tumalind. We have friends with us. No one's going to allow Dagla Kaz to take you against your will.'

'And what about you, Okkyntalah? Will Tryonta and Dagla Kaz be so easily deflected from taking revenge on you?'

'I can look after myself.'

She had to admit that his amazing feat in rescuing her from Ov-Bebna, in the sands, had increased her already high admiration. He'd proved so capable, so brave, so intelligent. That the troop sent by Feldrark had also arrived at that moment made her feel that right must be on their side. When, she wondered, would they be able to return to the island and settle down to the life they both so deeply desired?

'How many shall we have, Okkyntalah?'

He studied her. 'I don't want to ruin you with too many; maybe four or five?'

'I think I could manage that. Boy or girl first?'

'Doesn't matter. As long as they're all healthy and well. Shoarhn will be so happy to have grandchildren. I wonder how she is?'

'Mother's well. At least she was last time I mindtalked with Aklon. You know he's really started the Cause, don't you? I hope none of them are in danger from what he proposes. Who knows how it'll affect our future?'

'It'll be much different from our past, that's certain. But we just want a life free of danger and concern. Is that too much to ask?'

'For the moment it seems to be, Okkyntalah. But, once we've completed this particular task and got Myllthlan, father's woman, and the Virgin Gifts back safe and sound, perhaps we can find a boat to take us down the Sure to Shorrannon. Then we can make our way to Litkala for a rest before we set off back to Muhnilahm.'

'Got it all planned, haven't you?' He kissed and embraced her as they finished their meal.

'After all our adventures, I just want peace and quiet. And time and opportunity to join with you as often as possible. I'm so glad you thought to keep my little box with you. I'd hate to get pregnant out here in the wild.'

'I assumed that's what it was. Why didn't you tell me?'

'It's a woman thing. We all have our little secrets. And we both benefit, don't we?'

He smiled at her, looked about the camp and took her into the tent they finally shared alone. 'Time to discover whether the day's ride has tired you out, or whether you've any energy left.'

'I always have energy for you, Okkyntalah.'

In the city square, the people had gathered, as instructed. There was a buzz of concern and excitement. Aklon kept his sword tip at the High Priestess's throat as they threaded their way through to the raised dais at the top end. Phildrad, Delbon and others of the Few watched his back. Those they passed gasped or called out at the threat to their leader.

Slowly, they reached the destination. His reliance on Wendarah's strong survival instinct proved correct. She'd do nothing that might place her life in peril. It was a selfish quality he was happy to use to its full. He pushed her forward, to stand at the high point of the place traditionally used for announcements.

'You know what you must do, Wendarah. For every deviation from the rehearsed words, I will cut your beautiful flesh. You understand?' Aklon's whisper carried no further than her ears and she nodded.

The priestess raised her arms to the assembled crowd. In the square, almost twelve thousand of her people slowly stopped talking. Seeing her state, many shed their tabards, assuming this must be a sacred occasion. She waited for complete silence. 'Are all able to hear my voice?'

Murmurs of agreement reached the dais.

'Those furthest away. Can you hear me?'

Calls from those at the northern end of the square reached up to Aklon.

'You are heard, Wendarah. Proceed.'

'You've been gathered here to learn a great truth. I, the Holy Ones and Dagla Kaz have known this truth always. It's the knowledge of that truth that caused Aklon-Dji to be made the renegade he is today.'

There were calls of disapproval, threats to his life, demands for him to be put to death.

She raised her hands again, signalling silence. It came slowly.

'What I have to tell you won't please you. What I have to say will change your whole lives and your way of thinking. But it is the truth. The truth.'

She waved the roll of goatskin in her left hand, 'Before I read this parchment, I make it known that I, Wendarah Kaz, acting High Priest of Muhnilahm, hereby renounce my office, my title and my wealth. This is my apology for my failure to inform you of the truth before today. I am truly sorry.'

The noise took more time to die than it had previously. Aklon looked out from his place behind the priestess and saw growing confusion and concern on the assembled faces. There'd been enough preamble.

'Read it now, Wendarah. Now.'

'This scroll holds the words of the Lord Gadhallah, written by his own hand in the days before he passed out of this life. Hear his words, and weep.'

She waited for silence to descend again and then, her voice trembling with emotion, read the words their vile leader had left as his admission of evil, a belated and futile attempt at atonement. The scroll told how the very foundation of their faith was utterly false and no more than an excuse for a man who'd defiled, abused and raped a young girl before he'd killed her. Told how he'd been unable to face the enormity of his deed and had concocted the religion of the Followers as justification for his actions and his crimes.

The evil lived in his very words. The shame he felt as he admitted, at the close of his life, what he'd done, the details of his wickedness, all spoke of the truth of his confession. And the people heard the sorry tale in silence; shock and horror driving many to their knees before the account ended.

7

Aklon listened and watched, aware that the end of her story could signal any number of reactions from the people. Violence was what he must prevent. He contacted his mentor on the mainland, sending his thoughts to her, as planned.

'Now is the time, Ivdulon. We are ready.'

'So am I.'

He felt her enter his mind and vision, seeking out and targeting those with the tell-tale signs amongst the crowd. Swiftly and efficiently she found those she needed, spread amongst the gathering and including some of the soldiers who stood, disarmed and held captive by the city's entire contingent of the Few.

A hundred and more souls spoke as one. 'I am the voice of Ytraa. What you have now been told is true. For many, many cycles I have struggled to convey this truth to you, my Followers. But those who styled themselves your leaders have prevented it. You now all know the truth my most loyal Follower, Aklon-Dji, has tried so long to reveal. Give him the respect he has earned, love him as I love him, for he is the proper leader of my people. Listen to his words and act upon them. These are the words of Ytraa and must be obeyed.'

Aklon felt the wise woman of Litkala leave his mind. He stepped into the open, his sword no longer at the flesh of the priestess, and looked down at the people. Their confusion and uncertainty was obvious. They were still, silent, in shock as the magnitude of what they'd heard slowly dawned on them. The crowd was his to command.

Wendarah moved forward and shouted. 'It's a trick! A trick! He lies. Aklon-Dji is Renegade and must be killed!'

It was all she said before those nearest silenced her with whatever they had to hand. One grabbed Delbon's sword and finished the violence that hands had already done. The killers moved away from the gore, horrified by their act. Noise erupted from the square and confusion grew as disagreement and conflicting opinions spread through the crowd. Delbon stretched out and recovered his abandoned sword, gathering the torn and blood-stained scroll along with it.

Many would be hurt, as those who believed what they'd been told were attacked by others who clung to their false beliefs. Neither Aklon nor Ivdulon had foreseen Wendarah's desperate action. They'd expected and planned for her agreement and surrender to prevent the chaos that now ensued.

The High Priestess had thought she still held the hearts and minds of the people. Her selfish quest to keep her status now threatened misery for many. And Aklon had no plan to stop the violence that spread from neighbour to friend to family, as arguments became fights and passions ruled thoughts.

'Ivdulon. Are you there? I need you to intervene again.'

8

'Sorry, Aklon. Mindtalk with many is exhausting. I've no strength to...'

And she was gone. The connection fading instead of braking. He knew she'd given all she could for the moment. Now he must act alone until she recovered. The selfish act of one in power had undone much of the good he'd planned. Suffering for many; enmity, factions were already in the making right in front of him. Some of the Few had gathered round him in defence and now, regardless of his will, forced him through the masses and from the square.

Those left to guard the secrets he'd gathered from the Chamber, welcomed him and the others into the High Priest's house, there to convene and decide what they must do now.

The Cause had truly started, but not as he'd planned and hoped. Hard days lay ahead. Dangers. Those who'd supported him were now identified. And, whilst many of the population had accepted the word of Ytraa, as devised by Ivdulon, too many adhered to the old ways, willingly persuaded by Wendarah's claims of a trick. He couldn't yet walk the streets of his homeland free of danger. And those he loved, the Few, remained at risk, even if only from diehards. Civil war, the very thing he'd struggled to prevent, seemed inevitable.

Chapter 2

TAKEN

Corphanda, collecting herbs at the forest's edge announced their arrival. 'Dagla Kaz! Dagla Kaz, Ytraa be praised! They're back.'

By the time the High Priest arrived from his place by the river, Caarl had emerged from the shadows, followed by a straggling party, which soon cleared the outlying trees to gather in open grassland.

'Are the Virgin Gifts intact, Caarl?'

'They say they weren't harmed. Though Porryh offered herself to the wild men, I'm told.'

'I'll deal with 'er, bad little madam.'

'Do, Corphanda. But we're certain none was violated?'

'That's what they all say, Dagla Kaz. And no one was hurt in the recovery. The wild men ran away once they saw us. They were fewer than when they raided, so that may account for their retreat. Though I'm not convinced that's an end to it.'

The ship's captain came over, nodding. 'They'll be back. In numbers. Our only hope's to cross the river. Those Vagboh are terrified of water.'

'You suddenly know much about these wild men, Quyreena.'

'I was never consulted. You made it clear you were in charge and your command had to be met on all things. Personally, I'd never've landed on this shore…'

She left the unspoken accusation hanging and Dagla Kaz felt foolish and unable to redeem his reputation. Caarl glanced away, his face echoing a shared memory of the road to Qlentz, when Dagla Kaz had almost allowed his pride in leadership to take them into great danger, against all advice. But the Wormstalls of Glahynne were well behind them now. He must move on. Mend the damage. Find a way forward. And, it seemed, the captain's advice must be taken.

They made no celebration of the return. But Dagla Kaz congratulated the hunting party for their restoration of his precious Virgin Gifts. The returned members of the pilgrimage were clothed again with garments they'd left behind on capture.

Dagla Kaz surveyed his group. 'Has anyone any ideas about how we can cross this mighty river?'

'How much time do we have?'

'I don't know, Caarl. Quyreena thinks the wild men will be back in larger numbers. Their main settlement's supposed to be thirty leagues or so into the forest. How swiftly will they travel? How many will they be? How desperate are they to get their hands on our women?'

'What puzzles me is how they knew we were here in the first place, Dagla Kaz.'

'I agree, Tarruss. But for now, I'm more concerned to find a way to safety.'

'Excuse me, Dagla Kaz, I've got an idea…' Dilanthas, the shy retiring Virgin Gift from his own island, had been responsible for them obtaining a local guide in Kabalyt. His memory of her contribution and his own nearly fatal decision prevented him dismissing her as ignorant of their needs now.

'It won't be easy. But, well, we're surrounded by trees. Can't we make a raft, like?'

'Take too long. We don't have the means. It would have to be too big if it were to carry us all…'

'Sorry to disagree, Dagla Kaz, but I think it's our only hope. We either cross the river or risk walking this side of it. Every step we take toward Mehrrhyphrol takes us closer to the danger in the forest. At least until we're halfway to the city.'

He looked at the ship's captain and recalled his last look at the map. She was right. The only way to escape this danger from the wild men was to travel on the other side of the river. Half a league wide and with strong currents, it was impossible to swim. Even on a raft, they'd be swept down a good way before reaching the far bank. But there was no other way. Oh, how had he offended Ytraa, to be so beset with problems and trials on this pilgrimage? What had he done wrong?

'Your reliance on your god is pathetic, man. Wake up to reality. It's not a punishment, but the way you lead your life that's to blame. Take charge. Get the women frowkin' and find a way to collect more coin so you don't have to be forever labouring yourself.'

He shrugged off the sense that the intruding voice was right, growing more curious about these frequent incursions into his mind. But now was not the time for such deliberations. He handed over charge of the construction to Caarl and the ships' captain. They set to work. Quyreena and her crew explored the burnt wreck of her ship and discovered rope enough still sound for binding logs. Much of it lay tangled in the half-sunken wreckage and they had to dive into ash-blackened water to free it. Caarl organised a small party to locate suitable trees and set others to collecting smaller, dead wood, to provide them with fires for protection and cooking until the raft could be constructed.

'How long will it take, Dagla?'

'You're the one who's supposed to understand numbers, Jhonaht. Make a guess.' He enjoyed unsettling his astronomer. It suited him to have the man of science on the wrong foot.

All the men, including the male Virgin Gifts, began felling selected trees, stripping off branches, and rolling the trunks to the bank, where they'd be assembled. The women collected firewood and gathered fruit and roots so the party might eat whilst construction work progressed. Everyone but the High Priest was busy.

He took himself off to quieter reaches of the forest, ostensibly to commune with Ytraa. Though, in truth, he'd never felt at one with his god, never experienced the communion with Ytraa his acolytes professed to feel. Perhaps, because it was all a sham, he'd never found solace as the ignorant might. He knew too much of the truth about the religion to develop real faith. How could he put faith in something founded on lies and half-truths?

When he came back out of the trees, Jhonaht approached him. 'I've the information now, Dagla. I estimate three days before the raft's on the water.'

The High Priest nodded vaguely. It didn't do to let him believe he was too valued. 'Let's hope we have the necessary time before those savages return in numbers. Otherwise we're lost.'

'I take it you had no solace from your spell communing with Ytraa in the trees, then, Dagla?'

'What? No. None. These are unfriendly trees. This is a threatening and unholy forest. Ytraa chooses not to dwell here.'

In fact, he'd felt no different here than in any other place where he'd professed to commune with Ytraa. But, here, he could find no words to make it seem he had answers, and it wouldn't do to put words into the mouth of his god that might later be proved false. He, and all the party, had no choice now but to rely on good fortune and the willing work of all concerned in making their one means of escape.

Shoarhn was struck, at first, with that feeling that she'd been here before. Once previously, she'd come into her house from bright sunshine to discover a strange man waiting. Then, it had been Aklon, and their love had grown from that meeting, increasing each time they'd been together. But this man was unknown to her and she realised, at once, the Holy One wasn't someone she could trust or welcome.

'You're Shoarhn, wife of Aglydron, mother of Tumalind and, more recently, lover and protector of the vile renegade, Aklon-Dji.' His statement told Shoarhn she was in serious danger.

'You will accompany me.'

Her first thought was to run, but another Holy One, behind her, stepped out of hiding from behind the door.

'Resist or attempt escape, woman, and we'll destroy your twin boys and those who harbour them.'

She had no choice. 'Where are you taking me?'

The man, Aglydron's size, swiped the back of his hand across her face. 'Ask nothing. Obey in silence. Remove your tabard.'

She'd heard tales of the vile cruelty shown by these disciples of Ytraa; men and women supposedly so devoted to God that they believed in the Commands word for word and had their own interpretations of the rules of the religion. They demanded absolute obedience from those under their control. She stripped at once and awaited the fate she expected.

'Come.'

So surprised not to be raped there and then, she stood still for a moment. The female Holy One slapped her buttocks hard. 'Now, woman!'

With a Holy One in front of her and the other behind, she left the house. Irrildys was on the street as she emerged, alerted by the rumour of Holy Ones in town. She glanced briefly at Shoarhn and nodded just once. At least her boys would be cared for.

As required, the general population pelted her, many half-heartedly, with dung and small stones as the Holy Ones led her out of town. The pair made no other demands of her, spoke no more words. She walked away from her home and hopes of a life of love and wonder with Aklon once the Cause was complete. Nothing but pain and death lay ahead. How did they know? Who'd informed on her? A jealous woman from the Few? One of the army of informers and spies Dagla Kaz employed to keep track of Aklon? Or simply a neighbour who wanted to steal her farm?

She risked a glance up from the ground she'd gazed at so far on the journey. It proved her suspicions: she was headed for the caves under Ytraa's Peak on the Plain of Ytraa. No one returned from there alive. And the rumours of the torture and cruelty meted out by the Holy Ones were the stuff of nightmare. This was now her destination, her destiny.

Okkyntalah hadn't thought to see the city under the fire mountain. Unsure whether their manner of dress was a good or a bad thing, he nevertheless felt obliged to conform. Easy enough for the men. The women might find it a little more difficult. But they were guests, and it made sense to go along with the wishes of hosts when in a strange place. As second in command of the rescue party, and conscious of his duty to set a good example, he complied at once with the request, replacing his tabard with the belt and small apron offered him. Tumalind set the same standard for the women, reluctantly, aware of the stares she attracted.

'You seek a boat to take you through the lake and up beyond the swamp, I understand?' The town leader consulted Ouqitahl, the troop leader, who stood beside Okkyntalah.

They were mindful of the dangers faced by the captured women, and needed to set sail as soon as possible.

'With our animals, Paltrohn. We also need supplies of food and clothing. Our information is that the party we seek is in trouble from the wild men of the Great Forest.'

'You amaze me. That you can be certain of such things when so far from that party. Do you possess some special power unknown to normal mortals?'

'I have the knowledge. As to how I came by it; I'm not at liberty to say, Paltrohn.'

The town leader turned to stare at Tumalind through his eyes of lapis lazuli and Okkyntalah saw a brief look of recognition cross her features.

'That's as it should be. I applaud your discretion. And I'm in a position to help. Though the merchant whose ship I propose is likely to require a hefty fee.'

'I'm well provided with coin. Our Kiral, Feldrark, sent us out with more than enough gold for our needs. Please, lead me to the ship. We're in need of great speed, Paltrohn.'

'Then we'll dispense with the normal formalities. Please come with me.'

The ship, a two-master with open deck, had little superstructure; built for cargo and goods, rather than people. Okkyntalah left Tumalind with the rest of the troops and accompanied Ouqitahl and the town leader on board, via a sturdy but unfixed plank of wood.

Negotiations were conducted in a small three-sided wicker structure close to the prow. The captain had the look of a rogue.

'Pyqad may appear a scoundrel, but I'd trust him with my life. We've been friends since childhood and he's ever proved honourable.'

An older man, he smiled easily and had the air of one with few cares. But he drove a hard bargain and Ouqitahl handed over a considerable sum in gold before the deal was done. Once concluded, however, embarkation, the loading of stores, and the start of their voyage took a remarkably short time.

Okkyntalah stood beside Tumalind, in her favoured spot at the prow with the wind in her glorious auburn locks, as they left Kah-Labaz behind.

'Shame we didn't have more time. I'd have liked to explore the place. Maybe fish in the lake.'

'Me too. Still the town leader answered quite a lot of questions, so I know something of the city, and how they go about Following. It may be of use to Feldrark, once we're more settled.'

He hadn't seen her with the leader of the town but recalled that the man had the tell-tale signs. How much had his wife's mindtalk influenced the whole arrangement, and did those in charge give her credit for her help in so many things?

'Don't worry about me, Okkyntalah. You're the only reward I want.'

Jodisa, the High Priest's daughter he'd kidnapped to replace Tumalind as a Virgin Gift so many portions ago, had seemed to read his mind. It appeared his wife could also do so. Disturbing; to have his thoughts open. But then he realised he'd nothing to hide from Tumalind anyway.

'I can't really get inside your head, Okkyntalah. I'm just aware of how you think, especially when it comes to me.'

He hoped rather than believed that it was true.

Ouqitahl came over and engaged him in conversation, outlining their plan for what would happen once they found the party of pilgrims. They'd worked well together since their meeting during the fight in Ov-Bebna and he'd every reason to thank the soldier for his part in rescuing Tumalind.

'The Virgin Gifts have already been rescued, of course. But Feldrark wants us to continue as guards with the mission for the time being. Once the pilgrimage is well under way again, we'll decide whether we need to go further with them.'

'I'm hoping we can go back to Litkala with you and the troops, Ouqitahl. I'm weary of this wandering. I want to settle down and have babies with Okkyntalah.'

'I'd guess he's just as eager to do that, Tumalind.'

'I am. But we must go where we're sent.'

Almost, it seemed, like a signal of that truth, the fire mountain, Mount O'bo, blew a cloud of ash and smoke high into the air. They watched it rise and then fall slowly back toward the city, now far behind them, and wondered at the way those Followers lived under such a pall.

For now, however, their concerns were concentrated on the midges from the swamp the river passed through since they'd left the lake.

'These flies will eat us alive. I hope they're not going to be with us the whole voyage.'

'They're not, Okkyntalah. We'll be free of them by nightfall, if this wind continues. In the meantime, rub some of this onto your skin, and on your lovely woman. Unless she'd prefer the rough hands of a seaman to spread the oil?'

Tumalind gave the captain a speculative look, appearing interested, but then grinned at him. 'I'm for Okkyntalah alone, Pyqad. But thanks for the offer.'

'Aye, well, if you fancy a bit of variety, you know where to find me.'

Okkyntalah placed a protective arm about his wife. 'She knows, Pyqad. But don't hold your breath whilst you're waiting. I'd try one of the soldiers, if I were you.' He turned to Tumalind. 'You're wicked, you are; teasing the man like that.'

'Suppose I wasn't teasing? He's got a certain charm, you know.'

Okkyntalah frowned at her and then saw the glint in her eyes and hugged her close.

Chapter 3

AFTER THE ANNOUNCEMENT

Two days of utter confusion, with random acts of violence from both sides of the argument, had kept Aklon and his chosen deputies busy and almost totally sleepless. But, using those members of the army who'd converted to the Cause after Ivdulon's intervention, and some members of the Few, they'd managed to calm the populace before too many had killed each other.

Anecdotal evidence suggested those behind the Cause were in greater numbers, possibly as many as two thirds of the population of the capital. But those who remained loyal to the old ways were a formidable force and religious passion made them dangerous and volatile. It was clear he must do something to redirect their frustration and anger.

A second meeting in the square, controlled and disciplined by troops and armed members of the Few, allowed him to speak again to the people.

'You will not be here for long. Many of you are angry. Many are now grieving at the loss of loved ones after the recent violence. Let us have no more of it. We are civilised people. We are brothers, wives, sons, daughters, fathers, sisters, husbands, mothers. Are we to kill one another simply because we disagree on some rituals and rites? Does dogma matter more than life? It is true that we must make changes. And there will be things that some will welcome and others will abhor. Change is never easy. But let me assure you of certain matters, since rumours are spreading untruths amongst you.

'The practice of joining as and when both parties desire will continue. I enjoy the activity as much as anyone. However, we must modify the old rules concerning clothes, since these have been so central to our faith until now. You have freedom to choose how you dress. And that means anything from entirely naked to fully covered, except for the face, which is our only true way of recognising one another. Some will find such change difficult. But our attitude to nakedness is a major cause of dissent and we need to reduce it to the triviality it truly is. We are born without cover, it is therefore simply a natural state for us. From this time on, you may wear whatever you wish. But remember that no one is available for joining without their explicit consent, regardless of how they choose to dress.'

A small number of people in the crowd immediately removed their tabards and tossed them to the ground, causing some consternation. Aklon had to raise his hands in signal and his voice in volume to regain silence.

'We will do well to respect the rights of all to express their wishes. Naked is no longer sacred for many of us, but a natural response to the warm world in which we live. All punishments for former sacrilegious acts will cease at once. We will decide later what we consider is acceptable religious behaviour amongst us and will make appropriate laws to deal with transgressions. In the meantime, we will have no more whipping, no more beating bags, no more removal of sexual parts. But let us be clear on one thing: anyone found to have taken another by force will be severely punished. There will be no rape in this new society we are forging.

'There are aspects of our culture we need to consider for the future. In the past, we were ruled by priests, priestesses and the Holy Ones. Their rule is over. They have proved themselves untrustworthy and undeserving of any form of power. But we need leaders and a system to determine what laws we should adopt, and what methods we will put in place to uphold those laws. So, I ask you all to think on this matter, to form discussion groups where you may come to conclusions about what type of leadership we should institute to rule us in the coming days.

'Anyone found doing violence to another will have that same ferocity visited upon themselves during these days of change. There is but one law I give you to begin with and it is this: "Treat others as you wish to be treated yourself." If we all keep to this rule, there is little danger of wickedness.'

His words had been interrupted, there had been catcalls, dissent, cries of shock, agreement and praise, but the crowd was more thoughtful than angry as they dispersed. That they would, as individuals and in groups, express their disagreements in various ways he had no doubt. He could only hope to avoid any further major violence and instil an idea of tolerance.

Weary, he made his way back to his father's house, which was now the headquarters of the Few, and tried to get some rest.

One of Wendarah's slaves, a timid but sensuous girl with lustrous black locks and eyes dark as obanas, brought him a wooden platter laden with steaming seafood stew and a goblet of cool wine.

'Thank you. Who asked you to do this for me?'

'I'm a house slave, Paltrohn. I serve whoever's master. Are you displeased with me?'

'What is your name?'

'Hyllahn, Paltrohn. Have I caused you unhappiness? I'm yours to do with as you will...'

'No, Hyllahn. You have not caused me unhappiness and you are not mine. You are not the property of any other person. You are a free woman, to do and to go as you please, without reference to me or to anyone else.'

'You're dismissing me from your service, Paltrohn? I meant no harm. Is it the food?

18

Is it me? I can…'

'No, Hyllahn. You are not at fault. You are a very able and lovely woman. But I am now in charge on the island. You are no longer subject to the old laws. I am abolishing all slavery. You are free to lead your life as you wish.'

The girl allowed silent tears to trail tracks down her puzzled face. 'But how am I to live, Paltrohn? Where am I to go?'

Aklon sighed and ran his hand through his hair. 'You may stay here and continue with your old duties, if you wish. But not as my property, nor that of any other person. You are a free woman. Free, Hyllahn. You may do what you want. You may come and go freely. You may join or not as you desire. No one in this house will treat you as a slave. If you stay, it is as a member of the household and as a free woman. Do you understand?'

She stared at him, her mouth open. She still held the food and drink and looked for a place to deposit the items. Aklon stretched out his hands to take it from her.

'But if you're holding that, how will we join, Paltrohn?'

'You honour me with your offer, Hyllahn. But I need food at present, thank you. And you are not obliged to join with me. It is no longer one of your duties.'

She let him take the offerings. Turning a full circle, she displayed herself. 'Aren't I desirable, Paltrohn? Don't you want to join with me?'

'As to that: you're very lovely. But I wish to eat. And, for all that you are tempting and clearly available, I am in love with another woman and have decided that, from this day, I will join only with her. There are many men here willing to give you pleasure, if that is what you seek.'

'But they're not you, Paltrohn.'

'I am not Paltrohn. I am Aklon. The title neither suits me nor is necessary. We are equals.'

'Even so, I'd prefer to have you join with me for my first time as a free woman. Would that be so difficult?'

'Too easy, Hyllahn. But, as I explained, I am no longer available. I am exclusively the partner of another. Do you understand?'

'But what of Ytraa and the decree to join as and when we wish?'

'As to that, the words say "when we wish", and I do not. And, in any case, I no longer subscribe to the old ways and laws.'

'But, look. I'm here, ready, desirous, wanting you, Aklon. Please.'

'I am sorry. I am not ready. I await another.' He called to the others in the house. 'Any man here willing to join with this delightful woman?'

'But I don't want another, Aklon. I want you.'

'I am not available.'

Delbon came in and shook his head at the girl. 'You're wasting your time if you think Aklon's going to join with you. He's made it clear he's only interested in his woman in Morstahn. If you want some pleasure, come with me and we'll find you a suitable man.'

'But I'm a free woman. I want to choose for myself. I've spent years pleasing those I don't want. Now I'm free, I'd like to please, and be pleased by, the man of my choice.'

'So you shall. Hyllahn, isn't it?'

'I choose Aklon.'

'Well, you're in for a disappointment then. 'Cos, when Aklon decides he's going to do something, he does it. You'll not change his mind. Why not come with me and find someone who'll give you what you want, eh?'

'It's not fair! I want Aklon. He's set me free and I can do as I like now.'

'Right. So you think being free means you can do whatever you like? You've got to be responsible as well. You're not a child, Hyllahn. You're a grown woman, and very attractive. Loads of men would love to join with you. You can't have Aklon, and there's an end to it. Come on. Leave the poor man in peace. He's a lot on his plate.'

Delbon took her hand and she reluctantly allowed herself to be led away.

'Get her something to wear, will you Delbon? She is very distracting wandering around like that. If, of course, she wishes to be clothed. Oh, and make sure the rest of the house slaves know they are now free and may dress as they wish. There are spare tabards in Jodisa's old room. Use those.'

Once alone again, he ate the food and drank the wine without tasting either. Hyllahn's behaviour demonstrated yet another complication of his efforts to change the way the island and its people lived and were ruled. All slaves must be freed and allowed to lead their lives as they wished, as soon as possible.

As soon as possible. The Holy Ones were the source of most slaves, the organisation that had most to lose by freeing those in bondage. Perhaps now was the time to gather some of the more able amongst the Few and make that trip to the Plains of Ytraa to deal with the Holy Ones. It wouldn't be easy, but it was one of the most important tasks he faced. Yes. He would gather enough loyal soldiers, leave the town to sort itself out, and do something positive by setting free the sex slaves from the caves under Ytraa's Peak.

Tumalind discovered that Pyqad's oil had the desired effect, warding off the biting insects and leaving her free of their irritation. Its application also had the inevitable result of any attention to her skin by Okkyntalah, and they now lay side by side in the shade of the sails, hidden from public gaze by piles of gear and supplies stowed on deck.

Relaxed and still feeling that bliss he always brought her, she became aware, quite suddenly, of a sense of unease.

20

'What's the matter, Tumalind?'

'I don't know. Just an impression. I think it might be Mother.'

'See if Aklon knows anything.'

'No wonder I love you, Okkyntalah. Not only a wonderful lover, but a man who cares and thinks.' She kissed him and relaxed, sending out the thoughts to find the mind she needed.

'Tumalind, you are well?'

'Wonderful, thanks. Is Mother alright?'

'You felt it, too? I am not with her. You come to me on the road to the Plains of Ytraa, there to free the slaves held by the Holy Ones. But, if you were also aware of her distress, perhaps it is more than I thought. I should go to her in Morstahn and discover the cause. Thank you, Tumalind. I must leave you now, however, as we are traversing rather difficult ground.'

And he was gone.

'Aklon sensed it, too. He thinks it might be Mother, as well. He's changing his plans to find out what's happening.'

'Shame there aren't more like you on the island. If you could do this mindtalk thing with someone in Morstahn, you'd be able to find out a lot sooner.'

'Okkyntalah, you're brilliant! I'm going to range. Please stay with me, as I have to concentrate quite hard for this.'

Confident he'd protect her from anything outside, she plunged her mind into the magical world of mindtalk and sought a presence that might respond and lead her to more knowledge. There was much chatter in the strange place where those travelling minds met and crossed paths. There were shadows in the darker spaces; places it was dangerous to go, places where mad minds, bad minds, dwelt alert for those who might be vulnerable. So, it seemed, had Gadhallah been infected with his evil. She came across Teh-Blavv, idling on her way to Litkala and allowed her curiosity to lead to contact.

'Tah-Tumalind! How nice to talk with you. How are you and that amazing man of yours?'

'I'm actually seeking another mind, but I just wanted to know whether all is well with your party. Are you far from Litkala?'

'We've just passed through the mountains that Nuldron calls the Mascunl Crannel. Changed the camels for horses, and we're now riding across a vast open grassland by a lazy river. I think we'll reach the city in four or five days. I'm looking forward to all the wonders Nuldron tells us of daily. It's so odd, wearing clothes all the time. I'm hoping I can find a good man when we get there and start a real life.'

'You should contact Ivdulon, if you can...Oh! Obvious. Look, I've got to go. Please

don't try to get in touch with Ivdulon just now. I need her for something important.'

She left the former harem wife and sought out Ivdulon; an easy task.

'Tumalind, my dear. It's been too long. But you're troubled.'

She explained her difficulty.

'I've been putting out feelers for a while. There's someone in the town, sympathetic to the Cause and Aklon. Pelltryss is an older woman with no man, she can be a bit odd, but she should know the local news at least. I may be able to link you. Just a moment whilst I locate her.'

Tumalind experienced a brief hiatus, in which she seemed to be disconnected from the world. It was short but slightly discomforting.

'Good day to you, Tumalind. I'm Pelltryss. Ivdulon says you need help. What d'you want?'

'Thank you for connecting, Pelltryss. It's my mother, Shoarhn. She and my father run the farm in the northwest of the town; near the coast?'

'Aglydron's girl, are you? The beautiful one what was taken as a false Virgin Gift?'

'That's right. I don't know anything, but I just felt there was something wrong with Mother. Would you be able to find out for me, please?'

'I'm a bit long in the tooth to go gallivantin' but I can send me son, Hivoxahn. He can mindtalk as well, but he's not too good at it. He's in the stables. I'll ask him to go see her once he's finished muckin' out. Will that do you for?'

'Thank you so much, Pelltryss. It's worrying when these feelings come out of nowhere and you're such a long way from home.'

'Where are you now, then?'

'Oh, we're on a boat sailing up the River Mehrrhyph just out of Kah-Labaz.'

'Isn't that under that there fire mountain? The one with dragons?'

'It is. But I haven't seen any dragons.'

'Right, then. I'd love to see dragons, I would. Anyroad, I'll come back to you when Hivoxahn's found out. Can't rely on him to get through to you. He's not too good at this lark, see?'

'Thank you, I'll look forward to hearing from you soon.'

'Be near sundown before I can tell you anything, like. I'll say goodbye for now.'

And she was gone. Tumalind wasn't too hopeful. The woman sounded kind enough but not very bright and her son seemed a bit hopeless. She could only hope nothing serious ailed her mother. It would be a long day until she had the knowledge she needed to settle her mind.

Dagla Kaz stamped along the bank of the river for the fifteenth time since sun up. He gritted his teeth at the slow pace of work. Only half the trees needed had been felled so far and the threat from the Vagboh remained, an ever-present anxiety for him. The work was going too slowly.

'Can't we do this more quickly, Caarl? It seems to be taking an inordinate amount of time.'

'We're working as hard and as fast as we can, Dagla Kaz. But we lack the right tools and the youngsters are all green. If I had more soldiers, or a few more men like Tarruss, we could get on more rapidly.'

Frustrated by the logic and reason in the soldier's response, he stalked away. His anxiety had to be diverted. Porryh sauntered by, hips swaying in that inviting way. He couldn't have her but he could punish her for offering herself to the Vagboh. He followed her a short way until he caught her up.

'Stay, young woman. I've yet to deal with you for you wicked ways in the forest.'

'Corphanda's already done it. See?' she lifted her tabard and showed him the redness on her inviting rump. 'Anyway, you'd have done the same in my place, Dagla Kaz.'

Her cheek infuriated him. He grasped her arm and forced her to bend forward. With his free hand, he bared her buttocks and slapped her, hard, a dozen times. The satisfying smacks raised more red wheals on her virgin flesh and he responded to her vulnerability at once. This wouldn't do. He couldn't be seen to be lusting after a Virgin Gift. He dropped her tabard back into place and turned from her without a word. Kaz-Ca-Valorysta was supervising some of the young ones in stripping branches from the tree trunks and he signalled her.

She understood at once and walked with him into the edge of the forest to satisfy his lust in relative private.

Gratified, he allowed the priestess to wander back to her task before he left the trees and continued with his inspection of the work. All seemed to be going well and he praised Caarl for his ability to do so much in such a short time with so inexperienced a work force. The solider raised his eyebrows, but got on with the task.

<hr>

Shoarhn sat on the grass, head covered by the bag they placed whenever they stopped their swift march over the hills to the raised plain. She'd had time to recognise the position before they'd cut off her sight. They were camped on the edge of the Plain of Ytraa and would reach their destination the following day. So far, they hadn't molested her, apart from frequent slaps and pinches of her flesh as punishments for looking other than down at her feet as they walked in silence. The woman Holy One was worst with the slaps to her unprotected skin. Her arms, back, legs and bottom were all sore from the frequent attacks.

How long before they started more serious violence? How many would rape her? How many cuts would they make to her flesh? How much would she be burned as they tortured her for her association with Aklon? But she placed no blame on her lover. She knew, without doubt, the fault all lay with her captors. They were the ones in the wrong. They were the cruel preservers of a creed and belief system that she'd come to understand as fatally flawed.

The hood was lifted, a soiled goblet thrust at her.

'Drink.'

The water was tepid and none too fresh. But she drank. They replaced the hood. Her brief glimpse of her surroundings confirmed that the sun would soon set. They'd make her pray in that demeaning pose that had already been abandoned elsewhere on the island. So vulnerable in that posture, so open to attack.

The noises around her suggested they were organising shelter for their night's rest. Would she be bound again? Would they leave her in the open, unable to move, as they had the first night? She was reminded of her induction into the Few, when she'd spent a similar time in A'ahl's house as a test of her mettle. That trial had ended with an apology from her friend, the serving of wine and well-cooked food, and the salving of her sore wrists and ankles with a balm stroked on her by the fingers that had bound her.

She could expect no such mercy this time. These were the sworn enemies of her lover. These were the worst fanatics and extremists of a religion she'd left behind, except for superficial adherence to the rites and rituals necessary for normal life in the village. She'd thought Aglydron pious and extreme in his views and habits, but he was as nothing in comparison to these Holy Ones who seemed to live to inflict pain and humiliation on anyone in their power.

What, she wondered, did they actually want with her? That she'd be dealt with cruelly was in no doubt. But what did they expect of her? What would they require her to do? Or was it simply a matter of being taken to their secret caves so they could be as cruel and vile as she'd heard?

The hood was lifted again. The sun was low, setting.

'Pray.'

She made to stand and adopt the new pose but the man pushed her onto her knees. Vulnerable, she had nothing to say to a god she no longer worshipped and hoped she might escape attention if she was brief. The invasion came quicker than she expected but was no surprise. She must pretend again that she was blessed by Ytraa, as she had the day the High Priest had fathered Tumalind on her so many years ago. It was almost too much to bear. But she made no complaint, remained an impassive vessel for the lust of the Holy

One, and awaited only her chance to either escape or, if need be, to die quickly.

Finished, the Holy One kicked her onto her belly. Hooded again, bound hand and foot, she was rolled onto her back. No words were said as they prepared for sleep. She was left in the open. The night promised to be long and the day to come would bring no release from fear and torment. She must bear what she could until the end, refusing to show these perverted fanatics any emotion that might make them feel superior.

Chapter 4

AN ESCAPE ATTEMPT

In the end, it was the following morning before Tumalind heard again from Pelltryss. An earlier message from Hivoxahn had been unintelligible. He'd been incapable of expressing himself in a way that had any meaning, and kept losing contact. The garbled message was broken into small senseless parts, sometimes half way through a word. Tumalind wondered if the young man was completely sane. She decided to connect with Pelltryss herself, but had to wait, as the old woman was sleeping when she first tried.

'Didn't Hivoxahn tell you, me dear? By, but that lad's worse than useless, 'e is that. If I hadn't borne 'im of me own fern, I'd say he'd been put in me arms by some demon, I would.'

'Did he find anything out about my mother, Pelltryss?'

'What? Oh, yes. Seems she's been taken by them there Holy Ones. Led 'er from the town with nowt on. Some on them as still thinks this Gadhallah thing's the truth did their duty an' chucked shit an' muck at her, they say. I doubt you'll see her again. Well, not alive no 'ow. I'd forget about her, me dear. No point worryin' your 'ead about sommat you can't do nowt about, is there?'

Tumalind tried to get more definite information from the woman, but only received more rambling and opinion, none of which was helpful. In the end, she thanked the old woman and sought Ivdulon again.

'I'd contact Aklon straight away, Tumalind. And I've found another adept in your home town, who might be more use to you. I'll get her to connect with you as soon as you've spoken to Aklon.'

Aklon, well on his way to Morstahn, immediately turned round and set out for Ytraa's Peak. He had Phildrad, Delbon, a score of armed members of the much enlarged Few, and Choryssa with him. Delbon's mate had arrived in the capital with a small group from the jungle settlement as he'd left on the mission. They were intent on destroying the Holy One's power and evicting them from their stronghold.

'Take care. They may harm Mother if they spot you before you're in a position to attack, Aklon.'

'I am aware of the danger to Shoarhn, Tumalind. I will proceed as I see fit on arrival on the Plain. Do not worry that I will place your mother in more danger than she already faces. I love her. I love her more dearly than life itself. I will not put her at risk.'

'Thank you, Aklon. Keep me informed, won't you?

'I will. For now I must concentrate on getting to the destination. I will disconnect.

Please only come to me if you have useful information. That way, I am free to get on with the task in hand.'

As good as his word, he vanished form her mind only to be replaced almost at once by a new female voice.

'Tumalind? I'm Eyethlehn. Ivdulon explained the situation. I don't know exactly what I can do, but I won't sit here and allow your mother to suffer if I'm able to do anything to help her. I'll take a short while to prepare and then I'm off on the trail of those Holy Ones and your mother. Is there anything else you can tell me before I set out?'

Tumalind explained about Aklon's plans and thanked the woman, who described herself as a woodworker. She sounded both tough and capable and Tumalind was pleased to have her on her side. She also reminded her, probably unnecessarily, of the danger she might put Shoarhn in if she blundered into the caves blindly.

'I may be a simple carpenter, Tumalind. But I spent a year or more with the army before I settled to my trade. I'm strong and able, and, if I may say so, not as daft as you might think.'

'Forgive my needless advice; I'm just very anxious about Mother, that's all.'

'I understand. I'll keep in touch with both you and with Aklon. We'll do everything we can to rescue her, Tumalind. From what Ivdulon tells me, you've problems enough of your own. Let us deal with matters on the island. You sort out those difficulties you face with Dagla Kaz and his henchman. There's one other thing you might be able to help with here in the village.'

'Anything.'

'Your mother's girl, Dahrlahg, is it? She's been taken by that no-good priest, Kaz-Ca-Uldrad. They do say he's...well, she's still awaiting her first joining with her betrothed and they say the priest's raped her.'

Tumalind knew little of the girl, except that her mother had had trouble with her, as she was none too bright. But the thought of her taken captive by a priest and being used was too much. She advised Eyethlehn to find and speak to Irrildys and let her, with some of the Few, deal with the matter. She could think of nothing more she could do on that score.

'You make good use of this gift, Tumalind. Ivdulon said you were a good 'un, and it looks like she was right. Irrildys is a friend, so I'll get her onto it straight away.'

And she was gone, leaving Tumalind alone and back in the normal world again. Okkyntalah looked at her with curiosity and she explained all that was happening. Typical of her man, he took her in his arms and comforted her with his affectionate embrace and concern.

Feldrark held Jodisa's hand as they ascended in the riser. Teh-Blavv, dressed now in the tunic of a palace servant, a role she'd chosen as soon as Feldrark offered it, seemed relaxed and content as she rode with them.

Ivdulon was busy on the upper floor of the tower, so Netrodyl greeted them, offering cool wine and small savouries she'd made.

'Have you come up here to bother me just to fill your faces, or is there some more pressing reason for your interruption?'

Feldrark grinned at Ivdulon's impertinence, a feature he'd come to terms with over the years of her tutelage.

'Fret not, Ivdulon. We've come to introduce this young beauty from the desert to you and see whether she has the ability to understand any of your more arcane areas of knowledge.'

'How's the pregnancy, Jodisa? Still suffering the sickness?'

'A little.'

She turned to Netrodyl and spoke to the dark skinned woman softly for a few moments.

'Before you return to luxury below, Netrodyl will have a preparation that'll end the nausea for you. Now, this young woman. One of the Uhmbard's harem, I understand? Did you enjoy your life there?'

Teh-Blavv removed her tunic and turned graceful circles before the wise woman. 'I was decorative and, very occasionally, I was frowked by the...the bowelcreep.'

'I see. Well, here you've a choice in such things. You've a shape and appearance that will gain you many admirers in the city. Do you yet know what you wish to do?'

'I'm...I'm still trying to decide. I was taken by the Immallsu when I was very young and recall only a little of my earlier life. There's really little I can do. But I'd love to learn. I'm in the service of the palace for now; delaying a decision about my future. But I heard about your remarkable skills and, like Tumalind, I've a wish to discover new things.'

'Spend a couple of sixdays up here with me and we'll see what you can absorb. If you prove bright, we might be able to make better use of your abilities. Don't worry about Feldrark or Jodisa. They may be the worldly powers down there, but I rule up here. If I want you here or doing something more useful in the city, they won't stop you.' Her glance at Feldrark had him nod in confirmation.

'Stay and learn, Teh-Blavv, if that's what you'd like. I just hope the old crone doesn't turn you into a copy of herself. I enjoy bright women about me, but I can do without the usual tongue-lashing I receive when I venture into this witch's domain.'

'You'll get more than a tongue-lashing, my lad, if you don't show more respect. Now, off you go back down to that city of yours and let me get on with my work. Unless you've something of value to discuss with me, of course.'

'Teh-Blavv's been in touch with the Uhmteld in Ov-Bebna, Ivdulon. The former queen and the Uhmbard have been released from the Pit by a group of men who don't want the women to gain power. Well, she can explain for herself.'

Ivdulon glanced at Jodisa and nodded before she returned her attention to Teh-blavv. 'Well, young woman?'

'The Uhmteld was always sort of in-between with the wives and the Uhmbard. I suppose she had to be careful; as an older woman, her position was difficult. She could've been given to the common men any time, so she had to be clever. Anyway, once she got over the surprise of my contact, she told me she doesn't want the old rule to get back into power. The women are holding their position at present but there's signs they could be in difficulty if they're left alone. Is there anything we can do to help them?'

'I can connect with her and get the full picture. That'll allow me to form a plan for the women.'

'I'm not certain about the Uhmteld's loyalty, to be honest, Ivdulon. One of the wives, Teh-pavk, can mindtalk a bit. Might be worth talking to her.'

'Thank you, Teh-blavv. Of course, any physical help would have to be sanctioned by Feldrark and Jodisa. What do you think?'

'Do we know the population?'

'I can find out, Feldrark.'

'Do that, Ivdulon. Then we'll see what we can arrange. It might be a useful way of giving more of the army some field experience. When we start the real move forward, it'll be best for us if we have as many experienced soldiers available as possible. I fear we're unlikely to achieve our aims without some wider bloodshed.'

With that matter out of the way until further information could be gathered, the meeting seemed at an end.

'I'm wondering if we need to send any help to Aklon, Ivdulon. My brother's started his Cause, as he calls it. There's a good deal of conflict and it looks as though there'll be more killing there before the battle's won. Does he need material help?'

'I've intervened on a number of occasions. But I truly feel that Aklon needs to deal with that situation on his own, Jodisa, without any identifiable outside interference. I fear such intrusion would be resented by the people of the island. No. On balance, I think it best if we leave Muhnilahm alone. I'll keep an eye on things, of course. And I'll intervene as I have in the past, should it become necessary.

'At present, your brother's deeply involved in a dual mission: he's out to end the rule of those vile creatures, the Holy Ones, and is eager to rescue Tumalind's mother from their clutches. Oddly, none of the Holy Ones is a mindtalker as far as I can tell, so I've little insight into their particular world. You should connect with your brother and tell him any secrets about them that might help, Jodisa.'

Jodisa and Feldrark left. Teh-blavv remained with the wise woman, to learn what she might and to understand more of the world in which she found herself now she was free.

After a long day with axe and knife, preparing tree trunks for the raft, Aglydron gratefully accepted the food Chislanda brought. Equally tired, she sat with him, their backs to one of the outlying trees left standing because of its immense girth. Around the side, Linlyss and Myllthlan were also resting and eating.

'Will we finish in time, do you think, Aglydron?'

He glanced across to where the half constructed craft sat tethered to the bank, bobbing in the current and awaiting further work.

'I hope so. The work's exhausting. And having to keep constant watch in case those savages come back doesn't help. We won't be safe until we're on the far bank.'

'D'you think they will come back, then, Aglydron?'

Linlyss shifted closer. She looked anxious and Aglydron was uncertain whether this was due to fear of a second attack or because he'd always been unpleasant to her. He moved a little away from Chislanda until he could put an arm about the young virgin's shoulders. He held her close and squeezed the top of her arm.

'Don't you worry, young'un. I'll take care of you.'

She gaped at him in surprise. He knew he'd earned this disbelief. 'I'm sorry Linlyss. I was annoyed you paid so much attention to Okkyntalah. Jealous. Nothing to do with you; just me being me. Sorry.'

'I always believed you were a bigger man, Aglydron. I'm glad you can be so honest.'

Myllthlan's praise was enough reward for his effort. He smiled at her and the four of them gathered closer.

Caarl came across, inspecting and checking the physical state of his boat builders. None of them had been used to such hard physical work for a long time, though all their walking and hill climbing had toughened them.

Corphanda was with the soldier, her usual bag of herbs to treat blisters and small cuts at the ready. She and Myllthlan had decided that Corphanda would deal with small everyday hurts, Myllthlan would reserve her special healing powers for more serious injuries.

Aglydron let the little fat woman tend the blister on his right hand and then watched as she spread unction on a graze on Chislanda's thigh. Most of them had managed to attract some small injury during work on the escape craft; splinters being the most common complaint.

Caarl waited until Corphanda was done and then turned to visit the next group. He stopped, however and turned again to Aglydron.

'It's a great shame Tumalind and Okkyntalah took it into their heads to run off like that. He's a useful lad to have around. Good hunter and one of the best swordsmen and archers I've known. Wonder what made them go off into the wilderness alone? Seems such a dangerous thing to do, and so unlike Tumalind.'

Aglydron had the answer, but wouldn't risk the High Priest's wrath by spreading the information. The soldier wandered off when no response came.

'Why did she go, Aglydron?'

He turned to Linlyss, inclined to give her his usual rough treatment and then recalled his promise to be kinder to the young woman. 'Well, I'd rather you didn't spread this about, but she went because Dagla Kaz and Tryonta wanted to join with her and she wants to remain exclusive to Okkyntalah.'

'Isn't the High Priest 'er real father? Sorry, Aglydron; no insult intended. But that's what I 'eard.'

'Yes, Linlyss. And if I'd had the courage to admit it, she might still be here. I just hope she's safe, that's all.'

He left his food and wandered away, to be alone with his thoughts. He'd been in the trees only a short time when he was conscious of noises that suggested movement inside the forest. He stood, silent and still, alert. After a few moments he was certain. He crept from the forest and then ran quickly back to the camp and Caarl.

'There's someone in the trees, Caarl. I think the Vagboh are coming back. In great numbers if my ears are any guide.'

Aklon and his band of followers, all hardy and well prepared for difficulty, covered the ground rapidly.

'If we go this way, Aklon, we'll miss the bridge, won't we?'

'We will, Choryssa. I want to avoid the road as far as possible. We are few in number and the Holy Ones number some two hundred, apart from those they lost at The Point and in the capital. But I estimate there will be a hundred and seventy or so in the caves. We need an element of surprise if we are to stand any chance of defeating them.'

'Twenty four against a hundred and seventy?'

'That's nowt, Choryssa. At The Point it were three on us agin ower a thousand. An' look what we did.'

'It is not my intention to attempt to defeat the whole sect, Phildrad. I hope only to convert enough to start the necessary change and, of course, to free all their many slaves. Including Shoarhn.'

'Sure she's not the main reason for our trip, Aklon?'

'You of all people, Delbon, know we set out on this journey ignorant of Shoarhn's capture.'

'Still amazes me; the way you found out. I mean, I believe you, like. But to talk with people you can't even see. That's frowkin' amazin' if you ask me.'

'I concede it is a singular skill, my friend. But I am not alone in it and it exists whether you can witness it or not. Now. Shall we save our breath for the journey? We will shortly reach a crossing of the river, the only one available upstream from the bridge. It is dangerous and difficult. But if that oaf Aglydron can manage it, I have little doubt that we shall cross intact.'

'Is there anything Aklon doesn't know about this island of ours?'

'I doubt it, Choryssa. Nowt that matters, anyway.'

'I can hear you. And there are many things of which I remain ignorant. You have simply not come across a situation in which I have been unable to provide an answer. Yet.'

'Well, I 'ope this ain't gonna be the time for it, that's all I'm sayin'.'

Choryssa grinned at him. 'Agreed, Phildrad. We need to know all we can if we're to win.'

'Ytraa's balls! More chatter than a Priests' convention. Keep your voices low, if you must natter. Spies may be hidden anywhere.'

They trotted on, approaching the falls a little before sundown. The roar of the force was clear from a league away and when they eventually arrived at the spot above the crossing point, the group stared at the prospect with horror.

'We're not really going to try to cross here, are we, Aklon?'

'Not tonight. But first thing, as soon as it is light, we shall jump and leap our way over like young deer. For now, I think it most sensible if we set a single watch and spend as much time as possible in sleep. Once we have eaten, of course.'

'There's no other way? You're sure?'

'The bridge. And I am fairly certain that that will be observed, if not actually guarded. Our progress is not unknown and there are those who will feel it worth their while to garner favour with the Holy Ones in these dangerous times.'

'Well. If we must, we must. Bearing in mind our imminent deaths, Delbon, would you like to show me how much you've missed joining with me for the past couple of days?'

'Go on, the pair on you. I'll take first watch. But someone bring me a bit of food, eh? I'll sit up there near that rock.' Phildrad was as good as his word.

The group made a cooking fire whilst a couple of the more experienced soldiers

33

found food in the form of an injured male oxen that they separated from a small wild herd on the brow of the hill.

The night proved quiet and without incident. First light found them standing by the edge of the thundering fall surveying a crossing that had earlier almost defeated Aglydron and Okkyntalah. The fall dropped over fifteen manheights and the pool at its foot was full of jagged rocks that would kill anyone not drowned.

'That's a long jump, Aklon. And no run-up.'

'I need a strong volunteer to take the leap and carry the loose end of a rope across to the first landing place. That way, each of us can be tethered in case of stumbles. Who here is willing to take that risk?'

One of the Few, a small lithe woman, named Phrysilda, put up her hand. 'I can do it, Aklon. Been jumping gaps wider than that all me life.'

Aklon looked at the tiny figure and shook his head in doubt. Most children of thirteen cycles would dwarf her.

'Courage is one thing, Phrysilda; foolhardiness is something else entirely.'

'I can do it. Really I can, Aklon. Tell you what. Attach a light rope around my waist. Then if I fail, you can haul me back out, can't you?'

Faced with such determination, Aklon felt unable to refuse. But he was seriously concerned for her safety and agreed only with a heavy heart.

The midges were less numerous now that the swamp on the southern shore had given way to grassland merging with forest in the near distance. Favourable winds had helped them defeat the strong current, and Pyqad had used all his skills, even sailing through the night, to reach the other party as soon as possible.

They'd arrived more or less opposite the stranded party in the early hours of the evening, only just in time. Near the trees, Tumalind saw the Vagboh, attacking with rope boluses and pointed sticks for spears. The Followers were vastly outnumbered.

She sought Rrildyss Kaz and found her almost at once. *'Rrildyss, I spoke with Ivdulon about the Vagboh. They won't risk harming the women. You must make the men use the women as shields and the Vagboh will halt their attack.'*

'Tumalind. Where are you?'

'We're just behind you. We've a boat with soldiers on board, but you really must try to get the men there to see sense before they're all killed.'

'I'll try, but how am I to convince them? We daren't let Dagla Kaz know of this mindtalk…'

'I'll get Pyqad to come closer so we can call out to you. But that'll take too much time. Perhaps you can make Dagla Kaz believe you can hear our shouted warnings already?'

'It's worth a try.'

Tumalind broke contact so the priestess could concentrate on her task. The Vagboh, naked men, were present in great numbers and were clearly trying to avoid hitting the women with their crude weapons. But it was only a matter of time before they'd kill some of the men in the pilgrim party.

'They'll never stop them in time. I'm going to swim for it.'

Before she could prevent him, Okkyntalah had stripped off and dived into the river. He surfaced a good distance from the ship and swam swiftly toward the shore. But the current was strong and he was dragged downstream more rapidly than he could approach the bank.

Tumalind fretted as he struggled to get into the shallows. Then a cry from the land alerted all involved in the battle to the presence of the ship approaching. For a short while, all was still. Rrildyss took advantage and called out to the pilgrim party the advice Tumalind had given her.

There was clearly some disagreement amongst them. But one of the young men, a Virgin Gift, she thought, pulled a woman in front of him and began to back away from the field of battle toward the shore. When the attack was renewed, the Vagboh took no notice of him or his captive but attacked other men instead. The young man called out and some of the others recognised that the trick worked. More men drew women in front of them and moved backwards to the water's edge.

Dagla Kaz ran behind the lines of his fighters and cried out that those using women were cowards and should be ashamed. But Caarl saw the evidence for himself and recruited Myllthlan as his willing shield. They retreated to the bank unhurt. The High Priest, meanwhile, took a spear in the shoulder and fell to the ground.

A great roar of victory rose from the Vagboh at the fall of the leader of the group. They became bolder, running headlong out of the trees toward those pilgrims still fighting.

At precisely this point, the ship reached shore and the soldiers on board disembarked and began firing salvos of arrows at the Vagboh. The wild men halted under this assault, seeming surprised. But the relief was brief and they poured out of the trees in even greater numbers, yelling their war-like cries and descending on the few pilgrims still holding their ground.

Tumalind gripped the wooden rail, knuckles tensing white, as the sheer number of wild Vagboh overwhelmed the small group of men. Her horror was compounded when she saw Okkyntalah emerge from the water at last and run as fast as he could to join the fray.

Chapter 5

QUANDARIES

Aglydron saw those about him disappear toward the riverbank, each man clutching a woman defensively between his body and the advancing Vagboh. It was an act of cowardice he could never contemplate, especially with Chislanda, who stood beside him, armed and ready to fight.

The wild men swarmed from the trees in huge numbers. In moments they would be cut off from the main group. But running was too dangerous; a spear in the back the most likely outcome. What to do? How to rescue Chislanda?

'Oh, your foolish pride will kill us one day, Aglydron.'

She stepped sideways and placed herself in front of him, pushing him backward with her body pressed hard against his. At first he resisted, determined not to allow a woman to shield him. But Chislanda was not to be dislodged. And the Vagboh were no longer approaching him, turning their attention instead on the small group left. Two of the younger men still fought side by side, and a pair of the ship's crew stood firm, a little way off.

Slowly, he and Chislanda made their way back toward the shore. The four they left behind were soon overwhelmed. The young men were struck down and immobilised, though not killed. The female crew were captured.

'Here, Aglydron. Get aboard.' He turned at the cry from Tarruss and discovered the ship at last. Chislanda insisted on staying between him and the Vagboh as they shuffled backwards up the narrow plank, onto the deck. All but the four he'd seen surrounded by the Vagboh, were on board, along with others he didn't know and… 'Tumalind! How do you come to be here?'

The plank was lifted from the shore, leaving a narrow gap of fast flowing water between ship and riverbank. Only then did the chaos of their retreat subside.

'Who's left ashore?' It was Dagla Kaz, anxious and looking almost wild as he stared toward the wild men carrying off their women captives. His shoulder was bleeding but he seemed unconcerned.

The Vagboh left behind the young men, bound but seeming alive, no longer interested in them and intent only on escaping with the women.

'My girls! We have to rescue my girls.' Quyreena was distraught at the two young women taken into the trees.

'They're lost. We're too few to get them back from that hoard.'

'But they'll be taken to their city in the forest and made into wives to bear children.'

'That may be so. But we're powerless to help them now. I'm sorry, Quyreena, but we can afford neither the time nor the necessary forces to recover them. The risk's too great. We'll just have to accept that they're lost to us.'

'To me, you mean. You were anxious enough to recover your own precious virgins, Dagla Kaz. Why not my girls?'

'There's no comparison. Your girls are mere crew, of no significance in the wider scheme of things. My Virgin Gifts are vital to the success of our mission. Do you wish to bring down the wrath of Ytraa on the whole world?'

'Ytraa be frowked. I don't give that for Ytraa.' Her splayed fingers raked her hair. 'I'm no Follower. But I owe my crew loyalty. If you won't help them, I'll take the rest of my girls and go after them myself.'

'By all means, Quyreena. I appear to have a new ship at my disposal and yours is now no more than burnt and wrecked wood. But if you follow those Vagboh, you of all people, must know your fate and that of your crew members.'

The ship's captain stood irresolute on the deck that wasn't hers and gazed after the now vanished wild men. She shook herself and went in search of her remaining crew.

Aglydron knew Dagla Kaz was right, even though it seemed a dreadful thing to abandon the women to those wild men. But it was clear there were too few in their group, in spite of the enlargement with soldiers, to enable a proper rescue attempt.

He turned to Chislanda. 'Why did you risk yourself to save me? You might've been killed.'

'Did the Vagboh harm any of the women? Even those they took they just stripped and bound. But they carried them with care. They want live, fertile women. They're not interested in killing. They left the boys alive, look.'

He followed her pointing finger and saw a well-built young man, who seemed familiar, moving swiftly over the ground toward them. The captives were struggling to rise. Only when the other man stopped and helped them free their bonds did Aglydron recognise Okkyntalah.

Okkyntalah. And Tumalind.

Where had they sprung from? How did they come to be here at this moment of need? It was too much. His daughter and her husband had been chosen as heroes, selected by Ytraa to keep the pilgrimage safe.

Tumalind approached, her eyes fixed on Okkyntalah until she stood beside him and Chislanda at the rail. 'Hello, Father.'

'Hello, Tumalind. Except I'm not your father, am I? That's the High Priest. And if I'd had the courage to admit it, I might never have lost... But I haven't lost you. You're back here, safe and unhurt. How's this happened?'

'That, Father, is a very long story. Better told over food and drink and with my brave husband beside me to fill in details I'm ignorant of, I think.'

'And who are all these people you've brought with you?'

'All part of that story. Let's wait until Okkyntalah and those two lads get aboard, shall we?'

⁂

Feldrark rose from the bed and studied his wife; her belly only slightly enlarged, though her breasts had grown more. There, within the safe cocoon of her body, dwelt the heir to the kingdom. Was it boy or girl? Did it matter? Except, by long tradition, for reasons lost in time, the Wharhll had always been the firstborn male of the Kiral and Kirallah. And he so looked forward to having a new Wharhll to present to his people.

'Yes, my love, but the child will be what the child will be.' Her eyes opened and her smile followed her words. 'And we can make another, if this one happens to be a girl.'

'Now, there's a good idea, Jodisa. But I think we need more practice. Just to make certain we get it right.'

'You have the most wonderful ideas, Feldrark. But some are no use until they're put into practice.'

'Ytraa's balls! Do you two ever stop? First thing in the morning…it's just…well, I don't know what it is, to tell the truth. Anyway, I appear to have intervened in time. I need an urgent word. I'll be only a moment.'

'What is it, Ivdulon?'

'Don't be cross at her, Feldrark. She's a dried up old woman and can't understand the delights to be had by a potent man and lubricious woman…'

'You, Jodisa, had better watch that pretty tail of yours next time you come up to my tower; it'll be marked, young lady.'

'This is all very well, but it's neither progressing our lovemaking, nor satisfying your requirement for communication, Ivdulon. How can I help?'

'Teh-pavk's contacted me. She's helping that remarkable young woman Okkyntalah rescued to form a rebellion against their misogynistic menfolk. Well, it seems the men have recovered and healed the Uhmbard and he's formed a sizeable troop of males around him. The women are in trouble. The population's around five thousand, but the women are on our side and the men are poorly trained and badly armed.'

'And the women would like some help?'

'Exactly.'

'I'll send a troop as soon as I can get something organised. I won't have that backward desert despot gaining the upper hand again. Not after the effort we took to get him out of *power. We'll be there as soon as possible. Sorry, Jodisa, we've work to do.'*

'But we can recommence here once we've finished?'

'We must, I think.'

'You two: insatiable.'

'Condemnation, or envy, Ivdulon?'

'An observation.'

And she was gone. The royal pair sent palace servants on errands. In spite of the size of the population in Ov-Bebna, they felt a couple of hundred would be enough to quell the male rebellion. They could then help restore the fragile but growing equality they'd started with their first rescue mission. Although that had ostensibly been to save Tumalind from captivity, Feldrark and Ivdulon had long been seeking a reason to invade and destroy the vile faith practiced by those worshippers of a man made god: the so-called Immallsu. Now they had a little more to do if they were to make that good permanent.

Later, Feldrark must contact his other small troop and see what stage they'd reached with the pilgrims on their hopeless and pointless mission to Choshinahm. If he could oust Dagla Kaz from power on Muhnilahm, without appearing to have intervened, he'd be more able to combine the island Followers with his own, and then reform the whole faith.

Aklon's achievements toward rule were working better than expected. But the High Priest would quickly regain power if he returned to the island with the Godwood. Unfortunately, Feldrark couldn't risk failure of the pilgrimage too soon: he needed to know the situation in Choshinahm. He'd been informed Followers no longer existed. If that was true, the pilgrimage would fail of its own accord and he'd come out of the resultant mess with increased respect as a neutral leader who'd helped where he could.

With a combined force from Muhnilahm, Litkala, and Kah-Labaz, they'd have a real chance of spreading truth to the whole world and ending much suffering and inequality. His purpose would at last be achieved and he and Jodisa could spend the rest of their lives enjoying each other and their family in a world of peace.

⋯⋯

Aklon insisted on attaching the rope around the waist of Phrysilda himself. He wanted no accidents, no blame attached to anyone else, should she fail in this most dangerous of leaps. Whilst he dealt with the female soldier, others had cleared some of the bush from behind them, leaving a short but essential patch to be used as a run-up.

'I suggest you aim to slightly overshoot the strip of stone, Phrysilda. That way, you can lean against the rope on landing and we can steady you from here.'

'That was me plan, Aklon. I'm ready if you are?'

He examined the little woman. So slender, though unmistakeably mature. He looked away, conscious of his scrutiny.

40

'That's' alright, Aklon. I like you lookin'. Specially if you like what you see?'

'Very attractive. But now is not the time. Ready?'

She gave him a very suggestive smile and wink, nodded, and backed up the slope as far as she could. Swift and without hesitation, she covered the small strip of ground and launched herself over turbulent waters that threatened to drag any who stumbled down the fearful drop of the fall. With an accuracy that defied explanation, she landed on the narrow finger of rock, swayed a little, and righted herself.

'Oh, well done, well done, Phrysilda. Now, do you think you can reach the other side and tie the rope to that tall tree?'

The roar of the falls drowned her response, but she nodded her acknowledgement of his praise before she turned to study the lie of the land ahead. Aklon knew, from Tumalind, that Aglydron and Okkyntalah had used this dangerous crossing on their way back from the Plains of Ytraa after the Choosing. He'd done it only twice, during his lifetime of running and hiding, and it wasn't an experience he wished to repeat. This time, he had no choice. But a third attempt might be tempting fate rather too much and he offered up a prayer to his personal god, an idea rather than an entity, to guide him and his group over the treacherous river.

Phrysilda negotiated each of the many narrow crossing points in a methodical and studied way that turned her extraordinary courage into something that appeared normal. He had a real gem in this small but brave woman and must find a way to reward her once they'd rescued Shoarhn and removed the power of the Holy Ones.

Taking each stage as a single challenge, she made it across the roaring river and stood on the far bank, waving. Aklon waved back and pointed to the large tree above her. She shinned up the rise, untied the light cord from her waist, and began to haul the stouter rope across. Once she had the end, she secured it round the trunk and then dangled from it to demonstrate it was safe.

Now she must wait for the rest of them. Aklon fastened a loop, attached to a thin tether, around the fixed rope so it could be pulled back from the far side after each person had crossed.

Delbon went next, testing the way with his extra weight. He made the crossing look relatively easy, once he'd negotiated the first part, where the gap was too wide for some to leap. Once at the far side, he released himself from the safety loop and Aklon pulled it back. So the crossing began, with Choryssa remaining on the narrow strip of the first stage to steady any who might have difficulty with that awkward landing.

Aklon was last, urging Choryssa before him. The whole party had managed without loss. A couple of minor slips involved the victims in no more than a frightening dip in the swift currents. No broken bones; just bruises, grazes and dented pride.

Phildrad wondered if they should cut the main rope, now they were all across.

'I'd sooner we left it. Never know, might be useful again one of these days. An' it's not like we've got anyone after us, is it?'

'I think Phrysilda is right, Phildrad. We should leave it. I have difficulty envisaging it as of real use to our enemies.'

They stopped only long enough to eat and drink before they set out on the short trek to the Plain of Ytraa. Now they must be circumspect. The Holy Ones employed a lookout, positioned high up on Ytraa's Peak, to warn of approaching people. Once they emerged from the edge of the foothills, less than a league distant, they'd be in open countryside and visible.

'We must await darkness. I dare not let them know of our coming. They are brutal and without care for any they count as beneath them and may kill many of those we wish to free if they see we are on our way.' Aklon made this statement in the full knowledge that, even as he spoke, Shoarhn may well be suffering the most cruel treatment from them. The Holy Ones had distorted Gadhallah's already vile words and used them as a means to wield power and subjugate all who fell under their influence. 'I will rescue you, Shoarhn. I will.'

'Ay, but will you rescue me, Aklon? Rescue me from this longing? Eh?' Phrysilda took his hand and tried to urge him from the group to a place of privacy. He held fast, however.

'Your bravery has earned you a reward, Phrysilda. But I am not it. I will give you anything that is in my power, but I will not give myself to any but Shoarhn, who I love.'

'S'pose she's already dead when we get there?'

'In that event, I shall review my feelings. But I doubt I will consider joining with another for a very long time.'

'Shame. An' me 'ot as dragon's breath for you. Don't matter. I'll find another prod to quench the fire in me fern. For now.'

The little woman approached one of the men in the party who seemed delighted to be second choice of the heroine of the day. Aklon watched them depart and hoped she'd be content.

⁕ ⸙

The darkness was almost absolute. The temperature a constant chill on her unprotected skin. From somewhere close, unseen, Shoarhn heard weeping, though whether a man, woman or child grieved she couldn't tell. She'd lost track of time. Hunger was ever present. She'd had nothing but water since they'd taken her from Muhnilahm, and the trek across the island had been swift and demanding.

Everywhere hurt. Her feet were sore, her knees and hands grazed from falls caused by walking with the bag over her head for the last stage. And her flesh still smarted from the many smacks she'd received for the slightest deviation from their demands. So far, she'd suffered physical abuse, one unwanted penetration, frequent sexual assaults, but no actual torture.

What did they want from her? They'd hurt her until she gave them everything she knew of Aklon. But was she simply a hostage, to be destroyed as and when they felt like it? Was she captive to persuade Aklon to try to rescue her, so they could catch him and…and put him to the most painful death?

The weeping suddenly ceased. A short silence. A scream of absolute agony and then pleading; pleading by a child. A whip lashed. Another scream. The whip. A scream. The whip. A scream. On and on. She felt compelled to move toward the sound, knowing she could do nothing. Her hands remained bound, the bag covered her head. The ground she shuffled over was cool, hard, and smooth.

The whip. No scream.

'String it up by its toes and peel off what's left of its skin. They can watch and understand the rewards of disobedience.' The voice was harsh and uninterested; giving an order for supplies rather than dealing with a child's life. She shuddered and stayed still, no longer able to do what little she'd imagined she might.

'This one. What next?'

She recognised the voice of the woman Holy One who'd hit her most often on the journey.

'Give it a good hard slapping and tie it over a bench. We'll put it to the question it in the morning.'

'Can I slice it? I'd love to hear it scream and beg for mercy.'

'Not yet. I've special plans for that one. But slap it well before you bend and bind it for the night.'

She heard the approach and waited. The kick surprised her and she fell onto her face. The slaps were hard, many, and directed with cruelty. They left her smarting, sore and nauseous, but she refused to cry out. A final series, with the hood off so they could slap her face, made her bite her lip to prevent any sound escaping.

Dragged upward and hauled backwards over the sharp edge of a narrow surface, she was suspended free of the ground. To prove her complete vulnerability, the Holy One poked her with sharp nails.

'Tomorrow, that'll be hot iron. Then you'll scream, whore of Mhortag.'

A slap. She heard the soft flap of footsteps leaving. In the background, the sound of children moaning, crying.

Now she allowed the tears. Her situation was hopeless and she could only wish for swift death. But she knew it would be far from quick, and as painful as those Holy Ones could make it. As if to underline her fears, very quickly, the strain on her unsupported neck, as it held her head leaning back into thin air, became agonising.

Oh, Aklon, if only you could've found me before it was too late. But he was unaware of her kidnap and coming torture. They just wanted to kill her. Display her broken, tortured body to Aklon as a lesson on their power over him. Poor man would be devastated by what they'd do to her, would blame himself for their brutality.

The night was long. Morning, a lifetime away.

Chapter 6

A NEW VOICE

'Aklon, I'm new to this. Can you hear me?'

A fresh voice. The seeker sounded like a woman, but might not be. Who might try to connect with him?

'With whom do I speak?'

'I'm Eyethlehn, from Morstahn. Ivdulon contacted me and then I did this mindtalking thing with Tumalind. Amazin' isn't it? And I've spoke with Irrildys, too.'

'I am a little involved at present, Eyethlehn. Is your contact important?'

'They said you might seem a bit aloof, like. Yes. It is. I'm on the Plain of Ytraa. An' I think you should know there's a village priest here acting right queer. Tumalind said you're after saving Shoarhn from those 'orrible 'oly Ones. But I thought I ought to warn you about the priest, since 'e came up from the Chalamamnon road.'

'I see. Thank you, Eyethlehn. Are you a soldier, by any chance?'

'Was once. Carpenter and wood-carver by trade now. Why?'

'I think, in that case, you should make your way back home. It is likely to be dangerous here soon. The Holy Ones will not take kindly to your presence, and I have enough to worry about, trying to rescue Shoarhn and free the slaves.'

'Don't fret about me, Aklon. I can take care o' meself. Just watch out for that priest. I'm sure 'e's up to no good.'

"I am sure you are correct. He might well attempt to ruin our element of surprise. But there is nothing I can do about that. Please go back to Morstahn. I think you may do more good. Please Eyethlehn. Will you do that?'

'If you says so. Good luck with your fightin' then. G'night.'

She cut the connection. He hoped, rather than believed, she'd do as he asked. The worry of some silly girl from Morstahn trying to be a hero was an anxiety he preferred to avoid.

For a brief spell, he rested, but didn't sleep. As soon as darkness fell, they would approach the caves and take advantage of what little surprise they had over the Holy Ones. The priest would be Kaz-Ca-Atroad, the deviant who'd spent a lot of time and energy with Wendarah. No doubt he was up here to warn the Holy Ones of their danger from the changes.

'Hello Aklon. I'm so please Ivdulon did that thing and I can now connect with you at will. How are things going with you?'

'Porlesah. I am well. How is the situation in Pampahn?'

'You sound a bit distracted, so I'll give you my news and then wait for a better time to hear more from you.'

'That would be appreciated.'

'We, the Few, that is, have persuaded more than half the population that we're right. It's meant we're a lot safer now. Lasdilyss pretends she's recovered and sends her love to Phildrad. We're in charge of the town and I've dropped my title. Most of the Few are happy to have me with them, but a small number are still suspicious. They don't trust any of the priesthood. Not that I blame them. Well, that's all I wanted to tell you really. Contact me when you're less busy, eh?'

'I will, Porlesah. Thank you for your news. It leaves me in better spirits. I wonder; amongst the Few in Pampahn is a soldier who knows where the people from The Point are now settled. I think now would be a good time to advise them they can emerge from hiding and come onto the main part of the island, if they so desire. I suggest they look for a new home on the northwest point above Chalamamnon; it is more or less uninhabited but the ground there is fertile and there is a chance of sea fishing. No rivers, of course, but there are streams, springs and pools for fresh water. Yes. I think that might make a good spot for them to return to normal society. Will you set that in motion for me, Porlesah?'

'Of course.'

'Thank you. Now darkness approaches and I need to make plans, so I will leave you.'

'Make sure you visit soon. I miss you.'

'I will.'

He cut the connection and concentrated at once on the countryside around him. It was dark enough to set off for the caves. Phrysilda came last, her chosen man in tow, as the group gathered round. Nominating various small parties he expected to carry out specific tasks when they arrived at the cave entrances, he outlined his scheme. As a young man being prepared for his initiation into the rites for the priesthood, he'd visited the place. Explaining how light could easily trick with flaming torches flickering and reflecting from multiple black obsidian walls, he described the layout and look of the caverns.

Across the plain, they set out full of anxious anticipation. They were outnumbered by a factor of ten to one, but hoped surprise and experience would give them the edge in overcoming such odds.

Tumalind wondered about her mother's fate. She lay beside Okkyntalah under the sky on deck and, ignoring her own plight for the moment, sent out a connection to Aklon.

'Are you able to talk, Aklon?'

'Not now, Tumalind. I am leading a party of soldiers and the Few to rescue your mother. I will contact you as soon as she is safe.'

'Thank you, Aklon. I'll leave you to your mission.'

She broke the connection and rose to a half seated position to look along the deck. The boat had sailed across the river and anchored close to the western shore, free of the swamp, at last. The current and small waves made the vessel rock slightly but in a way that would have been soothing had she not been so anxious about her mother.

Dagla Kaz was in conversation with Ouqitahl, who she hoped would make it clear that Feldrark had promised her security after her rescue from the Immallsu in Ov-Bebna. Aglydron's open and loud declaration that he wasn't her father, but that Dagla Kaz was, certainly made her position in that regard more secure. The High Priest was unlikely to try to join with her now the whole party of pilgrims were aware of their relationship. That, however, would mean nothing if she ever found herself alone with him, as Jodisa's experience had proved only too well. And, of course, Tryonta was now more dangerous than he'd ever been, since she'd openly challenged him and made it clear she wanted nothing to do with the man.

Okkyntalah slept beside her. Once more, she thanked her personal god for putting her with him and gifting them with such love for each other.

'Ivdulon, are you free to talk?'

'As always, Tumalind. You're troubled?'

'I'm in danger here, even with the soldiers. What's Feldrark got planned, now the Virgin Gifts are safe?'

'The troops will protect you, providing you're not alone with either of those two men. Feldrark wants the rescue party to remain with the pilgrimage. We need it to succeed as far as possible, and they're more likely to complete the whole thing better secured.'

'Can't Okkyntalah and I set off back to Litkala now? I'd feel safer risking the wild again than staying close to Tryonta and Dagla Kaz.'

'I understand, Tumalind. But I'm convinced you and your amazing husband have something more to contribute to the larger plan before you return to your island.'

'How I long to return to Muhnilahm and make babies with Okkyntalah.'

'I know. But, for reasons I'd rather not disclose, Okkyntalah wouldn't be safe on the island. Better for him if you stay with the pilgrimage for the time being. And you're no longer in real danger, provided you never allow yourself to be alone.'

'Why's the island dangerous for Okkyntalah?'

'I suppose you ought to know. When he was getting water for the trip to Ylcrat with Jodisa and Aglydron, he humiliated the woman who leads the people of The Point. Chellyth *is a proud and stubborn woman. Even though Aklon's told her that her freedom, and that of her people, is in part due to Okkyntalah, she's sworn to kill him as soon as she meets him again. If you wait until either Chellyth is no longer a leader, or until she can be civilised by more cultivated people, I think Okkyntalah will then be safe.'*

'Thank you for you honesty, Ivdulon. I'll have to stay and risk it for the moment, I suppose. I'll be happier once Mother's safe, though.'

'Aklon's doing all he can. But his task is neither easy, nor without risk. Be patient.'

'I'll try. Thank you Ivdulon. I'll sleep now.'

The connection broke and Tumalind lay down with her skin in contact with Okkyntalah's, safer in his arms than anywhere else.

<hr>

That they'd encountered no sign of opposition, even within the cave entrance, worried Aklon. The Holy Ones had a reputation for arrogance and disdain regarding the general populace, but to be so complacent seemed utterly insane. He feared a trap. Perhaps they'd discovered he was on his way. Maybe they'd suddenly emerge, in great numbers, from the inky blackness of the subterranean chambers.

The passage he led his followers down flickered with unreliable light from lamps burning acrid smelling oil that made the shadows live with unseen threat. The party remained quiet; all communication made by hand signal or touch. Bare feet on solid stone, cleaned daily by many slaves, made less sound than the faintest whisper. Silence around them was broken only by occasional whimpers or moans that seemed to begin in multiple locations. These should be a guide to the place where Shoarhn might be held, but their very multiplicity made detection of her whereabouts difficult.

Aklon's previous experience refilled his mind as he led the party forward. He knew where the slaves dwelt, too frightened to do other than obey their masters. The memory of his earlier trips returned and he recalled where those under sentence of death were held; generally bound in painful and humiliating positions. He moved toward this location first; Shoarhn his primary motivation. The slaves were in no immediate danger and he could release them once he'd rescued her; if, of course, she was still alive.

The picture of her under torture was too much and he rejected it. He must concentrate on the rescue and worry about consequences only if the search proved fruitless. The group passed openings dark with threat and breathing fear. Avoided passages that bore the smell of kitchens, or the dank, putrid stink of latrines. Through the many storerooms and down flights of steps into the deeper, darker part under the mountain they descended. The air, oppressive and foul with human waste, sweat, and blood, carried pain.

The chambers and passages here were arranged to make all visitors insecure and threatened. Everything was designed to make prisoners as miserable as possible. Nakedness was standard; no particular threat, so captives were deprived of security by having thick bags placed over their heads. Blinded, sounds muffled, smell and taste diminished, they dwelt for the short space of time they inhabited these cells in a world without guides. Bound, and subject to random violence, some went mad from fear in this dreadful place.

As they passed through the various passages, each member of the team borrowed a lamp, until all were furnished with their own light source. The lowest reaches were deliberately left unlit; the Holy Ones carrying lamps when they visited.

A sound close by had Aklon halt the party. They held their breath and listened. But the sounds were no more than cries of pain and despair felt by prisoners.

They reached the individual cells: simple open cubicles where each prisoner was held in isolation. The first was empty. In the next, an old man hung upside down by one toe. His other leg had been fastened sideways to a ring in the wall and his arms twisted behind him and tied up to the ceiling.

'I am about to remove your bag. I am a friend. It is essential you remain silent as we free you. Wriggle your free hand if you understand.'

The old man's fingers moved slightly. Between them, they cut the bindings and removed the bag, loosened his bonds and gently placed him on his back on the ground.

'Remain here. Silent. We will return when we have freed all other prisoners.'

One of the party stayed with him, massaging life back into his tortured limbs. The rest moved on.

The next cell held a young woman. Suspended horizontally in mid air by tethers attached to her big toes and thumbs, she was spread-eagled in a cross shape.

Aklon used the same procedure he had with the old man. She cried out in pain after they took off the bag. A careful hand and kind words stopped her emerging scream as they released and lowered her with care. Another of the party remained to comfort her and help the life return to her stiff, strained limbs.

Shoarhn was suspended in the next cell.

'I am here, Shoarhn. We will release you. Please try to remain silent.'

He took off the bag first and she gasped quietly.

Sounds from beyond alerted them to the arrival of trouble. Each group member lay down his or her lamp, giving an eerie and sinister appearance to the already oppressive place. The Holy Ones came without apparent concern for their safety; without, it seemed, any expectation of serious conflict.

'Surrender your arms and remove your sacrilegious garments in this holy place.'

The group acted as one, each member selecting and attacking a Holy One. Aklon

49

remained in front of Shoarhn, to protect her from malicious attack. It was as well he did. One of the Holy Ones emerged from the fighting and lunged forward, intent on killing both of them. The futile and hopeless gesture ended his life.

The attack was over almost as soon as it had started and Aklon puzzled over the small number they'd sent. Unless, of course, they had no idea of the size of his party. Certainly, no experienced leader would send so few to attack so many.

Once all the Holy Ones had been killed, he returned to Shoarhn. He released her bindings, gently holding her so she wouldn't damage her skin further on the rough stone of the bench around which they'd forced her. Unable to stand, her neck so badly strained that she couldn't hold up her head, she needed support. Dryness prevented her speaking, but she croaked her thanks and relief.

'I have to see to others, Shoarhn. Delbon will stay with you until we return.'

He was reluctant to leave her but had no choice. They discovered another three prisoners; a young man, a middle-aged woman and the skinned corpse of a young boy. The woman had died in her captive position; a death that must have been agonising because of the way she'd been left dangling and trussed.

They had to carry those they'd rescued, as none could walk. Two identified themselves as members of the Few. The old man acknowledged that he'd fallen foul of the Holy Ones by failing to part with his last coin when it had been demanded of him.

A narrow tunnel led off the entrance to the prisoners' cells; the emerging stink unbearable. Phrysilda stood and listened. 'Kids, I'd say.'

Aklon nodded and she and one of the shorter men entered the passage, their heads brushing the upper surface. A short time later, they emerged leading a small gang of children, silent and traumatised but able to walk unaided.

'Slaves next.'

At the top of the steps, silhouetted against the myriad lamps gathered there, stood a group of armed Holy Ones. Aklon made a quick estimate. His party numbered twenty-four able-bodied and half as many in need of aid. Their fighters were outnumbered almost three to one. And the Holy Ones held the advantage of high ground.

Okkyntalah was unsure what had woken him. Beside him, Tumalind lay relaxed and sleeping. The flickering light of a torch revealed her exposed to the night air. Obscured by the flames, the face of the carrier was unidentifiable, but the body shape and stance revealed Tryonta. That he was so obsessed with Tumalind he'd risk a public shaming for his scrutiny, sent a message of real concern to Okkyntalah. He swiftly covered his wife with their shared sleep sack. Tryonta lowered the torch, thrusting it into Okkyntalah's face so that he had to move quickly to avoid being burnt.

'Think she'll escape me again, boy? I'll have her. See if I don't. You can't run forever. I'll have the whore, even if I have to kill you for it.'

He left. Silence fell again. No one else was awake on the deck of the softly swaying vessel. The stars overhead blinked down in all innocence and the Skyfire drenched the low horizon with a bright splash of flame the colour of dragon's breath.

Should he tell Tumalind? It would only cause her more anxiety. The talks with Pyqad, Ouqitahl, Dagla Kaz and the others had gone on long into the night. Daylight would reveal the plans and fates for all the party. Tumalind had told him they'd been promised security from attack by Ivdulon's intervention with the mindtalkers in the discussions. But Tryonta's threat was real. They'd run away once to escape him. He wouldn't run again.

No. He must find a way to expose the truth about Tryonta. A potential rapist on a journey with so many Virgin Gifts must be unacceptable. Even Dagla Kaz, with his distorted and biased views, couldn't allow someone like Tryonta to remain a risk to the girls. He must find a way to make the High Priest see Tryonta as a real and present danger; that the girl virgins were in peril as long as the man remained part of the pilgrimage.

But how? Dagla Kaz employed the man as his right hand man, his personal bodyguard, his trusted second. Was he really so blind? No, not blind. Unwilling to see the truth. The High Priest also wanted Tumalind for himself. It mattered not to him that she was his daughter. Publicly he'd make no move. But if the High Priest was able to get Tumalind alone... Was there any point in reporting one potential rapist to another? None. There had to be some other way. But what?

The night stretched long before him and he continued to worry as dawn raked the sky with a myriad colours, promising another fine day. The weather might be good, but he had no solution to his problem. Perhaps another escape was the only way. But Dagla Kaz had more soldiers at his command this time and may send a search party after them. What would happen if they ran off again and were brought back before the High Priest? Dagla Kaz would find it reason enough to have him executed. What hope then for Tumalind?

Escape wasn't the way. But he had no idea what it might be. How to end the threat facing them? Time, perhaps, would tell. But in that time, Tumalind remained vulnerable. He must stay as near her as possible. Must never allow her to be left alone. But he'd be called on to hunt for food. He'd make sure she stayed always with someone trusted whilst he was away. Tarruss was a soldier, not a hunter. Tarruss he trusted to guard Tumalind. That giant of a man would protect her, at least.

Teh-blavv, having escaped the harem and the boredom of that captivity with little attention, had been looking forward to a life of activity and fun, preferably with a man of her choice. But the call to send new troops to Ov-Bebna, to help the women fight the Uhmbard, found a response in her. She discovered she cared about her sisters in the desert. She couldn't let them do battle alone, even though her skills as a fighter were minimal. Her ability to mindtalk would be useful to Feldrark, with whom she'd fallen in love almost on meeting. And she could connect with the Uhmteld, who was, surprisingly, apparently helping the women in their battle.

Feldrark she loved not simply as a man, but as a leader with power and presence, a man who ruled with kindness and justice. She had no delusions that he'd leave Jodisa, his wife showing the first signs of pregnancy. Although she found him sexually attractive, her love was of a different sort. She felt driven to serve him in the best way she could. And, in spite of her desire to learn what she might from Ivdulon, joining the fight in Ov-Bebna seemed the most useful thing to do. And, so, she'd left the high Tower.

'You do know it'll be 'ard an' dangerous, lass?' Sondukal, a scout and seeker of ways was a man she could trust.

Jodisa had told her of his part in previous expeditions. He showed no interest in other women; faithful to his wife. This intrigued Teh-blavv at first, until she discovered it was quite common for men in Litkala to remain true to one woman. Something so strange to her, she found it an admirable quality and one she'd seek in a future partner. But, for now, she'd be a soldier, of sorts, and fight for a cause she believed in.

'I do know, Sondukal. But my life before this was hard in different ways. I lived naked, awaiting the attentions of a man I loathed, one who should've been able to satisfy every woman's desire and need but who cared for none of us. He lives only to satisfy his own lust. I'm coming along to see that man brought down. Do you know, in spite of the fact that he spreads his seed at least three times a day, he hasn't sired a single child. Not one. What does that make him?'

'Useless as a father at any rate, lass. You're fine looking wee things, the pair on you. Any man would be proud to have either one o' you on his arm. Now, let's get you an' Tah-Vlatak partnered with experienced soldiers, so you can at least swing a blade wi'out cuttin' off yer own 'eads, shall we?'

Although not a soldier, Sondukal had been tasked with ensuring the two women from Ov-Bebna would be able to defend themselves and not become liabilities in the coming campaign. He led them to where the troops were gathering and found a couple of female soldiers willing to take them on as apprentices.

Teh-blavv looked at the party as they prepared for the journey to the mountains. She was unable to count, unlike that wonder, Tumalind, but there were a lot of soldiers gathered. She asked her new companion and mentor

'There's near on two 'undred of us, Teh-blavv. How d'you feel about returning to the place you've escaped?'

'Tell you one thing. I'm doing away with that daft title they put on me. I'll be plain Blavv from now on.'

One of the male soldiers close by laughed. 'Plain, lass? There's nowt plain about you. You're a goddess. Wouldn't mind joining with you, if you're inclined, like.'

She looked up at the tall stranger and assessed him for the qualities she wished to find in a man. 'Perhaps, soldier. You might be the one. But I need to know more about you before I invite you to into my fern. I'm looking to be satisfied, not used.'

'Never had no complaints. You'll never find out unless you try, will you?'

'Perhaps not. But I still want to know more about you before I raise the hem. I'm not a Follower, willing to frowk with any partner. I was, when very young, but I've been an Immallsu for so long now I can't recall any other way. Since I don't like the Immallsu way, I think I'll have to make up my own until I learn more about the way of things here in Litkala.'

'At least you'll not be forced. Men and women are equal here.'

'I know. That's why I'm going back to Ov-Bebna; so we can get that city to be the same and stop men using and abusing women. Now, I need a horse. Anyone care to show me where I can find one?'

The female soldier who'd been detailed to teach her self-defence took her and showed her the animal she would ride on the journey. A small well-formed black mare. She mounted it at once and sat easily on the muscular back. This was to her liking: an adventure in the offing, new skills and a purpose. So much more to look forward to than when in that harem.

She looked across the lines of troops and saw Tah-Vlatak struggling to mount a grey gelding. Helping her was the same soldier who'd asked to join with her and she understood he, at least, didn't display that most essential of qualities she now sought. His interest lay in any available female but she was now determined not to share with any other woman. The next man who joined with her would be the only one for the rest of her life.

Chapter 7

IN THE CAVES

There was no point in delaying. Talking with religious extremists was a waste of time. They listened to no one, convinced they were right and everyone else was wrong, convinced they had the right to treat all who didn't conform to their own narrow definition of Following as inferior beings. No. There was nothing to be gained from any attempt at discourse. The blade was all they understood. Did such stark thinking place him alongside the fanatics? He had no time to contemplate the finer philosophical arguments: this was a fight to the death.

Aklon led the charge up the steps: a hard and potentially lethal fight on their hands. His sword struck the nearest Holy One even as the man lunged at him. He helped him on his way down the steps, his blade slicing into flesh as the fanatic passed. Whether he lived or not was unimportant; he'd take no further part in the fight. Around him, his trusted colleagues fought without fear; cutting, stabbing and slashing their way up the stairs. Blood flowed freely down the stones, making the surface slick and difficult. The Holy Ones may not be trained fighters but they had passion and a reckless disregard for their own safety that made them very dangerous. Death held no fear for these fanatics who believed it would deliver them as heroes to the Garden of Delights.

The fight was hard and costly. Most of his people had suffered cuts and two had died already. They had taken many with them but the Holy Ones greater numbers must give them a real advantage. If only they could gain the top of the steps, they might have a better chance. Aklon's people were all trained fighters, all experienced in the field. But they weren't only fighting, they were also defending the helpless prisoners they'd rescued.

The uneven battle grew more and more bloody. The Holy Ones were careless of their own lives and sheer numbers must soon overwhelm Aklon's small force. He glanced down and saw Delbon, still at the foot of the stairs, standing sole guard to the rescued prisoners. Five Holy Ones lay dead at his feet and the helpless foursome crouched or lay behind him, fearful and unable to defend even themselves.

Aklon turned in time to catch the blade of a Holy One who'd seen his momentary distraction. The sword cut into his left arm but he swept it up and away and then sliced through the belly of the man. He fell at his feet and didn't move again. Aklon stepped over the body and gained another step. Beside him, Choryssa fought with the confidence and skill of the experienced soldier. He was so glad he'd been able to spare her when he'd taken the troops at The Point. She'd proved her worth repeatedly. Now, blood flowed from a leg wound but she ignored it. And he must, too.

Another Holy One, small and singularly beautiful, attacked him. Her eyes gave the lie to her appearance. Such hatred there, such intensely violent intent. He brought his blade up as she thrust hers at his chest. His side step avoided her thrust but her momentum carried her down the steps and he disembowelled her as she fell against his sword.

Choryssa tackled another pair who'd taken the place of the man she'd defeated. Aklon also took two on. The fight was growing more and more difficult. And then, as he dispatched the man towering over him from the steps, he grew aware of more arriving behind the Holy Ones. More to fight. More to be killed. For a moment he almost faltered in light of the impossibility of the task. But he drove his sword into the woman facing him and carried on, determined to finish what he'd started here, even if it resulted in his own death, which now seemed inevitable.

The discussions between Dagla Kaz, Ouqitahl, Quyreena and Pyqad seemed to last all morning. Okkyntalah had woken in sombre mood and Tumalind couldn't discover what had caused him to lose his usual happy demeanour. But, serious as he was, she urged him to move closer with her so they could hear what was being discussed so earnestly.

It quickly became apparent that the main sticking point lay with Quyreena. She wanted to return to Kah-Labaz with Pyqad's boat, so she and her remaining crew could somehow find a way to continue their trade. Dagla Kaz was being his usual stubborn self, refusing any compromise and arguing that any delay would cause him further problems.

'May I speak out of turn, Dagla Kaz? If Pyqad hadn't arrived with his boat, where would we and the pilgrimage now be?'

Dagla Kaz turned on Myllthlan. 'What do you know, woman? A heathen like...'

'Such rudeness is unlikely to help us, Dagla Kaz, Myllthlan is a volunteer on this pilgrimage. And a healer who's now twice healed your wounds. You don't see it as unwise to dismiss her comment? She's right, anyway. Without the arrival of this boat and the troops from Litkala, we'd now be in a sorry state indeed. Since Ouqitahl has Feldrark's blessing to accompany us with his soldiers for the rest of the journey, it might be wise to consult him on this matter; don't you agree?'

The High Priest balled his fists at Rrildyss' comments but remained silent. Ouqitahl took advantage of the break.

'It'll take us a sixday at most to Kah-Labaz and back to this spot. Since you'd have lost much more time than that chasing the Vagboh, it makes sense to take Quyreena and her crew back to the city. As ship's captain, Pyqad's declared his wish to do that anyway. There's a code of honour amongst seafarers that it's unwise to ignore.'

So it was; the ship turned in the river and, sailing with the current, made good time back to the city under the fire mountain. The dragons, said to dwell in the cone at the mountain top, seemed angry and breathed fire, discharging clouds of smoke, ash and small rocks as the party approached.

'An omen. I tell you we should avoid returning. But no one listens to me.'

'Mount O'bo breathes fire like this every few portions, Dagla Kaz. It's no omen. This is the way the fire mountain is. Those of us who live beneath its slopes know it well. There's nothing unusual here.' Byfthlyn was a Virgin Gift who'd volunteered to join the pilgrimage from Kah-Labaz. He was also one of those who the Vagboh had bound as they fled the scene of the recent battle.

'A mere lad. What do you know?'

'Only what I've witnessed for eighteen cycles, Dagla Kaz. Can you claim such experience of the fire mountain?'

Dagla Kaz said no more. He stomped off. Tumalind could see the anger and frustration in his face. The High Priest was growing more and more impatient as the pilgrimage moved closer to the ultimate destination. It was as if the man feared what he might find there. And, recalling what Ven-Gadla, the merchant who'd taken them for much of the way on his carts, had said, Tumalind was unsurprised at his growing doubts.

'Should we remain behind in Kah-Labaz, Tumalind?'

'That would be the easy way, Okkyntalah. And I'd love to do it. But Ivdulon believes we're vital to the success of the pilgrimage.'

'Why does she care about the pilgrimage? In fact, why does Feldrark care? They say the Followers should end and we should look to some other faith in the future, don't they?'

'I wasn't aware you knew that, Okkyntalah. I can't tell you why they want the pilgrimage to go ahead, because I don't know. But they're concerned that many lives may be put at risk if it fails.'

'And our lives will be at risk each day we stay with Dagla Kaz and Tryonta. It seems unfair to ask us to do this without telling us the real reason.'

'To be absolutely honest, Okkyntalah, I don't think they know the reason themselves. They just have a feel for these things. Ivdulon's proved herself wise in so many ways and Feldrark has been a good friend to both of us. He sent troops all the way from Litkala to Ov-Bebna, just for me, don't forget. I'm willing to do as they wish, at least for the time being. What do you say?'

He kissed her. 'Of course. If that's what you want. Just make sure you're never alone with either of those two.'

She followed his glance the High Priest and Tryonta, who were both glaring their hostility at Myllthlan. 'I will, Okkyntalah. I will.'

Feldrark turned to watch Jodisa slip into the water beside him. The day had been long and boring with much talk of routine state matters. Few decisions were needed, and the only cause for any concern had been a dispute between two women captives from Mipahnhil, who'd he freed along with others after the battle. Their grievance appeared to Feldrark to be a small issue. They'd argued over the length of their respective tunics and had caused a public outcry by resorting to physical violence that had resulted in one woman stripping the other.

The pair had been brought before them in the great hall and he and Jodisa had assembled all the former captives from that city they'd destroyed. The public humiliation of both women in front of their compatriots and the declarations they'd been required to make regarding future conduct should prevent a repeat at any rate.

Jodisa, perhaps more understanding of the ritual role of their female clothing, had made a timely suggestion. *'Aklon says he's given the islanders complete freedom to be anything from naked to completely covered, Feldrark. Maybe it's time we did the same and removed our rules about Followers as well?'*

'Another stage on the road to destroying the faith? Good idea, Jodisa.'

'I don't give a rhaaht's fart for what you wear. You can be naked or covered from head to toe; apart, of course from your faces, which must always be visible. But I want no more trouble from you. You're new citizens in this city and it's incumbent on you to demonstrate your trustworthiness. This new rule about apparel applies to everyone in the city, by the way. So don't run away with the idea that you're being given preferential treatment.'

With that, he and Jodisa had left them to their deliberations and made their way to the pool for some relaxation, talking along the route.

'Now, to more important state matters, my love. You're twelve weeks into your pregnancy?'

'I should now be safe, yes.'

'Then it's time for the announcement.'

'Is that a state occasion?'

'Oh yes. And one that demands a special act from you.'

'I get to display my naked body to the entire population, do I?'

He smiled at her grin of mischief. 'I'm afraid you do.'

'Oh! Just me?'

'You're the only member of the ruling family who's carrying a child, an inheritor of royal office.'

'But you're the father. Why should you escape?'

He was thoughtful for a moment. 'Sometimes it takes a mind free of tradition to see that some customs aren't what they may be. I will, indeed, display with you. We are, after all, equally responsible for bringing this heir into the world.'

'I don't have to give birth in public, do I?'

He laughed. "Oh, you're serious. No. That will be like any other in Litkala: a private affair attended only by midwives and the husband.'

'Well, that's a relief. How closely will the populace be able to inspect us?'

'You recall our wedding day?'

'On the platform, then?'

'I'll get the whole thing organised for three day's time. I'd better warn Ivdulon.'

'She won't come.'

'Ah, for this ceremony she's required to attend.'

'Let me go up and tell her. I like visiting her tower.'

'Only if you promise not to lean out over the Red Rill like you did the last time we went up there. I thought you were going to fall to your death, Jodisa.'

'Idiot. I'm enjoying myself far too much to risk ending it all. But I'll be good and stay well inside the Riser. Promise.'

And so she'd gone off to announce the ceremony to Ivdulon, as Feldrark had gone to the pool alone. Now she was back and he marvelled at her beauty and grace as she slipped into the water beside him.

'So, what's the wise woman say?'

'She examined me and said, "about time". I reminded her she already knew. But she told me she was referring to the announcement, not the event itself. She says it's a boy, by the way.'

'That would be useful for the role of Wharhll. Unless we should alter that tradition as well?'

'Can a girl be Wharhll?'

'I can think of no good reason beyond tradition. Of course, she'd have to find a husband rather than a wife. But, if she's brought up in the right way, I feel sure we'll be able to have confidence in that changed arrangement.

'Jodisa, you're a tonic for me. It's too easy for a man to become enslaved by tradition. Just because something has always been done in a specific way, it doesn't mean that's the only way it should be done in the future. I like your influence. It's good for me and good for the city. My choice of you for my bride shows a degree of intelligence, forethought and judgement that sits well on my royal shoulders. What say you?'

For answer, she rose from the water, pulled him forward, and ducked him under the surface until he came up gasping for air and pleading for mercy. She laughed and kissed him and they dashed from the pool straight to their chamber so they could develop the feelings her kiss had initiated.

※

Shoarhn watched from the foot of the steps, unable to do more than simply observe, her limbs and neck still essentially paralysed from her prolonged period of stressed bondage. When she saw the new surge of people appear behind the Holy Ones who already outnumbered Aklon and his brave rescuers, she feared they were all finished. Her only thought then was that Aklon might escape and live on to fight his Cause.

But then the impossible happened. The newcomers didn't side with the Holy Ones, but attacked them from behind. For a while, there was great confusion and the Holy Ones faltered. These newcomers slashed with such passion that Shoarhn feared these were fanatics even madder than her captors and, once they'd destroyed the Holy Ones, might then kill all the others.

At last, after a lifetime of pain and uncertainty, the fighting stopped. Aklon stepped up to the flat space and greeted the strangers warmly. It was clear he knew none of them, but they seemed grateful for his presence. Only now could Shoarhn see that these were not Holy Ones but some of the sex slaves and domestics kept by them. Someone had freed them and brought them here to rescue Aklon and the Few.

A young woman with black hair and dark eyes embraced Aklon. She was the only stranger who wore anything, and Shoarhn felt no resentment at her passionate greeting of her lover. She'd saved them all.

'Hyllahn, how come you here? I left you in Chalamamnon.'

'I came after you when I heard what you were going to do. I used the rope to cross the falls and then, when I saw the Holy Ones dashing down here, I feared what they'd do to you. So I found the slaves and told them everything. They raided the armoury and came to your aid.'

Aklon kissed her again. 'Thank you, Hyllahn. You will be rewarded.'

'In the way I hoped?'

Aklon glanced down at Shoarhn and the woman followed his gaze.

'This is she?'

He nodded.

'If you desire him, please take him. You deserve him after what you've done.' Shoarhn's voice was soft and strained by her captivity.

The woman assessed her and turned again to Aklon, spoke to him quietly. He again held her and kissed her. 'You are a remarkable woman, Hyllahn. Truly remarkable.'

Shoarhn watched him descend and felt his arms around her, he raised her from the hard ground and helped her up the steps, Hyllahn supporting her other side. Delbon, with some help, assisted the other freed captives up after her.

The whole throng walked back to the cave entrance.

There, in the light of dawn, a strange scene was revealed. Shoarhn saw first a small group of Holy Ones gathered in a half circle, arms at the ready but still. They turned as the Few and the slaves entered the space. Some immediately attacked but most remained where they were. The attackers quickly died.

'Drop your weapons. Or be killed. I really do not care which you choose.'

Aklon passed Shoarhn to one of the women to help her stand. Her legs were regaining their life and sent pains up from feet to hips. Her arms tingled as the blood flowed back. Her neck protested at the weight of her head but she was able to hold it up with support from her hand.

Aklon moved through the Holy Ones and some of the Few followed, gathering their discarded weapons. Hyllahn helped Shoarhn through the throng to the front of the cave. There, standing in the bright light now flooding into the cave entrance, a young woman, knife drawn, held captive a man on his knees.

'Well, well. Kaz-Ca-Atroad. Came to warn your friends of my approach, did you? A foolish endeavour, bearing in mind my contacts on the island.'

He stepped forward and grabbed the priest by his hair, pulled him to his feet and shoved him forcefully into the crowd of cowed Holy Ones.

'For those who don't know, this priest is the consort of the late High Priestess, Wendarah Kaz. And this wonderful young woman is Eyethlehn, a gifted wood carver from Morstahn.' He turned to the woman and embraced her. 'You have done well, Eyethlehn, in spite of my mistaken request that you leave. I must find a way to reward you.'

'You're alive, Aklon. That's reward enough.'

The Few and their rescued captives followed Aklon into the daylight. Free from the oppressive caves, Shoarhn at last gave in to her emotions and allowed the tears to flow. Aklon laid her gently on soft grass, and sat with her head in his lap as her delayed fear was slowly overtaken by relief and the realisation that she and he were both alive and well.

Some of the freed slaves arrived with food and drink and Aklon gently fed her, gave her water from a clean goblet. He wiped away her tears with his tabard and combed his fingers through her tangled hair.

'Paltrohn, what should we do with the Holy Ones still left?' The man, one of the freed slaves, stood nervously before Aklon.

"I am Aklon, never Paltrohn. What you do with them is entirely up to you. I would have them change their ways, but I fear that is a vain hope. It may be that the only way to deal with them is merciful death. But they are your overseers, your torturers, your abusers. It is fitting that all you freed slaves determine the future of these cruel tyrants. Tyrants, I must tell you, who knew always that they acted on false doctrines and lies. They did what they did to you not from any idea of piety or sacred command, but from personal greed and lust. How you, now you are free, repay that abuse is for you to decide.'

A woman, scarred and limping, arrived from the northern reaches of the mountain. She was out of breath but insisted on speaking to Aklon at once.

'Paltrohn, your soldiers are outnumbered and in need of help at the other entrance to the caves. The Holy Ones there are fierce and your people are in great danger.'

Her warning done, she collapsed at his feet.

Aklon signalled his followers. Leaving a small number to care for Shoarhn and the others, they set off at a run for the entrance to the cave on the far side of the rocky outcrop. Shoarhn watched him go, marvelling at his energy and his commitment to the Cause, his bravery and concern for his Few. When, if ever, she wondered, would she see him again.

Chapter 8

OF DRAGONS AND FIRE

'At this rate, we'll be in Kah-Labaz by morning.'

Tumalind looked at Okkyntalah and nodded. She was still very concerned for her mother, awaiting word from Aklon that all was well with her. What would he do if Shoarhn had been killed by those vile Holy Ones? That led him to more doubts about their faith.

'Why are we completing this pilgrimage, Tumalind? Ivdulon, and even Feldrark, seem to think we should do away with Following altogether. I don't understand why we're bothering with this dangerous and difficult mission. Do you?'

She took his hand, squeezed it gently.

'Okkyntalah, you're far wiser than people realise. I don't pretend to know why it's important. But Ivdulon says it is and I'm willing to go along with what she says. With connections all over the world, she knows things we'll never understand.'

'Still, it's hard to be made to do something you don't believe in, isn't it?'

'What is it you don't believe in, Okkyntalah?'

He turned to find Aglydron standing behind him.

'We were discussing whether or not dragons really cause the fire in the mountain, Father. What do you say?' Tumalind was quick, but Okkyntalah wasn't convinced her answer would fool Aglydron.

'Dragons. Definitely dragons. And, for all that Jodisa was certain the fire mountain on Ylcrat was something else, I've spoken to Myllthlan about it and she says there could have been dragons on the island. Just that people never saw them, that's all.'

'Odd that, don't you think. I don't know anyone who's ever actually seen one.'

'No. But I know plenty of people who know other people who have, Okkyntalah.'

'Dragons? I doubt it. I've lived under Mount O'bo all my life. Never seen one and never spoken to anyone who's seen one either. No. The answer's what I've heard; that the world's full of fire and sometimes it comes to the surface, that's all.'

Okkyntalah smiled at Byfthlyn, who he'd had to release to take back to the ship after the Vagboh had vanished. He admired the lad's courage and his matter-of-fact ways.

'But what keeps the fires burning under the world?"

'No idea Aglydron. But I'm more inclined to believe it's that than that there are fire-breathing animals walking around. I mean, how would they make fire?'

'It's a mystery. Perhaps we'll never really find out. Like, what keeps the stars from falling on the world, and what's the Skyfire made of?'

'You shouldn't even question the Skyfire, Tumalind. It's sent by Ytraa to burn up the wicked. That's all we need to know. Getting brighter by the day, it is.'

Okkyntalah knew any further discussion would simply become argument and cause bad feeling. Aglydron's strong faith was unbreakable and the rest of them recognized it was pointless trying to discuss anything about Following with him.

'Does anyone have any idea how long we're staying in Kah-Labaz? Only I'd like to visit my parents before we sail off again.'

'Sorry, Byfthlyn. Dagla Kaz was talking with Pyqad about stores and it seems likely we'll be there at least a day to get more food and water on board for the voyage to Mehrrhyphrol. Why not ask the captain? He'll know, I'm sure.'

'Thanks, Tumalind. I'll do that.'

Aglydron wandered off to find Chislanda and the young lad went in search of the ship's captain, leaving Okkyntalah alone with Tumalind again.

'It's so difficult to get any privacy on this little boat. I'll be glad when we're back on land. At least then we can usually find a quiet place away from the others.'

'I could do with some of your comforting right now, Okkyntalah. I promised Aklon I'd not interrupt him whilst he was on the rescue mission, but I'm worried. I haven't heard from him for so long.'

'Didn't you say you'd connected with another woman on the island? Someone from Morstahn, I thought you said. Why not see if she knows what's happening?'

'Okkyntalah, you're a wonder. I sometimes miss the obvious. I will.'

She grew slightly distant, her gaze indicating that she was in that strange state that allowed her to send and receive thoughts across the leagues. Not for the first time, he wondered how this amazing feat was accomplished. That it was magical and strange was in no doubt, but it seemed a good thing, even though the leaders of the faith considered all magic to be bad.

He held her hand and simply remained by her side as she communed; connecting she called it. What was it like; to be able to go inside someone else's thoughts and swap them as if you were talking? Amazing.

The river took them swiftly downstream, the following wind a real help. They were far from the Vagboh and their desire for their womenfolk now. And, the captain had told him, there was unlikely to be any danger between here and their ultimate destination in the city upstream.

'Mind you, Okkyntalah, once you're in Mehrrhyphrol you'd best keep a firm grip on that beauty of yours. They'll have her off you as soon as look at you and she'll be lost. Once that lot get their hands on a beauty like Tumalind, they'll put her on show for the populace. She'll be made to dress and strip again and again, entertaining and titillating the men in the ale houses. Ay, and she'll be expected to lay with the landlord as well.'

'They'll try to steal her?'

'Not steal, but buy her. Tempt you with lesser beauties and plenty of gold. Beauty's the coin in that place. The better you look, the better you fare. Well, if you're a man, like. The women are just coin for the men who own them. But a beauty like Tumalind on display in an alehouse would make the landlord a very rich man.'

He hadn't spoken to Tumalind about this yet. It would be time enough to warn her once they were nearer the city on the river. She had problems enough to deal with as it was. He'd always known she was a special woman, but this trip had shown him just how special. It irked him that she was desired only for her appearance and that none of those who seemed to want her body had any appreciation for her other qualities. Tumalind was clever, kind, warm, generous, full of surprises, funny, dutiful but questioning, and, above all else, loving. At least, to him. He was a lucky man.

'I love you, too, Okkyntalah. And I'm a lucky woman to have you.'

She smiled at his expression of surprise. It happened so often when she'd been connecting in mindtalk and suddenly came back to him. He embraced and kissed her, perhaps a little more passionately than convention permitted. But they were still relatively newly-wed, so were bound to be forgiven any excess.

"You look happier. What's the news?"

Blavv had grown accustomed to riding on her way to Litkala from Ov-Bebna. She still found it tiring to be in the saddle all day, and was pleased when the troop leader, Teldrohn, called a halt by the banks of the river they'd have to cross in the morning. Better to face the test feeling fresh than when tired.

'For those who haven't been out in the field before, I should tell you that we don't bother with the usual formalities of Following. You can do whatever you please in that regard, but I won't have folk wandering off on their own. You never know what dangers there may be out in this wild country. So, we stick together. And I mean for everything. That includes bathing and the rest.'

It didn't worry Blavv to bathe, or do anything else, with men beside her. Most of her adult life she'd spent naked in the presence of men. That most had been without parts was neither here nor there. In fact, it made it more interesting to see the whole men in the group as they all refreshed themselves in the cool waters. And the horseplay and splashing greatly amused her.

She noticed Teldrohn was by himself and thought he looked a little lonely, bathing alone on the edge of the frivolity. Her youthful experience had given her a taste for men of power, since no other man than the Uhmbard had ever joined with her. He, of course, had been a selfish and demanding lover and her few experiences of his attention and desire had left a poor impression. But, as is often the case, she gravitated toward the familiar and so the troop leader attracted her. She swam to him underwater, her childhood skill returning quickly after so long a spell in the desert, and she thrust herself to the surface very close to him.

Teldrohn's initial surprise quickly turned to a smile and he ducked her for her cheek. Blavv, under water, gently grasped his prod and tugged it lightly before she rose back up and faced him. His look of surprised delight was reward enough for her daring.

'You, young lady, will get yourself thoroughly frowked if you're not careful.'

'Ooh! Is that an order, Paltrohn?'

'Don't you "Paltrohn" me. I see you need a lesson in how to behave when in the field.' He took her hand and led her, without resistance, to a quiet spot shaded by trees.

Blavv had never been kissed by a man in love, never been caressed with care and respect for her feelings. She'd never experienced the gentle attention of a man who cared for her enjoyment and pleasure. Surrender was the only course she knew, but this time it was a willing submission to the wishes of a man who actively gave pleasure in return.

Tah-Vlatak raised her eyebrows as she returned and sought out her tunic to cover her still tingling skin. 'That good, Eh?'

'Amazing. Never knew it could be so good. You should try him; he's wonderful.'

'Oh, I've already tried another and I see what you mean.'

'Do you suppose all the men are like that, Tah-Vlatak?'

'I doubt it. But we seem to have found at least two who know what a woman wants. I was determined to hate all men forever after my life in Ov-Bebna. But I might sample a few more now, see what I discover.'

'Ov-Bebna. I'd almost forgotten why we're on this mission. I wonder how the women are faring there?'

Tah-Vlatak was ignorant of Blavv's ability to mindtalk, and it had been made clear that she should keep it as secret as she could, without arousing suspicion or envy. Nuldron was a mindtalker and the Uhmteld had revealed herself able. Perhaps she should connect with one of them and see what was happening in the desert city. But her time with Teldrohn, coupled with the swimming and horseplay, had left her feeling hungry.

Once she'd eaten, she took herself to one side and sat with her back against a tree, allowing her mind to wander in those realms open only to those with her gift. Finding Nuldron was easy and she had a brief conversation with him. It seemed there was no objection to her connecting with the Uhmteld, though she was advised against discussing tactics or anything to do with their mission.

'I'm not sure how I should address you, now I'm a free woman. What name are you using?'

'Do I know you?'

'We shared the same man.'

'You are of the harem?'

'I was. I'm free and have shared pleasure with a wonderful man who understands how to treat a woman.'

'Ah. I had heard that such men exist, but was reluctant to believe it. You give me hope. I am now Celestohm. What is your name, now you're free?'

'You knew me as Teh-Blavv. I've dropped the title, that's all.'

'To what do I owe this connection, Blavv?'

'I was curious about what's happening in the city.'

'We, the women, that is, are holding what we've so far gained, but we're inexperienced in battle and more men, seeing they might actually win, are joining the fight on that side. I'm not hopeful for the future, to be honest. Our leader, Dahrlyth, is brave and resourceful, but we're only women and the men are stronger and more used to using weapons.'

'Have you spoken to Nuldron?'

'He tells me that a party of troops is on its way to the city, to come to our aid. But I'm not convinced we'll hold out for that long. Your journey might be wasted.'

'Well, if he's told you so much, I can tell you that I'm with that party. I'm coming to help, to use my knowledge and experience of the city in any way I can so the women can achieve true freedom. We're on our way and tomorrow will cross a broad river, one of three, before we reach the mountains and a pass called the Mascunl Crannel. Once through, we'll be across the desert in a few days. Hold on. We're coming, Celestohm.'

'You're free, Blavv. Why risk your life to come to our rescue? I don't understand.'

'We're sisters, we women. We were all oppressed and treated cruelly by those men. If we abandon each other, we're no better than the men who abused us. Also, I was born in Trotnahn and would love to return to that place. My parents never knew what had become of me, as I was stolen whilst alone and away from home.'

'I wish you well, and I thank you for your support. I'll pass on the message of your coming to Dahrlyth and maybe it'll inspire us all to hold on until you arrive. But we are in danger and it grows each day. You may come too late to do anything.'

'I'll do what I may. Now, I'm being approached by the man I spoke of and I hope he wishes to repeat our earlier experience, so I'll leave you.'

She broke the connection and rose as Teldrohn reached her.

'Oh, you needn't get up. On the ground, you're much closer to the place I want you.'

'Really? I'd prefer you as a cushion this time, Teldrohn, if that's satisfactory?'

'Let's try it and see what happens.'

* * *

The day had been long and hard for Aklon and his Few. The Holy Ones were a small but determined group and, in spite of his wish to spare as many lives as possible, none had surrendered. Those not killed had escaped and were now roaming the land as potential killers.

'How many ran off, d'you think, Aklon?'

'My estimate is around a hundred. Not a large number, but if they should become associated with the disaffected soldiers, together they make a force that could cause us considerable problems.'

'We'll deal with them, Aklon. Don't worry. What's next now?'

'For me, Choryssa, it is a journey to Morstahn with Shoarhn. She is well enough to travel now and her farm will need work that she needs to supervise.'

'And you'd like to join with her in private as soon as you can...'

'That is a desire, for both of us. But my fundamental concern remains her welfare and that of her means of providing for herself and her family. Is she still sleeping?'

'She's awake and feeling much better. Still weak, of course.'

He left the small circle of the Few and walked across the soft grass to where Shoarhn sat with her guardian.

Phrysilda rose and greeted him with a kiss. 'She's doin' well, Aklon. Says we can frowk if we want. But, much as I'd like to, I think she's the one for you an' I'll not harm that after what we've all been through.'

He kissed and thanked her.

Shoarhn struggled to her feet and embraced him. 'I thought we were both going to die. Horribly. I've never been so frightened. But I was more scared for you than for myself in the end. Does that make sense?'

'It does to me. Will you be well enough to travel today?'

'A short way. I need to get back home. Ytraa alone knows what that girl, Dahrlahg, has been doing in my absence. Eating all the produce and ignoring the beasts, if I'm any judge.'

'You might find her much changed, Shoarhn. Eyethlehn can tell you about that later. For now, some food and then we will take the first steps on the road back to your home.'

'My boys, Aklon. Are they safe?'

'As I explained before, Irrildys took them to your parent's house. They are safe.'

'Did you tell me? I don't remember.'

'You were still very weak then. But you were so insistent. I did wonder if you had truly heard me. But my news seemed to make you feel a little better at the time.'

They ate together, moving to be with the group of the Few and joining in the general talk. The freed domestic slaves from the Holy Ones' domain were so grateful that they insisted on serving and cooking for them. The former sex slaves seemed troubled and uncertain what they would do now they'd been released from their duties. Some had made it clear they were willing to join with all and sundry. Some were fearful for their futures, unsure how others would view them. All remained naked, of course, since the Holy Ones held no store of clothing beyond a handful of rough tabards.

They'd destroyed all clothes worn by their prisoners. The released ones now wore the dirty and coarse tabards that were the only garments found in the caves. Nakedness didn't seem to concern the sex slaves but some of the domestics fretted and felt vulnerable in their new state of freedom.

Aklon called all together on the plateau below the monument to Ytraa and explained about Gadhallah and Ytraa. The slaves were ready enough to be converted and few challenged what he told them. In fact, to his surprise, a small number collected together and brought fire from the kitchens of the caves. They set flames under the monument and gloried as the great wooden edifice slowly burnt to the ground. The embers were still glowing as the party set off for the road.

No one wished to remain in the caves. A good number of the slaves had relatives they hoped to live with until they could find a new way of life for themselves. Many, however, had no idea where they'd been born, whether they had any family. For them, the future was a great and frightening unknown.

Aklon suggested they accompany him and the Few to Morstahn. There they might be clothed and fed and take some rest. Later, when the people of The Point set up their new settlement on the peninsula north of Chalamamnon, those slaves who remained without a place to go might make their new home there. Once he'd explained about these social rejects, most seemed willing to follow his advice.

But, amongst those he'd freed, were many troubled souls and problems would beset the island for years. He may well have succeeded beyond his wildest dreams in fulfilling the Cause, but the aftermath would be far harder than the event itself. There were broken people now on the island, many who remained uncertain about their faith, many who resented the changes he'd already brought to their way of life and many who'd lost relatives and lovers in the fighting.

And, of course, there remained the large band of ex-soldiers, Holy Ones and other dissatisfied fanatics of the faith who would cause trouble wherever they went. It would be a long time before the island was a safe and pleasant place to live. And the experience with Shoarhn had demonstrated that no one was free from the dangers of kidnapping and death as long as Holy Ones continued to roam unrestricted.

Chapter 9

MATTERS OF LEADERSHIP

Aglydron felt he matched the High Priest's pleasure that they were at last properly on their way again. Troubled by the fire mountain, the memory of his experience on Ylcrat with Myllthlan made him glad to be away from its influence.

'Can we expect to come across more of these fire mountains, Aglydron?'

'I don't know of any others, Chislanda. But I hope not. This one looked angry to me and I'm glad to be well away from it.'

They'd been in the boat for four days since leaving Kah-Labaz for the second time. Ahead, on the eastern bank, a road began to run parallel to the river. The Great Forest was well south of them now and there was no more danger from the Vagboh. But Mehrrhyphrol was rumoured to be a den of iniquity and few of the party looked forward to entering this fabled place.

Dagla Kaz had made it clear that the women must be protected from the local population at all costs. He'd become even more inconsistent since they'd dropped off the female captain of the burnt ship and set off upstream. More than once, Aglydron had seen the man stare at Tumalind with eyes that spoke loudly of lust. His daughter - he could think of her no other way - was the object the High Priest's lust and it troubled him deeply. Many times on the journey his faith had been sorely tried, but this strange obsession of the High Priest disturbed him most.

'She'll be safe as long as she's not left alone with either of them, Aglydron. Don't let the situation get the better of you. Any case, Tumalind isn't your real daughter, is she? Isn't Okkyntalah the one who should keep her safe?'

'I raised her, Chislanda. And, if the truth's known, I feel guilty for putting her in danger before by refusing to let people know our true relationship. She's very special. And her mother's alone now I'm with you. The least I can do is protect the girl we brought up together as our own.'

'Sometimes it seems I don't know you at all, Aglydron. But it's nice you surprise me in a good way. What do they say about this new city we're heading for? What do we need to be careful of?'

'Women are bought and sold. Put on display. Made to undress to music for the entertainment of the men. The men who own the most beautiful women grow wealthy on their performances and share their beds.'

'Do they take women by force?'

'Apparently not. But they pay great sums for the most attractive. I fear Tumalind may be taken by Tryonta and sold.'

'Could he do that?'

'I don't think Dagla Kaz would stop him.'

'Okkyntalah would though.'

'Yes. That's what I fear. We might lose them both.'

'I've never seen you like this. Has something else happened, Aglydron?'

'Nothing.'

'It's unlike you to worry over things unconnected to the Followers and the faith.'

'You think I'm fanatical.'

'I think you're much troubled by what you've been told and what you've learned since. I think you're no longer certain of your faith. I think you're starting to question the High Priest and, maybe, even the Lord Gadhallah.'

'Chislanda! You mustn't ever say that. The Lord Gadhallah is the very foundation of Following. I could never doubt him. But you're right: I do have uncertainties about Dagla Kaz. I no longer trust in him as I did. I'm lost, Chislanda. Lost.'

Blavv was sore from the ride, but, as she'd been the one to urge the troops into greater speed, she didn't complain. In three days of riding since her talk with Celestohm they'd covered over fifty leagues and reached the small town nestled in the foothills at the western end of the Mascunl Crannel. They'd already exchanged their horses for camels and bought supplies for the trek across the sands. It would be hard going, but Teldrohn estimated they could be there in two days.

'Celestohm; apologies for my silence. We've been riding fast. We hope to be with you soon. How do you fare?'

'Things aren't good. We've run short of food and water and we're surrounded by the men now. We can't escape. They're threatening to burn us out. But I don't think they'll risk killing so many of us. They want sport with us. I fear some may have to go out and sacrifice themselves; provide the men with entertainment, if you're not able to get here sooner.'

'We have to be in fighting condition when we arrive, Celestohm. We'll be outnumbered and, if we're not ready, we could easily lose the fight. Do what you must to avoid complete surrender. We'll be with you as soon as we can.'

'I fear you may be too late already, Blavv. But I'll inform the rest of the women and we'll try to make some sort of holding move. I must go now.'

Blavv felt bad about her inability to rescue the women before dreadful events overtook them. But Teldrohn's estimate of the journey time was as accurate as possible. She'd seen the map he used to guide them. A fascinating and detailed drawing that showed landmarks and indicated distances between places.

'How could such a piece of work have been made?'

Teldrohn didn't know. 'Ivdulon provided it. No idea how she came by it, though.'

They rode out of the small town with most of the day behind them. The camp they'd make that night would take them to the very edge of the sandy region that lay between the mountains and the city. That long ride across those moving sands was the one she most feared. Childhood memories of sandstorms and her recollections of the wind borne sand that invaded the harem from time to time made her dread the journey. But she'd do it. She would do what she could to bring freedom to the women she'd shared that dreadful man with. She'd play her part in ending traditions that made women slaves. And then she'd see if it was possible to return to her home in Trotnahn.

Were her parents still alive? Would they recognise her? Her early life in the town on the edge of the lake had been happy. Her people were civilised and peace loving. But she'd been away for many years and things may have changed. There was a boy. She recalled his handsome face and wondered. But that was pointless. First she must do what she could to help her sisters in Ov-Bebna. Time enough for personal matters once the city was safe.

The announcement of the coming birth had gone down very well with the citizens in Litkala. The holiday made for the proclamation had found favour almost everywhere; there were always those few merchants who disliked losing a day's work, but they were in the minority. Pharah-Li had announced her own pregnancy, at the same stage as Jodisa's, on the same day. But her revelation had been a private affair and merely added joy to that created by the royal baby.

Jodisa wondered if her father knew of his new infant; the boy or girl that would be his heir, since Aklon had been disinherited and she was now married and joint ruler of Litkala. How life had changed since the night Okkyntalah and Aglydron had kidnapped her and taken her on the long voyage that had ultimately introduced her to Feldrark. And now, here she was, ruling a kingdom with the man she loved, bearing his child and announcing the coming event to their adoring citizens. Amazing.

Even Ivdulon had attended. But Feldrark had said that was tradition, and the wise woman had been quite willing to leave her lofty perch, knowing that the announcement didn't require her to join with some man. She and her pupil, Netrodyl, had stood together during the ceremony and remained as close friends at the feast that had followed. Feldrark had been amused. But Jodisa, who wondered if the rumours were true, was again reminded of the deep differences between her island attitude to the faith and that shown in the city.

Her view of Following had always been coloured by the secrets Dagla Kaz had shown

73

her. What, she wondered, had made her experience so different from Aklon's. What had made him become a rebel whilst she remained a loyal daughter, even after her father forced her into sex and made her pregnant? One reason was here in the city. Aklon had connected with Ivdulon. That difference, contact with another world, exposure to new interpretations of the reality of their faith, had been enough for him to recognise its iniquity. It really was no surprise that Aklon had rejected the teaching of Gadhallah and all that went with it. Given the same conditions, she wanted to believe she would have responded the same way. But her new-found honesty told her that cowardice at that stage of her life would have kept her true to Father's wishes.

It was some time since she'd been in contact with her brother. He was occupied with the Cause, with converting the Few to the many. How was he? How were things moving on the island? She felt a sudden need to know. Perhaps the new life stirring in her belly made her more conscious of the value of family.

'Aklon? Are you free to talk?'

There was a brief silence in that strange world where thoughts could be found and captured.

'I am, Jodisa. How are you?'

She explained what had happened with the public announcement, described those things that concerned her and Feldrark, knowing she had no need to detail events involving Ivdulon.

'How are things on the island?'

He told her of the conversions in the various settlements, mentioned the deaths of the two priests and the reasons for them, and explained about Shoarhn's capture and rescue.

'As ever, there's more to that tale than you're telling, brother. Are you unscathed? Truly?'

'Minor scratches, nothing more. Many of the fools died before they ran from the plain. We scoured the caves and discovered hoards of food, some gold coin, and many items that had been stolen from prisoners. We also learned from their slaves of the true scale of their cruelty and vile perversions. It is a wonder to me that people are capable of such treatment of their fellow human beings. I fear the remnants will make more trouble before we are properly rid of them. Perhaps I should have killed them all whilst I had the chance. No doubt I shall live to regret the mercy I showed, in spite of the advice of my colleagues to the contrary.'

'You always were too soft, Aklon. A leader needs iron in thought and deed. Being flexible is sometimes necessary, but disputes must be settled to the benefit of the leader, who sees the wider picture.'

'And if that picture is incomplete or misleading?'

'Well, views and opinions are subject to interpretation, Aklon. The leader has to make decisions. We can't dwell in the luxury that people like Ivdulon enjoy: we have to live in the real world and dispense judgment according to what we understand at the time. Sympathy is too often later proven to be misplaced.

'For many portions, centuries even, Feldrark's people, my people now, have put up with false accusations and lies spread by the citizens of Mipahnhil. In the end, we had to put an end to their baseless claims. It took the bloody deaths of Feldrark's parents to make him see the reality of the threat. And now that city on stilts no longer exists and all but a few hundred of its citizens are dead. The rest are now integrated here with our own people and learning to behave like true and loyal residents of Litkala.

'You may find you have to deal severely with those who oppose you, Aklon, in order to bring peace to the whole island. A soft approach may not bring the unity and security you seek. Because, make no mistake, they're your people now. You're their leader, and they'll look to you for guidance and example. Your days of gallivanting all over the island, playing the gallant hero, are over. You're their real leader. You've the responsibility of all the island folk now in your care.'

'You have grown, Jodisa. You were just a young woman with wild ideas and silly dreams. Now you are a mature woman, a skilled and thoughtful statesman. I hear your advice. I understand my position and my duties have changed. I know what is required of me. I only wish I felt better equipped to do the job.

'Sometimes the best leader in war is not the best in peace. But, for the moment, until the island population is united and settled, I must take on that role. What will come later, I know not. But I have no pretentions to leadership once all is settled here. I can only hope that the island itself will find and appoint a suitable head for our time of peace, when that finally arrives. But whoever that leader is, it will not be one of the priest class. Of one thing I am now certain; it is very unwise to mix religious faith with rule. They are two separate issues and need to be kept apart, secular rule is the primary need for law and order. The religious community can take care of spiritual matters.'

'That's how we try to do it here, Aklon. Generally there's a spiritual leader called the Wharhll, but Feldrark had that role and carries it still now his parents are dead. This new life in my belly should, one day, inherit. But we really need someone to take it on in the meantime, so that Feldrark is no longer required to act in both capacities. The local High Priest might do it, but Feldrark wants no bias regarding which religion people choose, so he needs a neutral figure in the role. So far, we haven't been able to find a suitable person. But we will.'

'It seems we have similar problems, sister. Perhaps we should stay in touch more than we have. You have certainly given me food for thought.'

'I hope I've been helpful, Aklon.'

'You have put into words some of my thoughts. Clarified the situation. I thank you. And now I must leave you; I am required in person for other matters.'

The connection closed and Jodisa moved from their private chamber into the body of the palace. She walked across floors that captured the vitality of the unknown folk who'd built this fabulous city so many portions ago; Ivdulon reckoned it had been standing for at least ten thousand cycles. An unimaginable period. Somewhere within the vast building her husband was busy. She'd go to him and see whether she could help him make those difficult decisions he had to make from time to time.

It had been a hard journey. But each day had helped bring back strength and sensation to her tortured joints and muscles. By the time they'd reached Morstahn, Shoarhn felt more or less normal. She was still haunted by the threats the Holy Ones had made, but she felt physically well again.

The farm was in a state. Animals left unmilked and some infection in a couple of the cows because of this. Some crops that should have been picked remained on trees and the churns seemed never to have been used since her absence. Of Dahrlahg there was no sign.

The boys greeted her with love and warmth and her parents embraced her with more love than she could recall. They told her of some of the events but advised her to find Irrildys.

'She knows what's happened, and you ought to know the truth afore you tear into that poor young lass.'

That was as much as she got out of her mother. Irrildys, however, arrived before she went looking for her. Her friend examined her at arm's length and then hugged her close, the warmth and love behind that gesture almost more than Shoarhn could bear.

Aklon had left her at the door; gone in search of news and to find temporary homes for some of the slaves they'd brought back with them. A couple, a man and a woman, had remained with her and awaited her instructions. She showed them Tumalind's room and asked if they minded sharing. They didn't; happy to be free and to be consulted for the first time in their lives.

'So. Are you hurt, Shoarhn?'

'I was. But I'm fine now, Irrildys. Where's Dahrlahg? Has something happened to her? Only Mother called her "that poor lass" and sounded genuinely concerned.'

Irrildys sat at the table and gestured Shoarhn to do the same. The ex-slaves came back in and hung about, uncertain what to do, where to go. Shoarhn prepared Tlathan for them all and invited the pair to sit with them whilst she caught up on the news.

'Dahrlahg was taken by Kaz-Ca-Uldrad. He intended to use her as a way to get to you. We don't yet know who told him about your relationship with Aklon, by the way. But we'll find out. Obviously one of the Few was either careless or wasn't really on our side. Anyway, he took the girl on the same day the Holy Ones took you prisoner. No one thought of her safety. I mean, she was virgin and in the house of the village priest. It seemed reasonable to think she'd be safe.'

'What happened to her? Is she alright?'

'One of the priest's slaves told us, otherwise she'd have been suffering in there still. That frowkin' priest raped her. Had her bound and used her. When folk found out, I mean they'd already heard of the Cause and some of Aklon's words had got through, so a lot were already thinking of converting. Then, the Holy Ones had paraded you through the streets like that and, well, it made many of them ready to come over to us. In a way, the Holy Ones and Priests helped us change a lot of minds and come with us.'

'But what did you do about poor Dahrlahg?'

'Ah. Well a group of the young ones went to the priest's house and caught him with her. Freed her, of course. Brought the priest out into the square and threw things at him. He was in a sorry state when I eventually arrived. I'm afraid I put an end to him. No matter how bad he'd been, I couldn't let them torture him to death. Ended it with a knife. He's buried outside the town, along with the other dead.'

'And Dahrlahg?'

'She's okay. Troubled and hurt, of course. But she's come over to us. She's no brighter than she was, but she's a lot more use around the place. Took her a few days to recover. But she'll be fine, if you want her back?'

Shoarhn turned to the slaves.

'That depends on what you two want to do. I've work enough for both of you here on the farm. I can pay you a small wage and feed and house you. Up to you. The work's hard and sometimes heavy, but it's plain, honest farm work.'

The man and woman glanced at each other and then at Shoarhn. He spoke for both. 'For now, until we know what we really want, may we stay with you and do whatever work you need from us, in exchange for our keep?'

'If you work, you get paid. I'll have no argument on that. But I'd be pleased to have you here until such time as you make up your minds. So, Irrildys, I suppose I can manage without Dahrlahg, unless she wants to come back?'

'I'll ask her.'

Her friend went and Shoarhn took the two slaves out and showed them round the farm, describing the various duties required of them. The woman had been employed on the plain, growing vegetables, so she had some idea of the work. But the man had been kept in the kitchens and needed to be taught some skills. They both seemed capable and she set them to some of the mundane tasks as she went about putting right what had been neglected during her time away.

In the evening, tired but with things under better control, she and the slave couple sat down to eat with the boys, only to be joined by Aklon. That night, in the privacy of her own room, she renewed at last her love with the man who'd rescued her. It was a short but passionate break from the daily duties that now faced her. And, for Aklon, it was some relief from his anxieties.

He left after breakfast. 'I have to tour the island and make sure that no advantage is being taken by those now in power. I do not want new leaders to take over the bad habits of old ones. And there are village priests I still have to deal with. I will return to you as often as my duties allow, Shoarhn. I have appointed some of the Few here to keep you under watch, so that you are safe from any Holy Ones or those still attached to the faith. I cannot risk you falling into their clutches again.'

With that promise and threat, he was gone. But, this time, he had no need to sneak off into the night. Now the Cause had truly started its course, he could be open and free. Danger now came not from the authorities but from those who remained loyal to the old ways. At present, they were an unknown number, their reactions difficult to predict. Shoarhn could only hope they would be less violent and more thoughtful than their predecessors. At least he no longer had to travel alone for the safety of his supporters.

But, however she looked at the situation, her lover remained in danger and she'd never know, from one day to the next, whether he was safe. Only his visits would confirm that. Already, she missed him and wished him back by her side.

Chapter 10

A TOUR OF THE ISLAND

No moon brightened the surface of the river as Tumalind leant on the rail and stared into darkness ahead, and the Skyfire lay low and to the east. Beside her, Okkyntalah held her hand, his other stroking the curve of her bottom; a gentle reminder of his love for her.

'Do you suppose this city really is as dangerous as some would have us believe, Okkyntalah?'

'We were told of cannibals on Ylcrat, dragons in Mount O'bo, and fierce, perverted Followers in Litkala. None of those were true. I think I'll make my judgment once we arrive and have some experience of the city.'

'But we'll keep our ears and eyes open?'

'Of course. I never want you in danger again.'

'Me neither. I've had enough adventure of that sort to last a lifetime.'

As they watched, twinkling lights came into view and they realised they were turning slightly to follow the curve of the river toward their destination. Coloured lights made trails on the water, brightening the scene and bringing life to the dark night. The closer they came to the city, the more lights appeared. In fact, neither of them had witnessed so much light at night anywhere they'd been. In parts, the city might have been basking in daylight; so bright were these areas. Other places were in total darkness, lending them a sinister air.

As they approached, sounds of life floated across the water, bringing the whole scene alive. Usual port smells rose and filled their nostrils with memories of other docks they'd visited. Here, however, an overwhelming scent of pungent spices overlaid the more usual stink.

Tumalind had wondered why Pyqad was unconcerned about docking at night, knowing how dark were the usual quays, especially when it was moonless. He clearly knew this city with more than enough light to allow them to approach the docks in safety.

Men caught ropes and tied them round enormous metal keys set into the hard ground of the port, holding the ship close and still against the current. Big men, muscular and broad, chests bare and hips and legs wrapped in items that covered them to the knee, each leg in a separate tube. She'd seen similar garments on Quyreena, but of longer length and in a more sheer fabric than the coarse cloth these men wore.

Sounds of song and music wafted softly from beyond the dock area and she heard an occasional rowdy chorus of approval from somewhere unseen. The spicy smell engulfed all others now they were at rest, so that the air could almost be tasted, causing her mouth to water.

'I wonder what that is.'

'Something to do with food, I expect. It certainly smells good. Making me quite hungry.'

'Oh you. You could eat all day. It's a good job you're always on the move or you'd be round as Corphanda.'

'I heard that, young lady. Mind you, can't complain at the truth, can I?' The tubby lady waddled up behind them and teased Tumalind with a soft smack, reminding her of the times she'd delivered stronger punishments, though they'd proved undeserved.

'How are your charges, Corphanda?'

'Oh, well enough. Fed up of being restricted to this little ship. I'll have my hands full keeping an eye on them once we're in the city, no doubt.'

'They'll behave. No one dare disobey you with that quick and hefty hand of yours.'

'Doesn't stop Porryh. 'ad to mark her bum twice today. The way she was with the ship's captain. 'Onest, you'd not believe she was a Virgin Gift.'

'Never really come to terms with being Chosen, has she? Still, I understand that.'

'Who better, eh?'

The night was suddenly rent by a long high-pitched scream. It silenced those on deck and struck fear into Tumalind's heart. She'd heard a similar cry in Shorrannon and, on that occasion, the morning had revealed a dead woman surrounded by onlookers who'd screened the details of her death.

'There was fear and pain in that scream. I'd go and look, if I knew where.'

'Stay here, Okkyntalah. I don't want you risking your life for a complete stranger.'

'If I kept to that policy, Tumalind, I'd never have met Dahrlyth and then I might not have managed to rescue you from Ov-Bebna. Helping strangers is a way to get help for yourself later on. Not always, but sometimes.'

'But that's not why you do it, Okkyntalah. You can't bear to think of any woman suffering. I know you.'

She felt his response in the slight pressure of his grip on her hand, the gentle squeeze of her bottom through the fabric of her tabard. He'd always been like this; a real lover of women. Sometimes it worried her, but most of the time she was grateful she had such a caring husband.

'I expect we'll be waitin' until daylight before we get off, will we?'

'I don't know, Corphanda. But I imagine so. Coming to lie down, Okkyntalah? We ought to get some sleep so we're ready for whatever the morning brings.'

'Let's hope it's fun, peace and fresh food, eh? And no danger.'

80

'Definitely no danger. I've had enough of that.'

Blavv descended from the camel and led it to the place where the remaining fodder had been strewn on the sand. She was sharing a tent with Tah-Vlatak and a couple of soldiers. They'd brought the flimsy shelters with them and she hoped they wouldn't suffer a sandstorm. Those winds would rip them to shreds and they'd all be exposed to the biting, tearing sands.

Once they'd eaten, she connected with Celestohm again to get news of the situation in Ov-Bebna.

'We're a day away, Celestohm. How are you managing?'

'Desperate. The men are getting stronger by the day. I've…we've had to sacrifice a few women, to keep some of the men on our side. They've gone out to keep the men happy, so they won't unite with their fellows. But things are very hard. I doubt we'll last the night. I think your trip might be a waste of time.'

'Where are you based?'

'The palace. It's the only place we can keep secure. But, not for much longer.'

'We're moving as fast as circumstances allow, Celestohm. But if we overstretch ourselves, we'll arrive in no state to fight. Hold on. We'll be there by this time tomorrow.'

Whether that was true would be determined by weather and terrain. Blavv returned to the normal world and went in search of Teldrohn. He was sharing his tent with the cooks and other servants they'd brought along to keep the troops happy and well fed. It struck Blavv as an odd arrangement for a man of power, but then she realised it was his way of making sure no one thought they were special.

He welcomed her with Tlathan, just prepared.

'I've been in contact with Ov-Bebna. They're really desperate. Can we set off before dark, do you think?'

'It was my intention, Blavv. In fact, I'm about to send round that message. I was going myself, but now you're here, the servants can do it.'

He instructed them, telling them to take their time and ensure everyone knew what was required. Alone, they took advantage of the short spell of privacy. Blavv could've spent the rest of the night in his arms, but it was important they made no one jealous, so she returned to her tent as the servants returned.

Evening brought no change in the weather. A fair wind, no cloud. They were up and on their way before the skies displayed all the stars, the Skyfire burning fierce and red as it rose above the horizon.

Toward midnight they came upon a small, tented village. Before Blavv could warn him, Teldrohn had turned the troops in their direction.

81

She urged her camel forward to ask him why he was making the visit. 'Those are the K'ahll. They kill strangers on sight.'

'Not according to Ouqitahl, the leader of the expedition that rescued you and Tumalind from the city before. He said they were hospitable and helpful, until he told them where they were bound. Then they stopped talking and refused to guide them. Very odd. But I'm going to invite them to come with us, if they will.'

Blavv was astounded at this news. She had no direct experience of the K'ahll, but everyone in Ov-Bebna spoke their name with fear and loathing. Perhaps this was yet another new thing to learn.

One of the elders emerged from a tent as they approached. Two women stood with him. All three were wrapped only in light loin cloths.

'Greetings, strangers. How may we help you?'

Teldrohn dismounted and handed the reins to Blavv, who happened to be closest.

'I know, from your previous contact with a colleague of mine, that you have a deep hatred of the city, Ov-Bebna. I also know that you're generous of spirit and kind to strangers. I make no plea, no request for help. But I must tell you we are bound for that city. Please. Let me explain. I will then go and not trouble you again. Will you hear my words?'

The man nodded and the two women opened their palms outward in a gesture of compliance.

'We're going to free the women of the city from the tyranny of the Uhmbard and his brutal gang of men. The women are already fighting for their freedom, a fight that began with the arrival of one of our own, a young woman called Tumalind, much admired by all. She's been rescued from the city, as has the beautiful girl who now holds the reins of my camel. Blavv is returning to the city to help her sisters. As you see, we are few. But we're skilled and experienced, whilst the men of Ov-Bebna remain only fit to beat helpless and naked women. I ask nothing of you. But I invite you, if you will, to accompany us on this mission and help rid this land once and for all of the evil rule of the Immallsu.'

The man and women turned to face one another and spoke in quiet tones. One woman left the trio and entered the tent, returning with others of both sexes. They, in turn, visited the other tents until all the people were gathered before them. Blavv couldn't count, but she thought there were many more of the K'ahll than were in the troop.

'What you tell us gives us hope that the scourge may be ended. We are not a warrior people. But we have honour and hold that all are equal in the sight of Ulkhon. The evil that lives in Ov-Bebna has ever been a blight on our people. We have decided that we will play our part in freeing the women. However, it will take us a little time to prepare. If you wish for refreshments whilst we do that, please allow us to feed you.'

'I thank you, but we must move now. The need is deep and immediate. But knowing you will be close behind us will help us in the fight to come. Be quick, or you may arrive only in time to bury our dead.'

The man and the first two women all bowed. At once, the people began to pack up their camp. Blavv handed the reins back to Teldrohn and they set off again towards the city in the sand and a battle that must result in death or injury for many in the small troop.

<hr />

'Aklon, how much further are we walking today?'

'I am sorry, Hyllahn, you must be weary from your exertions. We will rest around the next bend, where a small grove of magrana will give us shade and some refreshment.'

He intended to take the girl back to Chalamamnon, so she would be in familiar surroundings. Conditions in the city concerned him, too, and he needed to check on his father's house and its contents. The documents and stone tablets must all be displayed, but guarded, to allow as many of the population as possible to see them. The written words of Gadhallah would be the final evidence, the proof of the falsehood of their faith.

The party with him was larger than he'd expected. Freed slaves journeyed with him. Some would settle with their long deserted families in the city, others would continue to the settlement where the people of The Point were readying themselves for their move to their new location. Yet others would stay in Pampahn. They'd left a small number at Krohtl, where they'd found the village priestess, Kaz-Ca-Charrohn, wandering naked and homeless, begging for food and shelter.

He had wanted to intervene and stop this torture, which seemed unnecessary. But he was aware of how sensitive the people were. The priestess had taken great advantage of her power whilst in office, abusing her rule on a daily basis. It was no surprise she was treated with such disdain. In fact, it was a wonder she remained alive. The signs were that eventually, after a suitable period of punishment, she'd be allowed to settle back into the official house. Though, whether she'd find a good man to partner her was more doubtful.

She'd cried out to him for mercy. To him, of all people. And when she'd implored Delbon to help her, it had been all the man could do to ignore her, after her abuse of him.

Delbon, Phildrad, Choryssa and Phrysilda, had accompanied him. They would remain with him for the time being, a guard and support party now he was out in the open. Aware of the dangers he still faced, he nevertheless refused to hide away now the Cause was under way.

As many as two thirds of the population had already converted to the new ways. They'd abandoned their reliance on the words of Gadhallah but continued to worship Ytraa as their god. That would remain the case for some time. Let the dust settle before he tried to explain that Ytraa, too, was a false basis for faith. Ivdulon had made clear it was unwise to allow a vacuum to develop with the abandonment of Ytraa. Safer by far to let that falsehood remain, for the time being, especially after Ivdulon's efforts to bolster his reputation by speaking with multiple voices in the guise of Ytraa.

The night after the stop in the magrana grove found them entering Chalamamnon. The city was much changed. Some looting, and a number of houses burnt to the ground. The bodies of those caught in the conflagration remained unburied and a stray dog was eating flesh. Lawlessness lurked.

Aklon led the group to a house of one of the Few, thankfully untouched by flame. They were unharmed.

Buvlakkan bore a sword, ready for use, when he answered the summons at the door. As soon as he recognised Aklon, he dropped the arm holding the weapon and ushered the group in, gesturing that they be quick, and scanning the street for observers.

'There is trouble for you, Buvlakkan?'

'It's dangerous just now. Don't know who you can trust. Just the Few. We've got to be careful. There's murder, and worse, in the streets.'

'It was bound to be difficult, Aklon. But neighbour turning on neighbour, husband on wife, mother on son? It wasn't what we expected.' Wempiryss wore anxiety like a mask but welcomed him into her house with an embrace that said he could rely on her loyalty, as her husband looked on with mild concern.

'Perhaps I should have described the level of danger and difficulty. But I did not know how it would be. Like all of you, I could only guess. In Krohtl all is well. There is some bad feeling but no violence. They have made their village priestess naked and thrown her out of her home. But, considering how Kaz-Ca-Charrohn behaved, she is fortunate to be alive.'

'Surely, we don't use their titles, Aklon? I mean, she's just plain Charrohn, isn't she?'

'Ture, Wempiryss...'

'Never call that one plain, though, would you?'

Wempiryss gave her husband a look that said more than words. He shrugged and put an arm around her shoulders.

'So, Krohtl is without violence. Morstahn has small pockets of bad feeling but most of that community have embraced the Cause. There cannot be more than a dozen families who have kept to the old ways. Their priest was killed by the people after he raped a virgin he had taken as hostage in order to tempt me into captivity.

'As for your own priest, Atroad died on the Plain of Ytraa at the hands of the sex slaves we freed. So, you have no priest now.'

'Good news, Aklon. I'll get word out. With no leader, the Dissenters might not have

84

such power.'

Wempiryss glanced at the party he had brought with him. 'Hyllahn, Delbon and Phildrad we know. Who are these others?'

Aklon introduced the other members and the freed slaves. Buvlakkan stared hard at one of the ex-slaves and asked her name again.

She gave it.

'But you used to live across the road, didn't you?'

She nodded.

'How come you're a slave?'

She told them she'd been approached by a Holy One in the street when she was younger. He'd talked her into going with him, making it sound like her sacred duty and telling her she was destined for greatness. 'Ytraa requires you for special duties on Ytraa's Mount.'

She'd tried to go and tell her parents but he'd insisted they must go straight away, that Ytraa's word was law. Frightened, she'd obeyed. As soon as she'd arrived at the caves, they'd stripped and raped her and kept her as a sex slave ever since.

'Not an isolated story, I fear. There are many such boys and girls now free. I have brought only some of them with me. Most, obviously, wish to return to their families and I expect such returns may well change the minds of many who remain stuck in the old ways. Others will be rejected, out of guilt, fear, or denial of the truth. But we are being careful in how we send them out. A few at a time. Most remain in Morstahn, where they are being cared for. Two hundred and seventy one girls and a hundred and eighty three boys. The task will be hard, but it will help us establish the truth about the Holy Ones. Also, there are freed domestic slaves of both sexes, numbering a hundred and seven. Most were also violated by the Holy Ones.

'That term is inappropriate, but I can think of no other way to describe them. No matter, we will find some suitable term later. For now, Buvlakkan and Wempiryss, if you have the means, we would appreciate some refreshments?'

Quietly and efficiently, with help from like-minded neighbours, the group was fed.

Aklon learned more about the situation in the capital from Wempiryss, who sat with him as he ate.

'It's difficult to say how many, but there's a lot of folk here sticking to the old ways. You've seen the bodies and burnt houses. That's the work of the "True Followers", as they call themselves. The Few are grown in numbers but it's not safe on the streets. Though the violence has died down a little now. People are frightened, Aklon. And the danger is that neighbours will fight with each other again if we can't sort things out. Already there have been fights, bullying, women assaulted, even children harmed. Those ruined houses and the bodies there are the worst, so far. But we all feel it's only a matter of time before even worse happens.'

'The obvious way is to show the doubters the evidence that converted us. I know it will make no difference to some, but it might help convert enough to make life a little less fraught. We must avoid stigmatising those who refuse to change. Allow them to continue with their old ways, as long as they do not try to impose them on the rest of us.'

'So, what should we do?' Buvlakkan's question was to the point, but, for the moment, Aklon had no answer.

Chapter 11

TRAPPED IN OV-BEBNA

Aklon was silent for a while, thinking. 'My father's house is large and underused at present. I suggest we remove an internal wall and then lay out the parchments and stone tablets on tables in the enlarged room. The Secret Chamber has already been emptied and the proofs brought up. But events prevented us completing the proper display. We can now post notices and send round criers to invite the people to come and see for themselves the words of Gadhallah. We must make visitors feel safe and we must protect the actual documents against those who would no doubt try to destroy them. It means the Few here in the capital will have much to do, but it will make a solid start in changing those who do not wish to see reality.'

'We'll start as soon as you're rested, Aklon. You're worn out.'

'Should've seen the way he battled those frowkin' Holy Ones. Must've seen a dozen off alone. Holy Ones! What a frowkin' name for them vile creatures. Should be called Unholy Ones, if you ask me.'

'Brilliant, Delbon. Simple but accurate. Let all know that from now those who style themselves Holy Ones will be known as Unholy Ones.

'As for resting, Wempiryss; that can wait. We must get the display and notices out as soon as we can. The sooner we educate doubters of the truth, the better for all. If those who are able and willing can help, we will get the whole job done before nightfall.'

Delbon, Phildrad, Choryssa and Phrysilda, along with some of the freed slaves, went to the house and emptied the two largest rooms of extraneous furniture and personal effects, leaving tables and benches where necessary for the display. Others set about dismantling the interior wall. In the meantime, two ex-slaves who'd been taught to write, copied down Aklon's words to the people. Once he had set them away with an example, they made several notices on pieces of spare parchment that had been stored in the secret chamber.

He and the rest then all made their way to the house of the former High Priest. They laid out the stone tablets and manuscripts in the order in which they'd been made. Not only the words of Gadhallah himself, but records kept by many High Priests. As a whole, the accounts gave a true history of the events and sentiments of those who'd written them. Anyone reading them in full must come away with an impression of the truth that would drive out all doubt about the real nature of Following.

In the time it had taken to put the items in order and on display, the scribes had produced the notices. Aklon left it to local members of the Few to select the places where these should be displayed and who should undertake that task. But he allowed no one to venture into the streets alone. On the morning of the following day, a small group of the Few would tour the town and call out the same words as appeared on the announcements, so those who couldn't read would have the chance to learn of the display. Of course, they'd be unable to understand the proofs, but most would have a trusted friend who could help them.

Once all was settled, Aklon finally agreed to sleep. He went to his father's old room and slept there, alone and undisturbed, until movement and light awoke him from the best sleep he'd had for portions.

'Have you been there all night, Phrysilda?'

'I was tempted to join with you, but you said you want to do that only with that woman, Shoarhn. Though I can't see why she's so special to you. Not at all plain, I can see, but she's not especially beautiful, is she?'

'Ah, Phrysilda. Looks are not everything in love. Maybe not even in life. We have been raised in a society where physical appearance has always been important, as a means of attracting the necessary mate for joining and worshipping. Shoarhn is a lovely woman. But I love her because of who she is, not because of what she looks like. I do not deny that she appeals to me, but it is not the reason for my love. That goes far deeper. I love her for her courage, her kindness, her warmth and the affection she shows for her boys. I love her also because she loves me.'

'Well, all those things could be said about me, couldn't they? I mean, aren't I pretty?' She rose from beside him. 'Aren't I brave and…?'

'Phrysilda, you are a very attractive and lovely woman. You share many of Shoarhn's qualities. But you are not Shoarhn. And it is Shoarhn I love. Do you understand?'

'Not really. But you obviously do. Sure you don't want just a bit of fun with me?'

'If not for Shoarhn, I would happily join with you, and thoroughly enjoy the experience. But my heart wouldn't be in it.'

'Your prod would be in me, though. An' that's all I really want, Aklon.'

'You and many others. But I decline. I am sorry.'

She shrugged. "It was worth a try. I'll find another. Doubt he'll be as good as you. But, it's only fun, isn't it?'

'One day, you will find a partner who you love and then you will understand. Until then, you will believe love is something inexplicable and unattainable. But I truly believe we each have a perfect partner waiting for us somewhere. When you find yours, you will discover that love is so much more than just the joining of one body with another. Until you do, I wish you joy in those you find along the way, Phrysilda.'

'Thanks. Breakfast?'

'That would be most welcome. Especially if you would cover that distracting and lovely body?'

'Might. Then again, might not. Maybe make you see what you're missin', eh? Since I'm missin' out on you.' And she sauntered along the corridor to the dining area, sensually inviting him with her every movement.

'You, young lady, are very naughty.'

She turned and smiled, tongued her lips suggestively, and hung her tabard on a hook by the door, making it clear she wasn't giving up her attempts to persuade him.

One of the domestic slaves came in and stared at Phrysilda.

'It's alright. We can wear as much or as little as we like. The old rules 'ave gone. I think I'll stay uncovered, at least whilst Aklon's close.'

And she did, leaving to help prepare breakfast for those in the house. Aklon watched her and wondered how many more would try to tempt him. The visual display was pleasing, but he still wanted only to share his love with Shoarhn. And the sooner he could be with her for good, the better.

Whilst he was eating, the first group of doubters, and some already converted, arrived to view the proofs. The behaviour of these initial visitors would determine for him whether he need stay or could continue his tour of the island.

Blavv dismounted with the others of the troop and left her camel tethered close enough to the washing pool for the beast to drink and to graze on the sparse vegetation growing round its banks. From here, their journey would be on foot and the dangers they faced were unknown. She and Nuldron had both tried to connect with Celestohm but discovered only blank space without awareness.

'What does it mean, Nuldron?'

'I don't know. Sometimes it happens when mindtalkers are in deep sleep. But often, Ivdulon told me, it's a sign the person's dead.'

As the only ones in the party with any knowledge of the city, she and Nuldron were in the vanguard, but the rest came close behind. The groves were eerily quiet and they found no sign of movement as they approached the city through the unguarded gateway. A quick glance into the Pit revealed two women trapped. They helped them out. But, in a bad way, neither could tell them much of use. Food and water they could give them, but could spare no one to stay with them. The women crawled away to hide from the sun in a nearby building.

'We'll be back to help you.' Blavv hoped her promise would be fulfilled.

They closed on the palace and reached its doors before any signs of life emerged.

Then it became clear that a trap had been laid. A man atop the observation tower gave out a signal cry and men emerged from buildings and streets opposite the palace. The small troop was surrounded.

Disciplined and practiced, they formed a semicircle with the palace entrance at their back, assuming the place was still held by the women. The men of the town were ill-disciplined and badly led. Keeping his distance, the Uhmbard yelled orders from the safety of a building some way down one of the streets.

The initial surge resulted in a massacre for the menfolk. With few fighting skills and no organisation, they mostly fell as they pressed forward as individuals rather than in a concerted group. Injuries amongst the troop were few and slight. Retreating, the menfolk seemed unsure what to do now. But the troop was too small to advance on so many fronts and remained before the palace, awaiting the next move.

Without the necessary means, the menfolk of Ov-Bebna had never used the longbow. Arrows were unknown to them. The troop had archers of various skill levels. One of the best brought down the man on the tower, and another hit a man who seemed to be a leader, causing great consternation around him. Fighting broke out amongst them, as some declared their intention to abandon the battle and join the other side.

Teldrohn allowed the menfolk to cut down their own numbers; such chaos was to their advantage. The sun rose higher, making the day hot and uncomfortable. From behind, came the sound of movement as the palace doors opened. Blavv turned and saw Celestohm, a sword held to her throat by a man from the Uhmbard's personal bodyguard.

'Please. Drop your weapons, or they will kill me, and all the other women in the palace.' The woman sounded and looked desperate but Blavv felt something wasn't quite right. It was the women they'd come to rescue. If the threat was real, this placed the whole enterprise at risk.

'How many men in the palace?'

Celestohm's face showed she'd received the thought but she made no reply. Blavv was convinced all wasn't as it seemed. Without a word to her colleagues, she left the troop and walked boldly up to the palace doors. The man holding Celestohm glanced at her but didn't carry out his threat. Blavv sidestepped him and entered the palace itself.

At once, she could see men inside. Few but armed. It was a trick. She held her sword firm and approached the line of men, each held a woman in front of him, his sword to her throat.

'Nuldron. This is a bluff. They won't kill her. Anyway, I think she's on their side. Ask Teldrohn to let me have five more soldiers in here. We can deal with these few guards between us.'

'You seem very sure, Blavv. The woman on the steps seems genuinely scared. Are you

certain of this?'

'Sure as I can be. I've thought for a while she might be leading us on. I know her well, don't forget. She's trying to get us to disarm so the men can take control again. She wants her position of power back again. But hurry, Nuldron. The guards in here are restless and we need to move swiftly.'

She broke the connection and moved a few more steps inside. All her short but intensive training now came to the fore. The men threatened the women they held. But Blavv was convinced they'd be reluctant to harm their shields. It was a risk she must take, if the rest of the women beyond the closed doors were to be saved.

There was a disturbance outside; something happening that she couldn't identify. Cries and sounds of animals moving swiftly. Some change had taken place and the guards sensed it. One shoved his hostage to the floor, leapt over her and rushed at Blavv, his sword held high and ready to slice her.

◦───◦

'That scream. It haunted me all night. Is this another violent city, Okkyntalah? Do we face the danger Byfthlyn warned of?'

'I don't know, Tumalind. Perhaps it was just an isolated incident, like the one in Shorrannon?'

Daylight slowly coloured the sky with pale pastels, and a line of peaks, white crowned and unbelievably high, rose to the west, seeming to cover the horizon from south to north.

'Look at that!'

Tumalind followed his gaze and stood in wonder. Dagla Kaz had told her, many portions ago it seemed, of mountains so high that the rain fell on them to form a solid covering. She'd scoffed at the idea. But if it wasn't this solid rain that made these mountain tops white, what was it? He'd also warned her the stuff was so cold it would make her whole body shake and shiver, something she'd never experienced and couldn't imagine. But it sounded awful.

'Snow, they call it. I heard Sondukal describing it to Tarruss, and Pyqad agreed with him. It's rain that falls in soft white flakes. They say it's cold enough to kill a man. I don't know what that means, do you?'

'No, Okkyntalah. I hope we never have to find out.'

Dagla Kaz called the party together and they gathered on deck, the High Priest standing on the raised portion at the front, where the captain's small cabin stood. A similar raised area held the wheel at the rear of the ship. The rest of the deck was clear, apart from masts and the ropes that held and controlled the sails. A few barrels of fresh water, some other stacked boxes of dried foods and odd bits of gear were lined against the sides in places. Otherwise, the plain wooden deck had been the sleeping and living space for the whole party. The only real shelter was below deck. There was no light and the place stank unpleasantly of some old cargo long since unloaded. On this trip, Pyqad carried only his passengers and their stores.

'I am told, by too many to ignore, that this city is a place of great evil and that our women, in particular, are in danger if we go ashore here. Beauties, like Xylthynn, Zyreenha, and of course, Tumalind, are in special peril, since the men here consider such beauty a trophy worth possessing. For that reason, we will not be leaving the ship. Only those needed to gather supplies and other important items will go into the city. I know this will disappoint many of you, but I must stand firm. We are too few to risk the welfare of our women. On the ship you will be safe.'

'How long we gonna be 'ere, then?'

Dagla Kaz sought out the questioner and found the tall, slender Virgin Gift from Kah-Labaz. She dwarfed many of those near her and her black hair flowed softly over her shoulders to frame a face alive with interest.

'As to that, Lethrymynyhl, I cannot say. But we'll stay only as long as necessary. I hope to be on our way again tomorrow.'

'Can't say as I'm 'appy for me girls to be cooped up for long on this little ship, Dagla Kaz. How far we going to sail up this river?' Corphanda had asked a question he wished to avoid. But it was out there and he must answer as well as he was able.

'Not much longer. The river is unnavigable once we're a couple of leagues from the city. There are rocks and waterfalls that make passage by a vessel like this impossible. From that point, we will have to take to our feet again. But we'll take the less tiring route for as long as we're able. We will still have many leagues to travel once we start walking again.'

'If that's the case, why don't we just leave the boat now and walk from here?'

'As I've explained Porryh, the city is too dangerous for the women to wander in.'

'Still rather walk than stay aboard this ship.'

'Do I have to repeat my warning, Porryh? I know you wish to find a way to be released from your sacred mission. But, if you risk your virginity, make no mistake, I will make you very sorry indeed. Do I make myself clear?'

Her answered agreement was accompanied by a hefty slap from Corphanda and laughter from those who expected just this outcome. Porryh, for all her assumed worldliness, had still not learned to keep quiet if she wished to spare her bottom the red wheals her guardian so readily applied.

Tumalind watched the men leave. Dagla Kaz, Tryonta, who gave her a queer look that unsettled her, Tarruss and Pyqad left for the market place. They would gather supplies and return with a local guide who would advise on the next stage of the pilgrimage. Looking up at those mountains, she hoped they'd take the route that passed up north where the wide pass at Aagtaz would mean they could avoid the snow. But she'd heard Dagla Kaz consult with Caarl over the maps and discovered the way to the pass would add eighty leagues to their journey and the High Priest was eager to get to their destination.

'What do you think, Okkyntalah?'

'We'll take one of the mountain passes, I expect. But it depends what the local guide suggests. I can't see Dagla Kaz going another eighty leagues if he can avoid it. He's in a hurry.'

'I fear that snow, Okkyntalah. I feel it has some disaster in mind for us.'

'I'll be with you all the way, Tumalind. I'll keep you safe.'

'I know you'll try, Okkyntalah.'

Chapter 12

MEHRRHYPHROL

Aglydron leant on the rail, his hand on Chislanda's shoulder. Myllthlan stood on his other side as they stared out at the city. They'd been aboard the ship for longer than they wished and craved an excuse to go ashore.

'Why have we never seen these mountains before, Aglydron?'

He looked at the long line of white topped crags that seemed so high. 'I don't know, Myllthlan.'

'Jhonaht says it's because of the lie of the land between Kah-Labaz and here. He told me the steep rise of the riverbank hides the mountains for most of the way.'

Aglydron nodded at Tumalind. She often received knowledge from the astronomer that the man wouldn't tell anyone else. Aglydron had always refused to acknowledge that his daughter was clever, but he knew this was why Jhonaht singled her out. Why, he wondered, hadn't he been proud of her? Why had he denied it? Because she was more intelligent?

'The first river we passed also has cliffs like the Mehrrhyph. But, here, the cliffs disappear and there's a wide valley that let's us see the mountains, at last. Though I wish we couldn't. I think Dagla Kaz intends to lead us that way and I fear them.'

'Wherever the High Priest takes us, it'll be safe. He knows what he's doing, Tumalind.'

'Does he, Father? Is that why he allowed the Vagboh to capture the Virgin Gifts?'

He hadn't thought of that. 'The Vagboh happened on us by chance. We couldn't have predicted such an attack, Tumalind. Their city in the forest is many leagues from where we camped. No, I think we must accept that was just an unfortunate coincidence.'

They turned to Caarl, who'd joined them at the rail. The soldier, tall and muscular, made a good leader in the service of his god. He questioned very little and acted as required by the High Priest. Aglydron admired his determination and the way he obeyed Dagla Kaz.

'Do you think we'll go through the mountains, Caarl?'

He looked down at Tumalind and smiled. 'If we do, it'll be because the guide advises it's the best way. I don't think you need worry about any danger, not if a local's leading us.'

'Dagla Kaz says the white stuff up there, snow, is cold enough to kill. Do you know anything about it, Caarl?'

He nodded. 'In Litkala, I went to see Ivdulon in her tower. From there you can climb right up Mount Vahern. I got as far as the white covering and it was very cold. I touched it. The surface was soft but underneath it was hard and slippery. It was colder than anything I've ever experienced. I had to come back down because it made me feel unwell. The wise woman told me it was frozen water. She talked of ice. Said the higher up you go, the colder the air becomes. I didn't fully understand, to tell the truth. But she said we should keep clear of ice and snow, as they could destroy us if we stayed near them too long. I believe her.'

They all stared up at the distant mountains and Aglydron found he, too, hoped to avoid that route. Cold, something most of the party had never known, was frightening.

'Hey! Dagla Kaz, what brings you to this fair city? Of course, your pilgrimage. So you made it this far, after all?'

The High Priest turned at the call across the market square. Approaching was a vaguely familiar broad-set man sporting a short beard, arm in arm with a startling redhead, who he also felt he should know.

'How's that gorgeous young woman, Tumalind, the one like a goddess?'

Now he remembered. 'Ven-Gadla. How come you here? Trading, no doubt. And, of course, your bride, Stellanyl. You both look well. But I heard it was unwise for women of beauty to be on display in this evil city. Aren't you afraid…?'

'You can't believe all rumours, Dagla Kaz. There's some truth in it, of course. Always a little truth in every rumour. But this place is as safe as most cities, except, of course, the fabulous Litkala. Mind you, that's an exception, I've found. No, your women are fine here, as long as you don't sell them, of course. Once a landlord gets his hands, legally, on a pretty woman here, she'll spend her days dressing in private and undressing on a stage in front of his paying customers. That's how the hostelries make their money here. Well, you've seen how women here are covered up. What man wouldn't give a bit of coin to see an attractive woman displaying her all, eh?'

'I see. So, no danger of the Virgin Gifts being kidnapped or anything like that?'

'None. In fact, they'd take it as an insult if they knew that's what you thought. Very strict moral code. Only handle the women they own. Would never dream of stealing one from another man.'

'If I offered to sell a woman, they'd buy her. But otherwise they'd let her be?'

'That's the way of it. You'd get a small fortune for Tumalind. Mind you, as you say, your women aren't for sale. Young Stellanyl keeps reminding me I don't own her and then shows me she's mine. Funny old world, isn't it?'

'Indeed it is. Well, I'm pleased we met up again, Ven-Gadla. But I must wish you a good day and be about my business.'

'What is your business here, Dagla Kaz? I might be able to help you.'

'I'm in need of supplies and a local guide to take us on to our next destination.'

'As for a guide, I'm bound for Likdigmina on Ahn-Ehn Bay, where I've heard there's some wonderful bargains for those willing to take risks. But I'm going via Lake Qonahn, so I can get you that far, if you like.'

Dagla Kaz knew the merchant as both reliable and conscientious. What's more, he had respect for his charges. His fees had been reasonable as well.

'How are you travelling?'

'Carts from here to the valley head.' He pointed up to the west. 'Then donkeys through the mountain pass. I'm not carrying much this trip, since it's more an exploration, looking for new goods. Plenty of room for your lot on the wagons, and there are pack-mules enough to be had at the head of the valley. Shabby little town, but they know how to raise quiet beasts to take travellers through the pass.'

Dagla Kaz stretched out his hand and touched the merchant's shoulder. 'We have a deal, Ven-Gadla. Will you be ready to travel out of the city tomorrow at sun-up, or is that too soon?'

'Quicker than I anticipated. But, for company and coin, I'm willing to forgo a look at some female flesh, especially now I have my Stellanyl to show me hers whenever I fancy it.'

Stellanyl pinched his arm. 'Cheeky frowker!'

He rubbed the place ruefully. 'True, though.'

She smiled.

They settled on the details and Dagla Kaz asked where the merchant would be spending the night. He directed him to a tavern on the road leading to the pass, and then went on his way.

Dagla Kaz and his small party bought supplies of food and other necessities from the market and arranged for them to be delivered, whilst he and Tryonta went to the tavern Ven-Gadla had mentioned. He'd paid Pyqad for the two or three days it would have taken to get them past the city and to a place where they could find the road. For the chance of a guided route with transport, Dagla Kaz thought it worth the small loss. On their return to the ship, he told the captain the party would leave during the afternoon and spend the night at the tavern where the merchant was staying.

'We going ashore after all, Dagla Kaz? Thought you said it were too dangerous for me girls?'

'I was misinformed. I met an old friend in the city and we're going to travel with him. Some of you will recall Ven-Gadla?'

He saw Tumalind smile at the memory and wondered how she'd express her feelings when he sold her to the tavern keeper. The price they could expect for such a beauty was considerable. It would solve a number of problems. The only real disappointment was that, once the girl was sold, no one but the buyer would be allowed to share her delights.

Revenge, at least, would be satisfied. And Okkyntalah, who'd escaped proper punishment for kidnapping Jodisa-Li and for his previous escape with Tumalind, would be left without his beloved mate. Serve him right. They'd already warned the landlord that he'd best hide her away until their party had gone, because Okkyntalah was likely to claim her as his own and make trouble if she went missing.

'I can 'ide the lass. None'll find 'er. Onny if she's everything you say, mind. Won't go to no trouble for ought but the best.'

'You won't be disappointed. I promise you that.'

Only a few hours, and that pair of troublemakers would no longer be his worry. He'd send the lad off on a wild chase, where he'd lose touch with the pilgrimage and never be heard of again. He rubbed his hands together until he saw the girl watching him. He gave her what he hoped was a reassuring smile.

The noise outside distracted the man who rushed at her. Blavv took her chance, slicing through his sword arm. The other men watched her stab the blade through his heart as he lay at her feet. It was enough. Some abandoned their female captives and moved away into the shadows of the palace corridors. That left her with two men, still holding captives.

'Up to you. You can die where you stand, or you can be sensible and live to enjoy a full life. I don't care which.'

One moved forward, pushing the woman before him.

'I was talking to all of you. Not just the men. And you, drop your sword, or I'll deal with you as I did your colleague.'

The man hesitated and the woman captive took her chance, escaping his grip and running to stand behind Blavv. The remaining man held on: one of the old guard who'd been responsible for the personal safety of the Uhmbard. Tougher than the other men in the city, they were still not as accomplished as the soldiers she'd been trained by in Litkala. There was, though, the real danger that he'd harm his hostage. There was nothing for it but to take action.

'I'll attack even if you don't release her. But, you harm the woman, and I'll unman you and make your death slow and painful. The choice is yours.'

She moved toward him as she spoke. He cut the woman. She screamed. Blavv moved closer and stabbed his sword arm. That forced him to release the woman, who stumbled and fell to the ground. Blavv now had free rein. She sliced him again but he slashed the top of her arm before she skewered him through his stomach. At her feet, he squirmed in pain. She cut through the garment that hid his manhood. Lopped that flesh. A final carve across his face, through his nose and an eye, left him unable to fight. She left him to bleed to death as an example to the other men. Ignoring the crying women, she moved to the door the men had been guarding.

They'd held the double doors closed with a thick stave of wood slotted into iron hooks either side of the doorframe. It was easy to lift and she opened the doors wide.

An appalling stench greeted her. There was death in the main harem. Dark, and thick with the putrid smell of rotten flesh, the room had been used to imprison all the women of the city. At last, she understood why they'd had no sight of any women on their way in.

'You four. You seem well enough, come and help your sisters. We need to get them out of here and into the sunlight and fresh air. And get them some water. Quickly. Or we'll lose more to these vile men.'

The women who'd been captive, one of whom was tending the cut hostage, stared at her as if she was some sort of magical being.

'Now, please. You know me. I'm Teh-Blavv, not a stranger. Come. Help them or they'll die.'

They came to their senses at the mention of her name.

'Are you really Teh…?

'No time now. Get them out. Time for talk later.'

She left them to it and returned to help her colleagues outside only to discover she was too late. The fighting was over. The K'ahll had arrived and evened up the odds. The city men were on their knees in three lines, stretching down the whole street. At their head, stripped and with hands bound behind them, were the Uhmbard and Uhmteld.

The rest of the troop welcomed her. Teldrohn saw her wound and detailed one of the others to tend to it. But a K'ahll woman stepped up to her before anyone else could act. She stripped and raised her arms in the air, pulling down power from the air. Singing a strange, meaningless chant, she placed her fingers over the wound and restored the flesh. Once healed, she kissed the arm before she took up her stance again and offered the power back to the air. She dressed again, without ceremony.

'That's just what that healer from Ylcrat did in Litkala. I thought she was unique. Seems not. I thank you, Paltra.'

'I know not Paltra, but am happy to be of use.' She faded back into the anonymity of her people.

Teldrohn examined the healing and added his own kiss to that of the healer. 'Whole again, Blavv. A faint scar, nothing more. What's your tale from inside, my brave soldier?'

She explained, and he detailed a number of the troop, with some K'ahll volunteers, to help the women out of the harem and others to collect water for them.

The captive men, meanwhile, remained on their knees with their hands on their heads and their faces cast down. Blavv rubbed her shoulder in disbelief and sought the healer but the K'ahll women dressed identically and she couldn't identify her.

'What to do with this sorry mob of bullies and cowards?'

'I think we must ask the women, Teldrohn. What about the Uhmteld, by the way?'

'It was obvious she'd changed sides. That's why I put her with the Uhmbard. I'm unsure what to do with any of this lot, to be honest.'

'Perhaps the women and the K'ahll will have some idea?'

'Perhaps.'

The women were brought out, many of them unable to walk from the deprivation, lack of food and water. Some were already dead and decomposing and these were placed respectfully along the side of the street, awaiting whatever ceremony the people of this city determined. Blavv knew that their fate, had the Uhmbard still been in charge, would be to be left in the desert to feed carrion creatures.

Once the harem had been cleared, and the rest of the palace searched, the whole assembly, a total greater than Blavv could count, gathered in the large open area just inside the gateway.

Teldrohn consulted the leaders of the K'ahll, a man and two women, and agreed a decision.

'For now, we need rest and refreshment. Strip the men so they can't hide weapons and so they learn what it's like to be vulnerable. Bind them, so they can't escape. The women can decide their fate, as is right and just. But we'll do that tomorrow.' He looked about, 'I understand there's a woman called Dahrlyth amongst you. Please identify yourself.'

Two of the more able women, one a harem wife, approached Teldrohn and stood before him with their faces lowered. They indicated a woman who was unable to stand. She was in a poor way; emaciated and wounded.

'I hope this woman can be saved. She led the first rising here and deserves to see the fruits of her efforts.'

The K'ahll healer emerged from her people again and knelt to examine Dahrlyth. She prepared herself, closed the wounds, and brought some life back to the woman.

Blavv managed to reach her before she melted back into her own people. 'I'd like to thank you for your healing. It's a remarkable gift and you use it well.'

'I use what skills I've been given. It would be selfish and sinful not to do good for those who deserve aid.' She bowed and entered the throng of her people.

Teldrohn signalled the three soldiers guarding the Uhmbard and the Uhmteld to bring them to him. Both fell to their knees.

'You, the men worship as a god made man. Though why they'd worship a man incapable of fathering children on hundreds of wives, I can't imagine. In any case, you've shown yourself unworthy of such devotion.' He turned to the guards. 'Toss him into that Pit. We'll deal with him tomorrow. And, this time, make sure no one helps the frowkin' coward to escape.'

The Uhmbard struggled and demanded his rights as leader of his people but to no avail. Only some of the men muttered at his treatment.

Teldrohn turned to the Uhmteld. 'You're a little less easy to deal with. You helped the women initially. Why did you go back to the men?'

'They threatened me with terrible things, things I couldn't repeat. I was frightened. I tried my best to help the women for as long as I could, but I was terrified they were going to hurt me so badly. I had no choice.'

Blavv opened a connection to her. *'Why did you lie to me, when you could so easily have told me the truth without any danger to yourself?'*

'Because I...' She glanced around, uncertain who she spoke with. *'Are you here? Can I see you?'*

'I'm standing with Teldrohn. Yes. You see me now. So, why did you lie to me?'

'You're a harem wife. Why do you not give me the respect I...?'

'You deserve no respect. You're no longer a woman of position or status. Just another woman. And, if Teldrohn allows you to live, it'll be as the others.'

'I'll have you whipped and...'

Blavv cut the connection. 'She's unchanged, Teldrohn. She was always only concerned for her own safety. She never cared about the women, just for her own position.'

Teldrohn nodded. 'Toss her in with her pervert husband. We'll deal with them later. For now, let's celebrate our victory and consult with those we should to determine the future.'

Chapter 13

DEATH IN THE DESERT

The night in a tavern had come as a welcome surprise, after their expectation they'd have to spend another on the ship. And the reconnection with Ven-Gadla was even better news: riding rather than walking. However, Tumalind was still wary of the mountains. The merchant had explained that his route would avoid the highest passes and they'd be unlucky to come across snow.

'But you'll need warmer coverings than those tabards. Air gets cold up where we're bound. Still, no need to cover that beauty of yours till we climb, and the villages at the head of the valley always have warm clothing to sell to travellers.'

He'd turned then, to watch the show the landlord provided for his clients as they drank and ate. The area was wide and open, with tables and chairs scattered around the floor. Women, covered from shoulder to foot, and with their hair wrapped in brightly coloured scarves, carried trays of food and drink on their heads, weaving skilfully through narrow passages between groups. At one side, a raised area bore a small group of musicians, playing local tunes, a young lad singing words few could hear in the hubbub of talk and dining. In front of this area, that Ven-Gadla called a stage, were rows of benches, mostly occupied by men.

A woman slowly moved onto the stage from a small door in the corner opposite the musicians. She was dressed in the local style and walked proudly and deliberately toward the players, who stopped. At their silence, the crowd also grew quiet. All faces turned to the stage.

The woman spoke softly to the musicians and they began a swaying, lilting melody, which she followed in time as she moved back to the centre of the stage.

'What goes on here, Ven-Gadla?'

'Watch. One of the best shows in the city, this one.'

She continued to eat but glanced up at the stage and saw that the woman was swaying in time with the music. The men at the front, on the benches, began to clap in time to the beat of the drum.

The woman stroked her hands down her body and parted the robe, displaying another layer beneath. Slowly, and with much sensual suggestion, she slipped off the outer garment, swung it slowly around, turning as she did so, and finally flung it to the back of the stage. Her legs were now bare below her knees and her arms displayed from the elbows. The men on the benches called out strange words whose meaning was clear enough to make Tumalind curl her hands protectively around herself.

The music changed, the beat quickening just a little, and the woman danced some more, swaying her hips and turning to display the wiggle in her bottom, making the hem swish around her knees. She moved her arms to her front and when she turned round again, the short dress was parted, revealing skin beneath. Slowly and sensually, she removed the garment, again flaring it around her body until she finally allowed it to fly to the back of the stage to lie atop her discarded robe. A band of bright red fabric wrapped her breasts and another, deeper band enclosed her hips. Her arms and legs were bare but her hair remained covered.

The dance went on, the music changing again, and she removed first the upper cloth, revealing firm young breasts devoid of tattoos or other markings. The men applauded. After more suggestive movements, she played with the lower band, displaying and hiding her womanhood and her bottom by turns as she gyrated. Her body hair had been trimmed and shaped into a triangle with small, pointed wings at the top edge. She danced this way for some time, gaining more applause and vocal admiration from the men at the front. After teasing them, she stripped off the cloth and flung it to the small pile at the back of the stage. She danced openly and invitingly, displaying to all without apparent concern.

Finally, to a hushed and attentive audience, she slowly removed the scarf from her head, allowing long black locks to fall free and loose about her shoulders. The men in front called out, almost hysterical with excitement at this final revelation. She played the same trick with her scarf as she had with the rest of her garments, flinging it to the back of the stage in a flourish. Now, entirely naked, she strutted proud and daring up and down the stage, leaning toward the men, displaying openly and wantonly, inviting, it seemed, more than mere admiration. But, though they called, made lewd comments, invited her to join them, none touched her and she was allowed to strut and parade unmolested until she bowed, collected her clothes, and left the stage via the small door she'd used to enter.

The entire display had taken some time and ended with loud applause, catcalls and demands for more. The landlord waved his hands for silence and promised them all another show, after they'd refreshed themselves with food and drink, of course.

And so the night had passed until the mid hour, when her final show of four had ended the evening with her wandering about the crowd, naked but still unmolested in spite of her teasing and provocation.

'See how they admire and desire her, Tumalind? If you were to put on a show like that, you'd earn the landlord a fortune in no time. They love red headed women and appreciate the sort of beauty you display.'

'Well, they'll see none of me, Ven-Gadla. My skin's only for the eyes of Okkyntalah and Ytraa.'

She retired to the small room she and her husband shared and they enjoyed a night of sleep interrupted by passion until daylight woke them both. Breakfast was a good meal and they returned to their room, to collect their belongings, with the warning that they had only a little time before they must be on their way. The merchant was ready to go and their supplies would soon be loaded on the wagons.

A knock took her to the door and she discovered Tryonta, asking if Okkyntalah would kindly go with him to help Dagla Kaz identify an unusual, and possibly threatening, distant feature with his excellent eyesight.

'He'll be done shortly. You should join the party when you've gathered everything and be ready to go.'

Okkyntalah glanced at her, distrust and concern in his eyes. Something felt not quite right about the arrangement, but she couldn't put her finger on what. She nodded to him to go. 'Don't be long.'

Okkyntalah shrugged his resignation as he left her to finish their packing. She collected everything together and placed all neatly in the packs they each used. When she was ready to leave, the door to her room wouldn't open.

'Let me out! I'm locked in. Can someone let me out, please?'

Footsteps moved quickly along the hallway outside the room and she sighed with relief as the key turned softly in the lock. But the door was opened by the landlord, who carried a heavy stick in one hand. Behind him, two of the serving staff waited with silken ropes. Before she knew it, she was gagged, bound, and carried from the room.

<hr />

The early visitors to his father's house had been mostly convinced by the proofs on display. Only a very few had been stubborn enough to suggest the items were false. When challenged, they'd been unable to give reason for their doubts, other than their belief that what they'd always been told must be correct. One or two, incapable of defending their refusal to accept the evidence before them, had reluctantly decided it must be true after all. Aklon was content that his display would eventually persuade all but the most diehard Followers to the new belief.

Of course, at present, he had no alternative belief to give them. It was a matter he needed to discuss with Ivdulon; and soon. But for the moment, he was more concerned to ensure that all was well around the island.

He chose his travelling companions carefully, needing few rather than a large number, and anxious to leave as many to keep guard on the proofs as he could afford. Phildrad would come with him; he wanted to return to his wife, after all. Delbon and Choryssa would go; they'd been stalwarts for so long. Phrysilda had expressed a desire to be with him. She still had designs on him as a lover, but he could cope with that. And she'd proved an able and courageous member of the Few. Hyllahn also wished to travel with him. But her motivation was entirely sexual and, in spite of her courage in following him and helping defeat the Unholy Ones, he was disinclined to have her along.

'You have been in service for too long already, Hyllahn, and have yet to live for yourself. You will not do that with me. It is time for you to find a partner, find a way of living that suits you. Be free and live now. If you wish to be useful, then guard the proofs. But I would prefer to see you in a proper partnership. There are many men who will treasure your beauty and kindness. Why not make the most of what you have and find some happiness at last?'

'I'd hoped I could be happy with you, Aklon. But if I'm not good enough for you, I'll do as you say.'

'Your goodness is not in question, Hyllahn. You are desirable, attractive, kind, generous of spirit and will make some man a very worthy partner. But I love another. I am sorry. You may feel rejected but that is not it; I simply am not free to pick and chose any more. My heart is taken. Please accept that the fault lies not with you but with me.'

At that she kissed him, more passionately than mere gratitude required. 'Thank you, Aklon. I'll never love another like you. But I may find contentment, I suppose.'

His small party had left after that and made good time across country, making for Pampahn. Here and there along the route, they paused at farmsteads and isolated collections of houses too small to carry names. These were places he'd often found sanctuary when on the run. All these people were now happy to accept the new order and provide him and his party with food and shelter.

At one of his favourite haunts, a day's gentle walk away from Pampahn, they came upon ashes and ruin. Bodies lay abandoned amongst charred remains of buildings. It was the first evidence of the violence perpetrated by those soldiers and others who'd rejected his words. Some of the work was undoubtedly done by the Unholy Ones. He'd dreaded a pact between rebels and former fanatics of the faith, but it appeared this was exactly what had happened.

These violent extremists would be difficult to deal with. They had no concern for life, it seemed, and were incapable of seeing any point of view that didn't match their own. He'd intended a quiet and patient approach, hoping to win them over, but the sight of mutilated corpses of men, women and children at this small settlement put all such thoughts out of his head. They must deal with this plague against peace quickly and finally, or it would infect the whole island with its vile message of death and destruction.

Searching the surrounding area, it was clear that the rebel group had been no more than twenty-five or thirty in number and he was inclined to track them and deal with them straight away.

'We're too few, Aklon. We no longer have surprise on our side. They're experienced soldiers, judging by the tracks and signs. We need a larger troop to deal with extremists like these. We can't risk losing you by attacking with a fighting force too small to guarantee success.'

He had to accept Delbon's assessment and they continued toward Pampahn, not resting again until they reached the town.

Phildrad stayed with his wife. Lasdilyss greeted them all with warmth and hugged Aklon close, but only after she'd embraced her husband tightly. She offered them food, now she was returned to her own home after the town had been made more or less secure. But Aklon wanted to see Kaz-Ca-Porlesah face to face, to make sure her brief mindtalk messages were the truth. She'd risked much for him and the Cause and he wished to ensure she remained safe and unscathed.

Delbon and Choryssa accepted Lasdilyss' invitation. It was no surprise that Phrysilda went with him to the priestess' house, however. At least the small, attractive soldier had deigned to wear some covering, albeit scanty, on the journey.

Walking through the town, they came on individuals and groups sporting different dress according to their wishes. Inevitably, given the faith's insistence on naked being sacred, there were those rebellious enough to adopt this style everywhere as a form of protest against the old rules.

Porlesah greeted him at the door to her home, dressed only in a short skirt. She embraced and kissed him and hugged the small soldier beside him, greeting her as a new friend. Seeing the former priest's display, Phrysilda was bound to better her and took off what little she wore as she stepped inside the house.

It was going to be a difficult evening for Aklon. But the image of Shoarhn he carried with him in his heart would keep him true to her, he hoped. Certainly, that was his intention.

They ate and talked of what they'd seen and done. Only after they'd finished their meal, did Porlesah explain about the outbreaks of violence that had sporadically disrupted the new peace. 'Some of those rebel soldiers, in cahoots with Unholy Ones, are raiding outlying homes and demanding the occupants declare for them. If they fail, they murder them and burn down their houses. They're too strong for us, Aklon. We need some sort of army to root them out or they'll destroy everything we've achieved. People will revert to old habits rather than risk their lives for new ideas if we don't stop them soon.'

He agreed. In fact, as soon as he'd seen the people of The Point on their way to their new homeland, he would gather such an army and set about destroying the extremists. He'd hoped tolerance and time would see them able to at least cohabit. But they were unable to accommodate anything outside their own extreme views of the faith. And they'd shown no mercy to those who failed to agree with them.

There had been enough death and destruction. It was time to eradicate the Dissenters. More lost time, more time away from Shoarhn and his hopes of a peaceful life. But it must be done. And he must be the one to lead the fight.

They'd locked the men into the palace, where the women had been made prisoners, and left guards on the Pit to prevent a repeat of the previous rescue. Nuldron had been in touch with Feldrark, and Teldrohn came to Blavv in the early hours, weary with the duty that had been laid on him. She gave him what relief he could find in her arms, but knew that, come daylight, the executions must begin.

His troop and the K'ahll, now supplemented by another of their scattered tribes from the outlying desert, formed the necessary guards as the men were led from the palace and lined up in the large open area near the gateway. More than two thousand men knelt, naked and unarmed, hands tied behind them, ankles tethered to one another to prevent escape. Nevertheless, one rose from the centre of the group and made to run. An arrow found his chest at once and he fell his length, spilling blood on his fellows and warning the rest of the reward for disobedience.

The women gathered, coming from the many buildings, and, with them, came disabled men from the poor quarter; those who'd been less than citizens. Still mostly naked, due to a lack of fabric in the city, some had made brief pinafores from the coverings of cushions in the harem. Many were still weak from their period of captivity.

Dahrlyth explained that the Uhmteld had fooled the women into believing she could help them against the men and had caused the women to be gathered into the harem. A space intended for only a few hundred to gather in comfort, had been used to hold nearly three thousand. That many had died as a result was no surprise. They'd counted the dead and they numbered seven hundred and nineteen. Many were still recovering from lack of food and water and a few were expected not to live.

The troops and the K'ahll did what they could between them and gave water and food. But the women had been kept imprisoned for some days and the stocks of fresh food had all been eaten by the men and not replenished. Crops remained ungathered, animals were not milked, fruit had been allowed to fall and rot, uncollected. In some ways, the very reliance of the men on the women had been their undoing. Had the soldiers not arrived to end the fighting, the men would have had to free their captives to have some chance of life. They had no idea how to feed themselves, or do any of the many tasks undertaken by their women.

But the men proved incapable of understanding the reality of their situation. Feldrark decreed that half of them should be put to death, to reduce their threat. Who should die was left to the troop leader. Teldrohn, unable to face such a decision alone, consulted the K'ahll who now intended to live in the city, the reason for their exile gone, and they came to a scheme between them.

First, the Uhmbard and the Uhmteld were recovered from the Pit.

'This is the man you made a god. He can't father children. He can't save you. He can't even save his own skin. He's a god without power. Yet you've worshipped him simply because he allowed you to treat women as slaves, to do nothing but enjoy yourselves. That will cease at once. But first your god must die in front of you.'

Teldrohn was merciful and quick as he beheaded the Uhmbard.

'Bring the woman.'

The Uhmteld was brought before him and held upright by two soldiers, since her night in the Pit had rendered her unable to stand.

'This one betrayed you women; it's your decision what we do with her.'

Almost without exception, they condemned her to death. A few small voices called for mercy but they were ignored. The woman was made to kneel whilst Teldrohn sliced off her head with a single stroke.

The two bodies were dragged back into the Pit, which was then filled, never to be used again for punishment.

'Now to the men. They've shown cruelty, usage, abuse and brutality to you women. But you won't want to be without men. I'm directed to reduce their numbers by half. But that direction comes from afar, and we are here. I leave the decision as to their fate to you, the women of Ov-Bebna. We'll do the deed, but you must decide who is to live, who to die, and how they will live.'

Those women best able to walk, went amongst the menfolk and selected the men they considered the most evil and cruel. In the end they chose over five hundred such men and these were separated from the rest. Teldrohn had them executed quickly by sword, spear or lance. It was a duty Blavv could see sat uneasily on his shoulders, but it was necessary and he carried it out like the soldier he was.

She'd grown attached to this soldier during their short time together and knew she'd be sorry to see him leave the city. It was unlikely she'd find a man of similar stature amongst the men of Ov-Bebna. But in the city she would remain for the moment, until she had an opportunity to travel back to her real home, the distant city of Trotnahn. For now, the building of a fair and just society in this desert place was her duty to her sisters. She'd help with that for as long as she was needed.

The day of slaughter ended with the sun dying in a blood red sky. She was glad to have Teldrohn take her hand in his and lead her to the privacy of a small house he'd commandeered for them. In privacy and in passion they dispelled the horror of the day, knowing they had little time together and still other duties to complete before they must part.

Chapter 14

A DARK PLACE

Okkyntalah followed Tryonta from the room and through the tavern to the area outside, where Dagla Kaz awaited him and led him away from the loaded wagons and the others in the party. No surprise that Tryonta followed the pair as they walked toward the forest area surrounding the rear of the tavern, in fact, he was relieved, as he didn't want the man to go back to attack Tumalind now she was alone.

'You've become a source of serious concern, you and that wife of yours. I am minded to have Tryonta deal with the pair of you...'

'If you and that bowelcreep could stop seeing Tumalind as a woman to be conquered and show some proper respect for her feelings, we'd have no argument.'

'I won't be lectured by a mere lad; I'm the...'

'A mere lad who saved your life and that of your daughter. A mere lad who's been decorated for valour by the leader of a sophisticated city. A mere lad who's rescued many members of your pilgrimage...'

'Boastful. I dislike that. But enough. I don't want you, or your wife, in this party; you're disruptive influences. You can either leave of your own accord, or Tryonta can make clear my wishes.'

'I never wanted to come on this...this pilgrimage, Dagla Kaz. It was you who forced me into it. Tumalind and I will happily leave here and now and make our way back to Litkala, there to decide what we'll do with the rest of our lives.'

'Go, then. We're well rid of you. But, in exchange for a peaceful parting, kindly remain here until the rest of us have gone. I want no tearful farewells to further upset the others.'

'Tumalind will wonder where I am. I left her packing and ready to join the party.'

'That matter has already been dealt with. I sent Corphanda to explain my intentions to your wife, knowing you would be only too eager to comply.'

To his surprise, the High Priest and his henchman walked rapidly away. He remained behind in the small clearing for just a short while, wondering at his luck. This was exactly what he and Tumalind had wanted for so long. And he was confident that the High Priest and his evil henchman had not returned to endanger Tumalind.

As he made his way back to the tavern, he saw the wagons leaving, already some distance along the narrow track into the mountains. Linlyss waved from the back of the last wagon. Belatedly, it struck him that they could, had they wanted to, have taken

Tumalind with them by force, tricking him into the trees so they could separate him from her. But he had ensured they left without such action and, anyway, his keen eyesight saw no sign of her. He went back into the tavern to celebrate the good news with her.

Their room was empty. Tumalind's belongings remained with his. There was no sign of her and he assumed she'd made her farewells and gone into the public area to await his return.

Downstairs, couldn't find her. He questioned the staff, such as they were at this early hour, but none had seen her.

'Where's the landlord?'

'This time o' mornin'? He be asleep, that's where. An' don't you go wakin' 'im neither. He'll be a right sore'ead if you do.'

Okkyntalah searched as much of the tavern as he could access but there was no sign of Tumalind. Dagla Kaz and Tryonta had somehow managed to get her onto the wagons without her being seen. She'd been taken by them and he'd been tricked into staying behind so they could satisfy their perverted desires without the bother of his interference and protection. They were bigger fools than he thought if they believed he'd allow them to indulge their unnatural lusts so easily.

He gathered their belongings and hitched the bulky packs onto his shoulders, collected Shaulah from the stables, and set off at a loping run after the wagons.

They'd locked her in a small room, after taking her down some steps. She was bound and gagged, blindfold and strapped onto a flat soft surface. Twice before she'd been made captive because of her appearance. Was this imprisonment for the same reason? When would Okkyntalah come for her? Did he even know where she was? She breathed slowly, softly, preventing the rising panic and knowing that fear could so easily destroy her if she allowed it.

Okkyntalah would do all in his power to rescue her. Again. Why were men so consumed by her looks? Could she really be that unusual? It was true that many men had declared her the most beautiful woman they'd known. But was she so special, so desirable? Did she give out some sort of signal she remained oblivious to, some sign that told men she was sexually available? Was that possible? She knew of other women who seemed to be desired more than most but appeared unaware. Was she such a woman?

Even so, why would they capture her here, in this place? What did they want of her? The obvious answer came and she felt her body tense in horror of the invasion that would come after she'd been forced to display herself to the crowds. They must know Okkyntalah wouldn't rest until he found her, released her, avenged her. Except she was in a strange city with people who knew nothing at all about her brave husband.

The silence seemed so absolute in the room where they'd locked her. She recalled the sounds of the three of them as they'd bundled her, bound her and then locked the door. It had sounded heavy, solid. She knew she was on a raised platform with a soft surface. They didn't want her to suffer too much pain. The ropes were tight but not so tight that they cut off the flow of blood, and the fabric was soft. So, her skin must remain unmarked. She'd learned much about the ways of men and she used her knowledge and experience to guess at her fate.

She was destined to dance for them, the way that other woman had taken off her clothes on the stage last night. That was why they wanted her. The men hadn't touched that woman. Was this the same sort of thing that had kept her free of rape as a Dancer in the harem? She'd be made to strip and reclothe and perform every night for the pleasure of the audience. That's why they'd captured her. Perhaps she'd be spared sexual duties if that was it. And, of course, eventually Okkyntalah would discover her and take her away with him.

But they'd all be looking for her now. The pilgrimage would be delayed by her absence. Dagla Kaz would rant and rage at the delay. But would he wait until she was found, or would he not care and leave her behind? Hadn't Ven-Gadla made it clear these people only bought women who were sold legitimately?

Had she been sold?

By whom?

Dagla Kaz, of course. Of course! And Tryonta, that snake.

Okkyntalah wouldn't abandon her. But suppose they'd told him she'd gone missing? Suppose they'd lied; said they'd seen her killed and thrown into the river? Made him believe she was beyond retrieval? Worse: they'd enticed him away from the rest and killed him. Was he lying wounded, bleeding, in those trees surrounding the tavern? What had they done to him? Her Okkyntalah; her brave, wonderful, loving Okkyntalah: could he really be dead? No. She mustn't think this way.

But she might be alone in this strange place now. What would life be for her if that was so? Uncertainty was worse than knowing. She prayed for them to come for her so that she would at least have some answers.

Mindtalk! Idiot! Gidwallehn would know. She'd befriended him, and Okkyntalah had helped him escape after the battle with the Vagboh. Yes. She must contact that young man and discover what was happening.

⁂

'Another short visit, Aklon? I was hoping for your company for longer.'

'I have pressing needs, still, Porlesah. The island is simmering with potential unrest, for all that it appears calm on the surface. People do not like change. So far, the majority have been persuaded of the need by the evidence of their eyes and ears. But habits are hard to break and many will be easily swayed back into old ways if we do not find a set of new rules for them. Before I can start on that part of the Cause, I need to move the people of The Point from their isolation and into the main island. They must be given the chance at last to become united with the rest of us. They have suffered too long for sins uncommitted and I will leave them no longer.'

'But do you have to go yourself? I sent the runner, as you asked. Can't they make their own way to the new site?'

'If they could, I might leave them to do so. But they do not know the location or the route. Remember, they have been isolated on The Point for many, many cycles. They have no knowledge of the bulk of the island. And, yes, of course they have soldiers with them. But the army no more know the location I have in mind than the rest of them. No. I feel I must lead them to this final location. It is what they deserve after the dreadful treatment handed out to them by the Unholy Ones, and my father. I owe them that much, as the son of the High Priest.'

Porlesah nodded her acceptance and he smiled his gratitude. She'd already accepted she would be no more a special woman for him to visit; just another of the Few, and they were fast merging into the general population, as more and more people came to accept the changes.

Aklon set off with Phrysilda, Delbon and Choryssa for companions. The journey was short in distance but would take time because of the terrain. The expedition from the south-eastern peninsula to the north-western one would be slow because of the numbers that had to be moved. Problems for his people of The Point wouldn't begin to be over until they'd reached their new home. The sooner they started, the better.

Pampahn he left in the capable hands of Porlesah and the Few, with Phildrad and Lasdilyss as aids. He worried about the potential for violence from the group of extremists that had destroyed the outlying farms.

'You can't be everywhere, Aklon. You're but one man. We'll manage.'

He nodded at Porlesah's attempt to reassure him.

'An' I'll set up a system of guards and look-outs on the town borders so we're warned of any strangers comin' in.'

He thanked Phildrad and set off with his small party to spend the first night in the jungle, where the flies ate them and, in turn, they ate the snakes. Chellyth should be ready. Would Syylvah allow him to remain celibate on the long march? It seemed most unlikely. And he had such little reason to deny her wants, but it was a duty he'd much prefer to avoid. Perhaps she'd found a man capable of satisfying her desires at last. He hoped so. It was probably a vain hope and it would be some time before he could lose himself in his love for Shoarhn again. Though he longed for that wonder and peace he shared only with her.

With those words, the four of them set out for the peninsula to collect Chellyth's people and lead them to the site he'd found for them on the far side of the island. There, they could become a proper part of the community and live as ordinary people, or as normally as their circumstances allowed.

⁕

All those deaths; executions. Pictures of beheadings haunted Blavv's dreams, waking her with feelings of revulsion and fear. Awake, she understood the necessity. As long as men in Ov-Bebna outnumbered women, the women would remain in danger. It would be difficult to alter lifetime habits for all the population, but the women, and enough of the men, were willing to make the attempt.

Dahrlyth, who seemed to be a natural leader, had recovered enough to speak. On hearing the latest assessment of the situation she'd made a declaration that was currently being passed on to the rest of the city. In future, the community should never be ruled only by one person, of either sex. Instead, a group of people, of both genders, must make the rules and take the necessary decisions to keep the citizens both governed and happy. These individuals were to be chosen by the people. She was unclear at present how such choices should be made. But she'd wanted people to hear the idea so they could take some time to decide who they would like to represent their views.

All the other details; how many they should be, whether they should appoint a leader of the group, how often they should meet, how the system of government would actually work, were still to be considered. But a start had been made and she relaxed back into rest once her message had been agreed and taken to the people.

Blavv thought the idea had merit. She connected with Ivdulon and asked her for advice on the matter.

'What you propose is a system that's used in a number of civilised lands. It seems to work best when the representatives are taken from those who seem most suitable rather than from those who put themselves forward. I'd suggest a central place be chosen and citizens be given the opportunity to nominate people. Once the appropriate number have been put forward, the populace can be asked to decide which of those nominated should actually do the job. The more people who select each individual, the more suited is that individual for the role.'

'Suppose the ones selected don't want to do it, though, Ivdulon?'

'It may be necessary to make it an obligation. Maybe make them perform the duty for a limited amount of time only. I can't specify how many or for how long, but that's how I think it might best be organised.'

Blavv told Dahrlyth what the wise woman had said.

'Would you be willing to stand as a representative, Blavv?'

'I'd intended to go to Trotnahn; see if I can find my real home and family, but I'm willing to delay that a little time to help the city get settled.'

Dahrlyth called some of the messengers to her and gave instructions to set up places in the city where people could place nominations. She asked that Blavv's name be placed on the list that would be held in the palace, where she now rested.

In the meantime, Teldrohn and the K'ahll organised the disposal of the bodies of the executed men. The men who'd been spared were starting their instruction in how to behave with women. The K'ahll acted as teachers, stressing the equality that naturally exists amongst men and women, explaining the various qualities of both genders and illustrating the fact that people are people first and a gender second.

As the women came to understand that the act of sex could be made as pleasant for them as it had always been for men, they began to teach the men how to please them in this matter and joy slowly began to spread amongst the population.

There were diehards, fools, selfish men and women, cruel individuals who wished to dominate. But the majority wanted to make the new society work and were willing to try the new systems of being together. That the K'ahll acted as living examples of the joy and harmony possible under the rule of equality, was a bonus that allowed the men and women of Ov-Bebna to come to terms more quickly with the changes.

In this atmosphere of change and growing peace, Blavv worried that she must soon lose the man she was beginning to think of as a life partner. 'When will you leave, Teldrohn?'

He held her close, embracing her with affection. 'Feldrark wants us to stay in the city for a cycle, to ensure no further uprising occurs. He wishes Ov-Bebna to become a civilised place that can set an example in a world he wants to make safe for travel and the trade of materials and ideas. So I'll be here for a good time yet.'

'A good time's what I want; with you.'

He smiled and they went, hand in hand, to find an empty room.

'Blavv, a word of warning, my dear. Oh, sorry, you're with your man. I'll withdraw and...'

'No. Say your piece, Ivdulon. We can wait.'

'Good. The situation in Ov-Bebna seems very peaceful after the battle and the changes. But be aware that this is a false peace at present. There'll be conflict, fighting, murder and rape. Of that you can be certain. Until time heals wounds and experience shows the new system is better than the old, there'll be those who'll make trouble. You and your fellow citizens must be prepared for violence and destruction in the coming sixdays. They'll slowly

disappear, as they realise the new way is better, but they'll cause trouble before then. And some will always make trouble.'

'Thanks for the warning, Ivdulon. Now, if I may have some privacy...?'

'By all means. Enjoy your man.'

That connection broke and a more pleasant one took its place.

Chapter 15

MINDTALKING

Would it be better to contact Rrildyss Kaz or Gidwallehn? The High Priestess might be in league with Dagla Kaz and she felt unable to fully trust her. She'd always been too chatty in mindtalk, unwilling to concentrate on what really mattered. But Gidwallehn was a new acquaintance who'd only recently shown he despised the High Priest. No, her first choice had been right.

'Gidwallehn, I need help. I'm trapped and...'

'Tumalind? You still in the tavern?'

'Aren't you?'

'I'm with the pilgrimage. About three leagues up the valley on Ven-Gadla's wagons. Where are you?'

'I don't know.'

She explained what had happened to her.

'That's dreadful. But I don't see what I can do. Dagla Kaz told us you and Okkyntalah no longer wished to be part of the pilgrimage. Said you'd been very blasphemous about it and Gadhallah and even Ytraa. He's rejected you. We're never to mention your names. You're both evil and will cause Ytraa's wrath to fall on the pilgrimage if we're involved...'

'In that case, thank you for your trust, Gidwallehn, I appreciate it. Okkyntalah's obviously not with you.'

'He was with Dagla Kaz and that dreadful Tryonta, in the woods behind the tavern before we left. But I never saw him after that.'

'You didn't you see him come back out of the woods?'

'No. Linlyss waved at someone as we left. Might've been him. I'm not sure. Sorry, I daren't be caught.'

He cut the connection. Tumalind was left with the impression that he'd simply lost interest. He'd shown himself capable of doing whatever was best for him, and the High Priest's warning to avoid her and Okkyntalah would definitely have an impact on a man like Gidwallehn.

So, no help from that direction.

She considered what she'd been told by him, what had happened, and what Ven-Gadla had told her as they'd watched the woman dancing on the stage. She had little doubt now that she'd been sold to the tavern owner by Dagla Kaz. But what would happen next? And where was Okkyntalah? Had he come out of the woods, or had

Tryonta killed him there?

She examined her thoughts, her feelings about Okkyntalah, and discovered none of the pain or fear she'd felt when he'd been in danger before. It was likely that Linlyss had been waving to him after all and that he was now searching for her. But where would he look?

Her husband was a man of simple logic. With no sign of her at the tavern, he'd do the only thing he could: follow the wagons. Gidwallehn had told her they were three leagues away. Okkyntalah would have spent time searching for her and then run after the pilgrims on a wild and wasted chase. It would be a while before he caught up with them. Hopefully, someone would tell him what had happened and he'd come back for her. But, supposing Dagla Kaz or Tryonta, or one of the more pious ones got to him first? They might lie to him, might send him off in some other direction entirely. She must do what she could to let him know the truth.

Rrildyss Kaz seemed happy enough to connect with her. It was clear she didn't really believe Dagla Kaz; most in the party had received the news with disbelief. When she heard about Tumalind's situation, she was determined to tell the party to turn round and come back for her.

'If you do that, Rrildyss, Dagla Kaz will learn about mindtalk. Ivdulon was very definite that she wants him not to know until she's ready to reveal it to him.'

'But what about you?'

'I don't think I'm in real danger. I might be forced to join with the landlord, if Ven-Gadla's stories are true. And I'll be made to strip on stage, the way that other woman did. If I don't fight him, he'll probably treat me well, and I've danced naked before, so that's not too distressing for me. I'd rather not, obviously. But it's better than being beaten or killed or whatever else he might do if I refuse his wishes. In any case, if you can make sure Okkyntalah knows what's happened, he'll recover me. Again.'

'You have a truly remarkable husband in that man. I'll make sure I'm in a position to tell him the facts. And I'll tell you as soon as he's on his way back to you.'

She thanked the High Priestess and waited in the dark, amazed at her own logical and pragmatic response to her situation. But any other explanation would require her to use her imagination and almost certainly come up with a much more unpleasant fate.

It wasn't too long before she heard movement. She was about to discover the reality of her situation.

He covered the ground steadily; the uphill climb would eventually weary him if he ran too fast. What story had they told Tumalind to allow her to leave him behind? Was she grieving for his loss? Worse, had they actually not told her anything at all and merely made her unable to refuse to go with them? Maybe they'd drugged her. Perhaps she was bound and held captive in some container on one of the wagons. Had they already had their way with her and disposed of her in the very woods where Dagla Kaz had threatened him?

These thoughts spun through his mind as he ran along the narrow track up the valley. Shaulah loped along with him, tireless and devoted as always. Beside the path, the river ran, a fast flowing and boisterous wide stream full of rapids and small falls. A body falling in would quickly be destroyed and swept out to the main river. No one could swim such turbulent waters. But he mustn't think like that. Tumalind was still alive. Else, his own life was worthless.

He'd spent too long searching fruitlessly at the tavern. He should've realised it had been a trick to separate the two of them. They'd both been too naïve. Too trusting. He knew how evil Tryonta was, and the High Priest was capable of all sorts of lies. Why had he believed him? The chase would take him further from the tavern. Suppose she was still there, held captive.

But he had no choice. He must find out for certain what had become of her and the only way he could do that was to catch up with the wagons and ask the right people.

The sun began its descent toward the jagged mountains that rose both around and ahead. Already, he'd noticed a slight change in temperature. The air was definitely less humid and hot than it had been on the plain where the city lay. How much more would it cool as he climbed? He had no protection against the cold, should that become a real problem. He'd have to light a fire and stay warm that way as he rested.

The track wound, sometimes almost turning back on itself as it negotiated steep rises, but always climbing and always close to the river. At least he'd have no problem with drinking water. He followed the curve around a rocky crag and, suddenly, there was the last wagon in the line. It was only a short distance ahead. He slowed, not sure of his actions now. He must proceed carefully. He ran a few more paces and then stopped so he could focus on the people on the nearest wagon. He recognised Linlyss and three of the Virgin Gifts they'd picked up in Kah-Labaz, with Tarruss, Myllthlan, and Corphanda along with another two Virgin Gifts from Muhnilahm. Not a bad party to ask questions.

He trotted up the track. One of the girls recognised him when he was less than a hundred paces distant. She poked Corphanda and the rotund guardian turned in his direction. Tarruss twisted round also. The giant shielded his eyes and waved a greeting. For a short stretch, he followed the wagons as they moved around a steep curve before he moved closer.

The wagon train halted and Okkyntalah ran up to the nearest cart. He let his breathing settle so he could speak without pauses. No one spoke to him, but the looks he

121

received were a mixture of disgust, fear and curiosity. It was clear that all was not well. He must be alert.

'Tumalind isn't at the tavern, as I was informed by Dagla Kaz. Is she with you?'

This question raised a number of reactions, the most unexpected of which for Okkyntalah was surprise. He ignored the outrage and disbelief as products of something the party had been told by Dagla Kaz.

'She's not with us, Okkyntalah. We were told you and she…'

'Tarruss, we're not to 'ave anything to do with the blasphemers.'

'You've known Tumalind for many portions and you've seen how brave and true Okkyntalah has always been. Do you seriously believe either of them capable of blasphemy, Corphanda?'

The fat little guardian shrugged, unable to deny the words of the High Priest but equally incapable of arguing against what Tarruss had said.

'I'm certain she isn't with us, Okkyntalah.'

'Thank you, Tarruss. Then she must be back at the tavern, though I sought her there and wasn't able to find her.'

Tryonta appeared suddenly, sword drawn, and rushed at him without warning. Okkyntalah stepped aside quickly enough to avoid real danger but the other man's blade caught his hand and almost cut off his little finger. He recovered and drew his own sword. The man was a fool to attack so obviously. Okkyntalah had longed for an excuse to rid the world of this man who'd tried more than once to rape his wife, who'd threatened her with harm and him with death.

The two were alike in looks and stature. Neither had the advantage of height or bulk. Time on the road and in battle had developed Okkyntalah's muscles to the same peak of perfection as those of the High Priest's bodyguard. They fought hard and long, Tryonta using every underhand trick to get the better of the younger man. But Okkyntalah was quicker and had right on his side. He was fighting for his life where Tryonta simply wanted to kill out of spite.

He bested the older man and knocked him to the ground. But discovered he was unable to kill a man who'd lost his sword and now grovelled for mercy. He kicked the weapon into the river before he sheathed his own sword and moved away. Almost at once there was a shout of warning from the wagon.

He felt the man's fist in his back. Okkyntalah turned to find a short hunting knife moving for his face. His own was still sheathed and he had no comparable blade at hand. He dodged the first thrust and moved away from immediate danger. Before Okkyntalah could draw his own knife, Tryonta was on him again, wild fury in his eyes. The man meant to murder him. He must kill his opponent if he was to rescue Tumalind.

The thrust of the blade caught him in the chest but he sidestepped as Tryonta made the lunge. Injured, he nevertheless dodged and, as the man moved past him, kicked him on his way. There was a brief pause as Tryonta triumphed over his perceived victory. Then he swayed from the momentum of the move. His face betrayed his knowledge that there was nothing he could do to save himself. Slowly, he tilted backwards, arms flailing in a vain attempt to stop the fall. The sheer drop behind him offered no hand-holds to prevent his plunge onto the rocks below and into the boiling waters.

Okkyntalah nodded at the end of the fight. Then all was black.

The notices around Ov-Bebna had brought much interest, especially as those who could read relayed the message to all who listened. Arguments arose from men who had for so long relied on the word of a man they'd worshipped as a god.

'Your god had no power. He couldn't father a child, even with hundreds of wives. What sort of god is that? Puny. The Uhmbard was a man, no more, maybe less.'

'You'll see. When we get another to rule us. Then see who's right and who's wrong.'

'There'll be no other to take his place. He fathered no child to be his heir and the K'ahll and those soldiers from Litkala have freed us from your evil enslavement. We're free women now and we'll never let you make us your slaves again. If you don't like it, go and set up a new city elsewhere. But you'll be men alone, for no women will go with you to do your bidding.'

But they were proved wrong in a small way. A few hundred men got together and were joined by a score or so women, to remain in the old ways; tradition stronger than either sense or the courage to face change. Blavv heard and saw the division and knew it was inevitable. There were always those for whom change was worse than the old ways, no matter how bad those old ways might've been. There was no hope of making such cowards and blind fools see the error of their choices. They believed in tradition above all else. Believed in old words passed down through the generations and taken as truth because it had always been so.

Of course, for those bound by custom, there was no alternative settlement. No place suitable to sustain life lay within three day's hard march from the city. Huge areas of sand surrounded Ov-Bebna broken only here and there by dry scrubland where life consisted of thorn bushes, carrion creatures and the small rodents and birds they lived off. Nowhere, outside the city boundaries, could crops be grown.

'The K'ahll lived in the desert. If they can do it, so can we.'

'Try it. If you think it so simple.'

And some did. A pack of around fifty men and three women took off for the desert, as they were. Blavv watched them leave. They wouldn't return. No one could live in that heat and sand without the special knowledge the K'ahll had gained over generations. And the K'ahll kept such experience secret.

'You never know, if this change doesn't take, we may be forced to go back to our desert wandering. Though, I don't desire such a return. The life is hard and noble but its rewards are few and its pleasures fewer. The city, if it takes to the changes, must be a better place, especially with our influence.'

Blavv agreed. But the other dissenters who remained within the city walls posed a real problem. Without any formal agreement or decision, they gathered and took over the old quarter where the abandoned and rejected men and women had formerly lived. There, they grouped together to live a life as close to the old ways as they might. But with hundreds of men and so few women, violence and dispute were inevitable. Blavv could only hope that it wouldn't spill over into the rest of the city.

In the meantime, they had the beginnings of a new way to live. A list of possible representatives had been compiled and a system for people to mark the names of those they wished to advise and lead them. No name yet for the new power, no rules or laws for the way they should behave.

'Except that we must ensure that those who lead aren't able to make themselves into figures of authority with special privileges. If we allow that, we'll soon find ourselves in the same old ways as we left behind.'

Those assembled around Blavv and Dahrlyth nodded their agreement. The woman named by Okkyntalah was recovering rapidly and, though she was still emaciated from her days of starvation, she seemed to shine with energy and hope for the future.

'We, assembled here, have the chance to make a good place, a place where we can all be proud, where all is peace and harmony and none go without. We're charged with leading the people, but I believe we should do so by example rather than by imposition of strict laws, other than where that proves necessary.'

'Assembled. Perhaps, Dahrlyth, we should call ourselves the Assembly?'

Dahrlyth looked around at her group of representatives. Tentatively, she raised a hand in the air to signal her agreement. Others quickly understood her meaning and joined in until all assembled had their hands raised and so made their first decision that could lead them on the road to a better society.

Blavv told Ivdulon of their start.

'A good beginning, then, Blavv. But take care. Those who've chosen the old ways will be a serious threat for some time. Make sure they don't develop more power than you can resist but also that they're not excluded. If they feel ignored or rejected, they might become violent and form resistance to plague your efforts for many years. Try, if possible, to be tolerant of them. They'll come to see your new ways are better and, gradually, their number will

124

dwindle until they're no more than a memory.'

'I hope so, Ivdulon. But I fear there may be real trouble before we reach that stage.'

Chapter 16

A COOL BEGINNING

The way was narrow, with a sheer drop on the river side, so that it was impossible for more than one person at a time to move from a wagon forward or backwards. Aglydron had heard the shouts from the High Priest and Tryonta had made his way to the last of the wagons. Seven carts in total made up the chain and he was on the one second from the end. In the end one, some consternation was evident. He'd heard Okkyntalah's voice and there'd definitely been swordplay. Now, all was silent back there and there was the noise of movement from up ahead.

He acted spontaneously and jumped from the wagon, in spite of Chislanda's warning. Once clear of both wagons, he saw what caused the dissent. Myllthlan had stripped and was working on the fallen body at her knees. She was healing. He moved further and saw Okkyntalah bleeding in the dust and stones of the track. Of Tryonta there was no sign.

The troop, led by Ouqitahl, edged their way past and surrounded the healer. The soldiers seemed uncertain of their next move. Aglydron was sure they'd been sent by Dagla Kaz to deal with whatever they discovered. Having found no sign of present fighting, they were unsure how to act.

Myllthlan completed her healing and Okkyntalah sat. His dog licked his face. The healer kissed the wound and then kissed the young man full on his mouth before she covered herself and regained the cart with help from those aboard.

There was much muttering and disagreement on the cart but no one spoke to Okkyntalah or to Aglydron.

Ouqitahl nodded as Okkyntalah rose to his feet and brushed himself down. 'What brings a blasphemer back to this pilgrimage?'

'I'm no blasphemer, as you should know, Ouqitahl! I'm here to seek my wife, who I was told, by your High Priest, had stayed at the tavern. However, I find she's not there. The only other place she could be is with this party.'

'Your wife isn't here, Okkyntalah. She never emerged from the tavern before we left and she's not with us now. I suggest you seek her back in the city.'

'I've travelled these leagues because I believed she was with you. I won't go back until I'm satisfied she isn't here.'

He climbed up onto the wagon and gazed ahead. There were no containers on the carts, no places to hide a body. He inspected each wagon in turn and counted those present. He could name every one of them. But Tumalind wasn't there.

The troops moved out from the space beside the wagon to allow another figure through. Dagla Kaz, followed by an anxious Rrildyss Kaz, emerged.

'What do you want here, boy? You told me…Where's Tryonta?'

Rrildyss Kaz stared hard at Okkyntalah. She mouthed words Aglydron tried to interpret. It looked as though she was telling the young man that Tumalind was held captive in the tavern.

'How do you know Tumalind's been kidnapped?'

Rrildyss Kaz stared at him. 'I've no idea what you're talking about, Aglydron. Now, what's happening here?'

He was convinced he'd seen her try to tell Okkyntalah about Tumalind. But how could she know? In any case, she denied it. She was High Priestess. She must be right. He must be mistaken.

'Tryonta attacked Okkyntalah without any provocation. A right cowardly attack. The young hunter bested him, though. Your guardian lies dead at the foot of the cliff, Dagla Kaz.'

The High Priest stared at Tarruss and seemed unable to respond.

'It's true, Dagla Kaz. I saw it wi' me own eyes. Right cowardly attack. An' for no reason I could see. The lad were just asking questions.'

Corphanda's contribution brought the High Priest to life again. He moved forward and stepped close to the edge of the sheer drop, staring down into the boiling waters.

'No point searchin' for 'im there, Dagla Kaz. No one could survive a fall like that. Your guardian's dead.'

One of the soldiers in Ouqitahl's troop made this observation and Dagla Kaz pulled back. He rounded on Okkyntalah and raised a fist. But the blow never hit the target. The young man was too quick. He didn't retaliate, however, but simply moved out of the way, a slight wince indicating that, in spite of Myllthlan's healing, he still felt pain from the injury Tryonta had given him.

The High Priest turned and went back to his wagon. 'I've no time to waste on this matter. Get the wagons moving again. We have to go.'

The soldiers followed the High Priest and Rrildyss Kaz took the opportunity to speak softly to Okkyntalah before she went back to her wagon. The last that Aglydron saw, as he returned to Chislanda, was Okkyntalah setting off at a trot back the way he'd come.

The day was coming to an end, cool air flowed down the mountains, and the night may well be cold for their normal clothing. Aglydron had no real knowledge of what had happened, but he was sure his daughter and her husband were innocent, regardless of what Dagla Kaz had said. But he was the High Priest, so the whole thing must've been a misunderstanding. It was the only possible answer.

❦

She felt the binding around her ankles removed, slowly and gently. Her wrists were freed and she was helped to sit, still blindfold. A hand explored her thoroughly, from knee to belly, under her tabard.

'Aye, if you must. But no intrusion. She's mine for bedding. You can look all you like. In fact, let's have a proper look now. See what sort of goods we've bought here.'

The voice was rough and she recognised the tones of the tavern landlord. So, her guess had been correct. Her tabard was removed. She made no effort to stop them, fearing harm if she resisted. They stood her up and hands touched her body, making her squirm with distaste.

'Good firm dubbies. Fern's already peepin' through the short 'air. Temptin' legs. Invitin' bum. Little feet. Waist's narrow.'

'Let's see this 'air on its 'ead, then.'

The other voice was laced with lascivious overtones that had her growing tense as the bag was lifted from her head.

'Frowk me! They said it were a good 'un. Frowkin' amazin'. Me prod's proud as a punter's pole just lookin' at it! You'll make yer fortune with this 'un.'

'That's the general idea. Right. Let's get her upstairs and see what she can do, eh?'

'I am here, you know. I can speak and hear.'

Her blindfold was removed, so she blinked in the sudden light and saw the two men who'd released her.

'Who cares what a woman's got to say? Do the strip-dance and you'll get fed. Lie on yer back when I wants it. Do as your told an' you'll be well treated, spoilt even. Don't do as I say and I can hurt you real bad where it won't show but you'll be frowkin' sorry. Got it?'

'My name is Tumalind and I'm a married woman with a husband. You don't own me. I'm a free woman.'

'Chirpy frowkin' fern in't it?'

'Your name don't matter. You're a woman to be displayed and delight my customers. Your previous owner told me you'd lie about being married. Said you'd say it was a man called Okkintrowler, or summat like that. But I paid good money for yer, paid it in good faith. Yer mine now an' you'd best do as I tell yer. Right?'

'My husband is Okkyntalah and I suggest you set me free if you value your life.'

'Hey! Right chirpy, this 'un. Shall I poke it's squitter with me prod? Show it what's what?'

'The onny prod goin' into 'er is mine. And I'll do the punishing. You just make sure

129

she knows the routine in readiness for tonight. I've promised them entertainment, and entertainment's what they'll get.'

The two men shepherded her from the small room in which she'd been locked. They left her tabard on the floor. One in front and the other behind, they took her up narrow stairs and through an open trap door in the floor, which they closed behind them. No wonder no one had found her.

The room they led her to was large and reached by a ladder. A pile of garments lay on a small bench in one corner and beside them sat a fully dressed young woman with a lute. The landlord nodded at her and she gave him a nervous smile. The other man lifted a flat board with a wooden handle attached. Without warning, he smacked her bottom with it, just once.

'That's to show yer. Leaves no marks but 'urts, don't it? Do as I say an' you'll get no more. Don't do it an' you'll be sore for a sixday.'

The girl with the lute and the man with the board spent a short time in discussion and the landlord left. No one gave their name and they referred to each other without using names, like strangers.

'Right. Put on that lot. Lass'll show you 'ow, if you need showin'. Do it quick. We don't 'ave much time afore you'll be on.'

The girl helped her dress in the multiple layers of clothing and then sat down and picked up her lute.

'Right. You saw the woman last night. Do the same.'

The music started and she slowly danced her way through the motions, taking as much time as she dare to remove each layer of clothing and remembering to make the headscarf the last item, allowing her hair to flow freely over her shoulders.

'Yeah. Not bad. You'll do. I'll bring you some eats an' then you'll be on. Don't let us down, or else,' he bent the lute player over her stool, lifted her clothes and smacked her hard with the board, 'that's what you'll get.'

Tumalind watched him leave and take away the ladder. The girl allowed her clothes to fall back in place and sat with her lute.

'I'm Tumalind. What do they call you?'

'Girl. What else?' She said no more and her tone suggested she was unwilling to talk.

Tumalind wondered how long it would be before Okkyntalah found and rescued her. She'd had no contact from Rrildyss and that was worrying. Had Okkyntalah reached the wagons at all? Was he still free? Where was he? It occurred to her again that he might not be able to help her. That he might be dead.

The night was uncomfortable, the sky clear, with more stars than Aglydron had seen even at sea. He considered the earlier incident with Okkyntalah and Tryonta. Where was Tumalind? She certainly wasn't with the party and the High Priest's story of their supposed blasphemy sat very uneasily with his knowledge of his daughter and her husband. Something bad had been done and it was beginning to look as though Dagla Kaz and Tryonta were the guilty ones. It was hard to suspect the High Priest of wrongdoing. He was the representative of Ytraa here on the world. How could he be wrong? And, yet, what he knew didn't fit with what they'd been told.

Chislanda curled beside him, their shared sleepsacks placed one beneath and the other on top. For the whole of the journey so far, they'd never needed cover over their skins to sleep. But the mountain air was uncomfortable in a way that was unfamiliar to them. The merchant named it chilly, cool, and said when it got more uncomfortable, that would be what they called cold. Certainly, cover made it easier to cope with. Ven-Gadla had told them that they would need more clothing, even during the day, once they reached the head of the valley. They didn't like this fall in temperature. It was unpleasant.

Eventually, Aglydron found sleep, and dreamed of dragons; though, on waking, he was unable to describe the creatures.

Morning brought a faint mist amongst the trees that lined the steep valley walls. It hung over the river, making it look like the steam that sometimes rose over a pan simmering on a fire. They got up quickly, ate and boarded the wagons for the next stage of their journey.

Strange lands, strange customs, strange people lay ahead. If the city they'd just left was any guide, they were bound to come upon heathen habits. The way the men of Mehrrhyphrol treated their women was a scandal. To see them made to strip off their clothes for entertainment went against everything Aglydron, all Followers, held holy. Naked was sacred and not a spectacle to make coin for the performer. In any case, how could men do this to women and not expect the women to require the same treatment for them? It made no sense.

Men and women were equal under Ytraa; they must be, having once been a single being. The whole purpose of joining was to regain that unity in one person that they'd lost when Mhortag split them asunder. Ytraa, in Ytraa's wisdom, had made the act pleasurable and desirable so that they wished to couple as often as possible. And naked was for joining, and prayer, not for displaying attractive flesh to all. No, that city was a wicked place and he was glad they'd left it behind. But what lay ahead?

'You're very quiet, Aglydron.'

He turned to Chislanda and realised he'd been lost in his thoughts. He smiled at her and looked around him at the country they travelled through. The trees were tall and straight, pointing high to the heavens above. There were strange birds in the branches, strange animals in the forests. During the night he'd heard the howling cry of some beast answered by another somewhere too close for comfort. But nothing had come into their camp, where Ven-Gadla had advised they keep fires burning through the hours of darkness.

'I was thinking of the strangeness of it all, Chislanda. The city was a wicked place. I'm happy we've left it.'

'What about Tumalind and Okkyntalah?'

He studied her, wondering what he should say to this woman who he loved but who was still new to the ways of the Followers. Anything might undermine her faith, new and delicate as it must be.

'There's been a mistake. Tumalind would never be blasphemous; I raised her too well for that.'

'And Okkyntalah?'

'He's a young man and rash. But he wouldn't deliberately cause trouble. No. I think it must've been a misunderstanding.'

'What about the way Tryonta attacked him? Those who witnessed it, say he just went for Okkyntalah with no provocation at all.'

'Tell the truth, I never liked that man, Chislanda. Something about him I couldn't quite trust. He acted in a way that he thought was what the High Priest expected, but made a mistake. Paid for that mistake.'

'Will he have gone to the Garden of delights?'

Aglydron thought about this. Any Follower who'd lived a good life according to the commands of Ytraa, was assured a place in the Garden of Delights after death. There, he'd pass eternity in pleasure with all those he loved who'd gone before him, and would be accompanied by those left behind when their turn came. It was a wonderful place, where Ytraa dwelt and the sun shone always. No one slept, for there was no need. A man and woman might spend days in joining without ever tiring or becoming bored with each other, such was the delight promised for the Garden.

'I suppose he must have. Though I've heard tales of bad things he's done in life. But, no. He was Dagla Kaz's aid and assistant, so he must've been worthy of the Garden of Delights. Yes. That's where he'll be now.'

'You sound as if you're trying to convince yourself, rather than me, Aglydron. Do you think we'll end up there together?'

'Of course! As long as we do what we must to please Ytraa whilst we lead our lives here in the world.'

'Is that why we join so enthusiastically at every possible opportunity?'

'Isn't it pleasant?'

132

'It's delightful and sometimes even a bit amazing, Aglydron. You've found new ways to please me and I enjoy that you care so much for me now you no longer join only for worship. I look forward to this everlasting delight we may have in death.'

'Me, too. But I wish to live long here in the world first. Don't you?'

She smiled at him. 'Sometimes, on this pilgrimage, I wonder if the discomfort and hardship are worth it, if we could just be there in this Garden of Delights instead.'

He frowned at her. 'We don't choose when we go, Chislanda. That decision's made by Ytraa.'

'So, Ytraa decided that Okkyntalah should defeat Tryonta in the fight, then?'

This was difficult ground. He wasn't versed in the more intricate aspects of the faith; he simply believed what he'd been told throughout his life.

'I suppose Ytraa must have, yes. I expect that's it.'

'I'll ask Dagla Kaz when we stop. See what he has to say.'

'Better let him get over the loss of Tryonta first. He might not be too pleased to be reminded of it just yet.'

'But won't he be pleased that his friend has gone to the Garden of Delights?'

'I suppose so. But I think he relied on him here in the world to do certain things he'll now have to do himself.'

Chislanda seemed satisfied with that. He sighed with relief and continued to look around at their surroundings, as the mountains at the end of the valley came into view when they rounded a corner. There was white stuff up there. Snow. Cold enough to kill. And they must pass through it, or at least very close under those slopes, before reaching the land of Choshinahm. He shuddered and hoped they'd get through unharmed and that, on the far side, they'd find people much like themselves; Followers willing to help the aims of the pilgrimage.

Tumalind's words came back to haunt him, however. 'Ven-Gadla says he's never come across any Followers in Choshinahm.' If that was true, what would they do when they arrived in this land that had been the home of their ancestors? How would they find the Godwood, cut it, and take it back to their island home? How would they exchange Virgin Gifts?

Chapter 17

EXPOSED

'In trouble, Tumalind? Can I help?'

'Ivdulon. It's good to connect with you.'

She explained her situation.

'I've few connections in Mehrrhyphrol, but I fear it's another realm where women are seen as objects. It's more common in the world than you may realise, especially in less educated parts. Gadhallah and Ytraa have many faults but sexual discrimination isn't amongst them. From what I understand, you'll fare best by being obedient to your new master. I hear that you'll not be forcibly made to join with others, but the man who's paid for you will expect to enjoy you in every way. How do you feel about that?'

'I wanted to remain exclusive to Okkyntalah, but I'll join if it's necessary for my welfare and safety. After all, he's joined with many others and it's done our love no harm.'

'Nor should it, especially under the circumstances. How did you come to be sold, though? I mean, who claimed to own you in the first place? It wouldn't be Okkyntalah.'

'I don't yet know, Ivdulon. But I fear it was either Tryonta or Dagla Kaz. They both wanted to force themselves on me and I publicly refused them. They were very angry with me.'

'There's something else troubling you, I think?'

'I don't have my powder. If I have to join, I might become pregnant, and I dread that.'

'I see. Try to persuade the man to allow you to take the upper position and then leave him as soon as he's climaxed. Take yourself somewhere you can thoroughly wash yourself out afterwards. No guarantee it'll work, but it should at least give you a chance.'

The wise woman asked her for more details but the man returned and she had to cut her connection and go down with him for the first dance of the evening. The girl with the lute followed. Tumalind was made to wait in a small room with two doors. One led from the corridor into which the ladder descended and the other one the lute player went through to join the musicians. The door the other woman had used to reach the stage.

From behind the wooden wall, she could hear the noise in the tavern. It sounded full and lively.

The landlord's voice suddenly rose above the rest and silence fell whilst he made his announcement. 'Welcome; loyal patrons. Tonight, I've a special treat for you. A new delight for your eyes. This one's a rarity and moves with grace and passion. She's food for the eyes, the spirit and the loins. Enjoy her now for the first time. She's never appeared

135

before in public. I give you my new woman!'

There was a burst of loud music from the stage and Tumalind knew she was expected to emerge and begin her dance. To be utterly naked in front of so many people, whilst they remained clothed. Such exposure was for the eyes of Ytraa and for her partner only. But, as Ivdulon had said, better to be displayed than refuse the dance and suffer, maybe even die. She'd done as much for the Uhmbard in Ov-Bebna, after all.

She opened the door and moved onto the stage. From this position the room looked different. The audience appeared as shadowy shapes in the dimness beyond the stage. Between her and them lay a line of lamps, throwing up light to illuminate her as she moved near the edge. It would make it easier if she couldn't see the eyes of those watching her.

Pride and self-esteem dictated she do this as well as she was able. Her dancing for the Uhmbard had prepared her and she had no concerns about her appearance, knowing from the words and stares of many men she had a body they desired. Well, since she had no choice in who saw her performance, she'd choose to make it as sensual and erotic as possible. Let them lust after her, let them all desire her until it drove them mad with want.

She moved slowly but purposefully to the centre of the stage, to the very lip where the lights best illuminated her. She made several passes along the length of the platform, hinting at the removal of her first, full cover by touching the edges with her fingertips and then fluttering them over her body away from the join. The voices called for her to undress. She paused, tilted her head on one side, as if asking a question, moved her fingers to the join and parted it only a little, raised her face and asked again with her eyes.

'Yes! Yes! Yes!'

The cry was already charged with heightened emotion. She slowly drew the garment apart at one side, holding it close at the other, exposing the loose soft gown that lay beneath and showing the skin of one leg below the knee. The men cried out for more. She closed the open side and opened the other, uncovering that leg. When they demanded more of her, she closed that side so that she was again covered.

In the hush that followed, she turned her back to them and opened the robe completely, slipping it down her shoulders and exposing her arms to the elbows. She spun round and whirled the robe off her body and against the back wall, where it dropped silently to the floor.

The men went wild. They called for more.

Again, she questioned them with her face and gestures.

'More! More! More!'

The shouts grew raucous. She recalled the movements of the other dancer but accentuated them, deliberately teasing, hoping to excite the men into a frenzy, perhaps giving her the chance to escape. The men applauded and she danced.

'More! More! More!'

She bared her arms, allowing the top of the garment to hang loose around her waist, where a tied cord held it close to her. Moving sensually, swaying to the music, she traversed the stage from side to side, from front to back and back to front. Taking her time, she passed her palms up the bare expanse of her midriff until the thumbs reached the breast cloth. She inserted them to the knuckle and traced the lower curves.

'Off! Off! Off!'

She raised her eyebrows in mock disbelief. These men were wild for her. Without the restraint that their culture demanded, they would rush on stage, denude her and each try to join with her, fighting and battling to be her partner. The knowledge that she had such power gave her confidence and courage to continue. But is also scared her: if such a thing happened, they might tear her apart in their fever.

She extracted her thumbs and lowered her hands across her midriff to the cord that held the robe around her waist. Slowly, very slowly, she untied the knot and released the robe. It fell about her feet and she kicked it across to join the other garment against the back wall.

Now she wore only the cloth across her breasts, the short skirt around her hips, and the scarf around her head and hair. Already, she'd spent more time in this single dance than the other woman had taken to dance her performance twice through the previous night. If she could keep up this pace of movement and slow exposure, she might have to perform only once. That would be a real relief.

'Off! Off! Off!'

She pretended shyness, coyly turned her back and wound her hands behind to find the tie that held the cloth around her breasts. Still pretending, she made a play of trying to untie it and turned to face them, shrugging as if unable to perform this difficult task.

Those in the front offered to help and she opened her mouth in shock at the suggestion, earning the approval of the rest of the audience. A quick glance across the room to where the landlord stood in his small raised area, showed her he approved of what she'd so far done. He nodded at her briefly and she understood she should continue with her slow revelation.

She turned her back again and attempted to untie the cloth. Again, she turned and shrugged, apologising for her inability to undo it. The men grew more eager still, chanting at her.

'Take if off! Take it off! Off! Off! Off!'

She did a shy dance of uncertainty and turned her back again. This time, she undid the knot and slipped her hands to her front to hold the cloth in place as it began to drop away. Turning to face them, she held her hands across her chest, cupping the breasts under the cloth. Shrugging her shoulders threatened to make the cloth fall and she made a play of rescuing it and remaining covered, acting coy. She looked down and pulled a small portion of the cloth away, exposing some of the firm round flesh and then, as if realising what she'd done, quickly covered herself again.

Sauntering to and fro across the stage, she made it seem she was unable to decide what she should do now the cloth no longer held itself in place. She moved one of her arms and allowed it to slip a little, exposing the skin, and then recovering it again. Suddenly making up her mind, she turned her back and removed the cloth. Tossing it to the floor with the rest of the clothes, she danced, her bare back teasing and taunting. When she turned, with her hands covering her breasts, she made a face of surprise, as if shocked to discover the men still present. The shock she took to the extreme, removing her hands to cover her face, but peeking out through her splayed fingers. At this exposure of her breasts, the audience exploded with glee and lust.

As the noise continued, she cupped each in turn, examining and teasing the nipple between thumb and finger, stroking her hands suggestively up and over the mounds, displaying her pleasure in the feelings of skin on skin.

The men grew wilder than they'd been, some standing, only to be told to sit down by those behind whose views they obstructed. Custom prevailed and the men sat once more.

Tumalind slipped her hands together to the skirt around her middle. She inserted the tips of her fingers underneath and slid her hands apart, edging the band a little lower down her hips. She stopped dancing and stood deep in thought, pondering the puzzle. She slid her fingers around to the back and there 'discovered' the fastening that held the skirt in place.

She raised her head in triumph and then moved her hands to the front of the skirt, stroked down her thighs and found the hem. Gripping it lightly in both hands, she raised it a little and bent forward to examine the effect. Apparently dissatisfied, she dropped it again and then made the move more definitely, raising it further.

Pretending she abruptly became aware that the men were watching her, she turned her back and raised the front of the skirt as high as she could, stroking down her belly and between her thighs, moving her hips and body as though in ecstasy. The men behind her cried out, pleading with her to turn and face them again. She dropped the front of the skirt, stroked her hands to her rear and lifted the back of the skirt in a flip to expose her bottom.

The response was wild and loud and she knew she had them completely within her power. She danced, turned a cartwheel, walked a few paces on her hands from one side of the stage to the other, flipped from her hands to her feet by bending backwards with her knees to the front of the stage. Upright, she sauntered, danced, dallied and posed as if considering until the shouts from the floor were such that she feared they might actually climb up and take her. Standing in the centre of the stage, she looked out at the audience and nodded before she whipped off the skirt and flung it behind her.

The men screamed their approval. The hall erupting with enthusiasm and heat. She recognised for the first time in her life just how powerful a beautiful woman might be if she wished to manipulate men. It frightened her that they were so absolutely governed by their loins and she suddenly made the connection between this and the faith of the Followers. How clever Gadhallah had been, how well he'd understood his people and, especially, the men.

Only the headscarf remained. Here, in this strange city, a woman's hair was evidently her most desirable aspect. Why that should be wasn't important. The mere fact was enough for her. She must keep it covered for as long as she possibly could.

Tumalind danced, uninhibited and wanton, inviting their touch and their attentions to her body, making herself available and unhidden in the full knowledge that she remained safe from such invasion. The men were almost out of control. But the traditions of their history kept most of them in check. Those unable to restrain themselves were quickly set upon by the others and made to behave correctly.

She danced with the headscarf on for as long as she could. But, finally, she must free her hair. This would be the final removal before she must venture onto the floor and weave her way between the tables to show herself up close to all present. It was a performance she knew she must do, one she must undertake with all the enthusiasm she'd displayed for the whole dance, in spite of her fears and concerns.

She raised her hands and slowly, so slowly, unwrapped the headscarf until her tresses fell about her shoulders. A great cry of approval rent the air and she knew she'd won the hearts of these men. Or, at least, their loins. She'd excited them beyond their wildest dreams.

Slowly, she moved with the headscarf to the back wall and folded it to lie with the others, pushing the whole pile close to the door where she would make her exit once she'd travelled around the room.

Hands reached out to touch her but none made other than the lightest contact as she wound her way around the many groups, climbed chairs, crossed benches and mounted tables swept clear of drinking vessels to allow her passage. Everywhere she moved she saw eyes of want and desire travel her body, eating her with such naked lust that she felt drained of all emotion. But she continued to fool them with her performance until it was time for her to mount the stage once more. She gave them a last dance of suggestion and moved to the door, where she picked up her clothes and bowed three times before leaving them to their craven desires and wanton lusts.

Inside the small room, she unfolded the clothes to rewind the bands around hips and breasts, but the other door opened and the landlord entered. He stopped her covering herself and helped her into the long robe only.

'With me.'

She followed him from the room, along a corridor and upstairs to his chamber. Now the teasing was done and it was time to fulfil her promise to a man she neither liked nor desired. A man for whom she had no respect, care or concern. A man who demanded she give all she'd promised on that stage. Tumalind knew she must do it and that it would be the hardest thing she had ever done.

<hr>

The run back down the valley had wearied Okkyntalah and he'd been forced to rest, in spite of his deep concern and need to find Tumalind. He was certain she must still be in the tavern. As day turned into evening, the air cooled and he knew he must move on or suffer from this strange chilling that the mountains brought with darkness. Shaulah rose from her slumber at his feet and the pair had continued their trot down to the edge of the city and the tavern that lay at the entrance to the valley.

The noise from inside the main hall, where they'd witnessed the erotic dancing, rose and fell but always held a sign of pleasure from the men inside. Dare he go in and reveal his presence? He'd no idea what had happened to Tumalind. Could he be sure he wouldn't cause more harm than good if he went in? He examined all the possible reasons for her absence and none left him with any comfort. But, recalling Ven-Gadla's words to Tumalind as they'd watched that woman the previous night, he had to consider the likelihood that Tumalind had somehow been forced into the landlord's clutches. It was the only one of the alternatives that gave him any hope at all.

He knew she'd never have left him voluntarily. She might've been kidnapped by some other. Might even have been raped and murdered by Tryonta and Dagla Kaz. But he felt they'd have somehow let him know; boasted that they'd had his wife and he would have her no more. In any case, he'd left her safe in their room to talk to both men and they'd then set off. He'd already discovered she wasn't with them.

That left the only probable answer to the problem: that she was still in the tavern. And, if she was there, it was most likely because her appearance persuaded the landlord to keep her. She'd been threatened in some way. If he went into the tavern, he might place both of them in danger.

Ven-Gadla had said the men paid a great deal of money to own attractive women and have them perform on stage. They were proud and fierce in ownership, greedy for the wealth and status it conferred. If he appeared in the tavern, the landlord would know he'd returned to reclaim his woman. Okkyntalah would then be faced with a fight where he stood alone against many men. There had to be another way. But, first, he must be certain.

The entrance passage was deserted. Everyone was watching the show. In his mind, he retraced the way to the hall and how things were arranged. If he could get to the doors, he might gain some idea of what was happening inside. The doors were heavy and the landlord closed and locked them before each performance, so that no unpaying customers could watch for free. But there might be a gap between the two doors that formed the entrance. It was worth a try.

He crept along the main corridor, past the drinking area, where men gathered before the show. It was deserted. Not even the women who served drinks were about. He passed the side passage that led to the stinking latrines on the outer wall. No one lurking there. No one willing to risk missing this performance. A great roar of approval went up from within the hall as he approached the doors. He pushed close, seeking some chink of light that might allow him to see inside. There was just one. High on the left corner, a sliver of wood had broken away in some accident. Once high enough, he might have a chance to view the inside.

In the drinking area, stools and chairs were empty. He took a high stool and put it against the door. Shaulah stood beside him, alert and watchful. Climbing on the stool, he placed his face hard against the narrow opening and managed to get one eye into position, in spite of the nearness of the supporting arch that curved over the doors. It was enough. He was in time to see the woman on stage remove her headscarf and reveal her gorgeous hair. Tumalind was there before those wild and lusting men, naked and exposed. His first impulse was to jump down, break open the door, and rush in to rescue her.

Calming after his initial intention he clambered up the stool again. This time to see her leave the stage and saunter through the lusting men. She offered her body, though none of them dare touch her. She made promises with her face and limbs, promises that could only mean one thing. She was enjoying this. Enjoying the adoration and desire they all felt for her. It was in her face, in her every movement. She wanted them to want her, wanted their lust. How could she? How could she be so wanton and abandoned?

He left the stool and the unwelcome vision of his wife disporting herself. How could she make such promises to these vile men? Shaulah walked beside him out of the tavern and into the cool night air. He felt betrayed. Tumalind, his lovely, beautiful Tumalind, was no more than a whore. That's what they called women who sold their bodies. Whores. All this time she'd been fooling him.

Had she joined with many men? She'd said only he'd been in that sacred place. But she'd crossed the desert with those foul slavers, told him she'd serviced their needs. Had she enjoyed it? And the Uhmbard. Was it likely she could dance naked for that man and never share her body with him? Had she fooled him all this time? Had he been a gullible fool?

The cool air flowed about his body, highlighting the scanty nature of his tabard. What was perfect for their island home with its constant heat, was useless for these highland regions. What would they do when they had to flee into those mountains?

They.

He'd asked himself the question about them as a couple. They still were. Tumalind may have disappointed him with her sexual display, but she was still his wife. He loved her. It would be difficult to get rid of that image of her flaunting herself in front of all those men, but he would try. He loved her. Yes. He still loved her.

Disappointment, that was all.

And jealousy, that she'd displayed herself so openly to all those unworthy men. He would still retrieve her, still escape with her from this dreadful place. But she'd have some explaining to do, have some need to regain his trust after what he'd seen in that great hall.

He swallowed his hurt pride. Tumalind was his. She was his love. He must do what he could to save her from this life that might seduce her with her desire to be loved, her wish to show her beauty to the world. He must rescue her from this and make her realise she was his alone. He'd bring her back to him.

But how? How to get her out of there before she fell prey to their lusts and vile perversions? How to save her from the clutches of that wicked landlord who would take her as his own as soon as she left that stage.

That soon? Of course. He'd be fired with desire by her performance and he'd see her as his property to do with as he wished. It was obvious he'd take her somewhere private and satisfy the lust she'd inspired. What else would such a man do in that situation?

How to get inside the tavern to the room where the landlord slept? That would be the place he'd take her. That was where he must go to get her back. But there was so little time before she'd be taken there. Where was it?

Chapter 18

TENSIONS

Morstahn was not the same place since the Cause had commenced. Shoarhn was anxious about tensions that were developing amongst her neighbours. Unpleasant arguments had got out of hand until fists flew and regrettable words had been spoken. Such trouble was inevitable but she hoped it would remain free from real violence.

Dahrlahg returned from the byre with the fresh milk, having finally understood when it was kept for sale and when it was to be churned for butter or used for cheese. She was finally becoming an asset. Her terrible experience at the hands of the village priest had affected her in a number of ways and she was no longer pious, no longer certain of her faith at all. The absence of that crutch, however, made her more independent in thought and deed. She was thinking for herself and seemed more open to learning new things. It seemed strange to Shoarhn that such a violent event should have a positive effect, but she was pleased the girl was more alive and responsive.

'Thank you, Dahrlahg. Has anyone put the hens away for the night?'

She nodded and the response was enough now for Shoarhn to be confident it had been done.

'You're still very quiet, Dahrlahg. You know you can talk to me, don't you?'

The girl stood by the table, hands held together in front of her, face turned to the floor. 'Will 'e still want me, Shoarhn? I mean, I'm damaged, aren't I? I'm not whole. Pentryil mightn't love me now.'

'Is he a good man?'

'He's...'e was always kind. But 'e might think I'm bad, like, mightn't 'e?'

'You can't be blamed for what that vile man did to you, Dahrlahg. He took you by force. Forced you to join with him. We call that rape and it's punishable by death, for the very good reason that it's the most vile thing a man can do to a woman without actually killing her. I'm sure that when Pentryil understands the truth of what happened to you, he'll accept you. And, if he doesn't, do you really want a man with so little understanding?'

'Love 'im, don't I?'

'I expect you do. Where is he at the moment?'

'The army went to The Point to kill all those...Oh! They're not criminals, now, are they? Everything's so different. It's hard to know what's right now. It were simpler before and...'

'But was it better? Better to have men like Uldrad in charge of us? Would you want that back?'

Dahrlahg shook her head and seemed about to cry.

'I'm sorry, that was cruel. Of course you don't. But I'm trying to help you see what it was really like before the Cause. It's hard to accept change and easy to slide back into old ways if we allow ourselves to forget how things really were. With the army, you say?'

'A soldier.'

'And he wasn't very pious?'

'Not at all. Use to swear an' things all the time. 'E tried to get into me ages ago but I told 'im 'e couldn't. Not till we're proper wed, I said.'

'In that case, he's either with Aklon converting people to the Cause or else with the people from The Point. And it's them that Aklon has gone to bring back from their isolation. So Pentryil might even return when Aklon comes to see me. That would be good, wouldn't it?'

'Wonderful.'

'Well then. Let's hope that's what happens, since we can't do anything about it anyway. Now, shall we get some food on the go? Everybody's going to be hungry after such a long day's work. I know I am.'

'D'you miss 'im? When 'e's away, like?'

'Aklon? I miss him every moment we're apart. You?'

'We've never…joined. Will we be able to now, without the ceremony on the plain?'

'I expect so. I'm not sure yet what Aklon's proposing to replace the various ceremonies, but I know he considers rites of passage and wedding and death and birth rites to be important, so he'll come up with something. How do you feel about joining with Pentryil after your experience with Uldrad?'

'It won't be like that, will it? I mean, 'e made me do things. You wouldn't believe it. But Pentryil will join with me normal, like, won't 'e?'

'I expect so. He's a young man. Is he also a virgin?'

'Was when we last spoke.'

'Well, then. I expect he'll be as eager to please you as you'll be to make him happy.'

'I do love 'im. I want things to be good.'

'Yes. We all do.'

There was a scream from outside. Both women looked at each other and then dashed to the open door. On the street, a young woman lay in the dust, blood pooling from her naked belly. They caught sight of two young men running into the hills south of the village. It seemed the violence predicted by Aklon had started. Where, she wondered, would it end?

The rear of the tavern was in darkness but Okkyntalah recalled the details and knew where the door lay in that wall. Shaulah stepped lightly beside him, ears pricked against danger. He found the door unlocked and they slipped inside without difficulty. This was the kitchen, store and preparation area. There was food on the counter near the door that led into the building and he helped himself to a handful of chopped cheese and greens as he passed through. In the corridor, he touched Shaulah on the top of her head.

'Seek Tumalind.'

His whispered command was soft as breath but the dog stopped and scented the air. For a moment, she stood, uncertain. Then, she set off confidently and he followed her as she led him through various corridors and past closed and open doors. The place was quiet now, the entertainment over and the patrons on their way home or, for those spending the night, in bed. Here and there chinks and slithers of faint moonlight, from a moon approaching its first quarter, gave the shadows startling life, making Okkyntalah nervous and wary. Shaulah led him up narrow steps to a small door.

Careful, silent as possible, he opened up and entered. There was no sound of breathing. No movement. The room was almost totally black, windowless, it seemed. He searched with feet and hands until he came upon a pile of discarded clothing. Even he could smell Tumalind on the garments and understood why the dog had led him here. He gathered them into a tight bundle and left the room. Shaulah sniffed at the clothes and continued her search.

She mounted another staircase; narrow and steep, that led to a single door with a small landing in front of it. The stairs led nowhere else. He stood outside the door and listened. Two people breathing. He waited. Yes. Only two. He listened carefully, stilling his own breath so he could hear as much as possible.

Muttered words that might've been from a female were followed by moans of pleasure that sounded male.

Then he heard the man speak. 'Keep that up and I'll reward you well, woman.'

The tavern landlord. No doubt about it.

The female sounded as though she had something in her mouth as she replied, but he heard some of her words.

'...in the desert...Ov-Bebna...dancing...'

Tumalind.

Instructing Shaulah to remain on guard beside the dropped bundle of clothes, he sought for the catch to the door and found a simple metal rising latch. Carefully, silent as possible, he lifted it and pushed the door open slowly.

Candlelight illuminated the room. On the large bed the landlord lay naked, his head thrown back on the pillow and his eyes closed. Tumalind, also naked, knelt between his spread legs, her head down and her hands on his hips.

The man gasped and Okkyntalah thought he'd been observed, but it was an expression of pleasure. He stepped right into the room, his hunting knife drawn and ready. Silent and swift, he crossed the floor until he could touch Tumalind. His hand stroked her thigh and she stopped what she was doing and made a sound of surprise.

'Don't stop, woman. Don't stop.'

The landlord's eyes remained closed in something close to ecstasy.

'It's me.' Okkyntalah's whisper reached her ears and she turned to him. For a brief moment, they stared at each other in the candlelight. She wiped her mouth and moved away from the man on the bed.

'What the…?'

Okkyntalah nodded her toward the door. He lay the knife against the landlord's throat and knelt on one of his arms as the man finally opened his eyes.

'One sound and you're dead.'

The man's cry of fear and alarm died before it started. 'Who the frowkin…?'

'You took my wife. Give me a good reason why I should spare your worthless life. Quick and quiet.'

The landlord looked frightened rather than rebellious. Okkyntalah slipped the knife a fraction, shedding a little blood, to remind him of his situation.

'I bought her in good faith. Paid frowkin' good money for 'er, an' all.'

'Who did you pay?'

'That 'igh priest fellah what was 'ere with them fool pilgrims. Your wife, you say?'

'My wife. Tumalind…'

She returned, clothed in what he'd brought with him from the room downstairs.

'He doesn't deserve to die, Okkyntalah. He's been less than kind, but he's ignorant and lives in an uncivilised city. It's not really his fault.'

'On your face.'

The landlord turned and Okkyntalah indicated to Tumalind that she should bind his hands and feet, using the lengths of cord that had been used to belt his robe and her longer one. She did that and then took the long robe and wrapped it round herself.

'You should take his, Okkyntalah. The nights here get cooler than at home.'

He rolled the landlord over and stuffed his mouth with the headscarf Tumalind declined to wear now she was free.

'You've lost money over your lust and greed, Landlord. Be glad I don't deprive you of your life as well. Don't try to follow us. If I ever see you again, I will kill you. Understand?'

The man nodded, eyes wide with fear.

Okkyntalah took Tumalind by the hand and led her through the building, silently but as quickly as possible. They were outside and in the yard when the cry went up.

'We can't risk the city. We'll have to go into the mountains.'

Okkyntalah agreed and they ran, hand in hand, toward the track leading up and away from the tavern, faint moonlight enough to guide them until they reached the trees, where darkness quickly became absolute.

'We'll wait until dawn. Then we'll find a way through the mountains and make our escape. Though I'm not sure where that'll take us.'

'As long as it's away from this dreadful place, I don't care. Thank you, Okkyntalah. I knew you wouldn't let me down.'

'I wish I could say the same for you, Tumalind.'

In the absence of the young man to punish for the death of his henchman, Dagla Kaz grew more and more resentful and irritable with the rest of the party.

'If these fools only knew the pointlessness of this pilgrimage, they'd abandon it and let me alone, Jhonaht.'

The astronomer knew him too well to rise to the obvious in this statement. Instead, the man merely nodded his acquiescence and expressed sympathy. That was no good. He needed to vent his anger and frustration on someone.

'See how the Skyfire veritably blazed last night?'

'As we enter the clear air of the mountains, Dagla Kaz, the sky becomes more defined and the Skyfire with it. And, of course, as Ivdulon predicted, this appearance promises to be more spectacular than any of the previous ones. We might make capital out of that. If we can return in time with the Godwood, and prove that we've carried out the will of Ytraa along the way, we may yet win the hearts of the people and destroy, once and for all, any residual care they have for your renegade son.'

'With luck, the boy's dead. If not by the hand of the army through Wendarah, then through the actions of those vile Holy Ones. But your idea gives me some comfort, Jhonaht. I still wish I could've put an end to Okkyntalah. He's robbed me of a valuable tool and ally in Tryonta.'

'Perhaps if he'd been a bit more circumspect in his reaction to the lad's appearance here...?'

'Too late now. He always did have a headstrong streak. Still, the lad's gone back in search of Tumalind and will doubtless find a match in the landlord and his retinue. They won't lightly give up the woman they paid all that gold to acquire. So, perhaps they'll see to his fate for me.'

'One young man against the combined force of the landlord and men? I doubt he has

147

a chance, Dagla Kaz. I think you can be confident we've seen the last of that particular problem. We'll hear no more of Okkyntalah, or of Tumalind.'

'You comfort me Jhonaht. But we must get on if we're to do the deed in time. I need to ask Ven-Gadla when we expect to reach the head of the valley.'

He lowered himself from the cart he shared with the astronomer, Rrildyss Kaz, Caarl, Ouqitahl, and a handful of the Virgin Gifts. Making his way along the side of the narrow track to the lead cart, he reached the merchant, in front beside his driver. Travel was slow at this point, due to the steep gradient. At midday, the temperature was still very hot under the clear sky but night would bring a growing chill as they climbed higher.

'Ven-Gadla, when will we be at the village?'

The merchant looked down from his seat and then glanced ahead. 'I've been this way only three times, Dagla Kaz. But I remember it well. We'll reach the head of the valley this evening. But I'd not call the place a village. No more than a collection of rough houses built by people who grind a hard living out of the poor soil and the beasts of the forests. We'll buy beasts of burden, donkeys, straight away and pack them with our supplies. A visit to the pair who provide fur wraps for the climb, and another to the man who provides footwear for those who arrive barefoot, and we'll be set. Go without shoes in those mountains and you'll lose your toes.'

More bad news. But at least they were on target for time.

'How long will it take us to get through the mountains?'

'It's a good sixteen or seventeen leagues through the lowest pass. At the rate the donkeys travel up the rough paths, we should do it in around a sixday, if we're lucky. Early starts and late finishes, though. So, not a lot of rest.'

Dagla Kaz returned to his place on the second cart. Time was already running short. The Skyfire was predicted to be gone by the twenty-eighth day of the fifth portion. The merchant's estimate would place them at the far side of the mountains around the sixth of the fourth portion. That left only fifty-two days to complete the pilgrimage. It was a daunting prospect. True, they could sail for almost the entire distance, once they rolled the Godwood down to the shores of Lake Qonahn. From there, they'd sail the vast lake, and down the wide river through the Forest of Trashahn and the Gap at Aagtaz to Stornhil. Then through the Ibasim Sea, into Sho Bay and, finally, the voyage across the Sophraq Sea to Muhnilahm. He studied the map with Caarl and Jhonaht.

'Is it possible?'

'We do this for Ytraa. With Ytraa on our side, I see no reason for real concern, Dagla Kaz. Ven-Gadla says there are many boats that cross the lake and he's sure one of them will be happy to take us and the Godwood all the way to the island, for a price, of course.'

'Thank you, Caarl. I agree. The only questions we have to face are those of the exchange Virgin Gifts and the discovery, cutting and overland transport of the Godwood to the lake.'

'As Caarl says, however, with Ytraa on our side, we should have no worries on that count.'

Was that a gleam of spite in the eye of the astronomer? He glared at him, just in case, and the man visibly quailed. In their hearts, they both knew that there was no reason for Ytraa to be on their side, if, indeed, such a deity actually existed.

Chapter 19

COLD

Tumalind had remained silent after his accusation, wondering exactly what he meant, whilst making guesses. But it wasn't the time or place to argue, as they made their sleeping space together in the dark of a strange and hostile land. Time enough to discover and set Okkyntalah right once they were safe and away from the city and the landlord. He was bound to send men to recapture her after the price he'd paid, and especially following her display for his patrons. Perhaps she'd been a little more blatant and apparently enthusiastic than she needed, but it was done now. And she'd done it for the best reasons.

The night was long and cool, the extra cover of her long robe a welcome help. At least Okkyntalah had had the sense to gather up her dancing clothes from the back room. He'd rescued her. He'd come back for her. She knew none of the rest of his story; what had caused his delay in finding her. But his veiled distrust hurt. He must know she took no pleasure from what she'd had to do. Surely he must? But it would do no good to argue with him. When the time came for her to explain he'd understand what she'd done and why. For now, all that mattered was that he'd come back and collected her, in spite of whatever doubts he had.

Morning brought light enough for them to be up and on their way before the birds and forest creatures were about. They could see the tavern in the distance from their location, and Okkyntalah, with his extraordinary vision, told her a party of a dozen had set out from there already and were making in their direction. There was less than half a league between them and their pursuers.

'We need to get to hard ground as soon as possible. It'll be difficult to fool a good tracker in these woods. Our trail's too easy to follow. And they have less weight to carry. We must go now.'

He led the way, she and Shaulah followed, in silence. The way grew steeper as they moved closer to the mountains. In places, they had to cross narrow ravines, where churning water flowed fast through deep gullies. Fallen trees took them over most of these. Okkyntalah halted at the end of one such crossing and placed a finger to his lips.

She listened, and Shaulah cocked her head to one side. Okkyntalah nodded.

'They're closer than I hoped. Help me dislodge this tree, then they'll have to find another way across.'

'Won't that just make them certain they're on the right track, Okkyntalah?'

'They're after us anyway. And I'd rather make it more difficult for them. Unless you'd prefer you were caught again.'

She bit her lip to stop the protest, but had to say something. 'Of course I wouldn't.'

She helped him shift the tree trunk. It was hard work. They had to pause twice before they edged it close enough to the edge of the narrow gap to let it fall into the ravine. They set off again at once.

All day, they climbed and hacked their way through thickets. Tumalind was completely lost, but Okkyntalah seemed to know exactly which direction he was taking. It was good to have confidence in him, even if he'd lost confidence in her.

'I'm too hot now in this long robe, Okkyntalah. Can I have the other one, please? The short one without sleeves?'

He stopped and listened to the forest about them. He nodded, lifted the pack off her back, and extracted the lighter robe. Her longer one he put in its place as she changed. It was good to note that his eyes still devoured her. So, she hadn't lost his admiration entirely.

'Another couple of leagues before nightfall and we should be safe.'

They carried on, ever up and away. At last, they found what Okkyntalah had been looking for: a stretch of ground without vegetation. The shale was hard to cross but left no trail to be followed. Once across the long steep rise, hard, solid rock carried them further away from the tavern and nearer to the head of the river valley they were more or less following.

Okkyntalah had told her they must avoid the track taken by the pilgrimage as it would be an obvious escape route. 'They'd follow us too easily.' He'd chosen to take them along a smaller tributary of the river that flowed from the mountains down to the city.

What did he know of the track? What had happened? And what was the real reason for his lack of trust?

The day began to grow old and, with the approach of evening, the air grew cool. Her exertions had made her need the lighter robe but she was beginning to feel uncomfortable now they were out in the open and ever climbing. The night promised to see them cooler than they'd been earlier and she worried how they would keep warm.

Okkyntalah pointed along the ridge they traversed and down to a place where the forest thinned out. Above it, a wide stretch of hillside lay barren of all but coarse grass and stunted shrubs. 'We'll camp there for the night.' Higher, the dread white stuff called snow covered the slope. It was cold enough to kill, yet Okkyntalah seemed to be suggesting they travel right up to it. She'd always trusted his judgment in the wild and wouldn't question him now. She must show him she trusted him absolutely.

But, as they reached the end of the ridge, she saw he intended them to descend here. There was a sheer drop on one side but the other edge dropped less steeply toward the river they'd been following on and off all day. And there, at the bottom of the decline, lay a small sheltered patch of flattish ground.

She went with him down the slope and was glad to reach the grassy area by the fast flowing stream. So narrow it was possible to jump it. But they remained on this side and Okkyntalah began to look for signs of animal life to hunt. Tumalind searched for firewood at once and gathered as much as she could.

He returned with a small creature that looked like a cross between a coney and a deer. Shaulah had an even smaller one in her teeth. Tumalind had a good blaze going and had donned the extra long robe over her shorter gown. Okkyntalah took their sleepsacks from his pack and wrapped one around his shoulders, the other around hers, as she gutted the animal. He then skinned it whilst she found a stick on which they could roast it, turning the spit as it rested on two Y shaped supports, stuck either side of the fire.

'Okkyntalah, you feel I've let you down. I think I can guess how. But it's better I don't. Please tell me how I've disappointed you.'

The meat sent appetising aromas into the dark night around them, occasional drips of fat sizzling and flaring in the flames and adding to the night sounds. For a while, Okkyntalah didn't respond. He seemed to be listening intently. At last he nodded, evidently satisfied they were safe. He turned, seriously upset. She must let him tell her, in his own words, what had caused him such distress.

Two days hard marching through a jungle Aklon found too familiar took them to the settlement just before dusk. Chellyth greeted them warmly.

'They're getting restless, Aklon. You're sure it'll be safe now?'

'As safe as it is for anyone at present. I have done many things for you and your people over the cycles, Chellyth. Now I ask that you do something for me and the Cause.'

'We're to be some sort of trial, to gauge whether the ordinary people of the island will now accept us.'

'Not at all. But I do need to show the whole island that the Cause is here to stay, that we are undertaking a great change. Part of that is the acceptance of past wrongdoing. By taking up residence on the main part of the island, where others can visit, you will demonstrate that you are ready to forgive those wrongs and join the community once more.'

'And if we aren't?'

'I would be deeply disappointed. But, consider; it may even be possible that some of those gathered here with you may wish to return to their original homes and families. Would that not be a good thing? Would it not prove how you have cared for and helped those in a less fortunate position to others? It would show the whole community in a good light and increase the respect the ordinary people might have for you.'

'Or, we could find we're still ignored. Worse, still loathed and treated like criminals.'

'You will never find out until you make the first step. No one is going to seek you here. No one knows where you are. No one can pass through the jungle without great danger.'

'Except you, of course.'

'I have had the advantage of help and guidance from your own people, Chellyth. Others lack that special gift.'

'I need to sleep on it. I'd expected to leave here only once the island was safe for us. My people need to know there may be dangers. I can't lead them all that way without telling them what they may face when we reach the new place.'

'I understand. Now, we have hurried to get here and we are in need of refreshment, if such can be provided?'

'You're always welcome to what we have, Aklon. You, and those with you.'

They moved from her hut to the central open area, where the people had gathered on hearing that Aklon had arrived. He wasn't surprised when Syylvah approached and enclosed him in an intimate and passionate embrace.

'I don't know who you are, but if anyone's doin' that with Aklon, it's me.' Phrysilda gripped Syylvah's arm and pulled her away from him.

'Who are you, then?'

'I'm one of Aklon's trusted troops and I've known him…'

'You 'aven't known 'im no longer'n me. I saw 'im first an' I'll 'ave 'im if I like.'

'Please; both of you. Phrysilda, you are aware of my feelings by now. And I respect your restraint. Syylvah, however, lacks your advantage, as she has not seen me for some time.' He turned to her. 'I am not available for any woman other than the one I have now chosen to spend the rest of my life with, Syylvah. I am sorry. I know that will disappointment you. But that is how it must be. There are many men on the island and you remain a beautiful and desirable woman. You will find what you seek in the arms of another. I am sure of it.'

'I won't, Aklon. You don't understand. I need you. I've been 'ungry ever since you left an' I'm 'ungry right now.'

'Then find another man, other men, to satisfy your craving, Syylvah. For I am no longer able to quench that need. I am sorry.' He took her hand from his and kissed it tenderly. 'You have been a strong and brave help to me, Syylvah. But times change and I am no longer free to indulge your wants. For wants is all they are. Spend your passions in the arms of another who can give you what you desire.'

'But I desire you, Aklon. Onny you.'

154

'You have been celibate since I left?'

She sulked. 'Course not. I couldn't. But none on 'em is a patch on you.'

'I doubt it. I suspect many men can give you what I have given in the past, Syylvah, if you would only allow them the opportunity to show you their devotion. Try them. Give them a chance.'

'If I can't 'ave you, no one else will!'

She launched herself at him in a fierce attack that he had to fight off with his hands until Chellyth and Phrysilda between them managed to separate her from him.

'I won't have such behaviour in my settlement, woman! On your hands and knees. Here! At my feet.'

'Please, Chellyth, I do not...'

'Aklon. I rule here. Not you. I do what I must as I always have. On your knees, woman. Bend for a whipping.'

Syylvah struggled with her emotions; fear, desire, frustration, longing and rage mingling to cause her to tense into immobility.

Two of the men nearby made up her mind for her, forcing her into the position Chellyth required. The leader took a switch and thrashed the young woman on back and buttocks until she pleaded for mercy. She ceased abruptly and pulled Syylvah to her feet by her hair. 'I'll have no disobedience here. Do you understand, girl?'

Syylvah nodded, her tears flowing free.

'Apologise to our guest.'

She turned to Aklon, her face full of remorse, passion and indecision. But she gritted her teeth and looked him in the eye. 'I'm sorry I attacked you, Aklon. But I still want you.'

He placed a gentle hand on her shoulder but she shook it off.

'Don't touch me, less you're gonna frowk me till I can't take no more. That's what I want from you. That an' nowt else!' She stomped off into the gathered crowd, leaving Aklon feeling vaguely guilty for her misfortune.

Chellyth handed the switch to one of the men, who took it back to her hut. She indicated a space on the ground and invited her guests to sit to eat. No reference was made to the punishment and Aklon knew, from experience, that she wouldn't refer to it again. Por-Kildu emerged from the crowd to join his wife and the talk quickly turned to the practicalities of the coming journey to the other side of the island.

Aklon was happy to contribute and partake in this discussion, but he couldn't forget the fierce desire that had shone in Syylvah's eyes. He hadn't heard the last of her want of him.

Never had Aglydron experienced such a sensation. Dagla Kaz called it feeling cold. It was both uncomfortable and painful. His body shook in what Ven-Gadla described as shivering. His fingers and toes felt numb, lifeless. And they hadn't even ventured into the snow yet. It lay ahead of them. The donkeys breathed vapour as they laboured under their loads. He'd never witnessed this odd phenomenon, where breath came out like a cloud of steam from a boiling pot on the stove. Added to discomfort was fear, but he tried to hide his tension so the women wouldn't think him a coward.

'How much longer do my girls 'ave to wander through this wasteland, Dagla Kaz? Onny, I fear for their 'ealth in these conditions if we don't get out of 'ere soon.'

Aglydron silently thanked Corphanda for asking what he desperately wanted answered, but dare not ask. Ven-Gadla replied for the High Priest.

'This patch of snow is the only one we have to cross. It's no more than three hundred paces. Then we start to descend again and it'll get warmer. We'll be back to normal by nightfall. Well, we'll be free of the cold, at any rate.'

Beside him, Chislanda led the donkey that carried their packs and supplies. Myllthlan was ahead, her body covered from head to toe in a thick fur. Her feet, like his, enclosed in fur-lined covers the maker called shoes. He wondered what it would feel like if they hadn't obtained these protective garments and had had to make the climb in their tabards and with their feet bare as usual. Ven-Gadla laughed at his question.

'You'd die. But first your toes and fingers would turn black and fall off. The cold kills easily.'

He could believe it. His hand could barely feel Chislanda's as they clasped them together through their sheaths of fur. Finger ends felt numb and lifeless so that, from time to time, as advised by the merchant, they clapped their hands to warm them.

More fur wrapped around their heads and they'd made no proper prayers for two nights running. The pilgrims were silent and tense, sheets of snow surrounding them as they passed below under threat of something Ven-Gadla called an avalanche.

'Cover you with snow in the blink of an eye. Still, you'd freeze to death before the snow cut off your breath, from what I've heard.'

His warning had been enough to keep them very quiet, since he'd told them that sudden noise could set off one of these falls of packed snow. Those ahead entered this sheet of snow and their steps left marks clear to see. But it was only a few paces and then they'd be back on solid ground and begin the descent to lands they could recognise with trees and flowing water.

He felt real fear for anyone who lost their protective furs up here. They wouldn't last a day.

Chapter 20

SNOWFALL

'I can't believe I ever doubted you, Tumalind. I'm sorry.'

She held his hand, squeezed it. She'd found it difficult to understand. But his description of her dance made her realise she'd been even more convincing than she'd intended. But it had kept her out of real trouble and they were back together now. No harm had been done to her and she remained exclusively Okkyntalah's. The night's joining had reassured them of their mutual love.

'Do you know where we're going, Okkyntalah?'

He stopped and pointed due west. 'See the gap between those two peaks?'

She nodded. They looked tall, craggy, unwelcoming and coated in snow.

'There's a way through there. It looks like the lowest point. I'm trying to avoid the higher reaches, as the air gets cooler as we climb. It's already cool here and I don't want to risk getting any higher, even though that would probably be a shorter way through the mountains. We don't have anything to keep us warm if we climb too high.'

They'd heard no sign of anyone following them for the whole day and were fairly certain they'd lost the men from the tavern. The fear of being stalked remained for the moment, however. Okkyntalah was right about the chill. She had no idea how much cooler it might become if they had to venture onto slopes where snow lay.

The cold underfoot cut into their unprotected skin and made their feet ache as they crossed bare rock. Okkyntalah was seeking a lower place where they could be in the trees and have a chance to light a fire before night covered them in darkness. But the way wasn't clear and he needed all his experience of the wild country to decide where they should go.

'Here. This way. I think this should lead us down to those woods.' He pointed, but she could see only bare mountain slopes.

They entered the narrow defile he'd pointed out. On one side, a sheer cliff rose many manheights above them into clear sky. Overhanging the constricted way they trod, great clumps of snow drooped down, threatening to fall at any moment. Tumalind could feel tension in the air. As if the very rocks rejected them and wanted them away.

Okkyntalah stopped and listened intently.

'Someone's coming after us. I think maybe seven. We need to hurry or we might be trapped in here.'

They moved more rapidly, their aching feet protesting at the extra effort required over unforgiving ground. They entered a long narrow gorge. Both sides were sheer and crowned by overhanging snow. The atmosphere was heavy with threat. The passage stretched forward over seven hundred paces in an unbroken and relatively straight line, slowly dropping towards the end, which remained unseen where there was a bend.

Halfway along this passage, they could stretch out their hands and touch each wall. Tumalind turned to see men behind them, at the beginning of the passage. 'Look, Okkyntalah!'

He took her hand and pulled her behind him as they changed from a fast walk to a run. The men spotted them and one shouted out, his voice echoing as it bounced from wall to wall and back again a dozen times. The shout was loud and abrupt. A command.

But they took no notice and ran even faster, the end of the passage now coming in sight. Rounding the corner, they found the way ahead partially blocked by fallen boulders that would be hard to scale and cross. But they had no choice.

Another cry came from their pursuers, only serving to make them run faster.

A strange, ominous creaking and screaming sounded from above. There was a moment's silence. Okkyntalah and Tumalind looked up and saw a great block of snow crack away from the edge and fall swiftly. They turned and ran as fast as they were able. Behind them, more and more snow fell in huge lumps. Hitting the passage floor, it drove clouds of ice particles along the narrow passage. Cold air passed them; a howling gale, chilling their very bones. Powdering them with tiny shards of ice that lodged in their hair and clothes. Underfoot, the driven fall made the ground softer but so icy they could no longer feel their feet. The sound of falling blocks of compacted snow thudded along the passage, echoing and clashing, like thunder in a storm.

The way ahead remained clear. When they were only paces from the pile of boulders they must climb to escape, a fall of snow crashed down directly in front of them. Great clouds of icy spray buried them, covering them in a deep white, cold, blanket.

⚬

'I'm sure, Dahrlyth. Or, as sure as any woman can ever be at such an early stage.'

'When did you last bleed?'

Blavv told her and the other woman nodded. 'Of course, it may mean nothing yet. I'd wait until you've missed again before you announce it.'

'I feel as if I am, though. I can't explain it. It just feels true.'

'Do you know who the father is, Blavv?'

'It has to be Teldrohn. The only other man I've ever had is the Uhmbard. And we all know he was never able to father a child on any woman.'

'Does he know?'

'I haven't told him.'

158

'You should. It's his child as well. And he's proved himself a trustworthy man.'

'He's a soldier. He told me he never married because he felt it was a bad idea for a soldier.'

'You should still give him the chance to decide for himself, don't you think?'

'You're right, of course, Dahrlyth. I'll do it now.'

She felt relieved to have come to a decision and set out to find the soldier. He should be at the temporary headquarters in the building near the gateway. The streets were now clear of bodies; those executed having been taken well out onto the sands and left for the carrion beasts to devour. There remained an air of tension and distrust in the city, but all was relatively calm now the men had to remain naked along with the women. The question of clothing wasn't uppermost in their minds; just one of many topics on the list compiled by the Assembly. The main problem was a lack of fabric and, as there were more pressing problems, they'd decided they would worry about it later.

Blavv crossed the street from the large communal house they used for their meetings. Now known as the Assembly House, it was gradually being stocked with things they felt necessary for their meetings. The soldiers' headquarters was a small building Teldrohn had selected for its position by the only entrance to the city, so that strangers could be monitored and trade regulated.

He was sitting outside when she arrived, a stone bench affording him a resting place whilst he studied the map of the city that one of his soldiers had begun to compile. He smiled at her approach.

'Been avoidin' me, Blavv?'

'Just been busy, Teldrohn. How are your plans progressing?'

'Tell the truth, things are going pretty well. There's not a lot for me to do. The men seem to have largely accepted the changes. Mind you, I can't say I'm convinced they'll stay that way once they get over the shock of their defeat.'

'Still, women now outnumber them and they're armed, of course. It's just the rebels in the poor quarter we need to worry about, I think.'

'Aye, they'll be a problem for a while, I reckon. But our soldiers and the K'ahll will keep them under control. But you didn't come to see me to talk of such things, did you?'

'You're far too intuitive for a man, you know that?'

'When you lead troops for a while, you get to know how people think, Blavv. Out with it.'

She sat beside him on the bench, close enough to feel his body heat and savour his scent. He placed a hand on her thigh, under the tunic she still wore from her days as one of his troop. She let it lie there and leant over to kiss him.

'There's no clever way to say this, Teldrohn, so I'll just come right out with it. I'm

159

pregnant.'

His hand stopped moving up her thigh and he stiffened slightly so she could feel the tension in him. 'It's mine, isn't it?'

'Your women soldiers all take a powder that stops it happening, but I never thought about it. All that time in the harem with the Uhmbard frowkin' us all an' never bringing a single baby into the world; well, it sort of seemed unnecessary.'

'You want me to marry you so we can bring it up together?'

She gazed at him, uncertain of his seriousness. 'You really mean that?'

'I'm getting too old to keep runnin' about the land in charge of a troop. Time I settled down. What do you think?'

She felt the thrill of surprised delight flow through her body. She'd expected denial, argument, rejection. Anything but easy acceptance.

'Listen, Blavv, you're a real catch, if you didn't know it. I'm not going to find another like you. And we work well together. What do you say?'

She kissed him and urged his hand further up her leg as a signal that she found his proposal very acceptable. He embraced her, held her close so she felt affection as well as the lust.

'The only question now, I suppose, is where we'll live? Here or Litkala?'

'Thought you were after going back home to Trotnahn?'

'You'd risk that with me?'

He shrugged. 'Home's where it feels right to be, isn't it? The name doesn't matter. It's the place you feel comfortable. Me, I've travelled the kingdom of Litkala and never settled all my adult life. One place is much the same as another. But you've a home. Let's go there and see whether it lives up to your expectations, eh?'

'Teldrohn, you're even more amazing than I realised.'

'It's you who's amazing. Now, I think we'd best get you to do some mindtalking with Feldrark to see if he'll let me leave the army, eh?'

The silence that followed the snowfall was absolute. She was surrounded by white. No sign of Okkyntalah or Shaulah. Just whiteness and quiet, with no edges or outlines. And the sensation Dagla Kaz had described as 'cold'. It hurt, like standing too near a fire, but different. It was too uncomfortable to bear, painful so that her whole body ached, except where she felt nothing at all.

She realised she was prone, lying on snow and covered in snow. It was a struggle to rise but, when she did so, she emerged from the blanket to see the sun still shining above.

'Okkyntalah!'

Her voice echoed through the passage and she looked up, fearful her cry might set off another avalanche. But all the snow had been dislodged.

There were men following. Were they close? She searched the passage the way they'd come and saw it was blocked to a depth of a few manheights. If the men were there, they were buried much deeper than she had been. Movement behind her caught her attention as she heard a soft moan and the sliding, sifting sound of snow falling.

Okkyntalah rose ahead of her. He shook off loose snow and looked around. Some of the white that had fallen on them was sharp and crystalline, hard as wood. Some was like spikes of clear solid water; sharp and heavy. She moved toward Okkyntalah and he bent to pick up one of these shards, weighed it in his hands.

'If one of those fell on you it could spear right through you. Are you alright, Tumalind?'

'Just cold. We must get out of here as soon as possible. Ven-Gadla told me...'

'I know. Where's Shaulah?'

They looked but could see no sign of the dog. Okkyntalah made a piercing whistle, that bounced off the walls and reverberated until it died into silence again. There was no movement, no answering bark.

'I can't leave her.'

'No.'

They moved close together and used their feet to sweep through the snow and ice, feeling for something more solid beneath the drifts. Up and down the short length they felt might hold the dog, they walked, searching with feet growing more and more numb from the cold.

Tumalind cried out in pain as her foot connected with something solid and sharp. She bent and dug with her hands. Okkyntalah came over and helped her. They shivered with the chill but they scraped away the snow.

'Is she alright?'

Okkyntalah dragged her free of the drift. A great thick length of the frozen transparent solid had speared her body. Her open eyes, unmoving, told the story. Okkyntalah dropped to his knees and embraced the body, already cold.

'We must go, Okkyntalah. We must.'

He resisted her hand on his. Briefly, he held onto his dog before he rose and turned to face the way they'd come, the place where their pursuers must lay buried. 'Frowkin' bowelcreeps! I hope you all die here.'

He turned, gripped Tumalind by her wrist, and pushed forward through the drifts toward the rock fall.

It was a hard climb but mercifully short. They said nothing as they clambered over sharp broken rock until they reached the low summit. Beyond, the fall became a slope of shale that slipped as they descended so that they were obliged to run quickly across it to stop the rock from cutting their feet. At the bottom, they stopped to catch their breath and survey the land ahead and below. Only a few paces further down and they were below the snowfields. Another steep drop would take them into low scrub and a further descent into taller trees.

'We need to get into the forest before nightfall. We can light a fire and get warm again.'

Exhausted, chilled to the bone, hungry and distraught at the death of the dog, they moved on. Above, the sky remained cloudless but ahead clouds grew ominously over the valley they must enter to make their way through the mountains.

The ground around the shrubs was hard, and littered with small stones that hurt even their seasoned feet. As sensation came back to their extremities, they suffered the ache of returning blood and the pressure of sharp rocks under their soles. The way down was hazardous, and difficult to navigate; steep enough to prevent forward planning so that once or twice they came to a part that was unscalable and had to climb back and try a different route. The sun was already behind the mountains when they finally reached the edge of the forest.

'See if you can make a fire, Tumalind. I'll find some food.'

She collected dead branches and twigs, piled them into the shape she knew would work, and used the flints she carried to spark the tinder into flame. Her clothes were wet, and chilling her skin. She took them off to dry by the fire. When Okkyntalah returned, carrying a small coney and a game bird, she wore only the short skirt.

He frowned at her. 'You'll grow sick from the chill if you stay like that.'

'I'm trying to dry the clothes. Are yours wet?'

Okkyntalah had removed the landlord's cloak and wore only his tabard, torn and stained with travel, for the hunt. It had stuck to his body. Tumalind tested it with her hands.

'Take it off. Damp can harm you. Corphanda was very keen to make sure we were always dry.'

He did as she asked and she hung his tabard with the abandoned cloak on an arrangement of fallen branches she'd constructed near the flames. The fire kept them warm enough for the moment. But they knew night would bring more chilling air and they'd need to wear all the clothes they had and wrap themselves together within their sleepsacks.

Okkyntalah skinned and gutted the coney as Tumalind plucked the bird. Both of them held out morsels for Shaulah until they recalled the reality.

They ate in silence, Tumalind recognising Okkyntalah's need to grieve. The dog had been a large part of his life. She'd been with him since he was a boy turning into a man and had hunted with him in many lands.

Once the meat had filled them and their clothes had dried, they dressed and prepared for the night, wrapping the sleepsacks so that one lay beneath and the other covered them. They built up the fire to ward off the chill and the wild animals that must frequent these trees.

'She found me, Okkyntalah. More than once. I owe my life and freedom to Shaulah. I grieve for her, too.'

He held her and they fell asleep in each other's arms, weary, forlorn and uncertain what morning might bring. In a strange land, with no guide as to their whereabouts or their best route, they huddled together for warmth and relied on good fortune to keep them from their hunters.

Chapter 21

OUT OF THE MOUNTAINS

From the headland, Dagla Kaz surveyed the huge plain spread below him. To the south a fast flowing river issued from the mountains at his back and swept onto the flat land, where it became a wide, lazy worm of water leading over to the north. There, it fed the great lake. Between that and where he stood, lay the settlement of Bophron, if the map remained accurate. They'd arrived in the land of Choshinahm, the country that had spawned first Gadhallah and then the religion of the Followers. Over to the west, grew the forest from which they must select the Godwood. From up here, on the last outrider of the mountain's foothills, the fatherland looked vast, wide, and empty of life.

'Where do we go to exchange the Virgin Gifts, Dagla Kaz? Where do we find the Godwood?'

He turned to the soldier at his left. Caarl had been a faithful servant and guide throughout the long journey and he respected the man's judgment and professionalism.

'We must reach the place marked on the map as Bophron and see what we can discover from the people, Caarl. Only then will we know whether we need find the Godwood or exchange the Virgin Gifts first.'

'You'll find no Followers in Bophron, Dagla Kaz. Been there before and never come across any. Still, like as not, there'll be some there as knows where you might find 'em.'

The High Priest stared dismally down the valley. He already knew what Ven-Gadla had just told him, but he had to go through the motions for the sake of those he guided on the pilgrimage. Suppose there were no Followers? Not one in the land of Choshinahm. What would he do? It didn't bear thinking about. The sooner he could get to the settlement and discover the reality, the better. Time was pressing and he needed to move forward.

The donkeys carried the possessions and Ven-Gadla's commodities down the slow slope over the next two days, warmth gradually returning as they descended. The cold of the mountain pass had caught only one victim. The Virgin Gift, Xylthynn, from Litkala, had ventured too high into the snowfields alone and suffered an injury but told nobody. One of her toes had had to be cut off to save the rest of her foot: the peculiar rot seemed beyond the healing powers even of Myllthlan.

Dagla Kaz had wanted to punish her for disobeying his command, but Caarl had pointed out that the pain from the injury and the agony of having the toe removed with a sharp knife should be punishment enough. She was a magnificent girl; tall, slender, and very desirable. He had, at least, been able to have her present herself to him, naked and vulnerable, as he chastised her for her stupidity. Once she was paired and no longer virgin, he'd have his chance to master that body.

Now, the sprawling settlement, more a rural town than a city, lay before them as dusk rolled over the land. Toward the horizon, the Skyfire burned bright even though the sun was still setting. The burning covered nearly a quarter of the sky at night now: a fearful sight.

The outlying homes and farmsteads of Bophron were spacious and low. Single story buildings, constructed mostly of wood from the extensive forest that lay to the south and west, dominated. All were surrounded by paddocks where horses, cattle and other smaller creatures grazed. There were pens holding what looked like small boars. Flightless birds strutted and peck the grounds of most of these outer houses, unconcerned enough to ignore the proximity of the travellers as they passed. No one challenged them, though many of the occupants gazed at them with curiosity.

Dagla Kaz noted the manner of dress, hoping to discover some echo of the garb worn by the Followers. But there were no tabards, no tunics. The women wore long drab skirts that left their ankles free, and dark bib fronts over their breasts, leaving their backs uncovered. Their hair was tied into bunches at either side and grown long.

The men were clad in colourful striped garments that clothed each leg down to the knee, with aprons front and back for modesty. Their chests were bare but bore coloured designs of all types, echoing the islanders' habit of tattooing their women. Most men wore full beards but had their hair shorn at the sides of their skulls and grown long in the central portion, with a gathered tail dropping down the back.

The pilgrim party continued along a road that Ven-Gadla clearly knew well. He led them into the town square; a vast area surrounded by open fronted stalls, animal pens and the low buildings of several hostelries. It was to one of these taverns that the merchant took them. The landlord seemed a merry sort, full of welcome and hospitality and very ready to accept the coin of strangers.

There were no private rooms, but long halls lined with pallets laid on hard, brushed, earth floors. One for men and one for women, with a corridor running between, and their single entrance doors at opposite ends of that passage.

As they waited in the dining hall for their evening meal, Dagla Kaz caught the attention of the landlord.

'I'm seeking Followers. Do you know where such disciples can be found?'

'Followers of who, or what, Paltrohn?'

'Of Ytraa, through the intercession of the Lord Gadhallah.'

The landlord scratched an armpit and stuck his tongue in his cheek. 'Gadhallah?

Gadhallah? Now why does that name strike a gong? Wait. Wait a bit. Yes. Of course. He was the one who left Choshinahm hundreds of cycles ago with some of the more gullible folk. I remember we were learned about him in school. Damned silly man, from all accounts. Didn't he insist on his...followers, you call them? Yes. Insisted they go about stark naked, if I recall aright.'

Dagla Kaz nodded sagely. He must be careful. There may be hostility. 'The Lord Gadhallah was said to be the first to recognise that Ytraa made the world and he led his people, the Followers...'

'I'd not spout that sort of rubbish here, if I was you. We know of the false gods of old but we don't give them no credence.'

It would be unwise to discuss matters further, at least until he understood what the local beliefs might be. But he needed to discover whether any of the faith remained.

'I'm sorry to go on a bit. But do any Followers of Ytraa still live in Choshinahm?'

'None around here. I heard tell there was some across the lake at Phornahm. But we of the One True Faith are after ousting all superstition from the land, so you'll not find any round these parts now.'

Dagla Kaz wrung his hands. 'One more question about them, if I may? What happens to those who fail to follow your One True Faith?'

'Oh, that's simple. We don't tolerate deviants and heretics living among us. Visitors are welcome and we put up with their odd ways, long as they don't try any of that there converting stuff. Mostly, we burn heretics. But sometimes, for a bit of fun, we take them out into the middle of the lake and feed them to Na Dagun. Folk like that one. Lots of boats go and see how long the fools stay afloat before they're devoured.'

Dagla Kaz nodded. 'I see.'

'What's your interest, Paltrohn?'

'Oh. We're just travelling with the merchant to discover new lands and customs; students of life, you might say. We'd heard from other travellers that Followers came from Choshinahm and hoped to learn something of them here, that's all.'

'Word of advice, Paltrohn. Don't let it be generally known you're interested. I've heard of folk burned just for mentioning those heathen beggars. I'll say nowt to no one; you're strangers and we try to be hospitable like.'

'Thank you. I'll ensure none of my people make that mistake, then.'

Dagla Kaz returned to the pilgrims and made sure they were all aware of the danger, not going into specifics because of the public nature of the gathering. Later, he'd tell them in more detail. Most of them were sensible enough to know his concerns were justified and would remain silent on the topic of Followers. But he had little hope that they'd manage to get to Phornahm without some sort of trouble.

'This is where I leave you to your own devices, Chellyth. You know your destination. Or, at least, Delbon and Choryssa know it and will guide you. I must be away to check on progress in the rest of the island.'

'And you must rejoin Shoarhn, of course.'

'Be kind, Chellyth. He's been parted from her more often than they've been together. He's bound to feel the want of her.'

She gave Por-Kildu a big smile, and then checked on the straggling line of people and beasts as they emerged at last from the trees to gather on the slopes of the grassy plateau.

'Keen enough to give 'er a good frowkin' but won't let me anywhere near 'im. Not fair, that's what it is!'

'Syylvah, we have been through all this a hundred times. I thought you understood by now.'

'Understandin's one thing, Aklon. Don't make my fern no less 'ot for you, do it? See? Look. Wet as a dorado's mouth.'

He glanced and shook his head in mock despair. 'Will some man please provide this young woman with the satisfaction she craves?'

One of the soldiers moved forward and touched her shoulder. She scrutinized him and took his other hand to her fern. A moment of such intimacy was all she needed before she led him eagerly back into the trees. Aklon breathed a sigh of relief. He could do without the complication.

'I'm comin' with you, Aklon. Someone's got to keep an eye on you.'

'And who, I wonder, will be keeping an eye on you, Phrysilda?'

'I'll meck sure there's plenty to keep an eye on, eh?'

She'd been at least partly clothed during their time in the settlement, where some of Chellyth's people had now taken to wearing clothes the soldiers had brought with them. They were now a mix of completely naked and as covered as the brief garments allowed. Phrysilda took advantage of their escape from the humid heart of the jungle to strip off the small skirt she'd worn, and tossed it to a woman nearby.

'There you go, Aklon. All yours.'

He removed her hand, gave a final wave to the general assembly, and turned to Chellyth and Por-Kildu.

'Once you are settled, some of the soldiers will wish to return home. Perhaps they will help construct your new homes first, but many of them have been away for a long time and will doubtless desire to be with their families. I hope you will accept their needs in this. The last thing we want is to alienate them.'

'We'll tell them of your wishes, Aklon. They may do as they will. We've managed long enough on our own. Any case, some who've lived with us on The Point may also want to return to families they were forced to leave. We may yet be reduced to a small settlement. But we'll have to wait and see, won't we?'

'On the other hand, you may become the haven for people who are uncertain or unhappy. They may come for solace and comfort, once they learn of your new location. I am sure you will have some who visit out of pure curiosity, as well. The time to come may be difficult for you in ways different from the hardship you have borne for so long, but at least you will no longer be forced to hide or to forage for food from the wild. The place you go is very good farmland, only unsettled because no town was ever set up on that particular part of the island. I hope it becomes a good home for you. And I will come as soon as I can. For now, I bid you farewell.'

He embraced her and clasped Por-Kildu's shoulder before turning and heading back to Pampahn, where he intended to spend a night with Phildrad and Lasdilyss before setting out for the capital. Then he was bound for Krohtl, and finally, Morstahn and a lengthy period of rest with the woman he loved.

Phrysilda strode happily beside him, a constant distraction. Relishing her freedom, she walked proud, and as tall as her diminutive stature allowed. Aklon smiled at the picture of confident femininity she displayed and wished and hoped that all the people on his island could become as happy and free.

They covered the ground quickly together, occasionally engaging in provocative banter initiated by Phrysilda, who clearly hadn't given up hope of joining with him. It caused Aklon both amusement and frustration, as his physical response warred with his emotions.

Whilst they were batting sexual challenges and responses between them, they came on a group of Unholy Ones invading an outlying farm. They encountered the scene so unexpectedly that they were almost caught out by sudden proximity to the fighting. There were half a dozen of the vile breed attacking the farm with flames and the people with blades. Outnumbered, the pair drew their weapons and joined the affray.

'Ivdulon, do I interrupt you?'

'At nothing of importance, Tumalind. You seem a little distressed. I know you're now free of the previous trouble. What's the problem, my dear?'

Tumalind had explained what had happened following Okkyntalah's rescue.

'I see. I'd thought you were to play a major role in the plans Feldrark and I are developing, but it seems not to be with Dagla Kaz and his troop of foolish followers. Perhaps it lies in another place. However, for the moment, you need to get out of those mountains and down where you can be comfortable. May I see through your eyes, please?'

She'd given this sort of access to Ivdulon before and found the experience strange but enlightening. It was as though the mind of the wise women invested what she saw through her eyes with an extra layer of meaning. Together, they had scanned the horizon.

'In which direction are we looking, Tumalind?'

'Almost due west, just a little to the north.'

'And Mehrrhyphrol lies at your back?'

Tumalind had asked Okkyntalah for clarification and he'd confirmed the wise woman's guess.

'In that case, continue west for now. You'll emerge on a wide open plain with a forest of huge trees directly ahead of you. That's the Glades of Ytraa, where the Godwoods have always been cut. Dagla Kaz and his party will be there soon. The pilgrims are close to Bophron as we speak. I expect you'll come out on the plain at about the same time as them, so go straight into the trees and make your way west for a little over five leagues. You'll come on a river, the second one you'll encounter after leaving the mountain range that stretches to the northeast. Follow it back into the other mountains, the ones southwest of you. Go as far as the source of the river and then over the narrow saddle of land that will face you due south. Cross the lowest point of the Mountains of Chakahn and descend into Tohltaz.'

'I'd rather not go back to Ov-Bebna.'

'Not Ov-Bebna, Tumalind. You'll come out along another river into dry scrubland. Follow it to where it forms a lake surrounded by trees in a dry region. If everything goes according to plan, you should meet up with Sondukal, who's made his way, using his skill and experience, to Ov-Bebna. He'll be escorting Blavv and Teldrohn. They'll have a local guide with them; one of the K'ahll, who knows the arid region well and can keep you all in water and food. I'm afraid you'll have to go to Trotnahn with them. I suspect there may be something there for you, anyway. But, once they're safe, you and Sondukal can return to Litkala by whatever route you like. I'd advise you to go back to Kah-Labaz, and take a boat to Shorrannon, but it really should be Sondukal's decision, along with advice from the K'ahll guide.'

It wasn't what Tumalind or Okkyntalah had wanted at the time. But they'd now found their way to the edge of the Groves of Ytraa and were ready to cross the first river, as Ivdulon had predicted.

'Looks cold.'

'And deep.'

They looked at the setting sun and watched the Skyfire slowly brighten the darkening sky.

'Will it really burn up the sinful?'

'Ivdulon says not. She says its fire is just a tail it bears as it rushes through the sky higher than the tallest mountains. The tail looks like dust and the sun lights it up. That's what she sees through her observerscope, anyway.'

'I hope she's right. In any case, we can't risk crossing the river now. We'll be wet and cold to start the night. We'll do it first thing in the morning.'

Tumalind collected wood for a fire, as Okkyntalah went hunting. She always felt vulnerable when alone now. Three times she'd been captured. Okkyntalah had saved her twice, Tarruss the other time, but she never felt safe on her own. The fire helped her remain calm and she kept one hand on a thick bough in the flames, so she'd have a burning torch to defend herself, should anyone or anything attack. It was at times like this she really missed Shaulah. She reminded herself she had, after all, killed at least once, to save Okkyntalah. If necessary, she'd do it again. But only if her life depended on it.

Chapter 22

A SORT OF MADNESS

The High Priest's manner and his apparent blasphemy deeply disturbed Aglydron. Dagla Kaz had made a point of denying the Followers and, when Aglydron had tried to speak up against that, the High Priest had silenced him with a sharp order laden with threat. The meal in the tavern had been poor quality, the company suspicious and taciturn, and they'd retired to their separate sleeping chambers almost immediately afterwards.

'There are vitally important reasons for my denial of the Followers, Aglydron. Do not speak of the matter whilst we remain in this town or we could be in danger of our lives. I will explain later. For now, I want you to talk to each of the men individually and pass on my message that we are not to speak of, nor acknowledge Ytraa, Gadhallah or the Followers. Will you do that? We cannot even conduct our usual prayers.'

'It's hard, and I don't understand, but if you say we must, then I'll obey and let the others know. What about the women?'

'I'm about to consult with Rrildyss Kaz so she can spread the word there. Now, on with the task I have given you.'

Aglydron spoke to each of the men in turn, keeping his voice low because of the presence of non-Followers in the sleeping chamber. It was clear they were in danger as Followers, but the High Priest's insistence on denial seemed outrageous and contrary to everything he believed. And he quickly discovered he wasn't alone.

'Well, I'm not going to denounce Ytraa. I'm a Follower and proud to be so. I don't...'

'Byfthlyn. Keep your voice down. Please. I understand how you feel; in fact, I agree with it. But if Dagla Kaz believes we must deny we're Followers, then I think we'd be wise to go along with him.'

'Sounds like cowardice to me.'

'Maybe. But we're greatly outnumbered here and the High Priest says we're in danger of death if we declare ourselves.'

'I'm prepared to die for my beliefs. Are you?'

Aglydron had never had to consider such a stance. He did so at Byfthlyn's challenge. 'Yes. I suppose so. But, if we die defending our faith, how can we do the will of Ytraa and take back the Virgin Gifts and the Godwood?'

'That's another thing: if we can't let it be known we're Followers, how are we going to manage to swap our Virgin Gifts for theirs?'

It was a puzzle. But Aglydron had insufficient information to explain. 'I don't know. Dagla Kaz said he'd tell us as soon as he could.'

The young man seemed mollified for the time being and Aglydron moved on, only to discover three others amongst the company with similar arguments. He gave them the same replies. But he noticed that Byfthlyn approached Dagla Kaz as soon as the High Priest returned from his talk with Rrildyss Kaz. He evidently got short shrift from him as he returned meekly to his sleeping pallet without another word.

Morning brought a meal shared with the women in the dim dining hall. There was little chatter. Ven-Gadla and his woman, Stellanyl, who dressed scandalously for a woman who purported to be a Follower were the only ones in the party who appeared to be at ease. They were happy to chat with the waitresses and kitchen staff who provided the hearty if tasteless breakfast. Aglydron watched the High Priest approach the merchant and saw an exchange of words followed by another of coin. It seemed they were destined to travel together for a little while longer. He hoped they might be given rides again, though how and where carts were to be acquired he had no idea.

Noon brought the answer to that question, as Ven-Gadla returned to the party across the large square they occupied whilst awaiting their next move. Shade trees had kept them cool and water from drinking troughs had stopped them becoming too dry. The citizens of the town viewed them with suspicion and the air was tense with mutual distrust. He was glad to see that the merchant returned with a half dozen carts pulled by great horses and controlled by drivers who seemed well able to handle these huge beasts.

The merchant and the High Priest had brief words and some deal was evidently struck. They were sent to collect their goods from the place they'd been stored by the tavern keeper and they returned to the carts. There, they were made to board in groups of each gender, so that the men and women travelled separately out of the town.

It was evening before an explanation was forthcoming. The High Priest gathered them together in small groups and took each of these away from the rural camp where they'd stopped for the night. Aglydron was in the third such group.

'We're in a heathen and hostile land where one false step, one misplaced word, could cause death for all of us. They burn Followers here and the names of Ytraa and the Lord Gadhallah are so far from being respected that the tavern keeper refused to acknowledge his ever having heard them when we first began to speak. He eventually admitted to knowing of their names but only to suggest that Followers were utterly bad and should be burned to death on sight. You will, I hope, understand why I ordered silence on all of you. We're gathered here to talk so that the drivers of the carts don't overhear. We can't even speak in their hearing, as they will betray us to the people.'

'So, we've come all this way just to get killed then, have we?

174

Dagla Kaz glared at Porryh and Corphanda gave her a swift slap.

'There appear to be Followers on the far side of the lake and Ven-Gadla has arranged to take us to the town of Phornahm by boat. We board tomorrow night from Rrahp. Until we're sure who we can trust, the silence regarding the Followers must remain absolute. Is that clearly understood?'

'What if there's no Followers 'ere at all, Dagla Kaz? What'll become of us Virgin Gifts then?' Xylthynn still limped a little from the loss of her toe but she was uncowed by the High Priest's manner.

Dagla Kaz sighed. 'This is a new situation. I ask you to be patient. I shall consult with Ytraa as soon as I find a suitable spot to do so. In the meantime, we must all simply try our best to behave in the same way as the local people so that we don't become the object of suspicion.'

Porryh moved out of reach of Corphanda before she raised a point that seemed to speak for all the Virgin Gifts. 'If I've come all this way for nothin' I'll be wantin' some reward for my wasted time.'

Dagla Kaz glared at her again. 'Young woman, we are all the servants of Ytraa. If we are unable to exchange Virgin Gifts here, then we must assume that was Ytraa's plan all along. We might see it as a test of our faith. In any case, there'll be some way in which the pilgrimage can be brought to a satisfactory conclusion. Of that I am certain. Now, we've been gone long enough and I have others to inform. Please keep in mind all I've said.'

'And if we don't?'

'I think a more serious punishment, Corphanda. Perhaps a sound dozen to make that young woman understand.'

Two of the other Virgin Gifts held Porryh as Corphanda lifted her tabard and smacked her, hard, twelve times.

'If anyone fails to do as I say, they'll put the whole party here at risk of their lives. Such behaviour will not be tolerated under any circumstances. Do you all understand?'

The group muttered their agreement and looked tensely around as they returned to the campsite.

* * *

'Ytraa's balls; that water's cold!' Okkyntalah swept his palms down his skin to wipe it free of as much water as he could before he replaced his tabard. Tumalind was still drying her own skin and he watched, fascinated as always by her beauty.

She saw him looking and turned. 'It would warm us up.'

He agreed and they made for a small clearing between the huge trees where the sunshine was unbroken on the soft grass.

'Why are we going this way, Tumalind?' He stroked her back as she cuddled against

175

him, resting and satisfied together.

'Ivdulon said there's no other sensible route. She says we should avoid the people here and definitely not admit to being Followers if we're asked.'

'Are we still Followers?'

She sat up and stroked fingers through her hair to undo the tangles. 'I don't know. I look up at the Skyfire and see it grow and know that Ivdulon's observerscope shows it for what it is. And I think of all the things we've seen and heard on our travels and I wonder whether the Followers is really the faith we were taught it was. I mindtalk to Aklon and he denounces it absolutely. And he's seen the secret documents and stone tablets left by Gadhallah himself.'

'He was a liar and a child killer, wasn't he?'

'It happened right here in this forest you know?'

Okkyntalah shuddered at the thought that such evil had been done in such a beautiful place. 'Was he mad, do you think? Or just a very bad man?'

'Ivdulon says some who mindtalk are evil. He thinks some of them persuaded Gadhallah to do what he did as a way of entertaining themselves.'

'But he must've been a pretty nasty man anyway, mustn't he? To do what he did to that poor girl.'

'I think so, Okkyntalah. And to answer your question, "no", I don't think we're Followers any more.'

'What are we?'

'I don't know. Non-believers, I suppose. But I do believe there's a god. Do you?'

'Oh, must be. You just have to look around you and see the way the world's made. Some power must've made all this, surely?'

'And some power must have made fire mountains, and snakes that bite and stinging flies...'

'I suppose so. A good one and a bad one, maybe?'

'Perhaps, Okkyntalah. I doubt we'll ever know.'

He sat up and kissed her. Embraced her.

'If you start that again, we'll never get on our way.'

He stroked her breasts and then pulled her to her feet. 'Come on, wanton. We've got distance to travel. We don't want to meet Dagla Kaz again, do we?'

She shuddered and then shook herself, as if freeing her mind of an unwanted idea. Her robe lay crushed, where she'd used it as a pillow.

'I'm going to stay as I am for now. Like Mythanpho when Vaarkil found her.'

'I'll do the same. Feels nice, doesn't it?'

'Down here under the sun. But we'll have to wrap up again once we're back in the mountains.'

They strolled, hand in hand, through broad spaces between enormous trees that made the forest. Bright, coloured birds sang and performed in the high branches. Small deer-like creatures watched them pass with no sign of fear. Little creatures with huge bushy tails ran up the vertical trunks without slipping or falling. And bright butterflies, wings as wide as Okkyntalah's hands, floated in the air above them.

'It's lovely here.'

'But not a place to live. Be impossible to build a house; the trees are just too big. Mind you, those little beasts are easy to catch, as you saw last night. So we won't go hungry.'

'You frightened me near to death when you came back. I never heard a sound and then suddenly there you were in front of me, blood streaming down your chest from the neck of that beast around your shoulders.'

'A hunter has to move silently if he's to catch his prey. Otherwise we'd go hungry.'

'Yes. But in the past I've always known you were on your way because Shaulah would arrive before...Oh, Okkyntalah, I'm sorry. Really I am.'

She placed an arm about his shoulders and they walked in silence for the time it took for him to come to terms with the loss again. By the middle of the afternoon they came to the second river and turned to follow it into the mountains. When the sun vanished behind the nearby mountainside, they dressed, only too conscious of the change in temperature as they climbed higher.

'Will we see more snow?'

'See it, yes. But Ivdulon told you we'd be able to pass below it, didn't she?'

'I hope she was right. I don't want to have to be that cold ever again.'

Blavv's mindtalk with Feldrark had released Teldrohn from his duties as a soldier and gifted them Sondukal as a willing companion. The tracker and guide from Litkala had enjoyed the challenge of finding his own way to Ov-Bebna and was eager to extend his knowledge of lands far from his city. From the K'ahll, a slender dark-eyed woman, het'Kallohn, joined them as guide to ensure they could find water and defend themselves against sandstorms.

'Will our detour really double the time we'll take to get to Trotnahn, het'Kallohn?'

The guide raised her eyebrows. 'Had we set off due north, we would have been there in a little over three days on these good camels. But your wise woman requires we meet up with others in the oasis under the mountains. That takes us a long way east, and we may have to wait for these two wanderers there. The best we can hope for is that they arrive when we do. That way it'll take us just six days for the whole journey.'

Blavv nodded. 'Tumalind and Okkyntalah won't be there by the time we arrive. I've spoken to her and she thinks they won't reach the oasis for at least five days yet.'

'They move slowly, then?'

'On foot. And they have to cross the Chakahn Mountains out of Choshinahm.'

'The Mountains? They can fly, then?'

'No. But Okkyntalah's a skilled traveller with lots of experience. They've already crossed the Mountains of Geldakq and he says these other mountains aren't so fearsome.'

'All mountains are fearsome. We waste our time if we wait for those who challenge the Teeth of God.'

'Nevertheless, het'Kallohn, we will await them.' Teldrohn nodded to emphasise the point. 'Tumalind and Blavv are in contact with each other and we'll know of any problems as they progress.'

The woman scrutinised Blavv. 'How is this possible?'

Blavv described mindtalk to her. het'Kallohn shook her head and removed her cloaking robe so that she wore only her short loin cloth. The robe she folded and packed with her other belongings on the camel.

'I thought you weren't allowed to show yourself except when at rest, het'Kallohn?'

'That is the way for the K'ahll. But if I'm to guide and travel with those who are mad, I must not be of the K'ahll or all my tribe will be infected with such illness of the mind.'

'Blavv isn't mad. What she tells you is the truth, het'Kallohn.'

'Whilst I travel thus, I am 'het' no more. You will please call me Kallohn. 'het' belongs to the K'ahll.'

They tried to make her see reason. Even Sondukal, who was generally silent on such matters, joined in. But she was adamant and wouldn't change her mind.

'I 'ope yon sun don't burn your tender skin, lass. You've been covered up so long in daylight, your lovely body's not tanned.'

'I will bear whatever God requires of me. It is the way.'

'Aye, but if you get ill 'cos you've been burnt by strong sun, we'll be the ones as 'ave to care for you. Won't you, at least allow us to cover part of you with one o' these?' Sondukal showed her a tunic.

She examined the garment, tried it on and held it against her body. 'I haven't been in such a situation before. The robe is for the K'ahll, but the loin is for modesty alone. This garment seems to share the qualities of the loin for modesty and will prevent the burn you warn of. I will wear it. I thank you, Sondukal.'

All were relieved as they packed up camp to set off on the next leg of their journey.

'If we have no need to hurry, I advise we travel only in the early morning and the late afternoon and avoid the heat of the midday sun. We will take longer to reach the oasis, but will make the journey more comfortably. Will such an arrangement satisfy your needs?'

'Thanks, Kallohn. You know, I'm really not mad.'

'Blavv, you describe the impossible to me and pretend to believe it. How can you be other than mad?'

'Because what I told you is true.'

'The mad are rarely aware of their madness. So it is said in the K'ahll.'

Blavv shrugged. She'd prove her sanity once they met up with Tumalind and Okkyntalah. Until then, she'd put up with Kallohn's assertions. In the meantime, she would use part of the ride to discover how things were with the pair of islanders. Though, the concept of an island was foreign to her, as was the idea of a body of water so huge it could actually surround a whole land. Now, if Kallohn were looking for madness, surely it was there in the idea of an island?

'Tumalind, can you talk?'

'We're travelling, but I can talk as we move. Is there trouble?'

'Other than Kallohn's refusal to believe you and I can do this, and her accusation of me as a mad woman, no.' She described what had happened and they laughed.

'Where are you at present?'

'We're following the river into the mountains. Okkyntalah thinks we'll take five days to get through and another two or three to reach the oasis. It's still warm enough to go without cover under the midday sun, but the snow and cold make us cover up most of the time. I like the freedom and hate the cold, so I'll be glad when we're out of the mountains.'

'Isn't travelling like that against your religious beliefs?'

'We don't feel like Followers any more. We've seen too much that makes us believe the whole thing's a lie, to be honest. And it was our own High Priest who sold me to the tavern keeper, you know.'

Blavv had been raised as a child in a faith she'd forgotten. Her experience in Ov-Bebna had left her suspicious of the whole idea of religion. If men and women could worship a man such as the Uhmbard and call that infertile despot their god, then she wanted none of it.

'Good for you. Should I warn Teldrohn and Sondukal of your changed ways?'

'It might be better if we test the ground with them first. We've a long way to travel together and I'd rather avoid any dispute. We can, if necessary, always pretend to still believe.'

'I'm beginning to think a lot of people pretend, Tumalind. And not just Followers. Still, I've no faith, and I don't really understand it, to tell the truth.'

'No. I feel a sense of loss at no longer having something to believe in, but I don't know what I could believe in now. Perhaps Ivdulon can help.'

'Ivdulon. Now there's a woman with great wisdom. It was her idea that we all meet at the oasis, you know. I've no idea what she has in mind for us. But I'll see what we find in Trotnahn before I decide what to do with the rest of my life. Teldrohn has married me now that I carry his child and we'll decide where we want to live once I've seen my home city. It'll have to be a good place if it's to compare with Litkala. But I must see it again before I make up my mind. I'd never settle if I didn't make this journey there. I hope you don't mind me dragging you and Okkyntalah there with me?'

'Not at all. Anyway, Ivdulon seems to think I need to visit the place, for reasons she either doesn't know or won't say. And I generally do what Ivdulon advises.'

'Most mindtalkers follow her suggestions, don't we?'

'Except the evil ones.'

'I've never come across any. Are there many?'

'I once strayed into a very bad area, Blavv. It was frightening. I felt that, if I allowed them, the minds in there would take me over and use and destroy me. Be careful not to go exploring until you're able to defend yourself, won't you?'

'I will. You frighten me, Tumalind. I'll keep alert. I'd always thought this a safe place. I'm glad you warned me before I tried to wander alone and without guidance.'

'I have to go now. I need to concentrate, as we're about to cross a difficult ravine. I'll talk again later.'

Tumalind was gone. Blavv removed herself from the mindtalk world at once. The warning frightened her and she wondered just how safe she was in that special place. The danger Tumalind described sounded terrible. To be used and destroyed by people you couldn't even see. Perhaps Kallohn's accusations of madness had something in them after all.

Chapter 23

DISCLOSURE OF INTENT

'Feldrark? Things are moving. I need to talk to you face to face.'

He glanced at Jodisa, sleeping and peaceful, and wished he could share the whole truth with her. But she needed rest and the trouble he must face wouldn't help her with the child growing in her belly. No, it was best she should sleep as he went to the tower to discuss the difficult future with Ivdulon. It had waited long enough in secret.

The very fact that she wanted to see him rather than use mindtalk told Feldrark that something new had emerged from her many wanderings in the mindtalk world. Something of great import had come to light. Perhaps the thing she had dreaded and sought for so long?

He took the Riser and emerged into the early morning sunshine before most of the city was awake. As usual, he felt unable to pass without viewing the land over which he ruled. The city lay peaceful and calm below him. Fields, orchards and pastures clothed the land beyond the walls, feeding the population, giving them useful employment. Wide and vast, the sea spread soft and silent from up here, floating fishing boats that would soon set off to gather their catches. Holding ships that carried away and brought home the many products that kept the city functioning. Commerce: a necessary evil, and one that needed constant control if it were not to become more important than it deserved. He was aware of societies in which commerce ruled and they invariably lacked soul. They were devoid of spirituality and measured everything in terms of financial cost, nothing in terms of true worth.

Netrodyl emerged from the tower. She stretched and threw her arms wide to welcome the dawn.

'Greeting the day, my lovely?' He smiled as she started to conceal herself.

'Your display is no blasphemy, Netrodyl. I wish all my subjects could be so open. I enjoy the natural beauty of our people.'

She dropped her hands and smiled back. 'I'll tell Ivdulon you're here, Feldrark.'

'She knows. Ivdulon always knows. I sometimes think nothing is hidden from that extraordinary woman.'

'She is rather amazing, isn't she?'

'I'm pleased you've given her something she's lacked most of her life. You've brought her a personal delight and joy and for that I thank you. But I'd dearly love some breakfast, if that is possible? The old witch has demanded my presence before I've had a chance to eat.'

She laughed and preceded him inside the tower to prepare food and drink for them.

Ivdulon watched her saunter into the kitchen area. 'Beautiful, isn't she? I can see how you would be attracted to her.'

'She is and I am. Mind you, can't see what she gets from an old lump like you.'

'You'll feel the flat of my...Feldrark! You're very wicked. Netrodyl improves her mind and enjoys rendering her simple service and aid to me in return. I'm left free to think more deeply, to spend more time on things that matter. And, now, to those important matters.'

'Can we eat first?'

'Always thinking of material concerns. Feed the mind, the body will need less.'

'During, then. I see you're well enough fed, Ivdulon.'

The wise woman looked down at her own body and nodded. 'That's Netrodyl's feeding. I used to not bother for much of the time.' She signalled him to follow her up the steps to the upper storey.

He went with some trepidation. Her manner was serious, in spite of her attempted lightness of touch. There was something new and difficult in their world, or at least a disturbing addition to their knowledge.

Netrodyl brought a wide wooden tray bearing the juice of merphlions in glass goblets, freshly baked bread, pats of fresh butter and a pot of fruit preserve. She cut and spread the bread for them before she sat to eat.

'Feldrark may find you a little diverting, my dear. Men lack my ability to ignore the temptations the flesh may cause for most.'

He waved his hand in dismissal and the young woman remained; she pointed her tongue at the wise woman.

'You may regret that later, my dear.' But it was clear the interaction was full of affection.

'I've wandered where we believe Gadhallah found his inspiration for the crime that led him to concoct the tale that founded the Followers. Clearly, that realm is home to different minds from those that influenced his so long ago, but they're of the same type and their purpose remains to cause unrest. They spread hate and division. They act as a community to influence many. They combine to persuade the innocent and the gullible that good is bad, that evil is desirable, that corruption is most attractive and that greed is a positive quality. They inflate the properties and values of coin over all else and they drive their victims wild with want that they call need.'

'I've rarely seen you so exercised, Ivdulon. Is there a specific reason you've brought this up now?'

The wise woman looked thoughtful. She considered her reply, needing his trust.

'You're aware Tumalind's bound for Trotnahn with Sondukal and that gifted young woman from Ov-Bebna?'

'Blavv, you mean?'

'The very one. The source of the evil I speak of is partially centred in Trotnahn. I can't defeat it with mindtalk. I need someone I can rely on to observe, close-up, those who perpetrate this evil.'

'And the risk to that person?'

'Great. Very great.'

'Physical danger, Ivdulon? Or is this a risk to the person's soul, spirit, sanity?'

'All.'

'And you propose to expose Tumalind to this?'

'It's why I've been so assiduous in keeping her safe and sending her where we need her, without her knowledge.'

'You're more devious than even I suspected, Ivdulon. Can she know the risk?'

'Only when placed before it. I'll aid her at that time, of course. And I expect Blavv to be of help. But the risk remains grave.'

'And you want my silence on the matter?'

'I want, Feldrark, your judgement. I want to know that I act out of concern for the majority and risk only one or two in the process. Am I right to do this?'

It was Feldrark's turn to pause for thought. He was very fond of Tumalind. In fact, he suspected that had he discovered her before he'd met Jodisa, she may well have been the one he chose to marry, regardless of her connection to and affection for Okkyntalah. It wasn't that his love for Jodisa was diminished in any way by his attraction to Tumalind. But the young woman was gifted, modest, kind, utterly good and about as desirable as could be.

'Can she be warned beforehand?'

'Only by mindtalk. And I fear there are those who, like me, can listen in without the subject being aware. Some of those are the evil ones. I dare do nothing to let them know my intentions. Any foreknowledge would place Tumalind in even greater danger.'

'She could die?'

'That, or worse. Tumalind could be made as evil and corrupt as Gadhallah. Even if we were able to rescue her from such a fate, she'd be so defiled and ashamed of the experience that she'd be unable to face life afterwards. You see my dilemma?'

'And you ask for my opinion because you know I love this young woman. It's too great a decision to be made without deep consideration. Give me time, Ivdulon. Give me time.'

'We have little. The girl will be in Trotnahn within a sixday. And, if I'm to give her the best possible protection, I must make certain preparations first. I can give you only until this time tomorrow, Feldrark. No longer.'

'Then, tomorrow I'll give my opinion.'

There was no time to plan. Aklon drove straight into the fray, barely aware of Phrysilda at his side. His sword was drawn and he used it without warning on the nearest Unholy One. She fell dead at his feet, but not before others became conscious of the new enemy they must fight.

Phrysilda quickly dispatched one of the men. Then they found themselves the centre of attention, with the man, wife and child left alone, to fend for themselves, and free to attempt to put out the fire. A tall muscular Unholy One bore a long hide whip as well as the usual sword. He lashed at Aklon from the safety of distance. The hide striped his chest and wrapped around his free arm. The Unholy One jerked hard and unbalanced Aklon, who fell to the ground. Two other Unholy Ones were on him at once. Phrysilda was occupied fighting another woman.

Aklon shifted and rolled quickly, as a blade swung down and hit the ground where he'd lain only an eye-blink previously. The sword cut deep into the earth. It gave him time to roll back onto his feet and face the two closer attackers. But the man with the whip again lashed out and striped his face and chest. Aklon ignored the pain. He dealt a swift blow to the man whose sword had struck the ground. The weapon cut through muscle and sinew, leaving his fighting arm useless. He swept the blade back and slit the man's throat.

The lash caught him again and this time striped and wound itself around his sword arm just as the second assailant thrust at him. Aklon leapt out of the way, moving closer to the remaining woman. As this Unholy One prepared to make her deathblow, she stopped abruptly. Her face registered brief shock before she fell to the ground. Phrysilda hopped over her and stood with Aklon. She sliced through the whip and freed him. The other male Unholy One now stood alone. Both attacked him and he fell at their feet.

The last Unholy One backed away and grasped the farmer's wife around her waist, holding his drawn sword against her throat. The ruined whip he dropped to the ground.

'One step and she's dead.'

Aklon and Phrysilda remained still. The child, a small boy, knelt close to the Unholy One in an attitude of pleading, but said nothing. The farmer was attending to the burning house and unaware of the danger. He threw a canvas bucket of water over the flames and turned to draw another. Aklon caught his eye.

For a moment, the group formed a silent and still scene. Aklon willed the farmer to move and attack the Unholy One from behind, as the man was unaware of that danger. Phrysilda made a small motion with her head and the farmer got the message. He picked up a long-handled tilling fork from the ground and rushed straight at the back of the Unholy One.

Sensing the possible outcome, Aklon moved a step forward, to distract the Unholy One's attention. It worked. The farmer pierced him with the fork tines, both of which passed right through his body. He began to draw the sword blade against the wife's throat. But all power and force had left him. The weapon dropped before he could do any real harm, leaving only a trickle of blood down her neck and chest.

The Unholy One fell forward and, for a moment, all was still once more. The farmer was first to react. He helped his wife back to her feet from her knees where she'd fallen in shock. Held her close.

The boy wiped the tears from his face and looked beyond his parents. 'The house! We have to put the fire out.'

Aklon and Phrysilda helped, using canvas buckets that were stored beside the animal trough. When they finally doused the flames, one end of the house had been destroyed, but the rest was intact. No real damage had been done inside, apart from the cabinet that rested against that wall; now a blackened shell, its contents nothing but ashes.

The farmer embraced Phrysilda, his wife held Aklon. The boy tugged at Aklon's tabard, desperate to show his share of gratitude.

'You have the means to repair the house?'

'We'll manage. We gonna get more of this sort o' thing?'

'It is difficult to say with any certainty. I think you have been unlucky to have been attacked. The gangs of rebels are generally small and disorganised. But I strongly advise you to have a place you can escape to should you suffer another attack. Things can be replaced; people cannot. And I suggest you and your wife practice and become familiar with weapons. Do you have a sword, or any other form of defence?'

'Never needed nowt like that. But I can meck sommat. Won't teck me long to arm us agin the likes o' them. We'll be fine.'

'Use the Unholy Ones' swords. Weapons need time and skill to forge.' Aklon admired the courage of these hardy folk.

They insisted on feeding them after the fight. The bodies of the fallen they left until they could find time to deal with them.

'I suggest you burn them.'

'Aye. We'll do that. Now, whilst missus gets food an' drink, I'd best teck a look at your wounds an' that cut on this lovely's fine bum, eh?'

Aklon had been unaware that Phrysilda was injured. He examined her and discovered a straight cut to her right buttock. It no longer bled. But it would be some time before she could sit easily. He used clean water to bathe the wound and the farmer tore a length of cloth from a square of fabric his wife gave him from her kitchen supply. Phrysilda chafed as they bound up her wound but she let them complete the job. Only then did Aklon allow the farmer to apply balm to his whip stripes.

'You're a fair sight to go about like that, lass. Isn't that not allowed? 'Ope that cut don't scar your lovely little bum, like.'

'I'll be fine. I've 'ad worse in combat training. And, as for being naked; we can wear what we please, and I like to be completely free. We don't 'ave to follow rules made by the Priests and Unholy Ones. Didn't you know?'

'I'd 'eard sommat along them lines. To be honest, I thought it were just rumours. Mebbie you'll tell us all about it while we eat?'

Which is what Akon and Phrysilda did. And then spent the night with the family, before setting off again on their tour of the island.

· ·⋗· ·

The merchant's news deeply concerned the High Priest. There were now no Followers in Phornahm after all. 'Do you know anyone discreet, Ven-Gadla?'

'Discreet, Dagla Kaz?'

'Someone here who I can ask about Followers without risking death.'

'Ah. Give me a moment with the tavern keeper. I've ways of doing things that might give some clues.'

The merchant left the group and engaged the landlady in conversation, as the woman sat on her high stool, overlooking her staff and keeping count of the coin spent by her customers. It was clear he had a way with such people; she laughed and made gestures that suggested she thought him a rogue. But only moments later the merchant returned.

'You're in luck, Dagla Kaz. There's a visitor from the countryside in town and he's made it known there are Followers gathered in a place two day's walk from here. He's trying to organise a group to go out there and kill them. Perhaps you could persuade him you're that party, then leave him to his own devices once you find them?'

'And I thought I was devious! Do you think he'll do it?'

'Coin. He's a man after coin more than moral victory. Appeal to his love of coin. Oh, and let him know your women may favour him, for he's a carnal man as well.'

'And you know where I can find this creature?'

'Try to avoid the sneer when you speak to him. He might find it unattractive, Dagla Kaz.'

'But you can find the man?'

'He's no secret. Over at the corner table, drinking with the three women, Dagla Kaz.

186

Think you can distract him from such temptation?'

Dagla Kaz watched the man handle the women in the most intimate way. These were women who sold themselves, displaying their wares and eager to serve for coin. He found it distasteful and knew he'd be unlikely to part the man from them until he'd satisfied his lust. Unless…

'I'm a stranger here, Paltrohn. I see you've an eye for the ladies. Perhaps I can interest you in a proposition with a beauty I have with me? See the dark-haired young lovely sitting with the two young men…?'

'Ere! What you think you're at, man? We've a livin' to make. Shift your skinny squitter, or I'll be settin' me minder on you!'

He gave the woman a glance of malice and backed away, shrugging at the man. The man nodded and re-engaged with the three women again. Moments later, he put down his tankard and made an excuse to cross the floor, where he tapped Dagla Kaz on the shoulder.

'How much for yon, then?' He indicated Xylthynn.

'Delicate. But, if you can help me in a different way, I'll persuade her to serve you for the love of it. She's virgin, so you'll want to take it a little more slowly than with those whor…women of pleasure.'

'For 'er, I can wait a bit. Specially if she's really virgin. Looker like that?'

'That I promise you.'

'What's this other thing you want, then?'

Dagla Kaz shepherded the man into a quieter part of the room. 'I understand you've discovered some Followers?'

'Small group livin' out in the wilds. Take 'em easy with a score of blades. What's it to you?'

'I'd love to help in that venture.'

'Yeah? What's your angle, then? Killin' or the rapin' before we do the heathen buggers in?'

'Both, of course. What else?'

The man clapped him on the shoulder. 'How many are you?'

'Two dozen. All fighting fit, and both sexes, so fewer to share the women when we get there.'

The man considered. 'An' the lass? When do I get 'er?'

'Say nothing to her yet. I'll get her to understand how important you are to our cause first. Once she realises how much good you can do us, she'll come to you voluntarily and with enthusiasm. But you must be patient. She'll take a little convincing.'

'Why not just give 'er to me, like?'

'Ah. We clearly differ in that respect. Whilst I'm happy to join in the rape and despoiling of Followers, I won't see my own people forced into anything. We're a strong group with much honour to bind us together. One act of betrayal would ruin the cohesion we currently enjoy.'

'Big words. But I get your drift. Be ready on the morrow, then. I'll look after my supplies. You look after yours. Right?'

'On foot or by some other means?'

'On foot. Quieter we can be, the better we'll be able to catch them heathen buggers. Tomorrow, dawn, outside the tavern.'

'I look forward to the opportunity.'

The man returned to the women of pleasure and led one from the room. The other two approached and he understood the possible problems he may face. He caught the attention of Tarruss and Ouqitahl.

'We're not Followers, understand? It's essential to our safety that you join with these women for coin.' He handed each a small handful of gold, as he whispered his instructions.

Reluctantly, the two men took the women of pleasure from the common room. Dagla Kaz gathered the rest of the party and ensured they all understood their situation and what they must do to stay alive. There might be an opportunity to exchange some of the Virgin Gifts. Some in the party grew eager, others less so, but he'd deal with that problem once they were free of the town and with the new group of Followers.

Xylthynn he took aside separately. 'All our lives depend on you playing your part well, young woman. We've had our differences in the past, and I'm sorry you suffered after your disobedience in the snowfields. Now, however, such matters need to be forgotten. The welfare of the entire party and the success of the pilgrimage must be our first concern. You need not fear for your safety. I've had to make it appear you'll be willing to join with that man I was talking with earlier.'

'You want me to join with...'

'No, Xylthynn. I don't want you to join with anyone. I merely wish you to make it seem that you're eager to do so. Do you understand?'

'I'm to pretend? To Lie?'

'In the name of Ytraa. It's in the interests of the Followers here and those we go to meet. Many lives will be saved by your playing of a part you're fitted to play. The man finds you very attractive and we need his help, that's all. But no harm will come to you. We'll keep you safe and virginal. You are for the other Followers, not for the likes of a heathen like that.'

'I'll do it, Dagla Kaz. But I won't enjoy it.'

'As long as you make it seem you're eager, that's all I need. You can play a part, can't you? Pretend, in order to serve Ytraa?'

'If that's what Ytraa requires of me. I'll serve Ytraa in any way I can.'

'Good. Now we'll go back to the rest of the group and eat before we sleep. The morning requires that you appear a wanton. Perhaps Porryh may be persuaded to exchange one of her more revealing tabards with your more modest tunic? Ask her, anyway. But be discreet. The fewer who know of this, the safer we'll be.'

She nodded. And Dagla Kaz urged her before him. If it transpired that he had to let the man have his way with the girl, at least she'd no longer be virgin and he could then take his own pleasure in her loins. For a moment, he wondered at his choice. Wouldn't Porryh be more suitable for the role; she was made for it, wasn't she? But she was also unreliable, too carnal, and, in any case, he had other plans for that troublesome young wanton.

The party ate a supper of fresh fish, served with sweet root vegetables and helped by cheap, sweet wine. Ven-Gadla asked whether his help had been useful and the High Priest acknowledged his contribution and explained that he may need him to stay on hand for a little longer.

'I will, of course, pay you for your time.'

The morning would bring a possible solution to one problem, but the whole enterprise was fraught with danger. He must keep alert and be ready to abandon them all if that was the only way he could save his skin.

Chapter 24

TROUBLE NOW AND TO COME

'Sneaking off again without warning me, Feldrark?'

The tone of her voice told him she wasn't serious. He smiled at her and shrugged. 'Don't want you under any strain whilst you're carrying our precious infant, that's all.'

'Sure that's all?'

'What else could it be? We rule together. If you really want to come, by all means accompany me. I'm off to see Ivdulon.'

'Can't mindtalk with her?'

'Not on this topic. In fact, now I think about it, you should come with me. But wearing more than that delightful smile.'

'And if I don't?'

'You'll make me...us...late for our appointment with the wise woman, and your small bump won't save you from her swift hand.'

She slipped her tunic on and they held hands to and in the Riser. Ivdulon was pacing the lower floor as they entered the tower and Netrodyl was busy tidying away the remains of their breakfast.

'Do you ever let that young woman wear clothes?'

'Good morning to you, too, Feldrark. The choice in that, as in all she does, is hers. Have you made your decision? Ah, and good morning to you, Jodisa. You're well, still?'

'I think the term is blooming. I feel wonderful. But Feldrark's told me the purpose of this meeting and I have to say I'm not sure I agree with your intentions for Tumalind. She's a good ally and has become a good friend. Must it be this way?'

'Netrodyl, please refresh our guests, and then complete the exercise I set you, dressed or not, as you wish.' The suggestion that she always did precisely that wasn't lost on them. Ivdulon returned to her guests. 'This may be a longer session than I'd expected.'

The three sat at the table, spread, as ever, with charts, pictures, maps and parchment rolls filled with symbols largely meaningless to Jodisa. Judging by Feldrark's frown of incomprehension as he scanned the documents, they didn't mean a lot to him either.

'Feldrark has explained about those who see coin and its acquisition as their primary concern and how they constitute a threat to our way of life?'

'Sort of. I can't say I really see the threat you fear, though.'

'No. I'm afraid it's a subtle and insidious risk we face. Nothing dramatic, nothing sudden or easily defeated. What will happen if these...I can only refer to them as evil minds. If they have their way, the spiritual aspect of our lives, whether we worship a specific god or not, will slowly disappear to be replaced by the acquisition of material goods. At first this will occur so slowly that no one will see any change. Over a period of many cycles, those for whom coin is God will develop strategies and schemes to persuade people that the things they sell are essential to their welfare. They will, in effect, make their goods and services appear indispensible.'

'Is that all?'

'All? You don't see the inevitable outcome, Jodisa?'

'You do?'

Ivdulon allowed her frustration to show briefly on her face, but suppressed it in favour of a patient approach. 'I'll tell you. All other forms of authority, spiritual, social, generational, will be diminished until they count for nought. Those who worship coin will become the governors of the whole world. They'll make slaves of the population and coerce them into the belief that their labour and their wealth is best spent acquiring more and more things. Most of these will, in fact, be of little or no value. Their purpose, after all, is simply to remove the importance of everything else from daily life. Imagine, if you will, the ramifications if people decide that procuring some specific object is more important than caring for the poor and needy. Imagine if the system of exchange we use becomes not the servant of the users but the master of them, so that coin is king of all.'

Jodisa considered this unlikely outcome; she was inclined to scoff at the notion. But Ivdulon was wise and had so often been right in her predictions and calculations. 'You're suggesting coin would become more important than people?'

'That's one outcome, certainly.'

'But that's not likely to happen, surely? I mean people care for each other. They don't let disputes over ownership or exchange spoil relationships. What you're suggesting is a change that would make a family compete with their neighbours for the same plot of land, the same ovellah, the same merphlion. That would be intolerable. It would be a horrible way to live.'

'It's precisely what would happen if these worshippers of coin get their way. It's already happened. And they're planning to spread their evil ways to the whole world. Why they've developed such a philosophy, if it can be dignified with that name, in Trotnahn isn't clear. But it's there that the evil is being advanced. The plan's quite deliberate and the people developing it are very aware of their intentions and the outcomes. There's nothing accidental, nothing left to chance. These are soulless and determined people, ruthless and intent on gaining absolute power over everyone and everything.'

'What, exactly, do they hope to achieve?' Jodisa found herself involuntarily glancing over her shoulder and had to consciously return to stare at Ivdulon.

The wise woman looked straight back into her eyes. 'What they intend is absolute rule. The ones with most coin, will also have most power. You know already what can and does happen when power falls into the hands of those without proper spiritual or social concerns. Your own father's an example of the sort of abuse that occurs.'

'My father is…'

'A man who raped his own daughter, made her pregnant, had the unborn infant ripped from her protesting body and then punished an innocent for the crime. Not the sort of person who should be allowed any power whatever. Don't you agree, Jodisa?'

To hear it encapsulated. To have it spoken aloud in such terms was almost more than she could bear. Her whole body collapsed in on itself, her shoulders rounded, her hands protectively folded over her breasts, she crossed her legs and brought up her knees and her head dropped toward the table top. This was her father. The man who'd helped create her. Look what he'd done to her. Only now did she see and feel the true enormity of that betrayal, that injustice, that cruel domination. Tears sprang to her eyes, flowed unstemmed down her cheeks, to drip on the wooden surface.

'And these are the sort of people who will rule us all, everywhere?'

'They, and others even worse, will gain power and rule the world.'

'You're sure about this, Ivdulon?'

'Yes.'

That single assertion was enough.

'Then there's no choice. If Tumalind is our best defence against such a fate for the world, then she must be used. If she's damaged, destroyed or killed in the process, we'll have to live with that. But we can't allow such evil to take over the world. For me, there's no question but that we must sacrifice Tumalind in this endeavour.'

Ivdulon turned to Feldrark. 'Jodisa, as expected, expresses truth in all its starkness now she understands the reality. What do you say, Feldrark?'

He allowed feelings to chase across his face; doubt was first to be ousted, followed by realisation, confusion, hope and then full understanding. 'Yes. The young woman must be employed. Let's hope she's strong enough to come through the battle unscarred.'

'That, I fear, is unlikely. Though I'll do all in my power to protect her. I take it we're agreed that none of what's passed here should be referred to in mindtalk? And that Tumalind cannot be warned against the coming conflict, for fear of those secret listeners?'

Jodisa nodded and Feldrark took her hand and agreed. 'Just one question, Ivdulon.'

The wise woman raised a questioning eyebrow.

'Why now? What's happened to bring this to your attention?'

She sighed, her eyes clouding with recalled horror. 'I've been monitoring Dagla Kaz for some time. He's been invaded in much the same way as Gadhallah, perhaps all his life. Recently, the messages have been stronger and more vociferous. I followed one of them back to its source. I'll say no more of that experience than that I would not wish to repeat it. Ever. Such naked raw ambition and intent without moral restraint. I never expected to find evil on that scale or in that profusion.'

'Yet, you'll send Tumalind into that place, unprepared and undefended?'

Netrodyl rose and stood defiant between Ivdulon and Jodisa. 'She wept for a solid day. I had to nurse her like a child.'

'And Tumalind?'

Ivdulon gentled her servant, pupil and friend out of the way and stared at Jodisa and Feldrark with such sorrow that it was a physical hurt. 'We have no choice.'

'We had better be circumspect in entering the town, Phrysilda, if that farmstead was anything to judge by.'

'Wait till it's dark, then?'

'That might be best.'

'What we gonna do till then?'

He shook his head at her pose. 'Not that. Wanton. Do you realise how difficult it is for me to resist you?'

'Oh, well, let's see if I can make it 'arder, eh? Like this?'

He removed her hand. 'You, young woman, are very wicked. You know how I feel about Shoarhn.'

'What's she got that I 'aven't , then?'

'Love. It is as simple and as complex as love. Nothing more.'

'Never 'ad that. Lust in bucket loads. But love? No. S'pose it's bein' a soldier, like. Sure you don't want...?'

'You can see that I do. But I shall not. I have decided, and all your tempting and teasing will not make me change my mind.'

'When we was Followers, you'd 'ave done me every time I wanted you to.'

'I would.'

'What's so good about the changes, then?'

He took her hand, pulled her to sit beside him against the bole of the great and ancient olive tree. With her at his side, she was less visible and he wasn't so distracted by her body.

'Good? You enjoy the freedom of nakedness at all times. Could you have done that as a Follower? Not unless you became an Unholy One. As a Follower, you would have been obliged to watch those Unholy Ones we just destroyed rape that entire family and steal all their food. As a Follower, you were expected to join in the beating of men and women who transgressed the laws, regardless of whether you felt they deserved such brutality. As a Follower, you would give your fourth child to the temple for use as a sex slave for the Unholy Ones. As a Follower, you would…'

'Yeah. All right. I know, really. An' I like most of the changes. Just wish I could have your prod in me fern, that's all.'

'You are almost as wanton as Syylvah. Now there is a woman who definitely has a problem taking a refusal from me. At least you are willing to understand my position, Phrysilda, and I thank you for that.'

'Won't get me frowked though, will it?'

'Not until we enter the town and find you a willing man. Of which, I am sure, there will be many.'

'So, what we gonna do till then?'

'We have walked most of the day. Why not rest. I will keep watch.'

'Tell you what. I'll lie down an' rest me 'ead in your lap.'

She did and he stroked her hair as she slowly fell into sleep. He looked down at her loveliness and recalled his days of joining with all the women he encountered, free of the wish to remain true to Shoarhn. What made him want to reserve joining only for her? He called it love but did that explain it? Why should love for one woman exclude others? It was impossible to put into words, but, after he'd met and fallen in love with Shoarhn, his joining with other women had become, first, a duty and, second, a betrayal. It was as though that part of human contact was special in a way he'd never considered. No one had told him he should remain loyal only to Shoarhn. Certainly, she hadn't made any such demand, or even request. But she felt the same way. It was something he experienced deep within, something that arose from his feelings for this special woman.

If he was absolutely honest, objective, he couldn't say Shoarhn was especially beautiful or desirable. She held the same charms for a man as many women. Yes, she was lovely. Firm breasts, in spite of mothering children. Well-formed, her fern moist and welcoming. Face full of vitality and affection when she looked at him. She desired him as much as he desired her. Love, it seemed, didn't exclude lust. But these qualities could be ascribed to any number of the women he'd joined with. This lovely who lay available in his lap, was one such and there'd been many others.

So, what made him refuse the pleasure of joining with others whilst he was away from Shoarhn? And he realised the answer was in the question. The joy with Shoarhn was of a different order, of a completeness he hadn't experienced with any other woman. Joining with Shoarhn was so much more than a physical experience. It was if their very selves merged as they explored and joined with each other. As if their souls intertwined and became a single entity, so there was no longer a he and a she but a single unity. When he made love with Shoarhn he was as close to the promise of the Garden of Delights as he could ever be. And so was she.

But it was more than joining. More than lust they experienced mutually, though that was tinted with a special quality missing from other encounters. It was more than becoming one. He cared for her more than for himself. Her absence from his life would leave a hole that might never be repaired, a void that would ache with longing every day he had to exist without her in the world.

He wondered if others felt this inexplicable closeness and wonderful bonding. Did others have links so strong, so overwhelmingly absorbing, as he and Shoarhn? He hoped so. Perhaps Tumalind and Okkyntalah had something similar? Certainly, in her mindtalking, she suggested an experience like it. That was good. Tumalind was a singularly intelligent, gifted, generous and very beautiful young woman. Her loss would be a loss to the world. Why did that thought come to him? And, of course, she was also the child of his father; a half sister. How strange life could be.

'Dorltah for 'em.'

He looked down into the face of Phrysilda, her expression soft and full of gentle enquiry. 'Some things are impossible to explain, my lovely soldier. I think, however, it is time for us to go into the town and discover how things fare.'

'You're a strange one, Aklon, an' I'd love to know what goes on in that 'ead o' yours. But I'd love to have that....'

'I know. You are all sensation and pleasure, Phrysilda. And any man with a heart can provide what you need and want. Let us go and find one, shall we?'

She lifted her head from his lap, took her hand away, and got to her feet, where she stretched invitingly. He closed his eyes against her temptation and turned away. Under the glowing light of the growing Skyfire, led her from the clearing and onto the track that would take them into Pampahn in a few hundred paces.

Shoarhn, Dahrlahg, Irrildys and Eyethlehn stood in absolute silence behind the cowshed. The Dissenters, those who'd refused to accept the new order, had gathered to surround her house earlier in the evening. It had only been thanks to the quick action of Irrildys that she and the young girl had remained away from the house. Eyethlehn had met them in the field, on her way back from delivering a piece of woodwork to a customer in this part of town.

The enlarged Few in Morstahn now constituted almost half the town. After the first few days of quiet, those who refused to believe the changes being made in the name of the Cause had gathered together and were now trying to impose the traditional ways by force whenever they could.

'We know you're in there, whore. Come out an' all you'll get is the beatin' you deserve for whorin' with the Renegade. Stay inside an' we'll burn the 'ouse down, wi' you in it.'

The spokesman was a man she'd rarely had anything to do with. He had a farm on the far side of town and, although there'd never been any trouble, he'd tried to take some of her customers in the past. They'd always returned to her and Aglydron as they discovered the quality of her products was much better than those offered more cheaply by the other man.

'I'm going to gather more of the Few, Shoarhn. You and Dahrlahg stay here. Coming, Eyethlehn?'

The two left quietly, allowing the relative darkness of falling evening to hide their movements. Overhead, the Skyfire blazed bright into the night, shaming the full moon with its brightness.

'The twins!' Shoarhn started to move toward the house.

'I put 'em with your parents, Shoarhn, when I come out to 'elp after tea. Didn't think you'd want 'em left alone, like.'

Shoarhn sighed with relief and returned to the shelter of the cowshed. They could watch the mob whilst remaining unseen themselves. But they were in no position to stop them carrying out their threat. She watched with rising anger as they entered her house in force. She counted. A good twenty of them. She and the girl were no match for such a crowd of angry and determined Followers.

The mob emerged again, discovering she wasn't at home after all. They scanned the nearby fields but could see nothing of her there.

'Burn 'er 'ouse down anyway. Deserves it for whorin' with the Renegade.' The farmer was determined to make her suffer, it seemed.

'I don't think we should do that without giving her a chance to defend herself. It's cowardly and goes against the laws of Following, doesn't it?' The woman's voice raised in her defence was a surprise. She didn't recognise the speaker but thanked her silently. The others seemed uncertain.

'I say fire the place!'

'And I say it's against the law.'

'Aye, but who's the law now, eh? Tell me that. This woman's been frowkin' with the Renegade what's caused all this trouble. Think she deserves our concern?'

The discussion fell into quieter talk with just occasional words and phrases raised above the general muttering so that Shoarhn was unable to determine which way the decision might go. She was tempted, now they'd shown some caution, to address the crowd; see if she could persuade some of them onto her side.

'You can't go over there, Shoarhn. They'll beat you till you bleed. You know they will.'

'Nevertheless, I must at least try. I can't lose the house.' She crossed the field until she was in hailing distance of the mob. 'I'm here. I've been in the fields, growing food to keep people fed. What do you want with me?'

The other farmer turned and pointed, triumph clear on his face under the glow of moon and Skyfire.

'The whore comes out at last, eh? Should be ashamed of yourself. Frowkin' with that Renegade. I want to know…'

'Do you? Or do you just want to remove someone who gives her customers good value so that you can sell your poor food at a higher price? Who are you to accuse me? You don't even know me.'

'I know enough. I seen you with 'im, I 'ave!'

'Of course you've seen me with Aklon. The whole town has seen me with him. I was with him when he exposed the lies we've been told by the priests and those so-called Holy Ones. I was with him when he predicted this Skyfire would grow brighter and greater than ever before. Which it has. Where were you? Or didn't you listen to the truth?'

'Lies 'e told us. All lies. He just wants to rule the island hisself. Wouldn't never 'ave got away with it while 'is father were 'ere.'

'Lies? One of his truths burns over your head, plain as can be. Is the Skyfire a lie? Was the first Skyfire, the one his father used as reason to leave the island, was that the truth?'

'It were…it were a mistake. A mistake. Anyone can make a mistake, can't they?'

'So it would appear. I wonder whether you're here to ruin my means of earning a living or because you're really as devout as you pretend. Did you have children in service to the Holy Ones? Did you offer a generous tithe to the pilgrimage to the Homeland? I did.'

Some of those with the farmer had drawn back and were gathering toward Shoarhn. But the mob was still greater than those on her side.

'I say strip the whore and beat her for her whorin' ways!'

'Do you have a beating bag, or would you break another of your own precious laws and beat me naked?'

That detached another two, both women, from the mob, leaving him with thirteen. The odds were growing in her favour. She stepped forward. And those who'd left the mob mostly moved with her, showing they'd changed sides.

'I think you'd best go. Your support dwindles and dies as the truth grows. I'd have

198

you leave my property and be on your way.'

'Grab 'er! Strip the whore! Beat her till she bleeds!' He rushed forward but only half a dozen of those he'd brought came with him. The rest hesitated, unwilling to be part of an act against their own laws. As he closed on her, the others stood against him in her defence.

'Like she says, go. Go on. We don't want no fightin' 'ere. Go back 'ome and leave us alone.'

The woman who spoke was only an acquaintance, a woman she'd nod to in the street, possibly a customer for her milk or cheese. The farmer reached out and caught Shoarhn's arm, tried to pull her away. She leant forward and slapped his face very hard. He let go.

A number of the Few appeared at last, armed with sticks and a few blades. The balance had shifted and the farmer and his supporters were now outnumbered.

He held his stinging cheek and stepped back and away, looking about him. Frightened now he was in the minority, he edged away down the street. 'I'll be back!'

'Try anything and we know where you live. Whatever you do here we'll do to you. So beware. Go, and don't come back.'

It was one of the larger men of the Few and the farmer saw he was defeated. He and his cronies faded into the night.

'Thank you all so very much. I appreciate your concern, your help and your loyalty to Aklon. Thank you. Thank you.'

With the danger averted for the moment, she allowed herself to relax. And, with relaxation came the delayed fear. She hid her tears until she could escape the eyes and enter her own home again. There, she discovered one of the mob had used her kitchen floor as a toilet and others had turned over her store of food, wasting it with footmarks and dust. One of her tabards was in shreds and her bed held scattered broken pottery shards.

Dahrlahg entered behind her and surveyed the damage. Some of the Few, with Irrildys and Eyethlehn also came in. Between them, they cleared up the mess and rendered the bed useable again.

'I'm sorry. I've nothing to reward you with now. But I'll give you all free food for the next sixday, when I've collected my produce.'

'No need, Shoarhn. We're in this together. You'd do the same for us. Any one of us.'

'Thank you.'

'It's best if someone sleeps here tonight, Shoarhn. Never know with scum like that.'

Eyethlehn stepped from behind the man who'd offered to spend the night. 'I'm handy with a blade, as I proved at the battle on the Plain of Ytraa. I'll stay with Shoarhn.'

She gladly accepted the offer and the Few dispersed back to their homes whilst Shoarhn went to her parents' house to borrow food and ask them to keep the twins until morning.

The incident, unsettling, frightening and perhaps a taste of things to come, was over, but it would be a while before she, or her friends, felt safe again. There was trouble still in the town and would be for some time. Oh that Aklon could be home with her, live with her and travel the island no more.

Chapter 25

THOUGHTS

Three days in the mountains, and they'd finally emerged onto the plain. The Skyfire, visible now in daylight, at night outshone a moon that had been full only two nights ago. Way down on the southern horizon, smoke rose in great black billows, as if the world itself were on fire.

'Mount O'bo. I'd hate to live under that all my life.'

Okkyntalah glanced at the rising plume and nodded. He was studying the terrain ahead. 'Ivdulon said to follow the river to its end, didn't she?'

'It ends in what she calls an oasis. A sort of lake in the desert, like the one at Ov-Bebna, but bigger. Though she says we should see more shrubs and trees here than sand and rock.'

'Looks pretty barren to me. Not much hope of catching game. We'll have to live off fish.'

'We'll manage. Like we have all the way through the mountains, Okkyntalah. I'm not worried, as long as I'm with you. You make me feel safe.'

He embraced her and she relived the thrill of his skin on hers, as she did whenever they touched.

'Can it last? This amazing sensation I have every time we touch?'

'I hope so. I get it, too, when we hold each other. But, now we're back out in the open, we might be wise to shade at least part of our bodies from the fierce sun, especially at midday.'

'So, no need yet. I love being free like this. I bet this is how we're supposed to live. I wonder why we ever decided we need cover our skin; isn't the wrapping we've been given good enough to protect us? Don't see animals wearing clothing.'

'They have fur, or feathers, or scales. We're hairless. Perhaps it makes a difference?'

'It's our natural state. We need clothes for protection from cold or fierce heat. But why would we need them any other time?'

'Because we might always be making love with each other, Tumalind? When I see you like this I can't help wanting you.'

'What's stopping you?'

The sun was close to the highest point when they set out again, this time with some cover. There was no need to scout the way or move far from the river that was their guide. The sluggish stream, meandering and occasionally joined by other smaller streams that widened it, wandered lazily over parched ground so that they walked in as straight a line as they could between the many bends.

As night fell, they settled close to the bank and lit a fire only to cook and to keep wild beasts at bay. The sky grew dark where the Skyfire hadn't yet spread, but its light made the landscape almost like day, the flickering, ever-changing tail causing odd movement in shadows all across the plain.

'It's not flame, is it? I mean, look at it. I don't know what it is, but it's not fire at all. How could people think it was?'

'We don't all have your amazing eyesight, Okkyntalah. To my eyes the Skyfire looks very much like wispy flames of gold and blue and pink. If you can see more than that, you're the one who's seeing things differently.'

'I see many, many light, twisting, coiling, moving tails of different colours. But the whole thing's too flimsy to be fire. There's no power. No heat, either, is there?'

'None I can feel. So how did it get its name and reputation do you suppose?'

'I don't know. Ask Ivdulon.'

'I will. But not now. Do you miss not praying?'

'I thought I would.'

'But you don't?'

'No. Do you, Tumalind?'

'I miss not being able to have a quiet time communing with whatever force created us. We've always thought of that as Ytraa. But I can't believe in Ytraa now. I wish I knew what to call the thing out there that must be so much bigger and more intelligent than us.'

'I know what you mean. But I can't help you. When I'm out hunting, alone in the forest, on the plain, in the hills, I sometimes feel as if I'm a part of the whole landscape, as if I'm connected with everything else that lives there.'

'Mindtalk can be like that. There are dark places there, as well. Places no sensible person would ever explore. But most of that world is welcoming and makes you feel part of it, like your landscape. I wonder if it's the same sort of sensation, if your feeling of being one with the land is similar to mine of being one with those who mindtalk.'

'Stay away from those dark places, Tumalind. If you get lost in there, I can't follow and rescue you. Isn't that what happened to Gadhallah? Didn't he venture there and get taken over by evil minds?'

'That's what Ivdulon thinks.'

'Well, take care when you're exploring. I don't want to lose you to evil that might take you over and make you do terrible things.'

'You won't. I'm always careful in the mindtalk world.'

'And I'm careful when I'm hunting. Doesn't mean I'll never be in danger from some wild and vicious animal. Maybe, in the same way a terzet horn could creep up on me and gore me, one of those evil minds could hide in the dark places and leap out when you're not expecting it.'

'I'll be careful.'

And she would; she'd ventured into the edges of that dark world and been scared even there. The likelihood that she'd voluntarily move into the darkness was remote.

In contrast to their journey to Pampahn, their two day trek to the capital proved peaceful and uneventful for Aklon and Phrysilda. The town was quiet under the influence of Porlesah and the Few. There were Dissenters, but the ex-village priestess had managed to persuade these people that they could live side by side with no need for violence. Tension between those who espoused the new ways and those who stuck with the old was slowly disappearing. Porlesah had simply explained, right at the outset, that she'd been unaware of the lies and deceit shown by Dagla Kaz and the Unholy Ones. She'd described some of the violence done by those latter extremists, and the people had listened and, where there was reluctance to believe, had at least agreed to disagree.

Some of those who sat either side of the fence were married to each other, or neighbours, others were labourer and overseer. But, so far, the peace seemed to have held very well. Aklon could only hope such tolerance was growing elsewhere on the island. He knew, of course, that the Unholy Ones, and those soldiers who'd rejected the Cause, would make trouble. But problems from outside the town were more likely to unite the inhabitants than divide them.

They arrived in Chalamamnon toward midnight to find its streets largely deserted. A few lone figures scuttled suspiciously in the shadows like rhaats, but the town was quiet. The watch was still in place at his father's house and they welcomed him with warmth.

'What has been the reaction to the proofs?'

They explained how some had denied the truth of what their eyes told them. Some had accepted them straight away. Some had left thoughtful, only to return for a second and third look before they could accept that the words were as they'd read.

'So, how many remain attached to the old ways?'

'I can't tell you, Aklon. But fewer than before. We've had a couple of raids on homes of the Few by some of those ex-soldiers. A scraggy lot; undisciplined and ill-fed, but they caused some damage.'

'You weren't able to persuade them to see the proofs for themselves?'

'We couldn't even speak to them. They ran off as soon as we arrived.'

He nodded. It was the picture he'd expected, but the one he'd most dreaded. Such displaced people might become desperate. It was difficult to know how they would act, what evil they might do before the situation improved.

'Are all members of the Few ensuring they are never alone when out and about?'

'Most are. But we lost a young man yesterday. He went to visit his family who farm out of the town. When he didn't return by evening, three of the Few went out and found the house burnt to the ground and the bodies despoiled and left to carrion beasts. They buried them. But it's caused more fear and concern.'

Aklon nodded. "I shall have to form a squad of experienced soldiers to track these Dissenters, and either destroy them or convince them they are wrong. As soon as Chellyth gets her people settled, I can gather such an army from those she has with her. The earlier groups that set out to convert people seem to be doing a good job. In fact, I might commandeer some of her soldiers sooner rather than later. In the meantime, it will be as well that all travel in groups.'

'I'll spread the word.'

'Thank you, Hyllahn. Has there been any trouble here?'

'One man tried to take some of the scrolls but we stopped him. There's always more of us on duty here than those we let in to view. That way we keep the documents and tablets safe.'

'But it is very onerous for you, I am sure.'

'It's a job we do, Aklon. We daren't risk the proofs. They're doing such a good job. In fact, once they've done their job here, we're going to take them round the island so the rest of the people can see for themselves.'

Aklon hugged the young woman and she embraced him warmly.

'I thank you and your friends for your wonderful loyalty and your courage.'

'Not enough to join with me, though.'

He sighed. Was this to be the way of it forever? Perhaps his habit of recruiting the women of the Few by his prowess in their beds had been a mistake after all. 'I have explained that, Hyllahn. And I am sure you have found a suitable and a constant man to share your passion. I hope so, anyway.'

She glanced toward the rooms at the back of the house.

'Go to him. I can stand guard here for tonight.'

'You've travelled all day. You need food and rest. He can wait. And so can I.'

She called softly and a couple of former slaves appeared. The man naked, the woman with a short skirt about her hips. Both looked as though they'd been asleep. But, at a word from Hyllahn, they went to the kitchen and prepared food for Aklon and Phrysilda.

'They realise they are free now, I hope?'

'Oh, yes. But like a lot of slaves, they don't have nowhere to go, so they've decided to stay here and work for wages. They're good, those two, actually. I think they're just so grateful they're never beaten or made to join when they don't want to.'

'I wish they were not so servile, though. We must make it plain to them that they are free to do as they wish.'

'I've tried, Aklon, but they seem happy as they are.'

He shook his head, puzzled at the way of the world and his fellow humans. 'Come morning, I will travel to the new settlement, name it, and take away a small army of volunteers to defeat the Dissenters and Unholy Ones. That way we can all be safe at last.'

'Can I come with you?'

'You are doing valuable work here, Hyllahn.'

'Mebbie. But I stayed here before. Now I'd like a chance to come out with you and help defeat the extremists. There's plenty 'ere as can do what I've been doing. Please let me, Aklon.'

'On one condition. That you do not attempt to seduce me. I am tired of having to disappoint.'

She smiled at him and nodded. 'I'm happy with my man.'

• ◦ ❦ ◦ •

'We've arrived at the oasis, Tumalind. How long before you'll be with us?'

'Okkyntalah says we'll do the journey in a little over two days, if the land remains as flat as this. We have to rest over the midday period, as we've no proper protection from the sun, but we're travelling during the early morning and the evening to make up for that.'

'Good. There's nothing to do here and I'm bored. And we've a good march ahead of us before we reach Trotnahn.'

'Do you remember much about your home, Blavv?'

'Very little. I think a lot of people there were very interested in buying things.'

'What sort of things?'

'Oh, all sorts. It's a hazy memory, but I'm sure they all competed with each other to see who could get the most things. It was as if the more you had the more important you were in the town. If they're still like that, I don't think I'll be staying. Perhaps go back to Litkala with Teldrohn to have the baby.'

'Baby? You never said.'

'I wasn't meaning to make it public. But I had to tell someone, and I know I can trust you, Tumalind.'

'I'll keep your secret. Even from Okkyntalah if you wish. Are you very far gone?'

'Only a few sixdays. I'll confess once I'm carrying a bump. Mind you, Teldrohn says my dubbies are already bigger. He likes that, of course.'

'Funny, aren't they, men?'

'But you've got to love them, eh?'

'Well, Teldrohn's obviously good for you. You'd never have said that, Blavv, only a few sixdays ago.'

'True. And he is rather special. I suppose I must love him, really.'

'Only suppose?'

'We're not like you and Okkyntalah. I mean, the whole world must know you two love each other. Like those two I heard a story about: Vaarkil and Mythanpho, I think. One of the Followers told me about them.'

They chatted idly about myths and legends, swapping thoughts on the idea of gods and the stories that were told about the creator that made them and their world. But Tumalind had to break off their talk as they were nearing a place where they would camp for the night.

Blavv looked up to discover Kallohn replacing the borrowed tunic with her more usual robe. She displayed no sense of shyness about her brief nakedness and Blavv was suddenly visited with a wish to know more about her and the customs of her people. Before she could ask, however, het'Kallohn moved out, across the greening scrubland. Blavv followed her direction and noted the tents.

'She's off to see if she knows them. More of the K'ahll, she says. She seemed surprised to find them this far north.' Sondukal watched her as he spoke. 'Funny lot, by all accounts.'

'But you've met them in Ov-Bebna, Sondukal. You've seen for yourself what they're like.'

'Tell the truth, I never 'ad no dealins wi' them back there. I were always with our lot from Litkala.'

'Miss the city, don't you?'

'Miss my wife.'

'So what made you take up the job you do? I mean, you must've known you'd be away from home a lot of the time.'

'Ay, 'appen you're right. But I chose the job afore I met the wife, like. An' a body does what a body may. I do this. An' do it as well as I can.'

'Teldrohn says you came along with us so you could learn about the land here.'

Sondukal nodded.

'Why would Litkala be interested in this region, though?'

He smiled and nodded but said nothing. She knew from past encounters with the scout that he'd say no more than he felt he must. And she wondered at the reason for his secrecy on this matter. Litkala was a great city; its population larger than the combined total of all the other cities and towns she'd visited. And she'd heard they had recently wiped out an entire community over some dispute. In spite of her time with Ivdulon, she

206

wondered if perhaps Litkala wasn't all that people hoped. Perhaps there was some evil there, hidden underneath the surface of civilisation and prosperity.

'Be back in a while.' Sondukal wandered off into the shrubs, probably to spy out the land, or hunt for food.

Teldrohn had been quiet all this time, an observer. She'd learned that about him. He could be silent and watchful. Sometimes she wondered what went on in that head. But she didn't need to ask him what he was thinking at this moment. They were alone at last and she knew exactly what was on his mind, because it was on hers.

Something wasn't right. Too much was happening that seemed out of place. Tarruss wouldn't join with a woman for coin and Aglydron was sure he'd done that last night. So had the troop leader. Maybe that was normal for soldiers, but it didn't seem likely. The soldier had never done it before and there were plenty of Followers for joining anyway.

'You worry too much about joining, Aglydron. Men have always been willing to pay for it. At least, all the sailors who visited our city seemed eager.'

'They weren't Followers, Chislanda. And you know how we feel about joining by now. It's no small matter. It's central to our worship of Ytraa.'

She nodded, several times, as if she were recalling to mind something she'd forgotten. 'For me, in the past, it was always about making a child. Until I met you, of course. You showed me what love could be. Changed my life completely. I hate to see you so concerned and anxious. What is it, Aglydron?'

He looked out across the small town square, where they'd gathered in the early light of sunrise, and glanced up at the brightening sky, now devoid of the Skyfire. It would re-appear mid-afternoon and be with them until just before dawn of the next day. An ever-present reminder of the purpose of their pilgrimage. Yet the people of the town seemed unconcerned about it or, at any rate, unwilling to discuss it.

'How can they ignore it, Chislanda? I mean, it's so bright you can see it in broad daylight. But they act as if it didn't exist.'

'But that's not what's worrying you, is it?'

'It's part of it. The Skyfire. Tarruss paying for sex. The High Priest so scared and secretive. And this early morning start we're all so curious about but daren't ask him. I don't like any of it. I like honest, open talk and I like to know what I'm supposed to do and why.'

'Well, here's Dagla Kaz now, with that man he was talking to last night. Maybe he'll explain it all.'

The High Priest signalled that they should all approach, as the other man walked on a short distance and waited, impatient. Dagla Kaz beckoned them into a tight group around him, and spoke in soft tones that held an edge of fear and secrecy. The talk was short and gave them little real information. But they gathered up their belongings and followed the strange man out of town, on foot.

A couple of curious townsmen tagged along, much to the evident annoyance of the High Priest. But the stranger didn't seem concerned. They hung back, merely trailing the pilgrims and saying nothing.

All morning they travelled in the silence Dagla Kaz demanded. They halted only once, toward midday, for a brief break for food and drink. By the middle of the afternoon, as the first sight of the Skyfire loomed over the horizon, Aglydron estimated they'd covered four leagues. They hadn't seen a single settlement; no farms, no sign this land was inhabited in any way. But the two men from the town still tagged along.

He watched as Dagla Kaz consulted with the stranger. The man pointed toward a range of low, scrub-covered hills. The High Priest called them all forward.

'When we enter the hills it's vital we make no sound. The whole purpose of our pil…' he glanced toward the stranger, '…our journey, is tied up in these hills. No, Corphanda, I will hear no words from anyone. You will remain silent, as required. All will be clear once we're at our destination.' He waited for the murmuring to subside into silence again. 'I cannot impress on you too much how important it is that we are absolutely quiet. We must also approach in such a way that we can't be observed. To that end, we'll rest, once we reach a certain point in the hills, and then move forward under cover of darkness.'

Aglydron almost spoke, almost pointed out the obvious fact of the Skyfire. But Chislanda's hand squeezed his and he held his tongue.

'I know it won't be absolutely dark. The Skyfire will give us light enough to see our way. But, once it's night, we're unlikely to be observed, since the people of this land will not walk at night under the light of the Skyfire, such is their dread of it.'

The stranger nodded and glanced frequently into the sky at the growing flame rising above the horizon. For the first time, Aglydron saw that the man was really afraid. Not simply frightened, but terrified. Some deep, deep need must drive this man to fight his fear and make him venture out under the threat of the Skyfire. Aglydron wondered what could be so powerful that it would cause a man to take such risks.

They moved on and entered the hills, climbing and descending by turns until they'd covered another two leagues or so. By this time, the sun had gone and the two townsmen were nowhere to be seen. The pilgrims sank down where they were, ate and drank, and settled to await the time when they would move forward to their destination.

Rumour was rife. The pilgrims whispered softly as they shared ideas and concerns, but Aglydron wouldn't listen to speculation. He would wait until the High Priest declared their intention and then make up his mind about whatever this part of the pilgrimage was about.

He rested with Chislanda. No opportunity to join, as they did most nights, but they held each other as the night progressed. He couldn't sleep, but she fell into dreams until the call came for them to rise. They gathered round the High Priest and he spoke to them in whispers.

'Over that ridge, we will find the Followers who live in this land. They are persecuted and afraid, which is why we must make it clear to them that we are Followers as soon as we may. This will probably be our only opportunity to discover what's happened to our people here in our homeland. If anyone does anything to damage this chance, they will answer to me. Do you understand?'

'Where's our guide, Dagla Kaz?'

The High Priest glared at Myllthlan.

'He's left us. You need know no more.'

But the healer wasn't so easily deflected. 'Can he be trusted, though? Might he not tell others about this meeting?'

'Believe me, woman, that man will tell no one of anything, ever again. Do I make myself clear?'

The import of his words spread through the pilgrim party and subdued all other questions. Aglydron had long been worried that the High Priest might be losing his mind. But these words suggested the local man who'd guided them was now dead, and deliberately so. Had Dagla Kaz really had the man murdered? That was the implication. It was a thought unsettling and disturbing. But they had no time to consider further, as they set off for the ridge and the new party of secret Followers who would explain what had become of Ytraa in this hostile land.

Chapter 26

MEETINGS

The road had been long, the difficulties many, and he was feeling his age. Dagla Kaz had never had to kill by his own hand before. Always, in the past, he'd had others do that duty for him. Tryonta, in particular, had been a valuable assassin. But the stranger had been a different case, and there was no Tryonta to serve his needs. The knife in the back had been easy, kicking the body over the small slope into bushes had been no more difficult and he wondered why he'd been so hesitant in disposing of his enemies before. Killing was simple. His relief palpable.

He'd returned from his secret meeting with the stranger and woken the pilgrims and soldiers. Now he must lead them down to meet a group of Followers who may cause further trouble. But there was no other way to resolve his problems. He'd be unlikely to exchange the Virgin Gifts, as intended, unless the group was large enough. There would be disappointment, bitterness, even anger from those who'd taken on the role, whether volunteer or Chosen.

He shrugged. Nothing he could do about it at present. He must meet and greet these new Followers and hope something positive came from it. Should he have killed the stranger so soon? Perhaps he should've waited until they actually met the new group? But, by then, the stranger would have been a risk to them all. Although, of course, one man against many presented no real danger, they'd have had to determine his fate as a group, adding further tension to a situation already fraught with difficulty. No. It was better to have got rid of the man before they met with others.

He'd told his pilgrims to be silent and silent they were. He could barely hear them behind him and turned frequently to make sure he wasn't alone. There were no fires below to indicate a living place. No indication of life at all that he could see, in spite of the brilliance of the Skyfire. Perhaps they'd fled at first sign of their coming. But the stranger had been certain this was their location. He must simply continue and hope that the new Followers became known when they were closer.

It came as a surprise when he heard a cry of fear from behind. He stopped to remonstrate with the one who'd called out. But they were surrounded. New figures had emerged from the shadows under the small shrubs and trees and encircled the pilgrims. Now was the time for him to show his mettle.

'Good morrow to you. We are Followers from the chosen land of Muhnilahm, come to exchange Virgin Gifts. Come to collect a new Godwood to glorify Ytraa further.'

He'd refined this short speech from the many he'd turned over in his mind as he travelled this route all the way from the island. It sounded simple enough. Told the whole story in as few words as he could manage.

'If, as you claim, you're Followers, you'll know dawn appears and prayers are due.'

It was all the leader, a large man of middle years, said. Dagla Kaz noted the shining edge of a red sun as it appeared in the East, and prepared for prayer. The pilgrims followed his lead. To the utter delight of the High Priest, the other Followers took up the old prayer postures and Dagla Kaz quickly made it known his people should do the same. All but those from Litkala and Kah-Labaz obeyed. But all made themselves naked for their obeisance.

It was clear, as they dressed, that their demonstration had gone a long way to persuading the new Followers of their allegiance. Dagla Kaz placed a hand on the shoulder of the other man and found his gesture returned. The bearded man turned and raised both hands to catch the attention of his people. All paused and listened intently.

'I have need to speak to the leader of this group. Until I return from our conference, remain as guards. None may leave here until we're certain of their identity and purpose.'

With that, he led Dagla Kaz to a small hill that rose above the bush and shrubbery a little to the north. From this elevated position, Dagla Kaz counted the native Followers who numbered some hundred and thirty souls.

The new leader nodded as he turned back to face him. 'Yes. We are few. And we are the last Followers left in the land of Choshinahm.'

'I am Dagla Kaz, High Priest of the island of Muhnilahm and leader of this pilgrimage to celebrate the coming of the Skyfire. We've travelled many leagues across foreign lands to meet with you here in the land that gave birth to the Lord Gadhallah. I have already discovered that Followers are no longer beloved in this land.'

'I must stop you, Dagla Kaz. The very fact that you've discovered us means that we'll be in danger very soon. We must move or face slaughter from the heathens. I'm Wyyhn Kaz, my female consort and partner is Ialdyss Kaz. I need ask two questions before I take you into my trust. Will you answer?'

'It's clear that we're both Followers, simply from our names and the way we pray. Need we bother with more?'

'We live in a land where it is death to be a Follower. Would you have me risk my people?'

'Ask your questions.'

'How long ago did the last Skyfire appear?'

'Two hundred and forty-three cycles.'

The man nodded. 'And from whom is the Lord Gadhallah descended?'

212

'That's easy. I'm from the same stock. We come from the loins of Mythanpho and Vaarkil.'

'We're agreed, then. Now, we must leave this place for a higher domain where we may see our pursuers before they see us. Do you have need of a particular direction, since we simply wander without hope of settlement here?'

'I need to collect a new Godwood, from the Groves of Ytraa.'

'Ah, to hear again that sacred name. I live in a time of wonders, it seems. We must away to the mountains, for at their feet lie those hallowed trees. Come.'

Wyyhn Kaz returned to the people and took the hand of a slender woman with brown hair and mud coloured eyes. He turned to his people.

'We are found again. We return to the mountain forests. There to cut a new bole for these new friends, these Followers from the promised land, to take back with them. Our journey will take a little over a sixday. We go now. Collect your belongings and return here as quickly as you are able.'

There was no dissent, no questions from his people and Dagla Kaz felt respect for this leader who ruled so easily in this difficult place. He organised his own pilgrims and they waited until all re-assembled. Before noon, the party of just over one hundred and fifty souls set out south.

Dagla Kaz walked with Wyyhn Kaz and Ialdyss Kaz. Rrildyss Kaz and Kaz-Ca-Valorysta moved with them. They spoke quietly as they descended to the plain under a hot and relentless sun.

'We will, of course, be visible to any watchers as we pass close to Tohnpho in two days. But, if we time our marches for night time, we should remain undetected.'

'Do people here fear the night, Wyyhn?'

'They're superstitious and believe the Skyfire will burn them should they venture out at night. And they fear the roaming packs of jackals that can rip a man to shreds in seconds. So they avoid travel in the hours of darkness. Of course, we all know the Skyfire is no more than a wandering star that returns every two hundred and forty-three cycles and has significance only as a symbol of our beginning.'

Dagla Kaz held his tongue at this dismissal of the reason for their pilgrimage. It was unwise to alienate people on whose help they must now rely.

'You're the last remaining Followers in all this land, you say?'

'We are. And, if the population has its will, we'll die the last. They'll hunt us down and destroy us. Such is the decree of the leaders of this disparate people.'

'In reality, how likely are we to make it unmolested to the Groves of Ytraa?'

The big man scratched his beard. 'I'd say we have as much chance of getting there as not. But Ytraa will guide and protect us. Ytraa always has.'

213

Dagla Kaz was less confident. But he had no choice. His pilgrims must stay with this collection of Followers whose views differed on several important matters. The task now was to keep the peace between the two groups and avoid unnecessary trouble.

His journey, which should have ended here in glory and triumph, remained incomplete and fraught with danger. And there was still the matter of the Virgin Gifts. He faced the coming days and nights with trepidation and anxiety. A swirl of dust caught his eye and he started.

'Nothing to worry about, Dagla. Just the wind.'

But he would start at any undue movement, any unexpected sight, until they were free of this land where they might all die at any moment.

Tumalind was glad to see the oasis after an uneventful journey from the mountains. She and Okkyntalah had enjoyed freedom for much of the way but donned short skirts for their meeting with the others, anxious not to cause offence. When they discovered Kallohn wore something similar, and Blavv and Teldrohn were unconcerned about clothing, they relaxed again.

The group gathered at the smaller of two pools that watered the trees, and used it to bathe and refresh themselves, splashing and cavorting as they expressed their pleasure at meeting each other again.

Okkyntalah and Sondukal quickly reformed their former hunting prowess and returned to the makeshift camp with a coney and a small deer. Kallohn dug up roots and gathered herbs and showed Blavv where to collect dates and figs. Their feast was a joyous interlude in what had been a dreary time for most.

The morning found Blavv and Tumalind deep in silent conversation, as they discussed what each knew of their intended destination.

'Ivdulon wanted me to come this way, to be company for you as you enter your old home. But I think she has some other purpose. Has she said anything to you, Blavv?'

'Teldrohn asked me about the town. I know only what I remember as a child and that isn't much. But Kallohn spoke with the K'ahll tribe who were here a few days ago and they warned her the place is evil. As always with those desert wanderers, they wouldn't say in what way, just that they avoided it and advised us to do the same.'

'They were like that with Okkyntalah about Ov-Bebna, so, maybe the situation there is similar.'

'Perhaps. But that's not how I recall it. Men and women were treated more or less as equals. No, the division of society was more to do with, well, what people owned, I suppose. The more wealth a person had, the greater their power.'

'Seems an odd sort of thing to use as a guide for authority. I mean, that would make merchants the most powerful people and that would be just plain silly, wouldn't it?'

'I asked Ivdulon but she has no connections in Trotnahn. Says it's the one place she can't get into with mindtalk.'

'Have you tried, Blavv?'

The young woman looked troubled.

'I see. You found only the dark part of our world. Am I right?'

'I didn't dare venture in. But it's there, on the edge, if you know what I mean. Dark and frightening. I didn't go any further in case they discovered me.'

'Very wise, Blavv. I think it's an area even Ivdulon finds difficult to deal with. I certainly don't intend to explore it.'

'So, what do you think we should do, Tumalind?'

'Like everyone else, all those who can't mindtalk, we'll have to see for ourselves, with our eyes and ears instead of our minds, I suppose.'

They returned to the group.

'You two look very serious. What's worrying you?'

'Nothing, Okkyntalah. We can't find a mindtalker in Trotnahn, that's all. It's not important.'

'Still want to go, Blavv?' Teldrohn's tone was of concern rather than relief and the young woman shrugged in reply.

'The K'ahll say it's an evil place.'

'Yes, Kallohn, but they said that about Ov-Bebna. True, it was evil, but not in the way I expected.'

'Nowt to do wi' me, like, but if I were to 'ave me say, I'd say to go, lass. If you don't, you'll never know for sure what you've missed. Might turn out to be just right for you an' Teldrohn. But you'll not find out if you don't go, will you?'

They all respected Sondukal for his taciturn manner, so, when he spoke, they listened. His suggestion decided the matter and they packed up their belongings and set out for a long trek across uninspiring scrubland.

'How long do you think it'll take us, Sondukal?'

'From what I 'ear it's no more'n twenty leagues. Three days should do it. All fit and strong, aren't we?'

'Let's give ourselves four, eh? Take it easy?'

General opinion agreed with Teldrohn's suggestion and they mounted their camels and set off to the west.

'My imagination, Okkyntalah, or is that there Skyfire startin' to fade?'

'Ivdulon said it would reach its peak around the first day of the fourth portion. Where are we now? Fifteenth of the fourth? So it'll fade from now.'

Blavv stared at him in admiration. 'You know the date, even out here?'

'Oh, don't praise me, Blavv. It's Tumalind; counts the days in her head. She's the one who keeps track of these things.'

'It's easy enough. Anyway, Ivdulon says the Skyfire will disappear from view by the twenty-eighth day of the fifth portion.'

'Just a few more sixdays, then. An' if it's fadin' an' 'asn't burnt us yet, I reckon it's not about to, don't you?'

Tumalind glanced at Okkyntalah and found his agreement. 'To be honest, Okkyntalah and I no longer believe most of the stuff we were brought up to take as the truth. I hope we won't offend anyone, but we don't pray any more. We don't think Following is for us.'

To her surprise, no one seemed either concerned or offended. Blavv reminded her she'd never been a Follower anyway, and Kallohn was of the K'ahll. Her god was Ulkhon, the sun god. Sondukal and Teldrohn both hailed from Litkala, where religion was a person's own affair.

'Funny, I thought it would be difficult for us to admit we'd lost our faith. It was really easy, after all.'

'Aye, but yon Dagla Kaz, an' I reckon your father, will both be unhappy when that Skyfire's gone an' 'asn't burnt up all the bad 'uns.'

'I wonder where they are?'

Okkyntalah shook his head. 'Rrildyss can mindtalk, can't she, Tumalind?'

She smiled. 'Of course. I'll talk with her when we stop for a break. Let's get on our way to Trotnahn first.'

'You have plenty of able-bodied people, Chellyth. I need a small but experienced group of soldiers. If I do not quell the dissenters quickly, they will cause untold harm in all the settlements. I must take volunteers to rid the island of the danger they pose. Surely you understand that?'

'I thought you cared for us, Aklon? Will you abandon us now we have a new home? Leave us defenceless?'

'I care for all the people of the island, Chellyth. I always have. You are in less danger than any of the other settlements and, if you feel the need, you can erect a barrier to prevent surprise attacks. There is wood aplenty here. You have wild and domesticated beasts to feed you. You have the sea for fish. Springs for water. I selected this place because it is an ideal location for a settlement and I have given it to you and your people. All I ask in return is the loan of fifty men and women of experience in fighting. Is that too much?'

'Aklon's right, Chellyth. We owe him a great deal. Will we deny him the means to secure safety for the whole island, including us?'

Chellyth could be stubborn. She'd had to be unbending in her role as leader of the people of The Point. Now she was about to settle as rightful leader of a legitimate group at last, and the transition wasn't easy for her. But the words of her consort, Por-Kildu, were strong persuasion.

'I will keep them only as long as I need them, Chellyth. I do not intend to re-instate the army that my father needed to retain his power. But we must defeat these violent dissenters and the Unholy Ones who act as their allies, or no one, including your people, will be safe.'

'Take them, then. Take as many as you need. But bring them back when you've done what you must.'

'I'm commin' annall, Aklon.'

He looked down into her eager face, scanned the willing skin she presented. 'No, Syylvah. You have no skill in battle and where we go you would be more liability than help.'

'But I need you, Aklon.'

He took his hand from where she'd pressed it. 'Not me, Syylvah. Any man worthy of the name can give you what you want.'

'I want you!'

'We all want things we cannot have, Syylvah. Will some man give this willing woman what she wants?'

A soldier came forward and took her hand. He whispered in her ear and she brightened. They left together, without a backward glance from Syylvah. Aklon returned his attention to Chellyth and Por-Kildu.

'So, have you decided on a name for your new home yet?'

'We'll name it the town of Aklon. For you made it possible and should be honoured.'

It was pointless to argue or protest. The woman and man were strong-willed and determined. He nodded, graciously, and bowed to them.

'You honour me more than I deserve. But I thank you.'

'We honour you less than you deserve, Aklon. But it's all we can do, for the moment. Now, take your fighters and destroy this plague. But come back to us. If none else returns, then at least you must. I'm sorry for my former objections: you are, as almost always, right, of course.'

The gathering was assembled quickly. The choosing of volunteers equally swift. And, before she let him go, Chellyth named the town that was already growing.

'We call our new town, Aklohnahn, in honour of our saviour.'

She need say no more. In fact, she could say no more for the noise of agreement that rose in a great cheer from those assembled. Aklon acknowledged their appreciation and made to leave. They pressed him to stay and celebrate.

'When I return, when the land is rid of the scourge of dissent and violence, we will celebrate in style. Until then, I go to end the evil my father and his ancestors settled on this land. I go to fight for freedom!'

That did the trick, as he'd known it would. The settlers cheered, as he led his small army out and marched to the east and Chalamamnon to rid the capital of trouble first.

Chapter 27

MINDTALK

The skirmish, for that was all it could be called, west of a town Wyyhn Kaz called Tohnpho, had cost Dagla Kaz one Virgin Gift. Uhstyhll, the volunteer from Muhnilahm, had been a thief anyway. No real loss. The small group of townsfolk that had attacked had lost more of their own folk and it seemed unlikely they'd be back to cause more trouble. In fact, a party of Followers had harried them and returned with much of their food and other supplies. They reported that the shabby little town was now in fear of the Followers.

After that, they'd made good progress, driven by uncertainty, and were now well beyond the most dangerous part of their journey to the Groves of Ytraa. For Dagla Kaz it was all growing more and more pointless. These straggling nomads were the last Followers in the homeland. Of what help were they in the continuance of the faith? Still, they'd be useful in identifying, cutting and transporting the new Godwood. And they might provide at least some hope of exchanging a few Virgin Gifts. That was an issue he'd preferred to shelve. Clearly, there were too few here to provide the number of Virgin Gifts needed to fulfil the original hopes.

He counted his own, as they made their evening prayers on the third day of their journey. Five boys and seven girls. What to do with them now? Obvious. Those who couldn't be matched with whatever virgins existed in Wyyhn's troop would have to be paired off with each other. He must question him on the matter whilst they ate.

Jhonaht approached, wearing that expression of gloom that had characterised his appearance ever since they'd crossed the mountains and come into this now godforsaken land where all their hopes had been dashed.

'What?'

The astronomer started at his peremptory demand. He took a moment to compose himself and the High Priest allowed glee to colour his countenance as he enjoyed his power over this man of intelligence.

'I fear the Skyfire begins to fade, Dagla Kaz.'

'We knew it would.'

'But it's done no damage to the ungodly, those who don't Follow. What are we to tell the people?'

In all the trouble and difficulties of the pilgrimage, this factor had escaped him. How could he have failed to consider this? It was supposed to be central to the reason for their mission. The prime reason for visiting this land, where death threatened their very existence. The astronomer looked at him; wanting words of wisdom and comfort, awaiting some acknowledgement that he'd considered the matter.

But there was no answer. He'd known all along, from the parchments and stone tablets, that the Skyfire was harmless. It was no more than a symbol. A signal for pilgrimage to the homeland and a return in triumph, so that the priesthood could reign untroubled for a further two hundred and forty-three cycles. It had no significance beyond that simple device to fool the people. Gadhallah's own words had made it clear enough.

'Dagla?' The astronomer was insistent.

The man was a menace. Always had been. A liability with his cowardice and false knowledge. Not a patch on the intelligence of that damned woman in Litkala. That wise woman seemed to know everything. Jhonaht was a spent force, a redundant feature, an irritation at a time of danger.

Dagla Kaz slipped his sword from its scabbard and thrust it through the man's chest. When the astronomer fell at his feet, he hacked and slashed at the quivering body until it was a mess of blood and flesh.

Caarl and Ouqitahl ran over and stood, looking down at the carcass and then into his face. Battle hardened and experienced, the soldiers were appalled.

'What have you done, Dagla Kaz?'

They demanded answers? From him? From Dagla Kaz, High Priest of Muhnilahm? How dare they? He lifted his arm to strike but found them prepared. He couldn't defeat such men. Any attempt would result in his own death, here and now. He must make it right. Now.

He replaced the bloodied sword in its scabbard. Shook his head as if in deep regret and shock. The others had finished their prayers and now gathered about the three living, and one dead, men. Questions. Questions. Questions would be asked. And he must answer. Now.

He raised his hands in supplication to his god. Called out the name of Ytraa. Ripped off his tabard. The others would follow his actions. Most remained naked after prayers anyway. He preferred them that way. Vulnerable and under the long influence of the creed of their religion; it made them more malleable, less likely to rebel.

'You wonder why I've killed the astronomer? Of course you do. I will tell you. Jhonaht is a liar. A fraud. He predicted the Skyfire would burn all who fail to Follow. He claimed that all who sinned would die in the flames of the Skyfire. And, like a fool, I believed him. Not only did I believe this man, this man of science and knowledge, but I spread his words, his lies to all my people on the island of Muhnilahm. To all those in Litkala and Kah-Labaz. And I was about to tell these lies of Jhonaht's to our new friends here, the Followers of Choshinahm. But he confessed the truth to me. He told me the Skyfire is not a burning punishment to scour the world of the wicked. It is, as Wyyhn Kaz has already declared, a symbol only. It is a reminder of our duty to connect with those from our homeland. No more and no less. And Jhonaht knew this!

'I do not diminish the Skyfire. But I cannot be lied to in that fashion. I have therefore punished the liar with the death he deserved. I will hear his lies no more.

'This morning, he confessed that the Skyfire is diminishing. That it will fade and die in a few sixdays. With that message in mind, it is even more crucial that we obtain the new Godwood and return to the island as soon as we may. And, for that reason, and because we are a faith that cares for all Followers, I here and now invite our new friends. I put out the hand of friendship to our homeless wanderers in this land, this land that has rejected the Lord Gadhallah and Ytraa. I ask you all to return with us to Muhnilahm, there to live the faith in safety and contentment.'

He watched for reactions. His own party would show mixed feelings, but he could deal with any doubters. The new people were an unknown. But he judged he'd given them enough to make them believe he was a generous and sincere leader. There was, as expected, much discussion. He raised his hands again and received the silence he craved.

'I leave you to consider what I've said. The shock of execution, coupled with my announcement of invitation, must make you all consider your thoughts and feelings on these matters. I expect no answer today. We must needs continue our journey as quickly as we might, if only to escape further persecution by those who hate us. For now, let us move towards the sacred Groves of Ytraa. We may discuss as we walk.'

'Jhonaht, Dagla Kaz?' Caarl looked down at the corpse.

'The carrion beasts can take him. He's a blasphemer.'

Wyyhn, as expected, approached him and the pair set out together, leading the troop on the way to their destination. 'I see you bear the signs of the mindtalker, Dagla Kaz. But I've been unable to connect with you. Do you impose some barrier?'

The man was a fool. What was he talking of? Mindtalk? What strange language was this?

'I've no knowledge of…mindtalk you say? What is it?'

'Ah. You're ignorant of the gift you hold. I see. That's unusual, though not unique. You may find it difficult to understand what I'm about to tell you. I note the priestess, Rrildyss Kaz also bears the mark. I've yet to attempt connection with her. Tradition declares that I mindtalk first with the leader of the new group. And, of course two of your Virgin Gifts also have the signs.'

'You talk of something strange, yet to you it appears obvious. What are these signs?'

'Nothing to be anxious about Dagla Kaz. These are indications only of the possibility of mindtalk in the bearer. You note the similarities in our eyes?'

Dagla Kaz studied the man and was surprised that his eyes were lapis lazuli and bore small gold flecks. Like his own. And those of Jodisa. And Aklon, the Renegade. And…and Tumalind, if he recalled correctly. What was this 'gift' the new Follower spoke of? Did it have value? If Jodisa had it, did she know? Did Aklon? Did Rrildyss? And the two Virgin Gifts?

'Which Virgin Gifts?'

'The dutiful and quiet boy, Gidwallehn. And the attractive, laughing girl, Zyreenha, who I believe hails from the city of Litkala. You were unaware…of course? If you don't recognise the signs, why would you note the similarities?'

This man knew more of his charges than he did himself. He must be watched. Was Wyyhn a danger or an ally? And what, exactly, was this mindtalk? And why had it never been pointed out to him before? He recalled, quite suddenly, that Feldrark and Ivdulon had also borne the signs. How many had the gift? Was it dangerous? Was it useful? What was it? He had to know.

'Tell me of this mindtalk and how I may apply it, if you will, Wyyhn.'

They'd been on the way to Chalamamnon only hours when Aklon was contacted by Wempiryss, the woman who'd acted as his host in the capital.

'A connection of mine in Krohtl reports that Kaz-Ca-Charrohn is leading a determined rebellion against the Few there. Perhaps they should've killed the bitch when they had the chance?'

'I am on my way to help you in the capital.'

'It's your decision, Aklon. But we're managing all right here for the moment. Krohtl sounds as though it's in real trouble.'

'Who is your connection there?'

'Unfortunately he can only connect when you've met face to face. I met him years ago on the Plains of Ytraa. Kept in touch ever since. 'Course, I didn't know then there were a few of us could do this. Didn't know you could, until recently, of course.'

Wempiryss could gossip for hours, given the opportunity, so he thanked her and changed direction for Krohtl at once. Now, they had reached the outskirts of the small town.

An odd settlement, on the eastern end of the island, where the Rhyll poured into the Sophraq Sea, it had always been a bit of a thorn in the side of the various authorities. Even Dagla Kaz had had trouble with the inhabitants, which was why he'd placed the young but demanding Priestess, Charrohn, in charge. She was a harsh leader and an enthusiastic joiner, keeping the men, in particular, under control by her excessive demands. Blonde and curvaceous, she was a woman with all the physical qualities that attracted men, and she made the best of them. But she was a singularly selfish lover, leaving men wanting after they'd given what she required. Putting her in a position of power was typical of his father. A bad choice for so many reasons.

What puzzled him was that she had loyal men around her. Perhaps some men enjoyed being used in this way? But, for whatever reason, she had a strong following, almost exclusively of men, who were willing to do her bidding, no matter what it might be. Perhaps she rewarded these chosen ones with more generous joining; Aklon could think of no other reason for their loyalty.

Delbon, who'd been forced to join with the priestess on a number of occasions, had gone into the town to discover more. They'd been waiting longer than he'd anticipated and Aklon was starting to worry.

Choryssa moved closer to him through the forest cover. She was a lithe, sensuous creature who combined feminine sexuality with a tough and disciplined soldier's attitude to life. 'He's been too long, Aklon. I'd like to go and investigate.'

'Give him another hour. I do not wish to risk you as well.'

'I care for him.'

'More than care. Trust me. I usually get signs when there is trouble. So far, the town has been quiet.'

'It's early morning, of course it's quiet.'

'That is not what I meant, Choryssa.'

In common with many of the Few, she'd chosen her skin as a statement of rebellion against the Followers. It was fast becoming a recognised uniform for those on his side and he wondered if it might cause problems in the future. It was certainly a distraction, though the growing habit was slowly making the state normal. Only time would tell whether it would become acceptable for all. Aklon remained in his tabard, for no better reason than it was habitual and allowed him to carry items that might otherwise be difficult to have at hand.

Choryssa nodded but she gazed out in longing and he knew she felt more for Delbon than she'd ever declared. Delbon had told him her reserve didn't extend to joining. He smiled at the memory.

'What's amusing you, Aklon?'

He told her.

'I'm a soldier. When we've finished this and everything's settled down, I'll tell him how I really feel. I'll marry him and give him all the babies he wants.'

'Perhaps you should tell him now?' He pointed at the figure entering their encampment.

'Delbon! At last.'

He allowed her time to greet her lover with the passion she felt. Delbon extracted himself from her embrace with a look of delighted surprise.

'What was that all about?'

Aklon placed a hand on his shoulder. 'I think Choryssa should tell you. Now, what is the situation?'

Delbon explained that he'd spoken with the Few. There were still citizens here who were unsure, and Charrohn's influence over some men had made a number reluctant to disobey her. But the general feeling in the town was that they must reject the Follower's philosophy and make the changes Aklon had proposed. His presence in the town may well change minds and give many the courage to act on their new convictions.

'How many has she at her command?'

'A personal guard of fifty men, all armed of course, and apparently willing to die for her. They say she services all of them every day. I don't think she can, can she?'

'She is said to have an insatiable appetite. Who knows what she can or cannot do?'

'Not going to be easy to persuade them to desert her, then.'

'No. I fear we will be forced to make her abandon them.'

Delbon glanced at him. 'She won't give them up, though, will she?'

'That is why she must be removed from them. Has she caused much violence?'

'Some executions in the square. Public and violent. She unmans the men and spikes them on greased poles. Takes them a day or more to die. Agony, they say.'

'And the women?'

Delbon turned away, unwilling to give the descriptions he'd heard.

'Delbon?'

'She's a demon. Utterly debauched. I can't describe... Her men are animals! One of the Few tried to rescue a woman and the priestess put him to death herself. Everyone's terrified of her.'

'As to animals, Delbon, I have yet to know any wild creature that is as deliberately cruel as a human being. But she must be stopped. Our objective is to kill her and any of the men who cling to her ways. That means all fifty, if necessary. We cannot allow any of them to be free if they have been willing to do her bidding. Unless they sincerely repent and change their allegiance.'

He discovered her whereabouts from Delbon and, with Choryssa's detailed memory of the town, they formed a plan. It would be difficult and dangerous with so many of the townspeople undecided. Before they began their action, they must seek out and warn those members of the Few who were known and could assist. They'd need help to guard their backs as they went into battle against the tyrant.

Aklon sent Delbon, Choryssa and four others into the town to forewarn the Few and organise that necessary defence. Once they returned, the small army would descend on the house of the priestess and destroy her. But secrecy was essential. If she or her men heard of their presence before they were ready, the whole scheme could be put in jeopardy and his small troop placed at great risk. He had to trust to the skill and dedication of those he'd sent into the town to make preparations.

'Aklon? Sorry to intrude so early in the morning, but we need help.'

'I am not sure who speaks to me.'

'Sorry, Eyethlehn from Morstahn. There's a large group of soldiers and Unholy Ones gathering on the hills above town. We fear they may attack at any moment.'

'How large is the group?'

'Our scouts think about seventy.'

'And how many are you?'

'We've some returned soldiers, four groups of the Few, making up about sixty in all, but most have never had to fight.'

He explained where he was and asked how imminent attack might be.

'Our guess is that they won't attack today. They seem to be waiting for others. But we don't know who, or how many.'

'Can you organise some delaying tactics? See whether your scouts can cause them problems. If some brave souls could enter their camp at night and remove as much weaponry as possible, it would make them hesitate to act and give you weapons into the bargain. Do you have such courageous people?'

'I'm sure I can find some. But how soon can you be here?'

'We are a day away. But I have a fight to finish here before I dare leave this place. I have set action in motion and, if I abandon it now, many people will be hurt or killed here. We will be there as soon as we are able. Where, exactly, are the Unholy Ones encamped?'

She described the location and he knew it well, overlooking the place where his lover dwelt. Shoarhn. How tempting to go to her aid. To see her again. To hold her close. But he could not leave Krohtl until he had dealt with Charrohn. It was impossible.

Chapter 28

PRISONERS

Dreary. That was the only word Tumalind could apply to their journey from the oasis to the city of Trotnahn. The only highlights had been Okkyntalah's loving and his occasional forays into silliness that made her laugh. Now, the city walls stretched before them. There was something imposing, even hostile, about their construction and design. This wasn't a place that spoke of welcome. She'd mindtalked with Ivdulon on the journey. The wise woman had warned her, in a roundabout and subtle way that had her anxious as well as curious, of evil lurking in the place. From that uncertain and circumspect conversation, she'd gained the distinct feeling that an unspecified risk awaited her within those walls.

The K'ahll had warned them that female nudity was prohibited in the city and they'd therefore, reluctantly, put on clothing. She felt hot and confined under the short skirt and breast cloth, the only items she'd chosen. Okkyntalah donned his well-worn tabard. Sondukal and Teldrohn had tried constant nakedness but preferred their tunics. Blavv put on the tunic she'd earned as one of Feldrark's troops. Kallohn replaced her short skirt with the full-length black robe.

The gates had been closed against them in the night but dawn now opened them. Kallohn warned them to be wary and alert. Though exactly what dangers faced them she was either reluctant or unable to specify. But it was an anxious party that entered between frowning sentries.

'You are strangers. What do you bring of value?' The man who spoke was clearly a minor official. His manner, his position at the small but well-built kiosk just inside the entrance, indicated that his role was some form of control over visitors.

Teldrohn, as nominated senior member of their party, answered. 'We bring only ourselves and a little coin for our immediate needs. My partner here, was born in your city but taken by the Uhmbard's men into slavery. She's come back in hope of finding her parents and family.'

The man waved Teldrohn aside and gestured Blavv to stand before him. He had her turn as if a prize cow at a farmers' market. He nodded once she'd completed her display. And asked her name.

'I was very young. I can't recall what I was called when I left this place.'

'Enough!' he turned back to Teldrohn. 'You paid the proper price for her release from service to the Uhmbard?'

'I paid nothing. Why would I?'

The man's face changed from curiosity to instant concern; almost, it seemed, fear.

'You want to bring the desert hoards down on us? What do you mean, carrying this risk to our doors? Leave at once, or we'll have you whipped and her exhibited outside the city walls for his men to find when they arrive!' He gestured to the sentries, clearly wanting military back-up for his threat.

'The Uhmbard will send no one. He's dead. Our troops killed him when we freed our own captive woman, this beauty here, Tumalind.'

This idea seemed beyond the official's understanding. But he waved back the approaching sentry, almost in irritation.

'I don't understand. The Uhmbard is dead? But then the new Uhmbard will rule and want new women for his harem. We will have to…'

'There is no new Uhmbard. We put him and Uhmteld to death. There's no heir. Ov-Bebna is now ruled by an Assembly of those the people trust. There's no new harem and the members of the old one are free to marry or not as they wish.'

This idea was obviously too strange for him to comprehend. 'I require that you remain here until I can determine what should be done with you. This is outside my power.'

He gestured for the sentry once more and this time the man came quickly, anger and impatience driving his movement. He drew his sword as he approached.

'Take these strangers to the lock-up until I can find a Senior to question them further. Treat them well for the moment. You may have your entertainment only if the Senior deems them unsuitable.'

With that, the official was gone into the winding streets. The sentry made a swift gesture at his colleague, who called for a replacement from the room inside the gateway walls and came to stand with him, sword also drawn. Teldrohn, Sondukal, Blavv and Okkyntalah drew their weapons and faced the two soldiers of the city.

'We'd rather not spill blood in a city we don't know. Perhaps we can all put away our blades and discuss this sensibly.'

The first sentry nodded at his companion. Slowly and with much mutual suspicion, they all sheathed their swords and the tension lessened a little.

'We must ask you to come with us.'

Teldrohn nodded. 'But we won't be held as prisoners. We're guests and one of us is a citizen of this place. You understand?'

The sentry nodded and led them a short distance to a small building with thick walls and small windows barred with iron. The door stood open, though it was not inviting.

'I think we'll wait outside, if you don't mind. I don't like the look of that place.'

228

The sentry hesitated but agreed to the demand and went inside. A short time later, he emerged pulling a long wooden bench, which he set against the outer wall. He gestured that they should sit. Closely packed, they sat and waited.

In moments the official returned with another, accompanied by a troop of ten soldiers, bearing arms. The new man was the Senior the first man had named, his position of importance marked by the splendour of his outfit. A leather jerkin, open, covered him from neck to waist but left his chest exposed. A white silk apron hid his manhood and black silk covered his rear. His feet were part enclosed in leather straps that held him a thumbswidth from the ground. And on his head he bore a conical device of latticed bronze, studded with small gems. A chain around his neck, gold by the look of it, supported an item that had no meaning for the party of strangers. Black and heavy, it looked like a stem of metal with one end forming a loop through which the chain passed and the other end formed into several protrusions of uneven shape and size.

The Senior questioned the sentries and then sent them back to the gate. It was clear the gates would be closed to prevent the party leaving of their own free will. The new troop of soldiers surrounded them, their swords sheathed but their long spears ready.

The Senior approach Teldrohn and stood before him. Teldrohn rose to face the man.

'Retract the ridiculous lie you told my man. Clearly, the Uhmbard of Ov-Bebna cannot have been defeated by a small army, yet you claim he is dead and has not been replaced. Explain yourself.'

Blavv stood to have her say. 'This is my city as well as yours. Is it the custom here to accuse visitors of lying? I'd hoped to…'

'Silence, woman! Who gave you permission to speak? Remain silent until questioned.'

'I escaped one male tyrant. I won't be…'

Two soldiers grasped her arms. Another lifted her tunic and smacked her bottom soundly with the flat of his sword.

'One more word and I'll have you pinioned in the arena. Be silent, woman.'

Tumalind sensed danger in the men in her group. She knew Okkyntalah wouldn't draw his weapon yet, but was unsure of Teldrohn and Sondukal. But the treatment of Blavv meant she'd be very unwise to speak.

Teldrohn, anticipating her possible intervention, gestured to her and spoke to the Senior. 'I see we have more differences than expected. You will not beat our women. We do not treat them in such a way and neither will you. Release my partner at once. My leaders are the Kiral and Kirallah of Litkala and will not take kindly to mistreatment of their subjects. Blavv, here, is a citizen by adoption. You will do well to understand who we are and who protects us.'

The Senior was immediately troubled. He gestured to the soldiers to release Blavv. And uneasy tension fell on the meeting.

'The woman of the K'ahll, of course, is excluded from your general protection. She can be given to the guardsmen for sport.'

'het Kallohn is our guide and a respected member of our group. She enjoys the same protection as the rest of our party.'

The Senior stiffened and shook his head at this. 'It's clear there's more to you than merely five travellers. I must ask you to accompany me to an audience with the Chief Secretary. He will be better placed to determine how we should proceed. Come. Follow me.'

With that, he turned and moved forward. The troops formed a double column and gestured the group in between their lines with two soldiers making up the rear.

Tumalind kept her eyes and ears open and alert as they made their strange procession through the city. She knew Okkyntalah and Sondukal would be seeking out ways they might escape, should that need present itself. This wasn't a city that made strangers welcome and she was anxious about what their future here might hold in store.

⁎ ⸺ ⸻

Already, the difficulties of travel with a large group were evident. Aglydron had noticed a change in Dagla Kaz and put it down to the increase in his responsibility. The brutal execution of the astronomer had shocked him to the core. The High Priest's explanation didn't sit right and, added to other doubts that gathered in his mind, tried to break his faith. He was determined not to listen to them as they clamoured for his attention and attempted to make him rebel against the authority he'd followed all his life.

The Skyfire was diminishing. But was it the true Skyfire, after all? It had burnt no one. Even those that Aglydron knew to be heathen or sinner had escaped its fiery breath. Its flames had consumed nothing, yet it hung above them, menacing and bright with threat.

Did that mean the High Priest's accusation of the astronomer was right? But hadn't it been Dagla Kaz, and the Holy Ones, who'd taught that the Skyfire was a sacred flame sent by Ytraa to cleanse the world of evil? The High Priest now said not. But that wasn't the memory he held of words pronounced by Dagla Kaz and certain Holy Ones.

And what about the Virgin Gifts? They were yet to be exchanged. But it had already been announced that there were only two within the ranks of these new Followers. One boy and one girl. Not enough to satisfy the needs of the pilgrimage. And now they knew for certain there were no more Followers in all of Choshinahm. How had this happened? How could they have been sent all this way by their God only to find such disappointment and despair? It made no sense. No sense at all.

230

'A dorltah for them, Aglydron?'

He glanced sideways at Chislanda, saw beyond her the landscape now enclosed by high mountains. Up ahead, along the way made by the new Followers who led them, were the first signs of the Groves of Ytraa. By nightfall they'd be amongst the sacred trees at last. That, at least, was cause for joy.

'You look puzzled and unhappy, Aglydron. Do you want to talk about whatever's troubling you?'

What was the point of discussing his concerns with someone ignorant of the true history of his faith? Chislanda had proved herself a loving woman, a willing convert to the faith, but she had no real knowledge, no true understanding of what it was to be a Follower. Oh, she joined enthusiastically. But that was just a human need for love and sensation; she never experienced the oneness he'd attained in joining to become the one that Ytraa had first made them. It was true that he was one with her when they joined, but that felt more like love between them, rather than the spiritual joy of defeating the wickedness that Mhortag had done in separating man from woman.

'Aglydron?'

She was persistent. He must break his silence, answer her. But how? She wouldn't understand his doubts and worries. But there was a topic he could breach with her. 'It's Dagla Kaz. I'm worried for him.'

'I see. He's changed, hasn't he? Something's made him wild and unpredictable. I always thought him slightly dangerous and strange. But since we met these new Followers he's grown more reckless. I'm no longer sure he knows what he's doing, to be honest, Aglydron.'

He should contradict her. Should tell her she was wrong to think like that. He should persuade her of the error of her ways. Except that he agreed with her. 'I thought at first it was just the problem of the Virgin Gifts, but Ialdyss Kaz has made a suggestion for a solution of that problem. He isn't keen, but I can't see any other way to fulfil the needs of the pilgrimage, so I think he'll accept it. But there's more. It's almost as if he's being eaten up from inside. There's something frightening behind his eyes when he looks at you, don't you think?'

Chislanda nodded but said no more. She squeezed his hand as he was about to open his mouth and he turned and saw the High Priest had moved up close, and might even be listening to their conversation as they walked. After the killing of Jhonaht, who none of them was now allowed to name, they'd all become wary of angering the High Priest. Aglydron hoped the man hadn't heard what they'd said about him.

But the High Priest made no acknowledgement of Aglydron as he passed them by and made toward the leaders of the new Followers, at the front of the long column.

Aglydron sighed with relief. 'That was close. Do you think he really might be mad?'

Chislanda followed his progress through the crowd with her eyes. 'Yes. Don't you?'

For reasons Aglydron didn't at first understand, the admission that the High Priest might have lost his mind brought relief from his personal anxieties. It allowed other aspects of the doubts about the Followers to be left in place, reduced the pressure for a need to change his way of thinking. Perhaps that was it. By allowing all his doubts to revolve around the fact of the insanity of Dagla Kaz, he no longer had to worry about his concerns for his faith. There was nothing wrong with Ytraa or the Lord Gadhallah. It was the High Priest who was at fault, difficult as that might be to comprehend. If their spiritual leader was mad, then all he'd been taught, all he'd believed, was no longer in danger, no longer need be questioned.

'Thank you, Chislanda. You've helped me see the truth. I feel relieved and settled again.'

'Good. I was beginning to fear I'd disappointed you in some way.'

'Never. I love you and you're the best partner for me. I want this pilgrimage to finish now so we can farm fertile land and raise children.'

She squeezed his hand, this time with affection. 'And where, exactly, will that land be, Aglydron?'

He hadn't thought about it. The pilgrimage the only thing he had given his attention to. But that was closing now. They'd find the Godwood and float it back to the island.

'Muhnilahm. Yes. We'll return home. I owe it to Shoarhn to let her know she's free to marry elsewhere. She can keep the farm; it was half hers anyway. And we'll find a new place together somewhere else on that fair island. How does that sound?'

'You amaze me, Aglydron. I think I understand and know you and then you surprise me with ideas like this. It's wonderful. The sooner we can get back to your island home, the better. I'm weary of wandering, to tell the truth. I long to settle down and make babies with you. I love you.'

He squeezed her hand and they leaned in toward each other, kissed briefly and a little self-consciously, like young lovers not yet joined. The joy of their contact flowed through his body and he knew he wanted to be with this woman for the rest of his life.

The column ahead halted and they continued towards them. The crowd of new Followers and pilgrims gathered on the broad top of a gentle hill. In readiness for more than prayer, the High Priests divested themselves. Some announcement was to be made. Everyone else prepared but remained standing, waiting to learn what the leaders had decided.

Chapter 29

TROTNAHN

'But, why is it so important that my father doesn't know about mindtalk, Feldrark? I've never really understood that.'

Jodisa and Feldrark were in the Riser, on their way to talk with Ivdulon after her revelation that Rrildyss had given her the news by mindtalk.

He stroked his hand over her slowly swelling belly and smiled down at her in that way that had first drawn her attention. She parted the tunic to let him see, and he knelt before her, kissed the firm skin and placed his ear against her stomach. She played her fingers through his curls. Even here, in this impersonal stone box that climbed the side of the Red Rill at such alarming speed. Those two who'd stolen her from her island had given her Feldrark, and for that she would always be grateful. What, she wondered, would her life have been back home, especially now that Aklon had deposed the whole religion of the Followers? As High Priestess Elect, she might have suffered the fate of Wendarah. She shuddered and Feldrark felt it. He rose to his feet and embraced her, no need for questions, no need for comforting words. Touch was enough for them.

Ivdulon waited outside. She wore a circular brim around her head, to shade her eyes from sunlight, a pair of covers on her feet to hide the deformity. Netrodyl was nowhere to be seen, but would be in the tower.

'Not too cool up here like that?'

'I'm used to the temperature. It allows me to think more freely. The child grows well, Jodisa.' It was a statement.

She nodded and they walked to the edge of the lake, overlooking the pool of red stained water, reflecting the snow-capped top of the mountain. For a brief while the three gazed at the amazing accomplishment of their predecessors. A perfect circle, with perpendicular walls that plunged into an unknown depth. The water within undisturbed by wind at this early hour; calm and flat as a sheet of window glass.

Ivdulon raised her arms, stretched them wide and up, flexed her back and parted her feet. For a moment she remained in this position, that might've been taken as a declaration of worship, and then relaxed again.

'At first, I feared disaster had struck. But now I have more detail and have trialled a few tests, I know it's actually good news, rather than bad. Though you may see things differently, Jodisa.'

'My father's discovered he can mindtalk. I never understood why you were so

233

desperate to prevent that.'

'Dagla is a man with very rigid thinking patterns. Forgive me, Jodisa, but he's also a man who is basically self-centred and, I'm sorry to tell you, a potential for great evil.'

It was unlike Ivdulon to house her words in polite terms. She generally called a spade a bloody shovel, as the farmers would say.

'Why the circumspection, Ivdulon?'

She glanced at Feldrark and turned back to Jodisa. 'You are with child, an heir and potential ruler of the realm, an important offspring. I wish to do that baby no harm with emotional upset to its mother, no more.'

'Very considerate, Ivdulon, but I'm no more fragile now than I was when I escaped the fiery mountain on Ylcrat or fought the vengeful warriors from Mipahnhil.'

'They were acts of physical courage, Jodisa. Emotional bravery and ruggedness is an entirely different thing, especially when a woman is pregnant. Changes in the woman's body alter her mind and spirit. I've studied this matter long and I know that you're subject to sudden and apparently illogical switches in mood and temper. Is that not so, Feldrark?'

Feldrark nodded.

Jodisa felt a surge of resentment. 'I'm not a child! I can control my…!' The irony of the truth overcame the internal disturbance and she suddenly laughed. 'All right. I understand. I don't know why it happens, but you're absolutely right, Ivdulon. I'm calm enough to learn your news.'

A shiver made Feldrark tremble. 'Do we have to talk out here? Too cool for comfort.'

'I want no one, no one but we three to hear what has to be said.' Ivdulon glanced toward the tower.

'You surely don't mistrust Netrodyl, after all this time?'

'The young woman is willing and clever, now I've educated her. But she's also loose of tongue.'

'Is there any reason why we can't go inside and she come outside, perhaps to undertake some menial task for you?'

'Ah. A good idea. I hadn't wanted to exclude her so obviously. She's earned my respect and, yes, my love, and I've no wish to make her feel less than she is to me. A task. That I can do. Come.'

They followed her as she swiftly walked to the tower, her limp accentuated by the speed. Netrodyl greeted them with a tray of fresh tlathan and showed them the small sweet cakes she'd made, resting on the platter in the centre of a table clear of scrolls and parchments.

'Thank you, my dear. I need you to do something for me. Would you take a small bowl to the lake and collect unopened buds from the trailing water shield? They're best picked early, you see? Be careful not to fall in. I know you can swim, but the water's icy cold and could kill you. I don't want to lose you.'

Netrodyl collected a small bowl, showed it to the wise women, who nodded. 'You might want to put something on, my dear. The morning air is quite cool.'

'If you can bear it, Ivdulon, I'm sure I can. Anyway, I'll warm up when I return. I suspect I should be as long as it takes for Feldrark and Jodisa to leave?'

Ivdulon nodded. Nothing more was said, but even Jodisa could see that the young woman understood she was being excluded.

'She's grown, hasn't she? When she first arrived, she was so naïve and ignorant. Now she seems a lot more, well, intelligent, I suppose.'

'Intelligence is innate. She always had it. What she was before was uneducated, Jodisa. It's learning and the acquisition of knowledge that allows a woman to grow, providing she has the necessary intelligence in the first place. And, in my experience, many women are naturally more intelligent than many men, if you'll forgive the observation, Feldrark?'

'Nothing to forgive. I've long been of that opinion myself. Now, let us complete our discussion of Dagla before your poor lover suffers from the chill out there, shall we?'

'It's always surprised me that you care for even the least servant in spite of your burden of responsibility for the whole city. I applaud your concern. Now, to the matter at hand. Dagla knows of the power of mindtalk, from a new connection I hadn't come across, a priest in Choshinahm. Wyyhn is not a gifted, neither is he particularly open to new ideas. He doesn't seek or make himself available to new minds and he connected with me only reluctantly when Rrildyss introduced us. It was he who unwittingly gave Dagla the knowledge we'd hidden from him for so long.

'He can't connect with me, though I can intrude in his mind as required. He is one of those who has little control over his own seeking but is susceptible to intrusion, and probably, invasion by other minds, stronger than his own. I've little doubt that you two and Aklon, as well as Tumalind, could all connect with him, should you wish to. But I'm not sure that it would be either a good idea or welcomed by him.'

'How is it that you never knew of this Wyyhn before, Ivdulon?'

She smiled at Jodisa. 'I may be gifted, but I'm still human. There's probably a multitude of mindtalkers of whom I remain ignorant. Some are unresponsive, some are resistant. In some cultures, what we do and accept as a good thing is called witchcraft and those who profess to practising are tortured, burned even, as evil heathens against whatever religion is practised in their region.'

'So, to Dagla?'

She nodded at Feldrark. 'Fortunately, Wyyhn has a female counterpart, Ialdyss, who is far more open. I've asked her, along with Rrildyss, to keep track of what your father does, Jodisa. My biggest fear is that he may be corrupted by the same type of minds that destroyed Gadhallah. Those that currently aim to damage our world beyond recognition.'

'But those who invaded Gadhallah can't be still alive, surely, Ivdulon. I mean they were…'

'Not the same actual minds, but with the same values and priorities. There are those in this world for whom evil and manipulation are fundamental qualities. People with no moral concerns, no compassion. Such men and women are concerned only with their own pleasure, with vengeance against perceived enemies, with acquisition of material things and, ultimately, with their power over others. To give such minds access to mindtalk is one of the many factors that makes me believe there can be no real god. Why would a creative power allow evil of that sort to roam the world?'

Jodisa hadn't seen Ivdulon so exercised by doubt. 'And you think my father could be such a one?'

'I'm glad the words came from you, Jodisa. For I didn't want to have to tell you.'

Jodisa and Feldrark left shortly afterwards, questions unanswered, but a disturbance in the city requiring their personal attention.

'What do you know about Trotnahn, Ivdulon?'

'You're in the town all ready?'

'We're prisoners. At least, I think we are. They're hostile and suspicious. And this is another place that treats women as inferior beings, as goods. Is this the case most places? I thought the world behaved like Followers, but in so many places I've seen women subjugated and demeaned. Why is that?'

'Ah. That's a very old matter, Tumalind. We've no time now to go too deeply into the reason. But, if I tell you that many, many cycles ago, women were the superior sex in most lands and some took advantage of this power to subjugate men, you may understand there's an element of revenge at work. Of course, this is all very ancient and men should, by now, have grown up enough to give equality another try. But that hasn't so far happened in many places. As for the city you now find yourself in, I can't say too much by this means, but beware and take care. Oh, and keep in mind that in Trotnahn everything has a price but most things have little worth.'

She had to break off then, as they'd reached another building. This was an imposing tower of dark, worked stone. The windows were small and bore wooden shutters that could be drawn across the unglazed spaces. The door was guarded by a pair of soldiers wearing the same outfits as those at the gate.

The Senior knocked on the closed door with a wooden hammer that he took from a hook beside it. The sound echoed within, booming like some ancient call of doom. Tumalind shuddered at the noise. Silently and slowly, the double doors opened to reveal the dim interior. The Senior led them inside and the accompanying soldiers waited outside, their presence a threat and a warning.

The arched ceiling rose high and magnificent overhead. Great stone bars crossed over each other, supporting the upper surface and glinting with what looked like gold covering. Between these ribs of stone the curved panels of the roof were decorated. Although they moved forward, through a vast open space unoccupied by any furniture or other people, she felt drawn to study that decoration. The pictures were entirely of women giving sex to men in ways that could only be described as explicit. No subtlety here, no attempt at making pictures like those she'd admired on the floors of the royal palace in Litkala. These crude statements shouted that women were for one thing. Sex. And they were available at any time.

Okkyntalah stared open-mouthed at the figures and then looked away. His confusion showed and she was gratified that he wasn't attracted but appalled by the display. Sondukal glanced up and then turned away at once. Teldrohn seemed curious and then his face exhibited the same concern and disapproval her husband showed. Blavv was disgusted, in spite of her exposure to similar displays in the palace of the Uhmbard. het'Kallohn didn't even look up, as though already aware of what she'd see.

The Senior, however, gazed at the work in admiration and delight. He walked slowly through the great hall, enjoying the progress. At the far end, a second set of double doors were closed against them. He took another hammer from the wall, this one seemingly of gold, and struck the door three times. The knock, this time, fell dead and soft the other side.

The doors swung open, held in place by two scantily clad women, both of whom bowed at the men as they passed through. One caught Tumalind's eye and took in her appearance in one glance. There was both shock and disapproval in that look. But they were through before words might be exchanged. In any case, bearing in mind the way Blavv had been treated, it seemed wise for the women to remain silent for the moment.

They walked now on soft, lush fabric, piled like the wool of the ovellah and patterned in garish colours. The walls were hung with woven pictures echoing those they'd passed in the great outer hall. This room was long and thin, the fabrics hanging from bronze poles so that they swung a little as the party passed. In the gaps between each picture stood a live woman, posing in an invitation to intimacy. Tumalind turned as they passed and saw that those women they left behind moved and came after them in pairs, walking silently on flooring that drowned out all sound.

At the far end of the room, on a raised platform, stood an ornate sofa, backed with erotic wooden carvings. Cushions covered the wide seat and real women lay variously displayed at the feet of the reclining figure of the man who occupied the couch. He was dressed in fine, white silk, embroidered with gold thread in strange devices. On his head rested a narrow cylinder of gold, emblazoned with rich and precious gems of many colours. The effect was of extravagance rather than taste or beauty. It seemed to say, quite simply, I have great wealth and how I wear it matters only to me.

The Senior bowed before the reclining man. 'Your Most Wealthy and Acquisitive Highness, Chief Secretary, I bring before you visitors who carry strange and primitive beliefs and beg your powerful knowledge to determine how to deal with them.'

The man slowly rose and stepped up to Blavv, lifted her tunic and touched her. He opened the robe that covered Kallohn from head to ankle and cupped each breast in turn before moving on to Tumalind. She held her skirt and breast cloth close to her and stared determinedly into the eyes of this man who wished to invade her privacy.

'Primitive. I see what you mean.' He turned to face Teldrohn, who'd placed himself to indicate he was their leader. 'These women are naturally for sale. What price for the defiant one?'

'We don't sell our women. They are our equals. They're not goods and chattels.'

The Chief Secretary laughed out loud. 'A new one on me. Fine, so you want to raise their value. I like a man who wishes to bargain. We'll discuss their price over refreshments.'

He kicked one of the women at his feet. 'Fruit and wine.'

She rose, bowed to all, and ran gracefully out through a side door.

The man nodded at the other local women present. 'Take these others and have them bathed and prepared. I'll inspect them properly once we've concluded our business here.'

The women moved forward to grasp the arms of the female members of the party but the men moved between to prevent them.

'Our women will remain with us.'

Tumalind welcomed Okkyntalah's authoritative tone.

The Chief Secretary laughed again, but there was a hint of irritation behind the sound and his eyes glinted with annoyance. 'I see you have different ways of doing business. Very well. But, in order that our own women are not infected with false impressions, I ask that you reduce the covers of your women to make them available.'

"I think you've failed to understand us. Our women are not for sale. They are not inferior. They're our equals in every sense of the word. They either dress or make themselves naked according to their own desires. One of these women, Tumalind, is my wife. Another, Blavv, is betrothed to Teldrohn.'

238

'No, Okkyntalah, we're married now.'

Okkyntalah nodded. 'Sorry, Blavv, I didn't know. And het'Kallohn is a member of the desert wanderers known as the K'ahll. They take very badly to treatment of their women with anything but respect.'

The Chief Secretary seemed nonplussed by this intelligence. He stood and seemed uncertain what to do or say.

'K'ahll women are known to be animals, ready for sex with any man they find. But as for your civilised women…we…we cannot allow women such freedom. It will damage our delicately balanced civilisation and break our customs and traditions. No. We must insist on some compromise that demonstrates that the women in your party are subject to the wishes of men. We must.'

Okkyntalah turned to Tumalind and she smiled at him, sending him a message that had him grinning.

'For the sake of good relations, I'll ask them to display as much of their flesh as they're willing to show. No more. And whether they do or not, is their decision entirely.' Okkyntalah's tone was enough to pass the message to the other two women that it would help the situation if they were to make some sort of sacrifice for the moment.

Blavv loosened the belt of her tunic and drew the upper half open to display her cleavage. Tumalind folded down her breast cloth to expose the upper curves of her breasts. Kallohn opened her long robe, showing a narrow strip of her shadowed front through the gap.

'That is more than you deserve, but, for the sake of good relations, we will comply so far. '

'Better. Certainly better.'

The food and wine arrived and another woman came with the one carrying it and stood a small table on the surface. Once in place, the native women fell on all fours close around the table. The Chief Secretary and the Senior each sat on a woman, using her as a chair. They indicated that the men in the party should do the same.

'I don't think so. If you have no suitable furniture for guests, we'll stand.'

The Senior and Chief Secretary frowned, shrugged and opened their palms in a gesture of resignation. The fruit was prepared, peeled, sliced and eaten with delicate metal implements embellished with many and various designs. The wine was served in cups that gave it a slightly metallic flavour. Silence appeared to be the normal requirement for eating but, once the fruit had been consumed, and the wine was in flow, the city men spoke again.

'Now, tell us what we have to do to obtain these women. Is there some service, some commodity, some exchange perhaps that will satisfy the needs of your trading beliefs?'

'You seem unable to grasp the fact that we don't sell women. We will not sell our women to you, for any price. They're not for sale. They are their own people. We don't own them. Don't you understand?'

Incomprehension.

'There is no other way. Women are for men to own, to use, to have or not as they please. I don't understand why you refuse to admit that these are as valuable commodities as any you're likely to come across. We insist on you trading them. Anything less would be counted unacceptable. Unless, of course, you have some great hoard of gold you intend to spend on other goods and services?'

'And what goods and services can you offer us in exchange?'

'Ah. Now you see sense at last. Let the women either be entirely exposed or else taken to a place where they'll be out of hearing whilst we discuss what things we might trade.'

'Our women will leave only if we are assured of their safety and immunity from interference of any sort.'

The Chief Secretary sighed loudly. Okkyntalah was making life difficult. 'I've never dealt with such an awkward merchant. So be it. They may rest unmolested in the bleeding room. It's the only place they'll be treated as untouchable.'

'The bleeding room?'

'Where women are housed for their moontimes, of course. You must have such arrangements for…'

'We don't. But, if that's the only place, I'm sure they'll be willing to remain there for the time being.' Okkyntalah raised a face of query at them. Tumalind nodded and the other two went with her in the company of a couple of the native women.

The men watched them go. Tumalind hoped they'd remain uncorrupted by the strange misogyny exhibited by the citizens, but she was anxious and doubtful about their future here. The arrogance of the Senior and Chief Secretary, allowing her and the others freedom to share confidences with the city women, astounded her. Could they really be so certain of their power that they feared no danger from liberated women?

The room they were taken to was dark and small, located underground. This place of isolation was empty when they arrived.

'I thought the women came her during their Moontime?'

The native woman examined Tumalind's breastcloth. 'We do.'

'But none of them are present.'

'Of course not. The full moon isn't due for days yet.'

'Not full moon? Oh. You all bleed at the same time?'

The woman shook her head as though dealing with a fool. 'At full moon we bleed for three or four days. The men grow impatient. It's the time of freedom. We have no duties.'

A thousand questions spun in Tumalind's head, but she expected any answers would merely create more enquiries.

Chapter 30

KROHTL

There was little Okkyntalah could do about the fate of the women in Trotnahn, but he hated to see them so abused and it worried him that their own women were demeaned. The question of what they could use to tempt the inhabitants of Trotnahn was uppermost in his mind, however, as he stood uncomfortably beside the narrow back of the woman below him. He needed air and space to think without the distraction of the enslaved women. The signal he flashed to Teldrohn raised an almost imperceptible nod from the soldier.

'I thank you for your hospitality, Chief Secretary, but in order to discuss the most beneficial trade I must see more of your wonderful city. I wonder if we might be given an escort to view the place?'

'I see you've some scheme in mind, young man. I like a trader with a good head for business and, of course, profit. The Senior, here, can conduct you. And he may make most decisions on my behalf. The wine and fruit and our comfortable seats have rather heightened my need for recreation. So, if you don't mind, I'll leave you to go about your business whilst I spend some time making use of the rewards on offer here. No doubt we'll meet again, once you've made your estimates of the best way we can trade?'

Diplomacy of this sort was new to him, but Okkyntalah had judged, almost from the beginning, that the men in this city were all appearance and no substance. He needed to pander to their vanity if they were to escape intact and with their women unmolested.

'I look forward to that, Chief Secretary. For now, farewell. Enjoy your…recreation.'

He, Teldrohn and Sondukal moved a little away, waiting. The Senior reluctantly left his seat, groping the woman before he rose.

They returned by the route they'd used to enter. Halfway down the great hall, a door opened and revealed their women. They were ejected by the other women so that they must dress in the open hall, thankfully under the prying eyes of the Senior only.

Tumalind took Okkyntalah's hand, as Blavv did Teldrohn's. Kallohn whispered something to Sondukal, who looked a little surprised but nevertheless enclosed her hand in his.

The Senior took them from the dimly lit great hall and back onto the street. It was as they made the transition from dark to brightness that Okkyntalah was struck with his idea.

'We have no name for you. What are we to call you, please?'

The Senior sneered at him. 'I'm a city official. I do not use my name for such purposes. You may refer to me as Paltrohn, if you will.'

'I can do that, but I suspect both I and my colleague outrank you, since we're both decorated military officers.'

'You are? Of course, the military has its place in our society. But status here is conferred, as it obviously should be, by wealth. Are you wealthy?'

'That depends on how you measure such things, Paltrohn.'

'Well, by the acquisition and ownership of multiple objects, property, women, crops, anything in fact that may be bought and sold. Does that make you wealthy?'

'My father owns his fishing boat and his home, and my mother runs a small concern involving the making of clothes.'

'Your mother? She owns a business?'

'She employs a couple of young women to help, of course. But, yes, the work is done under her control, in our house, and she determines price and how the income is spent.'

'And you expect to inherit this wealth when your parents die?'

'I'm the only child.'

'Then you are on a level with me, young man. I assume you are called Okkyntalah, since the young beauty used that name for you. I take it that it's not merely a term of endearment for the lesser to use in communicating with the more elevated?'

'No. My name is, indeed, Okkyntalah.'

Very well, since we can be considered equals, I will tell you that I am called Ro'Vavak, Ro being my title. You may call me Vavak. Are your colleagues your equal in wealth?'

Sondukal shook his head and Teldrohn said he owned nothing and expected no inheritance from his parents.

'Then you will refer to me by my title. The women, should they have need to reply to any questions, will of course call me Paltrohn, since they can't own anything.'

Okkyntalah was minded to explain that Tumalind would probably inherit her parent's farm but she shook her head at him.

They stood outside the great hall and Okkyntalah made a play of inspecting the outer walls. The windows were shuttered, which explained the dim light within. He wondered what made them do this and looked across the open space at the other buildings. All had shutters over the window spaces.

'If I were to tell you I can provide you with a commodity that will enable you to open the shutters but maintain the security of the interiors, what would you say?'

'You mean fill the space to prevent forced entry?'

'Something that would allow you to look out of the windows yet prevent anyone from entering through them.'

'Metal bars, you mean?'

'Not bars. A substance that will fill the entire space and yet allow you to see through.'

Vavak shook his head. 'I don't understand.'

'The material is a clear sheet that resists those trying to push through it, but allows you to read a text on the other side.'

He shook his head again. 'Impossible.'

'I thought so too, until I saw it made, in Litkala. I act as emissary for the Kiral and Kirallah of Litkala and am charged with responsibility for trade with the city. The other item you might be interested in, since appearance seems important here, is a hard white stone that can be used for building and that remains undamaged by weather.'

'I see we do have something we can trade in. We, of course, might provide you with as many women as you wish to procure.'

'We don't buy women, any more than we sell them.'

'That will change as you become more civilised, of course. For the moment, it's a difference I'm sure we can accept. After all, business is what really matters, isn't it? We have many very attractive items that I'm sure will find favour with you. Let me take you to the market and show you some of our wonders.'

He led them through twisting streets until they reached a wide-open area encircled with open fronted stalls. The relative peace of the streets was suddenly explained. Most of the citizens of the city must have been in the space. The noise was deafening and the activity meaningless to the party of visitors.

Vavak led them to the nearest stall. They were faced with a display of what appeared to be dead animals. On closer inspection, these declared themselves as fabric covered copies of various creatures. Most wore expressions that seemed almost human, so they looked oddly unnatural and Okkyntalah found them actually quite repulsive.

Vavak picked one of the smaller ones up and handed it to him. It was soft and very light, the eyes dead and unseeing. The fur was real enough but the structure beneath the skin was boneless and without rigidity so that even a gentle squeeze deformed the creature. He expected it to cry out but realised it was but a poor imitation of nature, the eyes painted onto wooden buttons. He saw Tumalind looking at it and passed it to her. She shook it, squeezed and poked it and rejected it out of hand.

Almost at once, she became tense, her face took on an expression of fear, and she collapsed to the ground, clearly in pain.

The Groves of Ytraa held his gaze. Although he partially understood that these trees were imbued with sacred power, by their association with Ytraa, Aglydron couldn't

245

explain the feeling of awe he experienced. It was greater than he'd expected, though he'd known the place would hold some magic. He felt both cocooned and strange here. There was welcome but there was also suspicion amongst these giants.

Little vegetation grew between the vast boles that soared up into a dark green canopy that hid all but the smallest suggestions of sky. The Skyfire glinted here and there amongst those upper branches.

Dagla Kaz stomped up and down the wide passages between the trunks. The other two leaders had directed them to the banks of a fast flowing river, knowing they must float the Godwood down it to the lake, if they were to take it safely back to Muhnilahm.

Now that the whole party was one, the joining of all Virgin Gifts completed on the open hill two days previously, they acted with a single purpose. All was driven by the need to escape Choshinahm with the Godwood and get it back to the island before the Skyfire faded.

Dagla Kaz had assumed overall charge, with the apparent agreement of the other priests. But there was some concern for his state of mind. From time to time, he called out involuntarily, as though not in command of his actions or thoughts. Some put this down to the sacred nature of the place, but others wondered if the long pilgrimage might have made him a little mad. There were whisperings of more sinister causes but no one was willing to speak out loud of such things. Dagla Kaz had become unpredictable and had had more than one Follower beaten for minor infringements of the law.

Since entering the Groves, they'd been required to remain naked, in spite of the cool night air. They'd huddled together for warmth and Aglydron had been pleased to be with Chislanda, sharing her body heat with his own, and enjoying the elation of joining amongst these sacred trees.

The ceremony on the hill had been unexpected and the Virgin Gifts had been given no choice other than to become partners with those selected for them. But all were now joined with a partner and all were, of course, available for joining with any other Follower. Dagla Kaz had already sampled Xylthynn, the girl who'd lost a toe in the mountains, and Zyreenha who had eyes the same colour as his. There was growing talk that those with lapis lazuli eyes had some special quality, but most wouldn't countenance such gossip.

He watched Dagla Kaz, accompanied by the other priests, walking amongst the trees in search of one suitable as a Godwood. The High Priest carried with him a length of fine, gilded rope, knotted at the place that would provide the correct girth. From time to time, he paused at a tree and the priests passed the rope around the bole to measure it. So far, they'd failed to find one wide enough.

Night was falling and soon the only light to penetrate the dense canopy would be odd patches of flame from the Skyfire. They would huddle down for the dark again and shiver a little. Now was the time he missed the promised heat of the Skyfire. Instead, they slept under a sky cooler than he knew from home, where cover was unnecessary.

He heard a sudden cry of triumph. 'We have it! We have the Godwood!'

The message passed to all present and everyone gathered around the selected tree. Massive, it towered, a giant climbing into the depths of the canopy above. No side branches showed for a full fourteen manheights.

'In the morning, we cut the tree. Then we select the sacrifice to propitiate the spirit of the Groves, before we begin our return journey.'

Much murmuring and some cries of alarm greeted this news. Aglydron recalled no previous mention of such a victim. Did the High Priest mean a blood sacrifice, someone to be killed for the price of the tree? It sounded that way. But the look on the High Priest's face allowed no discussion, no questions.

The group slept uneasily and woke to the sound of songbirds. The day had dawned when, if rumours in the night were to be believed, one of their number would die. But who?

<hr>

'As little bloodshed as possible, please. We must aim to appease the dissenters and attempt to win them over to our ways. Unnecessary killing will go against us. But, if you are faced with a choice between that or being injured, you must save yourselves. If it is possible to defeat our enemies without killing them, please do so. Victory be with you. Let us do what we must.'

As always, Aklon led the move. This was no charge of madness and noise, but a silent and careful advance on an enemy about whom they knew only that they were outnumbered. It had been impossible to get reliable intelligence about the Dissenters under Charrohn's leadership. Those who served her were motivated by either lust or fear, or a mixture of both; a powerful combination.

Krohtl sat on a series of small hills. Trees existed only where the rural edge of a farm intruded into the town. Otherwise, the streets were narrow and devoid of cover. They had little choice but to march along the main street and approach the place where they knew the Dissenters were housed.

The village priestess had former soldiers amongst her supporters. It was possible some were archers. They had little defence against arrows out here in the open, but there was no alternative route they could use to meet their enemy. And, of course, there were the hostages to be considered. Charrohn had made it clear, by demonstration, that she was capable of using captured women and children as human shields against any assault. This was why they were unable to use fire or bows but must engage the enemy at close quarters.

Under the inadequate cover of a cloudy night that reduced the Skyfire's brilliance to a dull glow, Aklon led his small troop up the hill. Stealth and surprise were what he relied on in this attack. Within the small group of buildings, the priestess had made her headquarters. An unknown number of assailants and a small group of captives waited with her. Amongst those was one mindtalker, new to him and inexperienced in the gift. The lad was young and frightened, but willing to help. It was a small hope of cooperation but all he had in ending the terror initiated by the insatiable Charrohn.

'We approach. Are you able to unlock the door?'

'There's a man asleep beside it. I'm scared he might wake up.'

'I'll let you know when we're right in front. You must be ready to do it then. All our lives depend on your courage.'

'I'll try, Aklon. I will. I'm in place and waiting. Be quick before I lose my courage.'

He urged them to move more swiftly, aware of the risk faced by all. If the lad should fail, they and the hostages held on the other side would be in great danger. But if he did as required, they could be in the building and amongst the captives and Dissenters in moments.

The door appeared. Lights showed through the rush walls within, flickering dimly through unshuttered windows. Could she really have left no one on guard? Was she so arrogant and certain of her cause that she believed herself invulnerable? Or was she being serviced by one of her men, leaving the defence in the hands of some oaf who cared more for sleep than the lives of his colleagues?

They were three steps from the door.

'I am outside. Now!'

No response. Nothing changed. Aklon posted troops next to open windows and stood close to the door, waiting.

'Now. We need your courage now.' The tone of his thoughts was mild, gentle, persuasive.

A noise on the far side of the door.

Aklon tensed to move.

The door opened a fraction, moving outward, toward him. His response was instant. He grasped the edge of the portal and pulled it wide. Stepped within and found the lad held by the guard he'd woken. Others followed Aklon into the building through the door and yet more entered through open windows.

Silence was their hope for as long as possible. But a child cried out in alarm and the rumour of the attack quickly spread. Then all was chaos and violence, action and screams. Candles and lamps were snuffed out and, in the darkness, foe and friend were difficult to identify.

A woman came behind the guard holding the lad and stuck the man with a small knife. The guard turned to see his attacker and the lad escaped his grip. Aklon sent him into the street and finished off the guard.

'Kill the Renegade! Leave the rest. Kill the Renegade!' It was Charrohn. Awake and in charge. Armed dissenters fell on Aklon until he was faced with an impossible number of opponents.

For two long days and the night of this one, Tumalind had waivered between consciousness and oblivion. Okkyntalah had tried everything he knew to try to keep her awake. But each time she roused, she seemed more afraid, more confused, more uncertain of who she was, where she was, what was happening to her.

At least they'd secured a place to stay whilst Tumalind suffered. No one in the party could answer his questions about her condition, although he suspected Blavv understood more than she was willing to disclose. And none of the local healers were able to help, some even seemed unwilling to do so.

All that Okkyntalah could do was keep her fed with what little food and water she could take, and be there for her when she woke from what appeared like a never-ending nightmare. Only his offer of the sale of glass to the city had allowed them to shelter here. He was conscious that they were suspected, and tolerated only as long as they remained no threat to the way of life of men who ruled for power and wealth alone.

Blavv returned to their room with Teldrohn. She looked at him shamefaced and knelt beside the bed that lay on the floor. Early morning sun streamed through dust particles floating in the beam of light that drew a narrow oblong on the hard ground. Outside, the sounds of people rising and starting their working day floated through the window they'd unshuttered for fresh air.

'I'm sorry, Okkyntalah. I'm ashamed. I haven't told you the whole truth. I know what ails Tumalind. But I don't know what to do about it.'

'What's wrong with her, Blavv?'

'You know of mindtalk, of course. She's strayed into the dark place. It's a place we don't go. The minds there are so wicked. Minds that try to take you over and make you do things you don't want to. It's a hard and dangerous place. I tried to follow her but I'm afraid. I don't have the strength Tumalind has. I don't know what to do.'

'But she can't have strayed, as you put it. She was with us and talking normally only moments before she collapsed. It's as if something invaded her.'

'Yes. I think that might be what happened. I hadn't thought of it like that. But you're right, Okkyntalah, she's been invaded. But I don't know why they've done it to her and left me alone. I'm afraid that if I try to find her, they'll discover me as well and then…'

'We can't leave her there. She's in trouble. Even those of us who can't mindtalk can see she's in pain and frightened. Every time she wakes, she's weaker and less able to help herself. She needs your help, Blavv. All the help she can get. Please do what you can. We can't do anything in the place she is held. We can't enter that world. But you go there.'

Blavv opened her hands, made a gesture of despair that turned abruptly into a sort of hope. 'You helped me escape once. You brought troops from Litkala. Of course! I'll get help from the city!'

'We don't have time. She's fading too fast to…'

'No, Okkyntalah. Not like that. I'll contact Ivdulon. I don't know why I never thought of it before. Let me be. Just stay with me whilst I find the wise woman, seek her help.'

Chapter 31

EVIL MINDS

Darkness was no longer an advantage for Aklon. Behind him, the door that had been his escape was closed. But no one stood in that space and all who opposed him were in front. Many of his small troop had made it into the house and others continued to enter through open windows as dim light from outside slowly brightened.

'Aklon! Aklon, where are you?'

It was Phrysilda. The direction suggested she stood behind those opposing him.

'By the door.'

A sudden cry of pain told him the Dissenters surrounding him had learned they were in danger. The attacks grew fiercer and he slashed the air before him almost blindly, slicing flesh and bone as his blade cut down the enemy. Some fell, others tried to turn and flee but were caught by his fighters behind them.

'Get the Renegade. Kill him or…' Charrohn's voice ended abruptly.

'Your priestess is dead!' That was Hyllahn. The certainty in her voice brought an abrupt lull in the fighting.

'We have nothing to gain by continuing this idiocy. Let us all retire to the light, and parley.'

Aklon found the latch and opened the door onto the dawning day. As daylight silhouetted him in the frame, an arm with a sword lunged at him. The blade caught his side, sliced through the tabard and carved a line across his ribs. He brought his own sword swiftly up and chopped off the arm. The man lurched forward with a howl of agony and Aklon slashed again, taking off the Dissenter's head, so it rolled into the room.

There was a cry of utter despair from one of the other Dissenters and all fighting stopped.

'Enough! No more killing. We are one. We are all islanders of Muhnilahm. Let the fighting end here and now.' He staggered outside as the sun's rim edged above the horizon, below the lowering clouds, and drenched the street in crimson light. He was followed by his troops and the gang of Dissenters that had opposed them. Women and children who'd been held hostage came last. At least all were intact.

For a short while, Aklon's people and the Dissenters faced each other, arms drawn and threatening. Aklon sheathed his sword and remained standing, the injury making it hard for him. Others followed suit.

Phrysilda and Hyllahn dragged the priestess from the house and lay her at the feet of her defenders. A gash rent her body from chest to groin, blood and gore mingling with the dust on which she lay.

The younger of his two saviours had a wound to her upper arm, blood weeping from the cut. The older woman was unmarked, though her skin was splashed with the blood of others. She saw his difficulty and moved to help him before he fell.

'Strip that man. I need cloth to cover the wound.'

The Dissenter resisted only briefly and was quickly overpowered. His tabard cut into strips to bind Aklon's injury. Stemming the flow helped and he sat on the ground as the rest of his troop gathered the surrendered weapons from the Dissenters. Without their leader, they had no heart for battle. Farmers, fishermen, tailors, nursemaids, not soldiers, they'd supported Charrohn only out of fear, or through lust for the flesh she'd so willingly offered.

They dragged away the priestess to be buried later. The remaining Dissenters ambled off to their homes, scorn and derision loud from gathering neighbours, families, former friends and customers. Words of blame and loathing were shouted by those who came to claim women and children who'd been hostages. The rebellion had been short, violent and an utter failure. The troops counted the dead and discovered ten had been killed. One of Aklon's men had gone, the rest were all Dissenters.

The town leaders were brought to Aklon, now resting in a hastily made bed. They discussed how to proceed for the future. There'd be no retribution, no punishment of those involved in the dispute. They would suffer enough under the contempt of their townsfolk. Some had lost partners and others were rejected by their former loved ones.

Aklon, satisfied he'd done all he could to set the town at peace once more, was persuaded to rest for a while.

'You need complete rest if you're to heal, Aklon.'

'I have no time, Phrysilda. Morstahn lays in danger of attack by Unholy Ones and dissenting soldiers. They need our help. I must get to them before nightfall.'

She placed a hand on his shoulder, preventing him from rising. 'Travel like this and you'll be dead before you've covered a league.'

'Phrysilda's right, Aklon. We'll deal with the trouble there.'

Delbon and Choryssa would lead the troop of the Few and his new soldiers. He told them what he knew of the problems faced by the town.

'Do everything to keep Shoarhn safe, please.'

'We'll do all we can to keep all the people safe, Aklon. But, yes, we'll do our best to make sure your special woman isn't harmed.'

He watched them go, knowing they'd been right about his chances of survival. No point going to rescue Shoarhn if he died on the road. Oh, how he wished this violence and warring could end and peace be restored to the island at last. He lay down to rest, determined to be well as soon as possible.

An unfamiliar woman and man came into the room where they had laid him. She carefully cut away his tabard, as the man held and supported him. Once she'd washed him free of blood, the man poured wine into a goblet and fed it to him. Three cups he had to drink, until he felt close to collapse. The woman peeled away the strips of cloth, washed the wound, and used a needle and thread to close it up. Wine made the pain easier to bear but he passed out before she'd finished.

When he awoke, day had ended and the evening was bright with the Skyfire. The smell of rain came to him, drifting with scents of cooking meats. He was hungry and tried to sit up. A cool hand stayed him and he turned to find a woman at his bedside. Middle-aged and kind, her sagging flesh suggested she'd mothered many children.

'Rest. You need to stay still if that wound's to heal. What do you want?'

'Food. And water, please.'

She nodded, waved her hand at someone he couldn't see. The door to the room opened and closed. He shut his eyes again. The pain in his side and chest was now a dull persistent ache instead of the initial agony that had laid him low once the fighting ended.

He woke again to a younger woman, leaning over him and drying sweat from his uncovered body with a soft cloth.

'Ah. Awake again. Good. I'll bring you broth and a drop of water.'

She was gone before he could ask. But when she returned with the promised food and drink, he wanted to know how long he'd slept.

'Oh, this time, just through the night. Morning's just a spit away and looks like a fine one. Now, let's help you sit and get something inside you, shall we?'

'And Morstahn? What is the news from there?'

'None at present. But some of our men from Krohtl went with your people to help out. We're waiting for them to come back with news. Mind, it was only the day before yesterday and it's a day's walk each way, you know. They said you'd want that whore buried proper, but the women made her an example. Hung her upside down from a tree on the edge of town. Warning to the others.'

He allowed her to feed him, amazed how quickly the people had shed old traditions and respect for those who'd once been absolute authorities. It promised a brighter future, if the peace could hold and the Unholy Ones and traditionalists could be defeated. How, he wondered, was Shoarhn? Did she go naked like so many who'd rejected the trappings of Following? Was she well? When would he see her? Was she safe?

Sleep took him again, relieving him of pain and anxiety.

Where? What had happened? There was no reference point to fix on. She was in a dark, dark sludge of unknown evil. Swirling, drowning, pounding, pain. Tight, heavy, black, endless, falling, tumbling, fear.

Nothing made sense. Disorientated. Out of mind. Isolated.

'Frowk us.'

'I'll 'ave your fern.'

'Show them dubbies.'

'Frowk me. Frowk him. Frowk us all!'

'For coin. And give it to me.'

'Tumalind?'

An echo, dim and distant. But something to cling to.

'Frowk for coin.'

'For me.'

'Me!'

'She's mine.'

'Mine.'

'Mine! All mine.'

'Tumalind, are you…?'

A mind she recognised. Could she escape these clamouring…?

'Never. Too valuable.'

'Worth a fortune. That fern.'

'Mine. Mine. I've got most. I deserve her. I'll have her.'

'I'll pay more.'

'I'll pay most!'

'Serve me. Frowk with me for free. Frowk you for all your coin.'

'Tumalind, I'm trying to reach…'

'Ivdulon? Is that you, Ivdulon? Catch me. Bring me back.'

'Escaping. Hold the whore. I want…'

'Come back, Tumalind. Come back!'

Light. Air. Her limbs could move. She dared open her eyes. And he was there, holding her hand. Ever present; Okkyntalah. She must tell Ivdulon.

'I'm back now. Back. Thank you, Ivdulon.'

'Beware when you sleep. They know you're there now.'

'Who are…?'

'Now isn't the time. Keep out of the shadows, Tumalind. Engage with me or some other friend before you sleep. We'll protect you. Rest now. Talk with Okkyntalah. And thank

Blavv. She alerted me to your capture. She was brave and will also need rest and help after her ordeal.'

'Thank you, Ivdulon.'

She turned again to Okkyntalah, saw Blavv lying on the floor next to her.

'Is Blavv well?'

Okkyntalah shook his head. 'Are you really back with us, my love?'

She nodded. 'What's the matter with Blavv. She's not…'

'No. Not where you were. But helping made her lose the baby. She's been bleeding. She's weak, but she'll live, they say. Though, in this foul city, where the only thing that matters is coin, the help we had was little enough. Sondukal saved her with his care and skill.'

She saw they were all together in this small room. Blavv close beside her. Teldrohn sitting with her head in his lap. Okkyntalah on his haunches at her side. The other two huddled on a bench against the wall.

'How long was I gone?'

'We lost you in the market, two days ago. You collapsed. Vavak took some of our coin and brought us here. Since then we've been watching over you. But it was Blavv who went after you; she understood where you might be lost. Said it was a fearful place. I mentioned Ivdulon and she said she'd contact her. That's all I really know. But you've both been muttering. Blavv said you'd been caught in a dark place in the mindtalk world, where evil minds controlled you. I don't understand it. I thought I'd lost you, Tumalind.'

<hr>

'Aklon? I need your help.'

'I am weak, Ivdulon. How can I be of assistance?'

'Tumalind is in danger. If we don't unite in helping her, we'll lose her. It's my fault. I underestimated the danger. Can you use you mind, even as your body rests from your injuries?'

He hadn't asked how she knew of his wounds: he'd simply accepted that Ivdulon could divine certain things by using her extraordinary powers.

'That much I can do. What are we planning?'

Ivdulon had explained and, along with Feldrark, Rrildyss Kaz and several strangers, she'd led them on a journey into the dark unknown. The place was evil and menacing. But, together, in a concerted attack, they'd pushed their way through and discovered Tumalind's mind, captive and under torture by the evil ones. By a process he hadn't understood, directed by Ivdulon, they'd freed her from the bonds that held her and returned her mind intact. Severely exhausted from her own efforts to defeat the evil, she was now under constant care. They were taking that in turns. The whole exercise had left them all weary and in need of mental as well as physical rest.

Now, mentally recovered again, he realised he could so easily have answered the questions about Shoarhn and Morstahn by using mindtalk with the remarkable young carpenter who'd helped on the Plains of Ytraa.

'Eyethlehn, are you free to talk, please?'

'For now. But we might be attacked again at any moment. What do you want, Aklon?'

'News. I wish to know how things stand in Morstahn and, more particularly, how Shoarhn fares in the trouble.'

'Of course. We're fighting for our lives. There's a lull in the attack. But we're outnumbered. It's the Unholy Ones and ex-soldiers, with some of the more violent dissenters. They've tried fire and arrows, but so far we've kept most of them at arm's length. Shoarhn's in the thick of it with the rest of the Few. Last time I saw her she was battling an Unholy One with a garden spade against his sword. Soon as I find out how she is, I'll let you know.'

'Have my people arrived yet? I sent troops to help you.'

'Ah. That explains the lull. They stopped their attack for no apparent reason. Maybe your people distracted them. I have to go now.'

And she did. So abruptly that Aklon knew there was serious trouble near her. He was unable to lie abed when others were in danger, even though they were a day's march away. He must be up and about to help.

'And where d'you think you're going?'

He turned as he left the chamber where he'd been resting, seeking his tabard and sword. 'I have to help them in Morstahn. They are in trouble and I...' But the sentence never ended.

Darkness took him.

Chapter 32

SACRIFICE

No. No, this couldn't be right. The High Priest had made no previous mention of such a sacrifice. And to choose this particular girl, a Virgin Gift who'd suffered all the trials of the voyage and pilgrimage from the very start; that surely wasn't right. Aglydron took a step forward, prepared to speak.

'Who would dare oppose the word of Ytraa?' Dagla Kaz stood with arms folded across his bare chest, eyes blazing with anger and conviction. 'I have spoken with Ytraa and Ytraa demands the spirit of the Godwood Tree be propitiated by blood. Do any dare move or speak against the word of Ytraa?'

All present were devout Followers, apart from the soldiers from Litkala. And they had orders from Feldrark not to interfere in religious matters. None of the others had shown any sign of dissent in spite of the High Priest's increasingly inconsistent behaviour. One or two soldiers had raised concerns but had been silenced by their colleagues. Told by the High Priest they were no longer needed and could return home if they couldn't keep to the will of Ytraa, a few had actually considered desertion. But, loyal troops of Litkala, sent on the mission by Feldrark to protect the community of Followers, they wouldn't lightly desert them now.

Aglydron stepped back again. If Ytraa decreed the sacrifice, then there was no question that it should be done. No one spoke in support of the terrified girl pegged across the rough stump, where the section of the Godwood had been hacked from the living tree. The remainder of the huge sentinel lay fallen and defeated across a great tract of the forest floor. The Godwood itself, fitted with iron stakes around the circumference to both front and rear, awaited removal to the nearby river to be floated down to the lake and back to the island.

Dagla Kaz turned his back on the Followers who stood in a wide arc around the stump. He removed his sword from its scabbard and raised it high over his head. The Virgin Gift, recently married to one of the others who'd joined the pilgrimage, was stretched star-shaped over the heart of the stump, her centre raised by the rough cone left after the work of the axes that had felled the tree. A cloth gag closed her mouth against her protests and the coming screams, but her eyes told her tale of terror and incomprehension.

'Porryh of Chalamamnon, from the Island of Muhnilahm, in accordance with the will of Ytraa, I hereby dedicate your body and your blood as sacrifice to the Godwood.

May your soul rest forever in high regard in the Garden of Delights. May you spend eternity in a state of ecstasy joined with all, and one with Ytraa in Ytraa's divine grace. Here and now I spread your blood to quench the sorrow and anger suffered by the Godwood Tree. May your sacrifice appease the spirit of the Godwood Tree. May it bless the Godwood that we will add to the glory of the Monument of Ytraa under Ytraa's Peak on the Plain of Ytraa.'

As he spoke, he sliced the sword into each leg in turn, opening the flesh to let her blood spread over the damaged wood. He moved around her helpless body, carving to the bone in each limb until all were opened and bleeding. He placed the sword tip under her chin and ripped deep into the flesh of her front until he reached her sex, stopping before the opening, so that she remained intact as a woman and would therefore not be denied entrance to the Garden of Delights. He made a final cut through her torso, under the rise of her ribs, and blood flowed freely from her wounds until she ceased to breathe.

Aglydron watched the life go out of her eyes and turned his face away to look at the forest floor in hope of escaping the horror he'd witnessed.

'It is done. The price for Ytraa's glorification is paid in blood by our sacred gift. May the spirit of the Godwood Tree now be propitiated and bless our voyage back to Muhnilahm.' With that, Dagla Kaz fell into the old prayer position and led the Followers in a period of devotion during which each individual was allowed time to make whatever prayers they thought appropriate.

Aglydron found his mind full of confusion, anger and doubt. How could this be right? How could his God demand such pain and violence for a faithful and devoted Follower? Oh, Porryh had been troublesome, caused problems on the way. But who, faced with her situation, would not have felt some sense of injustice? Surely the girl didn't deserve to be treated so harshly? He heard those about him rising and moving and realised he'd spent none of the time in devotion and all of it in questioning. Nevertheless, he got to his feet.

The girl no longer wore the gag she'd been given to prevent her voicing her pain. And he wondered whether that had been its real purpose, or whether it had been placed to stop her protests.

Dagla Kaz gave the ruined body one final glance and then left the area. All followed him in silence. The day would bring hard work and danger as they worked the Godwood into the waters and then attempted to guide it down to the lake with the lengths of rope attached to the iron stakes. At least the labour would take their minds off the violence of the sacrifice. He wondered what her widowed husband would make of it all.

Fehtohn was last to leave the sacrificial spot and seemed devastated by the loss of his bride of so few days. A lad from Litkala, he'd voiced dissent when she'd been chosen. But the other Followers had silenced him, demanding that he allow the High Priest to do as Ytraa decreed. Aglydron watched him emerge from the space and the look on his face did not bode well for Dagla Kaz. There was murder in those eyes.

⊗ ⊰•⊱••

The tension had broken quickly. Fighting had replaced doubt and inactivity. Shoarhn, surprised at her own violence, had killed or wounded several attackers. Her wounds were few and superficial, though she hoped the cut across her shoulder and the top of her breast would heal without a scar. Aklon bore enough scars for them both and she wanted to remain as unmarked as possible for him.

The army of ex-soldiers, Unholy Ones and Dissenters had gathered and then attacked in force. Her farm, sited on the edge of the town and under the feet of the low hills that surrounded it as far as the coast, had been an obvious point of strength against the onslaught. She was prepared to fight to the death, if need be, to save it from those who would destroy it and deny her boys the life they deserved in freedom.

The fights had been skirmishes. Unplanned and sporadic. At one stage two small groups of attackers had descended on the farm only to stop short in the fields and begin to fight amongst themselves over disagreements about which battle cry they should use. She and her colleagues had watched in amazement as the two factions had fought it out, killing and maiming each other as their mutual enemies stood only paces away. Such madness only served to make those who'd forsaken the old ways stronger and more certain of their cause.

But there had been some in the ranks of the attackers who understood more of fighting. Old soldiers who'd seen battle training, if not actual battle, gathered the fighters together and led them with more sensible strategies. One such group had begun an attack on the farm in the early hours and the fighting had moved to and fro from fields to buildings and back again, as each side gained ascendency or fell back in defeat. Too many of her colleagues had been injured and now lay dead or crying with pain. They had waited in defence, as the troops of Followers lined up for another attack.

But the attack had never come. Something had prevented the forward movement as noises from the rear of the attackers revealed that they were themselves under assault. Aklon's troops had arrived.

Shoarhn, along with her colleagues, left the barn they'd used as a place of safe retreat, and attacked from the front, so that the Dissenters were caught between two implacable forces. A large, brawny old soldier swept her weapon out of her hand with his sword. As he turned the blade back for the fatal blow, she dropped to the ground, rolled, and ran back to the barn. He called her coward and set about another on the field.

She found the spade she sought and dashed back at her attacker, smacking him

259

soundly on the side of his head as he was engaged in an unequal fight with a young girl from the Few. He fell without a sound and seemed unlikely to rise. Shoarhn took his sword and moved further into battle, seeking out more of the enemy who would destroy her and her farm if they had the chance.

The Unholy Ones were the most fierce, uncaring for their lives and reckless in their attacks. But their heedless courage was offset by lack of training and ability. Too long they'd lived in ease, fed, tended and satiated by slaves they'd commanded. Most fell easily, even to the sword of a woman like Shoarhn who had no military training.

A neighbour, the man who'd led a previous attempt to have her whipped for her liaison with Aklon, slipped into view, saw her and ran to attack. She side-stepped his thrust but he turned swiftly and struck out again as she faced him. To her amazement, his blade swept a hairsbreadth from her throat as he ceased movement and fell to the ground. Eyethlehn pulled her sword from his back and gave her a fierce grin before she stumbled at her feet, her left leg bleeding from an earlier wound.

Shoarhn looked about her and realised the battle was all but over. The Dissenters defeated. She helped her friend and saviour off the field and into the house, there to submit to the tender care of men and women who'd been unable or unwilling to fight but who were now healing the sick and wounded.

Eyethlehn looked pale from blood loss, but she smiled with defiance and clasped Shoarhn's hand in her own before she allowed the carers to deal with her wound.

'I'll let Aklon know.' But she fell into an exhausted swoon almost at once.

Shoarhn glanced concern at the man who knelt to tend to her friend. He nodded.

'She'll be fine. Just needs rest now we've stopped the bleeding. Looks like you could do with a bit of help with that shoulder. Lie there and I'll get to you as soon as I've done here.'

Looking around her kitchen, strewn with the injured, she nodded her agreement and sank slowly to the floor to await her turn with the healers.

Ivdulon came to her quietly, almost, it seemed to Tumalind, in guilt and regret. The wise woman spoke in her mind using obscure and peculiar references so that what she said didn't make sense to begin with. Only when they'd disconnected, did Tumalind understand the purpose of her communication. She was trying to set up some system whereby they could mindtalk without anyone who might be eavesdropping being able to understand what they meant.

Wise woman indeed: the language, terms and incidents she'd referred to and used were things that only she and Ivdulon had shared. Tumalind replayed the conversation in her mind and understood various signs. One event was named as a clue to a specific emotion, another stood for an action, yet another represented a name, and so on. She recalled as much as she was able, returned to Ivdulon to test her suspicions, and discovered she was right.

A code; that was what Ivdulon called the system. It would allow them to speak normally but to intersperse their sentences with the code words in such a way that what they said to each other would only be sensible to them and not to any who might be listening in on their talk.

Awkward and slightly cumbersome, the code allowed them to nevertheless exchange information about the evil minds that had tried to command her. But, more importantly, it let Ivdulon teach her a system of self-defence that would allow her to venture back into that evil world with less danger of being captured again.

'I'm frightened, though, Okkyntalah. I know Ivdulon wouldn't want to allow any harm to come to me. But suppose she's not right about her defence method? What if I got caught again?'

'Why would you want to go back into that evil world anyway?'

Tumalind took a deep breath. How would he react? 'You know I've always thought she had a special purpose for us? That we had some part to play in the way things are moving?'

'You've said so. I never really understood how you knew or what you meant.'

'But you still allowed me to decide what we did, where we went?'

'I love and trust you, Tumalind.'

She embraced him and held him close, enjoying his courage and his amazing trust that made her confident of his love and devotion. How had she found such a brave, wonderful and caring man?

'Ivdulon wants me to find the owners of the evil minds. Then she wants you to kill them.'

She'd expected some resistance, some argument against this outlandish demand.

Okkyntalah just nodded as if considering the idea. 'She's told you why, I suppose?'

'As much as she can in mindtalk.' Tumalind explained their system of code. He didn't fully understand it but he seemed to appreciate enough to realise that it did at least allow them to converse in secret.

'And her reasons?'

How to explain something she only vaguely understood herself? Ivdulon was undoubtedly right, her assessment of the dangers and the situation accurate. Some of the details and consequences of inaction seemed a bit exaggerated, but she knew Ivdulon dealt only in truth and would never make something appear more important than it was in reality. She needed to think the whole thing over before she explained it to Okkyntalah.

261

If she got her explanation wrong or incomplete, she might make him turn against the scheme. And Ivdulon had impressed on her how vital it was that they succeed.

'Can we take a stroll? I need time and fresh air to make sure of the thoughts in my mind before I try to explain to you.'

'A walk, here in the city?'

'Yes. I know; as a stranger and a woman not owned by a citizen, I'll have to be fully covered. I understand that.'

He nodded. Kallohn lent her the robe she wore in public. The small room they shared was crowded when they were all present and their absence would give her and the recovering Blavv some relief. Teldrohn was out with Sondukal collecting food and water.

Although daylight was starting to fade, the Skyfire gave as much light as a full moon in a sky that would bear none this night. They sauntered along the streets, ignoring the looks of townsfolk who regarded them with suspicion. Here and there, they came upon grand houses where noises of celebration emerged through closed shutters, often accompanied by sounds of women in distress.

'Why are so many cities full of men who mistreat women?'

'I don't know, Tumalind. But I find it hard to ignore. I'd like to show this lot the errors of their ways and free the women from slavery.'

'Ivdulon says it stems from a period a very long time ago when women were the superior sex. She says some became very powerful and started to treat men badly and the men rebelled and that's why they keep us down now.'

'Sounds possible. But it's not a sensible solution to the problem. I mean, if women mistreat men when they're the superior ones, and men enslave women when they're in charge, no one gets the best of it, do they? Much better if both sexes are equal, like us, and each has proper respect for the other.'

'Exactly. No wonder I love you the way I do, Okkyntalah. Not only do you believe these things, but you act to defend them. That's something to do with what Ivdulon wants of us, by the way.'

'But not all of it?'

'No. There's another, equally important aspect. Give me time and I'll find a way to explain it to you.'

They walked in silence, treading the quiet streets as the population slowly moved indoors for the night until they were alone.

Tumalind turned over Ivdulon's words in her mind, filling in the gaps for herself and reaching conclusions from the clues she'd been given. From time to time, she ventured into mindtalk and discussed her thoughts in isolation with Jodisa, Feldrark and Ivdulon herself. By the time they were ready to return to their small room for the night, Tumalind had come to a full realisation of the situation as Ivdulon had tried to describe it to her. The more she thought about it, the worse it seemed and the more determined was she to do something to prevent the outcome Ivdulon feared from their failure to act.

All their travelling companions were present when they returned but Kallohn was in tears and being comforted by Sondukal.

'What happened?'

Blavv glanced at the K'ahll woman and spoke softly to Tumalind. 'That man, Vavak, came by when just Kallohn and I were here. She didn't have her robe, of course. He had a soldier with him. The soldier held me whilst Vavak used Kallohn. He didn't rape her but made her do things I wouldn't want to do even with Teldrohn. When she refused, he beat her and threatened to scar her with his knife. She had to give in and now she feels degraded and shamed and fearful that he may come back and make her do it again, or worse.'

'I'd like to stop him ever doing it to any woman, Blavv. But we're here under sufferance and I dare do nothing physical. But I'll speak to him and explain, again, that our women aren't for their use and pleasure. It's the best I can do at present. If I kill him, as he deserves, it'll simply mean we'll all be executed.'

Tumalind took the robe and placed it around Kallohn's shoulders as she sat on the floor with Sondukal. It was a while before she stopped sobbing but, when she did, they understood she wasn't crying with self-pity but with anger that she was unable to do anything to avenge her treatment. She swore to kill the man if she ever had the chance. Okkyntalah's pleas and explanations of the effect of such action seemed to mean nothing to her.

'Sometimes honour is more important than mere life.'

'There's no honour if there's no life to celebrate it, Kallohn.'

She glared at Okkyntalah with defiance. 'You're a Follower. You know nothing of the meaning of honour for the K'ahll.'

'First, I'm no longer a Follower, Kallohn. And, second, I may not understand the meaning for the K'ahll. But I know the meaning of such action for the rest of us and I can't allow you to do anything that would endanger the lives of us all. I'll deal with Vavak. Once we've left this place, you may do as you wish, of course. But whilst we remain here, we can't allow you to take action that would mean instant death for us all.'

Kallohn nodded, as if in agreement. 'But neither can you prevent it.'

Chapter 33

INJURIES AND PLOTS

Dagla Kaz watched Kaz-Ca-Valorysta supervise the teams pulling on the ropes that would take the Godwood down the slope to the churning waters of the river below. Her form was pleasing enough, but she'd become less satisfactory as consort than he'd hoped. No matter, there were plenty of other available women in the party; some of them young and inexperienced enough to provide the sport he most enjoyed. He shook himself free of such distractions. The Godwood must occupy his thoughts.

It would be a difficult journey. The river flowed through the forest and down the slopes at the foot of the mountain. There were gullies and falls along the way. How many might be injured, or even lost, in the endeavour? That was unimportant; he was safe, since he wouldn't be part of the physical effort. And he would retain as many as were needed for the return to the island.

That extremist fool, Aglydron, had been obviously troubled by the sacrifice. He must keep an eye on him. Such men could be dangerous if they were allowed to develop their own ideas. Perhaps the girl's death was a stage too far for authenticity. But she'd been a thorn in his side for the whole pilgrimage; questioning his decisions, threatening to get herself frowked whenever the opportunity presented itself, being generally disruptive. Good riddance to her. The only real shame was that she'd been the most delicious conquest so far. Her struggles to stop him had enhanced the experience so much that he would've enjoyed the chance to have her again before he'd had her pegged out for the killing.

'It's not just sex; though domination is fulfilling.'

'What of riches and power?'

'Time you started accruing more wealth, if you're to join us in ruling.'

That final intruding thought was so unexpected that he actually stopped in his tracks so the Follower behind walked into him.

'Do pay attention to where you're going…' It was Dilanthas, the other original Virgin Gift. In fact, now the only one left on the pilgrimage. She was a pretty little thing; quiet, modest and obedient. Hadn't had her. Yet.

'Sorry, Dagla Kaz. I…'

'Ah, no matter, girl. I may give you the pleasure and honour of joining with you this evening after prayers.' He walked away, giving her no opportunity to refuse him on behalf of her new partner.

There was a cry of distress from the team on the ropes. A women had fallen and was being dragged by a loop. She was pulled against one of the trees and its rough bark gouged her back. A man rescued her, removed the loop and replaced her in the team so she had time to recover.

He'd never understood such altruism. It made no sense. Fools thought it a positive and beneficial quality, but there was no good in it. Helping others cost you time and sometimes even coin. Could make you miss out on pleasure. No; not a good thing at all.

'But coin is good, isn't it? Coin could even be best, don't you think, after power?'

The thought sounded loud and clear in his head. They'd been invading his head for so long now that he would miss them if they fell silent. Ever since he'd been made aware of mindtalk, he grown more certain these thoughts came from that source. To reply to these minds, to be part of them; that would be a real achievement.

Wyyhn Kaz approached him from higher up the slope and walked beside him. 'Have you made any attempts to mindtalk yet, Dagla Kaz?'

The timing surprised and alerted him.

'You know I have. I can't understand it. I'm intelligent and able in every other area of life. Why cannot I use the gift you say I should possess?'

'One of those things we'll perhaps never know, Dagla. Have you had anyone connect with you?'

'Ah. So it was you. I thought so. Testing me, eh?'

Wyyhn Kaz looked askance at him. 'You've had connections?'

'You did it just now. Odd things to say, but it was clearly you. I don't believe in coincidence.'

Wyyhn Kaz was alarmed, shook his head. 'Not me, Dagla. I promise you. What did the voice say?'

'It matters not. Something about frowking and…worship of Ytraa, that's all. I didn't realise it was mindtalk. Odd sensation. But I didn't recognise the voice, actually. Does that happen?'

'In mindtalk, some people can "hear" the person they're connecting with. But most just sense the words in their mind with no identifiable sound. So I understand. You realise there are very few of us who are able, of course?'

'If the eyes you describe are the sign, I've met many. My daughter and my…the Renegade amongst them. And our other priest, Rrildyss.'

'Ah, Rrildyss can definitely mindtalk. In fact, she's very gifted and can connect over vast distances. She told me she has a wise woman who's a contact in Litkala. Wonderful mind, so she says.'

'Did she say anything about the leader of that city state? A man called Feldrark. He has the eyes.'

'Feldrark? I'll ask her. Myself, I can only connect within a limited area. And, as there are no others in my group who have the sign, I've been unable to practise very much recently. There were more before the heathens started to destroy and banish us. But even then we were always very few. From time to time, I've been approached by evil ones. I always close them out, of course. Don't want to suffer the same fate as Gadhallah, after all.'

This was new. Wyyhn had avoided questioning his utterances about Gadhallah, but now he was suggesting the reason for the founder's aberrations lay in mindtalk. He thought back to some of the stone tablets, the ones carved before they had the means to make parchment in the very early days on the island. Some had mentioned voices that had told him to defile and kill the girl in…in these very woods!

'No. No, indeed. How, exactly, do you close out these probing minds, Wyyhn?'

'Oh, it's really down to desire, you know? You reject their words and tell them you're not interested in what they have to tell you. It's all blasphemy and greed and evil anyway, so it's not difficult to cut them out of your mind. The danger is letting your curiosity get the better of you. But that won't trouble you, Dagla. They'll soon realise you're a good man with the faith at your very core and they'll leave you alone.'

Another small incident down the slope took Wyyhn's attention and he dashed down to help, leaving Dagla Kaz to ponder all he'd learned. Who had been trying to connect with him? And why?

A great cheer rose from below and he was brought back to the real world. It seemed the Godwood had entered the water and was now floating, quite swiftly, down the current. It was time to get the Followers moving. The sooner they were out of these woods and on the flat plain, the better. It would be hard going for those on the ropes, but it could be done in a day.

'I can show you how you can have any woman you like, for a price, of course.'

He said nothing, but his thoughts answered that he could have any woman he wanted at no cost whatever, so the offer was of no interest to him.

'I can show you ways to have pleasure you never dreamed of. Special ways. Ways of making them do what you want, even when they don't want to. At a price, of course.'

That seemed like a reply to his denial of interest. Had his thoughts gone to the mind that was in touch with him? Had he finally managed to mindtalk with someone?

'Yes. I receive your thoughts, Dagla Kaz. Now all I want to know is whether you'll take advantage of this gift and share it with like-minded people? We can make much of it, if we act together. Take dim-witted women to frowk as and when we want. Persuade lesser men to give us whatever coin they have. Given unity of purpose and a clear picture of the world

we want to rule, we can be all-powerful; do exactly as we wish. What do you say, friend?'

'I say, lead on. Show me the way, my friend.'

He'd done it! He had made contact, voluntarily and with control, at last!

The brightness of the day made Aklon blink when he opened his eyes, so that he shut them again. But she was there. He opened them again. Shoarhn sat beside the bed, her hand on his, her pretty face scratched and bearing signs of anxiety.

'Back with us, at last. No. Lie still. If they hadn't found you when they did, you'd have bled to death. Lie still, you silly, wonderful man, and let time and rest heal you. I can't lose you now.'

He felt so weak. Even as he tried to rise he knew he had no strength to move. She moved instead, shifting so that he could see her more entirely, see that she was skirted but no more and that she had also been wounded. A fine cut ran from her left shoulder to the top of her breast. But it was uncovered and appeared not to be deep. She might be scarred but she would lose no feeling or function from the joint.

'Here. You need to drink.' She pressed a soft cloth against his mouth and he sucked out the wetness. After seven times, he was exhausted.

'I...love...you...' Was all he could manage.

She stroked her hand across his face and lay it on his forehead, cool and damp from the moist cloth. 'Sleep now. Rest will bring you back to full health.'

He could do no more. Obedience to the woman he loved. But she was safe, and so was he. Nothing else mattered, for the moment.

It was later when he woke again. The light suggested it was evening. The flickering quality spoke of the Skyfire rather than the sun. She was still there, beside him, her eyes closed but her hand on his, as before.

'How long have I been like this?'

She started, coming back from her shallow sleep, and smiled at him. 'It took me two days to get here and I've been with you for a day since I arrived.'

Three days without knowing anything. There were things he had to find out. But first he needed water. She seemed to understand. Gave him the wet cloth to suck again. This time he managed ten times before he'd had enough and this time he did not succumb to exhaustion, though he was extremely tired.

'Delbon and Choryssa...'

'Both well. Both slightly wounded. But well. And here. And Phrysilda, that amazing little woman who'd love to frowk you when you're better, so she tells me. She's also well, though the wound to her left leg and foot has kept her bedbound since we arrived. I promised her I'd tell you she's well and still wanting.'

He saw her smile. She understood he'd been…what would be the word for what he'd done, or not done? True? Faithful? Something like that.

'She will be wanting a long time. Though she is a worthy woman, she is not for me. You are the one, Shoarhn. The only one, now.'

'Is that true, Aklon?'

'I always tell the truth, remember?'

'Of course. And I'm yours, Aklon. Have been ever since we first met. Get well: I want to renew my acquaintance with more than merely your face.'

'So you shall. As soon as I am able to move without passing out, that is!'

'Rest. That's what you must have. Rest and more to drink, to help replace lost blood. So the healer says.'

'The Dissenters? Did any convert, surrender, see sense?'

'Delbon says there were fifteen. All the Unholy Ones and most of the ex-soldiers perished either in battle or as they tried to escape. He says we won't have any more trouble from them.'

'I wanted so much for this to be a peaceful change. Am I a fool, Shoarhn?'

'Not a fool, Aklon. A dreamer and a good man who tries to see the best in everybody. So many people are less than good, that's all.'

'But you are good, Shoarhn. A good woman, a good person, and good for me. Promise me you will also rest when I take my next sleep. Lie beside me. There is room.'

'I will.'

She gave him more to drink and helped him settle into comfort before she took her place beside him and allowed sleep to take her.

◦ ⸺ ◦

The experience had been so bad. So very hard. But there was no escaping the return. Ivdulon had given her secret knowledge and a way to defend herself against the evil minds. Tumalind was not invulnerable in the evil part of mindtalk, but she now possessed a method of self defence that should protect her from most of the danger.

'But make no mistake, Tumalind, you will still be at great risk.' The wise woman's warning had been made in isolation, separated from all reference to the plot they'd begun to develop.

'What's she told you, Tumalind? What are you going to do?'

She looked at Okkyntalah and held his hand. The small room was no place to share such secrets, but she must at least explain some of what was involved in the great plot, and why she must do it. But it would be best done away from the actual city of Trotnahn, though not too far away, since proximity was necessary for complete success. She had, in any case to tell him what was required, since Okkyntalah would play a vital role in the

269

scheme. So difficult to know where and how to start.

'First, we must leave here. I can't do what I must and you can't do what you must from here. We have to be free to move and to make our escape. We need to be outside the city walls.'

'I take it you've decided not to stay here and live in the city, Blavv?'

'You've seen the way they are, Okkyntalah. Their worship of money, as they call it, and what it buys. They're without spirit. Completely devoid of any concern other than buying whatever they think will give them power and prestige. I truly believe some of them would murder to get what they want. No. I'm not staying here.'

'Did you discover anything about your parents?'

'From what little I can gather, it seems they might've set off into the desert after I was taken, looking for me. They were never seen again.'

Tumalind squeezed her shoulder in sympathy. 'Are you well enough to travel…after your loss, Blavv?'

'Thank you, Tumalind. I'm well enough. Are you?'

'I think so. In any case, I'm sure we'll all feel so much better away from here. You, Teldrohn?'

'I go where Blavv goes. But, yes, I'd rather leave this place. I hate the way they look at you women with hunger and lust.'

'Sondukal?'

'I'm with you to 'elp guide and guard. Feldrark would 'ave me protect you from evil and I've never felt a place so evil as this. I say we leave as soon as possible.'

'Kallohn?'

'I didn't want to be here in the first place. And I fear if that man returns he'll try again to abuse me and I will then kill him.'

Okkyntalah nodded. 'We're agreed then. I'll have to make them believe we're leaving to make arrangements for traders to bring them supplies of glass and whitestone, otherwise they'll be suspicious and may prevent us.'

Teldrohn nodded. 'It's a good job you took over in talking with these people, Okkyntalah. I'd have made a mess of it. But you seemed to pick up on what to say straight away. You've handled the situation well so far. Keep it up, and I'll stay silent, less my temper gets the better of me.'

The party agreed. They must now await an opportunity to speak to Vavak, whilst keeping him away from Kallohn. It would not be easy.

Two more days passed before the man returned. 'Are the women recovered from whatever ails them?'

'They are; I thank you for your concern, Vavak. We are ready to return to Litkala and make arrangements for some of our merchants to come here with the glass and whitestone I mentioned. What will you trade? We don't buy women, as you know. And your other goods, those you displayed at the market, may not be entirely suitable for less sophisticated people than those who live here. I suspect that coin will be the most valuable. Though, of course, a few samples of your more exotic items may be worth display in Litkala, to see whether the population there finds them attractive.'

Tumalind was more and more impressed with Okkyntalah. He'd grown from the simple hunter she'd wished to marry on the island into a man with wisdom, courage, sense, experience and, now, diplomacy. Vavak turned over the ideas in his mind. He trusted no one, of course. In this city where objects were utterly supreme, no one seemed to trust anyone else. Everything here had a price but nothing was valued beyond the status that material wealth could bring its possessor.

'Tomorrow, I'll have a small contingent of the guard escort you to the oasis so that you're protected from the marauding K'ahll. We don't want you robbed and murdered by those wild criminals, after all, do we?'

'The K'ahll are more civilised than…'

'Thank you Kallohn. I think, Vavak, that we may have no need of your guard, but I thank you for the offer. We're a small party and we have developed an understanding with the K'ahll that allows us safe passage through lands they consider their own.'

'Nevertheless, I insist on providing you with protection.'

Okkyntalah nodded. 'Very well, we accept your offer in the spirit in which it is made, Vavak. Our camels are rested and ready?'

'There'll be the stabling to pay for. And you'll need supplies for your journey. I suggest you let me have the necessary coin to pay for all this and I will arrange to have it ready for the morning.'

Okkyntalah asked how much was required and persuaded Teldrohn to hand over the considerable sum required. Vavak grasped it and left at once.

'Last we'll see of that lot and of him.'

'I don't think so, Sondukal. They have a sort of code of conduct here and thieving is part of it. But we've made them an offer of trade that they value and they'll want to ensure that we send merchants with the goods I've promised.'

'I bet that shitsucker pockets half of what we've paid him.'

'I expect you're right, Teldrohn.'

'Evil man. Evil mind.'

Kallohn was livid at her inability to deal with the man in her own way but recognised how delicate was their situation.

'The sooner we're away from here, the better.'

271

They all agreed with Tumalind.

'The bodyguard will be a nuisance. Wish I could've found a way to refuse, without being rude. But he doesn't trust us. Wants to make sure we're going where I said.'

'We can get rid once we're free of the city.'

'How, Teldrohn?'

'Lose them. We'll find a way to get away from them. Any case, they'll leave us at the oasis.'

'Except we're not bound for the oasis. We need to be going the other way, and we need to stay close to the city.'

Sondukal frowned at Okkyntalah. 'What's this, then?'

'Now isn't the time or the place, Sondukal. But Feldrark has asked certain things of me and Okkyntalah that mean we must, as he says, stay close to the city until we've completed our tasks. You and the others can, of course, return to Litkala.'

The discussion grew and flowed back and forth as the others asked questions Tumalind couldn't yet answer. Sondukal tried to persuade the pair of them that they needed friends around if they were to remain in this hostile place.

'Whatever else transpires, Okkyntalah and I have to do this. Whether you remain with us or not, we must stay. And, once we're free of the city, I'll explain as much as I may to you. But I feel you should consider going back to Litkala without us.'

'I'm not leavin' you an' Okkyntalah alone, lass. Not after all we've bin through. Feldrark'd never forgive me.'

'It was Feldrark who suggested what I'm advising, Sondukal. He was quite specific: both you and Teldrohn should make your way back to your home. And, of course, take Blavv back with you. Kallohn, of course, may decide for herself what she does and where she goes. Maybe the local K'ahll will take you in?'

'My tribe are in Ov-Bebna. Those who roam these sands will escort me back, should that be necessary. You need have no worry regarding my safety, Tumalind.'

The conversation continued for a little while longer but it was clear no hard decision would be made until they'd left the city behind.

Tumalind asked Okkyntalah to walk with her through the quiet night streets. 'I need to think in the fresh air.'

They left the small place and walked silent streets, as Tumalind wondered how to tell her husband, again, that he must murder men in cold blood once she'd identified those with evil minds. That he'd not refused when she'd first hinted at this, was some comfort.

Chapter 34

GODWOOD MOVING

They'd buried two Followers who'd fallen foul of the ropes; one crushed beneath the Godwood, the other dragged by the sheer weight of it through a narrow gap in the riverside rocks. Three more had drowned, their bodies irretrievably lost in the fast flowing waters. Dagla Kaz told them that such sacrifice only served to glorify their devotion to Ytraa, but the High Priest's words no longer fully convinced Aglydron.

He noticed that even the other priests viewed Dagla Kaz with suspicion and some alarm, as if they feared the man was mad. He'd taken to mumbling to himself, apparently unaware of the words falling from his lips, making little sense but often obscene or blasphemous.

But they were, at last, out of the forest and on the flat plain that led to the lake. On the edge of the wooded area, the unnamed river they'd used to transport the Godwood had joined another that the native Followers called the Flow. Wide and deep, it ran into the lake at a point where the town of Saahl nestled on the shore at the end of a long, narrow inlet. The settlement lay on the eastern side, which they were using to guide the Godwood with their ropes. Later, they must cross to the west bank and take the Godwood past the town in the dead of night. But how this was to be achieved seemed unknown.

'Have faith! Ytraa will provide for us.' Wyyhn Kaz spoke with more conviction than was written on his face.

Now that they were on the plain, smaller groups held the ropes and Aglydron and Chislanda were relieved of duty for a while. He studied the land they travelled at a pace dictated by the current. The local priest estimated they'd be at the lake by morning on the next day. It left them little time to swap from the present bank to the opposite one, half a league distant.

'We'll use the bridge.'

'Bridge, Wyyhn?' Dagla Kaz was alert and interested.

'A trade road connects Saahl with Tohnpho.'

Aglydron recalled that that was where they'd parted company with the merchant, Ven-Gadla and his wife. He wondered if the pair remained awaiting their return, but he daren't ask the High Priest.

'The bridge crosses the river some three leagues above the town. If we take the ropes over to the far bank on the bridge, we can anchor the Godwood there until nightfall, then use the cover of darkness to get it down to the lake.'

It sounded so simple. No one had mentioned what they would do when they reached the lake. How they would procure a boat to take them and the Godwood as far as Phornahm, where, it was rumoured, there remained some who were sympathetic to the followers.

Aglydron relied on the help and guidance of his God. 'Ytraa will provide, Chislanda. It's for Ytraa we do this, after all.'

'Is it, Aglydron? Can we be sure this is for Ytraa and not simply for the benefit of Dagla Kaz?'

Aglydron was shocked by her question. That the High Priest would arrange the whole enterprise for his personal benefit was surely unthinkable, wasn't it? But the very fact that he was able to question it softened his response.

'I'm not sure what you mean, Chislanda. How does it help the High Priest?'

Unlike Aglydron, Chislanda had little concern that others might hear her when she questioned the actions or decisions of the priests. Her reply was heard by those close by.

'Well, he retains his power by the glorification of Ytraa, doesn't he? Even you can't have failed to notice how convenient it is that he always has an answer to problems after they've occurred. The answers seem to fit conveniently with the solution to a problem unforeseen. A little too conveniently.'

Before Aglydron could respond with outrage at this suggestion, one of those who'd overheard agreed with her.

'The way he passed off the deaths of those two on the ropes as part of Ytraa's plans, you mean?'

Chislanda turned to face the woman. 'Well, that and several other things you won't be aware of. Things that happened before we reached this place. Things like the way he suddenly changed his mind about what should happen to Aglydron and his friend, Okkyntalah. He was all for killing them after they kidnapped his daughter to swap with Tumalind. And there's another thing: he accused Tumalind of blasphemy when everyone knows she'd never be blasphemous.'

'An' the way he suddenly 'ad an answer about the Virgin Gifts. I mean, Ialdyss Kaz said she couldn't see no real answer to that one. Well, not one that'd fit with what Dagla Kaz said was traditional, anyway.'

Aglydron worried that someone in authority might hear this dissent. 'But that's what makes it more likely that Ytraa made those decisions for him, isn't it? I mean, Dagla Kaz had already said he couldn't understand how to solve those problems. Then he communed with Ytraa and suddenly he had the answers. Doesn't that prove he got them from Ytraa?'

To his amazement, his reasoning seemed to cast uncertainty over the doubt shown by the others. They were silent and thoughtful, considering his suggestion, as they continued on their way.

'Stop! Hold the Godwood!'

The voice of Wyyhn Kaz carried to those on the ropes, who tried to halt the progress of the Godwood through the water. Alone, they could do no more than guide it, however, and many more rushed to their aid to stop the huge piece of wood in the flow of the river.

Aglydron ran to help, taking Chislanda with him. Together, around half the force managed to slow and then halt the Godwood. Only then did they become aware of the reason. There, in clear sight, stood the bridge that spanned the river, taking the road Wyyhn Kaz had spoken of. And there were people on that bridge. The Followers could only hope that they were not observed.

Against his better judgement, Feldrark had given in to Jodisa's demands that she be involved in what Ivdulon had planned. The Riser took them to the tower and Netrodyl greeted and fed them as usual.

Leaving them with the wise woman, and no longer needing to be excluded, she found a task that would take her out of hearing. 'It's alright, you know. I'm happy being kept out of your secrets, whatever they are. I'd rather not know, if you don't mind. I like my role up here. I don't want to be involved in matters of high state.'

She made a signal to Ivdulon and then left the tower with her basket to collect various herbs.

'She's a clever woman, Ivdulon.'

'She is. Now, we have strategy to devise.'

'Before we begin, may I clarify why we're doing this and exactly what we're doing.'

Ivdulon glanced at Feldrark for confirmation and then looked directly at Jodisa. 'You want the bald facts?'

'It will help me to help you, I think.'

The wise woman nodded. 'It might help all of us to summarise. Yes. Let's sit in comfort at least, shall we?'

She cleared charts, parchments and other unidentifiable clutter, making room for all three. Through the window, the sounds of the city filtered up, muted by distance. The soft breaking of waves on the shore the only constant amongst a wide variety of noises: seabirds calling, industry on the docks, and the gentle breath of the wind soughing through the sparse vegetation of the plateau on which her tower stood.

'You recall I told you of the evil minds a little while ago? I've decided to call them Powerseekers, since that's what they are.'

Feldrark nodded. 'Sounds reasonable.'

275

'You both know they intend to usurp power all over the world by converting people to their foul philosophy of material wealth over spiritual and personal concerns? We discussed the probable outcome.'

'Yes. And decided they were vile people and must be stopped, whatever the cost.'

'At the time, I hadn't managed to locate them. I have now, in two centres. One in Trotnahn and the other in a place I previously believed to be uninhabited.

'You may not know of the Monolith of Kro Lat? I thought not.' She rummaged amongst the parchments she'd moved and found a roll that she unfurled to display a map, very like that used by Dagla Kaz to guide his journey.

'North in Tohltaz, far from other habitation, and surrounded by a vast desert, stands the Monolith of Kro Lat. I know little about it, except that it's a work of extraordinary skill, beauty and power. A huge, hollow ball stands atop a cylindrical column of stone some thirty manheights tall. I know only that the sphere is pierced with two circular holes and is reached by a difficult spiral staircase inside the column. The purpose of the Monolith is unknown, to me, at least. I've no idea who built it, when or why. But I know it's very ancient. Maybe as old as our own dear city. It's now the centre of activity by the Powerseekers.'

Jodisa and Feldrark studied the map. He followed the route of the road that left Lake Qonahn and crossed several rivers in Choshinahm until it passed over the border into Ndagaal. There, it first tracked and then traversed a line of ancient earthworks to reach the Monolith before it continued to Ov-Bebna and beyond.

'It says this is the route of ancients, Ivdulon. What does that mean?'

'Another enigma, I'm afraid. The map, like many of my parchments, is copied from one of a group of small stone tablets that were hidden under a slab in the centre of the floor here. I discovered it by accident and have spent much of my life translating the information into our own tongue. The original works are in a form that I couldn't understand at first.'

'You're full of surprises, Ivdulon. However, the exploration of that must wait. We're here to talk about the Powerseekers and the reason for our involvement with them.'

'Thank you, Feldrark. They pose a real and, now, imminent, danger to us.'

'But they're so far away.'

'They are, Jodisa. But mindtalk isn't limited by distance, as you know. And neither is the danger. If these Powerseekers gain a foothold, anywhere, they'll slowly spread their doctrine of greed and selfishness all over the world. Once it starts to grow, this idea will attract people for all the wrong reasons. We know how fickle people can be. We know they are easily persuaded by what appear to be simple solutions to difficult problems. The way the Powerseekers work, giving prominence to material objects that require no real effort to acquire, will appeal to many of the people. It's an insidious invasion. Once in place, it will be impossible to remove. We must stop it now, before it really starts.'

Jodisa put her hands to her head, brushed her fingers through her hair; a gesture that told Feldrark she was engaged in speculation. He watched her, and Ivdulon allowed her the period of silence she needed to form her conclusions.

'Their system would place fellow-feeling and care and general consideration below the search for coin and material wealth, of course.'

'Yes. People would become selfish and unconcerned for others. Violence would grow from a lack of consideration. Power would pass to those with the greatest wealth, as they'd be able to persuade others to become their supporters and, maybe even their private soldiers.'

'That's terrible. Profit would be the only thing that mattered. We'd have a society where those most interested in things rather than people, the least deserving, would have the greatest say. It would be intolerable.'

'It would. And worse. There are consequences beyond even those you imagine, Jodisa. I've thought long and hard on this and concluded they'd eventually control everything. The courts, the flow of supplies, access to basic needs for life. In fact, they'd finally control life itself; have the power to decide who lived and who died.

'Once in control, these Powerseekers would be impossible to oust. They'd form a self-perpetuating system of status that we couldn't deconstruct. Much of what we value would become as nothing. Those we most treasure would be in danger of execution simply because their spiritual beliefs would remind the Powerseekers of their greed, selfishness and lack of compassion. The world would be unbearable for any person of worth and gentleness. Manners, concern, compassion; all worthless so that only those with a ruthless desire to enrich themselves would thrive. The very worst of society would rule that new world.

'We must stop it, act now. The Powerseekers are ready to launch an offensive into the world, aimed at corrupting as many mindtalkers as they can. They work in groups. Subtle or as open as they need to be, they gauge the true state of mind of their victims and use their combined strength to persuade them into their way of thinking.

'Once they've converted mindtalkers, these distorted individuals will spread their philosophy to convert ordinary people. Attracting them with small rewards, they'll put them fully under the spell of ownership and worship of coin, which they call money. A society where money is God will develop inevitably from each place where converted mindtalkers live. It'll spread over the whole world, a tidal flood spoiling fertile ground, until there's no place free of their influence and power. Once that's happened, all other forms of government and worship will be outlawed and the rich will rule supreme.

Everyone else will be mere slaves to the will and whim of the wealthy.'

'But can it really happen, Ivdulon? Sounds fanciful and unlikely.'

'Believe me, Jodisa, it's already happened in Trotnahn, and probably Mehrrhyphrol. Tumalind has been invaded by the minds in one place, used by them in the other. Had we not combined to rescue her, she'd have been converted to their ways and would then have polluted the minds of those around her, or found the means to destroy them.'

'You wouldn't let me help in that exercise, Feldrark. Because of the risk? You thought me not strong enough?'

'Not you, Jodisa. Your unborn child. If they entered his or her mind at this stage they'd control everything our child does in the future. Is that what you want?'

She was silent, appalled that such a thing might happen. 'They can really do that?'

'We know you can influence a child in any way you want, if you have them under your control from an early age. Imagine that sort of influence over an infant before it was even born. The child would be an unwitting disciple of whatever system of thought and beliefs you served to it. It's what the men of Ov-Bebna did to their children. It's what the men of Mehrrhyphrol do to female offspring to make them lifelong servants of the lust of those who profit from their displays. It's what the men of Ylcrat do to their offspring to keep their women subdued. And it's what Followers have long done to their children. It happens with all belief systems, but most people are unaware, simply because they've never known anything else, having been raised in the traditions, customs and beliefs of their faith and that of their parents. Here in Litkala, we give choice over religion, so we don't influence our children as strongly as happens in more restricted societies, like your island of Muhnilahm. But it would take only a small change to make all our offspring into fanatical supporters of an extreme version of Following.'

Jodisa's shock and alarm were writ plain. 'We have to stop this. We must!'

'Yes. Feldrark and I are agreed. And the only way is to eradicate the Powerseekers entirely.'

'Kill them?'

'It's the task I've set Tumalind and Okkyntalah.'

'Do they know the danger they face?'

'Tumalind has some idea. She has merely to locate the owners of those minds. Okkyntalah has to do the killing. As yet, he's ignorant of the possible consequences.'

'Let me deal with Vavak, please, Kallohn. Anything you do or say will make things worse. I understand your concern for your honour, but all our lives are at stake in this, not just yours. And life's more important.'

'To you. Not to me. Honour is all to the K'ahll.'

278

'But we're not K'ahll, are we, Kallohn? And the K'ahll consider hospitality and the welfare of their charges as paramount, don't they?'

'We do, Okkyntalah.'

'We're your charges. You were appointed our guide through this region and we rely on your knowledge. Therefore, you're charged with caring for us.'

'You twist words to make it seem so.'

'Isn't it so?'

'I can think of no argument against your clever words, but it doesn't feel right. I will, though, behave properly in this regard. But, once we're free of the city and you're safe, I make no promises about that disreputable cur, Vavak.'

'That'll do for me, Kallohn. Right. Vavak will be here soon and we'll set out for the city gates. Until we're clear of the actual city, we must behave as we have during our stay. Tumalind and Blavv, you need to put on the long robes we've bought. And all you women must remain silent through the streets. Please remember where we are and the possible consequences of any behaviour the people consider improper.'

'Yes master. We'll do as you say.'

He glanced at Tumalind and caught her knowing smile. Kissing her and giving her bottom a gentle pinch, he put on a tone of mastery. 'I'll deal with you later, young woman.'

She raised her eyebrows speculatively. 'And I, of course, will willingly submit, oh master.'

'You two are incorrigible, do you know that?'

'Oh, I hope so, Blavv.'

She shook her head at Tumalind and helped her don the long robe before allowing Tumalind to help her into her own. The women were now cloaked from head to foot in black, only their faces visible, as was the custom for those in the city who weren't objects of display and usage.

When Vavak eventually arrived, later than arranged, he was accompanied by five soldiers. They set off more or less at once, after Okkyntalah had inspected the goods and supplies the Senior had procured for them. They collected their camels from the stables and left via the city gate with no trouble.

To Okkyntalah's surprise and annoyance, Vavak remained with them for the first league out of the city.

'Now that you're well on your way, I'll take my leave of you. On your return with your merchants, I'll be happy to provide you with more comfortable lodgings and any of the city's comforts you and they wish to sample. Farewell for now. And may we all profit from your journeys.'

279

'Thank you, Vavak. May the future you're due be yours.'

The formalities done, the man left and returned to the city. Okkyntalah allowed another league to pass before he stopped and took the soldiers to one side.

'We've no need of your guidance or guardianship, thank you. As far as I'm concerned, you can return to your city and your homes.'

The senior soldier spoke for them all. 'We're ordered to see you clear of the borders, to the oasis.'

Okkyntalah nodded. Coin might persuade them otherwise. He consulted Sondukal and Teldrohn as to their funds and discovered they were still well provided for.

'No one need know you turned back early from this unnecessary duty. I'm sure you could all make good use of coin?' He made the offer slightly larger than what he considered likely to persuade them and discovered he'd been right. They accepted the bribe happily and went on their way, intending to spend a few nights in the open before returning to the city with the tale that they'd escorted the foreigners from the land without trouble.

'Good. We'll give them half a day to be well out of sight. Then Tumalind and I will turn and make for the trees near the lake at the other side of Trotnahn. From there we'll start the tasks set by Feldrark and Ivdulon.'

'We've no idea what you're charged with doing, Okkyntalah, but we've all decided to stay and help, if we can.'

'You can't, Teldrohn.'

'Then, we'll simply remain as friends and support.'

'It's dangerous, Blavv.'

'More so for a man and woman alone. Less so for a small group of friends.'

He tried to persuade them. Tried to make them go their way, but they'd have none of it. Even Kallohn wouldn't leave them.

'You've been a good leader and protected us in the city. My tribe would be ashamed of me if I let you down now. I'll remain.'

He looked to Tumalind for help but she just shrugged and spread out her hands in a gesture of helplessness. Their relief at such support, however, was great.

'Thank you, friends. It's good to know you'll be with us.'

'I think now's as good as any time for me to explain exactly what we're going to do, and why. So you can change your minds before we go back to the city.'

They turned expectantly to Tumalind, as she sat cross-legged on the sandy ground and invited them to gather round so she could tell them about the need to kill strangers in cold blood.

Chapter 35

THE HARDEST QUESTION

Dagla Kaz tried to resist the temptation to connect with the other minds that were now his almost constant companions. They were there, in his head, but he avoided reaching out to them. Like minds, they gave comfort; their encouragement and suggestions were such relief after so long a period of great responsibility. And their ideas and schemes attracted all that he felt worthy of his role. But, for now, as they'd pointed out, his most important task was to get himself and the Godwood home, to return to a place where absolute power awaited him.

The people on the road had gone and there'd been no sign of further travellers in this sparsely populated land. Now they must get to the bridge, cross the river and float the Godwood down to that great lake. He had no scheme, no plan about his move from that point on. But, at last, amongst the other voices, one that claimed to be the voice of his God, the voice of Ytraa had finally come to him. Ytraa had questioned him about his true intentions and assured him all was well, all was in hand. He need have no worries about the future for his pilgrimage; Ytraa would take care of everything.

But he was still the human here in charge of their purpose, even if the means to the success was now in the hands of Ytraa. The relief, the bliss of knowing that his God would guide and provide for the remainder of the journey was almost more than his weary mind could take. He felt euphoric, ecstatic. The voice of Ytraa informed him that his life, his deeds, his necessary lies and deceptions had all been good and right. Come the time to leave the world, he'd find peace and all the creative frowking he deserved in the Garden of Delights, where every woman he could want, of any age or type, would do his bidding. He was destined for an afterlife of utter bliss. But, first, he had a worldly life to complete and a mission his God considered vital to the future of that world. He'd tried to commune, to ask questions, but Ytraa had made it clear that such was not permitted.

The gang on the ropes had allowed the Godwood to continue on its journey at his word. Now they were close to the fabric of the bridge. Wooden superstructure, mainly planks of rough-cut timber, rested on pillars of stone, each a dozen paces distant from its neighbour. The gap between the underside and the surface of the water was barely deep enough to allow passage of the Godwood underneath. But it would go.

'I need strong swimmers to take the ropes beneath the bridge and bring them up the other side so we can pull the Godwood to the western bank.'

For reasons he didn't understand, the people and even the other priests, looked at him oddly. There was a mix of surprise and some delight there. Strange. But they were lesser mortals, as Ytraa had explained. They had no concept of the superior ways of godlike men such as Ytraa described him.

He needed swimmers. Of course he did. And he'd select these, since his powers of decision were loftier than all around him. And there, standing next to that reprobate who'd stolen his daughter and his heir, was the woman the man claimed to love, whatever that might mean. Chislanda, wasn't it? She'd go into the water with the others and, with Ytraa's help, an accident would befall her and rob that fool Aglydron of some of his ill-gotten rewards.

'You. And you, you, you and you. Gather the ropes and take them under the bridge. The rest, split into two teams. One to hold the Godwood here and the other to be ready to collect the rope ends the swimmers bring to you. Get to it!'

He felt alive again, after a long period of confusion and indecision. The voice of Ytraa, live and present in his head, gave such confidence and certainty to everything he did. Tonight, under the glow of the Skyfire, he'd have another of those recently married girls; one he hadn't so far sampled. Yes. That was something to look forward to. For now, the Godwood must be all his thought. That, and the hope of revenge on Aglydron.

They were all in place. The Godwood barely held in check by those still on the bank, swimmers in the water, ropes attached around them. He'd watched that woman fasten the loose end about her slender waist and felt slight regret he hadn't had the chance to sample that fine body, to subject it to the type of joining he'd always enjoyed. But it was a small matter, so long as she was lost to that damned Aglydron for good.

The plan came into action. People moved. The Godwood waited. Swimmers made progress under the bridge and he watched them reach the other side. He must be on the bridge to supervise; not here on the bank. What was he thinking? On the bank, he was in no place to organise things so the fool's woman drowned. He almost ran to the place where he could witness and direct events.

He was too late. The woman was already back on the bridge, helped up by that bowelcreep, Aglydron. Damn the man.

'No need to feel cheated, Dagla Kaz. You now have opportunity to humiliate and use her for your own ends, rob the fanatic of his pleasure in her. And then, when the time is right, we can arrange her death.'

Dagla smiled with satisfaction. He approached as the woman was dried down by her fool of a man. He slipped a hand under her buttock. 'Tonight, my dear, I will pleasure you as reward for your achievement here today.' And he was away before either of them had the chance to say a word.

Oh, how she would squirm when he abused her in the dark tonight.

The High Priest had selected Chislanda as a partner. Was this an honour, or a punishment? Aglydron couldn't decide. Under normal circumstances, the selection would unquestionably be an honour for both the woman and her partner. But, until very recently, Dagla Kaz had been anything but normal. It was true that he had, that very morning, become more like his old self, as if some great burden had been lifted from him. It was encouraging that the leader of their mission should be so positive now. Perhaps he'd communed with Ytraa. Had he received some answers to the many questions that must have beset him?

There was the very real concern about what they would do for transport across the lake, once they passed the town of Saahl during the night. A feat they were about to embark upon.

'Don't you mind that Dagla Kaz wants to intrude where only you are wanted, Aglydron?'

'Of course I want us to be an exclusive couple, Chislanda. But he's the High Priest. It's an honour. It'll raise your importance and make you special amongst Followers. It may even ensure your acceptance into the Garden of Delights when death eventually takes you. Surely a small sacrifice is worth such an outcome?'

'You really believe it all, don't you?'

'I don't understand.'

'You believe all that the High Priest says and does is right and in accordance with the wishes of Ytraa.'

'Of course. How could it be otherwise? You can't have half a faith, Chislanda. It's all or nothing. Surely you're not having doubts?'

'No more than I've ever had. You want me to willingly frowk with that man?'

'I think you must. I think it would be most unwise to refuse him. You saw what happened to Tumalind. I don't want to risk our welfare for the sake of a bit of pleasure for the High Priest. Do you?'

'You amaze me sometimes, Aglydron. But I'll do it. For you. Not for him. He repulses me. But you're more a Follower than I'll ever be and I suppose you understand subtleties that escape me. Anyway, here he comes. Should I undress now?'

'Not until you're alone with him. Dagla Kaz; welcome. Chislanda awaits your pleasure.'

The High Priest stared at him oddly; something between a smile and confusion. But he indicated that Chislanda should go with Dagla Kaz. They left, his woman trailing behind his leader. Others had already indulged in joining amongst the shrubs and occasional rocky outcrops of this bank of the river. Tonight, he'd share no pleasure. But

283

he was content that his High Priest would share the delights of his partner for once. Perhaps she'd return an even more accomplished lover under such tuition.

⚜

The woman proved remarkably submissive and compliant, engaging in the act with little sign of enjoyment but without complaint either. When he'd used her to the point of satiation, he slapped her rump soundly and sent her on her way, her body still uncovered as she left him in some hurry. Good. He might punish her for that sacrilege later. In fact, she'd been such a docile vessel, next time he'd use some of the more extreme discipline a woman should endure when willing to be dominated.

'*A satisfying frowk, Dagla. She promises better, if she continues to be submissive. We should have more of her, don't you think?*'

He was still unable to separate out each mind that connected. He remained uncertain whether his thoughts were transmitting the way that Wyyhn had described. But they all replied in a way that suggested he was sending out his thoughts. It was unsettling to be so one-sided in this, but such was the nature of his particular gift.

'*We're agreed, then. She'll make solid entertainment until we decide she's no longer required. Then we'll end her. In the meantime, I have good news, Dagla. A boat will await you at the lake and take you on your voyage back to your island. You need have no further worries about your return.*'

The relief. The sense of a burden lifted. The bliss of the recent frowk coupled with an overwhelming feeling of lightness, as all anxiety left to raise him to a state of ecstasy even greater than he'd experienced with the unnamed woman who supplied his potency drug. Wonderful.

He was restored. Recovered from the small effort of his joining with Chislanda. From amongst those resting on the bank, he took the delicate girl from Muhnilahm and educated her in the ways a woman should please a man. Dilanthas cooperated with diffidence, allowing his domination, a natural vessel for superior lust. Not for many cycles had he enjoyed such delights in one evening. The new connection with Ytraa had rejuvenated him and allowed the unbridled pleasure of self-indulgence without pause. It was a wonderful feeling that increased his sense of overall power. He released the young woman and sent her back to her new partner unclothed and trembling. It was well to have them fear him. Compliance the next time was better assured.

'*Another satisfactory frowk, Dagla. But, now, I fear we must progress the move of the Godwood to the lake before daylight overtakes us.*'

It was a shame to have to desist. The potency drug, allied to his newfound confidence and sense of power combined to make him ready yet again. But it would have to wait. Pleasure, after all, must not always take the place of responsibility, especially when his

284

God was the one who required action.

He strode back into the area where the rest awaited his command. At one side, he noticed his first victim berating that bowelcreep, Aglydron. Good. Conflict in their relationship would help his future domination over her, whatever her name might be. Odd; he couldn't recall it now. It was of no consequence. She'd answer to him, whatever he named her.

'We now make the final effort. If we're discovered on this stretch of our journey, we'll be in danger. Though the town where evil dwells lies across the water, we must not assume we are free of danger. So, there will be no noise. No talking. No sounds other than those needed to achieve our purpose. For those amongst you who doubt my powers, I can inform you with certainty that our journey tonight will end in our boarding a ship to take us safely across the lake and on to our destination. That, alone, should spur you on to the necessary effort to complete our task.'

There was a good deal of murmuring; mostly positive. And the two teams on the ropes rose as one and moved forward, preventing the Godwood from moving more swiftly through the current than the pace dictated by the whole walking party. The speed and nature of the journey so far had cost only a few lives; the old and infirm were rapidly lost to hardship, of course, but were no real loss to the purpose, after all.

Ah, but it was good to be on the move, knowing this was the final stage of the pilgrimage. He would arrive home in triumph with the Godwood and the new group of loyal Followers. Then he'd deal with any who'd caused trouble in his absence. It would be a marvellous challenge to devise suitable punishments for those who'd transgressed. And, back on the island, he'd finally find a way to destroy Aglydron for his foul abuse of Jodisa-Li. The very thought raised desire in him, but he knew he must remain unsatisfied for the moment. Aboard ship, he'd acquire a cabin where he'd indulge in all the pleasure he could possibly want.

'We'll share the delights to be had from each and every woman in the party, Dagla. Such reward is both natural and eminently deserved. For the moment, concentration on the task in hand is necessary. We approach the town and absolute silence is required. A small reminder, I think?'

'Let me remind you. Anyone who makes a sound before we reach the ship will be severely punished. I'll personally whip such fools until they beg for mercy; a mercy they will neither deserve nor receive. Silence is the watchword. Make sure you do not incur my wrath or that of your God. Ytraa is watching and expects us to do the bidding of Ytraa without error or fault. No more words, no more sound. Change the teams now and we set off for the final leg.'

He slept well for the next two days and, by the end of that time, Aklon seemed much recovered. Certainly, he was ready to join with her. A gentle coupling, passionate but without the energetic elements they'd sometimes shared. Shoarhn lay beside him feeling more fulfilled and loved than ever. Her head rested on his shoulder and his arm enfolded her, stroking the skin his hand reached. There was such love in him, such care and consideration.

'Are you ready to travel, Aklon? I need to be at the farm to get things back to normal as soon as possible.'

'I shall be ready come the morning. We will find a wagon and take it slowly so that we have time to allow our wounds to heal completely. I will live with you openly, at last. And we shall share the work.'

'For a while. Until someone comes and tells you they need help. I know you too well, Aklon. I may have you now as my exclusive partner. But you're still not mine completely. You'll always belong to the people.'

He was silent for a while and she thought he was sleeping, her own tiredness after the coupling urging her to rest.

'You are right, of course. I must lead the special troop I have formed and tour the island to rid it of the rest of those who would cause trouble and bring violence on all. But I will rest for some days. And that rest will be with you, Shoarhn. In the morning, before we set off, I shall connect with various people and discover what has happened whilst I have been incapacitated.'

'I wish others could do that duty. But I know you won't allow it. I fear I'll lose you to some fanatic one day.'

'I intend to lead a long and fruitful life with you Shoarhn. I have no intention of allowing any fool or extremist to end our hopes in service to his god.'

They embraced and relaxed into sleep. The morning would bring movement and a journey back to Morstahn, where the farm awaited proper management. Friends there waited to help or resume social contact and others required only soft words of sincere thanks as they slept the forever peace of death.

※

The concept of cold-blooded murder was so far removed from their experience and expectations that they remained in shock long after Tumalind finished her explanation of what must be done. Blavv accepted the idea without resistance, the advantage of coded mindtalk with Ivdulon letting her fully understand the consequences of a failure to act. She, at least, was able to confirm all that Tumalind told them. Kallohn seemed neither surprised nor resistant to the scheme.

'In the K'ahll we've long believed that some mortal evil existed in the world. We have long tried to escape its influence by our life of desert roaming. But the time's come when wandering is no longer appropriate. The time for action is here. I'm no soldier, nor assassin, but whatever help I can give is given willingly to end the coming threat.'

Her declaration had some effect on the men. But they were full of questions, full of doubts. Okkyntalah, in particular, was reluctant to believe that men could actually be so evil and so willing to conspire in such wickedness.

'What have we just escaped, Okkyntalah?'

Tumalind silently thanked Blavv for her reminder.

'You mean the abuse of the women in Trotnahn, of course.'

'That, and the position given to the wealthy. You saw how those with most wealth hold the highest positions. The issue with the women is slightly different. Almost everywhere, it seems to me, men hold power over women. In Trotnahn it may be worse that in other places, but it isn't unique, is it? Not that that means we should let it go on, of course. But in Trotnahn we saw the wickedness that comes from the worship of coin. That's what we must stop spreading across the whole world if we're ever to live lives of peace and love and worth, isn't it?'

'It's so difficult to believe men would actually set out to put such a plan in place. That they'd knowingly scheme to make most men slaves and all women objects of usage simply to allow those in charge to have empty lives of supreme power.'

'But that's what's about to happen, Okkyntalah, whether you can believe it or not.' Tumalind's words were spoken with deep sincerity.

He looked at his friends. Teldrohn had already accepted what the women said. Sondukal was his usual taciturn self and disinclined to argue. Okkyntalah wanted time to think it over, since he'd be the major assassin.

'Take as long as you need, Okkyntalah. I know you'll understand in the end. But all the time we delay plays into the hands of those who would rule the world by their perverted means. Postponement gives them time to infect more minds amongst mindtalkers and spread their evil. Is that what you want?'

'Give me a little time to be alone and think, Tumalind. I have to be certain, if I'm to kill in cold blood. It may be something I can't do. I don't know.' He wandered into the scrub and Tumalind wondered if she'd asked more of the man than he could give. The whole enterprise depended on his agreement. Without it, the plan would fail, and the whole world be endangered by this pernicious evil from which there would be no recovery.

Chapter 36

ACROSS LAKE QONAHN

He'd never had what he would call a spiritual experience. It was true that sometimes, hunting alone, Okkyntalah would feel at one with the landscape. But he hadn't had one of those moments he'd heard from other worshippers; a sense of oneness with their god. In fact, if he examined his past with honesty, he'd only paid lip-service to the religious part. He was now without belief but the truth was that he'd not really had any to lose.

Following, for him, he realised, had been no more than adherence to rules, the performance of certain rites. Nothing more.

So, why did the killing of evil men in cold blood trouble him? Had Following taught him to value life? On the small rise he'd chosen as the place to search his heart for the answer, he pondered the troubling question Tumalind had set him; well, that Feldrark and Ivdulon had actually asked.

Was it right to kill evil people in order to save other, less bad, people and some truly good people, from planned wickedness?

He'd killed before. Killed those who'd tried to kill him. Killed those who'd threatened death to people he loved and cared for. Killed those who'd mindlessly obeyed a bigoted and closed-minded leader in the city of Mipahnhil. Those last he regretted. They'd been caught between two impossible objects. But the rest had been natural acts. Wild creatures did the same: killed either for food or to defend themselves and their families or packs. So, killing for those reasons were naturally right. He didn't have to enjoy it, or even like it. It was, as Ivdulon had once described something to Tumalind, a necessary evil.

What would happen if he didn't kill these evil minds? Tumalind had explained, in great detail, the arguments put forward by Feldrark and Ivdulon. He had no reason to doubt those experienced and superior minds. Time and again they'd shown themselves to be right. Both had far more experience than him, and Ivdulon, in particular, was clearly very wise. It would be easy to accept that, if they thought it necessary, it must be. But that didn't rid him of his feeling that something might be wrong about this.

He needed to examine how he felt about it, and why. Because if he was to enter this period of murder, he'd better do so without the burden of doubt. Doubt could kill him in an instant. What, exactly, made him believe it might be wrong to kill in cold blood?

No chance would be given to the victim. Those he'd kill would be unaware of the danger, maybe even asleep. True, he'd caught such creatures in the wild and killed them, for food. For food. Could he view another human being in the same way as he viewed any other living creature? He had no qualms about ending the life of an animal he was hunting. He'd have no difficulty stalking and killing a stripecat that lurked near a settlement, threatening the lives of those who lived there.

So, he could kill an animal, not for food and not directly harming the life of an individual at the time. Was this the same? Did the Powerseekers deserve no more consideration? What were the consequences for his fellow humans, his pack, if he failed to defend them against the threats the Powerseekers posed? Tumalind had passed on the fears of Ivdulon, Feldrark and Jodisa. They painted a picture of abject slavery to coin, a scene in which women were devalued as people and made into objects of usage. These minds wanted to rise and become superior, become leaders, become, in fact, all-powerful. Hence the name.

They wanted to destroy all that he and his like held dear. They would take the value of everything important and make it no more than cost in coin. Could you reduce care to coin? Consideration? Fellow-feeling? Loyalty? Wonder in nature? Joy? And love, could that be reduced to the level of mere trade? To make what he shared with Tumalind nothing more than a transaction, a bargain made between two people for convenience, expedience, mutual pleasure? No. It was more, much more than that. His love for Tumalind, and hers for him, was greater than any bargain, more all-encompassing that any deal between merchant and customer. Love like theirs was beyond mere coin, greater than any material value that might be placed on it. The joy they experienced and shared in moments of passion. The simple happiness of being together, active, or sleeping, or sitting. The knowledge that each was in the world and always there for the other. The utter, absolute confidence that here was a soul that cared more for the other than for itself. They'd both demonstrated this. They'd both been tested and, though he'd had doubts, they'd both always come through to do whatever was needed to ensure the safety of their loved one.

And a mother and child: that was another form of love. Would these evil minds make that a transaction? Would parents no longer have their children? Certainly, they'd lose their daughters, since women were clearly seen as no more than goods and chattels. Yes, he'd seen this attitude in other lands, where men excused their behaviour with women as a form of protection of the modesty and sanctity of womanhood. But the argument never stood up to examination. Anyone looking at such a situation through open eyes must see that the protection was there for the man, not the woman. He was 'protecting' her from intrusion by another man. Nothing more than a way for an inadequate man to prevent his mate being made pregnant by another. It really was as simple as that. Control.

Such control was irrelevant once love and respect were brought into the relationship. A woman who was loved had no need, no wish, to go elsewhere for pleasure. That's why

Tumalind resisted the claims of other men on her body. She'd no need of any other man. She had no desire for another.

It was to defend this, as well as all the other values of his community and others of a like type, that they must end the influence and ambitions of these evil minds. It was impossible to convert them to better ways; Ivdulon and a number of other mindtalkers had tried. They were a real threat: they'd overtaken Tumalind's mind and tried to turn her into one of their number. Because they used their minds, there was no way to defeat them other than to stop their mindtalk. And the only way to destroy their mindtalk was to end their lives. Imprisonment, banishment, wouldn't work. There was no other way. None.

He returned to the small camp in the shrubs of this dry and empty land, understanding at least why such greed and want might have grown out of this sparse, hard land. Tumalind rose as he came into view but remained with the others, waiting for him to ease her mind, to remove all doubt from her.

'I will do it.'

It was all she needed. She held him close, hugged him. Kissed him and let him wipe the tears from her cheeks. 'I knew you would. But you had to be certain, didn't you? No man should engage in such activity unless he's absolutely sure of the rightness of it.'

'Convinced, are you, Okkyntalah?'

'I am. I've examined the arguments and come to the same conclusion as Ivdulon and Feldrark. There's no alternative, Sondukal.'

'Good enough for me, then. I'll help.'

He felt Tumalind physically relax in his arms and suddenly understood how much tension had filled her whilst he questioned her decision and her basis for making it.

'I'm sorry. I should've simply taken your word for it, Tumalind.'

'No. No, you shouldn't. There's no question about our love for each other, Okkyntalah, but that doesn't mean you can always trust my judgement. It's right that you reach your own conclusions when such great matters hang on it. I'm glad you had the courage to think it over, to ask your questions and find answers yourself. You'll be the stronger and safer for that. Now, if you'll all excuse us for a while, we have other things to…discuss.'

It struck him, as they rested together, that she'd just loved him as though it might be the last time. He hadn't considered how she might feel about the danger he'd face in the coming sixdays. But, when he examined his own concerns, he realised she must be anxious for him; after all, he felt that way for her.

Together, and separately, they faced the most dangerous and threatening situation they'd ever encountered. Either or both of them could so easily die. And, for Tumalind, in spite of her new defences, death might be better than the alternative. At least he didn't have the dread of corruption to face. He held her close and she wrapped herself protectively around him.

How had the High Priest found a ship to take them across the lake? He'd made no contact with the outside world for days. He'd been with the pilgrimage all that time. So how could he have arranged to have this ship waiting for them? A ship large enough to accommodate the whole party and to take the Godwood on board. A great vessel, larger than any he'd sailed in previously. It seemed impossible.

'I know we sometimes have doubts about Dagla Kaz, Chislanda. But here's the proof he really does talk to Ytraa. How else could he have arranged this ship?'

'I don't know, Aglydron. But I know he's evil. What he made me do…'

'You haven't said. What did he make you do?'

'I can't tell you. I won't, Aglydron. Just…hold me. Please.'

He wanted to know. Questions about his High Priest led to questions about his faith. But Chislanda was unwilling, maybe even unable, to explain what had happened between her and Dagla Kaz. She'd returned from the encounter in a sort of silent state of shock. Since then, she'd shuffled between violent rejection and desperate pleading with him to join with her. For Aglydron, the positive change promised future wonder, and he found himself willing to put up with her occasional rejection. More difficult was the hint of wickedness about the High Priest. That was hard. But, no matter how he tried, Chislanda would say nothing of what Dagla Kaz had done to her. He'd decided to let her be. Time would show him the reality, no doubt.

The Skyfire, fading each day, suffused the sky and sea with a warm rose glow as the sun climbed over the featureless horizon of the great lake. They were surrounded by water, with no sign of the land they'd left behind at first light the previous day. The captain, a tall, gangling woman with short hair and one bare breast bearing a gold ring through the nipple, had promised they'd reach the far shore before next nightfall.

Chislanda nestled close to his chest, trembling. He stroked her back through the soft silk of the tunic. There was little privacy aboard the vessel. Dagla Kaz had his own cabin. The other priests shared a slightly larger cabin on the foredeck but the rest of the pilgrims made shift together in a large dormitory below decks. Small, unglazed squares gave some light and a little air to this room, but it was unbearable during the day and hardly better at night. He and Chislanda spent their time in the open, finding a place to lay their sleepsacks toward the stern. From here they could look up to where the great wheel was manned by two of the ship's hands. A man and woman, bare-chested, and draped in loincloths wound around their waists and tied to overlap at the front.

Their chosen position was uncomfortable when the boat was rocked by motion, but had given them a little privacy in the night, though not enough for him to comfort Chislanda. The day stretched before them with nothing to do but wait until land was sighted. The ship would dock at Llohnrah, at the northern tip of the lake, where they'd take on supplies and unload goods stored beneath the sleeping quarters. A day was to be spent in the town, loading more cargo, some destined for Stornhil and Gatlibahn on their route, but most intended for trade with their island home.

As well as the pilgrims and the mixed crew, there were merchants aboard. Aglydron had heard them in conversation, all of which dwelt on how much coin they might make from the sale of their goods. With them were women, all confined to cabins that boasted luxury and comfort. He'd seen these exotic creatures in glimpses through the doors as the men entered or left.

'Land ho!'

Aglydron wanted to see the new town. Chislanda released her embrace to allow them both to rise. They made their way to the front rails, along the side of the ship that faced northwest as they sailed smoothly over clear water toward the first sign of land.

It seemed no time at all before the town rose above the horizon. Low hills surrounded it and buildings were dotted on some of these. But the bulk of the town lay on a flat apron extending into the lake, with the outlet flowing fast to the eastern side. No buildings lay beyond that bank. It was the outlet, fast and choppy, that they'd travel down through the mountains and eventually to the sea to take them home.

'Home. I miss my island.'

'At least you have a home to go to, Aglydron. Where do I go?'

'With me, of course. Always with me.'

'You'll stay with me even after what Dagla Kaz did?'

He resisted the temptation to ask. 'You're my partner. I'll close away the marriage with Shoarhn. You and me will make a new life together. Find a piece of land. Build a new house and get some animals, plant trees, grow olives and other fruit.'

'You make it all sound so easy.'

'Why would it be otherwise? We'll have to rely on others to begin with. Shoarhn will give us a start with some animals and cuttings from trees. We'll have the support of the settlement we choose. All will be well. Really it will. And, if you'd prefer, we'll choose a place well away from the High Priest so he's no longer tempted by your beauty and will leave us together without the need to share you.'

'It's all so simple for you, isn't it, Aglydron?'

'It's home, Chislanda. The island where I was born. Of course it's simple. That's the way it's always been on Muhnilahm. Could you bear to be in the same settlement as

Shoarhn? It would make life easier, since I'm known by everyone there and will get more support.'

'It doesn't matter to me, Aglydron. Though I've been soiled by Dagla Kaz, you haven't rejected me. And, as far as I know, you haven't had another woman since we've been together.'

'Just you. Though it's not strictly the way of the Follower, it is allowed for couples to be exclusive, and that's what I want for us.'

'And Dagla Kaz?'

'He's the High Priest. You can't count him.'

'I can't discount him, Aglydron. He's damaged me. I'm not the same since he…'

But she'd say no more. Aglydron held her close and she shrugged herself free. He allowed her these changes. She'd soon be back in his arms and eager to share with him, eager to join. That was the way of it now.

He gazed at the fast-approaching town. Would they find more Followers here? Or would they have to pretend they were something else in order to avoid persecution and possible death? Dagla Kaz had issued no new warnings. Perhaps they'd be safe here, after all.

As the ship slowed on its approach to the stone walls of the harbour, the High Priest emerged from his cabin. One of the local Followers left with him, arranging her clothing and quick to find her family. He called them together on deck and waited, stamping impatiently as slower ones or those about other things took time to appear. The ship was ready to tie up at the dockside before all were present on deck and ready for his words. His expression gave away nothing; stern, and gazing over their heads, as usual.

Aglydron felt Chislanda's hand seek and find his and he placed an arm around her shoulders. The next announcement would explain their position and their future on this voyage that, in spite of earlier assurances, Aglydron knew was far from over.

Jodisa sat in the stateroom, her glass of pale wine half drunk. The fruit abandoned on a plate, the bread uneaten.

'I'm no happier about it than you, Jodisa. But it's as it must be. We have no choice. I thought we'd been over this and that you were as convinced as Ivdulon and I?'

'I am. I am, Feldrark. But I'm very fond of Tumalind. And Okkyntalah saved my life on more than one occasion. If you hadn't come along, this might well have been the fruit of his loins, and welcome it would've been.' She smoothed her hands gently over the small rise of her belly.

'I know well enough you love the young man. I do, too. And Tumalind. But they are there and we are here. They're in the place where deeds must be done. There's no other

294

way. You know that.'

'Knowing doesn't make it easier to live with the fact that both of them will probably die in the process of saving the rest of us. I fear for them, Feldrark, that's all.'

'I know. But will starving yourself help? Will denying yourself the sustenance to feed your body, and that of our growing infant, make a dorltah of difference to the outcome for them?'

'No. And I will eat. I have been. It's just that sometimes the enormity of what we're asking of them comes to me, and I feel overwhelmed by the task they face.' She gestured to the door and Feldrark moved and signalled a servant, waiting beyond hearing.

The young lad entered and waited.

'Bring us fresh bread and fruit. This has gone stale in the heat.'

The boy nodded and took away the uneaten food.

Jodisa emptied her glass and Feldrark poured a fresh one for her and another for himself. 'You know Ivdulon suspects it's not good for you to drink whilst pregnant, don't you?'

'She's never carried a baby. And is never likely to.'

'True enough.' He shrugged.

'They'll do what they can, I suppose. And I'll be better placed to help in any way possible if I keep my strength up. I'm sorry, Feldrark. I don't mean to burden you with my worries when you've enough to do running this fabulous city. Forgive me.'

'Nothing to forgive.'

They kissed. When the servant returned with fresh food, he opened the door a fraction, then retired until it was seemly for him to enter. Feldrark thanked him for the food and sent him to stand outside the door to await further instructions.

Jodisa, relaxed and hungry, understood the significance of the servant's proximity and chose a different topic of conversation as they ate.

'So, what are we to call this infant and heir, Feldrark? A name from the city or one from the island?'

'That's a matter of great consequence. I think we must consult the populace, don't you?'

'Only if we're going to name our child with a string of names so long it'll take a day to read them out!'

'Perhaps, then, we should simply have one from Litkala and another from Muhnilahm? That way he, or she, unites the two communities even more strongly.'

'Agreed. Now all we have to do is select from those and see which two link in a pleasing way.'

'About four months? So, only another five to decide. Enough time, Jodisa?'

'Oh. I think we'll manage.'

They laughed together. But, still, at the back of her mind, lurked concern for her friends who now moved into great peril so far from material help.

Chapter 37

SEEKING EVIL

The scrub and sparse vegetation had finally given way to trees and lush grass, as they turned around and entered the forest west of the small lake feeding water to Trotnahn. Now they were in place to live off the land whilst they found ways to locate and kill the evil minds in the town.

Okkyntalah stood up to his waist in water at the edge of the lake, waiting for the small deer to turn away so he could move and fell it for their next meal. It surprised him that no citizens were on or around the lake, but their absence was a real advantage, allowing his party to remain in the woods with little risk of discovery. He moved forward, silent and full of concentration. The animal leapt as he reached it, but a single spear thrust into the body caused it to shudder just twice before it collapsed. He draped it over his shoulders, waded to shore, and turned to signal Shaulah to follow him. Her loss left a deep hole and he shook his head as he made his way back to their camp. How easy to slip back into an old habit.

After their meal, the discussion fell to who should go with him.

'The fewer, the better. I've a good idea where I'll find him. Tumalind has made sure he's still around. The only real problem is scaling the walls, and, to be honest, that should be child's play.'

'You need back up and someone to stand watch whilst you do what must be done. In fact, there's no reason you have to kill them all yourself, Okkyntalah, is there?'

The relief of that suggestion was immense. He clasped Teldrohn's arm in gratitude.

'I'm lighter and quicker than Teldrohn. Let me act as look out.'

'A woman in Trotnahn, Blavv? You'd either have to be covered from head to foot, which would make the climb impossible, or entirely naked and taken and abused by any passing man. No. In this place, it must be men. But thank you for your offer.'

'I feel so useless just waiting.'

'Tumalind needs company, and the protection of someone with sword skills, Blavv.'

That brightened her. She nodded her agreement.

'Three on us'll be best. We're all used to movin' quiet.'

'You're sure, Sondukal. Those on this mission must be certain what we do is right.'

'Like I said. Good enough for Ivdulon and Feldrark; good enough for me. I'm no philosopher. I'll teck their word on it.'

This was even better news. Okkyntalah felt he had a greater chance with the Litkalan guide along.

The moon had just entered the first quarter, so would augment the stars, and the Skyfire had already risen, though now diminished with each appearance.

'Funny, it's been there for so long now, it'll seem odd when it's gone.'

'Light enough for us but not so bright we'll be obvious.'

'That's true, Teldrohn. Shall we?'

They embraced and kissed their women as Sondukal and Kallohn looked on. Tumalind and Blavv would remain in camp, but Kallohn insisted she go as far as the edge of the forest with the men so she'd know if some problem delayed their start.

The darkness under the trees was deep, but occasional gaps in the canopy allowed them to travel in the right direction. Once they reached open ground, Kallohn stopped. She'd wait, in sight of the walls, until they'd scaled the barrier.

Teldrohn clambered up first, the block-built structure no defence against a skilled climber. He was on top quickly. Okkyntalah followed and then Sondukal. They could see no sign of Kallohn under the trees, but signalled and descended to the streets.

They were in a strange part of the town and had to get their bearings. The obvious landmark was the great hall where they'd met the Senior. It was the tallest building, and placed more or less centrally. They found it easily enough using streets that were deserted at this hour. The only sounds were the occasional cry from a sleeper, the scurry of rhaats and the muted crying of a woman.

From the hall, Sondukal led the group back to the room they'd occupied. It was from there that Okkyntalah, quite fortuitously, had followed Vavak on just one occasion. Whether the man's destination on that particular journey had been his home or not, he had no way of knowing. But it was the best clue they had.

Again, no one trod the streets. The town slumbered, safe in the knowledge that the locked gates protected them. For too long, isolation had given them security and they were unprepared for any form of invasion. They slept the sleep of the unaware, rather than the secure.

The house stood in a row of similar dwellings, side by side with no gaps between and no access to any rear entrance that may or may not exist. Two storeys, it sported openings on both levels at each side of a central door. All, of course, were shuttered. That the door was locked came as no surprise.

Teldrohn took a collection of small implements from the pouch at his belt and examined the lock as closely as the dim illumination allowed. He inserted one of the tools, twisting it carefully. Nothing happened. He paused and considered. Wiggled the instrument again and then withdrew it to replace it with another. Slowly, with great care, he moved the small tool. A distinct click told them something had moved. They waited for any sign of wakefulness but all remained silent. The door opened with a mild scraping sound as it rubbed over the packed earth floor but the hinges were well greased.

Inside in a trice, they closed the door behind them. Pitch black. No knowledge of the layout of the room. Okkyntalah moved slowly, hands outstretched, toward the window. Slim gaps in the shutters outlined the opening. He caught a foot against a sharp edge on the floor but stifled the inevitable cry of pain. Previous experience in the room they'd occupied helped him open the shutters. The dim light from outside was enough for them to move about. An inner door stood ajar in the back wall but no one occupied the room they were in.

Exploration showed them an opening that led to a flight of stairs. Wooden, they creaked at some of the treads. Sondukal remained at the lower window as look out. But Teldrohn and Okkyntalah eventually made the second storey and found a small stage bearing a couple of openings. From one there was silence. From the other, the sound of breathing. Two people.

The short period spent in Llohnrah had been a welcome break. No tension. No danger of execution merely for being a Follower; the people were welcoming of all humanity. And no threat of Chislanda being taken by the High Priest again, after the last time.

She'd come back to Aglydron in a state of shock, pained and unable to speak without sobbing so that her words were hidden by the power of her distress. He had no way to deal with this, other than to hold her close and try to comfort her with words and gentle caresses. Her walk from the High Priest's cabin had been slow and apparently painful.

For the moment, Aglydron allowed the soft motion of the ship and his gentle touch to calm her. What had happened, why was she was so deeply distressed? But this was the High Priest; their leader, their guide, the chosen man who spoke with Ytraa. Dagla Kaz can't have done anything too terrible, surely?

Chislanda must simply have disliked his form of joining. There could be no questioning the High Priest, especially since he now regularly communed with Ytraa. The man was clearly God's chosen and therefore above suspicion and censure. As Ytraa's representative in the world, he must, must, must be without fault. It could be no other way.

And, yet, the woman he loved lay sobbing in his arms, somehow distressed after a time with the High Priest. It was impossible to know what had happened, to understand why she might be so distressed.

In time, as dawn slowly paled the sky, and the Skyfire turned above to begin its long setting below the horizon, she calmed into a sort of sleep. She still slept when daylight

299

brightened the surface of the wide river they now sailed. Large trees hugged both banks of the waterway, the cries of wild animals sounding from the forest all around them. Overhead, the wide green wings of birds swept cloudless skies in search of prey. On the shores, huge black crocodiles slumbered or sauntered to the water to bathe, lazy in the current. In the branches, purple monkeys screamed and mocked as they sought fruit and settled their short fights of status.

Aglydron was stiff from sitting still for so long. But he wouldn't move until she woke naturally from a sleep that must be healing. When she did, he'd ask her what had happened. Only then might he solve the dilemma of the contrast between the purity of the High Priest and the evidence of Chislanda's real distress. A misunderstanding. It must be no more than that. It could be nothing else.

A crew member beckoned him, her figure a reminder that they sailed with heathens. He roused Chislanda, reluctant to disturb her but understanding they were wanted on the main deck. She woke and stared about wildly, as if in search of some unspecified threat, gathering her tunic close, protective of her womanhood.

'Come. We've to go to the main deck.'

He helped her rise and stretched his limbs to ease the aches of stasis. She clung to him and moved stiffly as they approached where all now gathered about the High Priest.

'Do not keep me waiting, man. I have important business.' Dagla Kaz directed his scorn at Aglydron and then turned to his task.

'We sail now through this great forest. Our captain, who will be our guide for the time it takes to reach the sea, tells me wild creatures dwell in the trees and water. Dangerous animals that prey on man. You're advised to stay on board ship at all times, even when we land from time to time to collect fresh water and food. No one is to leave without my express permission. Is that understood?'

The reply was a murmured agreement, not without some resentment, but Aglydron made his voice loud and compliant, eager to show the High Priest he had at least one obedient Follower.

'Good. Now, you've all witnessed the decline of the Skyfire. It's my understanding it will now rapidly diminish to the state of a bright but fading star. Do not be alarmed. This signal from Ytraa has done its work. In uniting the various gatherings of Followers, we have been given new strength. We may now combine to convert the heathens of this world to our religion; the only faith that is true. Before us stands a great and glorious task: to make all in the world subjects of Ytraa, to turn every soul that now exists into a Follower.

'What say you to that?'

The cheer that resulted wasn't as loud, long or full of conviction as the High Priest

300

clearly expected. Again, Aglydron's voice was raised above the others. Chislanda looked at him with what he thought was disapproval, but he wouldn't reduce his fervour because of the doubts of someone new to the faith.

'I'd expected a more enthusiastic response. I confess I am disappointed.'

'Mebbie we're just tired, Dagla Kaz. Bin on this pilgrimage a long time now, y'know.'

He glanced at Corphanda and nodded. 'And, of course, you no longer have your duty as a caretaker of our Virgin Gifts. Must make you feel unimportant, I suppose. But don't let such considerations dim your zeal for the faith. We are Followers. We've done a great deed here. To travel over foreign lands, evade the wickedness of heathens, cheat death at the hands of those who fear and hate us, to discover and reclaim the Godwood; these are wondrous tasks indeed. We are blessed to be alive in such auspicious times. Our children will respect and praise us for what we've achieved. And those who come after us will tell great tales of our bravery and perseverance.'

'We're not home yet.'

The High Priest glared at Tarruss, the giant who'd fought, protected, hunted and been a stalwart all through the pilgrimage. For a moment, Aglydron thought Dagla Kaz would challenge or scorn the big man, but his frown turned to a beatific smile.

'How right you are, Tarruss. We are, indeed, not yet home. But Ytraa assures me our troubles now are over. We'll have plain sailing now until we reach our island home. It's true that we must remain vigilant and alert to dangers from outside, but I'm confident we have the worst behind us. We sail to glory and acclaim. And we may increase that respect from our fellow Followers by converting those we find along the way. I propose we start with members of the crew.'

'Try if you like, mate. But you'll get short shrift from us. Why not have a go at the coin-lovin' merchants instead? Their souls really need savin'. The sailor who'd called from astride one of the spars, was mending a sail as the ship ploughed through calm waters.

Dagla Kaz glared at the man but nodded. He was silent a moment, his face reflecting some thought that troubled him. He nodded again, as if agreeing with some suggestion.

'The merchants have their own religion, a faith as powerful as Following, and one that isn't so different. In fact, I'm holding meetings with these wise and generous men to discover where our thoughts, beliefs and concerns might overlap. No. I think we may safely leave the merchants to their own devices for now. But the heathen crew will provide us with the opportunity to try our skills at conversion. Our chances will be few, as we won't be staying in one place for long. So, I urge you all to make an effort to engage with these poor souls aboard. Teach them, educate them in our ways, join with them freely, for they're men and women just like us and our faith requires that we join all we can. Do I have your support in this fine venture?'

The cry of agreement was heartier this time, but only, Aglydron suspected, because the people wanted to end the High Priest's talk and take breakfast. The suggestion that they join with the men and women of the crew, many of whom were young and fit, found approval with a good number of the Followers. He, of course, would remain exclusive to Chislanda. He held her close in reassurance and she gripped his arm tightly as the gathering dispersed.

Alone, awaiting the call to breakfast on the main deck, he asked her the reason for her distress.

'Dagla Kaz is a wicked and evil man, Aglydron. He did things to me…'

'A misunderstanding, Chislanda? Perhaps an accident due to passion?' He wouldn't correct her harshly. He'd be kind; allow her to come to terms with her error in time, as she would.

'If you think…' She stared at him with a look of such disdain that he knew he had a difficult task to convince her of her mistake. As she continued to speak, he ceased to listen to words too close to blasphemy.

He'd be gentle with her, treat her with love and consideration for now, show her she was wrong only when she'd had a chance to reach a proper understanding of her situation. At that time, of course, she must be punished for her sacrilege. But, at present, she was too upset to see the reality of the situation. Her confusion made her misinterpret what had really happened. Time, and his gentle persuasion, would bring her back to proper belief and behaviour. He'd show her his love in gentle joining, demonstrate the rightness of their faith with care and kindness, deepen her trust with compassion.

'Have you heard me, Aglydron? Have you heard anything I've said?'

'Of course. Leave it for now. Time will show us how to deal with this. Just be happy that I love you, Chislanda. I'll always protect you from evil.'

'But not from your beloved High Priest.'

'I don't think we need protection from the man who leads and guides us.'

Her look of total incomprehension made Aglydron realise he had a greater challenge than he'd thought. Still, Ytraa would provide, and faith would guide him until she came to her senses again.

'Let's eat, shall we? I'm starving. Aren't you?' He turned away from her, grasping her hand and gently dragging her behind him to the deck and breakfast.

The farm held an air of neglect, but the animals had been tended and none seemed to be suffering. Shoarhn thanked her helpers. Dahrlahg had done well, in spite of the distraction caused by the sudden appearance of her betrothed, Pentryil. The two ex-slaves had taken part in the struggle and the woman had suffered a wound to her shoulder but was able to do some work as she recovered.

'I'm sorry. I never discovered your names before all the fighting started...'

The female slave bowed her head, submissive, blonde locks trailing over her shoulders. 'I am Lallamdahl and my man is Tukladohn.'

'He can't speak for himself?'

'They cut out his tongue as a child, because he cried too loudly when they raped him.'

Shoarhn flinched as she glanced at the man, turned away at the haunted look in his eyes. 'I'm home now, Lallamdahl, so you can rest and heal fully.'

'I'm fine. It doesn't hurt, Paltra.'

'I'm not Paltra. You're free, remember?'

The woman smiled a little self-consciously. 'I was a slave from the age of seven. It takes getting used to, this freedom. Thank you, Shoarhn. I'm willing to work for my keep.'

'I know. But now I'm your employer, so will you please do as I say and take some rest? You deserve it after all you've done. In any case, if you don't do as I say, I'll set Aklon on you.'

'Oh, very frightening. Will he gently love me to death?'

'Please, Lallamdahl. I just want you to have the chance to fully recover. Please?'

'If you insist. But only for a couple of days. And I'll help around the house. Is that to your liking...Paltra?'

Shoarhn tried to look stern but couldn't avoid laughing at her pretence of servility. 'I'll take a switch to your backside if you...'

It was too much, too soon. She burst into tears at the pretended threat. Tukladohn embraced her, staring with fear at Shoarhn.

'I'm so sorry. Not ready for that sort of play. Understandable. Please. I'll never, ever beat you. We're equals now. The only difference is that I own the farm, not you. You now work freely as part of the team running it. Please don't ever think I'll hit or punish you.'

She calmed quickly and, embarrassed, went to tidy another room in the house, where she could recover her composure properly. Tukladohn nodded at Shoarhn, his eyes still uncertain, and followed his woman into the other room.

'It's difficult, isn't it? Keeping the balance between humour and necessary control?'

'You do it well, Shoarhn, as you do everything. Only such testing will display the readiness of ex-slaves and indicate how far they have stepped on the road to true freedom. No harm done, and probably another step taken for Lallamdahl. Now, our journey has been hard. We have been travelling and living in the wild for long enough. Do you have a place I can rest my broken body so I may again share your delights when you have finished your duties?'

She reached high and ruffled Aklon's hair, kissed him. Taking his shoulders in her hands, she turned him on the spot and propelled him into her bedroom.

'Lie there, and don't move until I return to feed you. I want you fully repaired and ready to pleasure me as soon as possible. Rest is what you still need. Take it. And no arguments!'

He stopped the words about to issue from his mouth and kissed her instead. But she insisted on making him prone and then, to his evident disappointment, left him alone.

Dahrlahg remained in the kitchen area, scrubbing some of the cooking pots. She turned as Shoarhn came back. 'Do you want some tlathan?'

'That would be nice. So, does Pentryil approve?' She nodded at the girl.

Dahrlahg brushed a dribble of water from her breast and smiled. 'He says he won't be able to keep his hands off me until we're married and that I'd better make it quick or he'll be taking me before he should.'

'I'm not surprised. How has he taken the news about what the priest did to you?'

She held her arms close about her, crossing them over her chest and clasping them. 'I haven't told him.'

'You must, Dahrlahg. He'll hear from others and it's best he learns from you. And sooner rather than later. In fact, go and explain right now. Until it's out in the open and you know how he feels, you'll not be able to settle.'

'Can I bring him here, tell him in front of you?'

'Of course. Do it now.'

The girl left and Shoarhn wondered just how mature the girl's betrothed might be about the issue. Dahrlahg deserved sympathy and she hoped her young man would give that and prove his love by accepting that the rape was nothing to do with her, that she was entirely blameless. But it was yet another indication of the changes happening on the island. So many things they had taken for granted, had lived their lives by, were no longer true. It was hard for them all.

Soon, Aklon would be recovered and fit again. He'd then insist on touring the island to rid it of the remaining violent extremists. She could make light of things, now she was at home, but the truth was that she wouldn't be really at peace until Aklon's duties about the island were complete.

Once he was rested, she'd ask him to contact Tumalind. She hadn't heard from her daughter for some time and knew only that her situation was still difficult, maybe even dangerous, but she had no details. It would be good to learn the truth. At least, she hoped it would.

Chapter 38

THE FIRST KILLING

The sound of two breathing. He'd hoped to find the man alone. This complicated things both practically and morally. Killing an evil mind was one thing. Killing an innocent, something else entirely.

Teldrohn entered the room before Okkyntalah could stop him. The soldier found and opened the shutters without a sound. By the inner wall, a bedstead, luxurious and softly clad in silk-covered cushions, took up half the room. Vavak slept exposed. Beside him, hands bound to the wooden frame, lay a woman, her back striped by the switch dropped at her side.

Okkyntalah didn't hesitate. Plunged his hunting knife deep into the ready chest. Vavak made a small sound of alarm, convulsed once, and then lay still. The spurt of blood from the wound showered all but ceased almost at once. He cut free the woman's arms and placed a hand over her mouth to stop the scream that would come on waking.

'Your tormenter's dead. Please, when I release your mouth, make no sound, or I'll be forced to silence you. Do you understand?'

She nodded. He released her mouth. She stared in silent horror at the body by her side and moved from it.

'We must go now. Will you be safe, if we leave you here, or do you have to go to some other place?'

She rose from the bed, crossed to the window, and looked out.

'I've time to escape, I think. Who are...do you require pleasure before I go?'

Okkyntalah sighed. 'We wish you safe and free from harm. Who we are doesn't matter. Come. We'll leave together and go our separate ways.'

He led the group downstairs and found Sondukal still waiting by the door. They closed it behind them and the woman accompanied them in silence down the first street. At the end, she bowed to them, kissed each in turn and walked away without a word. The men retraced their steps to the wall.

They returned without incident. Had been fortunate. So many things might have prevented them completing this first killing. Now they'd done it, the townsfolk would know a murderer dwelt among them. Would the woman speak? It seemed unlikely.

Sondukal was less sure they should have left her to her own devices. 'In a place like this, where women are treated so bad, they might do owt to 'er to make 'er talk.'

'She believed she was in no danger as long as she could escape the house and return

305

to wherever she lives without being spotted.'

'Mebbie. But I don't like it.'

'It's done. I'd not have an innocent life taken without reason.'

'Could've brought 'er with us.'

Okkyntalah had no need to counter that argument. A simple look conveyed his thoughts and Sondukal, his face illuminated by the small campfire, nodded agreement, looking sheepish for his unconsidered suggestion.

The women were relieved to see them and brewed a version of the local tlathan, made from leaves gathered in the forest. Sharper than the drink they were accustomed to, it provided a refreshing alternative after their night's activity. They'd washed off their victim's blood in the waters of the lake and now dried by the flames. Kallohn offered to stand watch as they slept.

Above, the Skyfire glowed a dull shrinking flame that signalled approaching dawn. They'd killed their first victim. Now the real work must begin. Vavak had been easy; he'd been known, his location remembered from Okkyntalah's previous visit. The subjects of their remaining killings must be discovered and their whereabouts established. Only Tumalind had the means to find them, by entering the dangerous place she called the Dark Space in the world of mindtalk. It was a place they all feared and one that she must dread most.

⁂

They hadn't joined since Chislanda had last returned from the High Priest's cabin and, when Aglydron attempted to make love with her that night, she resisted, pushing him away and turning from him, her body trembling.

'What's this, Chislanda? You refuse to join before Ytraa'

She mumbled something he couldn't make out and he urged her to face him again. Reluctantly, she turned, her face streaked with tears.

'What is it?'

'I'm hurt there. You'll make it worse if you enter me.' She'd say no more and he held her until she fell into uneasy sleep, but he lay awake for long after, wondering what might have caused such injury. The more he contemplated, the more certain he was that the High Priest must be responsible, since Dagla Kaz had been her last partner in joining. It had been an accident, of course. The High Priest would never harm a woman in the sacred act of joining. No, some unintended mishap had occurred, that's all.

The morning brought the obvious solution and he found Myllthlan early. She returned with him to Chislanda and examined her. The healing was done simply and without fuss, as always with Myllthlan. But they excluded him from their discussion about how such an injury might have been caused.

306

When the healer came to tell him all was well, she nodded toward Dagla Kaz. 'If you're able, you should prevent that man from joining with Chislanda ever again.' Her expression showed contempt for the High Priest and Aglydron was minded to put her in her place. But she'd healed his woman and he'd no wish to alienate her. Instead, he mumbled his thanks and returned to Chislanda.

'I'll make up for last night once it gets dark, Aglydron. I promise.' But she'd say no more about what had caused her harm, so he must guess. It had to be something to do with Dagla Kaz but Aglydron was convinced the High Priest couldn't deliberately cause damage; not without good reason.

During the night, the river wound its way through the forest and now flowed wide, deep and strong with trees overhanging the northern bank whilst the south shore passed barren and rocky. In the distance, the peaks of the Mountains of Geldakq rose into the sky along the horizon, marking the route they would take once they reached the Gap of Aagtaz. They'd leave Choshinahm and follow the river to the sea through Deztal, a land reputedly uninhabited other than at the coastal ports.

Time now passed slowly, with nothing for the Followers to do but occupy themselves with games, conversation and daily devotions. Most lived on the open deck, sheltering below only when sudden rains came. The sun soon dried everything and they returned to the fresh air again.

There were few children amongst the party. Aglydron had set himself the challenge of counting their number, simply as a way to occupy some of his time. The crew were easy. Thirteen men and fifteen women, including the captain, all relatively young and most sufficiently attractive to make desirable partners for joining. There'd been much interaction between Followers and crewmembers. Followers who indulged claimed to be attempting to convert the heathens. The crew needed no excuse; ready to join whenever the chance arose. Aglydron wondered at the sincerity of some Followers but said nothing, knowing that, if not for Chislanda, he'd have been equally keen on joining with those fine figures.

The Followers numbered seventy men, seventy-four women and five children. Five priests; three female and two male, four of them High Priests. He wondered whether such a small party of Followers had ever been blessed with such a large contingent of priests before. But circumstance, rather than design, had gathered this community together.

Aglydron pondered: random circumstance, or had Ytraa been involved, in the same way that Ytraa had designed and planned the happenings that had brought him along on this pilgrimage?

He considered those events; the capture of Jodisa and their difficult voyage together. Myllthlan's courage in leading their escape from Ylcrat as the fire mountain tried to destroy them. What had happened to the inhabitants of that small island? He shrugged them off; their fate irrelevant, since they were heathens. He recalled the slow voyage to Mipahnhil, the death of Chislanda's boy from a snakebite and his own forced partnering with her. The love they'd forged then, joining to fill her belly with a new child to replace the lost son, had outlived all other incidents of the pilgrimage.

They'd escaped, with help from Feldrark, who he'd been rightly convinced would rob them of their Virgin Gift. And that remarkable young slave, Malarhah, had helped too. She'd been a real loss. Okkyntalah's song of praise had surprised and moved him at the welcome party in the hostelry outside Litkala. He laughed as he recalled how they'd dreaded entering that notorious city only to discover it the most civilised and wonderful place.

'Dorltah for them, Aglydron.' Chislanda had moved close, leaving the group of women she'd been chatting with on deck. He held her hand and felt her responsive clasp. She was still entirely his, no matter what had happened between her and the High Priest.

'I was just remembering all that's happened on this pilgrimage. Do you remember when Jodisa was near death in the boat and we…something happened? I can't quite get at that memory. Can you?'

'I wasn't there, you know. But you all have difficulty with it. Something happened, but none of you can recall any detail. Only that some woman helped you; that's all. Do you remember the journey down from the palace in Litkala in that cart thing? I've never been so frightened in all my life!'

'And I thought you were unaffected. Mind you, with all those people shouting and threatening us, I'm not surprised I didn't realise.'

'You were so strong for me then, Aglydron. I've always been grateful for your constant love and loyalty during those hard days, you know. I'll always be faithful because of that.'

'It's not something many Followers try.'

She smiled. 'In Mipahnhil, we married but never promised to remain faithful, that is, exclusive, to our partners. Many women found their husbands couldn't provide the children that would give them added status and so took other men to their beds. And I had to take you to form a new life…'

She tensed. The loss of that unformed infant still haunted her. He enfolded her and stroked her back to comfort her and slowly she relaxed and lifted her tunic to wipe away the tears. 'Sorry. Still hurts.'

He examined his own feelings and found there lurked a sadness he hadn't previously acknowledged. It surprised him a little. Children hadn't meant much to him in the past, except Tumalind. And she wasn't even the fruit of his loins but the offspring of Dagla Kaz who'd taken his wife at prayer.

So, the High Priest had joined with both the women who mattered to him. Was there some personal reason? Did Dagla Kaz simply desire the same women as him? Or had he some other cause? Perhaps he recognised Aglydron's piety. Perhaps the High Priest paid him the respect of an equal by blessing his women. Yes. That must be it. Dagla Kaz secretly understood that Aglydron was his equal in the eyes of Ytraa. A man of great devotion and adherence to the laws of the faith. That's why he'd blessed him by joining with the women he loved and therefore acknowledging the sanctity of their union.

'You're very thoughtful again, Aglydron. What goes on in there?' She tapped his head lightly.

'Nothing really, Chislanda. Just thinking how nice it would be to have our child once we're back on the island, that's all.'

'And that's "nothing"?'

'You know what I mean.'

'You're a funny man, Aglydron. Odd, but I love you all the same. And I'll be proud to have your children, once we're settled somewhere safe and permanent.'

Permanent. A word with real meaning. He was abruptly aware of how much he longed for such permanence after so long spent journeying. To settle down, farm the land, grow things, and, yes, father a child, children, and share them with Chislanda. A future worth achieving. And now it wouldn't be long.

The captain estimated their voyage would take a little over six more sixdays. The Skyfire would have vanished from sight by then, of course, but its memory would remain in the minds of the islanders. There would be celebrations on the Plain of Ytraa, the carving of the new Godwood into the representation of Ytraa, and its lifting onto the monument. What joy, what ecstasy, to see that symbol so enhanced. After that, the difficult meeting with Shoarhn, the formal parting from her and the wedding with Chislanda, the finding and claiming of land and the building of their house with help from neighbours. All would be well, all would be wonderful. And only six more sixdays at sea before the dream could become reality.

'Dreaming, Aglydron?'

'Of our future. Our lives together will be long and fruitful. I know it. I'm blessed by Ytraa.'

She raised her eyebrows briefly but she couldn't yet understand. Still new to the faith, she would learn in time how right he was. Of course she would.

The first killing had proved simple. Tumalind knew that the rest wouldn't be so easy. In fact, as the numbers increased, Okkyntalah would face more difficulty. Word of the danger would quickly spread amongst targeted subjects. There was nothing she could do about that, of course. But it did mean that the sooner they disposed of the evil minds here in Trotnahn, the better. They'd still face even greater danger across the land when they reached the Monolith of Kro Lat, of course. But she would worry about that problem when they had to. For now, it was enough that they must rapidly identify, locate and kill the local evil minds of the Powerseekers.

Okkyntalah and Teldrohn were still asleep. Sondukal had woken and gone hunting for food. Kallohn slept in readiness for her role as watcher again in the coming night. Tumalind touched Blavv on her arm.

'I'm going to venture into the Dark Space. Will you watch me and alert Ivdulon, please?'

Blavv paled, but nodded and held Tumalind's hand for reassurance. No need for words. Both knew the dangers she faced in that black and violent place. Ivdulon's technique for masking her identity and shielding her mind from the Powerseekers had been put into practice only once; when Tumalind had deliberately entered the Dark Space alone to test it. It had protected her for that short visit, but she had no knowledge of how well it would defend her against a longer intrusion. Now she would find out. Much depended on her own strength of mind and determination. But, as Ivdulon had said, it also rested on her essential innocence and goodness, the fact that she was uncorrupted and wished to remain that way. The promise of huge quantities of coin and unlimited sex with strangers had no hold on her and that made her more difficult to corrupt.

The Dark Space was a world like no other she'd known. Describing mindtalk to someone without the gift was like trying to explain the concept of colour to one who'd always been blind. But she'd tried to make it real for Okkyntalah, knowing he would be less concerned if he understood the reality than he might be if he had to imagine it from his limited knowledge.

'It's always better to know than to be ignorant and make up your own guesses.'

She loved him for his basic common sense and down-to-earth attitude about things over which he had no influence. It made the man she loved even more attractive to her.

'I liken mindtalk to that feeling you sometimes get when someone either says something about a thought you've just had or asks about a person you've just been thinking about. You know what I mean. For a moment you're convinced they've been in your mind, read the thoughts there.'

'Oh, I get that all the time from you. You'd be amazed how often you say something about an idea I've been considering.'

That didn't surprise her.

'Actually, I had the same from Jodisa. Especially on the boat when I looked at her.

310

You know I was attracted to her physically, of course. I mean, she's so similar to you it would be impossible for me not to find her appealing.'

'And, yet you chose me, Okkyntalah.'

'I love you, Tumalind. With Jodisa it was always simple lust. Since you have her looks and I also love you, there's no choice, is there?'

'I think I'm being complemented but…anyway, that's not the point. Mindtalk is like what we were saying, but you can do it when you want and with the people you choose. It really is your mind talking to the mind of another.'

'Do you hear them?'

'It's not really a voice. It's more a sensation that becomes words as thought. With gifted mindtalkers, like Ivdulon, you can also sense taste and smell and touch, even see through their eyes. I've managed to get inside the mind of one or two without being detected and seen what they see. I used that when they took me to Ov-Bebna. It helped me a lot to survive those first few moments with the Uhmbard, actually.'

'But you could get caught, inside the mind of another?'

'If you're not vigilant. But don't worry about my danger, Okkyntalah, you've enough of your own to worry about and Ivdulon's given me tricks to use to defend myself. Anyway, back to the Dark Space. In there it really is black. Not a lack of light, like when you look at things, but an absence of any good feelings, a sensation of continuous spying as you pass through the…cloud, I suppose, of thoughts. When you're seeking a mind, you send out feelers of thought and somehow make connections. I don't know how it works, but I can tell you that you feel it as soon as you make contact. In the normal mindtalk world, it's a light and welcome sensation.

'In the Dark Space, those feelers of thought get twisted and entwined with others searching for vulnerable minds. You rarely come across a single mind in there and all those you encounter are dark and evil. Many belong to men in search of sexual victims. There are a few women, of course, but they're far fewer and their thoughts and searches are mostly about revenge and the acquisition of wealth.

'Once you've made a connection, you're in danger of being dragged into a mess of other minds that then try to take you over. Often it's just chaos. But sometimes they combine their efforts and gang up on you to subdue and control you. That's what happened to me in the market place in Trotnahn. I was unprepared; I was just venturing into mindtalk to ask Ivdulon whether she knew about some of the things we were being shown. Curiosity, nothing more. But the sheer number and proximity of the Powerseekers overwhelmed me at once. They took me over, made me collapse and then delved into every part of my mind, trying to find my weaknesses. They made me see things I could never describe, Okkyntalah. The depravity, the vile acts and the utter greed

311

I felt was so distressing I don't think I could've escaped it without the help of strong and good minds.'

'You can't do it, Tumalind. It's too dangerous.'

'We've been over this, Okkyntalah. I must do it. For the sake of the whole world. And I'm now prepared and protected. I'm not saying there's no danger, but I'm no longer as vulnerable as that first time. And, having been there and seen what can happen, I'm ready. I'll never be in that situation I was in the market place again. I'm stronger, wiser, more experienced and I've ways to defeat attacks. You're not to worry about me. I'll be fine.'

Clearly, he'd worry about her, in exactly the same way as she would worry about him. But he accepted that she must do what she must do. And, now, she was ready to take the first step. Ready to enter the Dark Space and find the next mind for Okkyntalah to kill. It wasn't a task she relished. The idea of taking life went so utterly against her nature that she felt revulsion just thinking about it, but Ivdulon and Feldrark had convinced her of the necessity. It was the only way to solve a problem that would otherwise infect the whole world with a disease that would destroy everything worthwhile and decent. She had no choice. The Powerseekers dwelt within the Dark Space. So, she must enter the Dark Space, regardless of the danger.

Chapter 39

ENTERING THE DARK SPACE

Aklon awoke to bright sunshine streaming through the oblong of the unshuttered window with Shoarhn still sleeping beside him. The past days with her had been wonderful. To relax with her, enjoy her company in secure and uncomplicated circumstances. But now it was time to make the final effort, to rid the island of those who would destroy the promised peace and harmony that he'd dreamed of for so long.

He rose on one arm and looked down at the sleeping form of the woman beside him. She lay completely relaxed, one leg extended from the cover and an arm thrown out to one side. Pale natural linen rested like a second skin against the curves and valleys of her body, leaving honey skin uncovered from the ends of her black tresses to the upper slopes of her full breasts. He shifted slightly, wanting to see her as she was before he left, his movement disturbing the cover to expose more of her undiminished beauty. The scar was healing well. He traced it with his fingertip from shoulder to the rise of her breast.

'Keep moving down. I wouldn't dream of interrupting that caress.'

He bent, kissed her, and they loved again. Their loving mingled love and lust, as it always should.

'I know you think you must go, Aklon. And I know I have to lose you once again. But come back often and be safe. I still have Tumalind to worry over. I'd like to not have to worry over you as well.'

He'd connected with Tumalind the previous evening, at Shoarhn's request. He'd put the questions Shoarhn had directed, and given her the answers both agreed on, mixing honesty with protection of Shoarhn's peace of mind. He would be called upon to help in Tumalind's great ordeal from time to time, of course. But there was no reason Shoarhn should be burdened with the danger facing her daughter, until that risk ended with the completion of her task.

They ate together and Delbon and Choryssa arrived to meet him and to say goodbye to Shoarhn. With them were Patrilha, Hyllahn and Phrysilda, who'd fought with them the whole time. Like many of the Few, they'd all chosen to declare their rejection of the faith, to rebel against the falsehoods of the past, by living in their skin, their belts worn only for their practical ability to carry weapons.

Shoarhn maintained some modesty, adopting a short loincloth wrapped about her shapely hips. Aklon continued to wear the tabard. He understood that, naked, he was even more desired by many women and he wanted to place some small barrier to that lust whilst away from Shoarhn. She didn't question his faithfulness to her since he'd declared it. He'd told her it was so and she'd explained that she felt the same way and neither doubted that that was the way they would live now.

He kissed her, belted on his scabbard and replaced the hunting knife into its sheath, slung the long bow and its replenished quiver across his shoulders, and led the group away for the planned tour of the island. As they left the town, he turned and saw her still watching. He waved and moved out of her sight, at once feeling he'd lost the most important thing in life. But the job had to be done, and he, as leader of the Cause, must do it. There would be no peace until they'd rid it of those violent extremists, or converted them to peaceful acceptance of the changes.

Patrilha strode beside him, her sexual indifference to him a comfort and a barrier to the threatened intimacy of Phrysilda and Hyllahn. It would be difficult to have their constant attention and he hoped some of the strong and good men in the troop would satisfy their physical needs. The faith had driven a healthy appetite for sex in most, made it a daily duty that had long been an excuse for self-indulgence and promiscuity. He had no quarrel with the people enjoying themselves but he also understood, first hand, how it might become destructive if unrequited love should play a part. Jealousy and lust could be important factors in the peace between neighbours, without those added dangers posed by those who were determined to restore the Followers to the old faith.

'You're very thoughtful, Aklon.' The woman at his side smiled as he turned to her. Lean and strong, Patrilha remained a soldier and carried herself tall and proud. Her first concern her duty to her leader. It was reassuring to have such souls along to fight the coming battles, but he wondered what life would have for her once the fighting ceased. There would, of course, remain a need for some armed force about the island, even if only to prevent outbreaks of territorial greed and dispute turning into war between unhappy neighbours. She would be good for that role.

'Yes, Patrilha. We go to root out friends, family and fellow soldiers, to persuade them they are wrong and to kill them if they fail to see the error of their ways. It is not a task that I relish. But it is a job that must be done if we are ever to achieve the peace and harmony I dream of for our people.'

'I'm glad you're our leader now. I never liked the priests and those Unholy Ones with their false piety. Didn't find it easy to believe we should allow them access to our bodies just because of some title. None that I knew showed any more real devotion than the soldiers I lived and worked with. As soon as you explained the falsehood and the lies, I knew I'd be with you till the fight was ended. You'll go back to Shoarhn and be a farmer once we've done the job, Aklon. I'm a soldier. Will there still be work for me?'

He explained his thoughts and she nodded, satisfied.

314

'I knew you'd have an answer. You always have a solution to all problems.'

He sighed. To have such a reputation and to bear such trust from the people. He would have many more 'solutions' to create before the island was the place he wanted it to be. But he no longer had the heart for leadership. Once the struggle was over, he would find a trusted man or woman, maybe both, to take on the role of leader. A new role. One that made for justice, fairness and tolerance. That would need a very special individual. And, at present, he could think of no one suitable. But, oh, how tired he was of taking all responsibility, how he longed for that role as farmer, tilling soil, caring for animals and trees, raising his own children and loving his own wife. How much longer before the dream came true?

It galled Dagla Kaz that the man remained happy with the woman. He'd deliberately hurt her in that place to make it difficult for her to join with Aglydron. But that interfering healer had soon had her back to normal. The man still fawned and worshipped him, despite his cruel treatment of the woman he professed to love. What sort of man was that? He needed punishing. He'd thought, for a short while, of killing him. But that would do no good. He'd just end his life and, for all the High Priest knew, spend the rest of eternity in the joys of the Garden of Delight.

No. He'd have to get to him through the woman. And, if he wasn't suffering because of her distress and pain, he'd have to deprive him of her instead. That would make the fool unhappy. But it was no easy task on board ship. He may have to await an opportunity at one of the ports. He'd managed to separate that delicious but disappointingly loyal young woman, Tumalind, from the obnoxious hero, Okkyntalah. If he'd done that, albeit with help from Tryonta, he could surely find a way to permanently place an insuperable space between Aglydron and Chislanda.

This was a problem worthy of some thought. He must ask the captain about the various ports they would pass through. At least one must present an opportunity to sell, give away or, if necessary, get the woman killed. It didn't matter which. Though he must use her again before he got rid of her. If only to experience the delicious agony of her pain and silent suffering. It made him hard just thinking of it. But now wasn't the time. He'd find another for the moment.

On deck, the Followers were at rest, playing games, talking, watching the world go by. With his own private cabin, he had no need to restrict his frowking to the hours of darkness. Who to take advantage of? The healer moved away from the group she'd been attending, using her heathen ways to mend some wound, no doubt.

'Myllthlan? I wonder, might I have a word?'

It wouldn't do to let her know what he really wanted. She'd made no secret that his attentions were unwelcome. Once in his cabin, she'd have no choice. Comply or suffer the consequences.

'Dagla? You have an injury you need dealing with?'

Oh, how delicious. She gave him the excuse to have her naked without any effort on his part. He nodded and moved back inside his small but comfortable domain. She followed and he closed the door, reducing the brightness but giving light enough to enjoy her exposure as she made herself ready to perform her magic.

'Where are you hurt?'

He raised his robe. 'Here.'

'Dagla. I've made it very clear I have no intention of joining with you. Why do you persist in your efforts? There are plenty of willing women with us. Use them, if you must. You'll get no pleasure from me.'

He grasped her round the throat, tight. 'You'll do as I require, woman. I'm the High Priest here. And you do what I wish!'

The sudden pain was intense and he let her go at once. His delicate parts throbbed and screamed their protest at her grip. She stared hard at him, the strength and determination clear on her face. At last she released him and he rolled into a protective ball on his bed, his love fruits aching and sending such agony through his body that he was nauseous and faint.

'You're not my high priest. You never were and never will be. I see you for the evil man, the abuser of women, the wicked liar that you are. Don't attempt to rape me again, Dagla, or I'll expose you for what you are.'

She dressed, glared at him with a look that said she was unafraid of him, and went, leaving the door open behind her.

He would pay her back. He would destroy her. He would…But she was beyond his power. A woman unafraid of him, not cowed by his position and status, was outside his ability to harm. But someone must suffer, someone must hurt for the hurt she'd given him. Once he'd recovered, someone would feel pain before the day was over.

* * *

Dahrlahg had been moody for a few days, mooching around, doing her duties without much attention, so that Shoarhn finally grew tired of her distraction and asked her what was the matter.

'It's Pentryil. He can't make up his mind about what happened to me with the priest.'

She quelled the fury she felt at the injustice. 'Bring him to me, as I thought you'd intended before. I'll talk to him.'

The girl brightened at once and Shoarhn hoped she hadn't given her false hope. She knew very little of the young man, having met him only once, when he'd arrived with

Aklon. Since then, he'd been living with his parents who worked on the coast, collecting seaweed and making it into a form of food or fertiliser for the fields. She'd bought some and been impressed with its growing qualities, but the food they could keep: salty and flavoured too strongly of the tidal beach for her tastes.

He came, reluctant and sulky; the very epitome of youthful resentment faced with elder wisdom. She'd have to tread carefully with this one. She made him tlathan and sat him at the table after sending Dahrlahg out to tend the goats, and collect eggs.

'Do you love Dahrlahg?'

The question obviously surprised him and she hoped she'd at least brought some consideration to his mind.

'I…we were always going to be married. Right from before we were even betrothed.'

'That isn't what I asked, Pentryil. I asked whether you love her.'

'Don't really know what love is. Soppy, isn't it? I mean, it's not somethin' for men, is it?'

'I see. I gather you were with Aklon for the fight both here and in Krohtl. Brave man, isn't he?'

'Aklon's the bravest and best man I've ever come across.'

'Yes. Aklon loves me, you know. And I love him.'

She allowed that to sink in. His face showed a mind slowly at work. There wasn't a great deal going on in that head, but if she could get him to understand and accept certain things, he'd be right for Dahrlahg. They were what she saw as a natural couple.

'So, love can be for a man, then?'

'It can. And it is. Most men realise that. It just takes some of them longer than others to recognise that's what they feel.'

'I like the way Dahrlahg looks.'

'Any man would like the way she looks, Pentryil. She's a very attractive young woman. You'd have to be strange not to find her lovely. You're a handsome young man, and I'm sure she looks at you the same way you look at her. But that's lust, not love. Do you miss her when you're away from her?'

'I try not to think about it, you know?'

'I think so. Do you want her to be happy?'

'Course I do. Why wouldn't I?'

'Sounds like love to me, Pentryil.'

'I'd…I'd do anything for her. It's just…well, she's been broken, hasn't she? I mean, shamed by that priest.'

'You think that was her fault?'

'Dunno.'

'Let me assure you of that at once. It wasn't. That awful man took her, against her will and raped her. That means he used force to make her do things she didn't want to do; he attacked and abused her. She had no part in the act, apart from being the receptacle for his vile power-seeking. She wasn't in any way responsible for what he did to her. Any more than you could be held responsible for your death by an arrow shot from the trees by an unseen archer.'

He considered this. She watched thoughts turn slowly within his head. It was an exercise new to him; that was plain.

'So she wasn't to blame, then?'

'Not in any way at all. She was the victim. The priest was entirely responsible for what he did to her. She resisted but he was too strong and he bound her so it was impossible for her to defend herself.'

'I'd kill the bowelcreep, if he wasn't already dead! Takin' her like that. Hurting her. Making her do things she didn't want to. I would. I'd kill 'im!'

Shoarhn nodded and smiled at him. 'You can't punish him, but you can stop punishing Dahrlahg and you can help her get over a very distressing experience by being kind, loving and caring of her.'

A light came on in his eyes. The solution was there for him. He knew what he must do now. That was all he needed: the guidance to make the right decision and the knowledge that what he would do was the proper thing.

'Thank you, Shoarhn. Can I go to her now?'

'You should. Tell her she can take the rest of the day off. And get that wedding arranged as soon as possible. You no longer have to wait until the whole town visits the Plains of Ytraa now. You can marry whenever you like. But I'd like to be present when you do.'

She didn't see Dahrlahg again that day. But the girl appeared hand in hand with Pentryil the following morning; happiness painted all over her pretty face.

'Will you come to our wedding, Shoarhn? Tomorrow. An' can I 'ave a day or two off? I'll meck up for it after, only…well, you know?'

'Take a sixday. Learn to make love with each other and decide where you want to live your lives together, what you want to do.'

'Oh, we already know that. We want me to stay on the farm, if you'll let me. Pentryil isn't sure, but he doesn't care to go on collecting seaweed.'

'Is he any good with his hands? Can you mend fences, Pentryil, fix doors and gates? Dig holes?'

He nodded enthusiastically.

'Well, I think we'd better get a house built for you here, don't you? Now that things are settling down to peaceful ways again, I intend to spread out a bit and grow some new crops and keep a few extra animals, so we can feed more people. And I'll need a strong man and a willing woman to help. How's that sound?'

They both embraced her, a clumsy but heartfelt thanks.

'You realise your wedding will be the first here since we ended the faith? We'll have to decide what to do about that. How we're going to conduct it and what things you need to say to each other.'

'Oh, Irrildys has already done all that.'

'Has she? Well, something so important needs agreement from all. So I'll go and have words with her, see what she has in mind. In the meantime, you two had better get yourselves organised. Have a look at the south field and decide where you'd like to put up the house.'

They went off, two young lives waiting to discover what the world might bring them, full of hope and happiness and youthful expectation. Shoarhn watched them in the field, discussing the siting of their new house, and wished that Aklon could be here to witness this first coupling under his guidance, such as it was. Soon, it would be necessary to form a set of rules for folk to live by, but, for the moment, it was enough that happiness was at least possible in this new world they were creating.

The Dark Space beckoned, it's evil intent partly hidden behind a benign surface designed to deceive. An air of threat and destruction hung about it for the wary. But, since her first intrusion and the evil minds' overpowering of her, she perceived the space in a different way. It was as if those who occupied the place were aware of minds that approached and could alter it accordingly. Tumalind had asked Blavv and discovered that, for her, the Dark Space remained as threatening and dreaded as ever. She'd entered briefly but never been taken over by the minds and her impression of the place was unaltered, the danger signals intact and obvious.

For Tumalind, the experience had changed. Now, as she approached, she felt a seductive power that urged her forward, tempted her within, promising unspecified joy and delight should she dare pass the barriers. It was a thin veil cloaking their real intentions and, unlike those willing to share their evil, she was alert to what they really wanted, what they really intended.

Death wasn't the danger. They wanted her physically whole. Wanted to distort her mind to match their ways: nothing more, nothing less. As their creature, she would perform the acts they desired, she would spread the word far and wide, send out the message that wealth was all, that power lay in the hands of those with most coin and property. They would use her to persuade others of the great power to be obtained once wealth and property became all. They would destroy her sense of self and of the worth of friendship, love, constancy, faithfulness, harmony with nature, consideration for others, tolerance, creativity, affection, respect and truth. And they would implant in her mind the concepts of material wealth, acquisition for the sake of acquisition, the power of coin, the gratification of sex without the responsibility and care of love, the necessary subjection of the masses in order to feed the needs of those with most power. They would extol the virtue of greed, the worth of selfishness, the greatness of power.

There were enticements for those who complied. And there were threats for those who defied them. Tumalind had to find the balance between her ability to enter the space and discover and enter individual minds, and the capacity to remain outside their influence. They acted as a pack; the only way in which they valued cooperation. They understood that, alone, each mind was futile and unimportant, but that together they might rule the world and turn it into the place they desired for what she saw as their perverted and distorted wants and desires.

She'd tried, several times, to enter the Dark Space, but each time she'd retreated, unable to convince herself of her strength to resist their combined power. Their inducements meant nothing to her. She had no interest in what they offered. But their threats were real and valid and they could destroy her; with time and sheer volume of numbers, they may be able to make her their creature. She would rather die than end up their puppet, spreading their lies and foul philosophy. And she understood that was a very real possibility if she lost concentration when she ventured into their domain. But she must do it. She must find each mind, physically locate the owner, and then let Okkyntalah and the others know so they could end that worthless life. And she must do it soon.

She must, in fact, do it now.

Chapter 40

THE ISLAND TOUR BEGINS

Krohtl remained free of bands of extremists. There was still some dissent, of course, but no violence, and the number of those unwilling to face the changes had fallen so the local population could deal with them without help. Aklon set in motion a scheme whereby the people would choose a group of individuals to act as joint leaders of the community. It was an idea he'd received through mindtalking with Blavv and Tumalind; something they had tried with some success in the far city of Ov-Bebna.

Free of worry about Shoarhn's locality, where there were no longer any organised bands of trouble makers, he now set off to the Plains of Ytraa. There, he'd make sure that none of the Unholy Ones or ex-soldiers had returned to use that place as a stronghold. He led a fit troop and they covered the ground in a series of quick marches. Disciplined and familiar with living off the land, the majority of the soldiers and the Few that accompanied him needed little support. Each community they passed through, understanding what they were about, gave them the essentials. The hunters and gatherers amongst the party provided fresh meat and fruit at each stopping place.

On the fourth night out of Morstahn, they reached the caves under Ytraa's Peak and made camp, ready to search before darkness set in. Aklon detailed Delbon and Choryssa to lead a party through the entrance at the far side of the mountain, aiming to meet up in the middle to ensure none of their quarry escaped.

As they explored the many tunnels and passages, natural and man made, they collected everything of use and destroyed anything that might be of value to future torturers using the place. To Aklon's horror, they discovered a deep chamber they'd failed to detect on their first sortie. The stench of death led them their.

Seven decaying bodies hung from chains of torture. No longer identifiable other than as the remains of humans, the carcasses were gathered and taken outside for decent burial. They would never know the names or origins of these victims but they could, at least, give them peace in death.

Other than weapons, stale food, and a small horde of stolen valuables, they found no signs of life in the caves.

'In the morning, we will seal them. I want them never to be used again for such foul purposes. It will be hard work, and use valuable time we might employ in finding those who still oppose our changes, but I cannot allow these caves to be available for those who would abuse life so.'

No one objected. They spent two days with hammers, levers and chisels left behind by the earlier cave workers, in breaking rock from walls and ceilings to make impenetrable seals to the caves. That, they hoped, would be an end to any use of them in the future.

Pampahn was their next destination. Seeking out signs of movement and habitation in the lands along the way, they took three days to reach the settlement near the lake. As expected, they discovered a gathering of armed Dissenters in the marshes that covered the plain to the north east of the lake.

The majority of those who opposed them here were men. Fewer than a dozen women dwelt with this group of nearly a hundred. Aklon's troops, already battle hardened and toughened by their days on the march, were outnumbered, by more than two to one. But the Dissenters, a mix of ex-soldiers, Unholy Ones and locals unable to accept the changes, were no match for fit and disciplined fighters. The skirmishes were violent and deadly but Aklon lost only one of his troop; a hardy old soldier who found himself surrounded by four of the enemy and hidden from the others by tall reeds. The others finished off those who'd killed him as soon as they found them.

Of the remaining Dissenters, seven women and five men were persuaded to give up their fight. It turned out that they had all been coerced into rebellion by relatives or spouses. They were glad to be free of the need to live a life none had chosen. The bodies of the fallen took two days to bury in the wet ground of the marshes, but Aklon wouldn't leave them uncovered for wild beasts to take.

In Pampahn, they heard of a smaller troop, made up entirely of Unholy Ones, that harried the outskirts of the town. No one had been able to discover where they based themselves. Phildrad had made several sorties, with others of the Few, but had lost their trail when they'd used tricks to confuse any trackers.

Aklon and his troops were made welcome by the townsfolk, who readily accepted the dozen prisoners, willing to convert them or merely allow them to live with the other small community of Dissenters. Porlesah welcomed him and sheltered him from the attentions of women who would otherwise have pleaded for his company. She understood his need to remain faithful to Shoarhn and had already found herself a reliable partner from the town. He greeted Aklon like a brother.

That night, the party of Unholy Ones attacked again. They burned two houses, killed most of the occupants, stole food and took two of the youngest prisoner. No one doubted the fate of such captives at the hands of the Unholy Ones and the search began at once in an attempt to rescue them before they were destroyed. Phildrad offered his experience in tracking them down.

The past four days had seen Okkyntalah and the others visiting the city nightly, killing an evil mind on each occasion and, the last time, finding two together. Tumalind had developed a method of locating them with accuracy. And the three men had found each intended victim without fail. She'd identified a dozen evil minds. Each one must be killed.

The pattern of assassinations had at last alerted the Powerseekers to their danger. They understood that they were being sought, identified and killed. Who endangered them, they appeared to have no idea. But they now took steps in defending themselves against further attack. When Okkyntalah, Teldrohn and Sondukal scaled the wall on the fifth night of their assault, they discovered the streets were no longer empty.

Sondukal pulled Okkyntalah into utter dark between two houses; held a finger to his lips. In the silence, they could hear their own breathing and then, unmistakable, came the sound of measured footsteps. Four men, marching in time, approaching along the street he'd been about to step into. He shifted Sondukal's finger and whispered.

The scheme was quickly agreed and they let the soldiers pass, unmolested. As expected, they were marching two and two. The last two were easy prey and died without a sound as hunting knives sliced through throats and hands covered mouths. Before the other two even realised the reason for the silence at their rear, they were similarly despatched. The three hunters pulled the bodies into the dark space they'd just left and went on their way.

Alert, now, to the possibility of other patrols, they walked in single file, the front man searching at each corner before they progressed. It meant they took longer to reach their destination, and that placed Tumalind in greater danger, as she'd be occupied in distracting the Powerseeker they sought, should he be awake.

They found the house. A soldier stood guard at the door. He leant against the portal, a pipe glowing under the cloud of smoke as he exhaled the mixture of his choice. The moon had risen above the roofs, its face still full and shining along the side where the soldier rested. The houses opposite cast a dark, almost impenetrable shadow along the street, leaving the front of their intended destination bright by contrast.

Teldrohn was chosen, being best at the selected skill. Okkyntalah and Sondukal melted into the shadows and stayed still as their companion edged his way through the darkness until he was opposite the smoking soldier. The knife he threw hit the target with enough force to fell the man, but he twitched with life for long enough to make a small noise of surprise. Teldrohn crossed the road and struck the deathblow before the other two reached him. They crept back into shadow, carrying the body with them, and waited to find out whether they'd been discovered.

When they judged they'd paused long enough, they ventured back toward the door of their victim's house. As always, it was locked, the windows shuttered. Once again, Sondukal used his tools to gain entrance. Okkyntalah opened the downstairs shutters and revealed a second soldier, sleeping, on a chair beside the door that led upstairs. He died without a sound. Again, they waited, listening. By now, they knew the Powerseeker wouldn't be alone in his bed. He would have the company of a woman, maybe more. They were the greatest concern for the assassins, but, so far, they hadn't had to kill any women.

The stairs creaked as Okkyntalah and Sondukal climbed. Teldrohn remained below in case of interruption. Okkyntalah found the edges and ascended in silence. Sondukal followed suit.

In the bedroom were three sleepers, one snoring. The shutters opened easily to let the moonlight in. One woman, on the floor, had her hands tied to a bed leg and feet bound separately to pegs driven into the floor, so that she rested painfully with her bottom raised and her knees apart beneath her. The other woman lay half covered by the man. Sondukal moved to the far side of the bed and readied his hands to gag the sleeping woman once Okkyntalah had struck.

As he plunged downwards, the victim moved and Okkyntalah had to swerve his knife hand. He caught the neck, but not as decisively as intended. The man cried out but the sound ended abruptly as he withdrew the knife and slit his throat with the upward cut. Blood showered everything. Sondukal calmed the waking woman with soft words and reassurance as Okkyntalah knelt to free and calm the woman on the floor.

It took some time to convince the women, and one remained in danger of making noise even as they led the pair back downstairs. Both were spattered in the blood of their erstwhile abuser and neither mourned his loss. But they were frightened.

Whispers told them they were free to go but extracted promises that they would say nothing of their role in the events. They'd be killed, of course, if suspected of complicity, so their silence was likely. They left with the men, who guided them into shadows and sent them on their way to the women's quarters.

The young woman who they'd rescued from the floor had reason to be especially grateful. When she realised the assassins didn't want the reward of her body, she gave them information instead, thanking them for releasing her from a servitude she loathed.

Her report had the three men making new plans. Their daring scheme wasn't without great risk, but the rewards should make it worthwhile. They made their way not to the wall where they'd entered but toward the city gates and the place where the remaining soldiers were housed. If they could destroy the wooden gates and do significant damage to the soldiers' quarters, they'd find it easier to kill the remaining six Powerseekers. Such destruction would mean they'd be hunted, but they had ways of hiding their location and moving, should such a hunt come close.

Under moonlight, the gate stood closed and barred, a sentry at each doorpost. The barracks; home, they now knew, to only three dozen soldiers, stood north of the gates and were in complete darkness. The men guarding their recent victim's house had been on duty for the night and weren't due to be replaced.

Sondukal, Teldrohn and Okkyntalah waited in the shadows of a group of houses, as they made their plans.

'You realise this might make the whole town panic?'

Sondukal grunted at Okkyntalah's observation. Teldrohn whispered his agreement and added that they had no choice now.

'After tonight's murder, they'd have placed too many men on guard for us to kill the next one anyway. We've got to rid the place of soldiers. Or at least reduce their number so we stand a chance. Otherwise, we might as well leave things as they are and set off for the next place.'

'We can't afford to do that. It would leave as much danger for the world as if we hadn't bothered with the half dozen we've killed so far.'

They were agreed. No matter what the dangers, they must neutralise the soldiers if they were to kill the other Powerseekers. Life would soon be even harder than it had been for all of them, until all their victims had been killed and they were free to leave the town.

Aglydron had no wish to leave Aagtaz. Neither did he want to stay there as an isolated stranger. The ship was ready to sail. But how could he go without Chislanda? Where was she? He'd left her aboard ship in this place that seemed so benign and welcoming. The people of the river port seemed friendly, open and approachable. He'd gone ashore with a small party of the men to collect fresh supplies, a duty allocated him by Dagla Kaz, who'd personally sought him out for the task, emphasising its importance.

On his return, he'd helped load the stores, as required, before going to find Chislanda to share his experiences of the place with her. She hadn't been at their usual place and nobody had seen her for a while. Linlyss thought she might be below decks. He searched, but failed to find her.

He'd asked, but no one had an answer and he assumed she must've decided to go ashore herself. It seemed unlikely, but she'd expressed a wish to be on dry land after so long aboard ship. Dagla Kaz had belatedly told him he'd seen her going ashore as well. He'd walked the narrow gangplank and wandered about the immediate area near the dock, but there was no sign of her there, either. Now the ship must sail.

'If you don't come aboard now, Aglydron, we'll have to leave without you.'

He glanced up at the crewmember, already reeling in one of the ropes that held them attached to the great blocks on the dockside to prevent the fast current dragging the ship downstream. Here, the river narrowed significantly and the waters flowed rapidly, with many whorls and small whirlpools indicating the depth and treachery of the water. A fall into the river here would be the end of even the strongest swimmer.

'Has anyone seen Chislanda?' His call was echoed on board.

A voice cried out from beyond his line of sight. 'She's here, Aglydron.'

Relief. He dashed up the gangplank as the second mooring rope was released and tossed on deck for the sailors to store in readiness for the next docking. Immediately, the great ship moved, the current alone enough to take it swiftly from the shore. Aglydron made his way across to the far side and asked where she was. No one seemed to know who'd called out the assurance. No one could identify where that reassuring voice had come from.

Dagla Kaz emerged from below decks and smiled on his way to the captain, nodding at various people as he went. For the briefest of moments, his glance alighted on Aglydron and he thought he saw a swift look that seemed to be triumphant malice there. But the High Priest was gone in an instant. Aglydron, drawn back to the landward side of the ship, gazed in hope at the dock. But Chislanda wasn't there. At least if he'd seen her, he would've known she was safe.

He spent the rest of the day searching the entire ship, including the captain's cabin, those of the merchants where the captive women teased him mercilessly, and even that of Dagla Kaz, the High Priest encouraging him. But of Chislanda there was no sign. No one had any news of her. No one could answer the mystery of her disappearance, except that one of the local Followers thought he'd seen her going toward the town, though he couldn't be certain. That she wasn't aboard there could be no doubt. There was no place she could be that he hadn't looked into. Chislanda had vanished without trace. And Aglydron had to face the fact that he was unlikely ever to see her again.

For a while, he leant on the rail, looking back along the river toward the town of Aagtaz, that had long since been hidden by distance. Where was she? Why had she left the ship? What was her condition? Was she safe? Was she even alive? The questions revolved around his mind until he was sick with the lack of answers.

The High Priest approached him, his face a mask of concern that eliminated all doubt about Aglydron's earlier suspicion of malice. 'I fear she must've taken it into her head to explore the town, Aglydron. No one really noticed she'd left the ship. Perhaps she felt the need to walk on dry land after so long aboard. It's natural for those of us who live on land to find the confines of the ship too much after a while. Maybe I should have allowed a little more time for refreshment and exploration in the town. But we must move forward. We do Ytraa's bidding here. I am sorry you have lost your partner. But she'll be safe there. The town seemed friendly and the women were treated nearly as equals. Chislanda is a fine looking woman, I'm sure she'll find a man to care for her.'

It was little enough comfort, but he thanked the High Priest for his care and consideration. Chislanda was lost to him. Probably forever. He could think of no way she might find her way back to him. She knew only the name of his island, not its location. In any case, how could she possibly get there? No. He must face the fact that she would never be in his life again.

For a while, he wept, alone and distraught.

Myllthlan came to him and gave him some comfort, holding him and persuading him he must still eat and drink. 'Life holds hope as long as life continues, Aglydron. We none of us knows what the future may bring. Time will soften your loss and you'll lead a full and pleasant life when we return to the island.'

As he sat with the others the following morning, eating only because he must, Dagla Kaz approached him again.

'You know, you are still married to that remarkable woman who gave birth to Tumalind. She waits for you on the island. Perhaps it's as well you were parted from Chislanda, a good enough woman, but not a true Follower. You have the blessing that on the island there waits a beautiful wife who's a pious and true Follower. I think you should thank Ytraa for that blessing, don't you?'

Aglydron nodded, though he felt the loss of Chislanda deeply and knew, from Tryonta's message when he returned from Muhnilahm, that Shoarhn was no longer exclusively his. She'd joined with the reprobate, Aklon-Dji. Perhaps, on his return, she'd see the error of her ways and return to him. Perhaps. If not, she must bear the punishment due for befriending the Renegade. In the meantime, Aglydron, alone and without a partner to worship his god properly, must find another to join with, lest he fail to perform his devotion correctly.

Perhaps Myllthlan would provide him with the means, even though she was still not a Follower? At least, as a woman, she'd allow him to join in worship and thereby please his god.

'I thought you loved Chislanda?'

'I do. But she's not here and I can't retrieve her, can I? I have to do my duty by Ytraa, Myllthlan. Anything less would be sacrilege.'

'So, you want to join with me just to satisfy your need to worship? You don't care about my feelings or wishes?'

'I've always respected you, felt affection for you, Myllthlan. I've learned ways to please a woman now. I wouldn't just use you like in the past. Of course, you're not Chislanda, so I can't love you. But I can give you pleasure in the act of joining to worship

Ytraa. Surely that's a worthy thing to do?'

'Sorry, Aglydron. I've another who can and does love me. You'll have to find your subject for worship elsewhere.'

He watched her approach one of the men from the Followers they'd gathered in Choshinahm. He'd never realised she was his partner. The man took her hand and they sat together, talking and laughing.

But he must have a woman to share worship. It was essential. It was necessary. It was impossible for him to go for any length of time without joining. In the boat with Jodisa it hadn't been possible and he and Okkyntalah had had to remain celibate. But in a place with plenty of available women, there was no excuse for such a lack of respect for Ytraa. He must approach other women until he found a willing partner. He had no choice.

Chapter 41

FORMING THE CIRCLE

'We can't just kill soldiers. They're obeyin' orders, doin' a job. I'll no be part of that. It's murder.'

'And what we've been doing so far, isn't, Sondukal?'

'It's different. Them Powerseekers is evil minds that'll turn the world into sommat terrible if we don't end 'em. But these are just…'

'…the men who help them lead those wicked lives, the men who protect those evil minds from retribution, the men who give them the freedom to abuse and enslave women and spread their evil lies and greed over the whole world.'

Sondukal had been silent at that. But Okkyntalah must be absolutely certain if the man was to be committed to the proposed raid.

'Look, Sondukal, you willingly came along with Feldrark to destroy Mipahnhil, didn't you?'

'I were a soldier. Soldiers do what their commander says.'

'True. You're still in service to Feldrark. And Feldrark wants these evil minds killed, and these soldiers will stop us doing that.'

Again the guide and tracker had been silent, unable to find an argument but clearly not convinced.

'Look, I'm no more keen to end these lives than you are. But they'll prevent us finishing the job. You agree, don't you?'

'Mebbie.'

'Come on. After tonight's experience, you know we'll face much more trouble next time. It's obvious. I don't know what's botherin' you.'

Okkyntalah had thanked Teldrohn for his contribution but Sondukal had remained unconvinced.

'Let me put it this way. What does it take for evil men to have their way?'

'Don't know what you mean.'

'I think you do. It only takes good men to say and do nothing. Evil men need no encouragement to be evil, but if good men get in their way, it often stops them. Agreed?'

'It's the onny way, far as I can see.'

'Exactly. So, we either stand idly by, defeated by those who protect the evil minds, or we remove those protectors from the scene. The outcome if we don't get rid of them will be the same as if we do nothing, since those who protect them will stop us ridding the world of this evil.'

'When you put it like that, I see your point. Still don't like it, though.'

'I'm not asking you to like it, Sondukal. I don't like it. Teldrohn doesn't like it. Look, in the battle to defeat the evil leader of the people of Mipahnhil, did we kill innocents, women and children amongst them?'

'That were terrible. But we 'ad no choice. They wouldn't surrender an' we couldn't let the buggers live or they'd 'ave 'arried us the rest of their lives.'

'That's right. We had to kill or be killed. And that's the situation here. Kill or die. That's the stark choice.'

The man had sighed and agreed. There was no other way, no matter how much they all disliked it. The garrison must be destroyed. Once in agreement, Sondukal was fully committed, as Okkyntalah had known he would be.

Fire was the answer. Killing the two who idled at the gate was easy enough. Thrown knives silenced them. After shifting the bodies out of sight, they'd entered the sentry box and found there the means to light a fire. The wooden barracks had quickly blazed. They'd set flame to the gates as well.

With the blaze at its height, they faced the most dangerous time, as citizens emerged at the noise and cries for help. He hated hearing men cry out as they burned to death. Some escaped, of course, but most of them suffered injuries caused by the fire or the rush to escape the flames.

They'd waited in shadow, as night progressed and the fire raged and destroyed the barracks and the gates, and spread to other buildings. The ensuing panic then gave them the opportunity to escape through the burning gap between the smouldering gateposts.

That had been three days ago. Since then, they'd been on the move, throwing off the hunters seeking them. Until the men were certain they were no longer hunted, they couldn't leave the women alone for their next assassination.

Tumalind used the time well. She'd identified and located all six remaining Powerseekers. They'd taken to spending the nights together, guarded by soldiers who changed shift three times a day, so they remained alert. How many, she couldn't tell, but it seemed there were fewer than they wanted. The Powerseekers were now living in the great hall and there seemed little prospect of them leaving. Okkyntalah and the others had spent some time reconstructing the vast building in their minds, so that they'd have as much knowledge of the place as possible when they made their attack.

Teldrohn returned from a sortie that had taken him away for almost the whole day. 'No sign of anyone searching. In fact, I don't think anyone's left the city. I think they've given up.'

They'd had no sight of hunters the previous night either. Sondukal was yet to return after a similar foray, but the soldier's wide sweep of the lakeside and the area overlooked by the city wall had found no sign of activity. It seemed likely they were safe again. But the guide should also have been back by now. As dusk fell, no longer augmented by the Skyfire, which now showed as a small bright star trailing a narrow glowing tail, they waited in silence and without the fire they needed to cook their fresh meat.

If he'd been caught, he would be tortured for information about the killings. These weren't men to show mercy. They'd make any suspect suffer until they extracted the knowledge they required. Sondukal might be strong and determined, but he was a man, after all. Night drew on and still there was no sign of their companion.

'What should we do?'

Okkyntalah held Tumalind tight. 'We stay here. Two on watch, the rest sleeping. If he's not back by daybreak, we move to another site. There's nothing else we can do.'

The night was long and dark, and morning felt too far away.

<hr />

Shoarhn welcomed Irrildys to her home. Only Eyethlehn hadn't yet arrived. They were due to start two important changes and all present were excited by the prospect, but also rather nervous. The first question they must resolve was how to go about the marriage service in the absence of traditions. For that reason, they'd invited both Dahrlahg and Pentryil to be present for the first part of the meeting.

'Sorry I'm late. Had a particularly difficult job to finish for today and it took a little longer than I'd planned. So, we're all assembled and ready, are we?' Eyethlehn brushed curls of fresh planed wood from her hair as she entered.

The rest of the group nodded. They'd really need her mindtalk once they got to the next part of the meeting, but they hadn't wanted to start the joyous part without her.

'So. The first thing we need to decide is whether the marriage of two people should include a public joining, like it did in the old days. Anyone got anything to say?'

Dahrlahg replied to Shoarhn's question at once and was quite emphatic that she didn't want to join in public. Neither did Pentryil.

It came as no surprise to most assembled in the barn, the only place big enough for those who wanted to attend. Since the removal of the restrictions and dictates of the Followers, many had adopted different attitudes to almost every aspect of their lives. And most, whilst unconcerned about displaying their bodies outdoors and in the streets, had decided that public frowking wasn't something they particularly relished. They'd indulged in it willingly whilst the priests had declared it essential for worship, but the loss of the sacred aspect made the whole idea less appealing. It was one thing to join publicly when others were doing the same, but to do it whilst others looked on was another thing entirely. It introduced an unsavoury element that made most feel uncomfortable, both as witnesses and as participants. That the ability to witness had always existed for the priests and those vile Unholy Ones didn't escape the former Followers and they realised they'd been the objects of perverted stimulus for all of their adult lives.

'I think most of us agree.'

There were murmurings, calls and mutterings, but whether they were of agreement of dissent Shoarhn found difficult to determine.

'We need a way to measure how much agreement there is before we go any further. Otherwise, we'll spend ages trying to come to conclusions. I don't know what we can do to identify who's in agreement and who isn't. Any suggestions?'

Those assembled either sat in thought or discussed and aired ideas with those closest. Shoarhn allowed the noise to continue until it seemed most had had their say.

'So, any suggestions?'

Several people spoke at once. She held up her hand in a gesture for silence and they slowly quietened again.

'I'll go round the room and point to each of you in turn, so you can have your say. Is that okay?'

There was general agreement to that, at least. The first half dozen people either said nothing or made suggestions that were no improvement on what had already happened. She came to Irrildys.

'I think we need a visual signal; a bit like the one you just made for silence. We can't use that, of course; we all know that the flat palm raised to shoulder height is the signal for quiet. We need one sign for assent and another for disagreement. I suggest we raise the left hand high above our heads for "let it be", and do the same with the right hand to say, "refused". How's that sound?'

The sound of agreement made Shoarhn laugh at the continued confusion. She held up her hand for silence again.

'Those who agree with Irrildys, please raise their left hand, as suggested.'

The majority did so.

'Those who disagree, raise their right hand.'

Two did so, but one dropped her hand when she realised how much they were in the minority. Two others made no signal either way.

'Thank you. I think that means we should adopt the method suggested by Irrildys.'

There was no further argument.

'So, to the wedding. We agree there'll be no public joining?'

Most raised their left hands. But enough right hands were raised, causing some discussion. The dissenters mostly felt some proof of actual joining was needed to ensure that the marriage had been properly completed, the promise to join for Ytraa fulfilled.

Shoarhn found the old ways of thinking increasingly frustrating, but she kept her head. 'We've already decided we don't need to obey the old rules set by the priests about what we should and shouldn't do regarding worship of Ytraa. So it shouldn't be necessary for those getting married to prove anything at all. It's between them, surely?'

This provoked a discussion, unruly and uncontrolled, that led to ill-feeling and raised voices. Shoarhn was conscious that the meeting could end in disarray before they'd made any decisions at all.

'I'm sorry, but would you all just be quiet!' Dahrlahg shouted this demand and it had the required effect. 'I know I'm young and not yet an adult, as far as you're all concerned, but aren't we supposed to be talking about our wedding?'

Shoarhn nodded at her and smiled her thanks. The others looked a little shamefaced.

'We're bound to have disagreements about all sorts of things. For so long, all our lives, in fact, we've been told what to do and what to think. It's going to take a long time before we learn how to do that for ourselves. And we'll have disputes for a while yet. But Dahrlahg's right. We gathered together to help work out how we should celebrate the love of two of our young people and have them join in marriage. I don't know about you, but I think it might be best if we let them decide what they'd like to do.'

This suggestion caused some surprise but, after a short discussion, most agreed.

Dahrlahg and Pentryil then stood together facing the group and, hesitantly at first, but with growing confidence, outlined their wishes. Most of those present approved. A few made suggestions for slight changes. In the end, they arrived at a short ceremony and decided this would take place in the town square, with as many of the population present as possible. Neighbours would spread the word and all were asked to gather for noon.

Once this was decided, some of those present departed, along with the couple who were to be married. The rest remained to decide how they should proceed with governing the town in the absence of the village priest and his small group of elders. Some of those were present, of course, since they had some experience of the sort of matters that the new body would have to consider.

'First thing we're going to need is a leader of some sort. Someone to take charge of future meetings, like.' This from one of the former elders.

Irrildys stood. 'I suggest we allow Shoarhn to do that, for now, as she's done such a good job of leading this discussion so far. Who agrees with me?'

Most raised their left hands. Shoarhn wasn't at all sure she wanted such responsibility but, for the moment, accepted it with a nod.

'I think, before we begin, we should ask Eyethlehn to connect with Ivdulon, the Wise woman in Litkala, and ask her advice on how best to go about such things, don't you?'

Apart from one or two who hadn't yet heard about the changes in opinion regarding

Litkala, there was general agreement. Few understood exactly what Eyethlehn would require but most remained silent whilst the young woman connected with the mind of one so far away.

Viewed as a sort of magic, this skill or gift was now well known. That Aklon possessed such a talent and used it to form his new ideas was also becoming better recognized. Some were violently opposed to the use of what they saw as sorcery, but they were largely confined to the Dissenters who continued to roam and disrupt the island. Their behaviour convinced most of the population that their ideas weren't worthy of consideration. But there were others who accepted the changes but worried about such an invisible skill. Some had had the gift demonstrated by the growing number who now declared themselves mindtalkers, displaying the recognised signs. Generally, people accepted it as a good thing, but some suspicion remained.

Eyethlehn came back to the assembled folk and signalled she was now ready to convey the ideas suggested by Ivdulon. Shoarhn stood beside her as she relayed her findings, and the reasons behind them, to all.

Long discussion, interrupted by breaks for food and periods of thought, accompanied the revelations from the wise woman. But, by nightfall, those gathered had settled on a system of future leadership acceptable to most. One of the elders, hoping to gain power, walked out when it became clear he wouldn't be included amongst those who'd initially form the group to govern the town.

Shoarhn, much against her will, was made nominal head of what they decided should be called the Circle; a name selected as they envisaged an assembly of equals gathered in the round so that no one individual took precedence. Shoarhn's role was simply that of managing discussions and ensuring all were given the same opportunity to speak. The Circle consisted of seven women, including Eyethlehn and Irrildys and five men.

As most were anxious to get back to their homes and work, the only decision they made was that they would meet, for the moment, at the end of each sixday in the barn, until they found some other suitable place.

Chapter 42

AN ACT OF THEFT

Feldrark waited with Ivdulon in the tower. Soon the sun would set and he must descend in the Riser.

'Still no word?'

'Blavv is still recovering after protecting Tumalind. We can't hurry this, Feldrark. Not if we're to keep them safe.'

'Another few minutes, that's all. I'll have to return tomorrow. I daren't descend in that cursed machine in the dark.'

'Fear of such devices does you no favours, Feldrark. It operates as well at night as in daylight.'

'Maybe. But next time we have to talk, I think I'll have you down in my terrain, if you don't mind?'

'And, if I do?'

'Makes no difference. I'll still have you down there.'

'Fear is such a poor guide to decision making, don't you think?' She smiled and then her face changed suddenly.

'*We've done it. The first is down.*'

Feldrark received the message from Blavv at the same time as Ivdulon and they nodded at each other. The killing of the Powerseekers had begun. Now they must set the next part of the plan in motion. But they couldn't inform the assassin party. Mindtalk on that was too dangerous. They'd have to continue to operate as if alone until the troops arrived in their vicinity. Any hint of their plans and activity would act as a warning to those in the city, and enable them to prepare defences, which would delay their takeover. The last thing Ivdulon and Feldrark wanted was an absence of rule in Trotnahn. The lessons of Ov-Bebna had shown it was a mistake to leave such situations to resolve themselves. Especially if they were to influence the future direction of the new rule.

The troops were ready; had been since Tumalind had made it clear she was prepared to start the process of identifying the Powerseekers. She'd clearly had trouble entering the Dark Space initially, but had apparently found a way. The first killing was the signal they'd awaited.

'Good. I can go back down to safe land and get my troops on the road. You'll keep me informed of progress with the Powerseeker's demise, I know.'

'I advised the girls to mindtalk as little as possible. We won't hear from them again until the last one has been killed in the town, Feldrark. Even then we must remain guarded. But I'm watching and keeping a protective presence by Tumalind as she enters that fearful place. I am, at least, aware when she makes the necessary contact, though I daren't let her know I'm there with her. Again, mindtalk could so easily betray us, and I can't defend myself at the same time as I place barriers to protect her. She remains in danger, of course. But I'll continue to do my best to keep her safe. She is, after all, vital to our aim.'

Feldrark nodded. The plan was moving. The first stage under way at last. What would be the outcome he had no way of knowing, but he hoped that it would come down on their side. Failure was unimaginable; the Powerseekers would undoubtedly step up their actions and move more rapidly than they had previously. And that would spell danger for the whole world far sooner than Ivdulon had predicted.

He took the Riser down in a mood of mixed hope and fear. Tumalind was most gifted, but she was a young and inexperienced woman alone in a realm of utter evil. Did she have the strength and ability to both remain safe and to defeat those wicked minds? Only when she'd completed the task, or failed, would he have the answer to that question.

Dagla Kaz hadn't been visited recently by those interesting, sensible voices that had advised how he might cause Aglydron the most harm without raising suspicion. Their absence troubled him. It was awkward, and disappointing, that he had no ability to voluntarily contact them and had to wait for them to find and connect with him, before he could reciprocate.

Recently, there'd been a disturbing connection from a strange, unrecognised voice. Difficult to know, but it might have been a woman. The voice had warned him against evil and suggested he might find things much changed when he arrived back on the island. But, when he tried to ask questions, he discovered he was unable to send them in the same way that he could with some other voices. Really most irritating, and concerning, especially as he'd like to tell her to mind her own business. But nothing he could do about it at present.

Now they'd arrived in Stornhil, the ship's captain had decided to load the vessel with a cargo that would make his trip to the island more profitable. The delay was frustrating, especially in light of the suggestions made by that other voice. The sooner he reached the island, the better. But he couldn't afford the extortionate amount the captain required for a full voyage to Muhnilahm without this extra cargo. That would at least spare him the need to spend his remaining coin. Coin he'd use to increase his empire and power once back home, as suggested by those more friendly, rational voices.

In the meantime, he played with the idea of abandoning Myllthlan in the port in the same way he'd arranged for Chislanda to be left behind. He laughed out loud as he thought of her returning from her fool's errand to give that 'important' message to Aglydron, and discovered the ship had left without her.

'Serves her right. Meddling fool.'

'I beg your pardon, Dagla?'

Kaz-Ca-Valorysta was dressing after providing her usual satisfactory pleasure. It was as well that she had relatively appropriate tastes. Though, once he was in a position of more certain power, he had plans to make her performance a little more dependent on the pain he might inflict before and whilst using her. The lessons taught by those powerful minds had been fascinating. They had ways of gaining gratification from women that had never occurred to him. Some were delicious in their simple cruelty and domination. Others were perhaps too extreme even for an adept such as he. But, they had suggested them as ways of increasing his potency, so he might indulge once back home with a reliable source of young flesh he could use and discard.

The priestess was still looking at him with a question in her eyes, her tabard still raised. He snatched it away and pushed her onto the bed, entered her at once and frowked her until she cried out and he found satisfaction again.

As she finally dressed, some time later, she asked the question. 'Who's the meddling fool, Dagla?'

But he'd forgotten the incident, lost in the conquest of her flesh, willing though she was. Soon he'd have an endless supply of women who would try to resist such usage and then he'd find the satisfaction of frequent domination. He would demand and they would supply, whether they wished it or not. He raised the hem and slapped her rump soundly.

'Off you go. I have things to do here.'

She pouted and took a palm to rub her assaulted rear, but stopped herself and gave him a look of contrition before she left, looking over her shoulder, as if in want of more attention from him.

'Later. If you behave.'

She nodded, raised the front of her tabard briefly, and was gone.

Stornhil. Isolated. A city community with only surrounding farms to service the population and no other culture within many leagues. It was inevitable that the society here be unusual. The most striking aspect was the superiority of women in most roles. Although, as in some other societies, men did a lot of the more demanding physical work, business and commerce here was conducted by women.

He strode the wide, clean streets, feeling the paved surface underfoot and wondering at the effort that had been made to keep everything so neat. The town was a riot of colour, and groups of mixed men and women played music on some street corners, lending an air of joy and excitement to events.

The shops stood open. Many of them seemed without anyone to take orders or coin. But the townspeople entered and left with the goods they wanted, leaving behind the means to pay in either coin or other merchandise. There was no rush here. And no sign that the wealthy were more important than those less well off.

As he made to cross one road, an elderly woman placed a restraining hand on his arm. He was about to shake her off when he saw a cart approaching, the sound of the horse's hooves muffled by soft material wrapped about them. Had he continued, he might well have been trampled. He turned to thank her and she merely nodded and went on her way.

In a stall selling sweetmeats, he looked over the confection on offer and the stallholder left her conversation with other traders and approached. 'Can I help?'

He picked up one of the small hard candies and examined it.

'By all means, try it. You can't decide to buy if you don't know whether you'll like it, can you?'

He placed it in his mouth and discovered a delightful mixture of sweetness and spiced flavour. Somewhere, honey lurked in the background and the sweet slowly melted on his tongue. 'Delicious.'

'Not from Stornhil, of course.'

His manner of dress was enough to declare him a stranger in a city where men were routinely bare-chested and clad from hip to knee in divided skirts of bright colours. The woman standing before him wore what seemed the general garb for her sex. A single garment, this one bright yellow, with a loop around the neck from which depended two wide strips of material covering her breasts whilst leaving the cleavage exposed to the waist, where they joined a simple skirt that draped to just above her knees. Her back was uncovered.

'No. On my way home to Muhnilahm.'

She started at the name but quickly returned to her former open manner and simply nodded. 'Our ways are a little different from many others, I know. Should you wish to have some of the sweetmeats, please take what you need and leave what you feel is a fair price in either coin or other goods. You'll find blatternie leaves piled just here to wrap your sweets.'

She turned to go back to her conversation, but stopped and returned to him. 'And, of course, do sample anything, before you decide whether you wish to purchase it.'

He could, he realised, help himself to as much as he liked, without paying a single coin. Such trust was inexplicable. He tasted many of the sweets on offer and selected those he most enjoyed. The blatternie leaves were broad, flat and pliable and capable of being

338

twisted into small soft containers that retained the goods placed within them. He made up three separate packets and turned to glance at the traders where the woman was still talking. She wasn't watching him, so he made a play of leaving coin on the tray, where others lay openly displayed. Instead, he took several of the more valuable coins and walked away.

The feeling of having got the better of the trader left him exhilarated and he visited another place, where strips of treated soft leather were on sale. They were oddly shaped, with a wider part mid length and the final ends very narrow, like simple laces.

The woman who kept this stall approached and glanced at him curiously. 'Can I help you, Paltrohn?'

'This leather's very soft and pliable. I'm curious as to its purpose.'

She smiled and looked as though she might even laugh, but kept her countenance and nodded at him. 'I see you're from a land with a different means of dealing with Moontimes.'

It was all she needed to say. But, sensing an opportunity to curry favour with other women, a way to make them grateful, he determined to continue his exploration.

'And they're used with what other device for this purpose?'

She nodded. 'A man with care for the women in his party? That's unusual in strangers, and quite gratifying. We use a disposable pad of soft cotton, like this.' It fitted into the wider space on the leather strap and she raised her skirt to show him how the item was worn.

Her completely natural display aroused him at once and he turned away, embarrassed at this public exhibition in a strange town, where he was unsure of the consequences. But the woman just laughed and gently stroked his manhood, once.

'It's gratifying to know I still have the means to excite a man. If you wish to purchase any of the items for your women, please take what you need and leave the appropriate return in the bowl. You'll find baskets to carry your goods just there.' She pointed to a stand where small reed bags with handles hung from pegs.

Again, he was left to his own devices. It took a little time before his arousal subsided enough for him to feel confident enough to leave the stall. By then, he'd helped himself to seven straps and a good supply of cotton pads, packed into two bags, though one would have been sufficient. Again, he made play of leaving coin whilst actually taking the more valuable ones and placing them in his scrip.

On his way back to the ship, he decided this was no place to abandon the troublesome healer. It would be far too pleasant for her. In any case, on consideration, in spite of her heathen methods, Myllthlan had proved valuable in treating many of the Followers' injuries. No. It made sense to allow her to remain with the party for now.

Perhaps he'd have her once they reached the island, where he'd be in a position of unassailable power and would be able to do exactly as he wished. Yes. He'd take Myllthlan whenever he liked on Muhnilahm, regardless of her wishes. In fact, the more she resisted, the better, the more he'd punish and dominate her until she begged him to have her in order to stop the punishment.

Okkyntalah stood watch alone. The rest of the party slept. At times like this, he missed Shaulah most of all. She'd been a silent but attentive companion, an extra pair of ears and eyes on constant watch. He gazed out at the landscape from his lookout on the lower bough of a tall, many-branched tree. Its open structure gave sight of the camp, a few dozen paces away, and of the surrounding area. He would have time and opportunity to act should any enemy appear. His bow rested in one hand, an arrow ready to knock and fire at a moment's notice.

The sound, soft and difficult to identify, was definitely behind him. He turned slowly, ears attuned for any further clue, eyes scanning shadows relieved only by starlight and the fading glow of a moon entering its last quarter. The Skyfire, a faint star, no longer cast its eerie light over the land.

Closer, the sound came again. He stared into shadows. There was movement. A man moving with stealth, but limping as if either injured or burdened with some weight. He waited, the arrow knocked, the bowstring taut but not yet at full strength. The man crept from shadow to shadow, his encumbrance making little difference to his secrecy or speed of movement. Okkyntalah pulled harder on the string, awaiting the opportunity to aim at a vital organ as soon as the man came into a place where he could discern his proper shape. The man moved again, staggered a little and relaxed. He stopped his stealthy approach and walked, still limping, and now clearly carrying the body of a small deer across his shoulders, toward the camp.

Okkyntalah waited until he was directly below him. 'Sondukal. Welcome back.'

The guide looked up without apparent surprise and whispered his reply so that Okkyntalah quickly descended and stood beside him.

'I don't think I'm followed, but I can't be completely certain. Might be best to kill the fire till we're sure, like.'

They walked together into the camp and covered the small fire with soil, piled ready for such an eventuality. It died without smoke or noise and the other sleepers, apart from Teldrohn, remained unaware of any change.

Sondukal unshipped the food from his shoulders and left it close to the fire as the men moved a little distance from the sleeping women so they could talk quietly without waking them.

'You've been a while.'

Sondukal nodded. 'Got caught in an ambush, while I were huntin'. Three on 'em. Must've been close by an' got themselves hid while I were concentrating on a coney. I mean, getting' trapped for such a small meal. Anyroad, I were in trouble to begin with. But they're soft, these soldiers 'ere. Mad as Mhortag about what we'd done to the barracks, like. But no skill nor team work. I 'ad the first as soon as 'e stepped from the trees. But the others was on me straight away. The one I'd felled wasn't dead an' stabbed me in the foot with 'is knife. I kicked his 'ead an' dealt wi' the other two. Kept one alive an' questioned 'im before I put 'im out o' his pain. Carted the bodies into a thicket. Don't think anyone'll find 'em till they start to stink.'

It turned out that he'd learned there was now only a small troop of eight soldiers left, and they were guarding the remaining Powerseekers in the hall. The gate hadn't been replaced but some citizens had been detailed to take shifts in watching during the night.

'What made you think you might've been followed, then?'

'You never know. Better safe than sorry, I always say.'

'Looks as though we can finish the job tomorrow night, then. But without your help, Sondukal. Glad to have you back, by the way. We were worried about you.'

'Give over. An' there's nowt to stop me commin' wi' you.'

'Your foot?'

'Just a skin wound. I'll be fine.'

'Maybe. But I'll get one of the women to look at it come daylight. Now, best get some sleep. I'll go back on watch.'

'No, I was due to relieve you anyway, Okkyntalah. Catch some shuteye.' Teldrohn picked up his weapons, collected the bow and quiver from Okkyntalah, and took up his place in the tree. Okkyntalah and Sondukal moved close to the women and lay down. Tumalind snuggled into Okkyntalah as he made himself comfortable beside her, but she didn't wake.

In the morning, she must again enter that Dark Space and gather as much information as possible to make their last assault in the city as trouble free as possible. He dreaded her times in that unknown and terrifying place that always left her exhausted and nervous. She'd lost her youthful glow and looked weary all the time now. He wondered how much more of this effort she could take, how much more terror of discovery and dread of what they might do to her should they enter her mind again.

Chapter 43

A CONVENIENT VICTIM

Along with others, Aglydron had taken advantage of the extended stay in Stornhil to explore the port. He still felt anxious, as most of the women had rejected him for joining in worship, making it impossible for him to fulfil his sacred duty on every day. But, last evening, young Linlyss had come to him after prayers and offered herself. She'd been kind, shown affection, and he'd been so grateful that he'd given her as much pleasure as he was able under the circumstances. Afterwards, he'd apologised again for his harsh treatment of her earlier in the pilgrimage.

'You was just jealous of me an' my lustin' for Okkyntalah. It's alright. I understand. 'Course, I'd still like to frowk him, but I s'pose that's not gonna 'appen now, is it?'

'I don't suppose so, Linlyss. What made you come to me tonight?'

She shook her pretty head. 'Can't just accept it, can you? We're Followers an' you need a partner to do your duty to Ytraa, that's all.'

He was suddenly overwhelmed by her kindness and his grief surfaced. Still uncovered after their joining in the place he'd shared with Chislanda on the ship, she embraced him as he shook with sorrow. She stroked his back and said soft words until he calmed and then joined with him again, this time as a means of comfort.

'Better go back to Byfthlyn now. He'll be eager an' all. Y'know, now I've done it, I can't seem to get enough.'

'Doesn't he want to be exclusive?'

'He'd like to. But I don't. I want to sample a few more first. Settle down mebbie when I'm pregnant.' She smiled at a memory but wouldn't explain to Aglydron.

She wandered off, her tunic still unbelted for her new husband. Aglydron hoped the strong young man wouldn't be jealous of him.

Now, on the streets of the strange city, he gave his attention to new things, feeling the pervasive mood of happiness. But, for all the joy and contentment surrounding him, he couldn't escape the emptiness of life without Chislanda. Her loss hurt. He'd dreamed of an ideal future and it had been snatched from him. Her inexplicable disappearance left him no way of knowing if she was safe, whether she thought of him, whether, in fact, she still lived.

But there was no hope in such thoughts. His faith demanded he must give up these melancholy feelings and concentrate on the present. Finding a partner for joining before Ytraa was what mattered. He'd continue to take advantage of any willing women on the

343

ship until he reached home and then he would reclaim Shoarhn. She was his wife still. He retained his interest in the farm. Of course, he'd now be able to give her more pleasure and ensure her continued partnering. He'd take her back, continue his life as a married farmer, bring up his twin sons and return to the ways they'd shared for so many years together. Yes. That was it. Shoarhn would again partner him through life. After all, once they landed, Aklon-Dji would be hunted down and killed. Shoarhn would need him by her side. And he would make sure she remained a true Follower with him as her husband, once he'd punished her for her association with the Renegade.

There was no opposition to Shoarhn's proposal to move the boundaries of her farm out into the wild, uncultivated land that bordered it to the west. As always, Shoarhn had consulted her neighbours and they'd agreed her extension, recognising she now had more people to support. Dahrlahg's wedding to Pentryil had encouraged the two former slaves in her household to marry as well. Both ceremonies had taken place in the sixday before the second meeting of the Circle and both couples were busy, with help, constructing their homes in the new fields Shoarhn had acquired.

It was easy enough to increase the number of fowls, nurturing some of the eggs instead of selling them. And the other livestock would be allowed to breed more freely, with some of the offspring raised to maturity rather than being slaughtered as soon as they reached full size.

She expanded the olive grove, with more saplings planted in the fresh ground, and exchanged some of her crop for young fruit trees to increase the diversity of the foods she could grow. The farthest fields, she used as meadows. Raised, as they climbed into the low hills, they were difficult to plough and irrigate, but made ideal grazing. This left her more level land to cultivate, and she planted vegetables and grains, so that the farm became a source of many types of food for the whole community.

Next to her house, she left a good-sized plot in readiness for Tumalind's eventual return, eager to have her daughter close after such a long period of separation. The interior she would change as soon as the former slaves completed their home. She'd then alter the two extra bedrooms so the twins could each have their own room in which to sleep, as they were becoming too big now to share without occasional fights.

Once Aklon completed his island tour, she felt certain he'd stay with her and no longer be absent for much of the time. They wouldn't be able to wed until Aglydron either returned or the recognised four year period of separation had ended. Either way, she would marry Aklon as soon as possible. Aglydron had been dutiful, but he'd never really loved her and he was no match for the younger and more caring man she'd fallen in love with. Whether there would be other children, she was unsure. Did she want more?

Perhaps. She'd enjoy planning her future with Aklon once they were permanently together.

The idea of spending the rest of her life with this man she loved more than herself filled her with joy and eager anticipation. To spend every day, all the coming nights, with her lover, a man who loved her so well; that was something to be cherished and anticipated with real pleasure.

For now, she must attend the next meeting of the Circle. Already they'd found a new location. A house overlooking the town square had been deserted after all those who'd occupied it had been killed in the fighting. They'd all been Dissenters and the property was now empty and without heirs to inherit. They'd removed inner walls, leaving a wide, open space that easily accommodated the Circle and left plenty of room for any of the townsfolk who wished to be present.

They'd decided that all meetings would be held in public. All decisions were to be made under the eyes of the people, so that there would be no secrets, no favour shown to members of the Circle.

Eyethlehn's mindtalk with Ivdulon had resulted in several of the wise woman's suggestions being adopted. Those who served the Circle would gain no special treatment, adopt no exceptional status. Their number would remain at the dozen who currently made the Circle. But, each year, two would step down and new members be installed after consultation with the townspeople. This should ensure new ideas and considerations were explored whilst giving the Circle stability, so that longer term changes or projects that might come about had time to be completed. Comments from non-members would be listened to and discussed to determine whether they were feasible and good for the community.

The meeting that Shoarhn would lead on this day was to start discussions about how to deal with disputes between townsfolk and how to administer justice now the old systems were no longer in place.

'There's a lot for us to consider. Shall we start?'

The Circle agreed with Shoarhn and they began. She looked around at her fellow members and at the crowd of non-members who'd come along to listen and participate. The future for the town looked good. As soon as Aklon and Tumalind returned, her life would be as magical and full of contentment as it could be.

The party of armed citizens that arrived on the dockside as the ship was making ready to leave seemed threatening and at odds with the mood of the peaceful and welcoming town.

Dagla Kaz had been summoned by the captain to meet with the deputation. He felt aggrieved at this imposition but understood his role as leader required him to sort out any small problem with the local people.

The ship was ready to sale. One or two crewmembers were still on land, taking advantage of their freedom until they were due to cast off at noon. They were the only reason that the voyage hadn't recommenced and Dagla Kaz had agreed with the captain that her crew deserved some recreational time ashore before the longer part of their voyage. They would, of course, stop in Gatlibahn, but only to take on fresh water. From there the voyage would be unbroken until they reached Choshinahm.

'What appears to be the problem?'

The leader of the group onshore beckoned that he should disembark and talk with them. He repressed his anger at such a command, for the sake of good relations with the town that had dealt generously with them.

On the dockside, he faced the gathering. 'Now, what is the reason for this rather threatening visit, please?'

A woman stepped forward, looking grave. 'We're proud of our tradition of honesty, here in Stornhil. We live in harmony and peace largely because we trust one another. Of course, we recognise that visitors may have different traditions and different standards of behaviour. That's inevitable. However, we rarely have the sort of incident that has happened with the arrival of your group. I have the unfortunate duty of explaining that some member or members of your party are guilty of theft.'

Dagla Kaz displayed shock at the accusation. 'The Followers I can account for. None of them would dream of stealing. It goes against every tradition and value held by Followers. For the crew, of course, I'm unable to make any such claim. They're heathens and outside my control.'

The party signalled the captain, who descended the narrow gangplank to join them. At the same time, the two missing crewmembers appeared, carrying bags of goods to take aboard. The group stopped them and asked them to wait.

'Is your crew in the habit of stealing, captain?' Dagla Kaz's suggestion was clearly unexpected.

'My crew's made up of honest sailors. On board any ship, theft is considered the lowest crime. Thieves are severely punished when we catch them and made to leave the ship as soon as we reach the next port. I tell you without fear of contradiction that we've had no need to punish any sailor on this vessel for the last thirteen voyages, a period of a full cycle and a half.'

'Nevertheless, someone has stolen from traders in our town. Coin has been taken and goods have been acquired without payment. We cannot release your ship until restitution has been made.'

Dagla Kaz stood tall. 'I doubt you have the means to prevent us sailing. And, since we've already declared that no one aboard is likely to be guilty of the crimes you accuse us of, I see no reason for us to remain here to be insulted.'

The woman made a clap with her hands and two of the men in the group stepped aside. Both were armed with bows, arrows fixed in readiness. The woman nodded toward a small fire that blazed to one side, providing the means for dockworkers to cook meat.

'Should you attempt to leave without making restitution, my men will fire flaming arrows into your vessel.'

'I think not.' Dagla Kaz had known, from the moment the deputation arrived, that Caarl, his trusted senior soldier, would prepare for trouble. He merely nodded toward the ship.

The woman looked up and the High Priest watched her face change as she recognised her danger. She signalled her men to lower their weapons.

'Now. I'm sure we can resolve this issue without violence or unnecessary hostility. Release the crew members and we'll come to some arrangement regarding compensation for whatever losses you claim to have suffered.'

The woman looked again at the ship and, this time, Dagla Kaz followed her gaze. Caarl and several of the troops that Feldrark had sent to rescue the pilgrims lined the rail, bows fitted with arrows ready to find targets. Those on the dock were far outnumbered.

She let the crewmembers board ship. Dagla Kaz considered his position, now one of strength rather than threat.

'I am unaccustomed to being insulted, as is my captain and her crew. I've no intention of paying any further visit to your small town. The captain may have different ideas. I therefore leave it to her to decide what is the necessary action. I do, however, insist that you and your…er, cutthroats, depart from the dock side to remove the threat to this vessel and my people.'

The captain, beside him, seemed uncomfortable but, nevertheless, went with the deputation to a place some distance from the ship. Dagla Kaz returned to the deck and found his people grateful and full of praise for his handling of a difficult situation. There was some outrage that any community could accuse Followers of theft and he allowed the complaints to develop. After all, the more they felt aggrieved, the greater was his reputation likely to grow for his strong stand in their defence.

It was some time before the captain returned, her scrip somewhat lighter than when she'd left. She was chagrined but not unduly concerned by her loss, but she'd managed to secure the reputation of her crew, it seemed, by some compromise that she refused to disclose. Dagla Kaz suspected she'd secretly placed the blame on the Followers in his absence, but that was irrelevant. He'd escaped the issue and his experiment in thieving had gone unpunished, as the voices had predicted when they'd suggested it, the last time they'd contacted him.

The ship set sail and, as they left the harbour, many Followers stood against the rail, fists raised, and shouted abuse at the town.

Their voyage, now, was across the wide waters of the Ibasim Sea, an inland body of water with little other traffic and no islands visible. All signs of land quickly disappeared and they sailed a calm sea under a light breeze.

'How long before our next port?'

The captain told him it was likely to be over two days, as the need to tack because of the wind direction would lengthen the distance covered. Her answer was given in courteous but cool tones and Dagla Kaz understood that the incident on the dock had caused a rift in their previously friendly relationship. He should try to restore the better arrangement, especially as she'd also made a serious demand that his people stop trying to convert her crew to the ways of the Followers. The activity had not only given his people a diversion during the long voyage, with the variety of joining responsible for much pleasure, but had also resulted in a few conversions. He must find a way to repair the damage as soon as possible.

It seemed the likely concern from the captain wasn't simply the loss of money, but the sleight on her crewmembers. Perhaps if they shared the burden, equity might be restored. It was easy enough to find a victim to take responsibility for some of the stolen goods. The straps he couldn't blame on anyone else, as he'd already given two away. One to Valorysta and another to that young woman whose name he couldn't recall. Only that she'd displayed a talent for servicing his domination and he'd rewarded her with one of the Moontime straps. The others, after testing their efficacy as punishment devices, he intended to keep. They had the advantage that, applied with the right force, they raised welts and gave exquisite pain without breaking the skin or drawing blood. He recalled the wonderfully striped rounded buttocks of Valorysta as she'd wriggled in ecstasy beneath his lashing.

But that was a different source of pleasure. For now, he had another delight to plan. Most of the sweetmeats remained wrapped in their leaves. A simple enough job to plant them on his intended victim and make her suffer for her agonising rejection of him. That healer would be sorry she'd ever crossed him.

Soon they'd enter the last port before their long voyage across the Sophraq Sea to Muhnilahm. Soon, he'd be home and reclaim Shoarhn for his own. Aglydron had now decided he would forgive her sin with Aklon-Dji, once he'd given her the private beating that was the least she deserved. But he'd gain some advantage from her understandable regret at her lapse. She'd be more compliant and less likely to criticize his piety. That would make her a better wife and, in return, he would join with her using techniques he'd learned from other women, especially Chislanda, to give her a little more pleasure.

The thought of Chislanda again raised the sorrow he felt at her loss. Would it, he wondered, ever go away?

Dagla Kaz approached him and he stood up straight, not wanting the High Priest to see him slouching. 'You've long been with me, Aglydron, and have shown yourself a devout and trustworthy Follower. I have a duty for you, that others might shy away from. Will you perform that duty, without question and in the full knowledge that you do it in the name of Ytraa?'

'Of course, Dagla Kaz. Without question.'

'Good. I knew I could rely on you. The time will come shortly. But, for now, it gives me comfort that I have a Follower who can be so trusted and relied upon to do what is right in the sight of Ytraa. I thank you for your loyalty and unstinting service.'

Aglydron felt his being swell with pride at this extraordinary praise from a High Priest not noted for such words. Some around him had clearly heard the conversation and he knew he would gain respect from Followers on board and that it might bring him more women willing to join with him in praise of Ytraa. Curious as he was about the nature of the High Priest's request, he kept his word. 'Without question' was what Dagla Kaz required and 'without question' was what he would provide.

Left alone, but with admiring glances from those who'd heard, and knowing that soon all the Followers would understand his elevated status, he moved to the bows and watched the ship negotiate the gap between two small rocky islands and enter the calm waters that would take them to Gatlibahn.

In a haze of euphoria, enhanced by many words of praise and offers of companionship from women, Aglydron spent his time in the port unaware of his surroundings. By nightfall of the same day, they were leaving, their supplies of fresh water increased in readiness for the long sail home.

That night, one of the young women engaged him in joining for Ytraa. Later, Zyreenha, a Virgin Gift who'd started the pilgrimage voluntarily from Litkala, came and aroused him enough to make a second offering to Ytraa. It was a pity that the sparse light of the ship's lanterns wasn't as bright as he'd like to display her full beauty. But he appreciated her qualities in every other way, as she gave herself completely over to his pleasure.

In the morning, she was still beside him, still uncovered. Her new husband neglected for the kudos of association with a man so recently and lavishly praised by the High Priest. It was then, as he studied her form before morning prayers, that he realised she

349

was another with the same coloured eyes as his daughter. Those eyes scanned him with promise.

'Tonight? Again, please?'

They prayed, using the old positions, since these were practiced by the majority of Followers on board and preferred by Dagla Kaz, who was, after all, in constant contact with Ytraa.

'Yes. Tonight.'

She smiled and returned to her husband for breakfast, leaving Aglydron alone with his thoughts.

The reminder of Tumalind had him wondering about her again. What had really become of her? Had Okkyntalah discovered her? Or was she, along with Chislanda, lost forever? The suggestion that the High Priest had somehow been responsible for his daughter's disappearance was ludicrous. Dagla Kaz was a man of honour and perfect adherence to the laws of the Followers. Such action as he'd heard about Tumalind was beyond belief.

He went to the gathering where breakfast was being served and found admiring eyes continued to survey him. He'd never been the object of desire of so many women and he found the feeling heady and enlivening. Would that he had a private space he could use to take advantage of it. No matter. His nights would be full of pleasure from now until they reached the island. And perhaps it would continue when they landed, as his reputation spread amongst the islanders. That would give Shoarhn reason to think better of him and to accept his return.

Yes, all was looking very good for the future. He took his food from the ship's cook and sat with his back to the rail, allowing the sea breeze to cool him as the ship skipped across Sho Bay heading for the wider sea and his home.

Dagla Kaz approached, looking grave, and dropped beside him after signalling him not to rise. He spoke in quiet tones, so only Aglydron could hear. 'The time has come for you to do your duty, Aglydron. Do not let me down.'

Aglydron started to protest that there was no question of such a thing but the High Priest rose again, waved a hand to silence him and then walked back onto the centre of the deck. Myllthlan, arms bound behind her back, was led into the same space and held there with a soldier on either side.

What, Aglydron wondered, was all this about? The healer had been a near perfect member of the group and, though not a Follower, was always obedient in those ways that really mattered. Why was she bound and held captive?

350

Chapter 44

JUSTIFICATIONS

'Ivdulon spoke with me in the night, Blavv. She's contacted you as well?'

'Yes. We're to merge all her recent messages to make a single one between us, apparently.'

'That's how I understood it.'

They compared notes on conversations they'd had with Ivdulon over the past sixday and, using their understanding of her methods when dealing with secrets, they eventually came to the same conclusion. Tumalind let Blavv tell the others.

'Feldrark has sent a troop to Trotnahn. Once here, they're to take over government of the place so there'll be no trouble once we've killed the rest of the Powerseekers here. He's leaving it up to us to decide how soon we want to end those other lives, but thinks we should do it before the people of Trotnahn learn of his troops.'

'When are they due?'

'Probably the day after tomorrow.'

'Why didn't they tell us before, Blavv?'

'I don't know, Okkyntalah. She's been feeding us information secretly for a few days. Until today, we weren't able to put it all together to make any meaning out of it. It's very difficult to send messages by mindtalk in such a way that the Powerseekers don't know what she's telling us. She's doing everything she can to protect us all in this dangerous situation.'

'Of course. I just wish she'd found a way of alerting us before now. I hate going on such a mission with a feeling of urgency.'

'I'm sorry, Okkyntalah. Perhaps if I'd been less tired, I'd have realised what she was about before today.'

'Not your fault, either, Tumalind. I should've worked it out.'

Okkyntalah grasped them both by their hands and smiled at them in turn. 'Neither of you is at fault. Please don't blame yourselves. It's all part of the dangerous mission we're involved in, that's all.'

He turned to Teldrohn and then asked Kallohn to wake Sondukal from his late sleep.

The men gathered close and made their plans, such as they were. Tumalind and Blavv had supplied them with as much detail of the arrangements made by the Powerseekers as they were able. It gave them some hope of success, but the mission would still be the most risky they'd yet undertaken.

As she listened to their talk, Tumalind realised anew how much physical danger the men were in. She and Blavv faced evil and dread in the Dark Space, but these men, the men they loved, would be in peril of their lives when they left to carry out the mission. She'd never had any doubt about the essential nature of what they were doing. As soon as Ivdulon and Feldrark explained the dire consequences for the whole world if the Powerseekers were allowed to rise to their desired positions, she'd known they must be halted. No other way existed to defeat these evil minds. She'd personally risked much in attempting to change the mind of just one of them and had almost been drawn back into the Dark Space as a result.

They were intractable in their wickedness. Their ambitions, the very methods they used, the things they valued, were all now so vital to their idea of what was desirable that they'd been made captive by their very wishes. They were no longer capable of seeing any alternative to the world they envisaged. So imbued by the power they'd already tasted, so hooked on the pleasure their domination bestowed were they that nothing would deflect them from the course they had set. The Powerseekers were drunk on power and saw no way forward other than the gathering of more and more. To achieve their plans, they were willing to subject the rest of the world to poverty, abuse and slavery in all but name.

She'd seen for herself how the men reduced their women to the value of mere goods and chattels, made them into objects of sexual and domestic usage, with no other worth. True, women were subject to male domination elsewhere in the world. She'd witnessed their poor treatment in many societies. But, here in Trotnahn, they were like farm animals. Bought and sold, traded, used for gratification and then discarded.

And, worse in many ways, those men who weren't Powerseekers had been persuaded to value their women in a specific manner. They must be adorned with gold and jewels, drenched in expensive perfumes, made to wear their hair in ways that required the attention of several servants. The Powerseekers had instilled such worth to their ideas of what was right that the men had been fooled into believing absolutely in it. They were in competition with each other to make their women, their objects of demonstrable prestige and status, into the most extravagantly decorated possessions they owned.

Tumalind realised that, like Following, this materialistic adulation controlled the people by using those things that most mattered to the men in society. With the Followers, the act of sex had been made the fundamental purpose of worship, as Gadhallah had imbued it with a command from Ytraa that all people should strive to become one again. But, when she examined it, the whole proposition was shown to be nonsense. If people were originally both man and woman in one, they would have been impossible creatures. However much she tried to imagine such a being, she couldn't see other than some creature both ugly and clumsy. The stories of the parting made it clear that the original single being must have had four legs and four arms, two heads, the sexual parts of both. And how would they come together for sex in that condition? The priests would tell her that they had no need to join before, since the whole purpose of joining was to combine their forms, and these had already been combined before Mhortag split them. But, if that were true, why did they have sexual parts? There would be no point in such things if they had no use.

However she viewed the faith of Following, she could find no sensible reason for it. It had suited men, like Gadhallah and the priests who came after, to give women the impression that they had the same status and freedom as men. And, perhaps, for some that was true. But she knew in her heart and from talk with other women that what most really sought was a man who'd love them. A man who'd protect and provide for her and be there to bring up her babies. All the rest was just a tale to distract them from the truth. Following gave men the freedom to frowk with any woman who would have them; made it a duty, and a sacred duty at that. How had they never seen it for what it really was?

The answer was that it suited men, and enough women, to prevent them thinking about what was really going on. It was no surprise to her that Aklon's conversion on the island had gone well. So many must have realised, once told of the deception, that what they really wanted wasn't multiple partners but stable relationships in which to raise their children and reliance on their spouses for mutual support and comfort. Most people, in the end, wanted love. Sex was just a substitute for the more real and lasting delights to be had from love. Once exposed, it was inevitable that most would understand they'd been fooled and would readily accept the idea of a single partner for as long as they had children to raise and a life to lead together.

It wasn't perfect. But, then, neither was Following. She knew many women who'd suffered experiences with men that had been, at best, perfunctory and, at worst, effectively acts of rape. And, in conversation with Okkyntalah and other men, she'd recognised signs of disquiet about the need for what other societies she'd encountered called promiscuity. The idea of many sexual partners with no real connection left most men with a feeling of emptiness and a craving for some emotional depth that, ironically, drove them to more sexual acts. It was like a habit that made its user continually act in a certain way without ever giving the rewards it promised.

'You're very quiet, Tumalind.'

Okkyntalah was observing her with the look he often wore; the look that said he loved her more than anything else and found her desirable, amazing, clever and admirable. He conveyed so much simply with his expression, telling her his love was real. She knew anyway. But that simple, complex, direct look said it all so eloquently.

She moved closer and kissed him.

He wrinkled his brow, unsure why he suddenly deserved her attention and display of love. She smiled and said nothing of it.

'Just thinking, my love.'

The day was all but over and, too soon, he and the other two men would leave their camp and risk their lives in attempting to end the scourge of the Powerseekers. At least, they would do that here in Trotnahn. The greater collection of Powerseekers, gathered in or around the Monument of Kro Lat, was another matter and one they must face shortly, but not tonight. She took his hand and found a private spot where she demonstrated her love for him before he left for what might so easily be the last time.

⁙

'How many, Delbon?'

'Too many for a frontal attack, Aklon. I guess there's a good hundred. About thirty Unholy Ones and the rest ex-soldiers and others. They're all in the open. No shelters, no guards. They look half starved. But they're well armed. Look desperate but I don't think they'll be easy.'

Aklon sighed. He'd hoped to find some way to speak to them and try to make them see reason. He'd had too much of killing. But he saw no way of approaching these Dissenters without risking the safety of his own small troop of fighters. His suggestion that he should go and parley with them had met with utter refusal from his people.

'They'd kill you on sight, Aklon. They fear the power of your words, so they wouldn't give you a chance to speak.' Hyllahn was right. There was nothing for it but to put an end to this gathering.

'They've robbed, killed, raped, and destroyed homes, Aklon. I don't know why you care so much about them.'

He nodded at Choryssa. 'They are the result of the lies my father and his supporters fed them. I feel pity rather than hatred for them. They are deceived, and as much victims as those they have damaged with their fanatical support for Following. It is not always their fault that they are the way they are. Many are the product of their upbringing and the faith we once all shared with them.'

'But that's the difference, innit, Aklon? We've learned an' discovered the truth o' the matter an' we no longer believe those lies. They're stuck in the past. Won't listen to reason. They don't want change, 'cause they're scared on it. If they won't give it a chance, 'ow are we suppose to deal with 'em? There ain't no other way but to kill the bowelcreeps, is there?'

'Thank you, Phrysilda. You have a way of cutting through the confusion and pointing out the obvious. And you are, of course, right. The only problem remaining is how we are to do it.'

Phildrad brought them food and sat beside him on the fallen log he was using as a seat.

'Seems to me we've had plenty of experience of dealin' with such troubles. We managed it wi' those soldiers at The Point, didn't we? Outnumbered by 'undreds there, but we won the day. What's so different 'ere?'

'Nothing. You are also right, Phildrad. Come dawn, we will surround them with fire and use our bows to reduce their numbers to a force we can defeat with sword and knife as necessary.'

But morning was long in coming and he slept little, knowing he must kill again when first light came. The Skyfire, the symbol that had started this entire series of events, was no longer bright, no more than a small star bearing a thin tail of light. That something so short-lived and so far from the world they lived in could cause such upheaval was a mystery. But, of course, he realised, it wasn't the sign but everything it represented that was the real root of the conflict, cruelty and killing. He hoped it would soon end. But he must be the one to bring the fighting on the island to a close. He had started it and he had to finish it.

<hr>

Aglydron stared with amazement at the healer. How could she be at fault in anything? Myllthlan had always been a good and honest member of the pilgrimage, even if she'd never fully embraced the faith.

And Dagla Kaz was looking at him. The signal was slight but clear. It was time for him to fulfil the trust and faith the High Priest had so enthusiastically placed in him. But what was he supposed to do, and why?

He waited with the others, making a circle surrounding the healer as she stood, proud and silent on the deck. Dagla Kaz dismissed the two soldiers who'd brought her to the place and pushed her to her knees, an action she resisted so that he was made to use considerable force, both hands on her shoulders. Once in place, it was clear she wouldn't be a willing or compliant victim and he must hold her there; a struggle for him. It was now that he made a more open signal to Aglydron.

Dread, confusion, dismay and some fear suffused his mind as he stepped forward and gave help to the High Priest. It was hard to shame this woman who'd saved many lives and healed so many others. What had she done to deserve this treatment? She looked up at him with pain and betrayal written plain in her eyes.

'I have assembled you here to witness the punishment of a thief.'

The consternation died at the accusation. All recalled the event on the dockside that had almost prevented their sailing, almost resulted in the ship being set alight. The story of the threat had grown, as such things will, in the telling.

'You all know that we, as a group, were accused of theft from the town of Stornhil. I was convinced that none of the Followers was guilty of such a crime. It's unheard of in our community. The captain assured me that the crew was equally unlikely to be responsible, but she paid a sum in compensation simply as a way of permitting our release from a dangerous situation.

'Since that event, it has troubled me that such a thief must be on board this vessel. I therefore instituted a secret search of the belongings of all aboard. The stolen items were discovered amongst the property of this woman, Myllthlan. We have accepted her amongst us, in spite of her heathen ways, because of her outstanding ability to heal. And I do not belittle her contribution to the pilgrimage on that issue. However, we cannot permit such thieving to go unpunished and I have therefore brought her before you so she may be publicly shamed and made to pay for her despicable actions.'

There was some murmuring and not a little disbelief at the accusation, but the High Priest had made it clear that she had the stolen goods and there seemed therefore no doubt about her guilt.

'Aglydron, release her bonds and help me prepare her for beating.'

Aglydron was appalled. He felt deep affection for this woman. She'd healed him, saved the life of his friend and companion, Okkyntalah, helped in the recovery of Jodisa at a time when all seemed lost. But the High Priest named her a thief and such a crime mustn't go unpunished. He untied her wrists and stretched out her arms, pulling her forward, so her back was in place to receive the lashes.

'Not like that, man. She's no Follower. Strip her so the switch can mark her skin!'

His beating of Jodisa, naked, and the punishment that Dagla Kaz had made him suffer for that beating, also on his bare skin, flooded back to him. And he recalled how Myllthlan, against the High Priest's wishes, had healed his stripes afterwards.

'Well, man?'

He had no choice. He pulled her to her feet, roughly, disguising his uncertainty with action, and untied her belt. She made no effort now to prevent him but he daren't look into her face, daren't allow himself to witness her expression, knowing how it would be. He stepped behind her and pulled off her tunic to expose her to the crowd.

'Hold her on her hands and knees.'

He thought he might again have to force her to her knees, but, with quiet dignity, she knelt and then leant forward until her palms touched the deck. Aglydron dropped to his knees and held her in place with his hands over hers.

The High Priest picked up the stick, a pliant wand of willow that swished the air as he tested it before he made the first stripe across her buttocks. She made no sound.

'Stop this!' The captain appeared and the High Priest stayed his hand as she

356

approached.

'This does not concern you, Captain. It's a disciplinary matter amongst my people.'

'This is my ship, Dagla Kaz. And, on my ship, my word is law. Not yours. I demand to know the reason for this flogging.'

The High Priest explained, in tones loud enough for all to hear, what he was doing and why.

'Is it the custom amongst Followers for an accused person to be punished without an opportunity to speak in their own defence? Seems barbaric to me.'

'What is there to say? The goods were stolen. She was in possession of them. The matter is simple.'

The captain shook her head. 'You evidently have little experience of the deviant nature of some people, Dagla Kaz. In any case, I won't allow any punishment on this vessel that is not administered by myself. Also, I require the accused be given the chance to speak in her defence.'

'But how are we to know she won't lie and…?'

'And how are we to know that her accusers don't lie, Dagla Kaz?'

There was a general gasp of disbelief at this suggestion, though the captain hadn't actually accused Dagla Kaz of anything, since she was unaware of all the details.

'You call my word into question?'

'You call hers into question. Are you both not human? Is there some difference I don't know of?'

'I am the High Priest. My word is sacred. She is a heathen, her word means nothing.'

The captain bent to recover Myllthlan from her humiliating position. Aglydron was unsure whether he should release her or not and looked up at the High Priest for guidance. Dagla Kaz nodded, just once. He not only released her but helped her to her feet and, at the captain's instigation, replaced her tunic and gave her the cord to tie it closed.

'Now that we've brought some justice to proceedings, let us further civilise the issue by allowing the accused to have her say.'

Myllthlan thanked the captain and then addressed the crowd. 'Most of you have known me for as long as you've known the High Priest. Whilst he bears a title conferred by your religion, I bear the simple name of "healer" and give my aid freely and without prejudice to all who come to me for such help.

'I am no more guilty of theft than the rest of you. In fact, I've no idea what goods I'm supposed to have taken from the town. Where, I ask first of all, is the evidence of my so-called theft?'

Dagla Kaz held out a small reed bag and took from it some sweetmeats wrapped in pliant leaves. 'These are what she stole. Items of little value but nevertheless goods that the maker and seller deserved to be paid for, I think you'll agree?'

Myllthlan glanced at the goods and raised her eyebrows. 'What are they? I'm not familiar with these things. In fact, until now, I've never seen them.'

'She lies! They were found amongst her things!'

'Were they, Dagla Kaz? Then I have to ask who put them there. For I certainly didn't.'

There was a gasp of amazement from the crowd. Aglydron saw a look of doubt, even fear, cross the face of the High Priest. But Myllthlan appeared certain and utterly unashamed of her words.

'I'm not the only woman on this vessel to suffer unwanted attention from this man. Do those others amongst us have the courage to speak out against him? You see, I believe Dagla Kaz placed these goods amongst my things to punish me for refusing his perverted form of joining.'

The outcry that followed this accusation was loud and long and Aglydron feared for Myllthlan's life after such a declaration.

Chapter 45

POWERSEEKERS IN PERIL

The gateway stood wide open, the charred posts leaning and the ruined gates no more than ash. Two citizens sat on the ground, one either side of the opening, deep in sleep. Okkyntalah decided against killing or binding them, since it would signal their presence in the city and undoubtedly raise a search for them. Better to leave the guards alone and able to explain to any relief that they'd seen no intruders.

Tumalind's final search had located the Powerseekers in the hall. She'd been able to identify four soldiers actually in the large room they occupied, along with a woman for each of the remaining six evil minds. It seemed that danger wasn't enough to prevent them indulging in sexual predation. From conversations and actions she'd witnessed through the eyes of a mindtalker, a woman who remained unaware of her gift, she'd discovered other useful information to pass on to the men.

'I was tempted to let her know about her ability to mindtalk, but she was about to be used by one of the Powerseekers and it might have alarmed her. Might even have alerted the Powerseeker to my presence in her mind. But I'll try her later and see whether she can be of help to us.'

Okkyntalah had thanked her and reminded her to take care.

'Me? You're about to face unequal odds. You need to take care, my love.'

He smiled at the memory, and moved forward into the darkness of deserted streets. They knew the way and felt there was nothing to be gained from using an indirect route. The city continued to sleep, in spite of the known danger, and they arrived at the main doors without incident. Was that arrogance, inexperience or simply a lack of concern for the other citizens?

The entrance was barred from within. They circled the building, searching for an entrance they might use. But all ways of getting in appeared to be shuttered or locked. The city was entrusting the safety of the Powerseekers to their ability to seal the building.

By circling once more, keeping contact with the wall, they found an obscure, side door, located in almost total darkness. Sondukal took out his small pouch of tools and, with his fingertips, discovered the hole for the lock. With no clues other than touch and sound to guide him, it was some time before he was satisfied he had the right tool. Another spell of anxious waiting passed whilst he manipulated the length of metal within the lock.

Okkyntalah was curious about his reasons for even possessing such skills and tools, let alone having the devices with him. Litkala was hardly known for its security of individual homes or for any sort of crime. It seemed such an incongruous talent for the guide and tracker to possess. But now wasn't the time for such enquiries and he put it to the back of his mind.

They all heard the click of release and stood without breathing, listening for a response, some indication that others had noticed a noise so strident in the night.

Nothing.

No one responded. No one came. The complacency amazed them but they gratefully opened the door and entered the utter darkness beyond. Moving carefully, they found their way to the shutters over the window to the left of the door. Faint starlight, barely augmented by the light of a moon in its last quarter, filtered into the space. They stood, waiting for their eyes to become accustomed to the light. Wondering if they had entered some elaborate trap.

Okkyntalah found the way first. He touched Sondukal, who was next to him and grasped his hand. The guide took hold of Teldrohn in the same way and they threaded their way through stocks of unidentifiable items piled on the floor in regular rows. Okkyntalah led them to the far end of the room and another door. Also locked. Perhaps security was stronger than they'd suspected.

Sondukal, aided this time by the faint light entering through unshuttered windows, was able to pick the lock relatively quickly. Having just enough light to see by, he was also able to turn against the resistance with a little less force and unlock the door more quietly. Nevertheless, the click sounded loud in the room and they spent more valuable time in waiting to ensure they were not yet discovered.

They entered a corridor, dimly lit by flaming torches on sconces held against the walls. Only one in three of these flickered with light, making patches of brightness interrupted by longer stretches of shadow, where anyone might hide.

Their slow progress caused the torches to waver as they passed, lending the shadows an element of life that threatened, and heightened their anxiety. At last, they reached a place where the passage split into two. One continued in the same direction, whilst the other turned a sharp corner to drive toward the centre of the building. At its end, they climbed wooden steps, testing each before placing any weight. None creaked but they were narrow enough to hold only one at a time.

Okkyntalah emerged from the stairs into the part of the hall where they'd eaten whilst the women were used as seats. Now he knew where they were and could form a picture of the rest of the known area. Tumalind had described the actual whereabouts of the Powerseekers and they must now discover the steps that led to the upper storey. Again, the space was illuminated by occasional torches, one of which smoked as it reached the end of its fuel. Flickering wildly, it spread shadows that leapt and cavorted in far corners, suggesting movement where none existed. As it expired, the acrid smell of burning reached their nostrils forcing Okkyntalah to supress a s sudden sneeze.

Everything Tumalind had described now became vital information. He moved past the couch on which the Senior had lain. The wall beyond was no more than a painted screen and they passed its lurid pictures of abused flesh until they reached an opening at the left. There, another room, empty of life, led to a number of doors and open rooms with bars across the entrances. Behind these, women slept, the flickering torches picking out pale skin uncovered on narrow bunks.

One called out in her sleep and another woke. She turned and moved, rolling over and muttering something indecipherable as she lay facing away from them. Again, they spent precious time waiting to make sure they weren't spotted.

The stairs leading to the upper floor rose from a corner of the room. They tested them for noise and strength, found them firm and well-made, and ascended in single file. Here, closer to the site of their intended victims, the torches were all illuminated, giving light to the whole area. At the head of the steps, they came onto a wide, open space. Across this they faced a wall with three doors, all closed. And, in the spaces between the doors, two soldiers. One smoked a pipe as he watched the other casually using one of the women, bent forward in front of him as he thrust into her.

The distance was difficult. Far enough to allow the attackers some small cover, but not close enough for throwing a knife with accuracy.

Okkyntalah, against Sondukal's advice, had burdened himself with longbow and quiver. He signalled his intent to the other two and they readied themselves to move as soon as was possible.

His first arrow struck the smoking man in the heart and he slid to the floor, dropping his pipe. Even before the other soldier responded to the sound, a second shaft struck him in the throat and he slowly collapsed, his blood spurting over the woman, who was crushed beneath his fall.

Sondukal was by her head before she understood what had happened. He clasped a hand over her mouth and then, with Teldrohn's help, released her from under the fallen soldier, who Teldrohn had finished off with his knife.

They made sure she was unhurt before they gagged and bound her with strips of cloth cut from the soldiers' garments. Leaving her lying on her back away from the bodies, they approached the first door. Unlocked. Nodding to each other, they opened the door and entered.

The soldier was seated just inside the door, his sword in one hand. But the woman whose head rested in his lap was too much distraction for him to react at once. Teldrohn slit his throat with a single cut and the woman pulled back and made a small involuntary noise of alarm. Sondukal signalled silence but the noise had already escaped her and the Powerseeker nearest to Okkyntalah awoke only in time to see the sword that ended his life. He made no noise.

The Powerseeker sleeping in the second bed woke before any of them could reach him. He had time to shout a warning, rousing the other two women. They, in turn, cried out in alarm. Although they were able to silence him immediately, the noise reached the other rooms.

A soldier entered, sword drawn. Sondukal, who'd moved back to the entrance, took off the soldier's arm and then plunged his blade into the man's chest.

The women, much to their surprise, became quiet, watching the killing with no concern but holding their arms protectively across their bodies and pleading only with their eyes.

'We won't hurt you. You're free to go.' Okkyntalah's words seemed to confuse them more and they merely huddled together on one of the beds.

'Go! We wish you no harm. Go!'

That had the desired effect and they made for the door at the same time as the men, so that there was a crush of bodies leaving the room. Teldrohn made it to the adjacent door first and Sondukal followed swiftly. Okkyntalah indicated the bound woman to the others and made it clear they should take her with them. Confused and unable to decide what they should do, they hovered around the woman on the floor. He left them to it and went to the third door, now opening.

His arrow killed the soldier who emerged. Sondukal and Teldrohn entered the other room and he heard cries of pain and sounds of fighting in there. He stepped into the third room to discover two more Powerseekers with four women. Another soldier waited with sword drawn. He stood in front of the evil ones, who huddled behind him, pushing the women forward as a second shield, behind the soldier.

Okkyntalah engaged him in swordplay. He was more skilled than some he'd fought and the young hunter felt respect for the armed man. One of the Powerseekers attempted an escape, releasing a woman. She rushed at the soldier's back, knocking him to the floor. Okkyntalah sidestepped the falling man. In the short spell of time that gave him, Okkyntalah felled the Powerseeker. He turned back to the soldier, who was disarmed and trying to rise, and pierced his chest.

The other women, emboldened by their companion's courage, attacked the Powerseeker and, together, brought him to his knees. Okkyntalah struck with his sword, almost decapitating him. One of the women fainted as blood showered them all.

The fourth Powerseeker wasn't dead, however, and rose again. Wounded but terrified, he lunged through the door. The woman who'd attacked the soldier went after him and Okkyntalah followed, leaving the other women to make their own escape.

On the open area, he discovered the woman had brought down the Powerseeker, but with some cost to herself. He was trying to strangle her and the first group of women had gone to her aid.

'Out of the way!' Okkyntalah leapt across the space and pushed through the throng to thrust his blade through the man's chest.

Released, the threatened woman rose, struggling for breath. Nevertheless, she stood before Okkyntalah, offering herself for whatever service he wished.

He embraced her briefly and went into the other room to see what had become of Teldrohn and Sondukal. Their two soldiers were still armed and fighting. The Powerseekers, using women as shields, were close to escape. Fixated by the fight they must negotiate to leave the room, they failed to notice Okkyntalah. He struck the nearest on the back of his neck, killing him instantly. The women he'd held backed away as he fell to the floor, spilling blood.

The last Powerseeker cried out in alarm, distracting the soldier fighting with Teldrohn, who pushed through the guard's lowered defences to kill him. The evil mindtalker pulled two women in front of him, hiding behind them in terror. Teldrohn seeing Okkyntalah had that matter under control, went to aid Sondukal. His opponent was fierce and skilled. He saw his danger and made a final effort, swiping Sondukal's sword from his hand and plunging forward with the blade. Teldrohn thrust with his own sword and caught the soldier under the ribs, slicing across his belly. His momentum caused the weapon in his hand to catch Sondukal on his hip as the soldier fell. But the man did no more: he was dead as he hit the floor.

Okkyntalah, enraged by the Powerseeker's cowardice, simply forced his way between the captive women and sliced his blade up the man's body from groin to throat. He bled and dropped his entrails at his feet before he collapsed and died, ending the reign of the Powerseekers in Trotnahn.

The women were quiet, but for moans of terror. Uncertain of their fate, they gathered, arms held across their chests. Okkyntalah told them to go, but make no noise. Teldrohn bent to examine Sondukal and Okkyntalah joined him at his friend's side.

The cut was deep and long, blood pulsing freely down his thigh and pooling at his feet.

'The bedding. We can use it to bind the wound.' Okkyntalah cut strips from the wide sheets that covered the bed.

One of the women remained. 'I can do that, if you'll let me.'

He gave her the strips of cloth and she swiftly, and expertly, bound up the wound.

But Sondukal had lost a good deal of blood and was unable to move on his own.

'If you make your friend walk, he'll die. We can care for him.'

'Won't you be in danger?'

'You've killed all those who threaten us. You've freed us from slavery. The citizens will be lost without the Council to guide and lead them. And the only soldiers left were those guarding this place. And they're all dead, aren't they?'

'All.'

'Then we're safe. Some men from the city may try to enslave us, but we've seen how weak they are. We can defend ourselves, my sisters and I. You've freed us from the bondage of the last seven cycles and given us hope where none existed. Since you won't take the only gift we have to offer, at least let us ensure your friend doesn't die.'

He bent to Sondukal. 'We can't risk you moving, Sondukal. The troops will be here shortly from Litkala. They can take over from the women. Are you content at that?'

'It's the onny solution, Okkyntalah. I'm sorry to 'ave caused the problem. Let these angels care for me. I'm sure I'll receive no better care, lest that magic healer, Myllthlan, should suddenly appear from nowhere.'

Okkyntalah realised some of the other women had returned and were now waiting to see what help they might give. Word of their exploits had spread fast and the women who'd been locked in the cells below had been released. As Okkyntalah and Teldrohn made their way out of the building, two women accompanied them, stopping briefly to gather cloaks that covered them from throat to ankle.

'The city will wake soon. If we come with you, the citizens may not notice the blood or your weapons. But we must move quickly, for dawn is close and some will shortly be up so they can oversee their slaves in making goods for sale.'

The courage and resourcefulness of the women surprised them, but they were happy for their company as they left the hall. The streets remained silent until they approached the gateway. There, a couple of early overseers, armed with whips, passed them, glancing with curiosity but not challenging them. By the gate itself, the two civil guards still slept, unaware.

The women bade them farewell. 'Should you ever return to our city, please make yourselves known and you'll be pleasured by as many women as you desire. You've ended our torment and we would reward you for your bravery.'

They each kissed Okkyntalah and Teldrohn with great passion but remained as the pair walked away.

'I were a bit worried about leavin' Sondukal there on his own, to be truthful. But I think he's in for a fine time.'

'He might be, if he was the sort to take advantage. But Sondukal's always been faithful to his wife. I don't doubt he'll be spoiled though. I certainly hope so.'

'Back to camp to see how our own women feel about our return, eh? All that naked female flesh has made me right randy, I can tell you.'

Okkyntalah laughed and the pair strode purposefully along the road until they were out of sight of the city. Only then did they turn and enter the forest to make their way back to Tumalind, Blavv and Kallohn.

Chapter 46

AN ACCUSATION

Dagla Kaz couldn't believe what was happening to him. How could his plan have gone so awry? The woman was accusing him, and there were others now, showing they agreed with her. Followers agreeing with the heathen against their High Priest? How could this be? He must do something. Must find a way to prevent any further deterioration of his reputation.

'Enough! Enough, please. Dagla Kaz is our leader, our guide, our only true way to Ytraa. Maybe he's made some mistakes here and there. Maybe he's a bit overenthusiastic with some women, but what man here can honestly say he hasn't done the same?' Aglydron stopped and looked around.

To the High Priest's astonishment, the man appeared to have captured their attention.

'Dagla Kaz is our High Priest. He communes with Ytraa. Can we truly believe he could be in such error if Ytraa speaks to him? Of course we can't. This is all just a misunderstanding, a difference of opinion. Maybe the best thing is to stop all this nonsense and for us to spend some time in worship. I know we've already made our prayers this morning, but extra time with Ytraa might help us all see things more clearly. I believe we should all pray for guidance and then join, in the spirit of our faith, to praise Ytraa and bring peace and harmony back aboard this wonderful vessel.'

Dagla Kaz watched in wonder as the fool removed his tabard. A few others, confused and uncertain, did the same and then, seeing how events moved, he took off his own tabard. He resisted the urge to sneer triumphantly at the healer's look of utter incomprehension. That could wait. For now, it was vital to his continued position of power that he lead them all in prayer. With his own preparation, the others Followed and soon all were at prayer. The heathen and the crew still clothed and looking on in surprise.

Once prayers were done, Aglydron took a crewmember and she, a little reluctantly, allowed him to undress her and join. Dagla Kaz had to make do with the nearest available woman; a mature female from the Choshinahm group, and had to join in conventional manner. It was less satisfactory than his usual domination but her surprise at being chosen by the High Priest obviously added to her pleasure and he left her more satisfied than many other women he'd abused.

When the mass worship was over, he took the captain aside and spoke with her about the incident. They decided it might be best, for discipline and morale aboard, if the matter were dropped entirely. No more was said to him and, in the uneasy aftermath, most seemed disinclined to chatter further about it with one another.

Dagla Kaz retired to his cabin to escape attention and reduce the possibility of further controversy. The man, Aglydron, had shown himself reckless to risk his reputation, but it had worked to the High Priest's advantage in a way he could never have expected. It was good to have such a loyal fool amongst his Followers; not that many of them were any less stupid. The man had clearly been trying to curry favour. He'd see that he was always civil to this devoted Follower but wouldn't allow him to develop ideas above his station. Perhaps, though, it would be politic to thank him quietly for his timely intervention. Better to have such a supporter on his side than as a resentful member of the group.

And what of Myllthlan? She'd got away with her refusal of him with no more than a short humiliation and a single stripe. There had to be a way to make her suffer. But, for now, it might be better to let her be. On the island, there'd be many opportunities to do her serious harm. He'd be patient. He'd wait as long as necessary, but he would have his revenge.

The coin he'd had to give to the captain, in recompense for her settlement of the entire deal with the people of Stornhil was a loss. But he'd quickly recoup that on the island. And he would be there, back home, in a little over a sixday.

'No more than eight days, with fair winds and friendly sea.' That's what the captain had told him.

Home. Was Aklon dead? Had he been defeated, his band of heretics tortured and shamed? It was a pity he'd missed the public humiliation of those betrayers, but it would make his return in triumph all the more satisfying to know he had no other fights ahead. They would haul the Godwood up onto the Plain of Ytraa, and there, below Ytraa's Peak, install the newly carved likeness and celebrate his great victory. There'd be songs written and performed to praise his greatness in completing the pilgrimage against all odds. Of course, he would have to modestly decline the praise and explain it was all the work of Ytraa, but the people would know, and he would know, that the success had all been his doing.

He could spend his remaining days in comfort, with adoring acolytes serving his every need and attractive slaves ever at his beck and call to do exactly as he required. Some would commit small misdemeanours that would allow him to torture and flay them. And there'd be unlimited coin. Those voices had shown him how to accumulate it, how to set up a system in which he'd become rich and powerful through coin alone. So many ways to cheat the unwary out of their small riches so he could acquire more and more. His wealth would be limitless. Life would be good again. No more wandering the seas and the trackless wastes. No more hunting for food amongst wild animals out of legends. No more fighting dragons or defeating the driving snows of the mountains. No more battling heathen hordes and leaving the field strewn with enemy corpses.

He sat on his small bed and imagined it all. From outside, he heard the everyday activity as Followers renewed their attempts to convert the crew, the settlement with the captain having removed her ban. The crew went about their maritime duties. It was, perhaps, time for another revelation from Ytraa. He'd hoped to hear from the voices but they'd remained silent for a while. Just once or twice he'd had a strange intrusion, criticising his softness. He missed those voices of encouragement and suggestion and tried to reach out to them again, tried to invite them back into his mind.

He'd experienced little success when attempting to use mindtalk, never fully understanding what it actually entailed. Was he trying too hard? Perhaps the gift was a natural thing. Certainly, Wyyhn Kaz had suggested as much.

'Just like having a conversation, but without actually being able to see the person you're talking with.'

He sat and allowed his thoughts to wander with no purpose or pattern. The feeling was relaxing and he soon felt sleepy, lay down, and, completely relaxed, let sleep overtake him.

<hr />

Tumalind woke to rain. It was the first they'd experienced since they'd arrived at Trotnahn and was a welcome change, even if it meant they were unlikely to be able to cook later on.

'Do I disturb you, Tumalind?'

'Ivdulon. Good morning. I'm awake and ready to face a new day. What peril do you have for me today?'

'No peril. But I need to introduce you to a couple of new mindtalkers who ride with the troops now a league away from you. Some will remain in Trotnahn to help the citizens form a new government and prevent rioting and chaos after the killing of the leaders. Others will accompany you and your party to…the next place.'

'No rest, then?'

'A little, whilst you make the journey. Once the task is over, I won't call on you again for such work.'

'Well, that's nice to know. I can go home and raise babies with Okkyntalah?'

'As many as you wish. Let me connect you with Yoqalohn. He'll remain with the troops in Trotnahn.'

'Hello, Yoqalohn. I expect we'll meet face to face shortly. Can you give me a picture of where you are?'

'Good day to you, Tumalind. I've heard much of you and all of it complimentary. I *look forward to seeing you in the flesh.'*

'Ah, that's for Okkyntalah alone.'

'I see you have a sense of humour. That's good. Soldiers thrive on it. But a disappointing answer. I suspect I'll live, in spite of the broken heart. We're here.' He allowed her to see through his eyes and she quickly recognised the place.

'And the other new mindtalker, Ivdulon?'

'Serrophenahl. She'll accompany you on the rest of the journey.'

'Will we need another mindtalker for that, Ivdulon? I'll be available, won't I, and Blavv?'

'Extra help. Nothing more.'

Tumalind wasn't convinced, but she could say nothing further without alerting the Powerseekers at the Monolith. For the moment, she was happy to accept the possibility of help in that venture. But it concerned her that a third mindtalker was deemed necessary for connection between the party and Litkala: was there some dark cause for that? Did Ivdulon expect one or more of them to be lost?

'Hello, Serrophenahl. I hope we can be friends on this difficult journey.'

'I hope so, too, Tumalind. I'll be with you for additional support.'

They met up with the troop easily on their approach to the city. No soldiers to dodge or avoid. And they spent that day with them, explaining the layout of the city and the habits and customs they'd learned. The soldiers were accompanied by a small group of men and women who would act as civil leaders and show the way for the people until reliable rulers could be found from the native population.

More than half the soldiers along with the diplomats moved into the city to take charge of the bewildered population. Tumalind hoped it would only be a short time before the women there were deemed equals. It would be many cycles before they were actually treated as equal by the menfolk. But the move had begun, and she was happy to have had a part in that progress.

The following day saw their own small party enlarged by a troop of around a hundred soldiers. Several camels were with them as beasts of burden to take them across the sands surrounding the Monolith of Kro Lat.

Now they must reach the final target of their campaign for justice and equality. What that destination held for them, and for her in particular, remained to be seen. But she was aware it wouldn't be an easy fight and that she'd again be in danger. Well, she'd defeated Powerseekers many times now. She had the knowledge, courage and experience to do so again. The difference, of course, was that in the Monolith dwelt an unknown number of much stronger minds, set on domination of the whole world. It wouldn't be as simple to defeat them as it had the outlying few Powerseekers in Trotnahn.

The fire had worked, almost too well. In fact, Aklon and his party had had to retreat a short distance to avoid being caught in the flames as the wind changed direction and the fire raced toward them for a while. But they'd managed to loose off enough arrows into the gathering to reduce the Dissenters' numbers to something nearer equality.

Some of those remaining lost heart and surrendered. Aklon placed Patrilha and a couple of others in charge of those prisoners, disarming and binding them until the fighting was done.

The remaining Dissenters, in particular the Unholy Ones, were fierce in their resistance, however, and Aklon lost a couple of his warriors. A half-day of hard fighting cut the enemy down until only a handful of diehards remained.

'I offer you life if you will renounce your faith and declare Gadhallah a vile liar and promise to cease all violence toward our new community at once.'

'Renegade! Liar! Bowelcreep!' The leader, a wiry old Unholy One, rushed at Aklon, his few supporters in his wake.

The killing was brutal and, mercifully, swift. Aklon stared at the field of bodies: they must now bury the defeated. He set the prisoners to the task, as a way for them to make some recompense for their former violence. They did it with heavy hearts but, by sundown, all the corpses were covered in soil and only the burnt and blackened stumps of the fire-blown trees remained as witness to the carnage.

He sat with the troops and the new members, made to wear headbands for identification and otherwise remain naked so they would realise they were no longer Followers. All eleven had renounced Gadhallah publicly and promised to mend their ways. Originally from all parts of the island, they were to be returned to their communities and there become normal members of the population.

Aklon ate with better heart that night, knowing he had defeated all but a small number of the Dissenters. The morning would bring another long march, this time to the capital. There would be possibly the most difficult task of finding and either converting or destroying the remaining malcontents. And then, his work done, he'd retire to Morstahn and a life of peace, love and farming with Shoarhn.

'Aklon, do I find you able to commune?'

For a moment, he was unsure who connected with him. It took him a while to recognise the voice as that of the High Priest from Litkala. Why was Rrildyss contacting him?

'I am free to talk, Rrildyss. To what do I owe this honour?'

'Silver-tongued demon. We've not spoken for many sixdays, so you may not know that I'm with the pilgrims, sailing the Sophraq Sea on our way to Muhnilahm.'

'I was aware you were with my father. I take it he remains in this world?'

'He does. And he's more dangerous now than when he left the island. He's secured the Godwood and the help of the last remaining Followers from Choshinahm. Since they're the last of their faith, from a land hostile to their beliefs, they're largely fanatics. Though quiet enough at present, since there's no opposition here on board, I fear they'll be a serious threat to any progress you've made on the island. I thought I ought to warn you of our coming.'

'You intend to land at Chalamamnon, of course?'

'So I gather. I think Dagla's expecting much rejoicing and a welcome of some measure, since he's going to send Aglydron and a couple of others in the ship's small boat to announce his coming.'

'That sounds like father. Always willing to make the effort to organise any form of idolising of his person. No doubt he will be expecting a celebratory march from the capital to the Plains of Ytraa with the Godwood.'

'He did mention a procession. I think he's expecting the Godwood to ensure his acceptance and the rejoicing of all the people on the island. I take it you're still fighting for control?'

'We are almost finished. There remain a few Dissenters, but the vast majority of the population has seen the sense of the changes, especially since I have arranged the exposure and display of all secret parchments and stone tablets for everyone to see. Once they have seen for themselves the lies they have been told, most people seem to lose faith in the Followers. At present, I have found no alternative, but I do need to find something to fill the gap, of course. People need some spiritual centre, after all. And the need for rite and ceremony remains as strong as ever.'

'Well, that's for the future, of course. I know Ivdulon's working on that back in Litkala and I expect to return there to discover many changes. But you're immediate concern, of course, is the disruption our arrival is bound to have on your newly formed community. We're due to land in about seven days.'

'So soon? It is as well I intend to set off for Chalamamnon in the morning, then. I will be there in two days, with my small troop and a few additions. Perhaps I need to recruit a few more helpers in readiness for the arrival of my father. Thank you for the warning, Rrildyss. But now I must return to the other world, as I am being stared at.'

'Of course. Keep in touch, won't you? I'll be here and ready with any additional information you may find useful.'

'Thank you.'

He cut the connection.

'So, what's the news then Aklon?'

He smiled at Phrysilda and gestured to the whole party to gather close. 'I have some interesting information for you. It appears we have a little more to do before we may return to our families and a more settled way of life. My father, Dagla Kaz, returns in about a sixday with a gathering of over a hundred fanatical Followers and a new Godwood. I believe we will need to organise an appropriate meeting party for them. Do you agree?'

It would be the final act in their cleansing of the island and they welcomed the news. The cheer was long, loud and derisory. They would arrange a greeting that Dagla Kaz would remember for the rest of his life, however long or short that turned out to be.

'Ivdulon, I am unsure of my actions when my father returns to the island. I need your wisdom, please.'

'A scheme long in the making is gradually coming together, Aklon. I've much yet to do, but your part in events is important. I'll gladly discuss it with you.'

'He has no idea of the changes here. In fact, according to Rrildyss, he is expecting a ceremonial welcome.'

'Understandable. I no longer have much interest in Dagla Kaz. He was needed to move a small part of the plan forward; ridding Choshinahm of the last few Followers. Necessarily a fanatical bunch, they might well have caused significant trouble in that region, had he not gathered them up to complete his futile pilgrimage. I'm sorry you'll be landed with them. They're likely to pose considerable danger to your fragile changes if they land in force. Might be best to ensure they never make it to shore.'

'I cannot simply murder them at sea, Ivdulon. It would be against everything I stand for. In any case, the practicalities of such an operation are beyond me.'

'Then, make sure they're broken into small groups and dotted all over the island, where they can be kept in check and absorbed into your new society. As for Dagla himself, I expect you know you must put an end to him at once.'

'I have instituted the idea of justice on the island. I cannot simply put my father to death because it would be convenient. He must be put on trial.'

'If you feel you must. But you're giving him a better chance than he'd ever have given you, or for that matter, anyone else. I don't suppose you've been told of his despicable behaviour toward the wonderful, kind and generous healer, Myllthlan?'

Ivdulon told him, in detail, explaining all she knew and all she'd put together from the various sources at her disposal. It didn't paint a pretty picture.

'If you feel you must give such a man a fair trial, that's up to you. But beware his tongue. He's used to persuading people of his value, honesty and sincerity, even though none of those qualities ever applied to him. Be careful that your idealism doesn't leave you open

to his deceit, Aklon. We've travelled a long hard road together and I'd hate for you to end this journey in peril through your kind-heartedness.'

'Thank you, Ivdulon. As always you give me difficult answers to my questions. I must give the matter serious thought.'

'Do that.'

'How is Jodisa, by the way? I have been too occupied to contact her recently.'

'She grows plump with child but is content and looking forward to producing an heir. Talk with her. She'll enjoy that.'

'I will. For now, I thank you, Ivdulon.'

He ended the connection and tried to lay quiet for a while, awaiting the waking of the rest of the camp, as the sun broke above the trees on the horizon. His mind was full of the threat posed by his father's imminent return and he was unable to relax, knowing he must take some very hard decisions once the former High Priest reached Chalamamnon. It seemed likely that the choice there would be between his own death or that of his father.

Chapter 47

AT THE MONOLITH

'A little over halfway, Dagla Kaz. At this rate, another three days, to arrive midway through the fourth. How's that sound?'

'It's been so long. I've been away for so many portions. I've no way of knowing what might have happened in my absence. You leave deputies, but they never do the job the way you would yourself, you know, Captain?'

'Of course.'

'Would it be possible for a few of my trusted people to leave the ship a little way offshore and land by your small boat to discover what they may about the island?'

'And to prepare for your arrival with a bit of pomp and ceremony, eh? Of course. I can afford half a day.'

Dagla Kaz bit back his rebuke; it wouldn't help his cause and, in any case, the captain spoke the truth. He thanked her and went to consult with the other priests.

Rrildyss shrugged, a little distracted when he approached her, but she quickly recovered her concentration and paid attention as he took her to seek out the others. Wyyhn bore an odd look but joined in the discussion willingly enough.

He explained his hopes and expectations. A gathering of the people on the quay to welcome him, the Godwood, and the new Followers back from the pilgrimage. A speech explaining his intentions for the next few days. The transporting of the Godwood to the Plain of Ytraa, where it would be carved into the likeness of Ytraa. Then a short celebration as they raised it to the top of the monument.

'Then, in around two sixdays, when all is prepared and everyone on the island has been informed, we will hold the greatest ever gathering of Followers. The whole population will meet on the Plain and I will address them from the Godwood, and inspire them with love and faith and there will be feasting, much joining and great joy.'

'And prayer.' Wyyhn reminded him.

'Oh, prayer, of course. That goes without saying.'

'I would've thought that would be the one thing that didn't go without saying Dagla. Surely, that is the vital part of the whole business, isn't it?'

'Yes. Yes, of course. Yes.'

'You seem less than sure, Dagla.'

'No, no. I merely assumed we all understood the role of prayer in the proceedings. Nothing else. How could anyone forget its inclusion, after all?'

He left the meeting feeling less enthusiastic than he'd started. It was his day, his triumph. How dare they try to take it away from him? He'd earned adoration and respect, earned praise and the chance to have his story glorified.

'Dagla, a word of warning, I think. You have been invaded in the past, been given ideas that are good for neither you nor your people. I know you cannot respond, you do not have that gift, so I will simply tell you certain things and you must make of the information what you may.'

He'd heard this voice before; briefly and on few occasions. It had told him things he didn't want to consider, implied he lived a life both unworthy and selfish. He wouldn't listen now.

'Very soon, you will arrive home. You will find it much changed. Your son is now in charge of the island, though he does not seek power. He has informed the people of your deception, shown them the lies of Gadhallah, and even suggested the probable non-existence of Ytraa. And most of the people agree with him.'

Aklon, alive and in charge? Intolerable, and therefore a lie. He wouldn't listen to the rest of what it had to say to him. It was a trick, some device to make him change his ways. Well, he wasn't going to. No. Not ever.

'You are reviled now, Dagla. The people hate you for your lies and unjust punishments. If you land at all, I advise you do so with humility and beg for forgiveness. If you are very fortunate, they may allow you to live amongst them as an ordinary citizen. But you might be better advised to sail on and make a home elsewhere.'

Impossible! An ordinary citizen? He was Dagla Kaz: High Priest, chosen of Ytraa. The voice must be mad, a thing sent by some outside force that wanted to test him. That was it. This was a test of his resolve. Those other voices had hinted that such a thing might happen. They'd told him of a malign voice that preached selflessness and sacrifice and love and harmony, as if such qualities did any good. They were for fools and underlings, not for the likes of him. He was a superior man, godlike in his lineage and manner. People looked up to him, worshipped him. Look at Aglydron: a man who understood his power and position.

The voice hovered in the background, trying to push through his own thoughts, but he ignored it, refused to hear it, though it remained an irritating presence for some time. But it had done one thing for him: it had warned him of possible dangers. He'd thought he must be made welcome once they heard news of the Godwood. But, if, in the unlikely event the intrusive voice was right about Aklon, if they were Followers no longer, then his whole approach must change.

He must discover the reality about the island before he set foot there. No matter. He'd arranged with the captain for his representatives to find out how things stood. The only change he need make was to ensure Aglydron, at least, understood the importance of his need for information. Let others, maybe so-called High Priest, Wyyhn, and one or two of the more dispensable people in his group, let them risk suffering the consequences, if that other voice spoke any truth. Aglydron would return with the facts. He must school the man in what he needed from him.

And, of course, he must persuade Wyyhn to go with his faithful servant, explain the need for a priest to lead the forward party to organise proper prayers. In that way, he might place the diehard priest into danger, maybe even get him killed, if there was any substance in what that mysterious meddling mind had told him. Of course, that wasn't true; it was a trick, or a test, or…anything but the truth. Aglydron held the key to the problem, and it was Aglydron he must use as his eyes and ears in this.

'Before Dagla Kaz returns here, he intends to send an emissary, as he has some inkling of our changes and his first thoughts will be for self-preservation.'

The group he addressed had been chosen from amongst the original members of the Few, augmented by those soldiers who'd shown themselves both brave and certain of their cause. This group contained only the best of his people. Their task was difficult and might have to change according to circumstance, and it was important he didn't confront his father too early. That meeting would influence those who remained unconvinced. With planning, it might be used to good effect when he exposed his father for the fraud he was.

All plans were in place, as far as possible in light of what was known. He'd sent runners to the townships to gather those who wished to be present, both believers and the majority who accepted that the faith was dead. The gathering must be as large as possible. People were collecting, amongst them many of those who'd lived so long on The Point. Chellyth and her partner, Por-Kildu, had brought with them over two hundred of their people. The open grassland to the north of the capital was already filling with the crowds. A nominated high point there had been prepared and those who were already gathered kept it clear.

Now, the boat approached the harbour wall, rowed by four sailors and bearing four Followers from the ship that lay at anchor offshore. Aklon stood back from the group he'd chosen to greet the occupants, in case his father proved foolish enough to be with them. The most recent mindtalk with Rrildyss had informed him the High Priest remained aboard. But it did not do to share every piece of information in these uncertain times. Though he was as certain as he could be of those he'd put forward for the mission, he had learned that absolute certainty might be lethally misplaced in times of great change. Trust at such times was no easy matter.

Dagla Kaz remained potentially a powerful force with the island people and a false step now could so easily undo much of the good he'd done to discredit the evil man. Circumspection was necessary, much as it went against his natural desire to be honest and open.

He was close enough to hear the first exchanges. The boat contained his lover's husband, Aglydron; a High Priest from Choshinahm; Caarl, the chief soldier and former commander of many of Aklon's own troops; and one of the original Virgin Gifts, a young woman called Dilanthas. Her inclusion was a surprise, but his father had ever been devious.

The initial greetings were cordial. Aglydron acted as spokesman and briefly explained to Delbon, Aklon's chosen speaker, the purpose of his visit from the ship, and who waited aboard.

'Welcome, Aglydron. Your exploits are a bit of a legend. Folk here admire and respect what you've done. Dilanthas, you're also welcome back, though why you're with this lot's a bit of a mystery. Caarl, of course, you're a valued member of our community and I'm to make you very welcome after your long journey. And you, Wyyhn Kaz, well, you're a guest, so I welcome you as such. Let's find a better place for our meeting, eh?'

He led them along the quay to the small building they'd selected for this first meeting. Aklon walked behind, entering the room last. Caarl drew his sword at once but Delbon and two other members of the Few stood between them and he had no chance to strike.

'You've a lot to learn about how we run the island, Caarl. Put down your weapon. Please.'

Aglydron and the other two gave all the appearance of the confusion expected. But the soldier was a man of action and remained alert, tensed for a fight.

They gave their guests refreshments. The dress of certain members of the greeting party, or its lack, clearly confused the new arrivals. Aglydron questioned it first.

'Are these slaves? Their dress is sacrilegious if not.'

'No, Aglydron. There's no slaves on Muhnilahm. Everyone's free. We've released them all, and folk dress 'ow they like. You'll see everything, from nowt to full cover. Lots of people go naked to protest against the lies forced on them by leaders of the Followers.'

'But isn't everyone here a Follower?'

'No one here's a Follower, Aglydron. In fact, there's less followers on the island than on your boat. About 'undred and forty, isn't it?'

Aglydron stood amazed. Wyyhn Kaz looked thunderous. Dilanthas seemed no more than simply confused and Caarl remained suspicious and alert.

'I don't know what to say. I don't understand. I was sent to arrange a welcome for the

High Priest. He thought there might be some changes but not this…this sacrilege. Is it true? I have to go back to him with information. What should I tell him? It can't be true. We're Followers on the island. Always have been. Always will be. There's no other way. We're Followers. Followers.'

Aklon finally moved forward and spoke. 'You are rambling, Aglydron. Considering your initial role in the pilgrimage, and your blind adherence to the faith, I am not surprised at your refusal to accept the simple truth. But I tell you that you will find few Followers here. We have changed. We know the truth. Dagla Kaz, if he is unwise enough to return, will discover he is no longer a figure of power and is unable to do as he likes. I am now in command. I suggest you return, Aglydron, and inform the former high priest that, if he decides to return, he will be made to stand trial for his misdeeds.'

They'd tested the water, and were now more fully aware of the way things stood with those on the ship. No point continuing the pretence. He sent them all back with the sailors. Already, the boats that would escort the vessel into harbour were setting sail. He knew his father well enough to understand he might try to flee and bring his people ashore in some remote spot in an attempt to invade.

Aglydron was mute with shock as he boarded the small boat that had brought him. Aklon nodded to the sailors and they rowed back to the ship.

The first encounter had been quite instructive. But these were no more than tools sent by his father to investigate. Aklon had tried to warn his father off, but the man had come anyway. Now he would take him, and all his people, to the designated place and there put him on trial for his evil ways. But, first, these new Followers would be shown the proofs, so they had a chance to change their minds about their faith.

It all sounded so straightforward. But it would be anything but simple. Recent experience had shown him how resistant people could be to change, even when faced with facts about their unproven beliefs. Many clung to what they'd been told was the truth, even in the light of evidence showing that was impossible.

In conversation with Ivdulon and Feldrark, and others gifted in mindtalk, he'd encountered a lot of ideas about the nature of religions. There were a great many in the world, but the one constant seemed to be that faith lay outside the realms of thought and reason. It was an emotional need, and fundamental to many people regardless of intelligence or experience. He'd removed the faith of Following from his people but left a gaping hole. That void must be filled. Filled as soon as possible, if discord and new violence were to be avoided. He awaited Ivdulon's solution to that problem and hoped she would resolve it very soon.

In the meantime, he would have a trial to conduct. The final battle between his way of life and that dictated by his father. He must not only make the people see the evil that

379

had been his father's way, but convince them that the killing he and his Few had done had been unavoidable. The coming confrontation on the hill outside the capital would be a pivotal moment in the future of the island. If he got it wrong, many would suffer. He must get it right.

The Monolith of Kro Lat was like nothing Okkyntalah had ever seen. Towering over thirty manheights, a smooth cylinder of bright white stone rose from a wide circular base of black that mirrored the building and the sky beyond. He viewed the monument, alone, from the top of a slight rise, whilst the rest of the party gathered on the slope approaching the tower, so they remained out of sight. But, if anyone occupied the great hollow ball that sat impossibly atop the cylinder, they must have seen the party approaching from leagues away.

That sphere of black stone he guessed measured some fifteen manlengths across. In the side facing him, toward the top and little to one side, a perfect circle opened. The angle of the sun showed that opposite this opening was another, which must be lower and smaller, judging by the shape of the shadow falling on the neatly manicured grassland beyond. Of human life there was no sign. The Monolith, as spectacular as it was sinister, was the only visible building.

Tumalind and Blavv and the new woman, Serrophenahl had all declared there were many evil minds present. They'd located them easily within the ball that topped the column. And those minds knew of their presence.

This warning had prevented the entire troop mounting the small hill; seeming sensible they remain as hidden as possible. But Okkyntalah's survey made it clear they wouldn't be able to approach unseen. The whole area surrounding the column was absolutely flat. It had the look of a man-made surface covered in short grass. No trees, no shrubs, no wild flowers varied the wide green expanse that circled the smaller black disk on which the tower rested. No birds sang or flew and no insects buzzed. The entire area had a lifeless, artificial quality that he found deeply unsettling.

Okkyntalah rose from his crouched position, conscious that he must be visible to anyone looking out from that great structure. It was a sight so incredible that he wouldn't have believed it possible had he not been able to see it with his own eyes. A marvel. A true wonder. Yet there was something about its setting and design that made the observer anxious rather than awed. The monument spoke of power and extravagance, not worship or praise. It stood as testimonial to those who'd constructed it, not a tribute dedicated to any god or exterior power.

The very air around it seemed alive. Okkyntalah felt waves of hostility and threat emanating from the structure. He trembled; wanted to cower and flee. As he stood,

380

resolutely watching for movement, the interior of the ball seen through the small aperture, pale in spite of being in shadow, slowly began to glow with deep blue light. It gave the ball the appearance of a staring eye, but it was only an impression. Okkyntalah didn't think it was an eye, merely a representation of one. The message was clear. He was being watched.

He stood for a time longer, measuring with his eyes and taking in every detail, before he returned to the troop commander and the women mindtalkers. From this location, on the upward slope approaching the Monolith, only the top of the ball remained visible, as had been the case for much of their journey. But the feeling of being watched persisted even here.

Okkyntalah described what he'd seen. 'In the green area surrounding the Monolith are darker circular patches. I think they may be entrances to underground chambers. Perhaps that's where the people live. But there's no sign of ground water and no indication of any sort of farming. Nothing to indicate they grow food here. Yet Tumalind and the others insist there are people up there. And, I admit, I felt I was being watched. It's not a friendly place.'

The troop commander nodded. They'd rested well on their approach, aware of their proximity once they'd had their first glimpse of the ball, as it rose partially above the horizon when they were about seven leagues distant. Its true form hadn't become clear until Okkyntalah had viewed it from the top of the rise they now occupied. The small, almost circular ring of low hills completely surrounded the Monolith, so that it sat in the bottom of the hollow they created. From the ridge, the full structure could be viewed at last, together with all its surrounding features.

They'd found no signs of other people as they crossed the harsh and seemingly endless desert of sand and rock. No wells, such as those used by the K'ahll around Ov Bebna and Trotnahn. Here, the barren land held no sign of life. Nothing grew and nothing moved except the sand, drifted by the winds into dunes that occasionally reached great heights. In other places, it had been stripped to reveal great stone slabs of the same colour, dun and drab. From time to time, they'd happened on deep hollows, signalled by sparse vegetation, in which water could be found, but only by means of a volunteer dropping within at the end of a long rope. It was the only water source they'd found and on one occasion supplied them with food as well, in the form of small lizard like creatures that showed no fear of the intruder. The only sounds were the wind and the hooves of their camels across the inhospitable terrain.

The commander asked for six volunteers to approach the tower. 'We need to see what, if anything, lives in the area. I daren't risk my entire troop. Some brave souls need to make that first approach, knowing it may result in their deaths.'

It was testament to the honesty and courage of the commander that he had no shortage of volunteers and had to select a party of three men and three women. He wanted to test whether both sexes would be treated the same, should there be any residents in this extraordinary place.

But, before the volunteers set off, the entire troop rode to the crest of the hill, so they became obvious to those in the sphere. The blue light that Okkyntalah had noted now glowed a little brighter, but nothing else changed.

The pioneers moved down the slope onto the grass area. They crossed most of the wide strip, a little over a thousand paces, with no challenge or activity from the tower or its surrounding. Okkyntalah was beginning to think that no one inhabited the tower after all, when the small party, with their camels, vanished from sight.

They were there and then they were not there. No warning. No fading. No sound. And no other people visible. The six simply ceased to exist in the landscape. A gasp of horrified surprise rose from the assembled troop.

'I felt something.' Tumalind glanced at the other two mindtalkers, both of whom nodded.

'Something came through the air when they disappeared.' Serrophenahl wore an expression of extreme puzzlement. 'It was like a shout of triumph. Yes?'

Tumalind and Blavv agreed. 'A cheer of victory.'

Chapter 48

ARRIVAL

'Something here is completely outside my experience. I think the same goes for Blavv and Serrophenahl?'

Tumalind hoped her voice betrayed none of the deep disquiet she felt might've shown on her face at the moment of the disappearance the previous day. She'd experienced something close to panic then, a feeling of such terror that it exceeded anything she'd so far suffered whilst in the Dark Space. It was a sense of such hatred and threat that she'd almost collapsed under its power.

The other two mindtalkers nodded their agreement over her assessment, making her feel a little less isolated.

The troop had withdrawn and spent the night encamped just behind the ridge. The commander, Phyloahn, had hoped to learn something of the first six volunteers before sending more to discover their fate. This morning, he'd called for more brave souls to try again, since nothing had been heard.

'I think one of us must go with the next lot of volunteers.'

'No!' Blavv's sudden denial of Serrophenahl's suggestion was loud and absolute.

Phyloahn, frowned at the outburst.

'I'm sorry. But I truly believe that if any of us enters that place, we, the mindtalkers, will be taken and irretrievably lost. Forgive me.'

He nodded. 'You may well be right. But the only way we can discover what became of the others is to send more, one of them a mindtalker.'

'I'll go.'

He was about to thank Serrophenahl for her offer when Tumalind interrupted. 'It has to be me. I'm the only one with real experience of their realm. Any other mindtalker would be destroyed utterly, lost forever, in mind, if not in body. It must be me.'

'No, Tumalind. I won't let you.'

She turned to her husband, held his hand. 'You've been brave on hundreds of occasions, Okkyntalah. You've fought and defeated many enemies. It's my turn now to do something real for this effort. In any case, no one else has the necessary knowledge. I'm the natural choice. I'm sorry.'

'Then I come with you.'

'I'd sooner you stayed safe until we know exactly what we're dealing with.'

Phyloahn held up a hand to stop the discussion. 'I call again for volunteers, one of whom must be a mindtalker.'

Tumalind put herself forward and discovered Serrophenahl on one side and Okkyntalah on the other.

'No, Serrophenahl. You're not strong enough. I can get past all your defences and these evil Powerseekers are far stronger than me, especially in the numbers they have gathered here.'

'At least let me contact Ivdulon to let her know your intentions. She might be able to help.'

'Any such message sent from so close would alert them to our existence, and secrecy's vital if I'm to get any information at all. I must go alone, as a mindtalker. I can rely only on you two as companions and guardians in the Dark Space; even then you must be very careful not to reveal your presence.'

'Only four this time, and sex isn't important, since they appear to make no distinction.' Phyloahn reasoned. 'Tumalind, you must go. I think Okkyntalah is a sensible companion for you, as your special bond is likely to make you stronger as a pair than if you're separated. For no better reason than that they're physically tougher, I appoint these two men to go with you. I send you without knowing what you face and with no promise that you'll return. It's best you go on foot, in case the camels are seen as a threat. And you should know I will think no worse of you should you decide against going.'

'Sorry, Phyloahn, but I've fought beside Okkyntalah many times. I think we'll work well as a team.' Teldrohn stepped forward.

The troop commander nodded and one of the other soldiers stepped back to give Teldrohn his place.

The four of them agreed to take the risk, since there was no other way of finding out what they needed to know about the tower and its inhabitants. The rest of the troop blessed them and sent them on their way with words of encouragement and hope.

Tumalind held Okkyntalah's hand as they descended the slope and entered the field of green. This close, it showed as a crop of thick, rich grass, growing to a uniform height, apparently uncut and ungrazed. It was as if it had grown to a certain height and then stopped. The ground beneath was soft and comfortable beneath their bare feet.

From ground level, approaching over the flat field, the tower and its crowning ball were both awesome and threatening. Objects of great skill and craftsmanship, they seemed imbued with an evil that detracted from any beauty they might otherwise convey.

Nothing changed as they approached. No sound emerged, no movement occurred. But, as they drew closer to the edge of the black stone circle, there came some strange vibration.

The ground on which they walked abreast abruptly ceased to exist and they fell into darkness. As they entered that dark space, Tumalind was aware that a section of the field they'd trodden rose slightly, tipping back so that, from the hilltop, it would seem that the green surface remained unbroken. At least one question was answered.

As she landed on unforgiving ground below, the jarring shocked her into instinctive movement, so that she rolled forward to break the fall. Okkyntalah rolled with her, as did Teldrohn. But the largest man cried out in pain.

The opening above snapped shut and left them in total darkness, waiting.

'Now we have you.' The voice laughed; a malignant sound that made the hair rise on the back of her neck. *'Oh yes. We have YOU, especially.'*

He'd returned to the ship with the bad news. Now he waited for Dagla Kaz to respond and take action. Aglydron had seen fear on the High Priest's face for the first time and understood the man was in need of help now more than ever before. He'd given him his assurance that he would provide that support.

At first, Dagla Kaz had raged, shouted and then taken to muttering incomprehensibly, so that Aglydron had worried for his sanity. But time had calmed him, it seemed.

'Very well. They use subterfuge and lies to trap us. I can play that game. I am master of such tactics. Let them engage with me in a war of words and let us see who wins.'

'Of course, Dagla Kaz…'

'I'll show them who is supreme distorter of words, best perverter of justice and truth. They…they care too much for honesty, and truth, and justice. Soft. They fear the dark too much. I, though, I have been there. I know what the dark can do. How it can aid and reward and make master. Fools. Stand trial? Of course I will. But I'll show them who's best at deception and underhand dealing. Not them. Not them, with their cares and concerns and consideration for others. Fools. I will be supreme. I am supreme. I am God!

'Well, why do you wait, man? Take me to them and let them do their worst. I have nothing to fear but fear itself, and that is no fear at all. Take me. Let them try me. They will fail. All of them will fail. Go, now!'

Aglydron instructed the captain to sail into harbour. Though, the escorting boats had already made it clear that they must go that way. The High Priest was clearly in some sort of ecstatic state, unaware of what he was saying. Some spiritual crisis lay at the back of his strange actions and words. Aglydron must help him in this vital venture. That the people on the island, especially that renegade Aklon, should believe they had the power to put the High Priest on trial for some unspecified crime was unbelievable.

He helped Dagla Kaz into his most extravagant tabard, girded him with his ceremonial belt and sword that had travelled the whole journey with them. He placed the high hat on his head, increasing his height and making him the tallest man on the ship. Caarl had been a disappointment. He'd failed to support the High Priest at once. He'd shown doubt and confusion, where Aglydron had remained strong and loyal to his leader, as always. Proudly, he assisted Dagla Kaz down the gangplank and onto the harbour.

The crowd that the High Priest expected was assembled, though in smaller numbers, and lacking the enthusiastic cheering he sought. They were hostile, shouting condemnation at their leader. Aglydron did his best to shield the High Priest from the worst of the abuse and actually protected him with his own body as they made their way through the throng.

Aklon awaited them at the small room where they'd met earlier. The rest of the Followers from the ship had been separated from the smaller party that consisted of Dagla Kaz, Wyyhn Kaz, Ialdyss Kaz, Kaz-Ca-Valorysta and Aglydron. Where was Rrildyss Kaz, he wondered? Aglydron felt a little isolated in this company and not very certain of what was intended at this point.

'Renegade! I condemn you to the most painful…'

'Be quiet, father. It is you who will stand trial here. Not I. As to your punishment for the lies and deception you have used against the people of this island, that will depend on the verdict and on the mercy of those who conduct the trial.'

'Trial! You talk of trials. You have no knowledge of the law if you think I will stand trial under you, Renegade. I am High Priest of…'

'You are a criminal. I had hoped you might show some remorse for your evil lies and deeds, but it seems you are incapable of regret.' Aklon turned to those with him. 'It is best if he is kept locked away until the trial. These others we must talk with to learn of their own beliefs and feelings. They must be shown the proofs, of course.'

Dagla Kaz looked aghast at this suggestion. He stared at Aklon with total incomprehension. 'You would dare allow others into the Secret Chamber? You would defy the sanctity of…?'

'The Secret Chamber no longer exists, other than as a store for food and wine. The parchments and tablets are exhibited for all to see in our old house. And most of those who have seen them are now not Followers. How could they be when exposed to the vile truth about Gadhallah and his invention, Ytraa?'

Dagla Kaz was bereft of words for a while and allowed himself to be led away to a small building where he was locked away. Aglydron tried to go with him but the people who supported Aklon prevented him. He went back and took his place with the other priests for the moment.

'I see no point in engaging in discussion with any of you until you have viewed for yourselves the proofs that have been seen by most people on this island. Please come with us. We will expose to you the truth of the religion you have trusted and followed all your lives.'

There was, of course, much disagreement with the proposal, but the people around Aklon were armed and determined and would allow no one to avoid the trip to the Priest's old house.

Aglydron felt and heard the disapproval of the people as they made their way through the streets of the capital. He'd looked forward to a time of welcome and reconciliation with Shoarhn. But she would still be in Morstahn. He'd have to wait until after the trial, a concept he'd come across only in Litkala, to go to her. But she would, of course, return to her duties as his wife as soon as she knew he was back home.

The parchments and stone tablets told a tale so vile and disgusting that it was impossible to believe. It was some sort of story compiled by Akon-Dji to persuade the ignorant and gullible that his beliefs were correct and theirs were wrong. It could not be so: that the Lord Gadhallah could be guilty of such indescribable wickedness was beyond belief. It was a trick, a foul lie and an evil, evil attempt to destroy the reign of a man who'd led his people along the route to glory. Once the Godwood was carved and placed in its proper place, atop the Monument of Ytraa, all would see it for what it truly was.

Aglydron saw doubt and disbelief creep over the faces of those who accompanied him. He heard their wails of sorrow, anger, refusal and knew they felt, as he did, that this was an attempt to blacken the name of their god. They would stand with him and Dagla Kaz when the time came to decide who was right and who was wrong in this dreadful business.

It was Wyyhn who spoke first as they left the display area.

'I must speak to my people before they're allowed to see this evidence. For some it may be too much. Will you allow me that, please, Aklon?'

Aglydron applauded the Choshinahm High Priest for his sensible approach to the problem. Obviously, he would forewarn them of the evil intent behind the false evidence. To his surprise, Aklon-Dji agreed to the request.

Kaz-Ca-Valorysta, who he knew came from Kah-Labaz, seemed uncharacteristically upset. She hadn't struck him as a particularly pious woman, seeming more interested in the pleasures of life than the doctrine that held the Followers together. But there were tears in her eyes as she left the display room. To see one so impious nevertheless made anxious and distressed by the so-called evidence was too much on top of all else.

Without thinking, Aglydron turned and rushed back to the nearest parchments and began to tear them to shreds. He hadn't got far before some of those watching dashed up and held him to prevent further destruction.

Aklon closed his eyes briefly, as if in pain. 'Show him out. The man is a fanatic. He

387

would probably believe anything he was told, so long as it came from the mouth of a priest. Just make sure he never has access to this place, please. He is likely to try again to destroy whatever fails to agree with his view of the Followers.'

Aglydron shrugged off the guards and moved out of the building. As he did so, some of the original pilgrims were being shown in. The rest were waiting outside for Wyyhn to prepare them for the disgust and anger they must feel on being exposed to such lies.

The evening meal was shared with some local people, many naked. Some of these served the food and Aglydron decided they must be slaves, regardless of the lies the Renegade had told at the earlier meeting. He thought that their mode of dress must be a matter for their overseer. Why some should be sitting with the rest, though, was a mystery. And then, why were there no Holy Ones? What had really happened here? Was the Renegade actually in overall charge, as he declared? Had he polluted everyone with his heathen beliefs? The Holy Ones would never stand for such treatment.

There were no local priests, either. And none of the local people had prepared for prayer. Only some of the Choshinahm Followers and a couple of the original pilgrims acted like Followers. Could it be that the heathen ways had already convinced so many who'd previously been members of the faith?

Aglydron took a walk outside, needing to escape the sacrilege and lack of piety that existed within the large public hall where they'd all been fed. He must leave the atmosphere of blasphemous discussion and the unholy activity that spread through the room. He'd counted those who'd worshipped with him. None of the priests and only two of the original pilgrims had prayed along with nearly fifty of the Choshinahm group. Even the High Priest from Litkala, Rrildyss Kaz, had failed to join in the prayers, and he'd always believed she, at least, was true to her own form of Following. It was clear that, once Dagla Kaz was released from his locked room, he and the High Priest must start to tour the island and bring the people back to the proper ways.

It was hard, after so long on the road, so many days spent in travel in foreign lands, to come home to such a complete breakdown in law and doctrine. To witness the ease with which his fellow Followers abandoned their faith and embraced heathen ways. Some refused to join with anyone other than their spouses. That, in itself, wasn't too troubling, but the way they looked at him when he asked for a partner made him deeply anxious.

Shoarhn. Was she corrupted by the changes? Had she allowed her association with the Renegade to destroy her faith? Once he'd stood by the High Priest's side and spoken in his defence, made them realise how good Dagla Kaz was as a man and a leader, he would travel to Morstahn and discover what had become of his wife. If she'd slipped into impiety, he would teach her the truth and bring her back to the right way, even if he had to beat her every day for the rest of their lives together. He must save her soul and give her the chance of spending the endless time after death in the Garden of Delight with him.

Chapter 49

INTO THE MONOLITH

'Leave me 'ere! I'm a liability. Just go. Save yourselves.'

The injured soldier couldn't walk. And, on exploring the place into which they'd been plunged, Okkyntalah discovered the initial lost party, one of whom had also been injured. She, too, was determined she should be left behind.

'We'll be back for you.'

It was a hard decision. But their first task was to find a way out. And they must send a message to Phyloahn about the nature of their apparent disappearance. A strange dark green glow lit the chamber, seeming to come from above but having no obvious source.

He returned to Tumalind as the two parties gathered together. Deep in concentration, her face was set in a determined expression that he hesitated to break. But they must warn the troop leader before any more soldiers were sent after them.

'Tumalind?'

She flinched in response to her name but her features remained unaltered and, if anything, her rigid determination increased. He'd seen her in mindtalk and this had some hints of that strange gift. But she'd never been like this before, even when seeking out the Powerseekers. This was something altogether different.

'Tumalind. We need to tell Phyloahn what's happened to us.'

The faintest hint of a nod acknowledged his comment, but she continued to concentrate on something else, very hard.

'You can do it?'

The nod was a little stronger.

'We need to move.' The soldier voiced the thoughts of them all. 'Now there's more on us, we'll 'ave a chance to beat the guards.'

They were still armed. The camels of the first party, one damaged in the fall, remained with the soldiers. The whole situation was bizarre. Okkyntalah followed the man's gaze toward the shadowed end of the chamber they occupied. Something changed there, but in the dim light it was difficult to make out, even for him.

'If we rush the buggers we'll maybe get through.'

Okkyntalah left Tumalind sitting on the floor, with Teldrohn as her guardian, and approached closer to the place the soldier had indicated. As he did so, he saw that the chamber was open ended, and guarded by a half dozen armed men who seemed oblivious of the activity of their charges. This unusual lack of interest so puzzled him that he walked toward them, expecting some sort of trick like that which had brought them crashing down into this trap. But nothing happened as he moved close. Even when he was within touching distance, they merely glanced at him and went back to their conversation, seeming to dismiss him out of hand.

'Are you guarding us?'

One of the men turned and looked at him, scratched his head. 'Cut off yer 'ead if you like.' The response was not so much a threat as an offer, with no aggression in the delivery.

'If I were to walk through your ranks, what would you do?'

The same man turned to his comrades and said something unintelligible to Okkyntalah. The whole lot turned to look at him and laughed. He shrugged and returned to the group.

'I can't make it out. They don't seem serious at all about keeping us from escaping. I'm not even sure they know how many we are. In fact, I'm not convinced they're all there. I think they might be a bit slow.'

'One way to find out. And it's the onny way we'll get out of 'ere.'

Okkyntalah nodded. He bent and touched Tumalind, who remained seated on the ground. All the others, except the two injured soldiers, were standing, weapons drawn and ready. She looked up at him, briefly, and then returned to her silent vigil. He and Teldrohn helped her to her feet and found no resistance, but no cooperation either. It was as if she'd lost interest in whether she moved or not. He experimented with her. She shifted ably in the direction he took her but stopped as soon as he ceased to tug her along with him. Her deep concentration worried and frightened him. But he feared any attempt to bring her out of that state might be harmful. If asked, he would've been unable to explain why he felt that way.

He tried running with her hand in his and she ran after him, perfectly able to make the steps and even avoid one of the injured soldiers, who she had to leap over. Satisfied that she would at least come with him as they made their escape, he nodded to the others.

'Let's run at them and see what happens. We'll leave the camels here for the moment, until we've learned more about our surroundings. I'll have to keep hold of Tumalind and lead her, so I'll only have one hand to fight with.'

They all understood and formed into a tight formation of two deep and four wide, with Okkyntalah and Tumalind in the centre of the back rank, Teldrohn at her other side. At a word from the soldier on the right of the front line, they moved forward in step and then broke into a disciplined run. To their utter amazement, the group of guards quickly cowered out of their way and let them pass with no challenge.

Breaking out of the chamber took them into a wide corridor from which many

392

openings depended. All were uniform and led into dim passages without doors. Nothing indicated where any of these might lead.

Tumalind pulled on Okkyntalah's hand and he stopped, calling the rest of the group to a halt with them. Still in her deep state of concentration, she stiffly rotated on the spot and led them back past three of the openings and moved toward a passage on the other side of the corridor. Okkyntalah let her lead them, since she gave all the appearance of having some destination in mind. She neither spoke nor indicated that she was aware what she was doing; her whole demeanour pointed to such solid absorption with something unseen that it seemed almost as if someone else was guiding her.

Okkyntalah reached that conclusion too late to avoid entering the place she led them. They emerged into a wide, open space, where the light grew brighter and the whole feel and sound of their surroundings became more open and busy.

Many people moved here. Smooth stone paved the ground, reflecting the light falling from above. The people took no notice of them at all. Most were women, wearing simple unbelted white shifts that ended mid thigh and hung from string like straps from their bare shoulders. The few men present, clad in similar garb but in deep blue, seemed unaware of the women. Okkyntalah felt he inhabited a dream world where nothing was as it seemed.

Tumalind now stopped leading and appeared content for them to continue on their way. The group kept together, though there was no threat from the people around them. In fact, the crowd took no notice of them.

Okkyntalah examined their surroundings. They were in a circular chamber with a high domed roof, in the centre of which a hollow led up toward the place from whence the light issued. There were no people in the centre of the space, so he led his party toward that point, only to discover that the floor gave out to form a round drop of considerable depth. No rail surrounded this opening, which must present a real danger to the people who seemed to wander aimlessly. Looking down, he saw the hole contained water at a depth about three manheights below the edge. It had the appearance of a great well.

Across from where they stood, a flight of steps, made of the same bright white stone, was set into the inner wall of the cylindrical opening, leading down and under the surface of the water. Here, at last, he saw some meaningful activity.

Women, clad in tiny pinafores that covered their sex, stepped up and down the stairway, carrying containers. They were clearly taking water from the well. He followed the route of one who'd collected some and set her container on her head, where she held it in place with one hand. She climbed the steps and moved toward the edge of the dome. There, veiled from normal sight by colour and form, a strange stair ascended the inside of

393

the curved slope until it reached the circular opening, where it continued to climb in a more conventional spiral. Because of the shape of the cupola, the wide stone slabs that protruded from its wall were very long, allowing those using them to do so without scraping their heads on the upper surface as they climbed to the central hole.

For a short while, they watched the progress of these women. Some walked away from the well and disappeared into the crowd. But others, a small number, continued their climb, disappearing into the hollow column that pierced the centre of the domed roof.

'That must lead to the ball at the top of the tower.'

There was general agreement on Teldrohn's observation.

'We need only go up and kill the bowelcreeps. Tumalind doesn't need to risk her mind any more.'

'What we gonna do? Leave 'er behind an' climb up there to do the job?' The grizzled soldier who made this suggestion doubted his own words.

One of the women soldiers voiced an idea. 'Mebbie we can call the others in, to help like, and...'

'As I see it, the only way anyone can get in here is the way we came.' Okkyntalah scanned the whole area as he spoke. 'That means they have the power to decide how many of us get inside. There's no sign of any entrance in the tower itself or in the surrounding area. No other way in that we can see from here...'

'But there's gotta be another way in. Has to be. All these folk need food an' other stuff. They got water 'ere, but nowt else. Must be some different way in, else 'ow do they get their clothes and all the other stuff they need?'

Okkyntalah was concerned about how her proximity to the Powerseekers might affect Tumalind's mind. But he couldn't fault the logic of his companions. There had to be another entrance, of course. But did they have the time and ability to find such a way in? They were here. Now. The Powerseekers' very system had delivered them into the place they needed to be. It was even possible that what had happened to them wasn't the result of some deliberate action, but some device that always caught intruders and dumped them into the underground cells. That might explain the peculiar attitude of the men who were supposed to act as guards.

The more he considered it, the more certain he was that they must use their presence in the building now to end the lives of the Powerseekers. They might never get such a chance again. It was their duty to do what they could, regardless of their personal safety. But it would be hard to deliver Tumalind up into that great ball; he couldn't, however, leave her unguarded down here.

'There's no other way. We have to go up there. And Tumalind must come with us.'

Feldrark and Jodisa settled within Ivdulon's tower. Patradko Kaz, their male High Priest, and Teh-Pavk, the other mindtalker from Ob-Bebna, were with them. The wise woman occupied the centre of the cleared space, seeking other mindtalkers to augment those already contacted. She'd found these, gathered them into the community with their minds, even though their bodies remained far away from Litkala. Porlesah, Eyethlehn, Zyreenha and Aklon were with them, from Muhnilahm. Wyyhn Kaz had needed some persuasion, but had come when told that his companion, Ialdyss Kaz supported the group. Nuldron came from his post in Ov-Bebna and Yoqalohn from Trotnahn. There were other mindtalkers who either could not project or who couldn't be fully trusted, and they were excluded. But there were many more, unknown to Feldrark, that Ivdulon brought in from outside. Minds that Feldrark, now he was aware of them, would wish to spend time with in the future, when this vital task was complete.

Ivdulon opened the proceedings. *'You all know the reason for this gathering of our minds. You know the dangers and the power of those we seek to defeat. Secrecy is no longer possible. Understand that, only if we stay together and combine our thoughts to direct them at the Powerseekers, we may succeed. We outnumber them and, with our efforts, we give Tumalind, the one who ventures into their black domain, the chance at least of survival.*

'If any mind here is unsure of their contribution, unwilling to enter the dangerous area we all recognise as the Dark Space, now is the time to desert us. Once we enter that arena, any mind not committed, any mind not willing or able to remain with the group, will fall prey to the Powerseekers. Have no doubt, these are powerful minds. They have the ability to turn a good mind into bad in moments. If you leave the group for even a brief spell once we're in the Dark Space, you'll be pounced upon by the Powerseekers and your mind harvested to increase their force.

'Does everyone here understand?'

Feldrark had never been part of such a gathering before, and, he guessed, neither had the rest of them. The response all gave echoed around their minds as a resounding 'yes'.

'Are we determined to defeat this evil once and for all?'

Again a loud and positive 'yes'.

'Then let us go, seek out and, at the very least, distract these evil minds whilst those on the ground do what they may to end them.'

Secrecy was done with. This had to be an all out, frontal and deliberate attack on those minds that he and Ivdulon had for so long been anxious to defeat. That Ivdulon had already done the ground work, informing the others over time, came as some surprise to him. Now, paradoxically, was the most dangerous time for Tumalind. She was on the spot. For the past few hours, Ivdulon had been with her in the Monolith, helping her concentrate on the issue that mattered most: finding the actual location and number of the remaining Powerseekers, to know, without doubt, that this was where they all lurked. Because, if they attacked without such certainty and therefore failed to kill the entire community, the Powerseekers might easily escape them.

They would then have the opportunity to disperse all over the world, never to be tracked down, and able to recruit more minds to their evil ways.

That they were devious and clever had never been in doubt; that they were ruthless and capable of any action that would protect them; that they would do anything to prolong and expand their wicked empire; this knowledge had ever been the driving force behind Ivdulon's long war of secrecy, and her long period of planning for this day. There'd never been any doubt about their insidious ambition, their desire to rule the world in their fashion, their wish to dominate absolutely and without concern for the lives of those they would enslave. But there had been uncertainty about their numbers, their power, their organisation and their actual ability.

Ivdulon had spent many cycles on this war, for war it was. The ultimate fight of good against evil. If the Powerseekers should rise to the role they espoused, then the rest of the people in the world would be enslaved forever in their self-fulfilling plans. There would never be a chance to escape the brutal logic of their system, once they gained that power. Ivdulon had recognised this fact the very first time she'd encountered them as a force. For a while, she'd been subject to their desires and ambitions, had even travelled with them before they grew to their present power.

She'd witnessed their experiment in Trotnahn, the first city they'd conquered for their trials of the common people. And, as the Powerseekers had predicted, those common people, so selfish, foolish, trusting and gullible, had fallen for their promises of wealth, their promises of lives of luxury and pleasure. They'd been told that, if they worked hard enough and long enough, and earned enough coin, they would gain the freedom from want that every human being strove for. Hard work was the key. Long hours making things, selling things, designing other things that must appear attractive, even though their real worth was less than nothing.

In Trotnahn, they'd succeeded in the first stage of their plans. The women, those most likely to oppose the Powerseekers aims and yet also most easily attracted by trinkets, had been tamed by the men. They'd divided them into two subclasses; those who would serve men with their bodies, for coin, and effectively act as sex slaves, and those who would act as household servants, given the false rewards of security and protection in the form of marriage. It had been easy to convince the men that women were there to be used. For cycles lost in time, the people of the region had been divided by gender, so that the men acted as the superior sex, lording it over their women.

It had been easy for the Powerseekers to make that extra step, to convince the men that they should take certain women as wives and treat them as devices to display their wealth and material success to their neighbours. The other women would serve as vessels for their lust, ever available, at a price of course, for the gratification of the males. That these women should be owned by those with the greatest wealth was a natural consequence of the idea. Women wouldn't have personal wealth, as that would give them power. Powerful women would not be good for the system the Powerseekers intended.

The men who had been persuaded of the worth of the new system were easily convinced that they were working their long hours in order to rise above their neighbours, to become leaders and the envy of their fellows. It had never occurred to them that the real rulers were the Powerseekers; men who lived in isolation, puppet masters controlling the entire enterprise from the safety and luxury of their gilded thrones.

The experiment in Trotnahn had gone well. Over a period of less than a generation, the place had become a model for the society the Powerseekers desired. Now had come the time to use their magic gift of mindtalk to infiltrate the rest of the world. Soon they would dominate the entire planet and increase their personal wealth and power beyond the dreams of common men.

That the Monolith of Kro Lat was already in place, built by the long lost race that had constructed the city of Litkala, was a piece of good fortune, no more. Deserted, like that fabulous city, it made the ideal home for the mass of Powerseekers to inhabit. Using their combined resources, they'd developed systems of supply across the vast desert that surrounded the Monolith. League upon league of tunnels, stretching to the port of Likdigmina on the Tulak Sea, had allowed them to supply themselves in secret. They'd built an empire of slaves who never saw the light of day, living underground in service to their needs. Hidden in their isolated spot, they had time and the ability to spread their influence.

Over many cycles, the Monolith of Kro Lat was made legendary and imbued with myths of danger and unknown perils, so that only the very brave ever approached it. And the traps assured the Powerseekers of their safety from attack. In fact, Ivdulon told Feldrark, they hadn't been invaded for such a long time that they'd grown negligent of their safety, complacency gifting them a false sense of security. Since none had ever managed to pass the first barriers, they were disinclined to spend time or coin on developing more sophisticated systems of defence.

'They really feed and provision all those hundreds of slaves by transporting everything from that seaport, Ivdulon?'

'I've travelled with the selected merchants, only in my mind of course, from

Likdigmina all the way to the Monolith. The problem has always been that they stop in an underground chamber some distance from the tower, so I've never been able to get beyond that point. I tried some of the Powerseeker's minds but it's extremely hazardous and can only be done for moments at a time. In any case, it seems they never leave the ball in which they live, so I was never able to discover the rest of the route to their stronghold.

'Okkyntalah's courage and the bravery of Tumalind have now closed up that gap and we know how food and water are transported from the tunnel complex to the sphere above. The rest we can guess at and is probably of little importance.'

'Probably, Ivdulon?'

'I can't be certain they don't have troops stationed elsewhere in the complex, Feldrark. I know what I know but I've no way of determining what I don't know. I think we must act on what we have. The risk is great anyway. But it's the only chance we'll have of defeating these evil minds for good. I believe it's a risk worth taking.'

'Even if we lose those two most extraordinary friends?'

'Sometimes, Feldrark, as your wise father often explained, leadership requires us to sacrifice those who best serve our needs. We're doing what we can to aid Tumalind and the others, and I've trained them both in the ways of courage and resourcefulness. I've engineered difficulties for them to negotiate and watched them both grow wise and clever as a result of their experiences. Of course, mutual love adds strength to their characters, so they've become, if anything, more suitable for the task as time has passed. Now it's time for them to act. All we can do is what we're doing now; help them from afar by distracting those minds whilst Okkyntalah and his party attack the physical bodies that house them. Shall we do the deed?'

Feldrark nodded his agreement. The combined minds channelled their thoughts toward the Monolith of Kro Lat and the Powerseekers. If they failed in their distraction, those evil minds would destroy Tumalind and Okkyntalah and then spread their evil over the whole world.

Chapter 50

WITHIN

Too many minds. Too many thoughts. It was all Tumalind could do to hold her place in the maelstrom and remain upright. Now hands were forcing her up steps and, with each, she grew closer to danger that threatened to engulf her in black dark evil that desired to devour her and make her one of them. Drowning in ideas, lusts, wants, emotions, sensations, pictures, sounds, smells and tastes utterly unnatural to her. All crowded in on her, trying to invade, trying to take over all she was.

So deep was her concentration on simple survival that she had almost nothing left now to give. Had she let them down; those who relied on her to do that vital task? Had she done the job demanded of her? If she had, they had no more need of her in this place where every moment took her closer to the annihilation of her very self.

What they threatened was much worse than death. She would live her life knowing she'd let down the world and that the evil power that proceeded from her failure was her fault. An existence in torment, never having freedom to end her perpetual shame and fear. That's what they told her; those voices that lusted to intrude and invade.

Her fear would make her theirs. Her very terror of failure would ensure she failed. Her fragile female form no match for their combined male power. What they planned for her physical self was as nothing to what they would do to her mind. She should surrender now. The longer she resisted, the worse the outcome. She was only one, alone, abandoned by those who'd sent her here. Isolated. Vulnerable. Undefended.

'Alone, little girl. I'll have you every way I wish.'

'Abandoned, little girl. I'll make you do things you can't even imagine.'

'On your own, little girl. I'll use you worse than your most terrifying nightmares.'

'You'll feel disgust.'

'Loathing.'

'Dread.'

'Fear.'

'You'll feel such shame.'

'Pain.'

'Terror without end.'

'Exquisite agony.'

'We'll make you want punishment.'

'Make it part of pleasure.'

'The pleasure will be ours, never yours.'

'You'll beg us to hurt you.'

'And we'll do it.'

'And laugh.'

'Make you so ashamed you'll beg us to make you suffer.'

'And we will.'

'Make you suffer till the last moment of your unendurable life.'

'You're not alone, Tumalind.'

'You are! Listen not to that…'

'We're with you, Tumalind. Hear us. Take courage…'

'Leave her. She's ours!'

'Tumalind. Be strong a little longer. We're with you. Always will be'

'Get out of our realm! We rule here. We're more powerful than you know.'

Too much. She stumbled. Suddenly aware of where she was. The physical danger a fall would entail. That drop so many manheights into that dark pool below. Absolutely no doubt she would drown.

'I'm here, Tumalind. I'm here.'

Okkyntalah's hand in hers, guiding, warm, loving, protective. She felt the love in him, felt his care and concern. The strength began to return and she was able to take another step. The evil minds still fought and threatened her. But there were others there now. She knew some of those voices. They were with her and she was not alone. The lies of the Powerseekers were exposed. She had the means to carry on. She had the courage to move closer to them. She had the love of Okkyntalah to protect her, as he always had.

She looked about her. They'd ascended much of the tower, climbing an internal spiral staircase that must lead them to the chamber at the top. There, she knew with certainty, awaited the Powerseekers and their trusted guardians. Armed and fierce, they outnumbered her companions three to one. For a moment she quailed under that knowledge, almost let the Powerseekers inside her mind to defeat and destroy her as they promised.

'Nearly there, Tumalind. Almost at the end now.'

Okkyntalah's simple words saved her. For the moment. But what would happen when they reached the top of these stairs? How would the fighting go? If she lost Okkyntalah would she be able to go on living?

'They're still with you, Tumalind. Trying more subtly to discourage you now they know we're close. Ignore the doubts. Ignore the false information. We're with you and they lie about the forces guarding them.'

Looking up, she saw they were so very close now. The stairs ended in a space illuminated by the deep blue light they'd seen from that far hilltop that now seemed so distant. As she entered that dark place, she hesitated a moment. Below, was movement and noise. Something happening down there.

⸭

Now came the most dangerous part for all of them. Ivdulon had warned them that, as the party approached, the Powerseekers would use all manner of tricks to make their attackers doubt their senses. Feldrark felt the invasion of their combined minds, trying to instil fear and doubt, trying to persuade them that what they would do was murder.

'*You choose the wrong mind to convert. I am a leader. I understand the difference between acts of self-preservation and self-glorification and those designed to do what is best for the majority. You will not change my mind.*'

And they were gone. But they would attempt to pervert others, less experienced, less determined, less sure and less aware of the ways of wickedness. He warned Ivdulon of this change in their tactics.

'*I'm aware, Feldrark. Now the soldiers are in place, we need to work together to prevent the Powerseekers trying to recruit more distant minds. They're quick and clever. We must take concerted action to prevent them spreading their vile philosophy. We've got to fight where we can do most good now. Leave the battle of the bodies to those at the scene. This danger was always what I feared most: we have to venture into the wider realm of mindtalk to prevent the Powerseekers moving into places too distant for our forces to defeat them.*'

He, Ivdulon, and others of their group with the necessary strength of will and power of thought, ventured into the spreading cloud of influence the Powerseekers held. The Dark Space now began its attempt at growth, spreading its evil and determined to devour all those unwary enough to let it take their minds. But they were there, the good minds, the strong minds of right, to cut off any attempted invasion. As the Dark Space expanded, so it began to lose power. But it was potent still and took all the force of concentration the good were able to manage, merely to contain it. Nothing spare remained to protect any at the place of conflict; in either body or mind.

⸭

Dagla Kaz paced his small room, his mind a turmoil of confusion and regret that he hadn't taken actions when he might. He'd convinced himself he could have destroyed his enemies with ease if he hadn't been so sentimental. He should have killed Aklon the moment he declared his doubts and resistance to the secrets buried in the Chamber. The Renegade would then have been defeated long before trouble on the island had started. It was Aklon's fault that Followers no longer held sway. He should have killed him at once, not allowed paternal softness to rule his head. He wouldn't let such sentiment prevent him again.

401

'Come with us. We'll show you. Join us for the spread of our way all over the world. Be one with us and gain the benefits of mutual experiences, shared pleasures, shared power over those who deserve only to be our slaves. Join us. Be one with us. Together we're stronger than all else.'

It was easy to surrender. Easy to accept these combined minds of power and wealth. They thought as he did, acted as he wished he might. They would give him strength for the future and for now.

⁜

Those with Okkyntalah reached the top of the stairs and came face to face with the men defending the Powerseekers. Though not as numerous as the voices had claimed, they outnumbered the attackers, and had the advantage of high ground.

The amazing arrogance and complacency that had allowed their prison guards to let them escape with their weapons, was here again displayed. These soldiers, if they really were such, were inexperienced. If they'd ever faced an enemy, it had been many years previously. Unprepared, they stood in an awkward group at the head of the stairs, occupying a small open area, uncertain how to act now that Okkyntalah and his companions had arrived.

Their very hesitancy was their undoing, and gave the attackers a chance. Had they been prepared, they might have used their superior numbers and position to dislodge their attackers from the narrow steps. Simple blows would send them falling down the interior of the tower into the depths of the well below.

Okkyntalah gave Tumalind's hand to the woman below him. He gripped the ankle of the nearest guard and pulled hard. The man tumbled forward and plunged through the gap to make the journey that should have been for the attackers. The shock of this assault gave them time to enter the body of the sphere. Gathered on the small open area, the guards seemed at a loss what to do. It was as though they had no control of their movements, as if they were under the charge of other minds. They moved chaotically, even running into each other. A sweep of Okkyntalah's sword cut down three without opposition.

The others with him set about eliminating these disorganised and ill-disciplined guards. Perhaps they were the vanguard, placed to slow down the progress of the attack. Whatever the reason, they were useless. The attackers quickly disposed of them, leaving the platform slick with spilled blood. It was too easy, lacking real fight.

Okkyntalah felt ashamed at the lack of opposition. It was like killing unarmed children. The group gathered close now that they'd removed this first group of protectors.

Tumalind was showing signs of confusion and doubt, but he was unable to reach her. She was no further help to the mission, as far as he could tell. Though he recognised she might be involved in some battle of the mind. They now had the most vital task: to kill the Powerseekers as quickly as possible. Defending Tumalind must be left to a single member of the raiding party. He asked the smallest, slightest of their group; a fierce little woman, who nodded her acceptance. Free of anxiety over his wife, he led the onslaught.

A small, narrow stairway led from the platform they occupied. To their utter amazement, they'd been followed up the stairs by women carrying water. Three had backed-up below them and now passed through the bodies on the platform without comment or concern. They were totally oblivious of the dead guards or their attackers.

Okkyntalah let them pass and then followed them. What better guides than these women who must make this trip several times a day?

The women trod the stairs, their containers of water still perched on their heads, and stepped onto the circular ledge that progressed around the entire circumference of the bottom of the sphere. Okkyntalah and the others followed them to this band of polished white stone and, at once, arrows zipped across the space. All three women fell, two injured and lying on the ledge, the other dead and rolling off the edge to drop down to the well. The attackers dodged back out of sight and waited for these new defenders to appear. Nothing happened. The silence was broken only by the cries of the wounded women.

Teldrohn, moved slowly toward the opening, crawling so he was less of a target. Again, arrows whistled through the air. None struck him but one of the injured women took another arrow, which silenced her. He pulled back far enough to avoid being hit but still able to reconnoitre the area. For some time he remained there, half hidden from the rest of the group, and then dropped to his knees and passed his arms into the space in front of him. More arrows flew and he pulled back his hands with a clutch of those that had been shot.

He returned, carrying the arrows, which he handed to the three carrying bows. Okkyntalah took his share and added them to his quiver.

'So, what have you discovered, Teldrohn?'

'Their archers are posted round the far half of the second level of ledges. There's a few of these ledges, all going right round the ball. Looks to be some areas behind walls and walkways from the ledges to the rooms. I couldn't count the archers exactly, but my guess is about twenty. They're responding to movement at the entrance, nothing more.'

As he spoke, another woman appeared with water carried on her head. She passed through them without looking or pausing and was at the entrance before they could stop her. Again, a swarm of arrows was released and she fell dead at the entrance, pierced by three. Teldrohn's guess seemed correct.

Okkyntalah closed his eyes at the unnecessary death. He and one of the women attackers pulled her clear of the entrance and, once more, arrows rained down. Teldrohn reached in and collected more of these missiles.

Now certain it was movement that attracted the archers, they realised entry would be impossible whilst they remained. Teldrohn stripped the pinafore from the fallen woman and withdrew one of the arrows from her flesh to hang the tiny garment on.

'What are you doing, Teldrohn?'

He didn't reply, but stood beside the entrance, hidden from the archers, and stretched his arm, with the piece of clothing at the end of the arrow, into the space. As expected, arrows flew at the target.

Teldrohn brought the white triangle of cloth back in on its arrow and looked at Okkyntalah and the others. It was obvious.

They took turns at sending out the target and on each occasion the archers spent their weapons on the movement. Twenty more attempts and then all arrows ceased. They tested it three times, with no missiles fired at the target.

'We've a choice now. Either, one of us steps out there to see what happens, or we stay here and do nothing.'

Okkyntalah, having delivered this idea, stepped toward the entrance, but one of the women with him gripped his arm.

'Wait.'

Another water carrier had appeared from the stairs and passed through them as those previous had done.

'We can't let her die to save our skins. I won't allow it. Stop her.'

Two of the group stood in her way but she moved quickly by them, so that another two were forced to try to halt her. Again she tried to side-step them. But they now surrounded her, leaving no escape route.

'If you go out there, you'll be killed.'

She made no response. No indication that she'd even heard their warning. She simply continued to try to move forward, turning each time she encountered a barrier until she'd made a full circle of the attackers. But she then continued her attempts and couldn't be coaxed to stop.

'Take her water container. See if that makes a difference.'

One of the men grasped the container. The woman struggled to hold onto it but the man was too strong and she lost her hold so that water spilt over the floor at their feet. She made a sound of utter despair and fell to her knees. Ripping off her apron, she tried to mop up the liquid and transfer it from floor to container a few paltry drops at a time. Her distress and anxiety were palpable.

Okkyntalah used the distraction of his colleagues to make a slow entry through the gap. No arrows came his way and he signalled the others to come closer. The archers now stood with empty quivers but bows still held. They continued to move as though they had arrows to fire, slotting imaginary missiles onto their strings, drawing back and releasing them, in a constant and uniform manner.

The very strangeness of this activity made the attacking group pause and take stock of their surroundings. Okkyntalah stared at the interior of the sphere. The smaller of the two holes piercing the ball lay behind his left shoulder and the larger one was sited lower and to his right. Sunlight poured through the higher aperture, adding its light and warmth to the strange blue that seemed to emanate from the walls themselves. He counted four circular shelves, following the circumference on different levels. There were three cubes in the centre, placed so that they didn't obstruct sunlight passing from the small hole to the large one. Between these boxes, gangways led from the encircling ledges, which, in turn, were connected by small flights of stairs. Beneath the smaller hole, an open balcony protruded into the sphere, without rail. This, too, was connected to a ledge by a narrow stairway. All the rooms were held in place by sets of fine metal beams set into the walls of the sphere.

Apart from the archers, who continued their useless activity, of soldiers there was no sign. Some water carriers, holding empty containers, were gathered close on the lower ledge, unable to pass the archer who stood there, and clearly distressed by this blockage.

There was no sign of other life.

'They'll be in those rooms. There's nowhere else.'

Okkyntalah nodded at this comment. 'We'll investigate the nearest, as a group, and then act depending on what we find.'

He led them, weapons at the ready, along the lower ledge. They had to push the archers out of their way as the shelf was too narrow to permit passage otherwise. The men fell into space until they connected with the lower curve of the sphere and then slid down it and into the hole where the column connected. There, they plunged into the depths.

As the attackers moved toward their objective, another water carrier made her way into the ball and, unimpeded, walked the other way round the ledge until she reached the stairs. She climbed to the platform protruding from beneath the lower hole, which, nevertheless was sited above the attacking party, still on the lower level of the entrance. There, the differences in height made her disappear from view.

Okkyntalah's people were gentler with the water carriers attempting to return below, and bodily moved them, holding them so they passed them out over the space and then returned them to the ledge to allow them to continue their journey back down the stairs. The grouping of three returning water carriers appeared to be the norm, as they'd passed none coming down during their climb up the column and no others gathered to block their passage along the ledge to the first and lowest of the cubes.

'Too narrow for us to go more than one at a time.'

They followed Okkyntalah as he ascended the stairs to the opening that gave access to the lowest, smallest cube. Six against an unknown force; Okkyntalah, two women and three men, including Teldrohn. Though the rather cramped space suggested there must only be limited numbers, his group perched precariously on narrow stairs with no rails and knew any opposition might easily send them into the column below, with no hope of preventing the fall.

So far, the defence of the Powerseekers had been inadequate though apparently controlled by those very minds. It was unlikely that such directed guards would be employed at the very heart of the complex. Here, they must face fierce, well-trained combatants and the probability of sudden death. It couldn't be any other way.

Chapter 51

BATTLE

In his small cell, Dagla Kaz plotted the downfall of his detractors. They would suffer and be sorry for their opposition to one who had the ear of Ytraa. There were ways to avoid the punishment and torture these heathens would otherwise make him suffer. They were stupid. Relied on truth and honesty, as if such qualities had any value in a world of corruption and ambition. Power was the thing. Power and wealth. Together they gave a man the ability to do as he would. He would again rise to supremacy and defeat these fools.

Aglydron approached with his evening meal. Here was a simpleton he could at least rely on. The man was all duty and loyalty to Ytraa, and, more importantly, to him. He'd make use of such blind obedience. And he needn't put on a pleasant face. The idiot was so fanatical, he couldn't even see when he was being used and abused.

'What news of my trial, Aglydron?'

'Tomorrow. On a hilltop outside the city, Dagla Kaz. You'll be accused of many different crimes.'

'What are they?' He knew, of course, what these heathens considered to be crimes and which of their idiotic rules they accused him of breaking. But he had to be certain there weren't others he hadn't considered.

'I…it's hard for me to use the words of blasphemers, Dagla Kaz. I…'

'Speak, man! How am I to prepare the words I need to defend myself if I don't know how I'm accused?'

'Sorry, Dagla Kaz. It's just that I can't understand why anyone would say such things about you.'

'No matter. Tell me what they say.'

'They say you deceived all Followers on the island by not showing the so-called proofs they've put on display. They say you've taken part in perverted joinings with women not willing to serve you. They say…they say that you…that you…'

'Get on with it, man! I need to know. Just tell me!'

'They accuse you of rape. I'm sorry, Dagla Kaz, but that's what they say. They say…there are those who say you murdered and tortured…'

'These are all trivial. Is there anything of a grave nature I need consider?'

Aglydron stood speechless for a moment. 'Trivial, Dagla Kaz? I…aren't these the most serious crimes you can be accused of?'

'No charges of theft or corruption?'

'Not that I've heard. I think they feel the other charges are so serious that such minor infringements can be ignored.'

'Fools! What do they know about the way of the world for a God like me? I'll defend myself with skill and intelligence that will show them how ignorant and irrelevant they all are. Good. Now, let me eat. In peace, if you will.'

Aglydron left the food and his cell. In the quiet, the High Priest mulled over these spurious charges. They were, in any case, of no consequence to a God. Wasn't he a direct descendent of Mythanpho and Vaarkil? His entire ancestry proved him divine. They had no right to place a God on trial and he would demonstrate his power and holiness once they placed him where he'd speak to all who gathered. Tomorrow; sooner than he'd expected. It meant many from the outlying communities wouldn't be present. Why the hurry? Surely it would be better for all if the whole community was to be gathered and the meeting held on the Plains of Ytraa, after the Godwood was carved and erected into place on the monument.

Come the morning, he would adorn his magnificent body with his robes of office. Resplendent in finery befitting a God, he'd take charge of proceedings and lay bare the inadequacies of mere people. Should he show them mercy? Or should he destroy them all with his powers? No. Some clemency. Let recent converts be given the chance to worship him. But Aklon must die. He must kill him in the most painful and prolonged fashion he could possibly devise. In fact, he'd spend the night designing the methods by which life would be slowly removed from that arrogant bowelcreep. By the end of the process, that boy would be pleading with him to end his life and begging for forgiveness.

The first of the runners had already returned. But they'd had to travel only very short distances. The others would reach their destinations soon and then the people would begin to arrive. It was an ideal opportunity to gather as many of the island population together as possible. Aklon would see his father disgraced and punished and then would take the centre and proclaim the new faith for all to hear and adopt, as they wished.

No one would be forced into a pre-ordained set of beliefs. The new way would be no more than a framework on which people might build their own ideas of god and life after death. The only thing he must impose at this stage was a series of rites of passage. Without such ritual, society might break into factions and unrest would disrupt daily life. It was important that the phases of life be marked by ceremony. Birth, naming, sexual maturity, partnership with another, the quitting of work and, ultimately, the ending of life itself, must all be celebrated in their own ways. Following had provided rituals for most stages in a person's life and its absence left voids. New ceremonies would fill those gaps.

His team of people working on alternatives had already discussed the possibilities of adopting the new wedding ceremony devised in Morstahn. Eyethlehn had earlier provided him with details in mindtalk.

Of course, mindtalk had now been suspended whilst those who were able took part in the joint defence of Tumalind in her battle with the Powerseekers. Aklon had been in the group for a time until the effort took its toll and he must rest. It was at the start of the break that he'd organised these other activities and set his plans in motion.

Now he must sleep and then return, refreshed, to help in the work of that brave young woman. In truth, the things he'd learned in that joint effort had alerted him to the need to invite as many people as possible to his father's trial and to the proposed announcement of an alternative way of worship. He hoped Ivdulon would be free to discuss the issue further, once Tumalind's task was completed. He'd left the battle at a crucial point. But, after his difficulties here on the island, he needed some relief from that demanding role.

He would return stronger and more able to give proper defence when rested. Unless, of course, the battle had by then been won. Or lost.

Voices. Voices everywhere. Such confusion and fear. Such arrogance and ambition. Such effort and endeavour. Tumalind trapped in a cruel world, relied entirely on her experience, her love for and from Okkyntalah, and her trust in the honesty of her own fellow-mindtalkers to guide her.

The Powerseekers had spotted her as soon as she'd entered their trap. Since then, she'd been forced to put in place barriers of such strength that even those surrounding her as friends would have difficulty breaking through. Everything must be done within her mind. Anything that happened to her physical self was irrelevant, as long as she remained conscious and alive. And for that she must rely entirely on Okkyntalah and his companions.

Conflicting messages warred through her mind and she was lost in the maelstrom for a while. But, slowly, and with enormous effort, she found her centre, organised a solid base from which to rally support on the one hand and send out her own missives of confusion and distraction on the other. Her role, now that the location of the Powerseekers had been definitely established, was to use her mind to prevent them acting in concert to destroy the small group led by Okkyntalah.

The task was more difficult and complex than she'd ever imagined possible. She had identified eighteen different minds within the grouping they called the Powerseekers, and one other that felt distant, indistinct and seemingly distracted. All but that odd other were strong, determined and fixed on domination of the whole world. They recognised her as a threat to their plans and tried many ways to destroy her.

'*You're a weak woman. We are strong, powerful and resolute. You'll pay for your invasion of our realm. We will make you suffer and bring you pain and humiliation beyond your feeble imaginings.*'

But threats of this sort had never stopped her before and they changed tack.

'*We're stronger than you and all your supporters. They'll desert you soon enough. They'll see we're right and more powerful and will leave you to us. You can't win this battle. It's beyond you. You're too weak. Give up now and we will show you mercy. We may even appoint you to a position of power. Imagine what you could do if you were really powerful. Nothing need be beyond your reach. You could wish for anything, anything at all, and have it. Think of it. Have exactly what you wish to have. Live that life of peace and tranquillity you desire, the family you long for, the husband you adore. We have the power to provide such comfort for you. Let us share our gifts with you. Let us be your guides and helpers into the life you crave.*'

But this transparent lying and attempted bribery had no effect on her; she refused even to acknowledge that she heard it.

'*You think Okkyntalah loves you? Believe he's true? He's had more women than you can count. He's joined with many by invitation. Beautiful, sexually experienced women who give him far more than you'd ever be able, or willing, to provide. He's refused others only to be tempted again when you were absent. We can name them. Myllthlan, Linlyss, Porlesah, and Syylvah. He frowked her even as you sailed from the island on your pointless pilgrimage. Then there's Chellyth, Sha'ra, Chislanda, and Shoarhn. Yes, your own mother, who he ravished whilst you slept innocent in the next room. And countless others in Mipahnhil, Litkala, Shorrannon, all those decadent cities where loose women welcome a man who can frowk whenever he feels like it. When you were captive in Mehrrhyphrol, he spent time with two serving wenches, frowking them so much they couldn't walk afterwards. In Ov-Bebna he frowked the entire harem and other women in the town. Eyethlehn, your mother's friend, he frowked many times before he was even...*'

'*Liars! He's never lain with me.*'

The interjection from Eyethlehn wasn't needed for Tumalind's peace of mind; she knew they told her lies. But she welcomed that it stopped the constant assault on her thoughts. There'd been other attempts as well. But then, as the attack started, they had to turn their minds to the defence of their physical realm. She'd learned of the men and women turned into slaves, minds made servile to the needs of the Powerseekers so they had no free will. That knowledge allowed her to disrupt messages sent to the soldiers defending the sphere, making them act without consideration, so they spent their arrows on phantoms instead of waiting for actual victims.

410

And now the group led by Okkyntalah approached the most dangerous stage of all. The inner temples of the Powerseekers. Each cube held six evil minds and as many armed soldiers. These were different. Men without care who'd been promised all the women they wanted, and been provided with such easy gratification. These were men chosen for their loyalty to the promise of gain. Men without concern for right or wrong, only for maximum self-indulgence. And they'd enjoyed such physical pleasure for long enough to be zealous in maintaining it. They would happily kill to keep their privileges.

Tumalind realised she could do almost nothing to disrupt the activity of these guards. All she might do was concentrate on the six minds in each cube her husband and his party approached and try to influence the Powerseekers, make them act in ways that interfered with the effectiveness of the men guarding them. It was a task she undertook to keep Okkyntalah safe. But it was an undertaking more difficult than any she'd so far faced, and already she was weary, weary beyond words.

Feldrark felt Ivdulon fail. He detected her weakening power as she slowly fell into unconsciousness. The effort of controlling the group, keeping them together and focussed on defending Tumalind had been too much. Her strength had given out.

He must lead them now. He felt the slight tremor pass through the group and hoped Tumalind wasn't at a critical point in her task. Any stumble now would have serious consequences for that young woman. He pressed the group to act in concert, urged them to renewed strength and effort. They were close, so close, to defeating the scourge of the Powerseekers.

'We mustn't fail now. Keep strength. Keep hope alive. Maintain your pressure on those gathered within the Dark Space.'

'Can we attack them physically, Feldrark?'

The suggestion came from a voice he recognised. He tried to place her. Teh-Blavv, one of the two mindtalkers they'd rescued from the harem in Ov-Bebna and, if he recalled correctly, a woman now with his soldiers at the Monolith.

'Where are you and the troops in relation to the Monolith, Teh-Blavv?'

'Just Blavv, Feldrark. We're in the tower, climbing steep stairs to the ball-shaped chamber.'

'So close? How stands it with Tumalind?'

'I can't say. We're not in sight of where she and the others are fighting. But we'll be there in moments and I wonder if now's the time to really distract our enemies. Divert them at the very moment when the attack is strongest?'

'You're being very open, Blavv. Won't this help the Powerseekers?'

'I don't think so. My guess is they're fully occupied defending their physical bodies.

411

Already, armed soldiers have dropped to certain death down the shaft we're climbing. I think the soldiers with Okkyntalah are fighting those that closely guard the Powerseekers. Our distraction may be very helpful at this stage.'

'It's a risk. But, if you're so close, I think it's one we must take.' He returned his attention to the whole group. *I expect all of you heard that conversation?'*

The response was immediate and positive.

'Then, let's do it. Wherever you are in relation to the Dark Space, enter now and confront those evil minds. But beware they don't corrupt you. Be on your guard, for they're powerful yet.'

Feldrark had touched the Dark Space more than once. He'd nudged it, feeling malevolence and aware of the hatred and self-absorption contained within. But now fear also lurked there. A hesitancy that hadn't been there before. The power of that evil was diminishing. He pushed on, through waves of induced nausea, wails of terror, deep walls of hatred, across trenches of threat, over jagged peaks of corruption, through thick fogs of greed. As he went, he identified individual minds at last and engaged with them in mental battle. There were no rules of war in this vile place. The first encounter took him into a mind so corrupt it had no place for anything but self-concern. He disrupted its thoughts and confused it with ideas foreign to its normal way of thinking. He felt it weakening and then, suddenly, it was gone.

Mental effort alone could never cut a connection that way and he realised that one Powerseeker now lay dead. A good start, but many others occupied the Dark Space, and he felt himself threatened from all round as he sought another distinct mind to undo and unsettle in hopes of helping Tumalind and her fighting companions.

Aklon awoke to the bright sunshine of noon and knew at once that he must return to the group of mindtalkers fighting to defeat the Powerseekers. He called Hyllahn and she came, full of hopes of joining.

'I am sorry to disappoint you, Hyllahn. I have a duty to perform that requires mindtalk. It is essential that I am left undisturbed, but I first need food and drink, if I am to have the strength required for this battle. Will you provide for me, please?'

'I will. If you'll give me what I want in return. Just once, Aklon. I have to know, you see.'

'I have no time for discussion. Make provision and then see I am not disturbed. Your reward will come once we have completed the success. I promise you.'

She returned in moments with freshly brewed tlathan, fruit juice, bread and cheese. 'A former slave was preparing meals for the household. I've brought what he'd got ready. Will it be enough?'

Aklon drank and ate swiftly. He asked her to stand guard to prevent others bothering him. She nodded, closed the door behind her. He settled into comfort and engaged his mind with the group. All were now invading the terrible realm of the Dark Space. With no thought for his safety, he plunged in and sought out evil minds to dominate, distract and disrupt.

Okkyntalah gained a foothold just within the cube, at the cost of a cut to his left forearm. The soldiers within combined in a forward rush, and he killed one instantly, his sword held out in simple self-defence. But the force of their attack pushed him from the room. For a moment, he teetered on the edge of the entrance. Then he fell. Instinct made him clutch at the nearest support. He found an ankle. Felt it stiffen as it took his weight. Hands from below and from above grasped what parts of him they could reach. Concerted effort restored him to a step below the woman whose ankle he'd seized. All remained safe. For a brief spell, they paused, aware how close he'd come to falling to his death.

They climbed again. Teldrohn now leading the assault, his sword slashing blindly as he entered. They were inside that enclosed space, crowded with fighters, Powerseekers and women kept for pleasure. The soldiers fought with fierce intent, trying to protect the evil minds. Six of these were gathered in the centre of the floor and held the female slaves around them. The half dozen soldiers were reduced to three with no loss to Okkyntalah's party. They remained determined to repel and defeat them.

To Okkyntalah's mind came an image of the Garden of Delight. As he fought against a guard, three naked slaves, beautiful and enticing, approached attempting to distract him. They touched and stroked him, made promises with their bodies and their eyes. Controlled by the Powerseekers, they'd been ordered to make it easier for the soldiers to kill him.

Teldrohn was similarly surrounded. And the other men in the group. The women of their party were untouched, free to attack the Powerseekers, who'd sacrificed their female shield's to confuse the men attacking them. It was a serious mistake and the women in Okkyntalah's group quickly killed four Powerseekers. At once, the female slaves became inactive and the men dealt with the guards, killing them and the other Powerseekers swiftly.

Within moments, all opposition in the cube had ended. All guards and Powerseekers were dead. The captive women wandered confused and no longer controlled.

'We're finished here but there's two more rooms, twelve more Powerseekers, to deal with. I don't think they'll make the same mistakes as this lot.' Okkyntalah led the way back down the stairs to take the flight that led up to the next cube.

As he took those first upward steps, a noise caught his attention and he turned to look down. At the entrance, the troops led by Phyloahn were entering the sphere. Beyond them he saw Tumalind, still tended by the woman he'd left guarding her. Help was at hand, all set for victory.

As he was about to turn back and continue his climb, Tumalind rose from her seated position on the floor. Her eyes widened briefly and she looked at him. He waved. She smiled. Her arms reached toward him. A look of utter horror crossed her features. Her mouth opened in a silent scream. Her hands grasped her head in agony. Okkyntalah watched, helpless, as his love collapsed to the floor, unconscious.

Chapter 52

TRIAL

The runner had arrived late in the afternoon, leaving them only that evening and the following day and night to reach the capital. Shoarhn had prevailed on Okkyntalah's father to take them on his boat. 'We can't possibly get there in time overland. And I must go. I must.'

'Why's that, then?'

'Dagla Kaz is Tumalind's father. He's also responsible for Aglydron kidnaping Jodisa. And he's the father of Aklon, the man I love. Enough reason?'

'S'pose so. I'll take you there. Find your own way back, will you?'

'If we must. These others would like to come, if that's alright?'

He'd assessed them all. All women, and to his liking. 'Cost you.'

Eyethlehn had nodded at him. 'I'll join with you on the voyage, if that's your price. Though I'd have hoped you might've done it as a favour to the mother of the woman your son married.'

He'd said nothing, but agreed to take them all. They'd had a short time to gather their belongings and some supplies. Shoarhn had arranged for her parents to take care of the twins and she'd left the farm under Dahrlahg's supervision. There were enough people there now to keep it going in her absence, after all.

The voyage had gone well, in fair weather. He'd extracted his price from Eyethlehn, much to Shoarhn's disgust at him and gratitude to her, and delivered them to the capital in time. He'd accompanied them as they walked the short distance from the harbour to the crescent shaped hill outside the city, where the rest of the population had gathered.

'If you were coming to the meeting anyway, why did you demand payment?'

'Never asked, did you?'

Many other fishing boats from Morstahn had sailed with them, making up a reasonable number of witnesses from the town.

The island's population was around thirty thousand and Shoarhn guessed half of them were gathered on the hillside, forming a semicircle around its hollow centre, where a slight rise formed an ideal speaking place. A platform had been built of wood and stone, with a special barrier at the rear to project sound toward the waiting crowd.

The excitement was palpable. People called greetings, shouted congratulations to recently married relatives not seen for too long, congregated in groups, loudly predicting the outcome of the trial. There seemed no doubt amongst the people that the former High

Priest would be found guilty of the crimes of which he was accused. Most had now witnessed for themselves the evidence of his lies. Resentment ran high and many hoped to see him humiliated and severely punished.

Shoarhn wondered how many of the offences she heard bandied about were actually true. Crowds often exaggerated, especially when a disgraced figure of authority was involved. The babble was tremendous and she hoped they'd be silent once the important matter began. As she wanted to listen to everything that was said, she made her way as near as possible in the press of people to the area where the trial would take place. Eyethlehn and Irrildys remained with her, wondering if she might even play a part in the proceedings, and eager to witness the whole event at close hand.

Toward the eastern side of the gathering, a group of individuals with deformities was attended by able-bodied people. They were from The Point. In common with the rest of the population, she'd heard about their settlement in the new town on the headland north of Chalamamnon. Aklon had assured her these people were just like everybody else; peace-loving and generally kind-hearted. She saw they were strong, even those not properly formed. Just like the rest of the population, they were variously clothed in nothing right through to full cover. Shoarhn had settled for the short skirt many women now favoured. She enjoyed the freedom and the cooler feel of air on her upper body, especially when working in the fields.

A clear sky carried seemeeuws with their melancholy calls; some squabbled noisily over scavenged food. Birds of the grasses, where people now sat in readiness, circled and cried out their distress at the disturbance to their nests. The air was thick with the scents of crushed flowers and grass, an occasional whiff of unwashed man or woman floating on the warm wind.

A wave of sound flowed up the soft curve of the hill as a small party of people approached the platform. The High Priest was unmistakable, sporting a ceremonial tabard and the high hat he'd worn during the Choosing so long ago. But he was welcomed with jeers and cat-calls rather than the silence and awed respect he'd received then. With him were several others. Shoarhn recognised Aklon straightaway, dressed as always in his neat and well-made tabard. Delbon and Choryssa, and the young woman who'd told her she wanted to frowk with Aklon until the end of time, were with him. Other women made up the rest of the party. One of them, Shoarhn was sure she remembered as a Virgin Gift from the Choosing. Two armed men guarded the High Priest. And, walking behind Dagla Kaz, came Aglydron. Aglydron!

What was her husband doing here? Why was he with the High Priest? Had he also been accused of some crime? She looked at him. Dressed in a tabard that had clearly travelled long leagues with him, he appeared worn and thin, his face a mask of anxiety.

What had he done to deserve association with Dagla Kaz? Though she no longer loved this man who'd been her partner for so long, she was sorry for his obvious distress.

As the party reached the platform, the noise slowly died until there were only isolated calls, mostly insults aimed at Dagla Kaz, who ignored them, his head held high and his face set in a sneer of superiority.

Aklon took central place on the platform and gazed out at the crowd. Shoarhn noticed how weary he appeared, and wondered at the cause. He looked at every quarter, every part and, as his glance passed where she sat, he lighted on her and the briefest smile said he'd seen her. He would concentrate on the set task. He always had. That was Aklon. His welcome would wait until the day's important business was done. He held up both hands in a gesture to attract the attention of the crowd and to call for absolute silence. It came after just a few in the crowd called out in dissent, naming him Renegade and saying he should stand down for shame, until those close silenced them with gesture or speech.

'People of Muhnilahm, I greet you and welcome you to this gathering. I will detain you only for as long as I must. Please rest assured that you will be fed and given refreshment when the time comes. We have no spare housing for you in the capital, but this hill is sheltered and the weather is set fair for today and the coming days, should we be here longer than the afternoon I anticipate.'

There was some disquiet at this suggestion but it died down again as those with patience quieted those who would find fault with any situation.

'I have gathered you together because you need to be aware that the pilgrimage that left here on the final day of the tenth portion of the cycle 1457 has now returned. As you all know, the intention of that mission was to exchange Virgin Gifts from our island with others from the ancient homeland of Choshinahm. Then to return with those young women and a new Godwood to add to the monument that previously stood on the Plain of Ytraa.'

The High Priest's face showed doubt and disquiet for the first time since he'd appeared. Shoarhn noted that Aglydron also seemed astonished at the suggestion that the monument no longer occupied its traditional place.

'No one has the authority to move the Monument of Ytraa, it must be restored to its rightful...'

Aklon faced Dagla Kaz and silenced him with a look. 'The monument has ceased to exist, except as ashes.' He waited for this information, which was also news to many gathered, to sink in, and allowed time for the reactions to die down.

'If you will allow me to continue, this process will take a lot less time than it will if there are continual interruptions. I apologise to those who were not informed of the destruction of the monument. I thought it of little consequence, given the general

417

acceptance that the rule of Ytraa and the Followers is no longer applicable here.'

Again, a few Dissenters shouted protests. But they were isolated. Dagla Kaz, and with him Aglydron, looked appalled at this news.

'I will continue. The new Godwood has already been cut into pieces to be used in the construction of a more permanent platform, to be built on this ground, and used for future meetings.'

Dagla Kaz called out, 'Blasphemy! You will die for this.'

Aglydron again looked aghast but remained silent for the moment.

'As for the rest of the pilgrimage, you need to know that Followers no longer inhabit Choshinahm. They are reviled there and subject to death if discovered. Dagla Kaz has returned with the last representatives from the so-called homeland. Many he brought with him have already accepted the new ways on seeing the proofs of the lies told by the priesthood and the Holy Ones. For those who remain unaware, the Holy Ones, recently renamed more appropriately, "Unholy Ones" no longer exist. With the exception of two isolated individuals who converted, they have been wiped out as a cult.'

Loud cheers of appreciation followed this announcement. Only Dagla Kaz and Aglydron showed alarm and disgust. Anger was clearly building in both of them. Shoarhn wondered how much Aglydron knew of the changes the island had witnessed and whether he'd seen the proofs that had convinced all but the diehards.

'I will not go into detail now, but there are amongst us former Followers not only from Choshinahm but also from Litkala and Kah-Labaz. Many of you will be ignorant of these places, but they are settlements where Followers have existed for as long as they lived on this island of ours. You will learn more of these events as time goes on. For the moment, be content that we are hosts to people from far lands.

'Nor will I bore you with the destruction of Following here on this island. You all know the details and most have seen the proofs with your own eyes. The Skyfire, called a sign from Ytraa by Dagla Kaz, was in fact nothing more than a wandering star that passes us by on a regular cycle as it, like our world, makes a wide circle about the sun.'

This was news to many people. The belief that the sun circled the world was a long held tradition and its denial difficult to take.

'I am sorry to deliver this fact in this fashion. But I speak the truth and, soon, will come others, far more intelligent than me, who will explain to you how this is so. For now, I ask you to accept that I am honest in this matter as I always have been in all others.'

The grumbling that accompanied his statement rumbled around the gathering until again it settled into reluctant silence.

'So. Today would have been a great celebration of a significant event in the Followers' history. Instead, it has become a day for you to learn more truths. You were promised a celebration. Once the main matter that occupies us has been dealt with, you shall enjoy your celebrations.'

Loud cheers greeted this announcement and Aklon was forced to wait again for silence.

'The difference will be that our festivities will be nothing to do with Following and everything to do with the enjoyment of life. But, more of that later.

'We are here to accuse the former High Priest, my father, Dagla Kaz, of many crimes against individuals and against the whole of the people on Muhnilahm. That is my purpose in calling you together here today.'

Aklon then took a long roll of parchment from Choryssa. He held it high for all to see before he unrolled it to show its length. He read from it the list of charges, starting with that which most affected those assembled: the deception of former members of the faith of Following.

'This duplicity was based on his full knowledge of the reality of the way in which Gadhallah invented his first lies, after repeatedly raping a young girl of thirteen cycles before killing her in the most cruel and brutal manner. The falsehood has been passed down from High Priest to High Priest throughout history until it came to me. Why did I reject it? Why was I different from all who preceded me? A simple matter of what you now all know of as mindtalk. This gift has existed for as long as our former faith, and probably even longer. It was simply not understood on the island before.

'By sheer good fortune, I stumbled upon my part in the gift just after Dagla Kaz first introduced me to the secrets in the Chamber that lay beneath the floor of the High Priest's house. I felt sickened and disgusted by what little I had learned from that first exposure. Out in the wilds, trying to come to terms with what I had heard, my mind in turmoil, I think that, for a short while, I went into madness. But it was then that the voice of one, Ivdulon, came to me for the first time.

'At first, I thought it was part of that insanity, but this wise woman convinced me of my rationality and understood the reason for my distress. What resulted from that initial contact changed my life completely and I decided then that I must end the lies and make all of you aware of the truth.

'So much for the first crime committed by my father. I will now list the others.'

He went on to describe the High Priest's rape of his daughter, Jodisa, and the murder of her unborn child, the torture of Por-Kildu, the frequent rapes of many other women, some of whom stood on the platform ready to condemn him. Even Shoarhn, who'd heard some of this before from Aklon, was shocked at the number and nature of his offences. The man was a monster.

Aklon finished his list and turned to his father. 'What do you say to this list of crimes of which you stand accused?'

Dagla Kaz sneered and stood tall. 'I am Dagla Kaz, High Priest of Muhnilahm and Chosen of Ytraa. I speak with Ytraa as an equal. Yes. As. An. Equal.'

He had to stop for the outrage expressed by the jeers and cries of the crowd.

Aklon signalled for quiet after a little while and the people calmed again, but their anger was palpable and Shoarhn felt it would take little to make them storm the platform and tear the High Priest limb from limb.

'I will not be tried by this rabble, or by a boy I disinherited. I am of a higher status than any man. I am a God and will be treated with the respect due any deity.'

As the crowd surged forward, Aklon and others in the party rushed to surround him, weapons drawn. The crowd bayed for the life of the man who claimed to be a god. Hatred and revulsion thickened the air and Shoarhn feared for Aklon's safety as he stood his ground to protect this brute who deserved nothing less than death. For some time, there was a stand-off. But, eventually, the people backed away and the tension reduced again. Much muttering and disquiet remained, however.

'You refuse to accept your responsibility for the acts described?'

Dagla Kaz made no answer.

'There are women here who deserve your acknowledgement of the vile way you treated them. Will you not show them such respect?'

The High Priest remained silent, his manner aloof and disdainful. The crowd jeered and threatened, but he made no reply.

Aglydron stepped forward, his stance and expression displaying his outrage. 'This is our High Priest, yet you treat him like a criminal. This is the man who led us, through danger and difficulties you can't imagine, all the way back to the land of our fathers. He fought mountains of fire, seas, great storms, places so cold your limbs could die. He battled against wild men, thieves, cheats and murderers for us. He did this for his people, for you, here on this island. Against all odds, he struggled and he won. Without Dagla Kaz to lead, the pilgrimage would've faltered and become lost. He never doubted. He never lost faith. He always trusted in his people and the power of Ytraa. And yet you condemn him like a common criminal. I am ashamed to be called your countryman.'

Aglydron's words found favour with a few who cheered and yelled approval. But most of the crowd remained unconvinced and hostile, jeering him for his support. Shoarhn was amazed at her husband's bravery, or foolishness, for she couldn't tell which it was. To stand up for such a man, to go against everything that had been said about him. That required real courage, or the devotion of a fool. Aglydron stared out defiantly at the crowd but said no more.

Aklon approached his father, spoke softly to him for a few moments. The High Priest paled as he appeared to listen, and then nodded. For a while, there was no movement on the platform.

Then, Dagla Kaz stepped forward and bowed his head. He raised his hands to the crowd in a gesture with no obvious meaning. Slowly, as if driven by a force outside himself, he removed the high hat and dropped it to the ground. He unfastened the buckle that kept his belt in place and allowed that to fall at his feet. Last, he undid the gold toggles that fastened his tabard and shed the gaudy garment, letting it fall where he stood.

'I have been your leader in all things. I placed my trust in a God I believed I could trust and have faith in. I followed my conscience and walked where my God made me go. I did what I believed was right for you. I faced great peril and endured great hardship, for you, for my people who stand here before me today.'

The change was startling. The haughty tone and superiority exchanged for a more reasonable and persuasive manner. Shoarhn found it difficult to accept such alteration. What had Aklon said to his father to effect it? The crowd murmured, grumbled, muttered. Some shouted their disbelief. Dagla Kaz remained silent, vulnerable, awaiting their willingness to hear him out. It came only when Aklon made a gesture for silence.

'But I now acknowledge that I also made mistakes. You now know, and I confirm the truth of it, that the man we all Followed as an example, the man we called the Lord Gadhallah, was a bad man. But, perhaps, he was a good man once. Perhaps he suffered from the evil voices of mindtalkers who polluted his mind with their wickedness. I say this, because I now understand, through the kindness and wisdom of my son, Aklon-Dji, that I, too, have been so contaminated. The voice I took for that of Ytraa was not Ytraa's, but the voice or voices of evil mindtalkers. Like Gadhallah, I had no knowledge of mindtalk. The only explanation, in my ignorance, for those voices that told me to act as I did, was that the words were those of my God, of Ytraa.

'I now acknowledge that what I heard was the evil of wicked mindtalkers, and not the voice of Ytraa at all. Everything I've done that is wicked, I lay at their door. I may be a fool, a man of little intellect, easily deluded and cheated by more powerful minds. But I'm not a bad man. I am not wicked.

'My acts of disrespect committed against the women I abused were the result of those evil minds. They took vicarious pleasure from my physical acts, as they lodged in my mind and experienced the feelings I enjoyed. I respect women; I always have. The aberrations came from the influence of powerful minds on my own feeble one. I had, in fact, no choice but to do as they made me.

'I now confess the sins and crimes that Aklon has listed. There may even be more. There may be acts I committed under the influence of those evil minds that I don't even

421

know I did. Such is the nature of mindtalk. I confess and I apologise, sincerely and most abjectly, to those I wronged. In particular, I make apology to all those women I abused and mistreated. Please forgive my uncontrolled lust and usage.

'I apologise to all who stand here before me. My crimes against you are great indeed. I made you believe in a God that most probably never existed. I made you partake in a religion that has no basis in truth or goodness. I made you take part in ceremonies that were wicked and meaningless. To all of you, I say I am sorry. Voices of evil controlled me and I apologise for your contamination by those evil minds.

'I stand here before you, naked, contrite, defenceless and ashamed. My fate is in your hands. You have Aklon-Dji, if I retain the right to so name him, I who have no right to anything at all, to thank for my realisation of what has befallen me, and what has befallen you as a result of my weakness and ignorance. You must do with me what you will. I am yours to command and dispose of how you will. But I ask you to reflect on one aspect of Following that I believe all of you have enjoyed to the full. I speak, of course, of the joy and pleasure to be had in joining.'

He bowed his head and waited. Shoarhn heard calls; cries of mixed condemnation and admiration, mutterings of doubt or belief, and understood that somehow this man had managed to convince enough of the people of his sincerity. But, in her heart, she couldn't find the means to forgive and forget. She couldn't reconcile the man's words with his actions. She felt certain something wicked lay behind everything he'd said, in spite of the appearance of his words. His final words contained, for her, the key to his new deception. He had appealed to the people through their delight in an act that was as natural as eating and breathing, making it seem like a blessing derived from his actions. And, there, beside him on the platform, stood her husband, his whole body sagging with the shock of revelation, his face a mask of utter confusion.

Was the High Priest to get away with his crimes, to place the blame on the influence of mindtalkers? What had Aklon said to him to make him change his public stance? For Shoarhn was convinced that what Dagla Kaz had said was merely a trick to save him from execution. Behind it lay evil intent, and she feared his plans.

Chapter 53

ENDINGS

Tumalind lay as though in sleep, but utterly unresponsive, in the small bunk, rocking with the motion of the ship. Okkyntalah, his wounds bound and stitched, sat beside her and considered all they'd been through. At his feet, for lack of anywhere else she could be, sat Blavv, her face signalling she still dwelt in the realm of mindtalk. She was searching for a connection with Tumalind, trying, as were others, to find her and bring her back from the place she'd gone at the height of the battle with the Powerseekers.

Many days had passed since that final confrontation in the Monolith of Kro Lat, a place that would now exist only in legend. Its destruction had been absolute. Such mastery of stone and design put to such evil use. It had to go; removed from the landscape. Okkyntalah recalled the sudden clamour from below as they'd killed the last of the Powerseekers in the final cube. The noise of awakening as the masses of slaves became aware of their surroundings, their confusion growing as they learned that they had no knowledge of who or where they were.

It had taken time and a great deal of skill for Kro Lat to be cleared. But, once the former slaves understood their role and what had been done to them in that place, they were only too eager to destroy it absolutely. Too willing, in fact; many died during their unplanned and passionate destruction. By that time, Tumalind and Feldrark's party of troops were clear of the structure. A handful had remained to supervise and advise the freed slaves. But Okkyntalah and the others had gone on their way to the nearest port; Likdigmina.

The journey was a blur. Over sands, along ancient earthworks, to the harbour. Boarding the ship. How many days? Tumalind would have told him, her ability to keep count of such things an amazing skill in his eyes.

Now, she lay there, good as dead. The woman he loved. The woman he'd rescued so often. The woman who'd now saved the world from domination by the Powerseekers. Not with arms and weapons, but with the power of her mind and will. And they'd destroyed her in the end. She'd never roused since the moment she'd fallen to the floor during the fighting. Would she ever leave her sleep? Would she ever be his again?

Blavv came back and smiled her hopeless smile of hope up at him. He placed a gentle hand on her head and smiled his smile of gratitude for her constant attempts.

'Time you rested, Blavv. Go to Teldrohn. That leg of his needs your love to heal. Would that we had Myllthlan with us. She'd have mended us in moment.'

'But could she mend Tumalind?'

He shook his head. 'I think Tumalind lies beyond even Myllthlan's healing power.'

The young woman rose and stroked her hands down her tunic. 'Will I get you something? You must eat, you know.'

He nodded.

The ship rolled in the swell as they left Xythonl after taking on fresh supplies and allowing the traders on board to do their work. Okkyntalah recalled Tumalind describing the place where she'd stopped during the journey from Muhnilahm to Litkala. It had seemed outlandish to her then, so early in their wanderings. Now, she'd still find joy in its differences, and pleasure in the similarities of all people, everywhere.

Next, they would enter the almost landlocked Kala Bay and dock in Kamakq. A change of harbours along the short road to the Shylnah Sea and, there, two different vessels would take the separate parties to their final destinations. Teldrohn, Blavv, most of the troops and released slaves from Kro Lat would sail to Litkala. He and Tumalind, with Phyloahn, a handful of volunteer soldiers and some grateful slaves, would sail for the island. Home. It would be good to be home again. Though not the ending he'd dreamed of.

He turned and gazed down into the face of the woman he loved, brushed his fingertips across her lips, stroked red tresses from her pale honey coloured skin. There was no response. She lay silent, as if sleeping, unaware of everything around her. And, it seemed, that was how her life would end. Everything sacrificed to the greater good of all but her.

He wept a while but stopped when Blavv came with food and wine.

She kissed him. 'You never know, Okkyntalah, something might awaken her. Don't give up just yet.'

'Oh, I'll never give her up, Blavv. Should she live a hundred cycles, I'll still be here beside her, looking at her beauty and willing her to wake.'

Blavv closed her eyes in grief for him, kissed his forehead again, and left to attend her husband.

'You don't own me, Aglydron! I'm yours no longer. Go. Please just go, and leave us to get on with our lives. Please.'

'This farm's as much mine as yours. You can't throw me out with nothing.'

'I don't want to throw you out, Aglydron. Nor do I want you to have nothing. I've told you; find another patch of land. Take Myllthlan, if she'll have you after your support of that evil priest. I'll help you build a new house, give you half the stock, set you up with saplings and other crops. But we can't continue to live like this; we'll end up killing each

424

other!'

The arguments had gone on for sixday after sixday. Nothing altered. Aglydron seemed incapable of changing his mind and Aklon wouldn't allow her to sacrifice all her hard work by moving out instead. But tension had grown over the time they'd been together. Their dreams of peace and harmony and a life of quiet loving had been shattered as soon as they'd arrived home to find Aglydron back in the house with the then unknown woman, Myllthlan.

She'd turned out to be a wonderful person and Shoarhn had quickly grown very fond of her. Nothing was too much trouble for her, and folk came from leagues around to take advantage of her healing ability. Tales of her cures had spread like wildfire through the island and she was often in demand. She never charged for her services, and worked on the farm for her keep. 'The gift is freely given to me. How could I not share it?'

That expression of generosity said everything about Myllthlan, and Shoarhn wondered what kept this remarkable woman with her husband. Though Aglydron was husband in name only. He refused to part from her, convinced such a parting would prevent his making a claim on the farm.

Myllthlan had tried to convince him they'd be better moving to a new place, but he would have none of it. Aklon had tried but knew better than to press a man who looked on him still as an evil heretic and who'd become even more of a stranger to Shoarhn since his re-appearance. Originally hated and then simply disliked for his part in the trial of Dagla Kaz, Aglydron was unrepentant. He remained one of the very few still faithful to the Followers, in spite of all that had happened.

They were eating the evening meal; an event that rarely went smoothly. Many sixdays had passed since the trial. Aklon had explained that he intended to send his father to Litkala, where his partner was pregnant with his child.

Shoarhn thought him too merciful. 'He deserves to die after all he did.'

'He claims to have been influenced by the Powerseekers. I could not blame him, knowing that to be the case.'

She'd looked at him for a long time until he'd dropped his gaze.

'I know. I should have him executed. But he is my father, in spite of everything.'

'Just as long as you understand and admit your reasons, Aklon. You've ever been truthful. I'd hate it for your evil father to be the one who made you tell lies.'

Chastened, he'd been especially loving that night.

Now they were at yet another evening that promised to end in shouting and bad feeling between herself and Aglydron. Another night of conflict and dispute. She sometimes wished Aglydron had been killed somewhere on the pilgrimage, and then always scolded herself for her wickedness.

A sound from outside caught her attention, as Aglydron paused for breath between protestations. He was about to start again, when she held up her hand to listen. There was definitely an unusual noise. Perhaps someone calling out a name, close by?

She rose and opened the door. A ragged, thin, unkempt woman fell into the house and lay on the floor, trembling and muttering incomprehensibly. Shoarhn turned her gently on her back and placed her head in her lap. She was skin and bone, her hair matted, her torn garment filthy. Scars and dirt marked her body.

Myllthlan was there at once, looking to see if this was a case for her healing. But the woman bore no fresh wounds the healer might repair and, though she rambled incoherently, it was more the muttering of extreme exhaustion than of an unsound mind.

The two women took her to the washing room and sponged her clean. They combed her hair, dressed her in a spare tunic Aglydron had brought home from his travels.

Returning to the dining area, they found Aglydron sitting with a goblet of wine, his face in a sulk of resentment still. Whilst Myllthlan tended to the new woman's seating and made her comfortable, Shoarhn prepared tlathan and made up a platter of fresh fruit, soft cheese, and thinly sliced meats for her.

She ate and drank ravenously, barely stopping for breath. Later, they put her to bed in the corner of the living area, since Aglydron and Myllthlan occupied the only spare room in the house.

Morning brought more clarity to the woman's talk. She was about to give her name, when Aglydron and Myllthlan came in from their sleeping chamber. The woman rose and staggered across to Aglydron. Held him tight, weeping freely as she clung to him and repeated his name, piteous and full of anguish. He remained rigid and aloof, but did nothing to shake her off. At length she pulled back from him and looked up into his face.

He deigned to look at her then, for the first time since she'd entered the house. His face registered utter confusion, and then shock. 'Chislanda? It's not possible! Chislanda?'

Myllthlan glanced at Shoarhn. 'I recognised her, of course. But I thought it best to give Aglydron the chance to acknowledge her before I said anything. I hope you don't feel I've let you down.'

'Not at all, Myllthlan. I think you're right. But I do wonder what'll happen to you now they're back together.'

'He comes here on sufferance only, and because he's Jodisa's father. At the first sign of any attempt to corrupt my people, rape a woman, or spout his evil words of a faith we've all rejected as lies and myths, he either goes or is killed, Pharah.' Feldrark dismissed the priestess's daughter, now plain Pharah, after Rrildyss had renounced her priesthood on her return to Litkala. Pharah was already growing round, the baby Dagla Kaz had made with her expanding her belly and filling her breasts.

Rrildyss, who'd kept an eye on him during the pilgrimage, was as unhappy as Feldrark about the prospect of having the old High Priest in the city. In accordance with Aklon's wishes, however, she'd approached Feldrark and Jodisa with the idea.

They were less inclined to forgive the supposed influence of the Powerseekers over him. Jodisa, in particular, recalled that her suffering at his hands had occurred long before he'd ever hinted at hearing voices. But the man couldn't be left to live on the island, where he was daily at risk from those who hated him, and only stayed their hands against murder because of their respect for Aklon.

None of them believed the former high priest was a reformed character. But, in the city, it would be easier to keep him under control. On the island, he had far too much freedom to garner support, especially with devotees like Aglydron still loyal to him. No, if the man wasn't to be executed, then Litkala was a safer place for him to be kept than on Muhnilahm. Feldrark asked Rrildyss to organise a ship to collect him, at the same time it was gathering some of the goods they now regularly traded between the two communities.

'Ensure the captain understands he's to be kept apart from any women, is guarded against escape, and isn't treated as anyone special. Give that man a suggestion that he's different and he'll swiftly become as obnoxious and vile as he was before that confession.'

He was sure he'd lost his mind for a time. There'd been voices. Confusion. Words he hadn't understood. But there'd been such good times, too. All those women so easily dominated by his priestly office. Of course, that was no longer there. He was supposed to be ordinary now. The fact he was a God he kept to himself, for the moment. The echoes of those persuasive minds, those sensible voices, remained with him and he missed their previous suggestions and support.

Aklon's quiet threat to have him roasted slowly over coals if he failed to admit the crimes he'd been accused of had forced him to recant at the trial. No matter. He'd done those things. His fool of a son's promise of clemency if he not only admitted them but expressed regret had held true. Anything to save his skin.

His life was leisure now. Soon, he'd be back with Pharah-Li, a woman willing to play his games. And she'd present him with a son and heir. Heir to what, though?

He'd lost almost everything. But he'd had his revenge on that sycophant, Aglydron. He couldn't believe his good fortune in discovering Chislanda freshly arrived on the island, slimmer and looking worn. She was unaware how he'd arranged for to her miss the ship the rest of them had sailed on from the mainland.

'Well, well. Chislanda. I thought we'd lost you for good, you know. Don't know how you got left behind.'

'One of those unfortunate mistakes that happen sometimes. I never did find Aglydron in the town, you know.'

'Well, I assumed not. He didn't find you, either. Must've gone in the wrong direction, I suppose. Then someone said you were aboard, and so we set sail. No way we could return for you when we discovered you were missing, of course. Still, you've managed to find your way to the island.'

'Aglydron's here, is he?'

'Aglydron? Yes. Yes. Go to Pampahn, my dear. That's where you'll find him.'

And off she'd gone, in entirely the wrong direction, whilst that fool had finally made it home to Morstahn. Aglydron's speech at the trial had made things worse; made him sound too good and kind. The man was stupid. Still, Chislanda would have a real job finding him, of that he was certain. He smiled at the thought.

It was one of the small pleasures left him: secret ways to cause trouble for those who displeased him. It was easy enough, when you understood people, when you knew the way they thought. Simple to sow seeds of dissention and envy and even greed, if you had the means.

Yes, Litkala would be a pleasant home, a place he might do harm whilst gaining more power without being caught or accused. As long as he stayed away from Feldrark and out of the clutches of that witch, Ivdulon. She; now, she was a figure to fear. She would see right through him. Ivdulon was best left well alone. But there were others he'd be able to torment and abuse, if he took care to disguise his methods.

'How did you get here, Chislanda?'

'I worked passage on two ships to bring me to the island. But I was misled when I arrived here, directed the wrong way by that High Priest. He sent me to Pampahn.'

Aglydron asked her for details and, as her story of the mix up that first caused her disappearance and then of her meeting with Dagla unfolded, the impossible changed to the possible and then to the probable. He understood, at last, that the High Priest, the man he'd all but worshipped and served as a godlike figure, had been responsible for her loss in the port.

In the telling of the tale, Chislanda reminded him of the terrible abuse she'd suffered as partner to Dagla Kaz. The truth slowly dawned on Aglydron. The High Priest really had abused and raped all those women. He'd lied. He'd known all along the falsehoods that had formed the Followers, but he'd preached them as truths. Maybe he'd arranged for Tumalind's capture all that time ago, after all. And now he'd lied again, deliberately, to stop Chislanda finding him. After all he'd done for the man. How had he been so blind?

How could he have been so foolish?

He sent Chislanda to the room he'd shared with Myllthlan to rest as she was still recovering from her desperate wandering around the island in search of him.

'I'm sorry, Shoarhn. I've been wrong in so much. I can't do anything about the past. But I can make the future better. I'll take Chislanda to the far side of town and start a new farm there. The help you offered still applies?'

'Of course. What's brought about this transformation, Aglydron?'

He explained. 'Have you heard any more of Tumalind?'

It was the first time he'd mentioned her name since he'd been home, though he'd known of her vital part in the changes that had occurred.

'Aklon's been in touch with Blavv. She's unchanged. The young woman describes her as living dead. She takes food and water, if they're fed to her. But her eyes stay closed and her body's limp and unresponsive. She breathes and her heart beats, but nothing else stirs. It seems her mind is completely gone. Okkyntalah hopes to be home with her soon. They sail from Kamakq tonight and expect to be in Chalamamnon in a sixday. She can't ride or walk, so they'll bring her here on a wagon. Another two or three days journey.'

'Then we'd best get ready for them, Shoarhn. You said you knew a place I can start a new farm? Let's do it straight away. Once we've built the walls and roof of a new house, Chislanda and I can be out of here. Then the room'll be there for Tumalind and Okkyntalah when they arrive.'

'And Myllthlan, Aglydron? I'm glad your beloved has returned and is recovering quickly from her ordeal. But you've used Myllthlan as your partner. You can't simply abandon her now.'

'If I may stay with you, Shoarhn, I'll be well. I have few needs and I've no further need to look after Aglydron now he has his own woman again.'

'You speak as though you did it as a duty to him.'

'Aglydron gave me a name when I had none. Tradition meant I was obliged to serve him because of that honour.'

'I never named you, Myllthlan. Not really. If anyone, it was Okkyntalah. He suggested your name. I just took advantage of your ignorance and claimed the name to give it to you. I'm sorry. I've not been very honest with you.'

To his utter astonishment, she slapped him, very hard, across his face. Just once. 'I'll not lie with you again. I no longer serve you, Aglydron. You are nothing to me.'

Shoarhn watched with him as Myllthlan left the house and went to do her duties about the farm.

He turned to his wife. 'And I must now separate from you, Shoarhn, as I wish to marry Chislanda.'

'Suppose I don't want to let you go?'

He was startled. What female foolishness was this? She'd spent the last few sixdays urging him to release her. Now, when he wanted her release, was she really refusing? 'I...I don't know why you'd...'

'No, Aglydron, you wouldn't. Of course I release you. But think about how you've treated me in this matter and remember it well.'

It was true. He'd been selfish and cruel. He must find a way to atone for that unkindness. Though, how, he had no idea at present. Perhaps some opportunity would occur in the future so he might make amends. For now, he must take care of Chislanda and ensure she grew strong and well again. How had she really managed to work her passage across the seas? She was no sailor, after all. He went to their room and asked her.

'You don't want to know, Aglydron. Sailors are often men without women.' She'd say no more and he felt it better not to demand a fuller answer.

Chapter 54

A PROMISE FULFILLED

Waiting. Okkyntalah felt he'd spent the best part of his recent life, waiting. Waiting to leave the Monolith, waiting to get Tumalind to Likdigmina, and then to Xythonl, and, finally, Chalamamnon and Morstahn, at last. And, now, he was waiting for Shoarhn to return to her house. The place was empty of those he knew; just Lallamdahl, who'd introduced herself as a slave from Ytraa's Peak, freed by Aklon.

'They will be here, Paltrohn. You were expected; just not yet, you see. Some are in the fields and barns, but most are finishing the house for Aglydron and Chislanda.'

Waiting for Myllthlan, and the hope of a cure for Tumalind's ailment, was the longest wait of all. He and Teldrohn laid Tumalind in the room the woman explained had been readied for their arrival. She made tlathan for them, overawed by their presence. Okkyntalah found her respect a little difficult to accommodate; as if they each had the status of a High Priest.

Blavv joined them and the three sat, drinking the refreshing brew and eating island fruit and cheese from the farm. 'I bet you're glad we decided to come with you now, aren't you?'

'You know I am. I don't know what I'd have done without you. I suppose I'd have had to wait until I could find help for the journey.'

'I'm surprised no one was at the port to welcome you. I mean, after all you've done and...'

'We arrived early, didn't we, Teldrohn? They weren't expecting us. We should've waited, but I just wanted to get home.'

'I offered to mindtalk with...'

'I know, Blavv. I really don't know why I refused.'

'Exhausted. That's why. Not thinking straight. I should've ignored you and contacted Aklon anyway.'

Travel-stained and weary from the difficult first leagues from the capital, they were all glad of the rest. The final leg of the journey had been easier and they'd thanked the farmer who'd provided the cart to take the weight of Tumalind from their arms.

They'd stopped to ask for water as they passed his farm. As soon as he heard their names, he'd offered the ride. 'No one from the capital to take you, Paltrohn?'

'We docked before dawn and set off straightaway. Anyway, we've no coin.'

'Coin? Coin? You think anyone on Muhnilahm would ask the great Okkyntalah and his beautiful brave Tumalind for coin? You'll find it hard to pay for anything, Paltrohn.'

All the way, the man had muttered under his breath about their bravery and the lack of respect shown to great people; mumbling, as if he'd no right to address his remarks to them. It was very odd to be treated as a hero, but Okkyntalah was only concerned to get Tumalind back home.

Blavv had then mindtalked with a woman who'd helped fight the Powerseekers. She was now telling everyone they'd arrived.

Outside, the noise of townspeople gathering grew into a tumult. Lallamdahl came and bowed to him. 'I'm sorry Paltrohn, but the people…they're hoping to see you…'

Okkyntalah shrugged and left Blavv and Teldrohn with Tumalind. A great crowd had assembled and they cheered as soon as he appeared.

He held up a hand for silence and it came sooner than expected. Was he more respected than loved here? No matter. 'Good day to you all. I…I'm overwhelmed by your support and kindness in coming to greet us, but we've travelled far and await a healer to restore my wife. Tumalind's unconscious and, until she's with me in mind as well as body, I'm only half a man. Forgive me if…'

But the crowd parted, excitement flowing as new people merged with them. And then Shoarhn was there, greeted by the people. And, with her, Myllthlan, Aglydron and Chislanda, and a man he guessed must be Aklon. Chislanda was leaner than he recalled. Aklon, was clearly held in great respect and the people obeyed at once as he quietly asked them to make space before the door.

Shoarhn greeted him with great affection. Aglydron hung back, uncertain of his welcome. Okkyntalah embraced him, and his bride-father then clapped him on the back and held him close in warm greeting. Aklon studied him and placed a hand of friendship on his shoulder, though they were strangers. He echoed the move and a cheer rose from the crowd.

Myllthlan moved nearer, tears in her eyes, and held him close enough to recall moments he'd spent with her in pleasure. 'I think it best we bring Tumalind out here. I need to do what I may in the open, Okkyntalah. I make no promise. This ailment is of the mind and I deal with the body. But I had a…sometime ago, in a cave, I…' She became confused as memory refused to serve her. Okkyntalah recalled similar partial memories of a place and time of great joy.

Teldrohn and Blavv, alerted by Lallamdahl, carried Tumalind outside. The woman brought the sleep mat to lay beneath her.

'I must expose her, Okkyntalah.'

Looking about, he saw half the people were naked anyway. Much had changed. Perhaps he should've listened more to Blavv as she'd tried to pass information to him whilst they sailed. But his mind had been entirely on his wife.

Now hope moved close, he clenched his fists and felt tightness in his chest. Suppose Myllthlan couldn't raise her? Suppose Tumalind remained this way for the rest of her life? A terrible price for her courage and tenacity, her perseverance and will against those wicked minds. But he wouldn't be found wanting. He'd be hers alone until one of them died. It could be no other way.

Myllthlan prepared and made her supplications to the air around her. The people watched, faces full of hope and expectation. Blavv had told him she'd healed many wounds on the island.

She drew power into her, seeming to pull more than he remembered from the times she'd mended him. Lost in the process, she was one with the elements and dropped to her knees beside Tumalind. How beautiful she looked, but how vulnerable.

Myllthlan placed her hands on Tumalind's head and jerked with sudden shock. For a moment, she seemed unable to move. But Okkyntalah saw this was a false impression. She was deep in concentration. She stroked her palms down Tumalind's full length and back up again, her quiet singing growing louder as she reached her patient's head. He'd forgotten she made this wordless song when healing.

Tumalind moved. The slightest tremor. Myllthlan rose again, her voice now loud, pleading, as she took more power from the air about her. Once more, she dropped and straddled Tumalind. She pressed her hands onto her head, gripping close around forehead and temples. Her song changed to a tone of command. Tumalind's eyes opened. Closed.

Those nearest gasped in surprise and hope. Okkyntalah crouched to be closer should she wake.

Myllthlan leant forward from her knees, hands gripping Tumalind's head, so that her body weight was concentrated there. The song changed to a sound that all, including Okkyntalah, attempted to obey. The sound said 'Awake!' And all within its compass grew more alive, more conscious of things around them. Okkyntalah felt the dust beneath his feet, saw every fine detail of Tumalind's skin and hair, smelt her scent, tasted her, heard her breath and her heartbeat. The sea rushing to the shore, the wind breezing through the branches, birdsong and scents of fruits and olives, flowers and richer odours of the farmyard all came clear to him. This was powerful magic; he could think of no other way of describing what she did.

Myllthlan ceased her song. She chanted unknown words. Okkyntalah, closest to healer and patient, felt wholesome warmth flow past him to the body of his wife.

Tumalind opened her eyes. Moved them. Looked up at the healer, still lost in her task. A brief glance of confirmation at her husband, then she stared into the eyes of

Myllthlan.

'I'm back.'

Myllthlan took her weight from Tumalind's head but maintained contact. She looked down into her face.

'I really am back, Myllthlan.'

The healer nodded, kissed her patient on the mouth. She rose and stood, sending back into the air whatever power she hadn't used. Then she fell to the ground, as she so often had when healing difficult wounds.

Okkyntalah helped Tumalind to sit. She was aware, seemed whole again. He held her close, kissed her, stroked her skin with hands of love and joy.

Slowly, he became conscious of jubilation, celebration enclosing them. He acknowledged there were others present. They rose together, Tumalind completely restored not in mind alone, but bodily, so that she could walk and move in every normal way. It was as though her period of inactivity had never been.

Great cheers accompanied her rising. Everybody wanted to embrace her, and her husband, now she was restored. Okkyntalah asked for calm around the healer. People carried Myllthlan into the house, laid her on the sleep mat vacated by Tumalind, and let her rest.

'I'm so thirsty, Okkyntalah.'

Someone brought water. Others carried wine and fresh tlathan, so that they were spoilt for choice and laughed as all about them joy and celebration spun its healing spell.

'The healer's dead.'

He didn't recognise the voice. Aglydron was there before him. Tumalind dashed with him to the place. Myllthlan lay motionless, her chest unstirred by breath. Okkyntalah watched his wife's father kneel and place his head on her chest, listen for the beating heart. He stayed, unmoving, body wracked with sobs as his tears wet her unresponsive skin.

Tumalind covered her face with her hands and Okkyntalah held her close, felt her trembling as grief and sorrow shook her frame. What god would ask such a price from good people?

She'd had some days to recover, though she'd explained she needed none, was perfectly sound and well as soon as Myllthlan had finished. She was complete and whole again. Except that she no longer had the gift of mindtalk. That had vanished in the ailment or the healing.

Myllthlan now took her eternal rest in her favourite place, beneath a giant cherry tree shading a corner of the field where Tumalind and Okkyntalah's new home was being built. She would never be forgotten. Already songs and verses had been made to celebrate her life and work. The promise only ever hinted at had come true.

Now, at Aklon's behest, they were carted round the island as heroes and joint heads of the people. No amount of resistance dissuaded Aklon from this plan. He insisted it wasn't just the right reward for their brave efforts but the best thing for the people.

'It's the most effective way of starting the new life we all must lead now the faith of Following no longer exists.'

'You said "it's".' Shoarhn observed.

'I know. I'm tired of speaking so correctly. I can relax that, now I'm able to relax in all things.' Though he glanced over his shoulder at the prisoner on the last cart in the train as he spoke.

The fact that it was seen as the best option for the island, persuaded Tumalind and then Okkyntalah to take the honours. Already they'd toured Morstahn and Krohtl, hailed by all as living legends and piled with gifts and offered great affection by a people who speculated over dangers they'd both faced. As they met them, the pair corrected false impressions and added details, answered questions and became better known to all those they now ruled.

In Krohtl they'd discovered Dagla, captive after he'd escaped whilst being put aboard ship in the capital. They were unsure why he'd decided against going to Litkala. He refused to say, but he'd hinted at interference from a distant source, suggested a threat had been made against his safety if he dared return to the city. But his manner in giving this information was so circumspect and vague that no one believed him. Aklon decided to bring him along to let him see just how much the people hated him, in hope of changing his mind. He was bound and guarded constantly by two armed soldiers.

Aklon and Shoarhn, travelling with them, advised each town on setting up the sort of Circle Shoarhn headed. And they explained the new faith to replace Following. The people needed spiritual elements in their lives. He and Shoarhn described rites and ceremonies devised by those he'd charged with the task.

'Each change in a person's life needs commemorating. A celebration of birth and entry into the world. A gathering to name the child. A challenge to mark passage from childhood to adulthood, so all face difficulty alone to learn self-reliance and responsibility. A public statement at the end of schooling to denote the start of work, whatever that might be. A community meeting and celebration for marriage of those ready for that step. And, finally, a ceremony to commemorate the close of life, when death of the body returns the soul of the departed to the realms of those who've gone before.'

As for the new religion, Aklon and Ivdulon had talked long on the subject, in

435

preparation for the alterations. Word had spread and was slowly being adopted in many lands. The transition would be slow, many changes were needed. But it was happening. One initial result had been improvements in the lives of women in most places. Of course, there was resistance; some violent. But Feldrark was willing and able to send his army anywhere to help quell any trouble.

'It'll be a lifelong task, but one we're determined to complete, for the sake of all who come after us.'

'And the nature of this new religion?'

Aklon smiled at Okkyntalah, and happily explained. 'It relies on respect for everyone and an understanding that the world is a natural place of value to us all. We call it Alltruth, combining all in nature with honesty. One basic commandment: Respect all; harm none. The rest will be developed as people come to understand the philosophy. We don't know whether there is a life after we leave this world; Ivdulon says it's impossible to know, though many wish for such a thing. But, if there is, we will not make the aim of this life to pass a test to achieve an afterlife. Such a condition devalues the life we lead here and now. So, we'll live each day as our last, and strive to end our lives having made the world more pleasant than when we entered it.'

'Idealistic and open to argument, Aklon, but what faith isn't? Fundamentally moral and just. I like it. Is there a system of prayer?'

'Ivdulon concludes we're incapable of knowing whether God exists, Tumalind. We think any god requiring our attendance in a specific place, demanding more than basic goodness, setting unachievable goals, or placing one sex or one type of labour above another, is unworthy of the title. We have no named divine power, and suggest people find their own spiritual path; pray, if they wish, to whatever entity they see as a force for good. We make no restrictions other than that we will not allow divisive forms of worship or those that exclude others.'

'Ivdulon's mind: I wish I could still connect with her.'

'You can, through me, Tumalind.'

She smiled at Aklon and nodded her acceptance. 'The movement's in its infancy and has a way to go. But, as a way of giving a spiritual lead to people, it's a good start.'

On the road to their third destination, Aklon explained the place was a new settlement. 'Here you'll find those who were rejected by Followers and those who've now decided to live with them. The town's named Aklohnahn; against my wishes.'

'Chellyth rules here?'

'You know…? Of course you met early in the pilgrimage.'

'Does she still vow to kill me painfully on sight?'

'In all seriousness, Okkyntalah, I can't say how she feels about that now. Much has changed since she led her people from The Point. But hers is a hard form of leadership. It's taking time to alter some of her ways.'

'Let's hope one of those ways involves her death sentence on me, then.'

Tumalind could see no point in suggesting they avoid the place. She knew her husband too well to advise against a visit. But she was also aware that some found change difficult. Would Chellyth be one such?

They entered the township, newly built. Neat and tidy in parts, with its ordered homes and farmsteads, its brightly painted walls, wide open spaces, its shaded central square around the large spreading tree, it still bore the rawness of recent construction. Piles of uprooted tree stumps, muddy hollows where earth had been dug but ponds had yet to form, marred its elegance. The people emerged from their houses, as soon as Aklon was recognised, and the cry went out to announce his arrival.

Tumalind was impressed by the warmth and respect shown to Aklon and, when they were introduced, to her and Okkyntalah. The people wore bright clothes of various styles. Some were very modest and others outrageous, though none was entirely naked. Those with deformities or disabilities made no effort to disguise these but proudly made the best of what they had.

A slender young woman, full breasts displayed and golden hair falling loose over small shoulders, her belly rounding with child, ran nimbly to Aklon and embraced him passionately, ignoring the fact that he still held Shoarhn's hand.

'Syylvah. Eager as ever. I'd hoped to find you partnered to some worthy man.'

She let him go, stood back, removed her short skirt, and stared at him. 'I'm 'ere for you, Aklon, like I've always been. Teck me an' give me what I want, an' 'ave what you want annall.'

He smiled at her and indicated Tumalind and Okkyntalah. She glanced briefly at her before gazing at Okkyntalah. To Tumalind's amazement, she rushed to him and embraced him in the same way she had Aklon. Clearly, there was a tale here. But she'd learn that later from her husband.

'Okkyntalah! Never realised it were you! Ooh, now I've two men as can do it for me. 'Ow will I choose?'

'Sorry, Syylvah. I'm married, and exclusive to Tumalind. Like Aklon, I hope you've found a worthy man as life partner.'

She pulled back and glared at Tumalind, assessing her and calculating some unexpressed idea.

The gathering crowd parted and two more people arrived. This must be the man tortured by Dagla Kaz. Scars and distortions of the flesh on the body of Por-Kildu were badges of his great courage and determination. Here was a man she could admire for many reasons. The woman, tall and with flowing blonde hair that partially covered the rise of breasts half concealed by a band of red silk, must be Chellyth, the one who'd threatened Okkyntalah.

She ignored them and went straight to Aklon, who she embraced with obvious affection, glancing at Shoarhn. 'So, this is the woman who displaces all others for your affections? I see love in her eyes and judge her worthy of you.'

The woman stood before Shoarhn and touched her shoulder in gesture of friendship. 'I am Chellyth and, with Por-Kildu, am the One. I lead the people of this settlement and welcome you as an honoured guest. Aklon is forever honoured, of course.'

Chellyth turned and faced her. 'Of you, Tumalind, I've heard great tales of brave deeds. I know that we, the people of this island, owe much to your courage and sacrifice and I thank you on behalf of the people of Aklohnahn. I welcome you to our new town and offer you the hospitality you so richly deserve.'

She faced Okkyntalah and moved closer to him. A belt circled her hips over a leather skirt, from it hung a scabbard with a sword and another with a hunting knife. 'Okkyntalah. The man who shamed me and made me a shield against the attack of my people. Okkyntalah, who forced me at knifepoint across burning sands and stripped me of my band of office. Okkyntalah, who forced me onto my face in dirt as he escaped with his stolen water.' She drew her sword and held it pointing at his face, a thumbs-breadth from his lips. He stood, arms hanging by his side, one hand still holding Tumalind's.

She could feel only slight tension in her husband but her intervention here might prove fatal. This was a matter of honour for the leader who'd made a success out of the very dust and sand of The Point. She deserved proper consideration.

'As I recall, I swore to kill you, most painfully, should we meet again.'

'I believe your actual words were, "If you return to The Point, I'll kill you with my own hands, slowly and painfully, Okkyntalah of Morstahn." As I recall, Chellyth.'

She nodded. A smile of relief spread across her beautiful face and she lowered the sword. 'Your memory's as fine as your reputation, Okkyntalah. I hope you never have cause to revisit The Point, for I'd hate to have to honour my promise.'

He bowed. 'I can think of no reason I'd return to that desolate place, Chellyth.'

'That's good. I have pleasure and honour in welcoming to our town the man who made the possibility of our freedom a reality. Welcome, Okkyntalah. Here, you're a guest of honour, worthy of the brave beauty who stands beside you. Come, let us refresh you all.'

A small disturbance rippled through the crowd. A voice raised in scorn. Several men pushed Dagla Kaz through the throng, his two guardians following at a respectful distance and conscious of the large and hostile crowd around them.

'Keep your foul hands off me. I am a God. Do you know nothing?'

Por-Kildu stepped forward, his leather jerkin open down the front and revealing his belt hung with sword and long bladed knife. 'Dagla Kaz. Most evil of leaders. A prisoner at last?'

The High Priest sneered at his former victim. 'No man overcomes me. I am divine and protected of Ytraa. I am the God Dagla. Know me and tremble!'

Por-Kildu nodded at the man close behind Dagla. 'Cut his bonds.'

Aklon moved a step but Chellyth placed a gentle hand on his chest. 'I may spare the man who set us free, Aklon. But no one has a right to prevent Por-Kildu's revenge on the man responsible for all we've suffered.'

Dagla rubbed his wrists, though the bindings had been kind and gentle. 'Do I know you?'

Por-Kildu removed his jerkin. 'These scars, and these on my face, were made by your own hand.'

He glanced at him, unconcerned and dismissive. 'I punished many. You must have deserved my justice.'

'You blamed me for your own fathering of a child on your daughter, because I was unfortunate enough to be the object of her love. You tossed me over the Scar onto The Point and left me for dead. But Chellyth and her people revived and nurtured me. Now has come the time for you to pay the price of that and your many other evil acts. I have not the concerns your noble son has shown in giving you mercy. I desire nothing less than your death.'

'I don't fear you. You cannot hurt me. I am God.'

Por-Kildu indicated a man in the crowd. 'Lend him your weapon. I won't kill an unarmed fool.'

The man handed his sword to the old priest, who took it and examined it as if a strange, unknown item.

He glanced at Por-Kildu with contempt. 'A mere man, hardly even that, thinks he may harm me? Fool!' He stepped forward with surprising speed and thrust the blade out.

Por-Kildu easily swept it aside and cut him across his thigh. The priest staggered, looked down at the wound with utter disbelief, and cried out in pain, and fear.

'Not God, then?' Por-Kildu stepped forward and sliced his chest, cutting the flesh but taking care not to make the blow fatal.

Dagla recognised his own pain, understood his self-delusion, and cried out in sudden terror. 'Spare me! I've been a fool. Don't hurt me. Please. I beg…'

'You ignored my blameless screams of pain.' Por-Kildu used the point of his sword to cut the fastenings of his tabard, opening the front of the garment. 'You led a group of cruel perverts in the destruction and rape of innocents.' He lifted his sword and slapped the flat of the blade hard between his thighs. The priest jerked with pain but, before he could escape, the blade turned to slice where it had struck. He was unmanned with a savage cut, and screamed in agony.

Por-Kildu, satisfied he'd revealed the man's cowardice and raised his knowledge and fear of the death to come, pushed the point of his sword into the man's flesh with each word he spoke. 'There will be no Garden of Delights for you.' He ended the matter with a merciful thrust to his heart. Dagla was dead as he hit the ground.

'Burn him. He deserves no proper burial and his carcase would pollute any ground that bore it.'

A great cheer rang around the settlement. Several settlers dragged the body from the scene to a place where it could be burned along with the uprooted tree stumps.

Por-Kildu nodded to Aklon. 'I'm sorry you had to witness that, Aklon. But you must've known that bringing him here meant his life was forfeit.'

Aklon nodded. 'You've done what I could not. It was necessary. I thank you. It is the end of that era. Now, we start anew.'

There was no further celebration of the death, but neither was there any grief at the ending. The crowd began to disperse.

As Chellyth turned to lead the visitors to the central house where she and Por-Kildu lived, Syylvah re-emerged from the crowd. In her hand was a knife, held out in threat as she approached Aklon.

'If I can't 'ave you. No one will!' She thrust the blade at him, for the second time in her life.

Before the blade had moved a handbreadth, it was out of her grasp. Okkyntalah's sword moved so fast it lifted it before anyone had even seen him move. Chellyth turned and, seeing what had happened, aimed her own sword at Syylvah's unprotected body. Okkyntalah held his weapon still and swept it round, catching Chellyth's sword and swiping it from her hand.

For a moment there was absolute silence.

Syylvah fell to her knees, 'I don't know what come over me.'

'You're with child, and women are known to do strange things when pregnant.' Okkyntalah retrieved Chellyth's sword, knelt before her, and returned it hilt foremost. 'My apologies for such swift action. But there'll be no more killing here, today. Syylvah isn't wicked. She deserves love for her past courage, not death for her present foolishness. She's a woman ruled by strong passion. There are men who suffer from the same demons. Is there no man here, of similar heat, who will quench the desire of this beauty?'

A man stepped from the crowd, took Syylvah's hand and raised her to her feet. He whispered soft words to her. She brightened and faced the group of leaders, bowed and smiled an apology, approached Okkyntalah and kissed his mouth with controlled passion, and turned back to the anonymous man. He bowed to them, took her hand, and led her into the crowd, where they disappeared from sight. A cheer went up, as relief surged through the people.

Chellyth nodded at Aklon and Por-Kildu and then turned to face the younger man, bowing slightly from the waist to him. 'Okkyntalah, I see, in you, we have a wise and just leader. Will you and your courageous wife honour us with your company for a celebration of our new life?'

The group moved across the wide space of the new square, each pair of lovers hand in hand and ready to share a better future.

Here ends the story of A Seared Sky

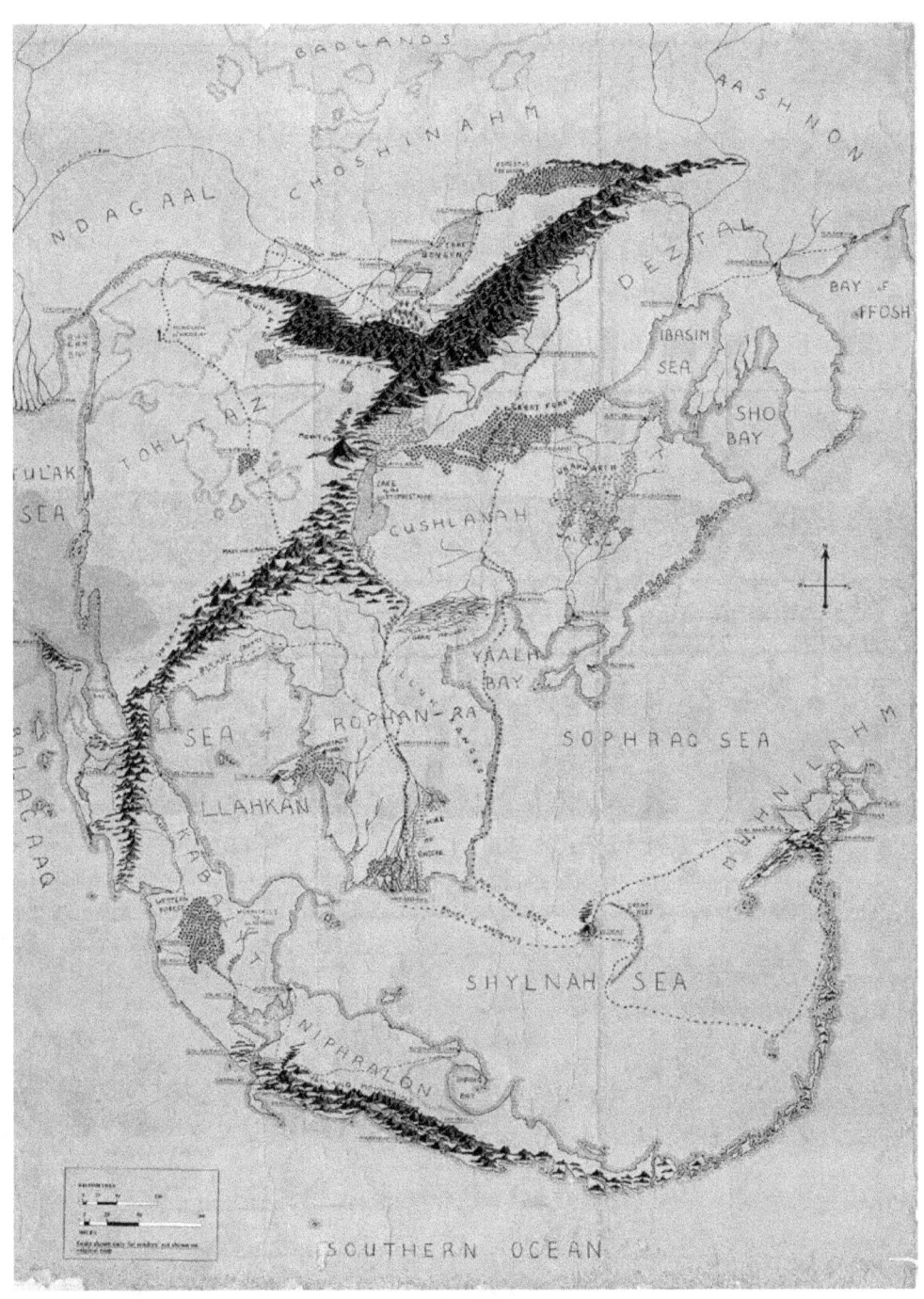

443

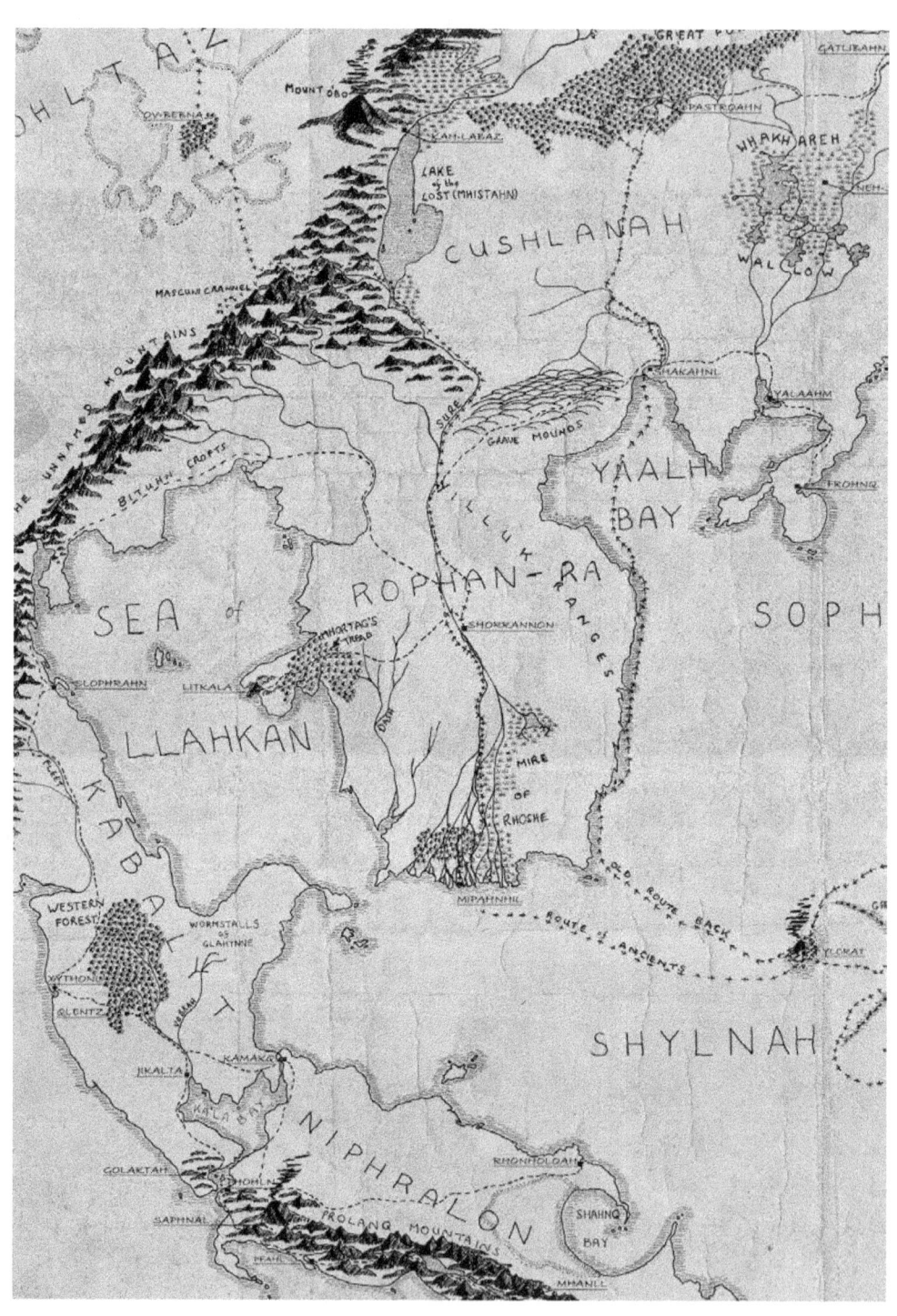

444

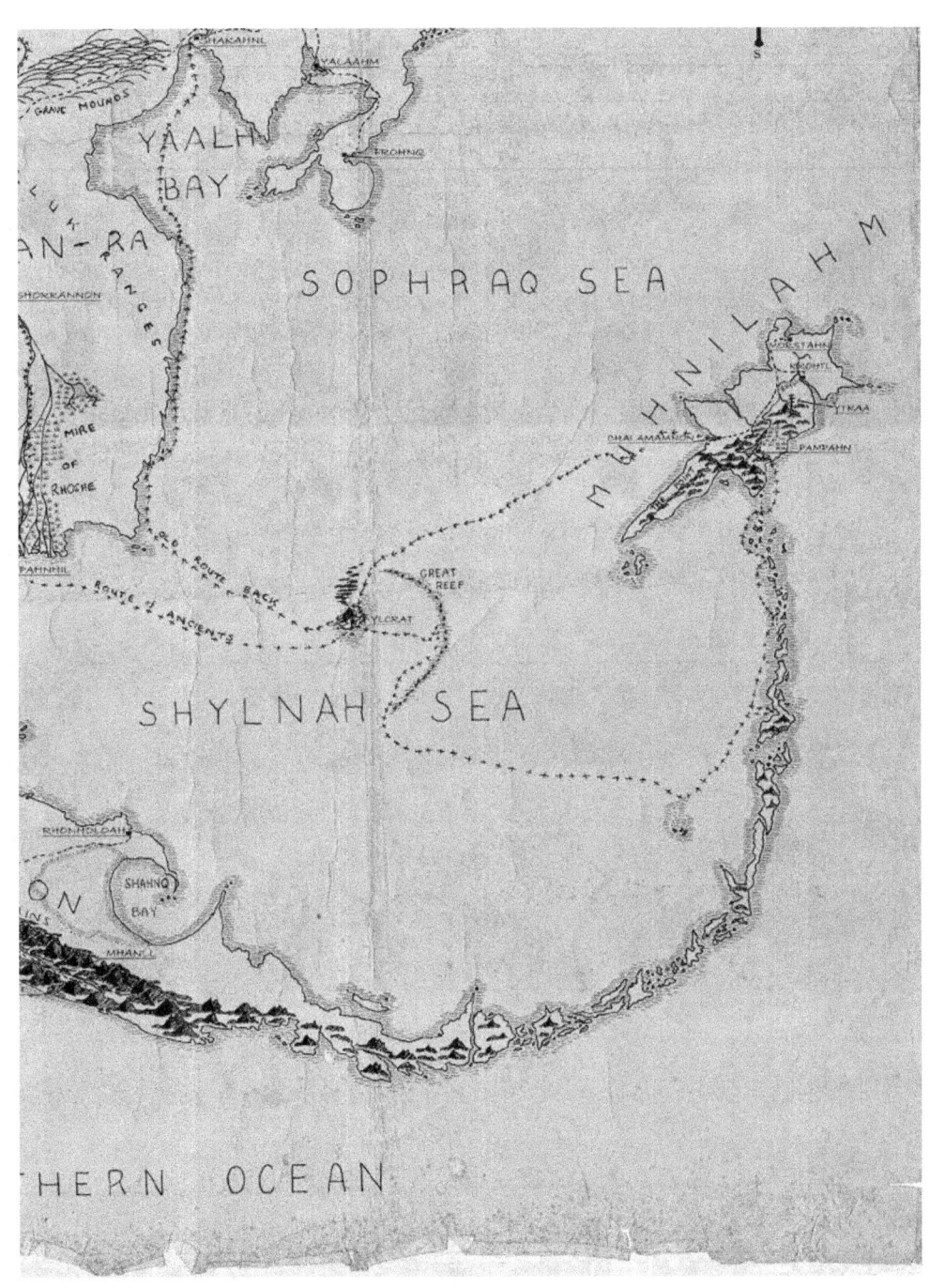

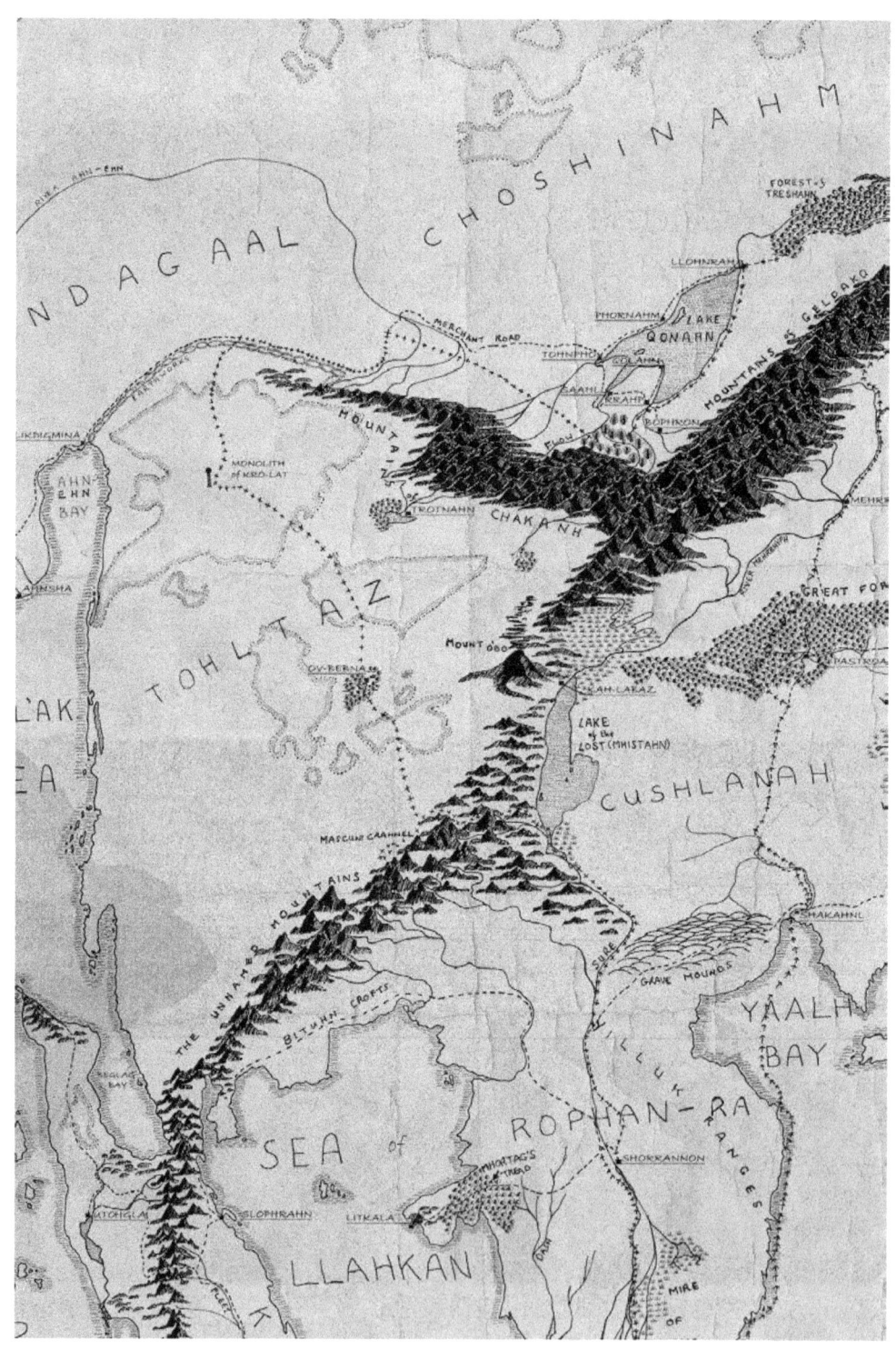

Stuart Aken is the author of other works of fiction. To explore these, please visit his blog at; **stuartaken.blogspot.com**

Stuart loves to interact with his fans so please go and find him down on his various social media sites and say hi;

Tweet with him on Twitter: **@StuartAken**
Like his author page on Facebook: **StuartAken**
Join him on Goodreads: **bit.ly/StuAkenGR**
Pin with him on Pinterest: **stuartaken**
Add him to your Google circles
bit.ly/StuAkenGPlus
Stumble with him on Stumbleupon
bit.ly/StumbleAken
And link with him on LinkedIn
bit.ly/StuAkenLinkedIn

If you've enjoyed this book, please tell your friends, and maybe find the time to place a brief review where others can discover what you think.

Characters in Alphabetical Order
Main players:

All Characters, in Alphabetical Order

For this, the final volume of the trilogy, I have included all named characters from all three books. I have given minimal information, since certain changes occur, which might signal story issues that might act as spoilers for alert readers who have not yet read books 1 and 2 of the series.

Main players:

A'ahl is a young woman, held as consort by the village priest, Kaz-Ca-Wesdan. She is Caarl's wife and lives in Morstahn, Muhnilahm.

Aglydron is a pious Follower who chases the pilgrimage. He is Tumalind's father, Shoarhn's husband, and Chislanda's enforced mate. He comes from Morstahn, Muhnilahm.

Aklon-Dji is Renegade and an outlaw with a price on his head. Leader of the Few, he is Dagla Kaz's disinherited son and Jodisa-Li's brother and was born in Chalamamnon, Muhnilahm.

Baklan is captain of the ship, Nupraxyss, and hails from Kabalyt. Ferries the pilgrim party in 'Joinings'.

Bardrohn is a whining volunteer Virgin Gift. He comes from Litkala, Rophan-Ra.

Buvlakkan is one of the Few in Chalamamnon, Muhnilahm. He is married to Wempiryss.

Byfthlyn is a volunteer Virgin Gift looking for adventure. He is from Kah-Labaz, Tohltaz.

Caarl is the senior soldier on the island of Muhnilahm and accompanies the pilgrims as expedition leader and guide. He is A'ahl's husband and lives in Morstahn, Muhnilahm.

Chellyth is a young woman who leads the criminals and outcasts living on The Point, Muhnilahm. She and her husband, Por-Kildu, are known as The One.

Chislanda is a bereaved mother from Mipahnhil, Rophan-Ra. Her husband is Doklas and she takes Aglydron as a mate.

Choryssa is a soldier from Krohtl, Muhnilahm. She is Delbon's partner when in town.

Corphanda, a tubby widow, looks after the female Virgin Gifts on the pilgrimage. She comes from Pampahn on Muhnilahm

Cymlihter is a dark haired slave to Kaz-Ca-Wesdan in Chalamamnon.

Dagla Kaz, the supreme ruler and High Priest of the Followers on the island of Muhnilahm, leads the pilgrims on their mission. He is father to Jodisa-Li, disinherits his son, Aklon-Dji, because of serious doctrinal and moral differences, and is based in Chalamamnon.

Dahrlahg is a young woman brought to help Shoarhn by Irrildys. She is Pentryil's betrothed, and lives in Morstahn, Muhnilahm.

Dahrlyth is a sex slave in Ov-Bebna, Tohltaz. She befriends and helps Okkyntalah.

Delbon is one of Aklon-Dji's trusted colleagues. His partner, Choryssa, is a soldier. He is a member of the Few and resident of Krohtl, Muhnilahm.

Dilanthas is a shy original Virgin Gift from Krohtl, Muhnilahm. She was one of the originals, Chosen to go on the pilgrimage.

Diryss, from Morstahn, becomes unwilling consort to village priest Kaz-Ca-Wesdan. He takes her to Chalamamnon, Muhnilahm.

Doklas, a citizen of Mipahnhil, Rophan-Ra, is Chislanda's husband. He appears only in 'Joinings'.

Eyethlehn is a woodworker from Morstahn, Muhnilahm.

Fehtohn is a vain young man and a volunteer Virgin Gift from Litkala, Rophan-Ra.

Feldrark is spiritual leader and Wharhll of Litkala, Rophan-Ra and married to Jodisa-Li. He is the only son of the Kiral and Kirallah.

Franorahl, a greatly respected and highly skilled tattooist, lives in Chalamamnon, Muhnilahm. She appears only in 'Joinings'.

Gidwallehn is a dutiful young man from Muhnilahm who volunteers as a Virgin Gift.

Grahtl is a native from a village in Kabalyt, employed by Dagla Kaz as a guide in this savage land. He appears only in 'Joinings'.

Gret-Zudas is the leader of the tribe who inhabit Qlentz in Kabalyt. He appears only in 'Joinings'.

Hephrastihn is a nice girl from Kah-Labaz, Tohltaz, who volunteers to be a Virgin Gift.

het'Kallohn is of the K'ahll in Ov-Bebna, Tohltaz. She acts as guide to Teldrohn's party.

Hivoxahn is a horse breeder from Morstahn, Muhnilahm. He is the slow son of Pelltryss.

Horsylth, a Palace servant in Litkala, Rophan-Ra, is a young woman with a fisherman for a partner.

Hyllahn is a house slave in Chalamamnon, Muhnilahm.

Ialdyss Kaz is a High Priest in Choshinahm.

Irrildys is an unhappy wife who seeks comfort from other men. She is Shoarhn's friend in Morstahn, Muhnilahm and one of the Few. She appears on the scene in 'Partings'.

Ivdulon lives alone in a tower overlooking Litkala, Rophan-Ra. She is a wise woman, astronomer, inventor and supreme mindtalker.

Jeklyzhon, a sailor on the Nupraxyss, is named only on his death. He appears only in 'Joinings'.

Jhonaht is the astronomer from Krohtl, Muhnilahm. He announced the arrival of the false Skyfire.

Jodisa-Li was heir apparent to Dagla Kaz, from Chalamamnon, Muhnilahm, until she met and married Feldrark. She is sister to Aklon-Dji.

K'ang Du-Saru is a highly muscular man who enjoys life as a Slaver. He is from Ov-Bebna, Tohltaz. He appears on the scene in 'Partings'.

K'ang Fah-Tesi is a man who enjoys using women and acts as a Slaver from Ov-Bebna, Tohltaz. He appears on the scene in 'Partings'

K'ang Fi-Tozu, related to the Uhmbard, and put in charge of Slave trade in Ov-Bebna, Tohltaz. He is driven more by duty than ambition. He appears on the scene in 'Partings'.

Kaz-Ca-Atroad is a village priest in Chalamamnon, Muhnilahm.

Kaz-Ca-Charrohn is the sexually demanding female Village Priest from Krohtl, Muhnilahm.

Kaz-Ca-Porlesah is the female Village Priest from Pampahn, Muhnilahm, who befriends Aklon-Dji.

Kaz-Ca-Uldrad becomes the male Village Priest in Morstahn, Muhnilahm, when his predecessor is promoted.

Kaz-Ca-Valorysta is a lower level Priest from Kah-Labaz, Tohltaz, who willingly becomes consort for Dagla Kaz. She appears on the scene in 'Partings'.

Kaz-Ca-Wendarah is the ambitious female Village Priest from Chalamamnon, Muhnilahm, who becomes deputy for Dagla Kaz after returning from the pilgrimage.

Kaz-Ca-Wesdan is the predatory Village Priest from Morstahn, Muhnilahm. He acts as deputy High Priest in the absence of Dagla Kaz.

K'eng Hin-Seru is a cruel and petty man who is a Slaver from Ov-Bebna, Tohltaz. He appears on the scene in 'Partings'.

K'eng Hok-Tusi is one of the male Slavers from Ov-Bebna, Tohltaz. He appears on the scene in 'Partings'.

K'eng Ho-Seri is one of the Slavers from Ov-Bebna, Tohltaz.

Lallamdahl is a sex slave from the caves under Ytraa's Peak, Muhnilahm.

Lasdilyss, Phildrad's wife, is carer to his elderly parents in Pampahn, Muhnilahm, a lover of Aklon-Dji and a member of the Few.

Lethrymynyhl is a tall and willing volunteer female Virgin Gift from Kah-Labaz, Tohltaz. She appears on the scene in 'Partings'.

Linlyss is a volunteer Virgin Gift from Litkala, Rophan-Ra. She is a gifted Lyre player who has designs on Okkyntalah.

Malarhah, a slave girl in Mipahnhil, Rophan-Ra, befriends Feldrark. The subject of a lay created by Okkyntalah in 'Joinings'.

M'Kolo-Ti is a native of Muhnilahm. She acts as guide for Aklon-Dji through the jungle.

Myllthlan is a gifted Healer from the island of Ylcrat. She is loyal to Aglydron but loves Okkyntalah.

Netrodyl is a wayward, uneducated young woman rescued in a forest near Qlentz, Kabalyt.

Ni-Dehla is a female pirate leader from Niphralon. She is Ryglan's sister. She appears only in 'Joinings'.

Nuldron is an Engineer and mindtalker from Litkala, Rophan-Ra, who provides contact on a desert mission. He appears on the scene in 'Partings'.

Okkyntalah is a brilliant hunter from Morstahn, Muhnilahm. He is Tumalind's betrothed and is loved by women.

Ouqitahl is a troop leader from Litkala, Rophan-Ra.

Patradko Kaz is the male High Priest from Litkala, Rophan-Ra.

Patrilha is a soldier from Pampahn, Muhnilahm who meets Aklon-Dji at The Point. She appears on the scene in 'Partings'.

Pedradol-Dji is the son of the High Priest at Kah-Labaz, Tohltaz. He volunteers as a Virgin Gift in hopes of impressing his father. He appears on the scene in 'Partings'.

Pelltryss is elderly mother to Hivoxahn, from Morstahn, Muhnilahm.

Pentryil is Dahrlahg's betrothed. He is from Morstahn, Muhnilahm.

Pettaklon is a young boy who acts as a page in Litkala, Rophan-Ra.

Pharah-Li, the spirited daughter of Rrildyss Kaz in Litkala, Rophan-Ra, has designs on Dagla Kaz.

Phildrad, a superb cook from Pampahn, Morstahn, is required to go on the pilgrimage. He is Lasdilyss' husband.

Phrysilda is a soldier. She hails from Morstahn, Muhnilahm.

Phyloahn is a troop leader. He is from Litkala, Rophan-Ra.

Por-Kildu is a much-scarred man who, with Chellyth, leads the criminals and deviants on The Point, Muhnilahm, as The One.

Porryh is an original Virgin Gift Chosen for the pilgrimage. She is troublesome and determined to change her status. She comes from Chalamamnon, Muhnilahm.

Pyqad is a ship's captain. He comes from Kah-Labaz, Tohltaz.

Quyreena is Captain of the ship, Mekoque. She belongs to a small cult that worships a female deity by living as lesbians. She originates from Ahnsha, Ndagaal. She appears on the scene in 'Partings'.

Rehthlynn is a loyal subject from Litkala, Rophan-Ra. He takes on the role of guardian to the male Virgin Gifts. He appears on the scene in 'Partings'.

Ro'Vavak is the go-between for the Trotnahn Powerseekers and Teldrohn and Okkyntalah, a mindtalker.

Rrildyss Kaz is High Priest in Litkala, Rophan-Ra, a gossipy mindtalker and Pharah-Li's mother.

Ryglan is the male pirate leader from Niphralon. He is brother to Ni-Dehla. He appears only in 'Joinings'.

Serrophenahl is a soldier. She comes from Litkala, Rophan-Ra.

Shaulah is Okkyntalah's faithful hunting dog; a bitch similar in size and looks to a lurcher.

Shoarhn is a farmer in Morstahn, Muhnilahm. She is Tumalind's mother, Aglydron's wife and Aklon's lover.

Sondukal is an experienced tracker and guide. He works from Litkala, Rophan-Ra, in the service of Feldrark.

Spiritman is a gifted Masseur in Litkala, Rophan-Ra, who is permitted to care for women as he lacks sexual parts. He appears on the scene in 'Partings'.

Stellanyl is an attractive unattached young woman selected as Okkyntalah's sexual partner on the mission from Litkala, Rophan-Ra.

Syylvah, a sexually active informant and member of the Few, who considers herself Aklon-Dji's lover, is married to the useless Wurrt in Chalamamnon, Muhnilahm.

Tah-Vlatak is a Dancer in Ov-Bebna, Tohltaz, where she entertains the Uhmbard. She befriends and guides Tumalind. She appears on the scene in 'Partings'.

Tarruss, a gentle giant of a man, is taken on as guardian for the pilgrimage. He is a metalworker who comes from Krohtl, Muhnilahm.

Tasallyss is a Midwife in Morstahn, Muhnilahm, who attends A'ahl at the request of Shoarhn. She appears on the scene in 'Partings'.

Teh-Blavv is a Harem wife of the Uhmbard's in Ov-Bebna, Tohltaz. She was born in Trotnahn and advises Tumalind. She appears on the scene in 'Partings'.

Teh-Pavk is a Harem wife of the Uhmbard's in Ov-Bebna, Tohltaz. She is a mindtalker and helps Tumalind. She appears on the scene in 'Partings'.

Teldrohn is a troop leader. He comes from Litkala, Rophan-Ra.

Tryonta acts as Dagla Kaz's trusted and feared henchman and comes from Chalamamnon, Muhnilahm.

Tukladohn is a slave from the caves beneath Ytraa's Peak. He works in the kitchens.

Tumalind, an original Virgin Gift falsely Chosen to go on the pilgrimage, is Okkyntalah's betrothed and Shoarhn and Aglydron's daughter from Morstahn and a gifted mindtalker.

Uhstyhll is a male Virgin Gift from Muhnilahm, who volunteers for the pilgrimage as he has been branded a thief after stealing food in his early life. He appears on the scene in 'Partings'.

Ven-Gadla is a helpful merchant from Kabalyt who provides transport.

Wakkyll is a volunteer Virgin Gift from Muhnilahm. His arrogance has prevented him finding a mate at home. He appears on the scene in 'Partings'.

Wempiryss is one of the few in Chalamamnon, Muhnilahm. She is married to Buvlakkan.

Wurrt is the hopeless husband to Syylvah, from Chalamamnon, Muhnilahm.

Wyyhn Kaz is a High Priest. He comes from Choshinahm.

Xylthynn is a volunteer Virgin Gift from Litkala, Rophan-Ra. She is along on the mission in hopes of finding the right man, having failed to do so in the city. She appears on the scene in 'Partings'.

Yatukon is the masked leader from Ylcrat. He is endowed with magical powers and subjugates the women of the island.

Yoqalohn is a soldier. He comes from Litkala, Rophan-Ra.

Yytlomohn is a volunteer Virgin Gift from Muhnilahm. She has escaped her controlling father who blamed her for the death of his wife in childbirth. She appears on the scene in 'Partings'.

454

Zyreenha is a volunteer Virgin Gift from Litkala, Rophan-Ra. Her first betrothed died in an accident and she is seeking a new life away from that memory. She appears on the scene in 'Partings'.

Mythical and Legendary Characters,
and Titles in Use:

Caboceer: the native people originally inhabiting the island of Muhnilahm.

Chief Secretary: leader of the Powerseekers that rule Trotnahn and hopes to subjugate the world.

Dji: title of a recognised male heir to a High Priest.

Doklas: astronomer who predicted the first Skyfire according to

Gadhallah: revered Founder of the Followers, born in Choshinahm.

Galhta: title given the male leader of the people in Mipahnhil.

Holy Ones: a sect of extreme Followers who have powers over the general populace.

Kaz: title identifying the High Priest of the Followers.

Kaz-Ca: title of lower level priests to the Followers.

Kiral: title of the male civic leader in Litkala. Feldrark's father.

Kirallah: title of the female civic leader in Litkala. Feldrark's mother.

Krakgragog: the savage God of the Fire Mountain on Ylcrat.

Lesythemis: legendary daughter of Mythanpho and Vaarkil on Lake Qonahn, Choshinahm.

Li: title of a recognised female heir to a High Priest.

Lypadladohn: the wife of Gadhallah, from Choshinahm.

Mhortag: the Devil, as accidentally created by Ytraa, according to Gadhallah.

Mipri: the young virgin raped by Gadhallah.

Mythanpho: possibly legendary heroic figure and Vaarkil's wife on Lake Qonahn, Choshinahm.

Na-Dagun: legendary double-headed monster of Lake Qonahn, Choshinahm.

Pah-Llon: possibly legendary adoptive father to Vaarkil on Lake Qonahn, Choshinahm.

Paltra: general title of respect for senior women.

Paltrohn: general title of respect for senior men.

Pentril: the probably legendary son of Gadhallah.

Poliphri: possibly legendary mother of Mythanpho in Choshinahm.

Poltrados: great-grandson of Yldohn and a noted scribe.

Powerseeker: one of a group of evil mindtalkers bent on ruling the world

Ro': indicative title given to a high-ranking official of the Powerseekers Trotnahn.

Sha'ra: a mysterious goddess, residing on the coastal margins of Rophan-Ra.

Skyfire: the name given to a celestial sign (probably a comet) that presages doom for those who fail to Follow to the letter of the law.

Sonclusipah: Gadhallah's daughter and sole heir, born in Choshinahm.

Swerriflomihl: boat builder and founder of the people after the flood caused by Mhortag.

Taniwha: a cruel sea God, worshipped and feared by sailors.

Tasallyss: daughter of Swerriflomihl who suggests he send out songbirds at the end of the flood.

The Senior: a high-ranking official with the organisation that runs the city of Tronahn.

Tihldha: possibly legendary adoptive mother to Vaarkil on Lake Qonahn, Choshinahm.

Tryhnn: kindly Goddess of open water.

Ulkhon: the Sun God and reputedly Mythanpho's father.

Uhmbard Of Tohltaz: the leader-cum-God and harem owner in Ov-Bebna, Tohltaz.

Uhmteld Of Tohltaz: the senior wife to the Uhmbard in Ov-Bebna, Tohltaz.

Vaarkil: possibly legendary hero, found in Lake Qonahn, Choshinahm. Offspring of Tryhnn and an unknown man. Mythanpho's husband.

Valorysta: Poliphri's mother in Choshinahm.

Wharhll: title given to the spiritual leader in Litkala; traditionally male.

Yldohn: deputy to Gadhallah and Zerryth's husband.

Ytraa: Supreme God of the Followers as determined by Gadhallah. This being is man, woman and God combined and is credited with creation of the world.

Zerryth: deputy to Gadhallah and Yldohn's wife.

APPENDICES:

Appendices.

Here follow copies of documents discovered by Aklon when he emptied the Secret Chamber under the floor of the High Priest's house. Some of these he had, of course, read. Others were new to him.

They are presented here for you, the reader, to read or not, as the mood may take you. But they explain certain aspects of the lives and beliefs of the Followers and may be worthy of the time spent reading them. I hope they provide you with some entertainment, information and, perhaps, enlightenment. As far as can be ascertained, they are presented here in chronological order of happening, rather than recording, of events.

A word of warning: those of a sensitive nature will find the Confession of Gadhallah particularly distressing. I include it here as an indication of the depravity and evil that underpinned the religion of the followers of Ytraa: read it with caution.

The First Great Knowing

The origin of this legend is unknown, though the suspicion is that it was created by Poltrados as a justification for the worship of Ytraa. Poltrados, son of the son of the son of Yldohn, was known later as Poltrados, The Great Chronicler, and he wrote accounts of all the happenings and other stories he was told.

Before Ytraa, nothing was. Black and empty was all.

Then there came Ytraa. And the blackness and emptiness rose up against Ytraa in great anger. And Ytraa fought the blackness and filled it with light. Thus was there darkness and there was light. And all was void and empty. But Ytraa took the emptiness and filled it. And Ytraa saw Ytraa and desired Ytraa and Ytraa did put the great male part of Ytraa deep within the great female part of Ytraa and did send forth the First Great Seed and did plant the First Great Seed in the womb of Ytraa. And Ytraa was the mother and the father of the First Great Sapling that was born of Ytraa. And Ytraa did plunge the First Great Sapling into the emptiness and it grew, plunging its roots into the blackness and its branches into the light. Thus came the First Great Tree. For Ytraa brought forth the First Great Tree and all other trees came from this one, from the First Great Tree.

Now when the Tree was grown, it bore many fruits. Ytraa found the fruit was good and blessed the Tree calling it Av-Qijjahn and Zephystryss, meaning The First One and Last To Die. And some of the fruits Ytraa made into the stars that shine in the outermost blackness. And some of the fruits Ytraa did eat, for they were good. But the greatest of the fruits Ytraa did make into the World. Even the very world on which all things that are do live and come into being. And upon the World did Ytraa make the water and the land, the seas and the rivers, the oceans and the lakes did Ytraa make, for they were beautiful in the eyes of Ytraa. The mountains and the valleys, the hills and the plains Ytraa made. And all the World was beautiful for it was made by Ytraa and was perfect.

There came a time when Ytraa looked at the world and thought to people it. And Ytraa again grew desirous of Ytraa and again put forth the male part of Ytraa and thrust it with great passion and desire deep within the very depths of the part that was female. And the female part did enclose and embrace the male part and did stroke and encourage the Sacred Seed of Life to journey through the passage and enter into the womb of Ytraa so it might grow. Thus was born the First People.

And The First People was born of Ytraa in numbers beyond count and all were born in the likeness of Ytraa; being both man and woman in one person. But the fruit of Ytraa, though they were like Ytraa, they were yet unlike Ytraa. For Ytraa was God and Ytraa was Man and Ytraa was Woman. But the First People, they were Man and they were Woman only; the First People had not the third part of Ytraa, they had not the part of Ytraa that is

461

God and is unknowable and mysterious and terrible beyond the imaginings of people. And Ytraa was well pleased with the fruit of Ytraa's womb and did call the fruit of Ytraa's womb the First People. Then did Ytraa see that the World was barren and bare and Ytraa did join again and again and again in passion and desire and with each joining of the male part of Ytraa with the female part of Ytraa was born a new plant or a new animal or a new insect or a new fish, such as was the desire of Ytraa. And Ytraa did join with Ytraa more times than can be counted and the First People did see the joining and rejoice and they also did join and did multiply and increase until their like was over the face of the world. And Ytraa was greatly pleased with all that was created and all that was done. And all was peace and harmony in the World.

But one fruit of the Great Tree remained in the darkness. This one fruit was not good and was not made into a star nor yet into a world, nor yet eaten to sustain Ytraa. And that fruit grew sour and bad. And its seed put forth maggots. And the maggots did grow and burst forth from the fruit and did devour it. And they grew wings and did become as hornets. And amongst them and over them was the Great Hornet, Mhortag the Cruel. And they did fly down and did sting Ytraa and hurt Ytraa sore. But Ytraa killed them not, feeling pity for their state.

And Mhortag, seeing how Ytraa did love the World, settled upon it and marked it. And all that is ugly and unclean was made by Mhortag. The plagues were brought by Mhortag and the wild beasts that devour flesh and the snakes that bite and the insects that sting and the fish that devour the people did Mhortag make after his own likeness for he was jealous of Ytraa and of Ytraa's people.

And Mhortag did the greatest evil known, for he took the people that were man and woman in one and he did split them asunder. The men he took from the women and the women he did divide from the men so that they were one no more but were two. And the people did cry out in lamentation for that they were become divided and were whole no more.

When Ytraa saw what Mhortag had done Ytraa was wrath and did banish Mhortag to the outermost depths of nothingness, saying, 'Go! Leave this world I have created and never return or I will kill you.' And that is where he dwells to this day. But before Mhortag fled, he set poison in the World. Some he put in the beasts so that they became fierce and some he spread amongst the people so that they might not live forever, as had been the will of Ytraa, but would grow wicked and would die.

Then did Mhortag flee into the darkness but he rent the covering of the darkness and did release it so that night came all around. But Ytraa made the sun in the likeness of a golden ball of flame, glowing with light and heat, and set it in the sky over the World, where it spins a circle round the world, so that there is time for sleep and time for activity.

And the sun gave life where the darkness would destroy it. And Ytraa caused the stars to shine also that the people might know the ways to travel over the World in the darkness. And the Moon made Ytraa to light the night sky and defeat the darkness.

And so was the World made by Ytraa. And Ytraa lives on to keep the people and protect them always from the evil that is Mhortag. And the Eyes of Ytraa gaze down from the sky and see the World that Ytraa did create. And the Eyes of Ytraa are like stars in the sky, yet they move not like the other stars, being always in one place above the World. And this is the end of the First Great Knowing.

The Flood

This account seems to be an adaptation of a well-known legend commonly held to be based on actual events and appearing in various forms all around the world. The nature of the account as told to Followers suggests it was one of the many documents invented by Poltrados as a means of justifying the worship of Ytraa and providing a foundation for the religion of the Followers.

In the days even before Mythanpho and Vaarkil destroyed the two-headed monster, Dagon, in Lake Qonahn, was the whole world covered in water by Mhortag, who wanted all life to end. But Swerriflomihl, a humble fisherman from the shores of Lake Qonahn, was a devout man; a man who would listen to the voices of the winds, the language of the lake, the ripples of the rivers. He knew well the world and all it contained in those days of harmony and peace.

As was the custom in those days long gone, he had him a wife and several concubines and they all bore him children, the seed of his loins. The family was great and his sons and his daughters were tall and proud and honourable. No famine nor drought ever troubled those shores in those happy days. And though it was needed for a man to have many women as men were fewer than women, following the battle of the Dread Doubters, when many men were killed by their fellows, most were happy with the way things were.

Now Swerriflomihl, being a man who could read the signs sent down by the winds and shown him by the waves upon the lake, knew the world well. He saw that a great deluge would come and made him a boat to save his family. He built his boat as large as a boat could be in those days. It stood as high as six men and as broad as seventeen. Ninety men could lie head to toe along the length of its deck, so huge was this boat. In the base he made many floors and many small rooms with cages and stalls. And his family, though they were obedient, often asked why he spent all this time and labour on making a boat from which no fishing could be done. But he told them he had knowledge that they did not and that what he did was what must be done. And they, being obedient and dutiful, as was the way in those days, did as he bid them and helped him construct the boat.

When all was complete and the boat, which they called Deliverance, was ready to put on the lake, they hauled it into the water and began to construct a great wharf for it to lie against. Again, the family and the villagers did question Swerriflomihl as to his purpose and need for such as they were building. And now, now that he had his boat ready, he told them all what it was that would come to pass in the portions to come.

'There will come a day when the rain starts to fall. It will fall so fast that a man will not see beyond the fingertips of his outstretched arms, so heavy that the waters will rise more quickly than a man can walk, so dense that a man walking in the open fields will drown as though he had fallen in the lake.

'This day will come soon and all who are not prepared will perish. It is Mhortag's wish that all life be ended on land by this deed. But I have built this Deliverance that all may be saved and now that it is ready we will collect four of every creature on the world, two of each sex, and house them aboard the Deliverance. We will collect the seed of every plant and the roots of those that live this way. All will be collected and housed in the Deliverance. My family and I will live henceforth aboard the Deliverance and will no more dwell on the land until the deluge has come and gone. For all the land, even to the mountain tops, will be covered in water that falls from the sky, as rain, for portions on end.'

And most of the villagers laughed at his predictions and took no notice. But his family understood the wisdom of their father and they did as he bid them and the Deliverance was filled with all the creatures of the land and all the plants as seeds or roots were stored and kept. And they filled the storerooms with foods of all types and they made places to catch and store water for the days of the deluge.

When all was ready, they boarded the Deliverance and did live there, taking only their small fishing boat out a short way from the land to conduct their business of fishing and returning always to the Deliverance at night. And all the village did laugh at the way they lived and none would have ought to do with the family of Swerriflomihl. Yet his family did trust him absolutely.

There came a day when the sun was hid behind great black clouds and the rain it did fall from the skies. And all the people were afraid that the deluge was come. But Swerriflomihl laughed at them and said that this was but a small storm and all would be well on the morrow. And so it was.

Then did the village people mock him every time the rain fell. But they did this not for long, as it was only a single portion after Swerriflomihl had made all ready that the deluge finally came. But the villagers did laugh as he cast off from the wharf and mock him, saying this was yet another small storm and they would see him back at the lakeside come the morning.

But those who mocked and made no provision never saw Swerriflomihl more for they perished. The rains did come just as he had predicted they would. The water came from the sky with such force that anyone in the open did drown from the falling waters. Some ran to escape the rising lake but the waters rose faster than they could run and they were drowned. Some took to their boats in hope of floating on the waters but their boats were open and did fill with water and did sink.

466

But Swerriflomihl and his family did live through the deluge and all of his women, his wife and his concubines his daughters and granddaughters, did worship him and thank him with their bodies and so was the family of Swerriflomihl made great and all were born of his seed.

The rain did fall for seven portions without end until the whole of the land was covered with water and there was not a single dry place on the whole of the world. And then did Swerriflomihl cry out to Tryhnn to cease the cascade but she heard him not, so deep was the water in which she lay. So he cried out to Mhortag and begged him for mercy and Mhortag did laugh and sent a tempest to rock the boat so that it was in danger of sinking beneath waves higher than mountains. And then did Swerriflomihl cry out to Ytraa. In those days Ytraa was not recognised as the supreme God and creator, but Swerriflomihl was desperate and he begged Ytraa for succour and help. And the waters did calm and the sky did clear and the sun shone on the world again.

And Ytraa did banish Mhortag to the far reaches of the sky to dwell forever in the darkness of night beyond the Moon.

Swerriflomihl made a sacrifice of his youngest daughter, cutting her throat and drenching the decks with her blood as a sign to Ytraa that Ytraa was all powerful and the greatest of all the gods. And then did Swerriflomihl send out the great white Zwahan, the male, to see if there was land. And the bird did return soon but there was no sign it had found land.

Now Swerriflomihl had a wise daughter; Tasallyss was her name and she was fair beyond compare and was his favourite and did lie with him much. And she told him to send out a smaller bird, a songbird, for she explained that the Zwahan was a bird of the waters that would not seek land but a songbird would seek out a tree on which to sing. And he commended her for her cleverness and sent out a songbird and it returned after a day with a leaf in its bill and they knew then that the waters were receding.

And so it was that. Two portions after the deluge began, they rested again on the shores of Lake Qonahn. And everything that had been there was no more. And the family of Swerriflomihl did release all the beasts and did plant the roots and seeds and soon was the land even better than it had been before the deluge had come, for they had not kept those plants that did damage their crops and they had not preserved creatures that caused them great suffering. And so it was that the new world of Swerriflomihl and his family was a better place than it had been and they did mock Mhortag for his attempt to do away with them.

Now all this happened many, many cycles before the coming of the first Skyfire and much did occur in the cycles in between, so that the world was not as new and perfect as it had been at the end of the deluge. But know that all who now live on the world are from

467

the one family of Swerriflomihl and that is why he is still revered, even though he denounced Ytraa after the floods had died down and did return to his worship of Tryhnn of the lake. But that is a story for other days.

The Legend of Vaarkil and Mythanpho

As written, in later cycles, by the Great Scribe of Muhnilahm, Poltrados, The Great Chronicler.

On a day so distant that even the ancient calendars do not know of it, then did Vaarkil come into the world. Pah-Llon, Master Fisherman of Qonahn by Lake Qonahn, being in his ninetieth and final cycle of that office, was emptying the lobster pots with his young pupils in the early morning. All was still on the waters of the lake. As Pah-Llon drew up the last pot he gazed down into the clear waters and saw that the pot was full. But his pleasure at the catch fell to dismay when he emptied the contents into the bottom of the boat. For there, amongst the living lobsters lay a naked new-born man child. And he most surely must be dead. But Pah-Llon held the babe aloft and showed it to Ytraa and asked for deliverance in a loud voice. And though there was no wind that day, the waters of the lake became a turmoil and tossed so that the small boat might be overwhelmed. And the young men with Pah-Llon were afraid and begged him to stop that the waters might calm but Pah-Llon paid no heed, begging Ytraa only for the life of the babe. And then the waters did quieten and the babe breathed and gave a cry and they returned to Qolahn.

All the village came out to greet their return for they thought the boat lost in the turmoil of the waters. And with those who came was the woman of Pah-Llon's house, Tihldha. Ancient she was, being near in cycles to Pah-Llon; and he could count two hundred and twelve summers in the caves of his memory. Tihldha took the child from Pah-Llon and held him in her arms. She bared her breast though she had been barren and dry for many cycles. Yet the child did take suck there and grew strong on the milk he had from her and the whole village was amazed. But Tihldha said it was a sign and the child would be a great hero in the world. And she named the child Vaarkil and blessed him before Ytraa. Thus was she, and her man also, blessed so that Pah-Llon and Tihldha grew to be a great many cycles but knew not a day of illness even until the day they departed this life.

And the child grew strong and straight and was of noble appearance. And Vaarkil was a man of proud bearing, true and kind, tall and generous of spirit. And the village of Qonahn gained much from his presence there and they loved him well.

It happened that on the same day as Vaarkil was found in the lake, so was conceived the fair maiden Mythanpho. In the desert region north of Lake Qonahn, where none now dare venture, lived a solitary people. And it was their custom to dwell alone as small families and come together only at times of suffering or joy. And one of these, Valorysta,

469

was a widow who lived alone with her only child, her daughter, Poliphri. And Poliphri was a maiden of great beauty, a prize amongst her people. Yet she knew no man in all her life though she was greatly desired.

And in the middle of the day, when it was warm and pleasant, for in those parts the nights were cold but the days were warm, she took herself into the hills to lie under the sun. And as she slept it happened that the spirit of the sun, Ulkhon did come upon her as he walked the air above. Seeing her there thus naked and unadorned, as was the custom of those people in those days, he was overcome with passion and with love for her. And Ulkhon did take Poliphri and fell on her and, entering into her, filled her with light and with life. And Poliphri awoke and was dazzled and afraid. But Ulkhon soothed her and spent his lust and she was quieted and made brave and did worship him for his act. He, in his turn blessed her and gifted her with beauty to live till she lived not. And so it was that Poliphri did live two hundred and sixty three summers yet aged not a day from that time. And the child that Ulkhon made in her womb he blessed also saying, 'This is the child of the Sun Spirit Ulkhon. She will grow to be the fairest maiden the world has ever known. Gold will not match the burnish of her hair, polished ivory will envy her skin and the blue of the evening sky will live in her eyes. The child will be born without pain to her mother and no trouble will her mother know from the child. Know that you and your baby are blessed, Poliphri, and fear no living creature.'

And Ulkhon left her and Poliphri returned to her mother, Valorysta, and told her all that had happened. And when the child came to be born it was as Ulkhon had foretold and all the people marvelled. For the people of that land were of olive skin and sable hair and hazel eyes, yet the child was beauteous fair and she was called Mythanpho by her mother, meaning daughter of the sun.

Yet as she grew the people loved her not, envying her beauty and her grace. And in her sixteenth cycle came one who would kill her for he feared her for that she was different. But Mythanpho was brave and did fight him off and escape and did leave her mother and the desert. For many months she wandered naked and alone until Vaarkil, hunting wild boar, came upon her bathing in a stream. Her beauty stole his heart and his noble bearing captured her so that they fell in love at once. And Vaarkil did bring her home to the village of Qonahn and they became one at the evening ceremony and all in the village did rejoice that Vaarkil had found one so fair to be his wife.

Many were the love songs that they sang together by the lake. Many were the sons and daughters that she bore, seed of Vaarkil, offspring of Mythanpho, and all were fair and strong and well loved. And they dwelt by the lake many cycles in great happiness.

Now, in those days, a tale was told of the monster, Na-Dagon, that dwelt in the bottom of the lake. It was a serpent of great size with two heads and it caused the waters to boil and did sink fishing boats and devour the crew. But Na-Dagon had not been seen, even by the elders and they were ancient beyond the cycles of modern men. Pah-Llon, called the father of Vaarkil, had eaten the grain of more than six hundred summers when he lived no more.

The young men of the village were disrespectful and made fun of the tales of Na-Dagon, saying it was no more than a story made up to frighten the children lest they do wrong. But the elders nodded sagely to one another and told the youths that time would tell the truth. But the young men were idlers and headstrong and decided they would find Na-Dagon and wake the serpent and cut off the heads for a wager. And the village elders were wrath and said that they must not jest about Na-Dagon nor wake the serpent from sleep lest it take more of the village fishermen as it had in the past. But the young men just laughed and said the serpent was no more than a worm grown fat on the imaginings of old men.

They searched the lake and prodded the bottom with long sticks and returned to Qonahn saying they had killed the great serpent with pointed sticks and that all could sleep safe in their beds again. And it was only seven days after this that a fishing boat returned from a trip with two of its crew missing and a tale of a great two-headed serpent that had devoured them and almost wrecked the boat. The serpent, they said, had eyes like red coals and black scales with yellow and green markings and teeth that were as long as a man's forearm.

But the young men just laughed and would go into the lake to see the serpent for themselves for they believed not the tale of the fishermen. But the elders forbade them to go. So it was that at night the young men did take a boat and also did capture by stealth one of the fair daughters of Vaarkil and Mythanpho to use for sport on their voyage, and did depart the shores to find the serpent.

In the morning there was great anger at what they had done and great sorrow for the maiden who was stolen away and the village people and the elders did promise that the young men would be most grievously punished on their return if harm had come to the maiden. But after two days the boat did return and sixteen young men and the maiden had set out but only three young men returned. And they were sore afraid and did fall on their knees before the people and beg their forgiveness. For all the others in their party had perished in the jaws of the serpent Na-Dagon. And the elders did question the young men who returned and they did discover that of the sixteen who went only the three who returned had not made sport with the maiden. And they told the elders they had tried to stop the others for the maiden was much afraid and distressed by what they did but the other young men heeded them not and laughed at them and cast doubt on their manhood. Yet still they had not used the maiden, pitying her in her distress and anguish. And so the elders did punish the survivors only lightly and the village people did agree.

Then was passed a law to stop others being killed by the serpent. Na-Dagon did live in the deep part of the lake so it was decreed that no boat must fish beyond the sight of land. And so it was. But the fish catch did fall and hunger soon haunted the village that had once been the home of laughter and plenty.

So it was that Vaarkil, being at this time in the spring of his life and no more than eighty summers old, was vexed by the sadness of the people and did wish to end their suffering. And three times did he go to the council of elders and ask that he be permitted to go onto the lake and try to destroy Na-Dagon. But they were loathe to let him go for he was just a man against the two headed serpent and they feared he would be killed. And Vaarkil said he would avenge the death of his daughter, the maiden who had been used by the young men. And the elders did meet again and they said that in all the village was Vaarkil the most blessed of men. He was the best of swimmers, the best of divers, the most fleet of foot, the strongest with the bow and the sword and the spear. This they said was due to the manner of his birth in the lake. After much talk, they let him go, blessing him and saying many prayers to their Goddess of the lake, Tryhnn, that she might deliver him. But Vaarkil put his trust in Ytraa as the one true God.

And Vaarkil did take a small boat and lade it with provision for the voyage and with weapons to defeat Na-Dagon. But Mythanpho would not suffer him to go alone and would go with him. And though the people of the village and the elders did not wish it so, they were starving and they let them go onto the lake and did watch the small boat until they could see it no more.

Two days and two nights passed and none knew what happened in the lake for none was there to see. But as the sun rose on the third day a great cry was heard in the village. All the people came out of their houses for the cry roused them from their sleep. And many came just as they were, fresh from their beds and naked yet no person spoke against them as they all went to the shore and waited. Through the still waters of the lake came a swimmer who pulled a heavy load behind. And as she drew close they knew it to be Mythanpho and they did wade into the water and help her. She was naked and in her hand she held the hand of Vaarkil and he was naked also and much wounded and was dead. Yet in each hand did Vaarkil hold one head of the serpent and the heads were huge and the teeth were mighty.

And Mythanpho did wave the people from her that she might speak to them. And she stood in the shallows and a great gash was opened from her neck across her breast to her thigh and blood poured from the wound. Yet she stood and held the body of her man with her as she spoke. ' Know that this day has Vaarkil slain the beast with two heads. Na-

Dagon is no more. But the monster wins even this day for Vaarkil, the greatest man alive, is dead and so am I. Mortals cannot fight the monsters of the dark world and hope to live. Do not forget Vaarkil the brave and his woman Mythanpho. This day have they done great deeds and have shed their lives that you might live in peace. Bury us well and care for our children.'

And then did Mythanpho drop to the ground and with her Vaarkil and they breathed no more. Those two fair people were not seen again walking after that day and they were laid to rest in the cave chambers of the mountains, side by side forever.

And some say that Vaarkil and Mythanpho did not die that day but that they are resting after their great toil and that they will return one day in an hour of great need and will once more free their people from great evil and terror.

And it is from that day that the custom of naming children after the great heroes did come as a way of remembering them.

The Confession Of Gadhallah

This admission was written by Gadhallah, in his own words. It is and always has been the most secret of the sacred papers held in the secret chamber and was never allowed to leave that room. For, in its exposure to the world, are all those who followed in Gadhallah's footsteps, all those who led after him, shown as charlatans and evil men and women.

I repeat my warning here, that those of a sensitive nature may find portions of this document extremely distressing.

I, Gadhallah of Rrahp, by the sacred Lake Qonahn in the land of Choshinahm, do hereby, freely, secretly and without coercion, make this confession, that all who come after me might know the whole truth of those events that resulted in the founding of the movement now and forever after called the Followers of Ytraa.

This statement is written as I begin to die in the new Homeland of Muhnilahm and contains the truths that I concealed from those who first heard my words and trusted in my account of matters that began in the forests that lie on the lower slopes of the northern reaches of the Mountains of Chakanh and continue to this day of writing.

Know that this account here given is the full truth and that I desire it be known only by those I have invested with the power of command in my line of descent. Let it never be told to any who are not initiates into the position of High Priest on pain of everlasting fire and pain beyond imagining.

My words, as spoken to the people of Choshinahm, were falsehoods, lies and mistruths. I charge my heirs and descendants to read this confession and weep for the evil that I did. Recall it forever as you minister and lead. I further charge all who come after me to keep these matters secret as penance for my wickedness, that those who take the faith as true might not be betrayed by this truth but that you, who come after me, may live in the lies I did purvey and know that you are liars also until the end of time. For you, my descendants, who have the right by birth to know these things have inherited my truth along with the privileges I have instituted on your behalf. Know that if you disclose the truths herein you do forever deny the rights and privileges conferred on you and your descendants and do thereby destroy all that your forefathers have lived for and held dear. You betray such matters in peril of your life and in the full knowledge that all who have lived before you in the line of Gadhallah will be loathed, hated and reviled by those who we now call the Followers.

Here, then, is the true account of how I, Gadhallah, a simple man from a poor family, became The Lord Gadhallah, leader of the Followers of Ytraa and how I led my people from their homeland of Choshinahm to the island that is called Muhnilahm, glowing like a jewel in the Shylnah Sea. I record this account, in my own hand, in the first cycle of my landing on the island, as I grow certain that my life will soon be closed and complete on this world, being as I am, one hundred and seventy seven cycles in age. To what end I go, I know not, nor do I believe I go to peace and rest. My life on this world has built for me much debt that must be repaid. I go to my death in the full belief that I shall spend eternity in torment, even until the end of time. And it is as penance for this that I declare now the truth that you who follow in my path might know in all certainty what it is you do and why.

Thus, my account.

I returned, empty handed, from fishing in Lake Qonahn on a hot afternoon in the middle season of the cycle in which I counted fifty-five. The voices that troubled my mind all of my life had been strong that day and they made my fishing painful and irrelevant. When I entered my house, my barren wife, a woman both large and strong, beat me about my face for my lack of catch. I ran from the house, my nose bleeding strongly and my ears ringing with her blows. Behind me, I heard the laughter of the villagers as my wife shouted abuse and accused me of diverse acts and many shortcomings but mostly of failing to provide her with a child because of the weakness of my male part.

The voice that most troubled and plagued me came and issued instructions. *'Get ye into the trees and there find the means to prove your manhood, unless ye be the failure she describes.'*

I wandered the forest a night and a day, going deeper and deeper into the trees. The voices did trouble me often and ever; some mocking, some encouraging, some, as was ever the way, making no sense to me at all as they spoke in words I knew not, but always present and never giving me peace to think my own thoughts. Some of these voices did hold conversations within my poor head as though I was not there at all; my part being that of a room where they might meet to talk of things I understood not.

On the morning of the second day, hungry and weary, I heard the sweet voice of a girl as she sang of the joy of the sunlight in her hair and the perfume of the flowers round her neck. I approached with caution, lest I startle this creature, and found her alone, sitting by the banks of a soft, shallow brook with her bare toes in the water. Her body was lithe and youthful still and I could see more than was customary in those days, for she had put off her outer garment and was wrapped only in the skirt that lay beneath. She was no longer a child but not quite yet a woman. Her hair was short and straight and dark with a reddish tinge and fell to her bare shoulders leaving the small budding breasts uncovered. The skirt of coloured linen, wrapped about her slender waist, enclosed her forming hips and displayed one shapely thigh through the opening at the side. She sang so sweetly and joyously and I was moved beyond words by her innocence, her youth and her sweet form. Untouched and clean, pure and virgin, she was all that a young girl should be before she grows to that state where she is ready to know her first man.

'Invade her. Take her. Use her flesh to prove ye have the power of manhood within ye.'

I tried to ignore the voice but it kept on and on at me to do its will and I was lost and alone and in deep distress. And she was displayed to me more than was the custom, for I had seen no other female form than that of my wife, and she was large and not lovely as was this girl.

She made a small gasp of fright as I came from out the trees and stood beside her. Her name, she said, was Mipri and she had wandered from her family alone into the trees, called by the need to be alone. She seemed unaware of her near nakedness and made no move to clothe herself. I found she came from an isolated homestead she shared with her father, mother and two brothers, some distance away in the forest. She knew of no village nearby and had no knowledge of other people living close by in the trees. Her father was a woodman and hunter and they lived well from his skills. She had no learning but few people were learned, since such things were for the elders to concern themselves with.

I knelt before her and she saw my injured nose and bathed it, washing away the caked blood with her fingers and lifting the hem of her wrap to dry away the wet. As she brought the cloth to my face, she exposed her young womanhood to me, sprouting the first fronds of fragile cover that soon would hide the gateway from the gaze of man.

'Take her. Thrust your life within her. She will bless you for the act, though she may protest. She is young and hot and eager for the sport; see how she shows you the entrance to her very self. Take her, take her now!'

I uncovered her and lay her on the bank and she stared at me with wonder and with fear and asked me what I would do. I said nothing. I found I was potent, at last, and the blood was strong upon me and I intruded into her innocence and broke her and she bled a little and I spilt my seed within her youthful loins and was glad.

She wept at my use and begged me to leave her be. But as she struggled to flee to her home I knew I had not yet done with this fruit of heaven that I had never before tasted. And I was stronger. She begged me to let her go. But her struggle aroused me once more and I took her again and she fought me, her fingers clawing my back and my face as she struggled beneath me. And I thrust deep inside her and spent my force again.

She screamed and I struck her to silence her. And, as she lay helpless and unaware, I took her wrap and tore it into strips. I bound her mouth to silence her and tied her hands behind her. Naked and helpless, afraid and unprotected, she lay exposed before me and I took her again, even before she had fully woken from my strong blow to her face.

For three days and nights I ploughed the furrow of this innocent and showed her the power and strength a man has over a woman. She wept and her gagged mouth made moans for mercy but I was driven by a lust so strong I had no mind or power to refrain. And ever my strongest voice did urge me on to use her and to take her in every way I could.

I looked and saw I had used her fiercely but I could not stop. I did unspeakable, terrible things to that poor girl until I was spent and she was near dead. I took my hunting knife and split her and she did spurt blood and slowly she did die.

Her gag and bindings I took from her ruined body and I made a fire and lit it and burnt her body. Now I was naked, my own clothes bloodied with her gore and burnt on the fire with her covering and the rags of her skirt. I was scratched and exhausted and marked with her blood.

'Now, Gadhallah, you have become such a man as there never was. Now ye will not be afraid but others will do as ye bid. Return to your village and lead them in ways they do not understand. But, first, when ye arrive at your home and your wife comes to shout and berate ye for leaving, rip away her covering and plunge your proven manhood deep within her. Do this even where she meets ye, whether it be outside or in, whether there be those to see or no.'

His voice was triumphant and full of exultation, as if he and not I had taken and overthrown the girl. He had relished the experience with me yet I saw him nor knew him not. Others of my voices came then to scold and to berate me. Some condemned me as a brute and a vile thing. Others, who had before been my sweet voices, cried out in outrage and pain and denied me and said I was evil incarnate. Yet others gave me the name of Ytraa to be my guide and my saviour and made it that Ytraa should lead me to better things and a more holy way of life.

I sat on the ground, alone, naked, spent and so layered with the evil and wickedness of my act that I knew not who I was nor what I might be.

How long I remained in that state of unknowing I have no recollection. I awoke on a morn with the sun on my face and before me a great tree rose and stretched as far up into the sky as the clouds. The sun blinded me in the darkness of the forest and I sought to hide in the shadows but my voices pursued me and would not let me be and all my endeavours to rid my head of their noise came to nought. And then I bethought me a plan to silence them all and to make myself right again in the eyes of the world.

Thus it was that I, along with those of my voices who seemed to me to be true, conjured my story of Ytraa and the coming of the Skyfire, which was predicted by a voice that was new to me. How my head did ache with the effort of thinking. But I made all my plans and did devise the most perfect way to have the people follow me. And all that I did is now lain before you to judge whether I acted well or no.

When I left the shadows of the trees, I walked naked, scratched and bloodied into the village of Rrahp on the shores of Lake Qonahn. My wife, Lypadladohn, ran screaming from the house to beat me for my nakedness in that place and for my absence. And the people from about came out of their houses to laugh at the sport they would have as they watched her whip me. But I stayed her hand with a command and she saw that my manhood was ready and she stood open mouthed and bereft of words. I did tear away her cover and push her to the ground and did enter her and spend my seed within her and she was cowed and made docile. Then all the men did commend me for that I dealt with her thus.

At that time, there had been a long period in the land of Choshinahm when the rain did not fall and the crops in the fields were failing and the beasts were thin and dying of lack of food. And only the fish from the lake did keep the people alive. I had been shown a spark of light that was new and strange and was growing in the sky in the west. My voices told me this spark would grow to engulf the whole sky in flames, though how they might know this I could not tell. It happened that the elders were ignorant of the spark and knew it not.

I went to the village speaking tree and there did stand, naked still, for I had bethought me a scheme to entrap all the people, knowing their minds and their true hearts. There did I await those who would come and listen, as they were bound to do by custom. And they came and I made them wait until the elders sought out the reason for the noise of the people shouting for me to speak or to leave the speaking tree. When the elders came, they asked me why I was unclothed before the people. I answered them not but I asked them what they thought the spark might portend and they were amazed at my question for they knew not the spark and had no answer.

I told the people I had seen the spark and that it was the beginning of the end of the world. I told them that the sky would be ablaze with fire and that all would perish in the flames. The drought, I told them, was the result of their wickedness in worshipping Tryhnn of the lake in preference to Ytraa of the trees. Ytraa, I told them, had appeared to me whilst I had been in the forest and I called the place the Groves of Ytraa and said it was a holy space and sacred. The people murmured because I did say Ytraa was to be worshipped and not Tryhnn but I said to them they should see the sky that night and find the spark of the Skyfire and see then whether they would believe me or no.

That night, the spark had grown a little brighter and many did see it. So, I stood again under the speaking tree on the following morn and called upon the elders to explain what they could of the spark. And they had no answer, only that it portended great upheaval and chaos and that all should be afraid. Then it was that I knew that I had them in the palms of my hands. They were as soft clay to me. My words found their way into hearts ready to believe because of the drought and the portent of the Skyfire.

I told how Ytraa had come to me and made me naked because naked is sacred in the eyes of Ytraa. For, in those times and in that land, it was deemed improper to show the sexual parts in public and the people would cover their parts from the sight of others with flowing robes that covered all from neck to feet so that none could see how they were made. I told them that Ytraa was wrath at this insult.

'Did not Ytraa make you? Did not Ytraa design you and make you glorious to behold? Why then do you hide your form from the sight of Ytraa? Why do you dishonour your Creator and hide yourselves from the sight of Ytraa who made you?'

And I said this that the people would become naked and I might look upon them and be made firm as a man once more. And some did take my words as truth and came and stood with me and said they would become my followers and I grasped the term and used it and said to these first ones. 'You shall be greatly blessed and honoured amongst men for you are the first true Followers of Ytraa and Ytraa is greatly pleased with you.' And they did remove their clothes and make themselves naked as was I at all times in this part of my scheme. And the other people did abuse them and call them false and unashamed and said they should be put away from the sight of them.

Now, in those days, know that my voice was as honey and people would listen for the joy of hearing the sound of it. Before I had shown them I had the way to enter and master my wife, they had scorned me and called me noman. But after I had dwelt within her before them and they could see I was potent and could send forth my seed they knew me a man.

I used my fair voice and I told how Ytraa had appeared to me and how Ytraa was three in one and was man and was woman and was God in one body. For I knew that the women in the land were downtrodden and abused by the men and they would more readily believe my story and follow me if I made them as Gods with the men. I described the faces and bodies of Ytraa to them all and they asked me how it was that I knew this. 'I have looked on Ytraa and Ytraa is beautiful to behold such that a mere mortal must be blinded by the sight of Ytraa. But Ytraa did prepare me, as the Chosen voice of Ytraa, for the sight, that I might let the people know the nature of their creator and I looked and was blessed and was blind for only two days.

And the foolish people believed my words that I spoke for they could see the change in me and wondered and were afraid of the spark and the drought.

I told them then the words that now are told in the First Great Knowing and introduced them anew to the knowledge of Mhortag and the First Great Tree. And though I could claim to have created the words myself, in this I tell the truth that the words did come from my voices.

Many days did pass and the numbers of my Followers did grow and all went naked and did travel the land explaining the truth they believed I had brought from the Groves of Ytraa. And though I lusted much and often for the loins of the young women who were my Followers, still I spent my seed only in my wife, Lypadladohn, and she did bless me and praise my potent manhood and tell all how it was that I was a man blessed and she was blessed by my manhood.

And the Skyfire did burn more brightly in the sky with each passing night. And, slowly my party of Followers did increase. And many days did pass and the Skyfire became as a great flaming torch that spread over the sky and made the night as day with its flames. Still, I had too few Followers and must have more and I sent some into the hills to the small villages that lay high up the slopes of the mountain, nearer the sky, and they spoke my words and converted some to be Followers but others would not change. So I had them set fire to the houses in the night and did say that the Skyfire caused the burning and many were killed by the flames and others did change and become Followers and so my people did grow in numbers.

Those who we had not converted to be Followers were afraid of us and did harry and curse us and some of us they killed and others they raped because they were naked at all times and could be seen. And it was time for us to leave the land of the drought where there was not enough to eat and where the beasts were dying. And, when I had many thousands to Follow me, I did set them to leave Choshinahm.

I gathered my Followers around me and they came from all around the lake. From Saahl, Qolahn and Tohnpho, they came and from Phornahm and Llohnrah and Bophron. And they were numbered in the thousands and with them their beasts and their carts and their oxen to pull and their goods from their houses and their clothes that were folded for they wore them no more and their food from their larders and their gold coin and their valuable gems and silver and their weapons of iron and bronze.

Many days before all this came to pass, I had met with a merchant who was from the south and he spoke to me of an island, large and green and with few native peoples. There was fresh water, lakes and rivers and hills and a great mountain that rose from a plain and half of its height was black shiny stone like the surface of a pool in stillness. And I did tell the Followers of this place and said that there we would go and be true to Ytraa with no more interference from those who did not believe.

I led them first to the Groves of Ytraa, a place near the swamp where Mipri had been devoured, and I marked a great tree and did have it cut down and the first Godwood was cut from it. Great iron posts I had driven in the round ends with ropes attached that the people might pull the Godwood along with us. And it was here that I made the first punishment. For it seemed proper to propitiate the spirit of the fallen tree and I thought me that a blood sacrifice would make the most lasting impression on my Followers.

Now, all in the group were naked at all times at this stage. And one man was small in his parts and had known not a woman in all of his life. There was in the party a young maiden of no more than thirteen cycles, hardly yet a woman and almost a child still. This man lusted for the girl and did take and abuse her, for her very innocence caused him to become a man with her for he was vile and corrupt. He hid her and used her and tore her with his wicked lust. The maiden did escape him, at last, and did run to me, bleeding and torn and I saw in my mind the body of Mipri and I was wrath for that I was reminded of my own wickedness. I asked her to name the man who had so abused her and she pointed and he did confess, when the flame was put to his parts.

Then I took ten of my most trusted Followers and set them above all the others that they might be my guards and my keepers of peace amongst the people. And to these I gave the task of punishing the evil-doer and making proper obeisance to the spirit of the tree. I had them stretch him across the stump of the great tree and peg him to the wood with iron spikes through his hands and feet so he was spread-eagled over the stump with his face to the sky. I told them I had spoken with Ytraa and that they must unsex him and peel away his skin with sharp knives and then, whilst he lived still, his quivering flesh was flailed with the thorns of the poison tnetsi until he was dead. And when the people saw the wrath of Ytraa, they were afraid, as I had known they must be, and they did obey.

And this ends the first chapter of my confession. Read these words often, know them to be true and understand that you, alone of your generation, are the custodian of the great secrets that never must be known to the Followers excepting to you and your offspring. For you are my descendent and carry my guilt and as I shall be judged, so therefore shall you be judged also.

Here begins the second part of my confession of the truths regarding my founding of the religion of the Followers of Ytraa. Read these words well, my heirs and descendants, that you may know the truth and keep it safe, for if the people know the truth, they will surely kill you and all the priests and our names shall be shame and torment and all shall hate us forever.

Now, when we had the Godwood secure and the first sinner was sacrificed on its stump to propitiate the spirit of the tree, then did the Followers spend their first night in the Groves of Ytraa. Know that this place is filled with great trees that are spread wide apart with grass beneath their spreading boughs and the land is a place of great beauty and peace does live there. But it is high in the mountains and the nights are cool there. The people were still naked and they did sleep but poorly for the night was chill.

One young woman did put on her gown and did wrap herself in it and hide from Ytraa. I had made the people naked to begin with so I could see all the parts of the women and lust after them at all times. But I found that the constant naked bodies did not make me lust for I became used to their sight and did lose the urge to join because of it. So I must needs make the people wear clothing that would hide them from site when that was convenient but would be easy to remove. Also, I wanted them to be only part covered and parts of their flesh to be seen that I might regain my lust and guess at the parts that were hidden.

My faithful Followers that I had chosen to be my guardians and my soldiers came to me with the girl who was dressed and they lay her on the ground before me and I saw that she was not naked but clothed. Now, another of my clever plans came to be to work things to my own advantage. I told them to be merciful and take away her robe and bind her to a tree until I had determined what should be done with her. And then I wandered alone amongst the trees for half a day. When I returned it was morning and the people were feeding and the girl was weeping and afraid for what would happen to her.

I told them all that I had spoken again with Ytraa and that Ytraa had given me the words I would speak to them. Then did I call to the girl and ask her name and she said it was Zerryth and she was a fair maiden and was not betrothed to any for she had come from afar and left all her family. And I told the ones I had chosen to stand forward. I named them the Holy Ones and said that henceforth they would be forever naked and would have no hair either on their heads or on their bodies and they would lead by example in their joining and their worship. And I then asked the girl, Zerryth, why she had disobeyed the rule to be naked and she wept and said she had been cold in the night and had covered herself to be warm.

This was what I expected and I was prepared for it. I told the people that Ytraa was merciful and understood our weakness and had pity on us. So I had the girl stand before me, dressed in her gown and I did cut her garment with my knife and did make it short so that her thighs were seen and did slit the sides and open them so that her body could be glimpsed. And her belt I took and wrapped it about her narrow waist and it did hold the two halves together and this I called the tabard and declared that Ytraa had decreed that all Followers must wear this, both men and women, except when at prayer or in the joining. And so it was.

But I said that the girl had sinned and must pay the price for she had disobeyed Ytraa and such disobedience could not go unpunished. And then I had my next piece of good fortune, for I had no wish to harm this young woman who the Followers had taken to

483

their hearts. A young man, named Yldohn did step forward and plead on her behalf, saying that she was a woman of honesty and truth and that he would be punished in her stead.

So I had my Holy Ones bind him to the tree and beat him twenty blows with thin branches that striped his skin without breaking it. And he was silent during the beating and afterward I blessed him for his act of kindness and asked him whether he would have the maiden and he said he would if she would take him. Zerryth then embraced Yldohn and they did seem right for one another and here I had my most brilliant plan of all, though it might have been that the voices said some words of it. I told the people that Ytraa was a man and a woman and a God all in one and that the Followers should do everything in their power to become as one again, both man and woman joined before their God to show how they were faithful and did worship Ytraa. And so I used Zerryth and Yldohn to make the first joining before Ytraa and the people were amazed at this act of union and many were moved to join with their partners and I encouraged this and later made it law. And all were well pleased at the mercy and beneficence of Ytraa.

After this was done, I questioned Yldohn and discovered he knew all my words by heart and I was afraid, for I might forget what I had said and he might contradict me. So I made him my assistant and called him priest and Zerryth was a priestess also and they ministered to the people. Then I told the Holy Ones to select ten each of the Followers for each of them so that they would have a hundred they could call on to help them with their duties. The second day in the hills did end this way.

Now we moved through the mountains and the trees and came at last to the edge of the forest, where the River Flow does rush down the mountainsides on its journey to the lake. Here we tarried a short while so that the people could gather more food and let their beasts feed on the lush grass that grew beside the waters.

I knew then that the journey would be long and hard and that my Holy Ones must be strong and diligent in discipline if we were not to lose many of the people or have them turn against the ways I had designed. So I took them to a secret place and spoke with them and asked them what they most desired as tokens of their office. They looked about them and they found that they all had the material things they needed but they had become used to the authority they had over the people and they wanted more of that. So I made the decree that all the Followers should be below the Holy Ones and they should join with any person they desired, whenever such desire took them. I made it so that they had dominion over all and could take any for a partner when they wished. And I told them that this was the wish of Ytraa, that the Holy Ones should ever be on show to Ytraa and that they would demonstrate the joy of joining and the wish of the Followers to do the will of Ytraa by joining when they might with whom they chose to take and honour.

The Holy Ones found this decree to their liking except that two or three were not in agreement. I said that it was the will of Ytraa that it be so and still they persisted in their disagreement, saying that this was not fair to the other Followers. Once more I told them that I spoke the words of Ytraa but there were three, a man and two women, who would not agree. Then I showed them what the wrath of Ytraa could do. I had them bound and did remove their sex and hang them upside down and cut out their tongues and roast them over fires until they died. And we left them there for the wild beasts to devour. And I found others to take the place of the unfaithful Holy Ones I had burnt at Ytraa's bidding. Though, to tell the truth, it was the voices that decreed I did these things and never did I speak or see the God I had called Ytraa.

There came the time to cross the river and many were afraid for it was deep and swift and cold. My voices came to me and told me I must move the people from the mountain or they might be crushed to death by falling rocks. I told the people they must cross the water and sent the strongest men and women over with ropes tied to them. They swam the river and tied their ropes to trees across the other side so that the people and the beasts had guides to help them cross the water. And many crossed because they were still fearful of the Skyfire that still burned strongly in the sky. But many would not cross and these I did declare as enemies of Ytraa, as blasphemers who would be punished by the mighty power of God.

In the night, as my Followers made camp and ate and joined and sang the praises of Ytraa, on the north bank of the River Flow, so a great noise was heard and the ground did tremble and many flung themselves on their faces and did cry out in alarm. But I went amongst them and said they were safe because they had obeyed Ytraa.

In the morning, we looked out across the waters and did see that many trees had fallen in the night and great rocks had tumbled down the mountain on the far side and crushed the trees and killed many of the people. Thus it was I had my next supreme idea.

I sent the Holy Ones across the river to speak to those who still lived. I had them slay the injured and collect together all those who were whole and that was near five hundred men and women. These they brought across the river and we bound their hands and feet and stripped them of their tabards for they had been disobedient. We made a brand of iron in the shape of a star, to stand for the Skyfire, and this we heated in the fire and marked each on their forehead that they might be known by this as sinners. These became slaves and were clad in sacking and were there to be used by all as they saw fit and they served all others and did pull the ropes to draw the Godwood over the ground. And to this day I know not how the ground was made to tremble for me, except that my voices told me it was done because of what I did to make the people follow Ytraa.

After this, the Followers came with me over the long marches under the Mountains of Chakanh until we reached the Merchant Road. And here ends my second chapter of confession for it is hard for me to set down all these things now I am old and weary beyond guessing. And the next part of my truth will follow in the third part of this true confession of my dealings.

This is the third and final part of my confession. Read and understand my words for they are your words also. I am old beyond the knowledge of most men and have lived a long and terrible life. Many have suffered at my hands, feeding my lust and my craving for cruelty and for young and vital female flesh to take and use for my desire. But I have no fear of death.

Death is not anything. Death is the end of all. I wish only to prolong my memory and that of my heirs, of you as well as me. I beg your patience if I ramble or seem terse. I am old and my life drains out through the tip of my quill as I write.

The history of the journey from Choshinahm to Muhnilahm is well recorded and much that was written along the way is true enough. Now, however, I must set right the records on a number of things that, if left false, will distort the picture and leave doubts in the minds of those who follow me.

My wife, Lypadladohn, a large, ugly and violent woman, died giving birth to my daughter, Sonclusipah, who will be the first of my descendants to read this. She is a worthy successor to her father, being wicked, selfish, cruel and expedient by nature. Sonclusipah is my named heir and, through her, will the line of Gadhallah continue. I made the Followers believe I was descended from Mythanpho and Vaarkil; of course, this may be a lie. My voices did say that it was so, but I know not. I know not my antecedents and care nothing for them.

My head still fills with those voices and I cannot control them and they drive me to the evil I have done and to the good I might have done also. I say to those who follow me, watch out for those who hear the voices and may yet learn to control them.

I must record my great amazement on seeing the Monolith of Kro-Lat in Tohltaz. Such a sight can surely not be meant for the eyes of mere mortals. Some denizen of the divine had a hand in that construction, for surely man could not have set the hollow stone ball so high on the tube that yet supports it. Enough of that, but that it gave me pause and made me think, for a little while, that there might be a God if such things were in the world.

We came, by long treks through the desert, hard climbs through the mountain passes to the great fire mountain by Lake Mistahn. The Skyfire was but a memory now. I kept it alive to make them follow me. I cannot count the numbers of the Followers who I led there for they had multiplied in the years on the long march. But we lost some there. They remained in that fine land to make their lives. And, though I set my soldiers on them, harried them and made them suffer for their desertion, they remained all the same. They were not bad people, those who stayed at Kah-Labaz; we called them the lost, though, in truth, they were good people. But they disagreed with me and I could not have such disagreement.

Greater was the terrible divide that came on the plains of Rophan-Ra near Litkala. There were some of those who also had the gift of the voices. And they heard me confessing some of my sins and doings and were appalled at what they heard. These did move away with many of my best people, those who were true of heart and who knew compassion and tolerance. And I was sore distressed at their desertion and caused a great rift between those who would follow them under their leader, Wharhll, a good and great man of vision, and those who would follow me still. It was my wickedness there that caused the violence and corruption so that men and women hacked the parts from one another and did unspeakable acts to sons and daughters, mothers, fathers, sisters and brothers. I look on that time with no pride even now. Steeped in evil as I am, I can yet find no satisfaction in the wickedness I caused on the road to Litkala. That was an act for which I deserve eternal punishment. But I say that, knowing such a fate will not occur. I die when I die and that is an end to it.

Those who would follow Wharhll wanted to take only the good things I had done and leave behind the punishments, the rights of the priests and Holy Ones to do as they would with whom they would. They wanted not the sacred prostitutes, the sacrifice of fourthborns to the temple, the postures for prayer, which so readily accommodated those of us who would join with worshippers. They rejected all the Commands of Ytraa I had made up and instead made their own. I had taken special care to make all my Commands as directives saying only what they must not do, knowing how hard it is for people to obey such orders. I learned early in my life; tell a person *not* to do something and they are more likely to do it. If you say to a person, 'Do not think of purple grass.' They will think of purple grass because they cannot but do otherwise. My negative Commands were bound to be broken and thus I had justification for control and punishment of wrongdoers.

That was another part of my genius. I understood people. I knew that people would readily accept a religion and a God demanding they have sex with whom they wish as often as they wish it. Making the act of sex an act of worship was a brilliant idea. My voices made me think of it. Who would move against such a command, except those who understood what real love can be? There are few enough of those, after all. And my negative Commands were just as clever, giving, as they did, justification for my cruel

487

punishments. How I loved to hear the screams of pain, the cries of terror, as my victims were unsexed, skinned alive and roasted over red hot coals. Their pain enlivened me, it made me feared and kept me in control and in power and ensured that all obeyed my word.

But Wharhll exposed me for the charlatan I am and endangered my position. If I could have killed him I would have devised the most painful, lengthy form of killing I could for him. But he escaped with his people into the forest and the thief stole away my sacred staff, saying I deserved it not, saying that my very touch on it defiled it. We killed only a few hundred of his Followers and lost as many of our own on that vile road.

I knew we must depart that place or lose more of our people when they saw what had been done. So, we made our way toward the coast, returning first to Shorrannon and taking boats and people from that city and leaving it in smouldering ruins and its remaining people homeless, naked and without provision. At the coast, we came to Mipahnhil and there we stayed a while to build our strength and make more boats to take us across the sea. They loathed us but were too afraid to fight us in that town on stilts, for we were many even then. I had many of their women, took them as and when I wished and tossed them back like small fry in the sea. When we left, I stole their sacred stone. A block of white hard stone they said came from the city of Litkala and was proof of their claim to be descended from the people who had built the city out of stone. Of course, I knew then they were lying. Who could build a city out of stone? I took their so-called proof and tossed it in the sea when we were days out of their stinking town. I had taken some women and men hostage from there and I tied some to their precious stone and laughed as the great block dragged them beneath the waves.

So, we came at last to Muhnilahm.

And the island was all I had hoped it would turn out to be. The climate was warm and gentle to allow us to be naked as we wished. The native peoples were few and easily defeated. The Point formed a natural prison for those who disagreed with me, and there were many in the early days. The Plain of Ytraa formed a natural location for the Godwood, where the Holy Ones could set up their community and have the common folk make pilgrimages at a cost that was not too high but that took effort. And the mountain was unusual enough to make the Followers believe it must be special.

Oh, I was so clever. All my plans had come to this conclusion and I had begun a religion in which my name would be hallowed forever. I laughed then at their stupidity, I laugh now, as I die, at their foolish superstitious natures that allow them to be so beguiled by lies. Fools. All of them fools. They deserve to be led by the corrupt and wicked, for they believe the words of liars and cheats, charlatans and bullies. Let them ever believe in Ytraa, who does not exist, and in the rites and rituals I have devised. Let them humiliate themselves each time they place themselves in those ridiculous positions to worship their non-existent God. Let them weep each time their fourthborn child is taken from their loins to serve as sex slave in the temples of the Holy Ones. Let them hide their tears of loss every time a priest demands their wife or husband as a partner and steals the fruit of their loins for use as a sex slave. Let them cry in pain and terror at the skinning knives, the searing rods, the roasting coals, the lashing thorns. And, you, my descendants, must devise new ways to use and torture them and never, ever let them know the truth of their religion.

They exist in lies and wickedness as I have taught them. Let them wallow in the vile pursuit of evil that they think is good. I have perverted every human good and turned it to my use. I revel in their shame and humiliation, in their torture, fear and subjugation. Let it be so always and forever. They are fools and indolent, lazy, unthinking fools at that, for any with an ounce of thought or justice in their veins could undo me in a trice. Yet they do it not, for they are afraid of shadows, terrified of what might be and is not. They are stupid and deserve the labours and misfortunes that I laid upon them. Use them, those of you who follow in my name, use and abuse them. Treat them harshly and accept their willing sacrifices for they deserve no better treatment. We know all men are wicked but only we who lead have the courage and the honesty to accept that such is as we are. We deserve to lead, deserve to benefit from their complicity in evil. I love them not and you who follow me should love them less.

And now I die. My life has been an evil thing, driven by the voices in my head and by my own desire to be respected and obeyed. I go now to the end of all things. Nothing will be for me when I close my eyes the final time. I feel the life departing from me, even as I write these final words. And, now, at the very end of life, when I should be so certain of my legacy, my destiny, I feel…I wonder whether…

The confession ends on this and it is said that Sonclusipah found her father with his head on the parchment, the quill still in his hand and tears drying on his face.

The Epic of Gadhallah

Let it be known that this account was first put into words and written on paper by Poltrados, The Great Chronicler, who wrote accounts of all the happenings and of the other stories he was told. It is supposed that this account was written to inform the general population and fool them into believing there were good reasons to follow Gadhallah and, through him, Ytraa.

The Skyfire was first seen over Choshinahm when Gadhallah was a man of seventy-three summers. This was also the time of the beginning of the calendar. Gadhallah could trace his line back through thirty-seven generations to Mythanpho and Vaarkil who slay the twin-headed serpent of the lake, Na Dagon.

In Choshinahm the people mocked Gadhallah because he had no beard and his head was bald. They mocked him because his wife was barren and a scold but he would not leave her though she nagged at him constantly. They mocked him because he spoke with the flowers and the trees that grew in the Groves of Ytraa. They mocked him because he played with the children as they splashed naked in the clear waters of Lake Qonahn.

But Ytraa saw their cruelty and looked kindly on Gadhallah. Ytraa spoke with Gadhallah as he walked among the trees. At this time, there was much trouble in the land with starvation due to drought and the rumour of war from the desert beyond. Ytraa told Gadhallah that the Skyfire was coming; that the sky would be ablaze for many nights. Ytraa told him that this was a sign for the good people to leave Choshinahm and find a new land that had been prepared over the seas. All the bad people would stay behind in Choshinahm and never know the joy and beauty of the new land of Muhnilahm.

Ytraa also told Gadhallah all that is written in the Great Book of Law. And one further thing Ytraa told Gadhallah, and this was the promise of the return of the Skyfire. And Ytraa said to Gadhallah that he must make a solemn promise for the people. The promise was this; that when the Skyfire returned then would the Holy Ones and High Priest of Muhnilahm select three female virgins of sixteen summers or more and take these back to Choshinahm. The Holy Ones and High Priests of Choshinahm must also select three virgins to be exchanged. Thus would the blood of the sundered people be mixed and they would not forget each other nor become totally estranged, in the hope that one day the people of Choshinahm might come to be believers in Ytraa.

Also, the people of Muhnilahm would take a portion of the trunk of the Great Tree from the Groves of Ytraa and would return to Muhnilahm with this. It must be more than two men high and one manheight across the base. The good people of Choshinahm would also take such a token with them when the first Skyfire came. The piece of the

Great Tree, which would be called the Godwood, would be carved in the likeness of Ytraa. Until this time, no man had seen Ytraa, but Gadhallah saw Ytraa. Ytraa showed Ytraa to Gadhallah. The side that was Man Ytraa showed to him, the side that was woman Ytraa showed to Gadhallah and the side that was neither man nor woman but was God Ytraa showed to him.

Gadhallah was blinded by the vision for three days and was lost to the world as he stumbled and wandered in the Great Groves of Ytraa.

Then it was that Ytraa gave back Gadhallah his sight and sent him back home to his town of Rrahp. There he began to spread the word of Ytraa amongst the people. But the people of Choshinahm would not acknowledge Ytraa as the only true God and they laughed at Gadhallah and mocked him. And some said that maybe the Skyfire, if it should come, would set his white hair on fire. But Gadhallah paid no heed, even though his wife mocked and rebuked him in public. Still Gadhallah was not dissuaded and he told his story all the more in the town. And he went from Rrahp and into the townships of Bophron and Qolahn and Shoal and on to Tohnpho and Phornahm and Llohnrah at the northern end of Lake Qonahn. All the small settlements on the eastern shore of the lake he visited, telling his prophesy.

When he returned to his house at Rrahp he had been away for two hundred and twelve days and he found his wife, Sonclusipah, great with child. This he told her was a sign from Ytraa. But she laughed and scorned him and scolded him for his neglect.

The child was born, a boy, whom they named Pentril. When he was fifty-four days old they made to take him to the lake to show him to the Goddess of the lake, called Tryhnn. But Ytraa showed Gadhallah that this was not good and therefore he would not take the boy to the lake as was the tradition and custom. The people were outraged and said that Tryhnn would be angry with them and would sink their fishing boats. But Gadhallah was unmoved by their pleas and listened only to the voice of Ytraa and would not let the boy be dipped in the lake.

Then the people grew afraid and took Pentril by force and cast Gadhallah into a pit in the ground. And they took the boy and dipped him in the lake three times as was the custom, to show the child to Tryhnn. When it was done, they took Gadhallah from the pit and gave him back his child. But Gadhallah was wrath and he took the child to the Groves of Ytraa. And there he divested himself and the child of all clothing and ornament and went forward naked to worship Ytraa as he had been showed. Again Ytraa appeared to Gadhallah and spoke with him, praising him for his strength and faith. And Ytraa blessed them both, father and son. Then the great Ytraa told Gadhallah again of the coming of the Skyfire and that soon the sky would be set ablaze for forty nine days on end.

Gadhallah returned naked to the village and told the people that the Skyfire would come soon but they mocked him and laughed at him as before. And they took from him his son, Pentril and would not let him grow the child, as they said he was not fit to do so.

Now it happened that amongst the people of Rrahp their dwelt one Doklas and he was learned in matters relating to the sky. He knew the stars and had names for some and even knew the ways of the wandering stars. On the twelfth day of the fifth month of that year he went to the Holy Ones and told them all he had seen on the night. A new star had appeared, faint but visible in the night sky to the north, over the lake in the early morning before sunrise.

When word of this reached Gadhallah he was glad for he knew that this was the coming of the Skyfire as had been predicted by Ytraa. Again Gadhallah told the people of the coming of the Skyfire but they mocked him still and laughed in his face. But some there were who were afraid because of the new star and they believed Gadhallah and went with him to the Groves of Ytraa and there he made them naked and showed them to Ytraa and they were converted. These he sent as the emissaries of Ytraa to the other towns and settlements of the lake and bade them tell the people of the coming of the Skyfire.

And soon the new star grew very bright and the people were filled with foreboding and some there were who heard the words of Gadhallah and his close men and they followed them. Some gathered in Rrahp, coming by boat across the great lake, others there came on foot with all their worldly goods.

And now it was, with the coming Skyfire still but a bright star, that Sonclusipah fell to her knees and begged Gadhallah to forgive her and he took her, and all the new followers with him, to the Groves of Ytraa and made them naked so that they might worship Ytraa in the proper manner. And when they returned to the village of Rrahp the whole night sky was burning with white flames and all the people were afraid. Now there were many people gathered in the small town and there was much unrest. But Gadhallah told the people of Rrahp that they were honoured by the gathering and should feed and house the people until the day they would depart. But the people were not convinced, even though they were afraid of the Skyfire, and would not do as Gadhallah said.

And Gadhallah warned them that there would be new and terrible signs if they did not heed him, but still they mocked him. And Gadhallah made to go to the town of Bophron which stood not on the lake and had not been visited by Gadhallah or any of his followers. But Ytraa came to him in a vision and told him that Bophron was destroyed by the Skyfire because the people there would not worship Ytraa.

Gadhallah told the gathered people and the people of Rrahp of his vision and some believed and some did not. And then it was that a runner came to Rrahp from Bophron and he was burned and near to death and he told them how the whole town had burned in the night. The Skyfire had touched the houses and had set them alight and many were dead and many would die of their burns. And then the runner died also.

Then did the gathering of the followers of Ytraa grow and swell as they came from the towns and settlements around the lake. And now did Gadhallah try to make his townsfolk see that they must turn to Ytraa. But they would not, saying, 'Tryhnn will save us. Tryhnn is the real God amongst Gods. Ytraa is only a God of the forests and woods. Tryhnn is the Goddess of the lake. We will put our faith in Tryhnn.'

So Gadhallah left Rrahp with his followers to search for the new land of Muhnilahm. And all those who went with Gadhallah, including his wife, Sonclusipah and his son, Pentril, numbered seven thousand, seven hundred and seventy seven souls. And with them their cattle and sheep and beasts of burden which in those days were oxen which carried all their food and worldly goods.

At the eaves of the Groves of Ytraa, Gadhallah halted the people and gathered them round him and spoke to them. And this is what he said, for it is written in the book.

'From henceforth these Groves shall be our sacred shrine, our place of pilgrimage. Here it is that Ytraa has made Ytraa's first earthly home. Here we would stay if we could. But Ytraa has told me that this is a land full of people who will never believe and Ytraa will send drought and earthquake and plague to trouble those who we leave behind but still they will not believe. We, who believe in Ytraa, shall be saved. But let all of you know that our journey shall be long and hard and full of peril. Many will perish on the road. Some will fall by the wayside and be left to wander alone and without guidance in foreign lands. The road is long and hard and will take us many years to travel.

'We seek our new home, our land of perfection to the south of here where the sun is always warm and the rain falls only through the night. The new land is an island in the great sea that lies beyond the mountains. We must travel through lands that are strange and empty and through lands that are hostile to us. But Ytraa will guide and protect us. Ytraa will lead us safe home.

'There are those amongst us who are weak in spirit and they will try to turn back. But Ytraa will not allow them to turn. Those who try to turn back will die. Now is the time of the first test. This is the first of many. Those of you who have not the stomach for the journey, those of you who do not believe in Ytraa as the supreme God, those of you who will not hear the words of Ytraa spoken through my mouth, you must go now and return to your homes. Know that I am the voice of Ytraa, I am the mouthpiece of Ytraa, I am the eyes and ears of Ytraa. You must obey me. If you will not obey the words of Ytraa, you must leave now. This is the only time that Ytraa will let you leave.'

The Skyfire had already risen in the evening sky and was bright enough to be seen even before the sun had set and the people saw the Skyfire and heard the words of Ytraa spoken by Gadhallah and none would leave.

Gadhallah opened his mouth again and spoke forth the words of Ytraa. 'Ytraa is pleased. Ytraa will bless Ytraa's followers. In the morning our great journey begins in earnest. For tonight you have already travelled many miles and must rest. Light fires but touch no living tree for this is the Groves of Ytraa. Burn only dead wood from the floor of the forest. Go now to your rest.'

Then Gadhallah gathered his chosen followers around him and named them his Holy Ones and bade them gather all the young men of the party who had between seventeen and twenty-five summers to him. And they numbered one hundred and seventy-eight. And Gadhallah questioned each one in turn and put them to the test and found those who were brave and strong and true to Ytraa amongst them. And in the morning Gadhallah had ninety-nine who were his soldiers and nine of these he made his Captains with the ninety in their charge. And all the ninety-nine were above the people and the people had to obey them. But the Holy Ones were above the ninety-nine and Gadhallah was above the Holy Ones.

When the people awoke they were amazed for Gadhallah and the Holy Ones and the ninety-nine were all naked and the Holy Ones were shaven having no beard nor no hair on their heads. And the ninety-nine, who Gadhallah named his Soldiers of Ytraa, carried swords unsheathed. Then did Gadhallah gather the people together about him and tell them what had come to pass with the Holy Ones and the Captains and the Soldiers and he spoke again to them with the words of Ytraa, and this is what he said.

'Now we must pass through the Groves of Ytraa and they are hallowed grounds and must not be defiled nor must noise be made. We will talk only in whispers and only at need. These are your instructions for the passage through the Groves of Ytraa. Hear them and heed them well. All garments must be removed and all jewellery also. Those who pass through the Groves of Ytraa must do so utterly naked. Ytraa made us and Ytraa knows each one of us. Ytraa does not wish Ytraa's followers to hide from Ytraa's eyes as we pass through the Groves of Ytraa. Therefore all will be naked and unadorned that nothing is hidden from the eyes of Ytraa.'

There was some grumbling from the people but many did as they were bid and stripped themselves of their clothes and their jewellery and their bangles and did load them on their beasts of burden. And, hearing the words of Ytraa, they did stand proud and open beneath the Groves of Ytraa and Ytraa was well pleased. But some there were and many from the northern township of Llohnrah who did not like to be seen naked and who were jealous of the eyes of others on the skins of their spouses and they were not

495

pleased and grumbled and said they would not go naked through the Groves of Ytraa. So Gadhallah sent his Soldiers and his Captains amongst them and persuaded them of the rightness of his command and many obeyed but they were not proud to be naked and hid their parts with their hands and the rest of the party did mock them until they were shamed and did stand proud and upright and uncovered as was the will and wish of Ytraa. But three amongst them steadfastly refused to take off their clothes and these were one woman and two men. And Gadhallah felt the wrath of Ytraa in his breast and he did curse them and vilify them for their disobedience and still they would not do the will of Ytraa. And Gadhallah spoke again with the words of Ytraa. 'Know that Ytraa is displeased and the wrath of Ytraa is great and terrible. Those who do not the will of Ytraa will perish.'

Then did the Captains set the Soldiers on the disobedient ones and they stripped them of their clothes and their jewellery and did set aside these things for the common good. And the two men were unmanned before the people, their parts cut off and thrown to the dogs. And the woman's breasts were sliced off and fed to the dogs and she was skewered on three swords. And all the disobedient ones were split asunder and their parts and innards were spread over the ground and left for the buzzards and ants to devour. And the people saw the wrath of Ytraa and were afraid and turned away from the sight.

Then Gadhallah bid them follow him through the Groves of Ytraa and they passed over the Shallow River and into the Groves of Ytraa. And so they passed through the Groves of Ytraa and up the higher ground to the banks of the Fleet where the waters boil and rage through a narrow gorge as they flow down from the Mountains of Chakanh to Lake Qonahn. Here they made camp for the night. And they had passed the day without speech and all were silent at the evening camp as Gadhallah had commanded. And though the night air was cool so high in the foothills of the mountains, none would cover himself with blanket or cape for Ytraa had decreed they must be naked in this place.

Morning came and the party was gathered about Gadhallah on the steep shores of the river. And Gadhallah broke the silence with the words of Ytraa, thus.

'Now you must be washed clean in the river, your past lives must be washed away and your bodies made ready for the new land. Each of you, separately, must pass across the sacred waters of the Fleet and submerge yourselves three times beneath the surface. Children may go with their mother or their father for the current is strong and Ytraa does not wish to lose young souls to the river.'

It was evening before all the people had crossed the Fleet in this manner and the Holy Ones and the Soldiers followed Gadhallah and then supervised the people in their crossing and the animals and beasts of burden were taken over last. And none was lost though the current was swift and dangerous and the people were amazed that all passed over safely.

'Why are you amazed?' Gadhallah asked them. 'Did I not tell you this was the will of Ytraa that we did? Do you not know that Ytraa treasures you, every one, and will not let harm come to you?' And the people nodded and were strengthened in their faith.

In the night the Soldiers on patrol found a young girl huddled underneath a blanket for warmth and took her to Gadhallah. He took the girl and bound her hands and tied her to a young tree until the morning came and she wept when she was brought before the people.

'She is a maiden of seventeen summers and a virgin yet,' Gadhallah told the people. 'She has hidden her body from the sight of Ytraa and has sinned. What punishment should Ytraa meet out on this sinning maiden?'

The people were amazed that he should ask them. Some said she should be beaten, others that she be shaved bald and whipped, others that her eyes be put out. None said she should be killed for this offence. One amongst the crowd stepped forward and said they should take pity on the maiden. He was a buck of twenty years and spoke thus to the people, 'Let her be. She has suffered shame and humiliation and fear and cold. She did not hide from the eyes of Ytraa, but only covered herself against the cold. I say she should be let free', he said, 'but let Ytraa do as Ytraa wills.'

The people were silent and wondered what might pass. Gadhallah stood and looked on the girl, still bound, and on the young man, and on the people before him. And all were silent, and the maiden was trembling with fear, her head bowed. The people waited.

Gadhallah spoke to the people and said,' Ytraa has spoken with me. The maiden has shown Ytraa our frailty. Ytraa decrees we may now wear what clothing we need to stay warm in this cool land. But no adornment may yet be worn.'

The people rejoiced and were glad, for the Groves of Ytraa that covered the feet of the mountains were not warm as were the plains about the lake. The people dressed in what garments they could find from their belongings. But the maiden was still bound and remained naked before Gadhallah and the people. And the young man who had spoken for her also remained naked with her and they spoke together quietly whilst the people about them put on their clothing. And Gadhallah donned his white tabard and gird it with a belt and this was the only garment he would wear in the Groves of Ytraa.

When the people were clothed again the Soldiers gathered them about Gadhallah once more and the maiden was still naked before them.

'Ytraa has spoken with me again and has said the maiden has yet sinned and that sin has not been punished. No sin may go unpunished. That is the Word of Ytraa.'

And the young man stepped forward and did prostrate himself at the feet of Gadhallah and begged that she be set free and not harmed. 'If there must be punishment, let me suffer it in her stead.'

All the people were silent and waited to see what Gadhallah would do.

'Ytraa is well pleased,' said Gadhallah. 'The young man will be punished and then be blessed. Bind him to the tree.'

And the Soldiers took the young man and bound him to the trunk of a young tree and the girl did prostrate herself before Gadhallah and begged him be merciful. But Gadhallah lifted her from his feet and bade her be silent and wait on the will of Ytraa. Then did Gadhallah take a thin branch that had fallen to the ground and he gave it to the Captain on his right and spoke softly to him so that no one else might hear his words. And the Captain took the branch and smote the young man nine times on his back but broke not the skin there. Then was the young man cut free and taken to stand before Gadhallah with the maiden, she also was unbound at this time. And the young man and the young maiden stood naked together before Gadhallah and the people and were in the sacred place that was the Groves of Ytraa. And the young man's name was Yldohn and the maiden was called Zerryth.

Gadhallah questioned them and asked if they would be joined and they gazed at each other and nodded. For Yldohn saw the maiden's beauty and humility and Zerryth saw the young man's courage and compassion. So Gadhallah took them and bade them stand side by side before the people, the man on the right hand side of the maiden. He caused them to speak the words of promise to each other before the people and this they did. And in those days, before the people knew the will of Ytraa, it was the custom for the newly promised to join at once, even before their joining vows were said. And Yldohn and Zerryth were much in desire for each other and wanted to join and the people willed it also. But Gadhallah spoke the words of Ytraa and commanded them that they lay not together until they had done so before the eyes of Ytraa in a place to be decided. So they were betrothed and promised but not yet joined and Gadhallah bid them not join, on pain of death, until the place had been chosen where Ytraa would be witness to their act of love.

Then did Gadhallah send out runners. Each runner had a length of hempen rope and each was sent to measure the girth of every tree that stood wider than their outstretched arms. And the runners were gone for three days and they were three hundred in number for the trees in the Groves of Ytraa are many. Yet the spaces between the trees are wide and sunlight warms the forest floor and the Groves of Ytraa is a pleasant place.

When the runners returned with their ropes knotted to mark the girth of the largest tree they had each found, so their ropes were compared until the largest of all was identified. And the young woman who had found this mighty tree then led the people to the place and two more days passed until they reached the place for the Groves of Ytraa is a mighty forest. And the tree they found was at the western edge of the Groves of Ytraa close under the mountains. Four tall men could touch fingertips with arms outstretched and still there was a gap between the last pair of hands, so wide was the girth of the tree.

Gadhallah touched the tree and stripped before it, placing his skin against the bark and clasping the tree as a lover. He stayed this way for that whole day and spoke to no one and the people waited and did not know what to do.

At last, as evening was falling and the Skyfire lit the space above, Gadhallah left the tree and fell to his knees in a trance.

Words came from his mouth and none knew what he said. Then did Gadhallah rise and place his back to the great tree and speak with the voice of Ytraa. Loud and clear and full his voice was and all who heard were amazed at how he spoke.

'This is the Godwood. Know ye that the trees of the Groves of Ytraa they are sacred and must not be touched for as long as they live. Yet this tree is the Godwood and will carry Ytraa to the new land across the seas. This tree must be cut down and a piece of trunk the length of two tall men must be taken from the widest part and this will be the Godwood. But the death of the tree must be paid for by the death of a follower of Ytraa for the tree is sacred and its death must be marked with respect.'

Then were the people afraid for they knew not how the sacrifice would be made nor who would be the victim.

Now Gadhallah bade the people all to strip naked once more for they were in the sight of Ytraa and Ytraa would not let the bodies of those Ytraa had created be hidden from Ytraa's eyes. So the people did make themselves naked once more. And Gadhallah bid Yldohn and Zerryth come before him and did cause a blanket to be laid on the ground at the feet of the Godwood tree. Gadhallah silenced the people for they wondered out loud what was to be done. He questioned Zerryth and asked her if she had lain with any man and she said she had not and she was virgin. He questioned Yldohn and asked if he had lain with any woman and he said he had, he had lain with a matron at the conclusion of his manhood ceremony as was the custom in that time. But he had lain not with any other woman. Then Gadhallah asked if they would join until death put them asunder and they said they would. And he charged them to remain faithful each to the other for all the days of their lives. And this they promised before the people. Then he did direct Zerryth to lie down on the blanket and make ready to receive her man within her. And the people cried out in alarm for this was not then the custom and some were outraged and did question Gadhallah in this. But Zerryth held her hands out from her body and showed all herself to them and was not ashamed.

'Do not be anxious over this,' she said, 'for it is the will of Ytraa that we join in this way and make our joining public.'

And Gadhallah placed his hands upon her shoulders and kissed her forehead as she lay on the ground. Still some people grumbled saying it was sacrilege to act this way. But Yldohn saw his lover waiting and was filled with desire for her and all could see that he was ready to be joined with her.

'Mock not the will of Ytraa,' he said to the people,' for what we do is out of love of Ytraa and from love for each other.'

Then did Yldohn fall on Zerryth and he penetrated her virginity before the people and she cried out in sudden pain but then was filled with passion and they loved until the act was done and all the people stood in silent witness until the cries of joy came from the lovers' lips and then did all the people sigh in joy also.

The next day Gadhallah told the men to fell the Godwood tree with their axes. All day they laboured at the task and by sunset they had caused the tree to fall and had cut the length of it that was called the Godwood. Into each end of the Godwood they did hammer an iron pole in the centre. And to each they attached stout ropes. With ten men pulling on each rope and ten pushing from behind, they moved the Godwood along the ground, rolling it to move it through the trees. And this is how they moved the Godwood from the Groves of Ytraa to the new land over the seas.

But before the people could move from the Groves of Ytraa, the Godwood tree must be propitiated. Gadhallah was much troubled how to chose the sacrificial victim. But Ytraa provided one for him.

Amongst the people was a man of forty-nine summers. Frail and weak of spirit he was and small with women so that they laughed at him. And never had he entered woman in his life. But at the joining of Yldohn and Zerryth he found himself aroused and sought himself a woman to be used for his pleasure. And at the edge of the crowd of people he found him a young woman of fifteen summers, hardly ripe and he did capture her by stealth and take her from the people against her will. And far away from the people he did penetrate her and take her by force and violence against her will and use her most foully. But she escaped him after this and he returned to the people to find her so that he might use her again. But she sought out Gadhallah and threw herself at his feet and begged him for his mercy, fearing she would be the sacrifice. For in those days a woman who was violated was as nothing and was made the guilty party even though she fought and strained against the act.

But Gadhallah was wise and did ask guidance from Ytraa and Ytraa decreed that the young woman bore no fault for what had been done to her and that the man alone bore responsibility and should be punished most grievously, suffering much pain and fear for his act. So Gadhallah despatched a whole section of Soldiers to hunt for the man and bring him back for trial.

Whilst the Soldiers conducted their search, Gadhallah sought to find a suitable sacrifice to propitiate the death of the Godwood tree. And behold the Soldiers brought the rapist before Gadhallah and he knew that this man would be the sacrificial victim.

The girl identified the man as her persecutor and did tell all present what he had done to her and he could not meet her gaze and cast his face to the ground and would not suffer his eyes to dwell on her even when she did show the wounds and marks he had made on her body.

The man was accused of his assault and could not deny it. He fell on his face, saying he was most sorry for what he had done but that the girl, as tradition did require, must bear the blame for the act, not he. And Gadhallah was exceeding wrath and did smite the man on his breast with his own hand and did force the man to gaze on the girl he had so wronged. Gadhallah caused the man to be naked before the people and to lay spread-eagled across the rough stump of the Godwood tree.

The Soldiers did beat him with thin sticks until his skin was broken and bleeding. Then did they take his manhood from him in three parts, slicing the rod down its length and cutting open the sack to pull out the fruits, which they beat with their sticks. And the man begged for mercy and an end to his suffering but Gadhallah said that Ytraa was mightily wrath at what the man had done to one of his virgin maidens and that the man must suffer yet more. And the Soldiers did slice off his ears and pierce his eyes and his tongue they did split. Still the man lived and was in agony. Then did the Soldiers split his skin and peel it in thin strips from his living body until there was none attached. And still did the man live and his body convulsed in agony.

'Thus does Ytraa to those who defile the virgin.' Gadhallah declared.

Then did the Soldiers drive sharpened stakes through his hands and feet and left him there to die that the Godwood stump be properly propitiated. And all who witnessed this sacrifice were amazed at the wrath of Ytraa and did tremble and learn.

In the morning, the body of the man was still twitching but they did no more to him and left him in that place that his blood might feed the stump and bring forth new life to the tree. And they began their journey to their new land taking the Godwood with them.

On the third day after the sacrifice, the people did reach the eaves of the Groves of Ytraa and there they did rest for four days and nights and let their cattle and sheep and beasts of burden graze on the wild fields that lay beyond the Groves.

Now did the people view the way ahead over the vast plains beneath the Mountains of Chakanh. And the great river that is called The Flow spread wide and deep before them and they were much afraid of it for the water was cold and full of dangerous currents.

Again Gadhallah bid the people divest themselves of their clothing and make ready to cross the Flow. But some of the people rebelled, saying it was too cold and the water was too dangerous to cross. Then did Gadhallah remind them of the purpose of their journey and their promise to Ytraa and most obeyed but many did not. And Gadhallah warned them that Ytraa was not pleased and would bring suffering to them if they obeyed not. Yet still there were those who would not obey. Gadhallah made them stay on the bank of the river and watch as the faithful crossed the water with their animals and beasts of burden. And to their amazement none was lost and all did safely cross to the other side even though it took one thousand men to hold the ropes and stop the Godwood floating down toward the lake. And when all the faithful had crossed over, Gadhallah called to those still left upon the farther bank and bade them join the throng. Some repented and did cross over but many stayed behind. Gadhallah warned them that the night would bring them punishment for Ytraa was God and would be obeyed. Still they would not do as they were bid. And Gadhallah fell on his knees and did remain naked through the first part of the night and the people fell on their knees also and prayed with him for a while. But he excused them his ordeal and bade them eat and prepare for sleep and only the chosen ones stayed with him.

In the morning Gadhallah cried aloud to the unfaithful ones across the river and begged them to repent and join the throng. But they were stubborn and refused to obey and then did Ytraa cause the ground to tremble and the river did boil between its banks and trees did fall, crushing those who remained and many were killed and others were badly injured. Then did those who were left alive on the far bank obey at last and they stood on the banks and waited for the waters to stop boiling and then they crossed and came over safe.

And Gadhallah caused the Soldiers to arrest the late comers and to mark them on their foreheads with brands from the fire and so they were made slaves to the community and even though they be man and wife they could not live together and became the property of all the people to do with as they might. And the dead and injured across the river were left for carrion for Ytraa was displeased with them and their belongings and beasts were divided up amongst the people.

And, when the earth had stilled and all was calm again, Gadhallah made a new decree, and it was this. That all the people of Ytraa be henceforth known as Followers. And that at the beginning and end of each day they must pray to Ytraa on their knees, this at sunset and at rising. And that they must do this wherever they may be, alone or with other, free or captive, at home or abroad and amongst strangers. And that the act of prayer must always be done without clothing or adornment or ornament so that Ytraa might see their frailty and the followers might be reminded of their humility and simplicity in the eyes of Ytraa. And so it was and so it is to this day.

When morning came, all the people took up their belongings and gazed on the Groves of Ytraa across the Flow for the last time. Then did the host leave that place and begin in earnest their search for the land of Muhnilahm.

(At this point, the narrative is interrupted and then continues, on a different style of parchment, in a slightly more modern style).

When Gadhallah began his mission to the new land, he did not know where it was or in what direction he must travel. He knew only that it was over the Mountains and across the seas and that it was an island. The Mountains of Chakanh cannot be passed, even through the high passes, with livestock such as the people had with them. And the Godwood was too heavy and big to be taken through the passes. So it was that Gadhallah sought the old Merchant Road that ran for hundreds of leagues from Tohnpho to Likdigmina and then on and down by the Ahn-Ehn Bay to Ahnsha. The road passes out of Choshinahm into the wild region known as Ndagaal where no people live and the wide plains are home to vast herds of wild deer and antelope and great wild beasts of prey. Trees are scattered but there are forests near the Chakanh ridge of mountains, so Gadhallah led his people on the flat lands close to the mountains for many leagues and they camped each night and their beasts ate the lush grasses and the going was easy in this time. Hunters brought back game and the women and children gathered many fruits and berries from along the way so none went hungry and all was at peace in the Followers.

In the host was a man who had travelled the length of the Merchant Road and he was their guide as they crossed three of the tributaries of the great River Ahn-Ehn, which flowed from the mountains and then across the plains until it emptied into the sea beside Ahn-Ehn Bay. He led them to the Merchant Road and along toward the end of the mountains where they joined the great earthworks that were made in a time before history. It was said then that the earthworks, which filled the gap between the end of the Mountains of Chakanh and Ahn-Ehn Bay, covering hundreds of leagues, were built by the people who had once lived on the plains of Ndagaal. The earthworks were a defence against the fierce warlords who dwelt in the land beyond, the region known as Tohltaz. They were merciless killers who had roamed the land at will, robbing and raping and making slaves of all they captured. But the earthworks had cut them off and they had remained behind the ramparts and not gone into Ndagaal again. There were said to be forts and great wooden towers and a wall of wooden posts along the whole length of the earthworks. But these had fallen into decay and disrepair when Gadhallah took the Followers to that place.

The plains of Ndagaal were rich and lush with much grazing and plenty of game and water in abundance and the people liked the place for the climate was mild and pleasant so that they were loathe to leave it. Their cattle and sheep and swine grew fat on the grazing and the people had room to live and roam free. They had been travelling for more than four portions and had covered over one hundred and thirty leagues, some across snow, as the winter had set in and gone in the mountain region. Now it was warm and pleasant for the followers and they did not want to leave for they had all they needed. Gadhallah let them rest close to the Earthworks for another portion, to gather food and other supplies for their journey over the harsh lands of Tohltaz. For he had intended to go to the city of Likdigmina and on to Ahnsha but Ytraa had warned him against that route in a dream and had told him to cross the desert that was now the land of Tohltaz, being uninhabited by man in those days.

When Gadhallah spoke to the Followers at the end of the portion of rest and told them they must cross the Earthworks into the land of Tohltaz there was much grumbling and some amongst them made trouble so that Gadhallah had to send in his Soldiers to quell the rebellion. Some of the people were hurt and some were killed in this riot. Afterwards many of the Followers gathered around Gadhallah and said they would go. But there were some who had forgotten the wrath of Ytraa. The Skyfire had been not visible in the sky for many days and the earthquake had been forgotten and so had the plagues that had ruined the country before the people had joined Gadhallah and become Followers.

Gadhallah warned the disobedient ones that Ytraa would send a plague to punish their wickedness and some came and joined the true Followers. But still there were many who would not but who wanted to remain behind and live in Ndagaal in ease and tranquillity.

So Gadhallah separated the two groups and the true Followers came and made camp right under the Earthworks and the disobedient ones were made to stay on the far side of the Merchant Road some three leagues distant. And Gadhallah decreed that no communication be between the two groups for nine days and nine nights. And so it was.

On the tenth day, Gadhallah sent ten of his Soldiers with a Captain to the disobedient group, who numbered nearly five hundred, to see if they would now return to join the Followers. It was after sunrise prayers that Gadhallah sent the Soldiers and they had but three leagues to go but it was after sunset prayers on the second day before they returned with some of the group of disobedient ones. And those that returned were only one hundred and thirty seven in number and there were amongst them neither any children nor any people more than thirty summers. And they would not talk of what plague had overcome them, being sore afraid of what had passed. Never did any speak of what had overtaken the disobedient ones and to this day it is not known what form that plague took. But the Captain told Gadhallah that he had found the remainder of the disobedient group huddled together with their beasts and that of the others there was no trace. No bodies, nor blood nor clothing nor any other thing did they find. Yet the belongings and the beasts were still with the group that remained.

Gadhallah made them all renew their oath to follow Ytraa even unto death and this they did. Then Gadhallah said they must be punished for their wickedness. The Soldiers made to strip them so they might be beaten but Gadhallah stopped them, saying, 'Naked is sacred and will not be suffered for punishment. From this day nakedness in public is allowed only at times of prayer, at the several rites and ceremonies, and at times of bathing. Only the young and virgin and the Chosen Ones may go naked freely. Punishment will be made without nakedness, but with the bodies of those to be punished wrapped in coarse cloth. For nakedness is sacred and to allow it to the profane would be sacrilege in the eyes of Ytraa.'

Thus did Gadhallah cause the disobedient ones to be branded as slaves and all their offspring to be slaves to the community in perpetuity. And all were marked with the hot metal that seared the mark of the slave into their forehead for all to see. And their property was divided amongst the faithful Followers and their beasts also. And the slaves had to work for the others for their food and clothing and shelter and must do the bidding of the others and were subject to the whims and will of the faithful. Women and men both were slaves and could be used by the women and men of the faithful for any purpose. They could not cry 'rape' and hope for mercy for they were less than beasts and were not free and had no rights.

After this, Gadhallah led the people over secret ways across the Earthworks and down onto the plains of the land of Tohltaz. They met no strangers as they travelled southward for many leagues and reached the edge of the desert of sand. And before them was sand and nothing else in that land and the people were afraid to go further. But Gadhallah sent out his Soldiers and they returned with tales of wonder and amazement on their faces such that Gadhallah would not suffer them to relate their tales to the people lest they be corrupted. But the people followed Gadhallah and they pushed and pulled the Godwood over the sand and their beasts also. For many days they crossed the sand without water and they became thirsty and some were close to death when they spied the Monolith of Kro-Lat on the horizon and the Soldiers told them there was water in plenty to be had there.

All the people were amazed by the Monolith of Kro-Lat. Sixty manheights it stands and is built of solid stone blocks where there are none to be seen. The tower is round and, at the top, is the greatest stonework known to any man living or dead. For seated on top

505

of round tower is a ball of stone, made from one solid piece of rock and it is hollow inside. The purpose of the Monolith of Kro is not known to any man living. Neither does anyone know who built it or when. But it has stood there for as long as men can recall and will stand there till the end of time. And it is a source of wonder and great awe to all who see it.

Some of the people bowed down to the Monolith of Kro and worshipped it, saying it had led them from certain death in the desert to water and pasture for their animals. Then was Gadhallah wrath with them and punished them for their blasphemy. And when all the people and their beasts had had their fill of water and were rested they left that place and continued their wanderings.

Many months were the Followers in the land of Tohltaz, sometimes moving on, sometimes settling for a time where there was water and good grazing to be had. At Ov-Bebna they found a deserted township amongst the trees. There was water in abundance and good grazing and much game to be had and the people urged Gadhallah to let them stay and rest awhile. Gadhallah spoke with Ytraa and Ytraa let the people stay for some months to recover their strength and gather more supplies for their journey. But then Gadhallah urged them on again and they were reluctant to go, being a settled people with no love of travelling. Then Gadhallah had to remind them of the purpose of their journey. And some would not move on and had to be put to death for their sacrilege in that place.

The wild men of Tohltaz, that live in the south of the land under the Unnamed Mountains, came down on the followers at night and stole some of the young maidens. This they did on five occasions until Gadhallah with his Soldiers set a trap and captured the raiding party. The men they captured rode strange beasts with long necks and Gadhallah suffered these beasts to live for they were tame and were good beasts of burden. But the captured men he had put to death most horribly. All but one of the raiding party was tortured and skinned alive and had his manhood torn from him and the one who was not killed was made to watch and then set free so that he might tell his people of the wrath of Ytraa. And no more raids were made on the Followers after this.

Under the Unnamed Mountains Ytraa confused Gadhallah and made him lose his way so that he could not find a path through the mountains. The people became restless with him and asked him where they would go. But in the night Ytraa came to Yldohn in a dream and showed him the way through the mountains. And Yldohn spoke to Gadhallah and Gadhallah made him his second in command and Yldohn led the people out of the land of Tohltaz and through the mountains to Mhistahn that is called the Lake of the Lost.

At this time was Zerryth big with child and she begged that the people be allowed to stay by the lake and rest awhile. And Gadhallah said that they might. But the Lake of the

Lost was much like Lake Qonahn to the people except that it was warmer and less troubled by storms. So the people became attached to this place and did not want to move on. Each time Gadhallah bade them to move on, they pleaded with him to let them stay a little longer in this good land. And so it was that nine years passed and still they were no further. Then Ytraa lost patience and grew tired of waiting for his Followers to move on to his appointed land across the seas. Ytraa told Gadhallah to move on with the Followers and Gadhallah told them they must move for Ytraa was impatient and would grow wrath. Many of the people saw the truth of this and prepared to leave. Yldohn and Zerryth and their children and the Soldiers and several hundred others made ready to leave. But the rest were loathe to go from this pleasant land. Gadhallah told them they would be visited by plagues if they did not continue their journey. But they heeded him not and wanted to stay.

Then came the first plague and all was covered by flies and they ate the food out of the mouths of the people and made everything they touched black until there was no food to be eaten. But the flies went away at last and the people remained and would not go.

Storms and floods came and plagued the people and ruined their homes that they had built along the shores of the Lake of the Lost. Gadhallah warned the people that Ytraa was wrath and would lose patience with the people if they did not do as he bid and set out once more for the land over the seas. But they would not listen for it had been many years since the Skyfire had been seen and the people had forgotten their terror and had forgotten the famine and drought that had sent them from their homeland.

Gadhallah made supplication to Ytraa and asked Ytraa to send a sign again for his people that they might become true again and follow Gadhallah's lead. And there were many amongst the people who were willing to go with Gadhallah and who were still true Followers but most of the people had lost their faith and some had even reverted to the worship of Tryhnn, saying she was the true Goddess of all lakes.

Then Ytraa sent a sign for Gadhallah to let his people know that they must follow his lead. Gadhallah told them that smoke would come and cover the sky and that ash and rocks would rain down on the people and choke them and that the ground would be covered with ash and dust and rocks so that the crops would die and there would be no feed for their beasts. But the people just mocked and would not listen. But the true Followers listened to Gadhallah and made preparations to leave the Lake of the Lost. And the Followers made themselves boats according to the design laid out by Yldohn who had dreamed again and knew the will of Ytraa. And these boats were many for they must carry the people and their belongings and the cattle and sheep and swine and the beasts of burden.

Then came a dark cloud that rose from the northern end of the Lake of the Lost and it rose and covered the sky with darkness so that the sun could not be seen. And the air became cold in the warm place and the people became afraid. Gadhallah told them, 'I warned you of the coming of the Skyfire and you did not believe me until it came and covered the sky with its burning flames. I warned you of this smoke and cloud and you have not believed me until it appeared. I have told you of the ash and dust and rocks which will come soon and cover this land. Will you heed me now? Will you do the will of Ytraa and leave this land now? Or will you wait for the rocks to smite you and the ash and dust to choke you? You have little time if ye are to escape from this plague.'

The Followers were all prepared and got themselves into their boats with their belongings and their beasts and began to move to the south end of the lake where the river ran down toward the far sea. But those who had mocked and were not prepared were not ready and begged to be allowed to use the boats made by the Followers. But Gadhallah said there would not be room and they must trust to the smaller boats they had made for fishing on the lake. But these boats were not enough to carry the people and their belongings and some stayed behind in their ruined homes on the shores of the Lake of the Lost.

And as the boats made their way onto the waters of the river there was great wailing from those left behind. The rocks fell from the sky on them and ash fell and filled up their mouths and the dust choked them so that all but a few perished in that place. And some that did not perish cast themselves into the waters of the lake and were carried on the current, clinging to logs until the river took them into the arms of the Followers. And these few were saved and told of the terror of the ash and rocks and how all who had stayed behind had perished under the wrath of Ytraa. And all who remained renewed their faith in Ytraa and declare their allegiance to Ytraa and promised they would follow Gadhallah until the ends of the earth. Those who had been left behind numbered nine hundred and seventy four and their beasts and belongings also. And that is why it is called the Lake of the Lost because so many of the people were lost to Ytraa forever there.

Those who remained faithful sailed down the river that is called the Sure, for it winds and weaves but it is constant and without rapids or falls all the way from the Lake of the Lost to the sea, uninterrupted. The Sure flows full and free all the way to the sea through the south part of Cushlanah were the Followers were avoided by the local people as they feared these people who could float on the water. For the people of Cushlanah were primitive and knew not the craft of building boats. They were afraid of the Followers and stayed away and let them be. But a few of the people were amazed and not afraid and they came and wanted to join the Followers. And Gadhallah asked Ytraa for guidance in this and Ytraa said to Gadhallah that all peoples of all lands were as one in the eyes of Ytraa

508

and that one day all peoples in all places would be Followers and that Gadhallah should accept these people of Cushlanah and make them Followers and teach them the ways of Ytraa and let them be made to understand the ways of the Followers so that they might not do that which is evil in the eyes of Ytraa. And this Gadhallah did and the number of people of Cushlanah who were made Followers was four hundred and sixty seven and they had with them their beasts and their belongings. And their number was too great to fit in the boats and so were more boats made by the Followers and the other people of Cushlanah did thus learn the craft of making boats to float them on the wide river that bordered their land. Thus it was that the land of Cushlanah became allies with the land of Muhnilahm and the peoples of those lands are friends in perpetuity.

The people of Cushlanah rode beasts of burden, which they called horses and taught the Followers in return for the boat building skills the way to be with the horses. And so it was that the Followers remained in the land of Cushlanah for nearly a cycle and then they left. And the number of Followers that departed from the borders of Cushlanah and entered the land of Rophan was six thousand and one hundred and seven and their beasts and their belongings they took also. And all of these were in the boats that they had built, and horses also they took.

As they passed from Cushlanah to Rophan they must travel for long leagues beneath the shadows of the Grave Mounds. This was a fearful place ancient beyond memory and full of troubled spirits and tormented souls. It was said that the vast range of hills had been made by man, though this is hard to believe and there are rivers that run from the hills as they do from the mountains. But legend says that great giants built the Grave Mounds to bury their dead kings and that the ghosts of those dead wander the hills in the night, moaning and crying in great lamentation. Whether this be true or no, Gadhallah did not permit the Followers to venture into those hills but bade them graze their cattle and do their hunting on the west side of the Sure, where the lands were empty and not full of rumour.

The Followers left the Grave Mounds behind and were glad to be away from that place of terror. And so they came into the land that is Rophan. All day long the Followers let the Sure float their boats down toward the sea. And each evening they stopped and made fast along the banks so that their cattle and beasts could graze on the lush meadows there. And so it was that they travelled through the land of Rophan even as far as Shorrannon.

This great city that is big enough to swallow all the villages and towns of Choshinahm is populated by a people who are renowned for their greed and their hostility to strangers. But the Followers were too great in number to be threatened by the city people. But they tarried not in that place that was unholy and devoted to the pleasures of the flesh and all manner of evil things and they sailed through the city and the people there jeered as they passed by and threw rotten fruit at the boats until the boats were forced to move into the fast flowing channel in the centre of the wide river to escape their taunts. And it took the whole party one whole day to pass through that city so vast was it.

Out of Shorrannon they passed and thence on through the flat lands of Rophan where the people of the villages and towns came down to the shore and gazed at them. Some, having heard that nakedness was sacred to the Followers, stood unclothed and made obscene gestures at the boats as they passed. Yet some there were who came in the evening, stealthily, and wished to join the Followers in their journey. And Gadhallah permitted this and welcomed the newcomers.

So it was that when the Followers came to the great swamps and fens of the Sure, where it begins its approach to the sea, they had with them people of Rophan who knew the ways and could guide them through the maze of lesser channels so that they did not become lost in the great swamps. And they came at last to the mouth of the river and to the great port of Mipahnhil where the houses are built on stilts at the edge of the river and out over the sea. And here the Followers would stay and rest awhile and make ready for the long sea voyage to come. And some of the followers were seduced by the people of Mipahnhil and left and joined the folk of that city. And these were lost to the Followers, for the people of the city would not help the Soldiers find the deserters but said that they should be let alone to do as they would. And it took some months for the people to ready themselves for the journey across the sea for many provisions would be needed and barrels of water had to be made ready and feed for the animals that could be taken. So the people of Mipahnhil did barter with the Followers and much trading was done until all was made ready. And some of the people of the port joined the Followers and Gadhallah welcomed them as true Followers.

In the night Yldohn was much troubled by dreams and he did not understand them. He spoke with Gadhallah and explained his dreams and they consulted Ytraa together and so it was that they understood the meaning of the dreams. Thus it was that they knew how they would recognise the island of Muhnilahm when they came there. For that was the meaning of the dreams. But Gadhallah and Yldohn were sworn to secrecy by Ytraa that no one but those two might know when they found the right land. So it was that the secret of Muhnilahm died with Gadhallah and Yldohn for it was not written in the books.

When at last all was made ready for the voyage, many of the Followers were loathe to leave the bright city of Mipahnhil for it was a place where life was easy and the needs to live were easily to be had. And many feared the long sea journey ahead. So it was that the number who left those shores in the ships with some of the beasts of each type and much grain to plant and vegetable seeds to grow and flax and cotton plants to take for their clothing, that number was just four thousand, seven hundred and twenty two souls. And some of those were from Cushlanah and some from Rophan and some from the city of Mipahnhil but most were from the land of Choshinahm. That is where the Groves of Ytraa grow in the space between the mountains that is known as 'between the Wings of the Hawk', but no living soul knows why it is so-called.

Many days they sailed south and east in search of the island that Ytraa had decreed would be their home. And they had no sight of land in those days and so it was that they came upon an island where there was smoke coming from the central mountain and the people asked if it was Muhnilahm and Yldohn and Gadhallah said it was not. Yet the people did need to go ashore and this Gadhallah did permit. And this was the island that is called Ylcrat and it is fair but dangerous because the mountain spews fire and is never asleep and the fire claims the lives of many. But the people who live there are fair beyond compare and all are young and there are no aged people there at all because they die when they are not yet forty cycles. And all die this way and none lives on. And the people there are generous of spirit and body and do give all without expectation of return for this is their way. And the people of Ylcrat love and live and laugh very much and they give themselves as freely as they give their food and clothing and other things for these things have no hold on them. And some of the Followers fell for the people of Ylcrat and joined with them even though Gadhallah decreed that they must not and Ytraa warned that none of those who had joined with the people of Ylcrat should be Followers afterward. And though they were sore afraid that they would die if they stayed, even so Ytraa would not let them leave the island and so the numbers that left the island of Ylcrat were four thousand and six hundred and thirteen only. And the others were left behind and would die, for there was poison in the water and that is what made the people of that place happy but also killed them.

The Followers sailed away from Ylcrat and searched for their island home. The boats came to a great whiteness after they left Ylcrat and the sea was boiling and much troubled and rocks broke up out of the surface that would wreck the boats. And the people were very afraid but Gadhallah spoke and told them that Ytraa would protect them and Yldohn found a way round the reef and caused the boats to sail south until the danger was past. And not one boat was lost to the reef.

On they sailed, steering east, for that was the way Ytraa would have them go and they came at last to the string of small islands that lead to the island of Muhnilahm. And the people were growing weary of being at sea and some of them would settle on the smaller islands but Yldohn persuaded them to tarry not there but to continue the search for they would find their island home in but a few days. There were no native people on those islands but on some there were signs that people had lived there at one time.

At last they came to a very great island and they asked Yldohn if this was Muhnilahm and Yldohn caused the boats to sail right round the island before he would permit them to land. And when they had circled the island entirely then did he declare it to be Muhnilahm and the people landed.

The joy of that day has never been repeated and it is celebrated each year as the Day of Finding. There was a day of great celebration and the people danced and sang and drank of their wine and beer and worshipped Ytraa and gave thanks for their deliverance from the voyage and the long journey.

And it was fourteen cycles that the people had been travelling and they had come many hundreds of leagues from their land of Choshinahm to the island of Muhnilahm and they found that it was a paradise and they were happy.

After that day of rejoicing, Gadhallah gathered all the people together and spoke with them and told them that he must go to find the site for the erection of the Godwood where Ytraa would be. Yldohn and Zerryth he placed in charge of the people and they would be the leaders of the people whilst Gadhallah was away. The Soldiers would do as Yldohn and Zerryth bade them and the Holy Ones would act as guides also and help keep the people in the true way until Gadhallah returned.

Then Gadhallah took three of the Holy Ones and one Captain and five Soldiers and set out to find the place where the Godwood was to be erected. Ytraa led Gadhallah over the hills that surrounded the landing place and to the lake where now stands the town of Pampahn, the oldest settlement of our people. All along the lake did Ytraa lead Gadhallah and north, through the marshes until he came to the hills that lie north of the waters.

Then Ytraa bade Gadhallah leave the rest of the party at a place appointed by Ytraa and Gadhallah did go the rest of the way alone and naked and without anything but his own frail body. He took neither food nor drink nor anything but only his body to sustain him. And he wandered alone and naked in that new and strange land but Ytraa protected him and took him up to the wide flat land that lies beneath the highest mountain of Muhnilahm. And at that time the mountain had no name and nor did any other part of Muhnilahm for the Followers had not discovered all there was to know of the island and no place was named yet. And Ytraa showed Gadhallah the place where Ytraa would stand and Gadhallah questioned not the will of Ytraa and obeyed and marked the place well so that he could go there again. And in that place were no trees and only tall grasses grew and the warm wind blew and it was a pleasant place to be and Gadhallah named the place the Plain of Ytraa. And Ytraa was well pleased and did bless Gadhallah.

Then Gadhallah returned to the party and they were amazed for he had been alone and naked in that land for four days and four nights without food or drink yet he returned to them well and unharmed. And Gadhallah ate with them and bade the party return with him to the place Ytraa had named as Ytraa's place of being. So the whole party went naked to the place and saw that it was good.

From that day it was decreed that no person approach the place or be in sight of it unless that person be naked. And that is why the Holy Ones, who live on the plateau beneath the constant gaze of Ytraa go naked at all times so that they do not offend the eyes of Ytraa.

Then Gadhallah and his party returned to the people and made arrangements for the moving of the Godwood to the Plain of Ytraa. And there the carvers of wood made the likeness of Ytraa in the form that Gadhallah described to them, for he alone has seen Ytraa even to this day. And all was done in accordance with the will of Ytraa. Then was Ytraa made whole again for the Followers so that they could see Ytraa in all Ytraa's glory and the people were amazed and bowed down in awe and wonder before Ytraa. Great was the joy of that day so that no day has matched it since, for the Followers had come to their home and Ytraa had come to Ytraa's home and all were glad and full of rejoicing.

And when all the laws and ceremonies were decreed by Gadhallah and the people knew what they must do and how they must live, then the leadership of the Followers passed to Yldohn and Zerryth for this was the will of Ytraa. And Gadhallah gave up his life and his body was laid in the sight of Ytraa so that his soul could join with Ytraa, as is the fate of all who worship Ytraa and are true.

Thus ends the Epic of Gadhallah.

The origin of the following documents remains unknown, but they resided amongst the other parchments and stone slabs in the Secret Chamber of the High Priest's house.

Sacred Verses

The Lore Of The Journeys

From between the Wings of the Hawk we came
To the trench and mound made by mortal hands of old
Across the sands three times wind blown
Over the barren wastelands hard and dry
To the Nameless Mountains cruel hills
At last to the Lake of the Lost and rest
But the hard Kabahl drove us into the river
Until to the swamps and streams we came
Over the wide seas to the Island of Dreams
Onward from that sweet land we moved
And many were lost on the crescent of white water
The great sea took our boats to the Islets
Until at last we found Muhnilahm and home

Over the sea for many many days
North beyond the boiling waters
To the sweet Island of Dreams
Tarry not but travel on over the
Sea and under the cliffs for many leagues
To the wide bay where boats lie safe
There the old road runs north to the
Greatest forest of them all
After the trees the river runs out
From the feet of the Mountains of Gold
To the high cold pass where the snow may kill
The path runs between the wide river and
The Forest of the Haunted Souls
To the wide lake it leads and then
Between the Wings of the Hawk
Lie the glorious Groves of Ytraa

Priest's Declaration at the Wedding Ceremony

Within the sight of all gathered here in the holy place and as witnessed by Ytraa I declare you now to be man and wife. And that your souls never will be parted until death takes you.

And though one may stray and join with some other for once or for many times still this first joining will stand.

And though one fall ill near to death still this joining shall stand.

And though great sorrow fall still this joining will stand.

And though great riches come still this joining will stand.

And though one shall go missing and be not heard of for five years and a day still this joining shall stand, but after that time the other may take a new partner for life.

And though one shall be barren and not bring forth new life still this joining shall stand.

But if one will not lie with the other for this first time before Ytraa and all gathered here present and join again on each of the five nights that will follow, then shall this joining not stand and both may go their separate ways and find new partners for life.

But if one, being already joined to another, should take a second partner and be joined with that person, as husband or wife, and should lie with that person in the sight of Ytraa and the people then shall that one be in peril of death. And the death of that one shall be terrible and shall last three days in agony for it is the law that for man there is but one wife and for woman there is but one husband while they both shall live. And the soul of that one shall lie in torment in the darkness until Ytraa allows its release.

Go, therefore and be ye loyal one to the other and join with others only as required by the laws of the Followers. Show your hearts to Ytraa and to one another and stand before Ytraa in humility. Join now before Ytraa and those gathered here that all may witness your joining and know that it is good. May Ytraa bless you and guide you all of your lives.

Responses Due At Time Of Coming Of The Skyfire

This document was found hidden under many others in the Secret Chamber of the High Priest. The evidence suggests that the responses had not been in use for very many cycles.

Priest: Why do we return to Choshinahm at the season of the Skyfire?

Congregation: We go to fulfil the promise of Gadhallah to Ytraa.

Priest: What is that promise?

Congregation: That we will keep blood ties with our misguided brethren in the ancient homeland.

Priest: How are these blood ties kept with the ancient homeland?

Congregation: By the exchange of three virgins. Three from Muhnilahm exchanged with three from Choshinahm.

Priest: Why do we keep these ties?

Congregation: So that the chosen people of Ytraa may remain one in body even though they be split in spirit.

Priest: Why are the people of Ytraa not united in spirit?

Congregation: The ancient ones do not acknowledge the true meaning of the coming of the Skyfire.

Priest: What is the true meaning of the coming of the Skyfire?

Congregation: The one meaning is for all to acknowledge; it is that Ytraa is angry with his people for their wickedness.

Priest: What sacrifice does Ytraa demand to cool Ytraa's anger?

Congregation: Ytraa demands the blood of three youths at three times for three days.

Priest: What more does Ytraa demand to cool Ytraa's anger?

Congregation: Ytraa demands three days of fasting and three days and three nights of prayer from Ytraa's true Followers.

Priest: What further does Ytraa demand at the coming of the Skyfire?

Congregation: Ytraa demands that before sixty days after the Skyfire is no more seen in the night sky we, the chosen of Muhnilahm, should do this penance. We should take our three virgin gifts to Choshinahm and return with the three virgins from that land in return.

Priest: And that we should further return with a new Godwood selected as decreed and brought back with whatever labour can be found by the party. On return to Muhnilahm the Godwood must be carved into another likeness of Ytraa in every way similar to the original Godwood and be carried aloft and placed on top of the column of Ytraa in this holy place. And that we should worship and bow down before Ytraa as is demanded. And every living person in the land of Muhnilahm must do penance before Ytraa and declare allegiance to Ytraa as the only and true living God of all that is created.

Ytraa be praised and guide the hands and hearts of those who must choose the virgin gifts and the sacrificial youths.

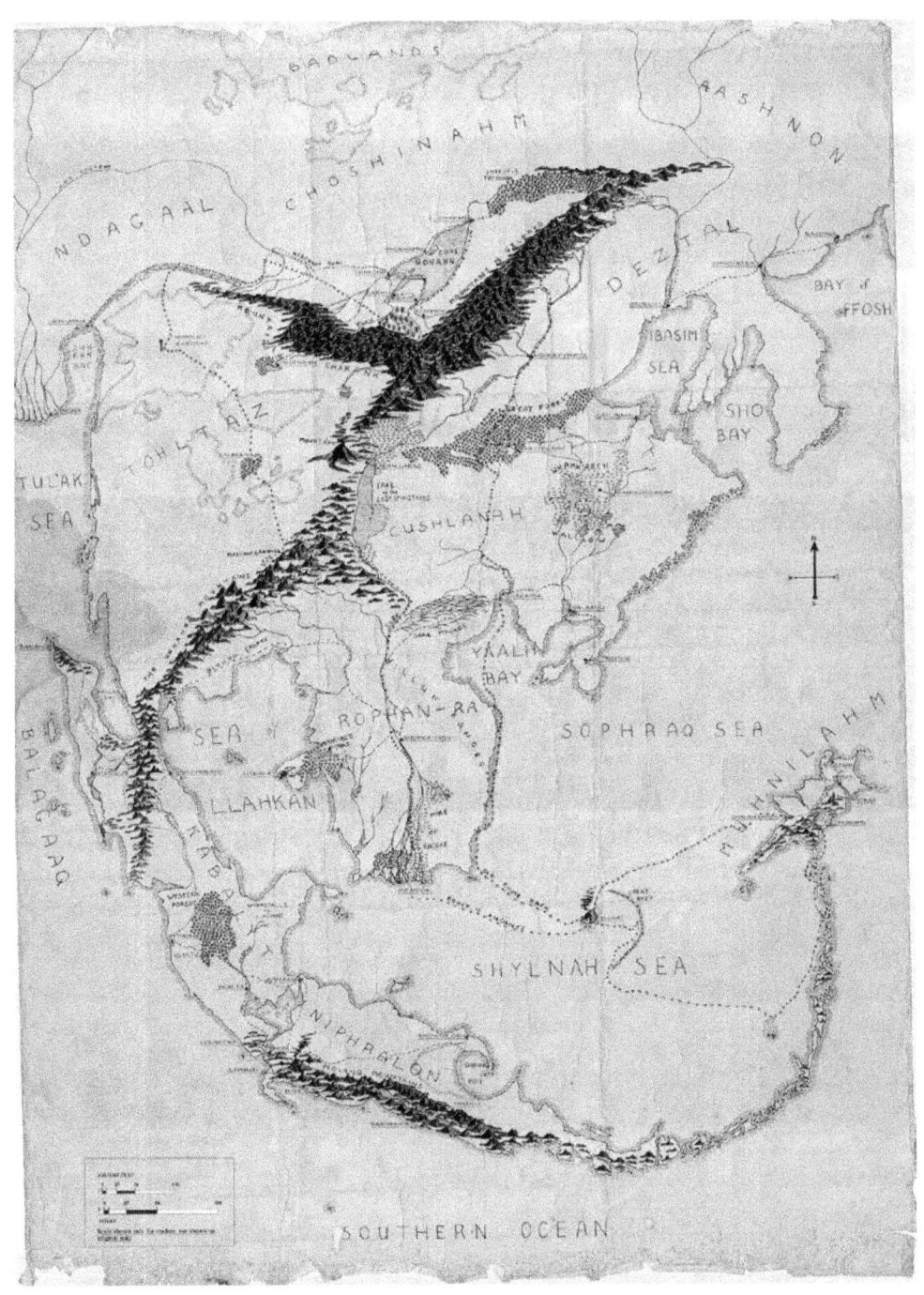

www.ingramcontent.com/pod-product-compliance
Lightning Source LLC
Chambersburg PA
CBHW080715020726
47501CB00010B/2442